CW00829470

The True Prophecies or Prognostications of Michael Nostradamus

Michael Nostradamus

Translated and commented by
Theophilus de Garencieres

To the Courteous Reader

Reader,

Before thou goest on further to the perusing of this Work, thou art humbly intreated by the Authour, to forgive him his Anglicisme; for being born a Forreigner, and having had no body to help him to the polishing of it, for several reasons, it cannot be expected he should please thine Ears, so much as he may perhaps do thy Fancy. Every Exotick Plant can hardly become Domestical under one or two Generations: Besides that, the Crabbedness of the Original in his own Idiome, can scarce admit a Polite Eloquency in another. The very Antient *English* Language in this refined Age, is become both obsolete and unintelligible, as we may see in *Chaucer, Gower,* and others. If you adde to this, that the Authours Nation hath been alwayes famous for its Civility to those that were Strangers to their Language, as not onely to abstain from laughing at them when they spoke amiss, but also in redressing them charitably to the best of their power. I may probably expect you will measure me with the same measure, as you would be if you were in my case.

As for the Errataes of the Press, I could not help them, being out of Town most part of the time that the Book was a Printing; when you meet with any, I hope your Charitable Pen will either mend or obliterate them, and not lay another mans fault upon me, who neither for pride nor ostentation undertook this laborious Work, but that I might give some Satisfaction and Recreation to the Learned and Curious, who have had a longing for it ever since its Birth.

Farewell.

THE PREFACE TO THE READER

READER,

Before I speak any thing of the Author, or of his Works, I think it convenient to speak somthing of my self, and of my intention in setting out this Translation, with my Annotations.

The Reputation that this Book hath amongst all the *Europeans*, since its first coming out, which was in the year 1555. and the curiosity that from time to time the learned have had to see the Mysteries contained in it, unfolded: is a sufficient warrant for my undertaking.

Many better Pens (I confess) could have performed this work with better success, but not with greater facility than I, having from my youth been conversant with those that pretended or endeavored to know somthing in it. Otherwise, it would have been impossible for a man of my profession to wade through it. This Book was the first after my Primmer, wherein I did learn to read, it being then the Custom in *France*, about the year 1618. to initiate Children by that Book; First, because of the crabbidness of the words; Secondly, that they might be acquainted with the old and absolete *French*, such as is now used in the *English* Law; and Thirdly, for the delightfulness and variety of the matter, so that this Book in those days was printed every year like an Almanack, or a Primer for Children. From that time, without any other Study than reading of History, and observing the events of the world, and conversing with those that made it their Study, (some of which were like to run mad about it) I have attained to so much Knowledge, as to bring it into a Volume.

The Book is written in the Nature of Prophecies, digested into old *French* Verses, most of which are very hard to be understood, and others impossible at all, whether the Author did affect obscurity, or else wanted the faculty to express himself, which is the cause that it could not be rendred into *English* Verses, it being troublesome enough to be understood in Prose, as the Reader will find. That's the reason that I have translated it almost word for word, to make it as plain as I could; as also because the Reader (if curious of it) may benefit himself in the knowledge of the *French* Tongue, by comparing the *English* and *French* together. The rest that can be said upon this subject, you shall find either in the Authors Life, or in the Appology made for him.

And because I have told you before, that many have been like to run mad by over-studying these, and other Prophecies, give me leave to give you this advice, that in vain, or at least without any great profit, thou shalt bestow thy time, care, and study upon it: for which I will give thee the chief reasons, that have disswaded me from it.

The first is, that the thing it self, which you may think to understand, is not certain in it self; because the Author disguiseth it in several manners, sometimes speaking a double sense, as that of the ancient Oracle.

Aio te Æacida Romanos vincere posse.

Which is to be understood two ways, and cannot be determined, till the event of it be past.

It is true, that the Author doth mark so many particular Circumstances, that when the thing is come to pass, every one may clearly see that he pretended to Prophecie that particular thing. And besides he doth sometimes deliver the thing in so obscure terms, that without a peculiar *Genius*, it is almost impossible to understand it.

The second is, that though the Prophecie be true in it self, yet no body knoweth, neither the time, nor how: For example, he plainly foretelleth, that the Parliament of *England* should put their King to death; nevertheless no body could tell, nor when, nor how, till the thing was come to pass, nor what King it should be, till we had seen it.

The third is, that he marketh the times with Astrological terms, *viz.* when such and such Planets, shall be in such and such Signs; but as those Planets are often here, and go out of it, and come there again, no certain judgement can be made of it.

The fourth is, that many times he giveth some peculiar Circumstances to those he speaketh of, which may be found in others. Thus *the Royal first born* might have been applied to *Lewis* the

XIII. to *Lewis* the XIV. to the first born of *Philip* the II. and *Philip* the III. King of *Spain*, and to Kings of *England*, Father and Son. Nevertheless we find that this word *Royal first born*, was intended for *Henry* IV. Grandfather on his Mothers side, as we shall shew hereafter. This being so, it cannot be expounded, but after the event.

The fifth is, that the knowledge of future things, belongeth to God alone, and no body can pretend by any study, to have a certain acquisition of it in all its Circumstances.

The sixth is, that the orders of Gods providence, which cause the several events in all States, will not permit that men should have a publick notion of his designs, sometimes he revealeth them to his Servants, or to some particular man as he pleaseth, but he will not have them to be known among the common sort of men.

The seventh, is the experience we have had of many, who pretending to understand the Author, have made a quantity of false Prophecies, expounding the Stanza's according to their fancy, as if God had given them the same understanding that he gave the Author, and what ought to confirm us more in this point, is, that they have expounded some Prophecies, as if they were to come to pass, which were past already, by which we see the darkness of humane wit, who without authority pretendeth to bite into the forbidden fruit of knowledge.

The eighth is, that this knowledge is no way profitable for the Vulgar; because those things being decreed by God, they shall come to pass without forceing our liberty, nor hindering the contingency of sublunary things, where we must observe that the Prophecies which were revealed to men, are many times conditional, as we see in that of *Jonas* against *Ninive*, but those that they have left in writing for the times that should come after them, are absolutely true, and shall infallibly come to pass, as they have foretold them. This no ways hindereth, but God may reveal some secrets of his to private men, for their benefit, and that of their friends, without imparting it to the Vulgar, who may be, should laugh at them.

The ninth is, that God hath peculiarly reserved to himself the knowledge of times. *Daniel*, by a special favour, knew the end of the *Babylonian* Captivity, and the time of the *Messiah*'s birth, and yet the interpreters can scarce yet expound clearly the meaning of the seventy weeks of *Daniel*, and we see, that since 1600 years ago, holy men, from age to age, have foretold the proximity of Dooms-day, and the coming of Antichrist.

The tenth is, that the foretelling of future things in this Author, is for the most part included in business of State, and one might be guilty of a criminal temerity, if he would discover things that concern us not, and the concealing of which, is commended by all prudent persons, seeing that we owe respect, love, and submission to those that bear rule over us.

For these reasons (dear Reader) I would not have thee intangle thy self in the pretentions of knowing future things. If you have light concerning them, keep thine own secret, and make use of it for thy self: Preserve peace, and let the Almighty govern the World: for he can turn all things to his Glory, and may when he pleaseth, raise up some Wits that will make known unto us, what we desire, without any further trouble to our selves. Before I make an end, I cannot but acquaint thee for gratitude sake, of my Obligation to several persons, which have lent me Books, to help me towards the finishing of this work, as namely that worthy Gentleman, and the Honour of his profession Mr. *Francis Bernard*, Apothecary to St. *Bartholemews* Hospital, and Mr. *Philip Auberton* Gentleman, belonging to the Right Honourable the Earl of *Bridgwater.* Farewell.

THE LIFE OF Michael Nostradamus,
Physitian in Ordinary to HENRY the II. and
CHARLES the IX. Kings of France.

Michael Nostradamus, the most renowned and famous Astrologer, that hath been these many Ages, was born in St. *Remy*, a Town of *Provence*, in the year 1503. upon a *Thursday*, the 14th of *December*, about noon. His father was *James Nostradamus*, a Notary of the said Town, his Mother was *Renata* of St. *Remy*, whose Grandfathers by the Fathers and Mothers side, were men very skilfull, in Mathematick and Physick, one having been Physitian to *Renatus*, King of *Jerusalem*, and *Sicily*, and Earl of *Provence*, and the other Physition to *John*, Duke of *Calabria*, Son to the said *Renatus*, whence cometh that our Author saith in his Commentaries, that he hath received from hand to hand the Knowledge of Mathematicks, from his ancient Progenitors. After the death of his great Grandfather by the Mothers side, who first gave him a slight tincture, and made him in love with the Mathematicks, he was sent to School to *Avignon*. After that he went to Mount *Pelier*, to study Philosophy and Physick, till a great Plague coming, he was compelled to go to *Narbonne*, *Thoulouse*, and *Bourdeaux*, where he first began to practise, being then about 22 years of age. Having lived four years in those parts, he went back again to *Monpelier*, to get his degrees, which he did with a great deal of applause. Going to *Thoulouse*, he past through *Agen*, where *Julius Cæsar Scaliger* stayed him, with whom he was very familiar and intimately acquainted, though they fell out afterward; there he took to wife a very honourable Gentlewoman, by whom he had two Children, a Son and a Daughter, all which being dead, and seeing himself alone, he resolved to retire himself into *Provence* his Native Countrey. After he had gone to *Marseille*, he went to *Aix*, where the Parliament of *Provence* sitteth, and was there kept three years at the City Charges; because of the violent Plague that raged then in the year 1546. as you may read in the Lord of *Launay*'s Book, called the Theater of the World, who describeth that Plague according to the informations our Author gave him. Thence he went to *Salon de Craux*, a City distant from *Aix* one dayes Journey, and in the middle way between *Avignon* and *Marseille*; there he Married his second Wife *Anna Ponce Genelle*, by whom he had three Sons and one Daughter, the eldest was *Michael Nostradamus*, who hath written some pieces of Astrology, Printed at *Paris* in the year 1563.

The second was *Cæsar Nostradamus*, who hath deserved to be numbred among the *French* Historians, by reason of the great Volume he hath written of *Provence*.

The third was a Capuchine Frier. *Cæsar* did insert in his History the propagation of that Order in *Provence*. The fourth was a Daughter.

Nostradamus having found by experience that the perfect knowledge of Physick dependeth from that of Astrology, he addicted himself to it, and as this Science wanteth no allurement, and that besides his Genius he had a peculiar disposition and inclination to it; he made such a progress in it, that he hath deserved the Title of the most illustrious one in *France*, insomuch that making some Almanacks for recreation sake, he did so admirably hit the conjuncture of events, that he was sought for far and near.

This success was the cause of an extraordinary diminution of his fame; for the Printers and Booksellers seeing his fame, did print and vent abundance of false Almanacks under his name for lucre sake, whence it came that his reputation suffered by it, and was the cause that the Lord *Pavillon* wrote against him, and that the Poet *Jodele* made this bitter Distichon.

Nostra damus cum falsa damus, nam fallere nostrum est, Et cum falsa damus, nil nisi Nostra damus.

To which may be answered.
Nostra damus cum verba damus quæ Nostradamus dat, Nam quæcunque dedit nil nisi vera dedit.

Or thus
Vera damus cum verba damus quæ Nostradamus dat, Sed cum Nostra damus, nil nisi falsa damus.

Nevertheless the Beams of Truth did shine through the Clouds of Calumny; for he was singularly esteemed of by the Grandees, Queen *Katharine* of *Medicis*, who had a natural inclination to know future things.

And *Henry* the II. King of *France*, who sent for him to come to the Court in the year 1556. and having had private conference with him about things of great concernment, sent him honourably back again with many gifts. He went from *Salon* to the Court upon the 14 of *July* in the year 1555. and came to *Paris* upon the 15 of *August*. As soon as he was come to Town, the Lord Constable of *Montmorency* went to see him at his Inn, and presented him to the King, who received him with much satisfaction, and commanded that his lodging should be at the Palace of the Cardinal of *Bourbon* Archbishop of *Sens*.

There he was taken with the Gout for ten or twelve days, after which his Majesty sent him one hundred Crowns in Gold in a Velvet Purse, and the Queen as much. Their Majesties desired him to go to *Blois* to see the Princes their Children, and to tell them his opinion of them. It is certain that he did not tell them what he thought, considering the Tragical end of those three Princes, *viz. Francis* the II. *Charles* the IX. and *Henry* the III.

Having been so much honoured at Court, he went back again to *Salon*, where he made an end of his last Centuries, two years after he dedicated them to the King *Henry* the II. in the year 1557. and in his Luminary Epistle discovereth unto him the future events that shall happen from the Birth of *Lewis* the XIV. now Reigning, till the coming of Antichrist.

While he was at *Salon* he received there the Duke of *Savoy*, and the Lady *Margaret* of *France*, Sister to *Henry* the II. who was to Marry the said Duke according to the treaty of the general Peace made at *Cambresis*, both entertained him very familiarly, and honoured him often with their presence. The Duke came in *October* and the Lady in *December*.

When *Charles* the IX. went a progress through his Kingdom, he came into *Provence*, and did fail not to go to *Salon* to visit our Author, who in the name of the Town went to salute him, and make a Speech, this was in the year 1564. the 17 of *November*.

The extraordinary satisfaction that the King and the Queen Mother received from him was such, that being both at *Lion*, they sent for him again, and the King gave him 200 Crowns in Gold, and the Queen almost as much, with the quality of Physician in Ordinary to the King, with the Salaries and profits thereunto appertaining. Being come back to *Salon* he lived about 16 Months longer, and died upon the 2 of *July* 1566. in his Climacterical year of 63. having all his senses about him: His Disease was a Gout at first, which turned into a Dropsie; the time of his death it seemeth was known to him; for a friend of his witnesseth, that at the end of *June* in the said year he had writen with his own hand upon the Ephemerides of *John Stavius* these Latine words, *Hic prope mors est*; that is, near here is my death, and the day before his death that friend of his having waited on him till very late took his leave, saying, I shall see you again to morrow morning, you shall not see me alive when the Sun riseth, which proved true. He died a *Roman* Catholick, having received all his Sacraments, and was solemnly buried in the Church of the *Franciscan* Friers at *Salon*, on the left hand of the Church door, where his Widow erected him a Marble Table fastened in the Wall with this Epitaph, with his Figure to the Life, and his Arms above it.

The Inscription of his EPITAPH is in imitation of that of *Titus Livius*, and is thus.

D. M.

Ossa clarissimi Michaelis Nostradami, unius omnium pene mortalium digni, cujus Divino calamo totius Orbis ex astrorum influxu futuri eventus conscriberentur. Vixit annos LXII. menses VI. dies X. Obiit. Salonæ CIƆ IƆLXVI. Anna Pontia Gemella, conjugi optimo. V. E.

Which may be rendered thus:

Here lies the Bones of the most famous *Nostradamus*, one who among Men hath deserved by the opinion of all, to set down in writting with a Quill almost Divine, the future Events of all the Universe, caused by the Cœlestial influences; he lived 62. years 6. Months and 10. days, he died at *Salon*, in the year 1566.

O Posterity do not grudge at his rest.

Anna Pontia Gemella wisheth to her most loving Husband the true Happiness.

He had a Brother named *John Nostradamus*, famous for several Works that he hath written, the Catalogue of which is in the Book of Mr. *du Maine de la Croix*, Intitled, the *Library*.

As for our Author, he hath left several Works, among which is a Book of Receits, for the preservation of health, Printed at *Poitiers*, in the year 1556.

Another concerning the means of beautifying the Face and the Body, that was Printed at *Antwerp* by *Plantin* in the year 1557. which he Dedicated to his Brother *John Nostradamus*, an Attorney at the Parliament of *Aix*.

Besides this, he Translated from Latine into French the *Paraphases of Galen*, upon the Exhortation of *Menedotus*, which was Printed at *Lyon* by *Antony du Rhosne*, in the year 1557.

But before we conclude, it will not be amiss to give some recreation to the Reader, by relating a merry passage that happened to *Nostradamus* being in *Lorrain*, for being in the Castle of *Faim*, belonging to the Lord of *Florinville*, and having in cure the Mother of the said Lord; it chanced one day that they both walking in the Yard, there was two little Piggs, one white, and the other black, whereupon the Lord enquired of *Nostradamus* in jest, what should become of these two Piggs? he answered presently, we shall eat the black, and the Wolf shall eat the white.

The Lord *Florinville* intending to make him a Lyar, did secretly command the Cook to dress the white for Supper; the Cook then killed the white, drest it, and spitted it ready to be rosted when it should be time; In the mean time having some business out of the Kitchin, a young tame Wolf came in, and eat up the Buttocks of the white Pig, that was ready to be rosted; the Cook coming in the mean time, and fearing least his Master should be angry, took the black one, killed it, and drest it, and offered it at Supper. Then the Lord thinking he had got the Victory, not knowing what was befallen, said to *Nostradamus*, well Sir, we are eating now the white Pigg, and the Wolf shall not touch it. I do not believe it (said *Nostradamus*) it is the black one that is upon the Table. Presently the Cook was sent for, who confessed the accident, the relation of which was as pleasing to them as any meat.

In the same Castle of *Faim*, he told many that in a little Hill that was near the Castle, there was a Treasure hidden, which should never be found, if it were sought with design, but that it should be discovered when the Hill should be digged for some other intent. There is a great probability in this prediction, for there was an ancient Temple built upon it, and when they dig there, many times several Antiquities are found. All *France* telleth several Histories foretold by the Author, but I am unwilling to write any thing without good warrant. His Stanza's are sufficient to prove the extraordinary Talent he had in foretelling future things.

CHAP. I.

It is not unusual for Calumny to follow the best Wits, and those whom God hath endowed with so extraordinary Talent, upon weak and slight grounds. It is not also unusual for Men to side easier with calumny against innocent persons, then with those truths that justifie them; therefore no body ought to wonder, if *Michael Nostradamus* hath been so much cried down and defamed by several Authors, being in the number of those extraordinary persons, whom God had priviledged with that grace so much desired by curious Men, *viz.* the knowledge of future events.

Besides that, there was four things in him, which might have been the grounds of this diffamation.

The first was the vulgar life which he led in the Roman Catholik Religion, which seemed to bear no proportion with such an extraordinary favour of God.

The second was his application to judicial Astrology, which is condemned by many learned Men, and detested by those that pretend to ignorant devotion.

The third was a suspition brought by his enemies, and many devout persons in his time, that he was a Negromancer, and had familiarity with the Angel of darkness.

The fourth was the obscurity of his Stanza's, which was made worse by the enormous faults of those that first Copied them, and by the carelesness of the Printers.

CHAP.   II.

How the first Objection hath caused the Author to be reputed a false Prophet.

In consequence of the first Objection, calumny hath endeavoured to place him among the false Prophets, because scarce any body can persuade himself, that there being among the Faithful so many Illustrious persons in Holiness and Learning, the Holy Ghost would have made choice of a common person, and to reveal him so many rare secrets, concerning the future Estate of his Church, and of those Kingdoms that acknowledge her for their Mother, seeing that the Holy Scriptures shew us, that the knowledge of future things (chiefly if it be extraordinary in its extent) is a special Priviledge wherewith God honoureth his most faithful Servants.

And to say truth, when the Holy Fathers and the Interpreters of the Scripture speak of the Prerogatives of the Apostle St. *John*, they make the chiefest to be that by which being full of Prophetical Spirit, he foretold the future Estate of the Church; and in the Old Testament, so many Prophets were so many Miracles and Prodigies of Holiness, and the only name of Prophet in the Scripture is the most glorious Title that is given to those that were Gods most faithful Servants.

If we find in the Scripture that *Balaam* hath Prophesied notwithstanding his perfidiousness, and that the High Priest *Caiaphas*, notwithstanding his wicked design of murdering Christ, hath also Prophesied; it was only for a few things, and in such cases where God would singularly shew forth his Glory, by those that would have smothered it.

How can we then believe the same of *Nostradamus*, who had not so much as an extraordinary atom of Christian piety, by which he might have been so much priviledg'd of God, as to know by his Divine Light the future Estate of the Church, her Persecutions and her Victories from the year 1555. to the end of the World.

Can it be possible that a Physician, an Astrologer, and one of the common sort of people should have been chosen of God among so many thousands his betters, to impart unto him those

Graces, which have been the reward of the purity and holiness of his Apostles, and of the faithfulness of St. *John* the Evangelist.

This seemeth altogether improbable to Christian piety.

CHAP. III.

The second Objection hath ranked the Author among Dreamers and false Visionaries.

Some are more moderate in the censuring of this Author, and being unwilling to call him maliciously a false Prophet, would have him to be a foolish Dreamer, who believed his own imaginations, and took pleasure in his own fancies, whence came that Latine Distick of the Poet *Jodelle*,

Nostra damus cum falsa damus, nam fallere nostrum est, Et cum falsa damus, nil nisi Nostra damus.

This Distick was so pleasing to the Wits of the times, that without further inquiry, since that time *Nostradamus* went for a Dreamer and a doting fool.

This opinion increased more and more by his making of many Almanacks, wherein every body may see how much he was taken with judicial Astrology; and we see often in his Stanza's the decision of the times, by the conjunction of the Planets with the Signs, and by the Eclipses, whence sometimes he doth infer some events that were to happen.

But what did undo him most, was the covetousness of the Printers and Booksellers of his time, who seeing his Almanacks so well received, did set forth a thousand others under his name, that were full of lies and fopperies.

From that time the Author went for one of those poor Astrologers, who get their living by foretelling absurdities; and pretend to read in the Heavens, that which is only in their foolish imagination.

CHAP. IV.

The third Objection accuseth the Author of medling with the black Art, of being a Negromancer, and a Disciple of the Devil.

If the precedents have been moderate in their censure; others have been more severe in delivering their opinion, accusing him to have kept acquaintance with the Devil, as the Negromancers and other Prestigiators of the ancient times did.

The reason that made them think so is, that seeing so many things come to pass, just as the Author had foretold; they could not attribute it to the knowledge of judicial Astrology, nor to Divine Revelation, and consequently concluded, that it must of necessity come from Satan.

They could not attribute it to judicial Astrology, either because they had no opinion of it, or that the greatest defensors of that Astrology do agree among themselves, that it cannot reach so far as to foretell a thousand peculiar circumstances, which depend purely from the freedom of Men, such as proper names are, and the like, which nevertheless our Author did foretell.

They could neither attribute it to Divine Revelation, for the reasons alledged in the first objection; moreover, because he was accused of a thousand falsities and fopperies, Printed in those Almanacks that went falsly under his name, whence they concluded that it could not come by Divine Revelation, seeing that the Holy Ghost is the Spirit of Truth.

It followeth then (say they) that it must come from the Devil, by the help of the Black Art; the Lord *Florimond de Raimond* a very considerable Author, was of that opinion in his Book of the

CHAP. V.

The fourth Objection maketh him the Head of those Seductors and Impostors, which are dangerous in a Common-wealth.

As Fame doth increase by continuation of time, so doth calumny increase by the multiplicity of opinions, she was not contented to deflour slightly the Authors reputation, by making him pass for some sottish Dreamer, and to rank him amongst the false Prophets, by accusing him to meddle with the black Art, but must needs also sacrifice him to the infernal Furies, by making him the Prince of Seductors and Impostors, that ought to be banished out of every Common-wealth. The fondamental reason of this was the obscurity of his Stanza's, where there was neither rime nor reason; the obscurity did proceed of abundance of gross faults, which the Copisters and Printers have inserted in them, from the omission of several words, from the changing and altering of others, and from the addition of some others, which did destroy the sense.

From this great obscurity, calumny draweth this argument, to ruine utterly the Author, charging him to be all at once a false Prophet, a dotish Dreamer, a Magician, and an infamous Seductor of people.

If God had inspired him what he hath written, he would have done it for the good of his Church and true Believers, seeing he never granteth this Prophetical Grace to any, but to that end as it appeareth in the Holy Scriptures.

This being so, what profit can any body draw from him, if the sense of his Stanza's be so obscure, as not to be understood? and although it should be granted, that some accidents that have happened in Christendom, may sometimes be found in his Prophecies, what fruit hath the Church reaped of it, seeing that those accidents that were foretold, were never known, till they had come to pass, and that there was no avoiding of them?

It cannot therefore be believed, that God should have been the Author of his Predictions, but rather the Subtle Spirit of Satan, with whom he was acquainted by such like black Arts.

According to those four Objections, the Lord *Sponde* in the third Volume of his *Annals*, made him this Epitaph in the year 1566. *Mortuus est hoc anno nugax ille toto orbe famosus Michael Nostradamus, qui se præscium & præsagum eventuum futurorum per astrorum influxum venditavit, sub cujus deinceps nomine quivis homines ingeniosi suas hujusmodi cogitationes protendere consueveruent, in quem valde apposite lusit qui dixit. Nostra damus cum falsa damus,* &c. In *English.* In the year 1566. died that Trifler so famous through all the World, *Michael Nostradamus* who boasted while he lived, to know and foretell future things, by the knowledge he had of the influences of the Planets, under whose name afterwards many ingenious Men have vented their Imaginations, insomuch, that he that made that Distick, Nostra damus *cum falsa damus,* &c. seemeth to have very well said.

CHAP. VI.

Proofs setting forth evidently that Nostradamus was enlightned by the Holy Ghost.

In consequence of these objections forged by calumny, *Nostradamus* name hath been so cried down, that I have thought me self oblidged to make his Apology, to give the greater credit to his Prophecy, the exposition of which I do here undertake, and to proove, that effectually he was enlightned by the Holy Ghost: first, by writting the History of his Life, as I have done in the beginning of this Book; Secondly, by answering to all the said Objections; Thirdly, by alledging the Elogies given him by several Grave and Authentical Authors.

First, I maintain that he was enlightned by the Holy Ghost, by an unanswerable reason, drawn out the Theology, but before we discourse of it, let us suppose that *Nostradamus* hath foretold many things, which absolutely depends from the free will of men, and cannot be known, neither by judicial Astrology, nor by Satan himself, such are for exemple the proper names of Persons, which nevertheless he doth in his Prophecies.

He nameth the Lord of *Monluc*, the Sprightful *Gascon*, the Captain *Charry*, his Camerade, the Lord *de la Mole*, Admiral of *Henry* the II. Galleys, *Entragues*, who was beheaded by order of *Lewis* the XIII. the Headsman of the Duke of *Montmorency*, named *Clerepegne*; the Bassa *Sinan*, destroyer of *Hungary*; the Murderer of *Henry* the III. named *Clement*; the Attorney *David*, the Captain *Ampus*; the Mayor of the City of *Puy* in *Gelay*, named *Rousseau*, under Henry the IV. *Lewis* Prince of *Condé*, under *Francis* II. *Sixtus* V. calling him the Son of *Hamont*; *Gabrielle d'Estrée*; the Lord *Mutonis* sent to *Paris* by those of *Aix*, under *Charles* the IX. the Lord Chancellor of *France*, named *Antony de Sourdis*; the Queen *Leuise*: *Antony* of *Portugal*: the Governour of *Cazal* under *Henry* II.

Secondly, The number of things is of the same nature: *Nostradamus* doth often calculate it; he reckoneth fourteen Confederates for the service of *Henry* IV. in the City of *Puy*: ten great Ships prosecuting extreamly the Admiral in the Battle of *Lepanto*: five Ships taken from the *Spaniard* by those of *Diepe*, under *Henry* II. nine hundred thousands *Mores* that went out of *Spain* under *Henry* IV. three hundred and fifty thousands killed under *Charles* IX. and *Henry* III. three saved at the taking of a Town in *Hungary* by the *Turks*: nine separated from the company of Seditious, that were to be put to death, three Princes of *Turky* Massacred, and the fourth being the youngest saved; thirty Conspirators upon *London* Bridge, against the Majesty of King *Charles* I. and such like.

Thirdly, We find in these Prophecies, the Prodigies that have no other causes in nature, then the meer will of God; such as Comets are, the casting of monstrous Fishes by the Sea upon the Land, the Armies in the Air, the speaking of Dogs, the birth of Monsters, and such like.

Fourthly, We find in those Prophecies those actions that are purely indifferent; for example, that the King of *England* did appear upon a Scaffold without his Doublet; that in the place where he was beheaded, another man had been killed three days before; that *Libertat* went a Hunting with a Greyhond, and a Blood-hond; that the two little Royals were conducted to St. *Germain*, rather then to any other place, and such like.

Fifthly, We find the Birth of several particular persons that were born after his death.

Sixthly, The Governments of Places given by the free will of Kings to such and such.

All these things cannot be known by judicial Astrology, seeing that in Heaven there is neither Names, nor Numbers, nor extraordinary Prodigies: seeing also that judicial Astrology presupposeth the Birth of persons, that one may foretel their future actions; the same things are also unknown to Satan, for the Angelical species know nothing of individual things, but under the notion of possible, and not of future.

Whence I conclude with this irrefragable Argument, that the Author hath known many several things that are not written in the Heavenly Book, nor represented to him by Angelical Species, therefore he hath known them from God himself.

The Author himself in his Epistle to his Son *Cæsar Nostradamus* confesseth, that he hath foretold many things by Divine Virtue and Inspiration.

And a little after he saith, that the knowledge of those things, which meerly depends from free will, cannot be had either by humane auguries, nor by any other humane knowledge, nor by any secret virtue that belongeth to sublunary things, but only by a Light, belonging to the Order of Eternity.

This is not a small Argument, to confirm what we have said, and to prove that the Author hath evidently been conscious, that his knowledge came from Heaven, and that Gods goodness did him that grace; for having rejected and abhorred other means, that Impostors make use of for foretelling something.

He writteth all these things of himself: First, in his Liminary Epistle to his Son *Cæsar*, he conjureth him, that when he should go about to study the foretelling of future things by Astrology, to avoid all kind of Magick, prohibited by the Holy Scripture, and the Canons of the Church; and to encourage him the more to it, he relateth what happened to him, *viz.* that having been Divinely enlightned, and fully persuaded that God only can give the knowledge of future things, which absolutely depends of the free will of men, he did burn abundance of Writings, wherein was taught the Art of Prophecying, and as they were a burning, there came out a great flame, which was like (he thought) to burn his House all to ashes, by which accident he understood the falsity of such Writings, and that the Devil was vexed to see his plots discovered; besides that, he confesseth that being the greatest Sinner of the World, nevertheless he got that favour from Heaven by a Divine Inspiration; and because no body should doubt of it, he learnedly expoundeth wherein consisteth that inspired Revelation, he saith that it is, *A participation of the Eternal Divinity*, by which we come to judge of what the Holy Ghost imparteth to us; by that participation of Eternity, the Author doth not understand a communication of the continuance of the Divine being, but a participation of the Divine knowledge, measured by its Eternity, as the Schools terms it.

Effectively, the Author compareth this participation to a glistering flame, which createth a new day in our understanding, which flame proceeding from Gods infinite knowledge, who seeth and comprehendeth what is Eternity, doth impart unto us what is inclosed in the volubility of the Heavens.

After this testimony, which wholly destroyeth the Sinister opinions that men had of his Prophecies, he sheweth how Judicial Astrology may agree with the knowledge of that which proceedeth from a Prophetical Spirit.

It is true, saith he, that sometimes God imparteth this Light not only to the unlearned, and to his Holy Prophets, but also to those that are versed in Judicial Astrology, making that instrumental for the confirmation of his inspired truths: As we see that natural Sciences, help the light of the Faith, and make a certain disposition in the mind fitter then ordinary, to receive those Divine impressions.

Thus (saith he) in the beginning of the Epistle, God did supernaturaly inspire me, not by any Bacchick fury, nor by Lymphatical motions, as he did the *Sybilles*; but by Astronomical assertions; that is to say, that God gave him that grace, not by any Extasy, but by studying those rules, which Astrology teacheth.

The same things he saith again a little after in this manner: the Astrologer being in his Study, and consulting the Astronomical Rules upon the motions of the Heavens, the Conjunction and several Aspects of the Planets, he guesseth at some future events, of which being not certain, this Divine Light riseth in his mind, and imparteth clearly to him what he knew before, only *Ænigmatically* and obscurely, and in the shade of that natural light.

Sometimes also (saith he) this Light cometh the first into the Astrologers mind, and he afterwards comparing the thing revealed unto him with the Astronomical rules, he seeth that they do wholly agree together; and this is the method that he hath made use of, to know whether the inspired truths were agreeing with the Astronomical Calculations; a method that he hath made use of some times, but not always, for he hath foretold many things, which he could not read in the Heavens.

By these testimonies of the Author himself, every one may see how he made use of Judicial Astrology, and wherefore he studied it so much; how far his knowledge did extend; the glory he giveth to God alone, for his Prophetical knowledge; what horrour he hath always had against unlawful means to attain unto it; how much he did value that Grace, considering his unworthiness; and the manner how the Lord was pleased to gratifie him.

CHAP. VII.

Answer to the first Objection against Nostradamus, which pretendeth to rank him among the false Prophets.

Let us see now what calumny pretendeth for the obscuring this Prophet of our days; the knowledge of future things (saith she) is a priviledge belonging to the Saints, and to those whom God hath endowed with an eminent vertue. I acknowledge, it is so commonly, and in the ordinary way of Grace, but if God be pleased to impart that priviledge to those that have not attained to that

Degree of Holiness, and that it really appeareth by the reasons of Theologie, that they have been gratified with it, we are bound to admire his Royal bounty, which giveth when, and to whom he pleaseth: for example, no body deserveth to be a Marshal of *France*, but he that hath been in several Battles, and at the taking of many Towns; but if the King be pleased to honour with that Dignity a Gentleman that never Warred but against the Deer, the Kings goodness is to be praised, which extendeth even to those that have not deserved it; it is the same reason here, it is visibly apparent that *Nostradamus* hath been enlightned by the Holy Ghost, and yet he hath not imitated the lifes of those great Saints of the Church: what can be inferred from thence, but that it was Gods pleasure to extend his bounty upon his poor Creatures, which is easie to be granted in this point, because the gift of Prophecy is not a sanctifying Grace, but a supernatural gift, of which a sinner is capable of, as we see in *Balaam, Caiaphas*, and the *Sybilles*, and much more in a Christian, who observeth Gods Commandments, and endeavoureth to keep himself in his Grace.

But (saith calumny) Christian piety seemeth to be repugnant to this Divine disposition, seeing that in *Nostradamus* time, there were thousands in the Church of God that were capable of this favour, and to prefer to them a Physitian, an Astrologer, and an Almanack-maker, is a thing that the Wits cannot apprehend so well, as to frame a good opinion for this Author.

Hold there Reader, do not enter into the Sanctuary of Gods secret Judgements, you should loose you self, and never find the way out: how many such questions might I ask you? why did God in former times chuse the Family and person of David, and preferred it to so many others of the Children of *Israel*? why did Christ raise *Judas* to the dignity of an Apostle, preferring him before *Nathaniel*, and so many others that lived Holily.

Bring therefore no more such questions, but say with the Scripture, *As it pleased the Lord, so it was done*: I will nevertheless give you some satisfaction in that point. There was two things in the Author which might have procured that blessing from God.

The first is, that having in his possession those writtings which promised the knowledge of future things, to which he was much inclined, he slighted and burnt them, being persuaded that God alone was the Author of this Grace; I do esteem that action very Heroical in its circumstance, because being inticed by a vehement curiosity to know future things, and having in his hand the means that opened the way to it, he did Sacrifice them to God, for which perhaps God was willing to gratifie him with this favour.

The second thing that was in *Nostradamus* is, that he had naturally a *Genius* for the knowing of future things, as himself confesseth in two Epistles to King *Henry* the II. and to *Cæsar* his own Son, and besides that *Genius*, the knowledge of Astrology, did smooth him the way to discover many future events. Having those two things, he had a greater disposition then others to receive those Supernatural Lights; and as God is pleased to work sweetly in his Creatures, and to give some forerunning dispositions to those Graces he intendeth to bestow, it seemeth that to that purpose he did chuse our Author to reveal him so many wonderful secrets.

We see every day that God in the distributing of his Graces carrieth himself towards us, according to our humours and natural inclinations, he employeth those that have a generous and Martial heart for the defence of his Church, and the destruction of Tyrants; he leadeth those of a melancholick humour into Colledges and Cloisters, and cherisheth tenderly, those that are of meek and mild disposition; even so, seeing *Nostradamus* inclined to this kind of knowledge, he gave him in a great measure the grace of it.

CHAP. VIII.
Answer to the second Objection, which would have him pass for a Doctor.

We shall not have much to say to these more moderate persons, seeing that we have already given the reason of it, *viz.* the covetousness of the Booksellers and Printers, who made use of the Authors name, for the better sale of their false Almanacks, therefore if *Jodelle* the Poet grounded upon this opinion, made that Satyrical Distick.

Nostra damus cum falsa damus, nam fallere nostrum est, Et cum falsa damus, nil nisi Nostra damus.

We answer him,
Nostra damus cum verba damus quæ Nostradamus dat, Nam quæcunque dedit nil nisi vera dedit.

Or thus
Vera damus cum verba damus quæ Nostradamus dat, Sed cum Nostra damus, nil nisi falsa damus.

CHAP. IX.

Answer to the third Objection, which accuseth him of the Black Art, and of Negromancy.

The more doth Calumny lift up her self against this great man, the weaker are her arguments, like the smoke which is so much the easier dissipated, as it ascendeth higher.

Her reason is impertinent in this distributive argument, he hath known those things (saith she) which he could not know by the Planets, and he had them not from God, therefore he had them from Satan.

And we answer this argument in the same way, he hath known those things which he could not know by the Planets, nor by Satan, therefore he had them from God; this Argument is concluding, but that of calumny halteth, for it ought to have proved that he had not his knowledge from God, and that all those things he hath known may be known to Satan, which two things we have manifestly proved to be false, therefore if the Lord *Florimond de Raimond* was alive, I believe he would correct what he hath written against him.

CHAP. X.

Answer to the fourth Objection, of Calumny, which brandeth our Author with the title of Chief of the Seductors and Impostors.

The Weapons of this *Medusa* are sharper in this point then in others, therefore our Buckler accordingly must be of the best mettle and temper.

We cannot deny but *Nostradamus* hath affected obscurity, himself acknowledgeth it in his two Epistles, in that to *Cæsar* his son, he saith, he hath done it, not only because of the times wherein he lived, but also by reason of those that were to follow, in the times wherein he lived the Case was as it is now, *Veritas odium parit*, and this hatred in powerful men is prejudicial to those that speak the Truth, he was also cautious in that, by reason of the times following; for if he had plainly declared what he meant, the Wits would have laughed at it, and would not have believed those strange revolutions that came to pass, and which our Author had foretold. In his Epistle to *Henry* the II he telleth him, that he doth purposely make use of obscure terms to express his mind, for the reasons before alledged.

Now *Calumny* saith, that this affectation of obscurity is a sign that God was not the Author of his Knowledge, seeing that by this obscurity they have proved unprofitable to the Church.

I answer first, that the consequence is false; for the Holy Prophets have spoken so obscurely, that a great part of what they had Prophecied was not known till after it had come to pass.

I answer secondly, that although Prophecies were not understood till after the fulfilling thereof, it doth not follow that they were unprofitable; because by their fulfilling in due time, we gather, that he who revealed them was the true God, Lord of times and Eternity, and therefore being the God of *Israel*, and of the Christians, he ought to be worshiped. By this principle *Cyrus* and *Alexander* knew the true God, *Cyrus* by having seen the Prophecies of *Isaiah*, and *Alexander* those of *Daniel*.

Therefore as the Prophecies of the Saints have not been fruitless, though not understood till they were fulfilled, even so we must not infer that *Nostradamus*'s Prophecies have been useless, though they have remained in obscurity so long a while.

Besides, there is no doubt but *Nostradamus* having Prophecied so many several things that are come to pass, but that hereafter when the Heathen shall see it they shall glorifie God, and shall acknowledge a true Religion, as did *Cyrus*, who many Authors believe to have obtained Salvation.

I answer in the third place, that God permitteth ordinarily that Prophecies lie long in the dark, and then raiseth the Spirit of some men to expound them, as he did that of *Daniel* to interpret the 70 Weeks of the *Babylonian* Captivity, Prophecied by *Jeremiah*, to incourage the faithful three ways.

First, in shewing them, that if the first Prophecies have been punctually fulfilled, the rest will likewise come to pass, seeing the same God hath dictated them.

Secondly, in unfolding to them the future wonders, of which they shall be partakers.

Thirdly, in giving warning how they may attain to them, and shew those accidents that might be an hindrance. Thus God did permit, that for the space of 100. years *Nostradamus* Prophecies should lie in darkness, and be contemned, but after that time God will raise some body to interpret them, whence the faithful seeing so many things foretold come to pass so exactly, will incourage one another by seing so many wonderful prodigies, of whom they shall be Eye Witnesses.

As for my part I have undertaken this Work, only to authorise the wonders that shall be seen in our days, and to invite the Christian Princes to the same design.

The conclusion of this discourse is, that our *Medusa Calumny*, must needs retreat in her dens, and that we ought to forgive those Authors that have spoken so ill of our Author, seing they wanted the Intelligence of his Prophecies, and that the Church did suspend the authorising of them.

CHAP.   XI.

Some difficulties against what we have said, drawn out of Nostradamus his own Epistles.

We have (thanks be to God) sheltered this famous man from the back-biting of *Calumny*, but that we may clear wholly the Heaven of this reputation, we add this Chapter more for the clearing of some words that are in his Epistles, which seem to contradict some of those things we have said; the Author in his Epistles to his Son *Cæsar*, after he had said that God had disposed him to receive thy impression of supernatural lights, not by a *Bacchant furor*, nor by a *Lymphatical motion*, but by *Astronomical assertions*, he saith in the same Epistle towards the end; *That sometimes in the Week being surprised by a Lymphatick humor, and making his Nocturnal Studies sweet by his calculations, he made Books of Prophecies, each one containing a hundred Astronomical Stanza's, which he endeavoured to set out something obscurely,* from which words it might be gathered, that he made his Prophecies by a Lymphatical Spirit, and by the only judicial Astrology.

And in the Epistle to King *Henry* the II. he seemeth to confess, that his Prophecie is nothing but a natural Genius, which he had by Inheritance from his Ancestors.

To these difficulties I answer, supposing first that anciently those were called Lymphaticks, who were mad for Love; because the first that was observed among the Ancients to be mad with that passion, threw himself into the water, which in Latine is called *Lympha*, whence all those that were afterwards transported with the excess of any passion, either of Love, Melancholy, Choler or Envy, have been called Lymphaticks.

So that in this place a Lymphatical motion is nothing properly but a deep Melancholy, which separating us from all Earthly things, doth transport the mind to extraordinary thoughts either good or bad.

This being suposed, I say that the Author confesseth, that his retreat, solitariness, nocturnal Watchings, and Melancholy, have disposed him much to the receiving of that Heavenly flame, which is the cause of Vaticination and Prophecie.

And because he did often spend the whole nights in this study, this Nocturnal retreat caused in him a retirement from all worldly things, at which time he felt a Divine elevating Virtue, that raised his understanding to those Divine Knowledges.

And because this elevating Vertue was caused in him by Divine operation, he doth attribute always his Prophecies to God alone; and by reason that this elevation hath some resemblance with that of the Lymphaticks, he saith, that sometimes he did Lymphatise not properly speaking, but by resemblance.

So that it is true, our Author did not receive his Prophecies by Lymphatical motion, or *Bacchant furie*, but from God himself, who did work in him while he observed his Astronomical assertions; and it is also true, that he felt this Divine operation by a kind of a Lymphatical motion.

Concerning what he saith to *Henry* the II. it is certain he maketh use of that Language as much by a motive of Truth to conceal that Grace which he had received from God, as of Humility.

By a Motive of Truth, because effectually; because all the *Nostradamus*'s had some tincture of Prophecie, and his Son the Capucin acknowledgeth it himself.

By a Motive of Humility; because acknowledging himself to be a miserable sinner, and seeing that this gift of Prophecie was not ordinarily granted but unto Saints. He chuseth rather to attribute his Prophecies to his Genius, than otherways to procure a Fame and Authority to his predictions.

In confirmation of what we have said, *That he was often in that transport*, many years before his death he made the Stanza of the Century, in which is contained all the great Works of the Philosophers, and foretelleth, that a great Divine shall attain to the perfection of that great Work, which Divine is called, the *Divine Verbe*, turning into *French* the Word θεολογος, which signifieth Divine Word or Verb. Nevertheless he never wrought himself at that Work, but got his living Honourably by his practise of Physick, by which we may see, that he did write some things which himself understood not, unless they were such general ones, as might be read in the Heavens.

CHAP.   XII.

Elogies given to Nostradamus by several Authentical Authors.

If several Authors either by envy or ignorance have defamed our Author, others of no shall repute have taken his defence in hand.

D'*Aurat* one of the most excellent Poets of *France*, living at the same time as *Nostradamus*, made a few explications of his Prophecies, which as the report goes, did please the Readers. I am sorry I could not get them, it would have been some ease to me; for it is easier to add than to invent. The first Volume of the Lord *la Croix du Main*, maketh honourable mention of him, the same saith, that his Motto was *Felix Oviam prior Ætas*, Happy the first Age that was contented with their Flock, shewing by that, what esteem he had of frugality and sincerity of manners, and what aversion he had against the Vices of his Age, the unruliness of manners, and cousenage of men. *Ronsard* the Prince of the *French* Poets singeth his praises: The Lord *Boucher* in that great Volume, intitled the *Mistical Crown*, in favour of the future *Croisade*, doth vindicate our Author from *Calumny*, and expoundeth some of his Prophecies pretty happily.

I will not relate here what his Son *Cæsar Nostradamus* writeth modestly of him in his History of *Provence*, under *Lewis* the XII. *Henry* the II. and *Charles* the IX. his Evidence may be suspected, because of the Consanguinity.

One of the greatest Wits of this last Age, who desireth to be nameless, giveth him this Character.

First, That God Almighty hath chosen *Michael Nostradamus* among the common sort of Christians, to impart unto him the knowledge of many prodigious and extraordinary future things.

Secondly, He maintaineth, that after the Apostles and Canonical Prophets, he is the first of all in three things, in his certainty and infallibility, in the generality and in the quantity. As to the first, he doth not doubt but the Abbot *Joachim* ought to give him place; for though he hath foretold some things that have come to pass, he hath written a hundred others which are meer fopperies.

Thirdly, He maintaineth that the Emperour *Leo* in his prophetical Tables is far below him;

for he doth only aim at those things which regard the Eastern Empire, as *Theophrastus Paracelsus* hath done for the Western.

Concerning the quantity of things, he maintaineth, that none of the others can dispute it with him; for *Nostradamus* hath made above a thousand stanza's (if we had them all) each of which containeth two or three prophetical Truths, some of which regard the East, others the West, others some private Kingdoms and States others private and particular things, and all with Truth and certainty.

CHAP.   XIII.

What these Stanza's Prophecie of.

The Author in his Epistle to King *Henry* the II. saith, that he treateth of things which were to happen in many Cities and Towns of *Europe*, and of a part of *Asia* and *Africa*.

And to say Truth, I have found nothing in them concerning the East or West, *Jappan* or *China*.

He treateth chiefly of *France* as of his Native Kingdom, and of his own Countrey *Provence*, and that which is next to it, viz. *Piemont*.

He speaketh amply of the Popes, and of *Italy*, *Turky* and *England*: As for the Empire *Spain*, and *Suedeland*, he doth moderately speak of them. Concerning *Æthiopia* and *Africa* there is some nine or ten Stanza's.

In all those places he foretelleth many things, not only general for every State, but also particular and individual for several persons. He also foretelleth many supernatural prodigies in the Heavens, the Air, the Sea, and the Land.

He hath inserted among his Prophecies four Horoscopes, the first of the Grandfather of the Lord l'*Ainier* in the Province of *Anjou*; the second of one called *Urnel Vausile*; the third of one *Cosme du Jardin*; and the fourth of one, whom he nameth not, but describeth him by his stature.

CHAP.   XIV.

Since what time these Prophecies began.

It is certain that they began in *January* 1555. because he dedicated the first seven Centuries to his Son *Cæsar* the first day of *March* in the said year, and consequently they were made before that time, and we cannot allow less than two Months to an Author for the making of 700. Stanza's: Nevertheless for a greater manifestation of his prophetical Spirit, I have not found any of his Prophecies that did come to pass before the first of *March* 1555.

As for the Eight, Ninth and Ten Century, there is reason to believe, that the effect of them doth not begin before the *27 June 1558.* which is the date of his Liminary Epistle to *Henry* the II. Nevertheless he saith in the same Epistle, that in a writing by it self he will set down the exposition of his Prophecies, beginning the 14 of *March* 1557. and in the Epistle to *Nostradamus* his Son, he saith in general that he hath composed Books of Prophecies, each one containing one hundred Stanza's, without specifying whether he spoke of the seven that he dedicated to him, or of all the others.

As for my part, I believe he had made them all in the year 1555. but that he had not yet examined the three last Centuries, according to the Calculation of his Astronomical assertions, as he seemeth to indicate often in his Epistle to *Henry* II. and to say the truth, I have found some Stanza's, which were fulfilled before the year 1558. though very few.

As for the extent of his Prophecies, it is certain, that it is to the end of the World, as I shall make it appear in the explication of the 48, the 49, and 56. Stanza's of the first Century, and the 72, 73, and 94. of the tenth, and all according to the Holy Scripture.

All these things being premised, we shall proceed to the explication of the Prophecies, setting first the Authors Luminary Epistle to his Son.

THE
PREFACE
Mr.
Nostradamus
HIS
PROPHECIES,

TO
Michael

Ad Cæsarem Nostradamum Filium vita & Felicitas.

 Thy late coming, *Cæsar Nostradamus*, my son, hath caused me to bestow a great deal of time in continual and nocturnal watchings, that I might leave a Memorial of me after my death, to the common benefit of Mankind, concerning the things which the Divine Essence hath revealed to me by Astronomical Revolutions; and since it hath pleased the immortal God, that thou are come late into this World, and canst not say that thy years that are but few, but thy Months are incapable to receive into thy weak understanding, what I am forced to define of futurity, since it is not possible to leave thee in Writing, what might be obliterated by the injury of times, for the Hereditary word of *occult prædictions* shall be lockt up in my brest, considering also that the events are definitely uncertain, and that all is governed by the power of God, who inspired us not by a Bacchant fury or Lymphatick motion, but by Astronomical affections. *Soli numine Divino afflati præsagiunt & Spiritu Prophetico particularia*: Although I have often foretold long before what hath afterwards come to pass, and in particular Regions, acknowledging all to have been done by Divine Vertue and Inspiration, being willing to hold my peace by reason of the injury, not onely of the present time, but also of the future, and to put them in Writing, because the Kingdoms, Sects, and Regions shall be so Diametrically opposed, that if I should relate what shall happen hereafter, those of the present Reign, Sect, Religion and Faith, would find it so disagreeing with their fances, that they would condemn that which future Ages shall find and know to be true; considering also the saying of our Saviour, *Nolite Sanctum dare canibus ne conculcent pedibus & conversi discumpant vos*, which hath been the cause that I have withdrawn my tongue from the Vulgar, and my Pen from Paper. But afterwards I was willing for the common good to enlarge my self in dark and abstruse Sentences, declaring the future Events, chiefly the most urgent, and those which I foresaw (what ever humane mutation happened) would not offend the hearers, all under dark figures more then Prophetical, for although, *Abscondisti hæc a sapientibus & prudensibus*, i. e. *potentibus & Regibus enucleasti ea exiguis & tennibus*, and the Prophets by means onely of the immortal God and good Angels, have received the Spirit of Vaticination, by which they foresee things, and foretel future events; for nothing is perfect without him, whose power and goodness is so great to his Creatures, that though they are but men, nevertheless by the likeness of our good Genius to the Angels, this heat and Prophetical power draws near us, as it happens by the Beams of the Sun, which cast their influence both on Elementary and not Elementary bodies; as for us who are men, we cannot attain any thing by our natural knowledge, of the secrets of God our Creator. *Quia non est nostrum nosse tempora nec momenta*, &c.

 Besides, although there is, or may come some persons, to whom God Almighty will reveal by impressions made on his understanding some secrets of the future, according to the Judicial Astrology, as it hath happened in former times, that a certain power and voluntary faculty possessed them as a flame of fire, so that by his inspiration, they were able to judge of Divine and Humane things: for the Divine works that are absolutely necessary, God will end. But my son, I speak to thee too obscurely; but as for the secrets that are received by the subtle Spirit of fire, by which the understanding being moved, doth contemplate the highest Celestial Bodies, as being active and vigilant to the very pronunciation without fear, or any shameful loquacity: all which proceeded from the Divine Power of the Eternal God, from whom all goodness floweth. Now my son, although I have inserted the name of Prophet here, I will not attribute to my self so sublime a Title, for *qui*

Propheta dicitur hodie olim vocabatur videns, and Prophets are those properly (my Son) that see things remote from the natural knowledge of Men; but put the case, the Prophets by the means of the perfect light of Prophecy, may see as well Divine things as Humane, (which cannot be seeing the effects of future predictions) do extend a great way, for the secrets of God are incomprehensible, and the efficient power moveth afar off the natural knowledge, taking their beginning at the free will, cause those things to appear, which otherwise could not be known, neither by humane auguries, or any hidden knowledge or secret virtue under Heaven, but only by the means of some indivisible Eternal being, or Comitial and Herculean agitation, the causes come to be known by the Cœlestial motion. I say not therefore my Son, that you may not understand me well, because the knowledge of this matter cannot yet be imprinted in thy weak brain, but that future causes afar off are subject to the knowledge of humane Creatures, if (notwithstanding the Creature) things present and future were neither obscure nor hidden from the intellectual seal; but the perfect knowledge of the cause of things, cannot be acquired without the Divine Inspiration, seeing that all Prophetical Inspiration received, hath its original principle from God the Creator, next, from good Luck, and afterwards from Nature, therefore cases indifferently produced or not produced, the Prophecy partly happens where it hath been foretold, for the understanding being intellectually created, cannot see occult things, unless it be by the voice coming from the *Lymbo*, by the means of the thin flame, to which the knowledge of future causes is inclined; and also my Son I intreat thee not to bestow thy understanding on such fopperies, which drie up the Body and damn the Soul, bringing vexation to the Senses; chiefly abhor the vanity of the execrable Magick, forbidden by the Sacred Scriptures, and by the Canons of the Church; in the first of which is excepted Judicial Astrology, by which, and by the means of Divine Inspiration, with continual supputations, we have put in writting our Prophecies. And although this occult Philosophy was not forbidden, I could never be persuaded to meddle with it, although many Volums concerning that Art, which hath been concealed a great while, were presented to me; but fearing what might happen, after I had read them, I presented them to *Vulcan*, who while he was a devouring them, the flame mixing with the Air, made an unwonted light more bright then the usual flame, and as if it had been a Lightning, shining all the house over, as if it had been all in a flame; therefore that henceforth you might not be abused in the search of the perfect Transformation, as much selene as solar, and to seek in the waters uncorruptible mettal; I have burnt them all to ashes, but as to the judgement which cometh to be perfected by the help of the Cœlestial Judgement, I will manifest to you, that you may have knowledge of future things, rejecting the fantastical imaginations that should happen by the limiting the particularity of Places; by Divine inspiration, supernatural, according to the Cœlestial figures, the places, and a part of the time, by an occult, property, and by a Divine virtue, power and faculty, in the presence of which the three times are comprehended by Eternity, revolution being tyed to the cause that is past, present, and future, *Quia omnia sunt Nuda & aperta*, &c. therefore my Son, thou mayst notwithstanding thy tender brain comprehend things that shall happen hereafter, and may be foretold by cœlestial natural lights, and by the Spirit of Prophecy; not that I will attribute to my self the name of a Prophet, but as a mortal man, being no farther from Heaven by my sence, then I am from Earth by my Feet, *possum errare, falli, decipi*; I am the greatest Sinner of the World, subject to all humane afflictions, but being supprised sometimes in the week by a Prophetical humour, and by a long Calculation, pleasing my self in my Study, I have made Books of Prophecies, each one containing a hundred Astronomical Stanza's, which I have joyned obscurely, and are perpetual Vaticinations from this year to the year 3797. at which some perhaps will frown, seeing so large an extention of time, and that I treat of every thing under the Moon, if thou livest the natural Age of a Man, thou shalt see in thy Climat, and under the Heaven of thy Nativity the future things that have been foretold, although God only is he who knoweth the Eternity of his Light, proceeding from himself; and I say freely to those to whom his incomprehensible greatness hath by a long melancholick inspiration revealed, that by the means of this occult cause Divinely manifested, chiefly by two principal causes, which are comprehended in the understanding of him that is Inspired and Prophecyeth, one is that he cleareth the supernatural Light in the person that foretelleth by the Doctrine of the Planets, and Prophecyeth by inspired Revelation, which is a kind of participation of the Divine Eternity, by the means of which the Prophet judgeth of what the Divine Spirit hath given him by the means of God the Creatour, and by a natural instigation, *viz.* that what is predicted is true, and hath taken its original from above, and such light and small flame is of all efficacy and sublimity, no less then the natural light makes the Philosophers so secure, that by the means of the principles of the first cause, they have attained the greatest depth of the profoundest science; but that I may not wander too far (my Son) from the capacity of thy sense, as also, because I find that Learning would be at a great loss, and that before the universal Conflagration shall happen so many great Inundations, that there shall scarce be any Land, that shall not be covered with water, and this shall last so long, that except *Ænographies* and *Topographies* all shall perish, also before and after these Inundations in many Countreys there shall be such scarcety of rain, and such a deal of fire, and burning stones shall fall from Heaven, that nothing unconsumed shall be left, and this shall happen a little while before the great conflagration; for although the Planet *Mars* makes an end of his course, and is come to the end of his last Period, nevertheless he shall begin it again, but some shall be gathered in *Aquarius* for many years, others in *Cancer* also for many years, and now we are governed by the Moon, under the power of Almighty God; which Moon before she hath finished her Circuit, the Sun shall come, and then *Saturn*, for according to the Cœlestial Signs, the Reign of *Saturn* shall come again, so that all being Calculated, the World draws near to an Anaragonick revolution, and at this present that I write this before 177. years, three Months, eleven Days, through Pestilence, Famine, War, and for the most part Inundations, the World between this and that prefixed time, before and after for several times shall be so diminished, and the people shall be so few, that they shall not find enough to Till the Ground, so that they shall remain fallow as long as they have been Tilled; although we be in the seventh Millenary, which ends all and brings us near the eighth, where the Firmament of the eighth Sphere is, which in a *Latitudinary dimention* is the place where the great God shall make an end of the revolution, where the Cœlestial Bodies shall begin to move again. By that Superiour motion that maketh the Earth firm and stable, *non inclinabitur in seculum seculi*, unless his will be accomplished, and not otherwise; although by ambiguous opinions exceeding all natural reasons by *Mahometical* Dreams, also sometimes God the Creator by the Ministers of his Messengers of fire and flame shows to our external senses, and chiefly to our eyes, the causes of future Predictions, signifying the future Event, that he will manifest to him that Prophecyeth for the Prophecy that is made by the Internal Light, comes to judge of the thing, partly with and by the means of External Light, for although the party which seemeth to have by the eye of understanding, what it hath not by the Lœsion of its imaginative sense, there is no reason why what he foretelleth should come by Divine Inspiration, or by the means of an Angelical Spirit, inspired into the Prophetick person, annointing him with vatication, moving the fore part of his fancy, by divers nocturnal apparitions, so that by Astronomical administration, he Prophecyeth with a Divine certitude, joyned to the Holy prediction of the future, having no other regard then to the freedom of his mind. Come now my Son, and understand what I find by my revolutions, which are agreeing with the Divine Inspiration, *viz.* that the Swords draws near to us now, and the Plague and the War more horrid then hath been seen in the Life of three Men before, as also by Famine, which shall return often, for the Stars agree with the revolution, as also he said *visitabo in virgâ ferreà iniquitates eorum & in verberibus percutiam eos*, for the Mercies of God shall not be spread a while, my Son, before most of my Prophecies shall come to pass; then oftentimes shall happen sinister storms, (*Conteram ergo (said the Lord) & confringam & non miserebor*) and a thousand other accidents that shall happen by Waters and continual Rains, as I have more fully at large declared in my other Prophecies, written in *solutâ oratione*, limiting the places, times and prefixed terms, that men coming after, may see and know that those accidents are certainly come to pass, as we have marked in other places, speaking more clearly, although the explication be involved in obscurity, *sed quando submovenda erit ignorantia*, the case shall be made more clear; making an end here, my Son, accept of this Gift of thy Father *Michael Nostradamus*, hoping to expound to thee every Prophecy of these Stanza's, praying to the Immortal God, that he would grant thee a long Life in Felicity.

From Salon this 1. of March 1555.

THE TRUE PROPHECIES OR PROGNOSTICATIONS OF

Michael Nostradamus, Physician to *HENRY* II. *FRANCIS* II. And *CHARLES* IX. Kings of FRANCE, and one of the most excellent *Astronomers* that ever were.

CENTURY I.

I.

French.

Estant assis, de nuit secrette estude, Seul, reposé sur la selle d'airain, Flambe exigüe, sortant de solitude, Fait proferer qui n'est a croire vain. **English.**

Sitting by Night in my secret Study Alone, resting upon the Brazen Stool, A slight flame breaking forth out of that solitude, Makes me utter what is not in vain to believe.

ANNOTATION.

In this *Stanza, Nostradamus* expresseth those Humane dispositions which he made use of to be favoured of God, for the knowledge of future things, to the benefit of the Publick.

The first Disposition, was the tranquility of Mind, when he saith, *Sitting by night*; Because a troubled Mind cannot see clearly the Things it is busie about, no more than tossed Waters can distinctly represent the Objects that are opposed to them. Thus we read in the Scripture, that the Prophet *Elishah*, being transported with Zeal against *Joram* King of *Israel*; and nevertheless willing to consult God concerning the event of the Warr against the *Moabites*, called for a Minstrel, that the Harmony of the Instrument might quiet his Mind, as it did happen. *And it came to pass when the Minstrel played, that the Hand of the Lord came upon him,* 2 Kings *chap. 3. ver. 15.*

The Author in his *Dedicatory Epistle* to his Son *Cæsar*, calleth this Tranquility of Mind, *A long Melancholick Inspiration*; because the Melancholick Humour and Mind sequestreth a Man from the concerns of worldly things, and maketh him present to himself, so that his Understanding is not darkned by a multitude of *Species* that troubles its Operation.

The Second Disposition, was, the Silence of the Night; For Man who is compounded of Body and Soul, doth notably intricate himself in External things by the commerce of the Senses with the Objects; which obligeth him to withdraw himself from visible things, when he intends to apply himself to some serious Study. And as the silence of the Night causeth in the Universe a cessation of noises and clashings in Business, Visits and Colloquies, the Mind is then more at rest. Besides that, Night covering with her Darkness our Hemisphere, our Senses are less distracted, and our Internal Faculties are more united to serve the Operations of the Understanding.

Therefore the Author in his two *Liminary Epistles*, makes often mention of his continual Nocturnal Watchings, of his Sweet-smelling nocturnal Studies, and of his Nocturnal and Prophetical Calculations.

The Third Disposition, was Solitariness; that is, having no other Conversation then that of his Books, being retired in his Study, Alone. For it seemeth that God commonly maketh use of Solitariness when he doth impart himself to Men, and revealeth them his Oracles: And the *Sybils* were chosen to be Prophets, as much for their Solitariness, as for their Chastity.

The Author saith, that with those three Dispositions he raised himself to the knowledge of future things; which is signified by those words, *Resting upon the Brazen Stool. Servius* in his *Commentaries* upon *Virgil*, speaking of this Brazen Stool, saith two things of it. The First, that this Stool was a Table set upon a *Trevet*, called by the *Greeks* τρίπους, and by the Latines *Tripus*. The Second is, that the *Sybils*, or the Priests of the *Delphick* Temple of *Apollo*, got upon that Table, when they went about to pronounce their Oracles. *Pliny*, in his 33. Book, Chap. 3. saith, that they called those Tables *Cortinas*, and that some were made of Brass for the use aforesaid.

From the use of that Brazen *Trevet* is come the Proverb, *Ex tripode loqui*. When one speaketh like an Oracle. Thus the Author willing to express, that being in his Study in the solitariness of the Night, he raised himself to the Knowledge of Future things, to write them, and transmit them to Posterity; he saith, *He was sitting or resting upon the Brazen Stool*.

Thus raising himself, and taking his Pen in hand to write what he should learn, he saith in the Third Verse, that *A slight Flame*, or small Light did insinuate it self in his understanding, by whose splendor and brightness he saw future things.

The Author in his Epistle to *Cæsar* his Son, expoundeth always this Prophetical Light, by the comparison of a shining Flame, and calleth it rather a Flame than a pure Light, because this Light doth not only discover the Mysteries, but more-over it lightens in us a certain Heat and Prophetical Power, as himself terms it; as if we should say a Sacred Enthusiasm, even (saith he) as the Sun coming near us with his Light, not only darteth upon all Elementary things the brightness of his Beams, but withal infuseth in them a certain quickning heat, which causeth the Vegetables to grow, and upholdeth the Being of all other natural things; Even so (saith he) this good *Genius*, as the Ancients term it; or as we Christians say, that Divine Spirit of Prophecy coming near our understandings, not only importeth a Light to them, but more-over a certain heat and Prophetical Power, which strenghteneth them in the knowledge of the aforesaid things, and causeth them to breath out, as by a Sacred Enthusiasm some Prophetical Verses.

Which happeneth to them (saith the Author) coming out of Solitude, that is to say, when their Spirit stoopeth down, and by degrees cometh down from that sublime Region and high elevation, taking the Pen to write down the future time. Therefore he with his dispositions participating of that *slight flame, coming out of his solitude*, began to write and to utter, *What is not in vain to believe*.

The things that the Author hath written, shall not be unprofitable as we have proved already, and the time will come, when by the means of Divine Providence the Church shall receive the fruit thereof, at which we ought not to wonder, seeing that God saith of himself in *Isaiah Chap. 48. Ver. 17. I am the Lord thy God, which teacheth thee to profit*.

The Author foretelleth many wonders, of which we ought to be certain by the verification of those that are already past, seeing that it is the same Spirit that shewed them all.

The same Prophecies are also profitable, in that every where the Author condemneth Seditious and Rebellious persons, and Prophecieth the Churches Victory over her Enemies.

They are also profitable for particular Men that understand the meaning of them, for by it they may provide for their own business, according to the storm, undertaking nothing but upon sure grounds, following always the best party, and disposing themselves to patience, when the calamities are general, and involve together the guilty and guiltless. Therefore our Author saith well, *A slight flame breaking forth out of that solitude, makes me utter what is not in vain to believe.*

II.

***La Verge en main, mise au milieu des Branches, De l'Onde je moüille & le Limbe & le Pied, En peur j'escris fremissant par les manches; Splendeur Divine: le Divine prez s'assied.* English.**

With Rod in hand, set in the middle of the Branches, With water I wet the Limb and the Foot, In fear I writ, quaking in my sleeves, Divine splendor! the Divine sitteth by.

ANNOT.

Amongst the customs, the Ancients observed, before they pronounced their Oracles; one was to take a Tuffie Branch of Laurel, and with it dipt in water, to sprinkle the edges and Columns of the Table, that was upon the Brazen Trevet, by which ceremonies they procured credit to their Oracles.

The Author willing to let us know, that his Verses were not only a simple writing, but also Prophetical and full of Oracles, doth represent them to us by this Metaphore of the Ancients, when they did amuse the people with their ambiguous, and many times fallacious Oracles.

Being then sitting and quiet in his solitariness; coming out of that great devotion of mind, animated by the virtue of his good *Genius*, he putteth first *the Rod into his hand*, that is the Pen, and putteth it *in the middle of the Branches*, putting it between his Fingers. Secondly he dippeth this Rod *into Water*, dipping his Pen in his Ink; with this Pen dipt in Ink, *he wetteth the Limb and the Foot*, writing upon his paper from one end to the other, and from the top to the bottom.

Which we must understand by this word *Lymbe*, which is a Latin word, signifying the long and narrow pieces of stuffe, which women wore at the bottom of their Petticoats, therefore the Latins called them *Lymbos*, from the Latin Verbe *Lambo*, which in matter of cloths signifieth, to leek or sweep; and because those pieces of cloath were in the bottom of their Garments, the word hath been afterwards employed to signifie the brims of some things, so that the Lymbs of a sheet of paper, are the two margines, and the top and the bottom, as if it were the four ends of a Quadrangular Figure.

The third Verse sheweth the internal disposition of the Author, after he hath described his external one; that disposition was a Sacred quaking, which putting his heart into a palpitation, caused his hands and arms to shake, as if he had been taken with some fit of an Ague. This quaking is the disposition which the good *Genius* causeth in Prophets, that they may be humbled, and not be puffed up with pride, when they come near the Majesty of God, as we read in *Daniel*, St. *John*, and the *4th.* of *Esdras*. Therefore the Author saith:

In fear I write, quaking in my sleeves. And because the Divine Spirit after he hath cast down those, to whom he will impart himself, doth afterwards quiet them; the Author therefore addeth, that a *Divine splendor did sit by him.*

III.

***Quand la littiere du tourbillon versée, Et seront faces de leurs Manteaux couvers, La Republique par gens nouveaux vexée, Lors blancs & rouges jugeront a l'envers.* English.**

When the litter shall be overthrown by a gust of wind, And faces shall be covered with Cloaks, The Common-wealth shall be troubled with a new kind of men, Then white and red shall judge amiss.

ANNOT.

The two first Verses signifie that a great tempestuous wind was to happen, in which a litter should be overturned, and every one should muffle his face in his Cloak, for the fierceness of the wind.

And that presently after the Common-wealth should be troubled with new Sects and Opinions, which may be understood of the beginning of Reformation by *Luther* and *Calvin*, which was about that time.

The last Verse by the white and red signifieth here (as it doth thorough all the Book) the *French* and the *Spaniards*, because the *French* wear white Scarfes, and the *Spaniards* red ones: and consequently the troubles and jars that happened presently between those two Nations.

IV.

French.

Par l'Univers sera fait un Monarque, Qu'en paix & vie ne sera longuement, Lors se perdra la Piscature Barque, Sera regie en plus grand detriment. English.

In the World shall be one Monarch, Who shall be not long alive, nor in peace, Then shall be lost the Fishing Boat, And be governed with worse detriment.

ANNOT.

That Monarch was *Henry* the II. King of *France*, who did not Reign long, but was unfortunately slain, running at Tilt against the Earl of *Montgomery* (as we shall see hereafter) and almost during all his Reign had Wars with *Charles* the V. Emperour, and his Son *Philip* the II. King of *Spain*; the said Emperour in that time did sack *Rome*, took the Pope *Clement* the VII. prisoner, which is signified here; as also in several other places by the loss of the *Fishing Boat*; the Roman Church being often compared to a Ship or Boat.

V.

French.

Chassez seront sans faire long combat. Par le Païs seront plus fort grevez, Bourg & Cité auront plus grand debat, Carcas, Narbonne auront cœurs esprouvez. English.

They shall be driven away without great fighting, Those of the Countrey shall be more grieved, Town and City shall have a greater debate, *Carcas, Narbonne* shall have their hearts tryed.

ANNOT.

Herein is nothing mystical, the meaning is that some of the Protestant party intending to take or vex the Cities of *Carcassone* and *Narbonne* in *Languedoc*, shall be easily repulsed, and shall afterward fall upon the Countrey round about, which shall suffer for.

VI.

French.

L'œil de Ravenne sera destitué, Quand a ses pieds les aisles sailliront; Les deux de Bresse auront constitué, Turin, Verceil, que Gaulois fouleront. English.

The eye of *Ravenna* shall be forsaken, When the wings shall rise at his feet, The two of *Brescia* shall have constituted, *Turin, Verceil,* which the French shall tread upon.

ANNOT.

This is a confirmation of the fourth Stanza, concerning the loss of the Pope, *Clement* the VII. who is called here the eye of *Ravenna,* because he is Lord of that famous City, which was once an Exarchat of the Empire.

The wings that shall rise at, or against his feet, shall be those of the Eagle, which are the Arms of the Emperour.

The two of *Brescia* were the Governour and Proveditor of *Venice* in that place, who would at that time have endeavoured to seize upon *Turin* and *Verceil,* the two chiefest Towns of *Piemont,* but were prevented by the *French.*

VII.

French.

Tard arrivé, l'execution faite, Le Vent contrare, Lettres au chemin prinses, Les Conjurez quatorze d'une Secte, Par le Rousseau seront les entreprinses. English.

One coming too late, the execution shall be done, The Wind being contrary, and Letters intercepted by the way, The Conspirators fourteen of a Sect, By the Red-hair'd Man the undertaking shall be made.

ANNOT.

The sense of the whole is this, there shall be fourteen Conspirators of one mind, and their Ring-leader, a Red-haired man, who shall be put to death, because their Reprieve could not come timely enough, being hindered by cross winds, and Letters intercepted. I could find no particular things in History concerning this.

VIII.

French.

Combien de fois prinse Cité Solaire, Seras, changeant les Loix barbares & vaines, Ton mal s'approche, plus seras tributaire, Le grand Adrie recouvrira tes veines. English.

How often taken O solar City, Shalt thou be? changing the barbarian and vain Laws, Thy evil growth nigh, thou shalt be more tributary, The great *Adria* shall recover thy veins.

It is hard to judge what he meaneth by the Solar City that shall be so often taken.

As by *Adria*, it is certain he meaneth *Venice*, that was so called anciently, because of its scituation in the *Adriatick* Sea.

IX.

French.

De l'Orient viendra le cœur punique, Fascher Adrie, & les hoirs Romulides, Accompagné de la classe Libique, Trembler Melites, & proches Isles vuides. English.

From the East shall come the *African* heart, To vex *Adria*, and the Heirs of *Romulus*, Accompanied with the *Libian* fleet *Melites* shall tremble, and the Neighbouring Islands be empty.

ANNOT.

This was a clear and true Prognostication of that famous Invasion made upon *Maltha*, by the grand Signor *Solyman* the magnificent, in the year of our Lord 1565. and just ten years after the writing of this Prophecy, wherein that Island, and some of the Neighbouring ones were wholly depopulated by the *Turks*, to the terror of *Venice*, called here *Adria*, and of all the Islands of the *Adriatick* Sea. For the better understanding of this, the Reader must observe, that *Punicus* in Latin signifieth *Africa*, so that the *African* heart signifieth the help the *Turk* had from *Tunis, Tripoly*, and *Algier*, Cities seated in *Africa*, and under the Turkish Dominion; by which not only *Maltha* (which in Latin is *Melita*) but *Venice* and *Rome* were put into a great fright; the conclusion of this Siege was, that after six weeks time, and the loss of 26000. Men, the *Turks* were constrained shamefully to retire. *Vide the Turkish History.*

X.

French.

Sergens transmis dans la Cage de Fer, Ou les Enfans septains du Roy sont pris, Les vieux & Peres sortiront bas d'Enfer, Ains mourir voir de son fruit mort & cris. English.

Sergeants sent into an Iron Cage, Where the seven Children of the King are, The old Men and Fathers shall come out of Hell, And before they die shall see the death and cries of their fruit.

ANNOT.

This Prophecy signifieth, that some Sergeants or Executioners shall be sent into a Prison, to put to death seven Children, servants of a King that were Imprisoned there, and that some old Men their Fathers, shall see their death, and hear their cries.

XI.

Le mouvement de Sens, Cœur, Pieds, & Mains, Seront d'accord, Naples, Leon, Sicile, Glaives, Feux, Eaux, puis au Noble Romains, Plongez, Tuez, Morts, par cerveau debile. English.

The motion of the Sense, Heart, Feet and Hands, Shall agree, *Naples*, *Leon*, *Sicily*, Swords, Fires, Waters, then to the noble *Romans*, Dipt, Killed, Dead, by a *weak-brain*.

ANNOT.

The two first Verses signifie the concord that shall be among the *Spanish* dominions, expressed here by *Sense, Heart, Feet,* and *Hands*. After which, the *Romans* or those of *Rome*, shall be evilly intreated, being *drowned, killed, and put to death by a weak brain*. I guess this to have come to pass, when the Emperour *Charles* the V. his Army sacked *Rome*, under the command of the Duke of *Bourbon*, who was killed at the Assault; and of the Prince of *Orange*, who permitted licentiousness to his Souldiers, and suffered them to commit more violence, than ever the *Goths* or *Vandales* did, and therefore is called here *weak brain*. This Prince of *Orange* was of the House of *Chalon*, after which came that of *Nassau*.

XII.

French.

Dans peu ira fauce brute fragile, De bas en haut eslevé promptement, Puis en estant desloyal & labile, Qui de Verone aura gouvernment. English.

Within a little while a false frail brute shall go, From low to high, being quickly raised, By reason that he shall have the Government of *Verona*, Shall be unfaithful and slippery.

ANNOT.

This foretelleth of a wicked person, who in a short time shall be from a low degree exalted to a high one, by reason that those that have the Government of *Verona*, shall be unfaithful and slippery. That person seemeth to be some Pope, who from a low degree shall be exalted to that dignity, by the unfaithfulness and slipperiness of the *Venetians*, who are now Lords of the City *Verona* in *Italy*.

XIII.

French.

Les exiles, par ire, haine intestine, Feront au Roy grand conjuration, Secret mettront ennemis par la mine, Et les vieux siens, contre eux sedition. English.

The banished, by choler, and intestine hatred Shall make against the King a great conspiracy, They shall put secret enemies in the mine, And the old his own against them sedition.

Although this Prophecie seemeth to be indefinitely spoken, because in every Countrey or Kingdom where there is banished people, they most commonly plot against their King and Countrey; nevertheless I find two remarkable Histories to make this good, one in *France*, and the other in *England*. That of *France* is thus.

The Cardinal of *Lorrain*, and the Duke of *Guise* his Brother, being in great favour with *Henry* II. the Queen Mother promoted them in the beginning of the Reign of *Francis* II. his successor, so that the Cardinal was made Lord high Treasurer, and the Duke General of the Armies, to the prejudice of the Constable of *Montmorency*. Those two favourites, fearing the persecution that is raised by envy, did remove all the great ones from the Court, whether they were commanded to do so, or whether they had any other pretences.

The Princes of *Condé*, and of *la Roche sur yon*, were sent into *Flanders* to *Philip* II. *Condé*, to confirm the alliance between the two Crowns, and *la Roche sur yon* to carry the Order of *France*.

Diana of *Poitiers* Dutchess of *Valentenois*, was banished from Court, and compelled to surrender to the Queen all the Jewels she had extorted from the King, besides the Castle of *Chenonceaux*, which the Queen took for her self.

The Marshal St. *Andrew* was likewise banished from the Court. The King of *Navarre* was in *Bearn*.

The Constable took also his leave, and surrendred to the King the Seal of his Office. On the other side, the Protestants began to stir notably, having on their part many Princes, as that of *Condé*, of *Porcien, Gaspard*, of *Coligny*, Admiral of *France*, d'*Andelot*, and the Cardinal of *Chastillon* his brothers, *Magdalene* of *Mailly*, their Sister, Lady of *Roye*, the King of *Navarre*. All these discontented persons, and the Protestants made a great conspiracy under pretence of Religion, and of freeing the King from the tyranny of the *Guisians*.

They did by *Choler*, the Protestants because they had been so ill used, in the time of *Francis* I. and *Henry* II. and lately by the *Guisians*. And the discontented, for to pull down their power, it was also by an *intestine hatred*, because the Constable could not brook to be dispossessed of his Office of great Master, which was given to the Duke of *Guise*; and the others to see themselves from the management of Affairs, and the Protestants by the spirit of a contrary Religion.

Their *conspiracy* tended to expel the *Guisians*, and to seise upon the Queen, the King, and his Brothers.

To compass their end, they secretly sent some trusty persons of their own, who nevertheless feigned to be their Enemies; insomuch that the King of *Navarre* sent them word, that he would be always of their party, though apparently he took the Courts part.

But *the Old his own*, saith the fourth Verse, that is to say, the Kings old friends shall raise *Sedition* against them, which happened in the year 1650. when the *Guisians* having discovered the conspiracy that was made at *Nantes*, the 1. of *February* 1560. whose chief Ring-leader was the Lord *La Renaudie*; they presently got the King out of *Blois*, and carryed him to *Amboise*, caused the Town to be fortified, and set strong Guards upon all the passages.

The day appointed for the execution of the conspiracy at *Blois*, was the 10th of *March*: But the King being got to *Amboise*, the Conspirators went thither in such great numbers, and under such specious pretences, that had they not been betrayed, no body would have suspected them. All the Suburbs and the Countrey Towns thereabouts were full of them. The Prince of *Condé*, the Admiral, d'*Andelot*, and his Brother the Cardinal, were all there.

Then the *Guisians* began to fall to work, and to set upon the Conspirators on all sides.

Abundance were taken, some in the City, some in the Suburbs, others in the Countrey round about.

Most of these were slain before they could come to Town, or be carried to Prison. And their process was so short that they were hanged in their Boots and Spurs.

The Scouts did every where kill those they met withall. To conclude, it proved a very Bloody Tragedy.

La Renaudie the Chief of the Conspirators, was met with by the Lord *Pardaillan* a *Gascon*. At the first approach *La Renaudie* killed him; but himself was killed by *Pardeillan*'s Servant, and his dead body brought and hanged at *Amboise.*

The second History is concerning *England*, which palpably makes this Prophecie good, if we make reflection upon what hath happened in this last Century of years, concerning banished people that have conspired against their King and Countrey, as we may see through all the Life of Queen *Elizabeth*, and by that famous Plot of the Gun-powder-Treason in King *James*'s time, which must be understood here by the *Mine*.

XIV.

French.

De gens esclave, chansons, chants, & requestes, Captifs par Princes, & Seigneurs aux prisons, A l'advenir par Idiots sans testes, Seront receus par divins oraisons. **English.**

From slavish people, Songs, Tunes and requests, Being kept Prisoners by Princes and Lords, For the future by headless Idiots, Shall be admitted by divine prayers.

ANNOT.

This is a prognostication of the beginning and increase of the Protestants in *France*, who began to sing their Psalms in *French*, and from time to time presented their request for tolleration. The Author being a zealous Papist calleth them *Idiots*, and that notwithstanding the persecution that should be against them, being put in Prison by *Princes* and *Lords*, they should at last be admitted by reason of their often praying to God.

XV.

French.

Mars nous menace par la force bellique, Septante fois fera le sang respandre, Auge & ruine de l'Ecclesiastique, Et par ceux qui d'eux rien ne voudront entendre. **English.**

Mars threatneth us of a Warlike force, Seventy times he shall cause blood to be shed, The flourishing and ruine of the Clergy, And by those that will hear nothing from them.

ANNOT.

The Author having premonished us in his Preface, that God having imparted to him the knowledge of many future things, he was curious to know if his Divine Majesty had written the same thing in the Cœlestial Book, as concerning the States, Empires, Monarchies, Provinces and Cities, and he found that it was even so as it had been revealed to him, so that the Book of Heaven, written with Gods own hand, in so many shining Characters, might serve to studious men for a light and a Torch to discover very near the common estate of the world.

He then having learned from God in his solitariness, the prosperities and afflictions of the Clergy, from the beginning of the year 1555. to the end of the world; he found that there was an agreement between his prophetical Knowledge, and the motion of the Heavenly Bodies; because having made the Systeme of the years after 1550. he found that *Mars* was in a dangerous Aspect to the Ecclesiastical estate, and found that this Planet by its position did presage a long, bloody and horrid Catastrophe in the world, by which the Ecclesiastical estate should suffer much.

To make good this prediction, the Author doth assure us in his Preface, that he had considered the disposition of this Planet, not only in the year 1555. but also in the years following, and joyning together all that he had found in his Ephemerides, he found that this Planet did on all sides presage most bloody actions. Although, saith he, the Planet of *Mars* maketh an end of its course, and is come to its last Period: nevertheless it will begin it again, but some gathered in *Aquarius* for many years, and others by long and continual years.

As if he would say that his prediction ought not to be rejected; because *Mars* ended his course, and cometh to its late period; for it would take again its Exaltation and Dominion with a worse conjunction, having his Astronomical dignities, with the Conjunction of other Planets in the Sign of *Aquarius* during many years, and in the Sign of *Cancer* for many years more.

Which maketh the Author conclude, that within the space of 177. years, three months and eleven dayes, the world shall be afflicted with Wars, Plagues, Famines and Innundations, that scarce any body shall be left to Till the Ground. By which prediction we learn that those evils began in the year 1555. the first of *March*, which is the date of the Authors Book, and shall last till the second of *June* 1732. abating the ten days of the Gregorian Calender.

During which time, he saith, that *Mars* threatneth us with bloody Wars that shall be reiterated 70 times.

This word seventy doth not signifie a determinate number, but a great number indeterminated according to the Phrase of the Scripture, which by the number of seven signifieth many times, and by that of seventy incomparably many times more. Thus the Scripture saith, that the just man falleth seven times in one day, that is many times, and our Saviour saith to St. *Peter*, that we ought to forgive our Enemies, not only seven times, but seventy times seven; that is innumerable times.

We have found the truth of this Prophecie to this very day. 1. In *France*, by the Wars between *Henry* II. and *Charles* V. and *Philip* II. 2. By the Wars of *Charles* IX. against the Protestants, wherein so much blood was spilt on both sides. 3. By *Henry* III. against the same Protestants, and factions of his time, and then against the *Parisians* and others of their league. 4. Between *Henry* IV. and those of the league in his revolted Kingdom. 5. By the Wars of *Lewis* XIII. against the Protestants, against the Duke of *Savoy*, in the *Valteline*, in *Piemont*, in *Lorrain*, in *Alsatia*, in *Catalonia*, in *Franche-Conty*, in *Flanders*, and for the defence of *Portugal*, which have been continued by his successor *Lewis* XIV. now Reigning.

Italy did also find the truth of this prophecie, by the Wars between *Paul* IV. and the *Spaniard*, between *Pius* V. and the *Turks*, between *Clement* VIII. and the Duke of *Ferrara*, between the Emperour and the Duke of *Mantua*, between *Urban* VIII. and the Duke of *Parma*, between the *Venetians* and the *Florentines*, by the revolt of the Kingdom of *Naples*, under the conduct of the Duke of *Guise*.

England hath had its share of it under Queen *Elizabeth*, by the revolt of *Yorkshire*, and some other Provinces, by the *Spanish* fleet of 88.

By the death of Queen *Mary*, by the revolt of the Kingdom against *Charles* I. And by the horrid perfidiousness of *Cromwel*.

Germany hath made it good by the War against the *Turks*, the Protestants and the *Swedes*.

Poland hath done the same against the *Russians*, *Tartars*, *Turks*, *Cassaks* and *Swedes*.

And *Venice* against the *Turk*, for the Islands of *Cyprus* and *Candia*, the Battle of *Lepanto*, and the Wars of *Dalmatia*.

This *Mars* besides presageth two contrary things, one is the *Auge* or Exaltation, the other the *ruine of the Clergy*: where it is to be observed, the *Auge* in tearms of Astrology signifieth mounting or ascending, and cometh from the Latin *verbe augere*, which signifieth to augment or increase. This augmentation and ruine of the *Clergy* is made good by the several changes that have been in the Ecclesiastical estate, in *France*, *England*, Low-Countreys, *Denmark*, *Swede*, *Poland*, *Hungary*,

Valachia, Transylvania, Moldavia, Dalmatia, Geneva, Switzerland, &c.

The fourth Verse saith. By those that will hear nothing from them: that is, by the Protestants that will hear nothing from the *Roman* Catholicks.

XVI.

French.

Faux a l'Estang, joint vers la Sagittaire, En son haut Auge de l'Exaltation, Peste, Famine, mort de main Militaire, Le Siecle approcher de renovation. **English.**

The Sith to the Fish-pond, joyned to *Sagittarius*, In the highest *Auge* of the Exaltation, Plague, Famine, Death by a Military hand, The age groweth near to its renovation.

ANNOT.

The sense of all this is, that when a Meadow that was a *Fish-pond* before, shall be Mowed, the Sign of *Sagittarius* being in its *Auge* or ascendant, then shall *Plague, Famine,* and *War* Reign, and that age (which a Century of years shall be near its end and renovation *viz.* of another Century.)

XVII.

French.

Par quarante ans l'Iris n'apparoistra, Par quarante ans tous les jours sera veu, La Terre aride en siccité croistra, Et grand deluge quand sera apparceu. **English.**

During fourty years the Rainbow shall not appear, During fourty years it shall be seen every day. The parched Earth shall wax dryer and dryer, And great Flouds shall be when it shall appear.

ANNOT.

The Interpretation of this is easie, and signifieth nothing else but that during 40. years the *Rainbow* shall not be seen, and during that time there shall be an exceeding great drought upon the Earth, and that for 40. years after the *Rainbow* shall be seen every day, which shall cause great flouds and innundations.

XVIII.

French.

Par la discorde, negligence Gauloise, Sera passage a Mahomet ouvert, De sang trempé la Terre & Mer Senoise, Le Port Phocen de Voiles & Nefs couvert. **English.**

Through the discord and negligence of the *French*, A passage shall be opened to *Mahomet*, The Land and Sea of *Sienna* shall be bloody, The *Phocen* Haven shall be covered with Sails and Ships.

ANNOT.

In the year 1559. *Sultan Solyman* called *Leonclavius*, according to the alliance made between him and *Francis* I. King of *France*, was desired by *Henry* II. his Son to send him some succours: Whereupon he sent some of his Gallies to scour the *Tyrrhenean* Sea (otherwise the Sea of *Tuscany*) to give a diversion to the *Spanish* forces in *Italy*, while the King by the means of the Marshal of *Brissac*, should continue his Conquests in the *Piemont* and *Milanese*.

All what this *Turkish* Fleet did, was to plunder and over-run the Island of *Elbe*, and to attempt *Piombino* without effect; and because these places were seated upon the Sea of *Sienna*, called in Latin *Mare Tirrhenum*, the Author saith that both the Land and Sea of *Sienna* shall be died with Blood, and at that time the Haven of *Marseilles*, which was called by the Ancients, Port-*Phocen* was full of Sales and Ships, as well to go into the Island of *Corse*, as for other designs. This History makes good that *Stanza* which saith, that through the *discord* and *negligence* of the *French*, a passage shall be opened to *Mahomet*, wherein it is to be observed that the Marshal of *Brissac* doing wonders for the King in *Piemont*, his virtue got him abundance of enviers and enemies in the Kings Councel, which was the cause of a great discord among them, by the diversity of opinions, and this diversity was the cause of a prodigious negligence in sending to him relief, as *Turpin* witnesseth in his History of *Naples*, and *Paradin* in the continuation of his History.

By this discord and negligence, *a passage was opened to Mahomet*, his Fleet going freely upon the *Mediterranean* Sea near the Coasts of *France*. And the reason of it was, because this discord and negligence did compel *Henry* the II. to ask succours of *Solyman*, that the *Spaniard* might be compelled to divide his Forces in sending some to the Sea-Towns, and so should not be so strong in *Piemont*; and thus must be understood the *French discord and negligence*, in the first and second Verse. As for the many Sails and Ships that were then in the Haven of *Marseilles*, to go into the Island of *Corsica*, the following Stanza's are full of predictions concerning it.

XIX.

French.

Lors que Serpens viendront circuir l'Air, Le sang Troien versé par les Espagnes, Par eux: grand nombre en sera fait tare, Chef fuit, caché aux Marets dans les saignes. English.

When Serpents shall come to encompass the Are, The *Trojan* blood shall be vexed by *Spain*, By them, a great number shall perish, Chief runneth away, and is hid in the rushes of the Marishes.

ANNOT.

By the *Serpents*, the Author being a Roman Catholick, meaneth the Protestants, who then began to appear numerous in the Reigns of *Francis* the I. and *Henry* the II. in whose time the Admiral *Coligny* was the chief among them, for his great feats in War.

These Serpents or Protestants begun to encompass the *Are*, that is to say, the Church and the Altar, which in Latin is called *Ara*.

And that happened when *the Trojan-blood was vexed by Spain*. By the *Trojan-blood*, the Author meaneth the *French* blood, according to the vulgar opinion, that the *French* are descended from the *Trojans*. The *French* were then vexed by the *Spaniards*, at the Battle of St. *Laurence*, and at the taking of St. *Quentin*, and other places in the Year 1557.

The third Verse saith *by them*, that is, by the Protestants *a great number shall perish*, that is to say, a great number of *French*. Among whom the Admiral of *Chatillon* having done what was possible to be done at the defence of St. *Quentin*, and seeing the Town taken, run away with three more, and hid himself among the Rushes that are in the Boggs about the Town, where he was found, and carried Prisoner to the Duke of *Savoy*, who received him very honorably, according to his valour and deserts.

Observe that the word *Saignes* here signifieth in old *Provencal* a *Marish*.

XX.

French.

Tours, Orleans, Blois, Angers, Renes & Nantes, Cités vexées par soudain changement, Par Langues estranges seront tendues Tentes, Fleuves, Darts, Rennes, Terre & Mer tremblement. English.

Tours, Orleans, Blois, Angers, Renes, and *Nantes,* Cities vexed by a sudden change, By strange Languages Tents shall be set up, Rivers, Darts, *Rennes,* Land, and Sea shall quake.

ANNOT.

All the Cities mentioned in the first Verse are seated by the River of *Loire,* and are threatned here of a sudden change, and that some strangers shall set up their Tents against them, and chiefly at *Rennes,* there shall be an Earth-quake felt both by Sea and Land.

XXI.

French.

Profonde argile blanche nourrit rocher, Qui d'un abysme istra l'acticineuse, En vain troublez ne l'oseront toucher, Ignorant estre au fond terre argileuse. English.

A deep white clay feedeth a Rock, Which clay shall break out of the deep like milk, In vain people shall be troubled not daring to touch it, Being ignorant that in the bottom there is a milky clay.

ANNOT.

It is a Rock in the middle of the Sea, whose Roots are fed by a white clay, which is at the foot of this Rock, in the bottom of the Sea, and therefore called deep.

This clay being softned, and dissolved by the Sea-water, shall appear upon the superficies of it like milk about the Rock. Those that shall see this wonder, *being ignorant that in the bottom there is a milky clay*, shall in vain be troubled at it, and shall not dare to touch it.

XXII.

French.

Ce qui vivra & n'aura aucun sens, Viendra le Fer a mort son artifice, Autun, Chalons, Langres & les deux Sens, La Guerre & la Glasse fera grand malefice. English.

That which shall live, and shall have no sence, The Lion shall destroy the art of it, *Autun, Chalons, Langres*, and both *Sens*, The War and the Ice shall do great harm.

ANNOT.

This is a great Riddle, which was never found out till now; and had I not been born in the Countrey where the History did happen, it might have been unknown to this day, and buried in oblivion.

The History of a λιθοπαίδιον or petrified child. In the year of the Lord 1613. which was that of my Birth. There was in the Town of *Sens* a Taylors Wife named *Columba Chatry*, who presently after her marriage conceived, and for the space of 28. years persuaded her self to be with Child, had all the signs of it in the beginning of her impregnation, and having gone her compleat time, she begun to feel the pains of a woman in Labour, with great gripings in the Guts. The Urine was suppressed for a while, but at last it broke out with a strong current. This quantity of water not coming so much out of the Bladder as was supposed, as from the womb, by the breaking of the Membrane, called *Amnion*, seeing that with those serous excrements, she avoided some conjealed blood. After that her breast begun to fall, and the Child had little or no motion, her pains being less than they were, which caused no small admiration to the Midwifes, who expected a safe deliverance. For the space of three years after, this woman kept her Bed, and was brought to Deaths door, complaining of gripings and a hard swelling, which she desired all the Physitians and Chyrurgeons to feel, having lost all appetite, but that little which she recovered by the use of sharp things, as Verjuice, Lemmons, &c. she was wont to say to her Neighbours, that she bare a Child that should be the cause of her death. After she was dead, her Husband got two experienced

Chyrurgeons to open her body, who having opened the belly, and taken away the *Peritonæum*, saw the Womb of several colours, as the flesh that is about the head and neck of a Turky-cock, but as it were of a Horny substance. They begun to make an incision in it with a Rasour, but finding it resisted the edge, they begun to use their Incision knives with all their strength; at last one of them by chance hit the Scull, and after that some Ribs, and then the Shoulder bone, by which, knowing that there was bones contained in that lump, with greater strength they made a deeper incision, and having parted the edges of the womb, saw in the bottom of the womb a Child, wrapped in the membrane, called *Allantoides*; at which the Chyrugeons wondering, sent for the Physitians to have their opinion in a thing that is almost beyond belief; in the mean time people flocking thither from all parts, and troubling the Chyrurgeons in their operation; they thought good to take away with their Instruments all that Lump, as a Tree from its Roots, and to carry it home, that they might with more time and leasure examine the whole Anatomy of it. In that hasty pulling out of the Child, they had no time to observe what Chorion it had, what umbilical Vessels, and what connexion there was of the Allantoides with the Womb, and with the Child, chiefly about the right hip, the Buttocks, and the Back-bone being all grown solid together.

The scituation of the Child was almost *Spherical*, the face leaning upon the breast, and the Nostrils upon the Knees; the bones of the Head were but thin, but very hard, and shining like Horn; the skin of the Head was hairy in many places; the head did hang so much upon the left arm, that the Ear, and part of the skull had given way to the Shoulder-bone; the Elbow was bent towards the Shoulder stretching only his hand, which was so close shut, and the fingers sticking so fast to the Palm of it, that although they did appear distinct one from another, nevertheless it was all but one and the same stone; the right arm did stretch its hand towards the Navel, which unadvisedly was broken by the wrist, and left in the Mothers Belly; the left Thigh, Knee and Leg were on the top of the right ones, with which they were so entangled, that the left heel, and the sole of the foot were planted upon the right foot, who seemed to have given place to them, and were almost inseparably joyned; for all such hardness of the matter, the body was not less than that of other Children of the same age, but kept a perfect fulness and proportion all the internal parts, as the Brains, the Heart, the Liver, had their natural shape, and were not altogether so hard as the external parts, so that to this very day this little body defieth all kind of corruption.

This Child was kept in my time by one Mr. *Michel* a Chirurgion of *Sens*, who kindly shewed it to all the strangers that came far and near to see it. The Fame of it was so great, that Doctor *Mayerne* coming from *Switzerland* to *England*, took his way through *Sens* to see it, and would have perswaded King *Charles* I. to buy it, as himself told me; since that I hear it was fallen into the hands of the *Venetians*. In this History there is two observable wonders. One, that the Child dying in the Womb, did not corrupt, and so cause the death of its Mother. The other, by what vertue or power of the body this child was petrified, seeing that the Womb is a hot and moist place, and therefore more subject to putrifaction. Those that will satisfie themselves with the reasons of it, and the truth of the History, may read *Johannes Alibosius* Physician of *Sens*, who was an eye witness of it, and *Sennertus* in his book of Sympt. *quam feminis in utero accidant.*

Now this accident being so rare, and without parallel, our Author thought fit to foretel it, and to cover it in abscure tearms, that he might not appear ridiculous in so admirable an event. When therefore he saith, *That which shall live and shall have no Sense*, he meaneth this λιθοπαίδιον or child petrified, which had a Life while it was in the Mothers belly, being tied to it by the several Vessels and connexions, known to Anatomists, and yet was senseless in that it was petrified. When in the second verse he saith, *The Iron shall destroy the art of it*, he meaneth that it should be spoiled by the rasour, in the two last verses he saith, that the Towns of *Autun, Chalons, Langres,* and *Sens* the Town in which this did happen should that same year suffer much damage by Hail and Ice, which did come to pass, as many persons may justify in that Countrey, that are alive to this day.

XXIII.

French.

Au mois troisiesme se levant le Soleil, Sanglier, Leopard, aux champs Mars pour combatre, Leopard lassé au Ciel esttend son œil, Un Aigle autour du Soleil voit sesbatre. **English.**

In the third month at the rising of the Sun, The Boar and Leopard in *Marth* camp to fight; The Leopard weary, lift his eyes to Haven, And seeth an Eagle playing about the Sun.

ANNOT.

This signifieth a particular accident, *viz.* that in the third Month, which is that of *March*, at the rising of the *Sun*, the *Boar* and the *Leopard*, that is, two persons of quality hidden under these names, shall go into the fields to fight a Duel. The *Leopard* one of them being weary, shall lift up his eyes to Heaven, calling upon God, and thereupon shall see an *Eagle* playing about the *Sun*, that is, shall get the Victory, of which the *Eagle* is the Emblem.

XXIV.

French.

A Cité nevue pensif pour condamner, Loisel de proie au ciel se vient offrir, Apres Victoire a Captifs pardonner Cremone & Mantoue grands maux auront souffert. **English.**

In the new City for to condemn a Prisoner, The Bird of pray shall offer himself to Heaven, After the Victory, the Prisoners shall be forgiven, After *Cremona* and *Mantua* have suffered many troubles.

ANNOT.

This name of new City is appropriated to several ones in every Countrey. The *French* have many *Villeneufuas*, the Germans many *Newstads*, the *Italians* and *Spaniards* many *Villanovas*, so that it is hard to guess which of them the Author meaneth. The missing of this dore makes the rest of the Prophecie so obscure, that I had rather leave it to the liberty of the Reader, than to pretend a true explication of it. I shall only say, that *Cremona* and *Mantua* are two famous Towns in *Italy*, which are here threatned.

XXV.

French.

Perdu, trouvé, caché de si long siecle Sera Pasteur demy-Dieu honoré, Ains que la Lune acheve son grand Siecle, Par autre vents sera deshonoré. **English.**

Lost, found again, hidden so great a while, A Pastor as Deme-God shall be honoured; But before the Moon endeth her great Age, By other winds he shall be dishonoured.

ANNOT.

The Prophecie is concerning the body of a famous Churchman, which was lost, and shall be found again, and worshiped as a *Demy-God*, but before the *Moon* hath run her great age, which is of 13 Months, it shall be vilified and dishonoured.

XXVI.

French.

Le grand du Foudre tombe d'heure diurne, Mal & predit par Porteur populaire, Suivant presage tombe d'heure nocturne, Conflit Rheims, Londres, Etrusque Pestifere. English.

The great Man falleth by the Lightning in the day time, An evil foretold by a common Porter; According to this foretelling another falleth in the night, A fight at *Rhemes*, and the Plague at *London* and *Tuscany.*

ANNOT.

This is concerning some great man, who being premonished by a common Carrier not to travel upon a certain day, did slight the advice, and was strucken by Lightning in the day time, and another in the night; at the same time there was a fight at *Rhemes*, and the Plague at *London* and in *Tuscany*, which in Latin is called *Etruria.*

XXVII.

French.

Des soubs le Chesne Guyen du Ciel frappé, Non loin de la est caché le Thresor, Qui par long Siecles avoit esté grappé, Trouvé mourra, l'œil crevé de ressor. English.

Under the Oak *Guyen* strucken from Heaven, Not far from it is the Treasure hidden, Which hath been many Ages a gathering; Being found he shall die, the eye put out by a spring.

ANNOT.

The sense of it is, that some body (who is named here *Guyen*) being under an Oak shall be strucken with the lightning, and that near that place there is a great Treasure, that hath been many years a gathering, and that he who shall find it shall die, being shot in the eye with a Fire-lock.

XXVIII.

French.

La Tour de Bouk craindra fuste Barbare, Un temps, long temps apres Barque Hesperique, Bestial, gens meubles tous deux feront grand tare, Taurus & Libra, quelle mortelle pique? English.

The Tower of *Bouk* shall be in fear of a Barbarian Fleet, For a while, and long after afraid of

Spanish shipping, Flocks, peoples, goods both shall receive great damage, *Taurus* and *Libra*, O what a deadly feud.

ANNOT.

      The Tower of *Bouk* is a strong place seated by the *Rhosne*, where it entereth into the Mediterranean Sea; it is said here that it shall be in fear of a Barbarian Fleet, and after that of a *Spanish* one, and that both the *Spaniard* and the *French* shall have great losses in Cattle, People and Goods, and this shall happen when the Sun shall be in the Signs of *Taurus* and *Libra*.

XXIX.

French.

Quand le Poisson, Terrestre & Aquatique, Par forte vague an gravier sera mis, Sa forme estrange suave & horrifique, Par Mer aux murs bien tost les Enemies. English.

When the Fish that is both Terrestrial and Aquatick, By a strong Wave shall be cast upon the Sand, With his strange fearful sweet horrid form, Soon after the enemies will come near to the Walls by Sea.

ANNOT.

      This signifieth no more but that after, a Fish, Terrestrial and Aquatick, that is which, liveth in Land and Water, called by the Greeks αμφίβιον, shall be cast upon the Sand by a storm, then a little while after, that Town which lieth near to that place where the Fish was cast, shall be Besieged by her Enemies, who shall come by Sea.

XXX.

French.

La Nef estrange par le tourment Marin, Abordera pres le Port incognu, Nonobstant signs du rameau palmerin, Apres mort, pille, bon advis tard venu. English.

The Outlandish Ship by a Sea storm, Shall come near the unknown Haven, Notwitstanding the signs given to it with Bows, It shall die, be plundered, a good advice come too late.

ANNOT.

      It is a Forrein Ship which by a storm shall be driven to an unknown Harbour, and notwithstanding the signs that shall be made to it with Branches, by those that are upon the Land to beware of the entrance of the Harbour, it shall be cast away, and plundered; thus a good advice shall come too late.

XXXI.

French.

Tant d'ans les guerres, en Gaule dureront, Outre la course du Castulon Monarque, Victoire incerte trois grands couroneront, Aigle, Coq, Lune, Lion Soleil en marque. English.

So many years the Wars shall last in *France*, Beyond the course of the *Castulon* Monarque, An uncertain Victory three great ones shall Crown, The Eagle, the Cock, the Moon, the Lion having the Sun in its mark.

ANNOT.

That is, the Wars shall last so long in *France* after the death of one King of *Spain*, till three great ones shall challenge an uncertain Victory, these three great ones are the Emperour designed by the Aigle, the King of *France* by the Cock, and the *Turk* by the Moon, and this shall happen when the Sun is in the sign of the Lion. I suppose that came to pass in the time of *Charles* the V. *Henry* the II. and *Soliman*. For the *Turk* had no great odds upon the Emperour, nor he upon the King of *France*.

XXXII.

French.

La grand Empire sera tost translaté, En lieu petit qui bien tost viendra croistre, Lieu bien infime d'exigue Comté, Ou au milieu viendra poser son Scepter. English.

The great Empire shall soon be translated, Into a little place which shall soon grow afterwards. An inferiour place of a small County, In the middle of which he shall come to lay down his Scepter.

ANNOT.

This is concerning the same *Charles* the V. Emperour, who about three years before his death, being weary of the World, resigned his Dominions of *Spain* and of the *Low-Countries*, to his Son *Philip* the II. and his Empire to his Brother *Ferdinand*, and retired himself into a Monastery of *Castile*, called l'*Escurial*, which after his death, was much enlarged and beautified by his Son *Philip*: and that is the meaning of our Author when he saith:
Into a little place which shall soon grow afterwards, An inferiour place of a small County,

For this *Escurial* being seated in a Desert place of a County of *Spain*, called *Castilia*, which the *Spanish* vanity calleth a Kingdom, (whose Use, Fruit, or Revenues, the said *Charles* only reserved for his maintenance) is now by the *Spaniards* accounted to be the eighth wonder of the World.

XXXIII.

French.

Pres d'un grand Pont de plaine spacieuse, Le grand Lion par force, Cesarées, Fera abatre hors Cité rigoureuse, Par effroy portes luy seront reserrées. **English.**

A great Bridge near a spacious Plain, The great Lion by *Cæsarean* Forces, Shall cause to be pulled down, without the rigorous City, For fear of which, the Gates shall be shut to him.

ANNOT.

The meaning of this is, that a great Captain, Commander of the Imperial Forces, shall cause a Bridge that was built near a spacious Plain to be thrown down. The City near the Bridge being terrified at it, shall shut up their Gates against him.

XXXIV.

French.

L'Oiseau de proye volant a la Fenestre, Avant conflict, fait au Francois parure, L'un bon prendra, l'autre ambigue sinistre, La partie foible tiendra pour bonne augure. **English.**

The Bird of Prey flying to the Window, Before Battle, shall appear to the *French*; One shall take a good omen of it, the other a bad one, The weaker part shall hold it for a good sign.

ANNOT.

It is a Hawk which in presence of two Armies ready to give Battle, shall fly to a window and perch upon it, in the presence of them all, one of the Armies shall take it for a good sign; and the other, for an ambiguous and sinister one. In Conclusion, the weaker party shall get the Victory.

XXXV.

French.

Le Lion jeune le vieux surmontera, En champ bellique par singulier Duelle, Dans Cage dor Lœil il lui crevera, Deux playes une puis mourir mort cruelle. **English.**

The young Lion shall overcome the old one, In Martial field by a single Duel, In a Golden Cage he shall put out his Eye, Two wounds from one, then he shall die a cruel death.

ANNOT.

This is one of the Prophecies that hath put our Author in credit, as well for the clearness as for the true event of it.

    Cæsar Nostradamus our Authors son, in his History of *Provence*, writeth that by this *Stanza* his father intended to foretell the manner of *Henry* the second's death.

The *French* Histories relate that this great Prince desiring to honour the Nuptial of his Daughter *Elizabeth*, married to *Philip* II. King of *Spain*, did appoint a Tournament to be kept in St. *Anthony*'s street in *Paris*, where himself would be one of the Defendants against all comers, and for that purpose chose for his companions and associates *Don Alfonso d'Este* Duke of *Ferrara*, and *Francis* of *Lorrain*, Duke of *Guise*.

The Tornament being almost ended, in which the King had shewed much Valour being mounted upon a Horse of the Duke of *Savoy*, *Philibert*'s, *Emanuel* his Brother in Law, this Duke intreated the King to leave off, because he had got the Victory; and the weather was hot, and the night drawing on: But this Martial King would need break one Launce more, and commanded the Captain *Gabriel de Lorges* to be called, a young and valiant Lord and Captain of the *Scottish* Guard. Being come, the King commanded him to run against him, which he refused a great while; but the King waxing angry, he obeyed, and set Spurs to his Horse, he did hit the King in the lower part of his Beaver, the Launce was broken into shivers, and the mean stump lifting up the Beaver, a splinter got in, and wounded the King a little above the right *Eye*, where finding the Bone too hard, it went very deep under the said *Eye*, and broke some Veins belonging to the Membrane, called *Pia Mater*.

The blow was so violent that the King bended his head towards the lists, and fell, into a Swound, being presently disarmed, they perceived the splinter of the Launce in his *Eye*, and his face all bloody. He lived ten days after, and died with great Convulsions, because the Sinews were offended, whereupon he suffered grievous Torment.

His death was also foretold by *Luke Gaurick* a great Astrologer, who being constrained by the Queen *Catharine* of *Medicis*, to tell her by what kind of death her Husband should end his days, told her it should be in a *Duel*, which made him to be hissed at, Kings being exempted of those accidents.

According to this Narrative the Author calleth the King an old *Lion*, and the Captain *Lorges*, since Earl of *Montgomery*, the *young Lion*; because both fought like *Lions*. The *young Lion* overcame the old one in *Martial field*, and in a fight of one against one, and consequently a *Duel*.

He overcame him by putting his *Eye* out in a *Golden Cage*, that is, in his Gilded Helmet.

Of which *Wound* there came another, because the blood of some broken Veins, creeping into the Brains by the vehement agitation of the head, caused an Impostume there, which could not be remedied: therefore the Author saith *two Wounds* from one, that is, one wound made two: and the King died of a cruel death, as we have said before.

XXXVI.

French.

Tard le Monarque se viendra repentir, De navoir mis a Mort son Adversaire, Mais viendra bien a plus haut consentir, Que tout son sang par Mort sera deffaire. **English.**

The Monarque shall too late repent, That he hath not put to death his Adversary; But he shall give his consent to a greater thing than that, Which is to put to death all his Adversaries Kindred.

ANNOT.

The words of this are plain, though it be questionable whether the thing is come to pass already, or not.

XXXVII.

French.

Un peu devant que le Soleil sabsconse, Conflict donné, grand peuple dubieux, Profligez, Port-Marin ne fait responce, Pont & Sepulchre en deux estranges lieux. English.

A little before the Sun setteth, A Battle shall be given, a great people shall be doubtful, Of being foiled, the Sea-Port maketh no answer, A Bridge and Sepulchre shall be in two strange places.

ANNOT.

The two first verses I believe are concerning the Battle of Saint *Denis*, which was fought in the Evening hard by *Paris*, and where the Constable of *Montmorency* was kill'd, which made that great people of *Paris* to be doubtful.

The other two Verses I leave to the interpretation of the Reader.

XXXVIII.

French.

Le Sol & l'Aigle Victeur paroistront, Response vain au vaincu lon asseure, Par Cor ne cris, harnois narresteront, Vindicte paix, par Mort lacheve a l'heure. English.

The Sun and the Eagle shall appear to the Victorious, A vain Answer shall be made good to the vanquished, By no means Arms shall not be stopped, Vengeance maketh Peace, by death he then accomplisheth it.

ANNOT.

This Stanza being full of Figures and Equivoques, I will not interpose my Judgement in it, lest I undertake too much, and perform too little.

XXXIX.

French.

De nuit dans le lit le supresme estranglé, Pour avoir trop suborné blond esleu, Par trois l'Empire subroge Exancle, A mort mettra, Carte ne Pacquet leu. English.

By night in the bed the chief one shall be strangled. For having too much suborned fair Elect, By three the Empire subrogate Exancle, He shall put him to death, reading neither Card nor Packet.

ANNOT.

The Author hath purposely obscured this Prophecie in the third Verse, to take away the Knowledge of it from the Reader; because the parties concerned were then alive, *viz. Philip* II. King of *Spain*, who caused his only son *Don Carlo* to be strangled in his bed, for suspicion of being too familiar with his wife *Elizabeth* of *France*, and Daughter to *Henry* II. The last Verse saith, that he was so implacable, that he would read neither *Card* nor *Packet*, that is, no requests.

XL.

French.

La tourbe fausse dissimilant folie, Fera Bizance un changement de loix, Istra d'Ægypt qui veus que l'on deslie, Edict, changant Monnoys & alloys. English.

The false Troup dissembling their folly, Shall make in *Bizance* an alteration of *Laws*. One shall come out of *Ægypt* who will have untied The Edict, changing the Coin and allay.

ANNOT.

There is two things in this Prognostication, the first that in *Bizance*, which is *Constantinople*, a *Troop* of tumultuous persons gathered together, and dissembling their folly, shall cause an alteration in the *Laws*.

The other, that some *Bassa* come out of *Ægypt*, shall perswade them at *Constantinople* to alter their *Coin*, and the allay of it.

XLI.

French.

Siege a Cité & de nuit assaille, Peu eschapez non loing de Mer conflict, Femme de joye, retour fils, de faillie, Poison & Lettres caché dedans le plie. English.

A Siege laid to a City, and assaulted by night, Few escaped, a fight not far from the Sea, A woman swoundeth for joy to see her son returned; A poison hidden in the fold of Letters.

ANNOT.

After the taking of *Vulpian*, the *French* came to *Montcalvo*, and in the night surprized it by *Scalado*, and *Paradin* saith, that not a drop of Blood was shed on either side.

The Town being taken, the Citadel did hold out a good while, and at last did surrender, *Don Arbre*, who was in the place of the Marques of *Pescaire*, and of the Duke of d'*Alva*, knowing that the besieged had not made a sufficient resistance, caused the Captain, and eleven more of the chief ones to be hanged; because the place was of consequence, and those within had not made a sufficient resistance.

The Author saith in the first Verse, Siege was laid to a City, that is, it was resolved to besiege *Montcalvo*, as the Martial of *Brissac* had advised. In the execution it was assaulted by night, in the taking few escaped; for they were all taken, and yielded to the Victorious. There were none killed or wounded, all were taken, except few who ran away, and carried the news to the *Spaniards*.

At the same time *a fight not far from the Sea*, that is, at the same time there was another Battle by the Sea, between the *Spaniards* and the *Pope*, as we shall shew hereafter.

The third and fourth Verses are concerning a particular accident, which happened presently after the taking of *Montcalvo*, which is, that a woman seeing her Son come back safe, fell in a swound, or died for joy, because knowing the danger wherein he was, she had lost all hopes of ever seeing him. This fellow had brought Poison in a Letter to give to one that had not rewarded him according to his desire. His wickedness being discovered, his Master put him in Prison, whence he escaped, and came back again to *Montcalvo*; the Author speaketh of the same in another place, which we shall set down in its order.

XLII.

French.

Les dix Calendes d'Avril de fait Gothique, Resuscité encor par gens malins, Le feu estaint, assemblée Diabolique, Cherchant les Os de Damant & Psellin. English.

The tenth of the Calends of *April*, *Gothik* account, Raised up again by malitious persons, The fire put out, a Diabolical assembly, Shall seek for the Bones of *Damant* and *Psellin*.

ANNOT.

The tenth of the Calends of *April* is the 23. of *March*, *Gothik* account signifieth the old account of the Calendar, before the reformation of it by Pope *Gregory* the XIII. which old account is called here *Gothik*, because it is kept still by the Northern Nations, which do not acknowledge the Pope, as *Sweden*, *Denmark*, *Holland*, *England*, &c. at that time saith our Author, a Magician shall be raised up by malitious persons; which fire or tumult being put out, that Diabolical assembly will go about to seek the bones of two famous Magicians, *viz. Damant* and *Psellin* that were dead before.

XLIII.

French.

Avant qu'aviene le changement d'Empire, Il adviendra un cas bien merveilleux, Le Champ mué, le Pilier de Porphyre, Mis, translaté sur le Rocher Noileux. English.

Before the change of the Empire cometh, There shall happen a strange accident, A field shall be changed, and a Pillar of *Prophyry*, Shall be transported upon the Chalky Rock.

ANNOT.

This will not seem incredible to those that have read the *English* Chronicles, who relates that in a County of *England* (I think it is *Herefordshire*) there was an Earthquake, which transposed a large piece of ground in another place, with the Trees that were in it, and if I remember well, half a Chappel, those that have the Books may examine the truth of the History, and satisfie themselves better.

XLIV.

En bref seront de retour Sacrifices, Contrevenans seront mis a Martyre, Plus ne seront Moins, Abbez ne Novices, Le Miel sera beaucoup plus cher que Cire. English.

Within a little while Sacrifices shall come again, Opposers shall be put to Martyrdom; There shall be no more Monks, Abbots, nor Novices, Honey shall be much dearer then Wax.

ANNOT.

This is a true Prophecy of the miserable condition of the Church and Clergy in our Fore-fathers times, and chiefly of *Henry* the II. in *France*, and *Henry* the VIII. in *England*, when in the beginning of the Reformation there was such a confusion of opinions, and such unsettledness in Ecclesiastical Government, that sometimes the Popish party prevailed, and put to death the Opposers; at another time the Protestants, who drove away the Monks, Abbots and Novices, as is expressed here, and proved true in *Henry* the VIII. time. As for what he saith, that *Honey shall be much dearer than Wax*. It is to be understood of the downfal of the Romish Religion, who maketh use of Wax Candles and Tapers in their superstitious ceremonies, as if he would say, that the Romish Religion being down, Wax shall be cheap, and Honey dear.

XLV.

French.

***Secteur de Sectes, grand paine au Delateur, Beste en Theatre, dresse le jeu Scenique, Du fait antique ennobly l'Inventeur, Par Sectes, Monde confus & Schismatique.* English.**

Follower of Sects, great troubles to the Messenger, A Beast upon the Theatre prepareth the Scenical play, The Inventor of that wicked fact shall be famous, By Sects the World shall be confounded and Schismatik.

ANNOT.

      The Author being a Papist, is probable that in this Prophecy he aimed at *Luther*, after whose coming the world hath been full of Sects and Schisms.

XLVI.

French.

***Tout aupres d'Auch, de Lectoure & Mirande, Grand feu du Ciel en trois nuits tombera, Chose adviendra bien stupende & mirande, Bien peu apres la Terre tremblera.* English.**

Near *Auch*, *Lectoure* and *Mirande*, A great fire from Heaven shall fall three nights together, A thing shall happen stupendious and wonderful, A little while after, the Earth shall quake.

ANNOT.

      Auch, *Lectoure* and *Miranda* are three Towns in *Guyenna*, a Province of *France*, the chief City whereof is *Bourdeaux*. The rest is easie.

XLVII.

French.

***Du Lac Leman les Sermons fascheront, Des jours seront reduits par des Sepmaines, Puis mois, puis an, puis tous defalliront, Les Magistrats damneront leurs Loix vaines.* English.**

The Sermons of the *Leman* Lake shall be troublesome, Some days shall be reduced into weeks, Then into months, then into year, then they shall fail, The Magistrates shall condemn their vain Laws.

ANNOT.

      The *Leman Lake*, in Latin *Lacus Lemanus*, is the Lake of *Geneva*, therefore it is palpable, that by this Prophecy, the Author aimeth at *Calvin*, and his Successors, who began the Reformation in that Town. I leave the rest to the Readers Judgement, it is enough I have opened the door.

XLVIII.

French.

Vingt ans du Regne de la Lune passez, Sept mil ans autre tiendra sa Monarchie, Quand le Soleil prendra ses jours laissez, Lors accomplit & fine ma Prophecie. English.

Twenty years of the Reign of the Moon being past, Seven thousands years another shall hold his Monarchy, When the Sun shall reassume his days past, Then is fulfilled, and endeth my Prophecy.

ANNOT.

All this signifieth no more, but that the Authors Prophecies extend to the end of the world.

XLIX.

French.

Beaucoup, beaucoup avant relics menées, Ceux d'Orient par la vertu Lunaire, L'An mil sept cens feront grands emmenées, Subjugant presque le coin Aquilonaire. English.

A great while before these doings, Those of the East by the virtue of the Moon, In the year *1700.* shall carry away great droves, And shall subdue almost the whole Northern corner.

ANNOT.

I desire Posterity to take special notice of this *Stanza*, that in case it should come to pass, our Author may be admired for the specification of the time, which is so punctually set down, here that it admitteth no ambiguity. The plain meaning is, that the *Turks*, which he calleth those of the East. By the virtue of the Moon, which is their Ensign and Badge, shall in the year 1700. carry away abundance of people, and shall subdue almost the whole Northern Countrey, which to them is *Russia, Poland, Hungary, Sweden, Denemark*, &c.

L.

French.

De l'Aquatique triplicity naistra, Un qui fera le Jeudy pour sa feste, Son Bruit, Loz, Regne & puissance croistra, Par Terre & Mer, aux Orients tempeste. English.

From the Aquatick triplicity shall be born, One that shall make *Thursday* his Holiday, His Fame, Praise, Reign, and Power shall grow, By Land and Sea, and a Tempest to the East.

ANNOT.

The meaning is, that at that time, as such conjunction of Planets shall be, which he calleth here *Aquatick triplicity*, there shall be born upon a *Thursday* a famous man, such as he describeth here, who shall be a foe and a terrour to the *Turks*, signified here by the *Orients*.

LI.

French.

Chef d'Aries, Jupiter & Saturne, Dieu Eternel quelles mutations! Puis apres long siecle son malin temps retourne, Gaule & Italy quelles emotions? English.

Heads of *Aries*, *Jupiter* and *Saturn*, O Eternal God, what changes shall there be! After a long age his wicked time cometh again, *France* and *Italy*, what commotions?

ANNOT.

This signifieth, that when *Jupiter* and *Saturn* shall be in conjunction in the head of *Aries*, that then shall be great commotions in *France* and *Italy*.

LII.

French.

Le deux malins de Scorpion conjoint, Le grand Seigneur meurtry dedans sa salle, Peste a l'Eglise par le nouveau Roy joint, L'Europe basse, & Septentrionale. English.

The two malignants of *Scorpion* being joyned, The grand Seignor murdered in his Hall, Plague to the Church by a King newly joyned to it, *Europe* low, and Septentrional.

ANNOT.

This third position of the Celestial bodies foretelleth the death of the great *Turk*, who should be murdered in his own Chamber, as happened to Sultan *Osman*, who was strangled in his Chamber, by the command of *Daout Bassa* great Vizeir, about the year 1622. *vide* the Turkish History.

The rest of the Prophecy is concerning a King, who being newly joyned to the Church, (I suppose of *Rome*) shall bring much mischief to it, and in his time *Europe* shall be brought very low, and in a manner confined to a corner of the North, which hath relation to the foregoing 49. Stanza, which see in its place.

LIII.

French.

Las, qu'on verra grand peuple tourmenté, Et la Loy Sainte en totale ruine, Par autres Loix toute la Chrestienté, Quand d'Or, d'Argent trouve nouvelle Mine. English.

Alas, how a great people shall be tormented, And the Holy Law in an utter ruine; By other Laws, all Christendom troubled, When new Mines of Gold and Silver shall be found.

ANNOT.

This is a true Prophecy of the mischiefs that have happened in the World by the finding of the Mines in *America*; first to the *Indians* themselves, called here a great People, by the cruelty of the *Spaniards*, and then to all Christendom besides, by the evils that this Idol *Mammon* hath brought into it.

LIV.

French.

Deux revolts faits du malin facigere, De Regne & Siecles fait permutation, Le mobil signe a son endroit s'Ingere, Aux deux egaux & d'Inclination. English.

Two revolts shall be made by the wicked Link-carrier, Which shall make a change of the Reign and the Age, The moveable Sign doth offer it self for it, To the two equals in inclination.

ANNOT.

This obscure Stanza must be interpreted thus.

Two revolts shall be made by the wicked Link-carrier; that is, *Paris* which is the *Link-carrier* of *France*, and whose example the rest of the Towns follow, shall revolt twice, the first revolt was against *Henry* III. in the time of the *Barricadoes*, the second against *Henry* IV. his successor.

Which shall make a change of the Reign and the Age: This happened when the house of *Valois* was extinguished, and the house of *Bourbon* came in, and that is *the change of the Reign. The change of the Age*, was, because this did happen about the end of the year 1599. and the beginning 1600. which was a *change of Age.*

The moveable sign offers it self for it: That is, the position of the Heavens was such as to forward these accidents.

To the two equals in ambition: That is, to *Henry* III. and *Henry* IV. who both intended, and went about to reduce *Paris* to obedience.

LV.

French.

Soubs lopposite climat Babilonique, Grande sera de sang effusion, Que Terre, & Mer, Air, Ciel sera inique, Sectes, Faim, Regnes, Pestes, Confusion. English.

In the Climat opposite to the *Babylonian*, There shall be a great effusion of Blood. Insomuch that the Land, and Sea, Air and Heaven shall seem unjust Sects, Famine, Reigns, Plague, Confusion.

ANNOT.

There is nothing difficult here, but what *Climat* is that is *opposite to the Babylonian*, of which every body may satisfie himself by perusing the Globe.

LVI.

Vous verrez tost on tard faire grand change, Horreurs extremes & vindications, Que si la Lune conduite par son Ange, Le Ciel sapproche des inclinations. **English.**

You shall see soon or late great alterations Extreme horrours and revenges, The Moon leaden by her Angel, The Heaven draweth near its inclinations.

ANNOT.

I conceive there is some things omitted, and corrupted by the Press in this Stanza, which rendreth it so difficult, therefore I had rather leave it to the decision of the impartial Reader, than venture my opinion upon it.

LVII.

French.

Par grand discord la trombe tremblera, Accord rompu, dressant la teste au Ciel, Bouche sanglante dans le sang nagera, Au Sol la face ointe le loit & Miel. **English.**

By great discord, the Trumpet shall sound, Agreement broken, lifting the head to Heaven, A bloody mouth shall swim in blood, The face turned to the Sun anointed with Milk and Honey.

ANNOT.

The words and sence are plain, and I cannot believe that there is any great mystery hidden under these words.

LVIII.

French.

Trenché le ventre, naistra avec deux testes, & quattre bras, quel qu'ans entiers vivra, Jour qu'Aquilare celebrera ses festes, Fossan, Thurin, chef Ferrare fuiera. **English.**

Slit in the belly, shall be born with two heads, And four Arms, it shall live some years, The day that *Aquilare* shall celebrate his Festivals, *Fossan, Thurin,* chief *Ferrare* shall run away.

ANNOT.

In the first Verse the Author speaketh of a Monster that had two heads, and four Arms, and the Belly slit, that is to say, it was a female.

His Son *Cæsar* in his History of *Provence,* saith, that in the Town of *Senan* in *Provence,* a Child was born with two heads, and that it was foretold by some that were skilful in Astronomy, by which words I guess he spake of his Father, sith the Astrologers cannot foretel the birth of a particular Monster, and therefore *Nostradamus* only was able to do it in those days.

He saith in the same place, that it was born in *February* 1554. and was brought to *Salon* to be shewed to his Father, and thence was carried to *Claudius* Earl of *Savoy* Governour of *Provence*, who commonly had his residence at *Salon*.

He maketh no mention if he had four Arms, nor what Sex it was of, it may be that being in swadling cloths, nobody took notice of the Arms or Sex.

The Author Prophecieth that it should live some years, it may be two or three, and that is was preserved to see, whether in time it should have the use of its Senses, of the Tongue, and understanding of its two Heads, to see whether there were two Souls, or onely one, and to say the Truth. I think that in such an accident both Heads ought to be Baptized, that in case there should be two Souls, both should partake of the blood of Christ, for their Eternal Salvation.

I do not find in the same History how long it lived, it being a thing not much material to History. In the third Verse he marketh, *The day that Aquilare shall celebrate his Festivals*; and in the fourth he saith that *Fossan, Thurin, chief Ferrare shall run away*.

To understand this, one must suppose here that the Town of *Cazal* is called here the chief of *Ferrare*; because it is the chief City of *Montserrat*, and as *Paradin* saith, is called *Cazal* St. *Bas*, a handsom and strong place, honoured with many Nobles and antient Families, as of the Earls of St. *George* and of *Biandratte*.

Secondly, We must suppose that in the year 1554. the Lord *Figuerol*, Lieutenant to the Governour of *Milan* did command in that place. Of this *Figuerol* I find in the Author of the four Volumes of the States and Empires, (when he speaketh of *Spain*) that the House of *Figueroas* was the root of that of *Aquilar*, which hath several branches, out of which came the Duke of *Feria*, and the Marquess of *Pliego*, so that *Figuerol* and *Aquilar* is the same thing.

If it be objected that *Figueroas* and *Figuerol* are not the same, *Paradin* teacheth us, that this *Figuerol* was bred up amongst the *Genoeses*, and the corrupted *Italian* of *Genoa* may have named the Captain *Figuerol* in stead of *Figueroas*.

Thirdly, We must suppose here that *Cazal* was taken in the night that is between *Shrove-Tuesday* and *Ash-Wednesday*, and that from *Shrove-Sunday* to that day there were great rejoycings, because of a famous Marriage that was made between two persons of quality, where the Lord *Figuerol* was one of the chief persons invited.

Fourthly, That these rejoycings were the occasion of the taking of *Cazal*; because the Lord *Salvaison* Governour of *Verrüe* hearing of this Feast, resolved to be among them, though with a different intention. He had before hand made himself sure of one *Fontarole*, who under pretence to sell fruit, went up and down the Town to spie what was a doing.

Fifthly, The resolution of surprizing *Cazal* was agreed upon, and the time appointed to be the night between *Shrove-Tuesday* and *Ash-Wednesday*, when the Governour, Inhabitants and Souldiers should be buried in sleep, weary of debaucheries committed the day before.

Sixthly, This resolution was so happily put into execution, that *Figuerol* hearing the noise of the *French* being in Town, came out of his house, having only his night Gown upon him, and a Halbert in his hand, to quiet those whom he only thought to be some drunken persons; but hearing the cry of *France, France*, he presently retired into the Castle, with all those that were come to the Nuptials.

Seventhly, The Marshal of *Brissac* coming about seven of the Clock in the Morning, caused the Tower of *Cazal* to be assaulted, which was taken with a considerable loss of the *French*, and after that the Castle which held out 12 days.

All this being supposed, mark what the Author saith in the third Verse.

The day that *Aquilare* shall celebrate his Festivals, that is, the day that *Figuerol of the house of Aquilare shall celebrate his Festivals*, not only one Festival, but his Festivals, that is of three days.

Fossen, Thurin, saith the fourth Verse, *Chief Ferrare shall run away*.

Fossen, Thurin, doth not signifie two Towns, but one onely; for although *Fossen* and *Thurin* be two Towns, of which *Fossen* in the time of the Wars in *Italy* under *Henry* II. belonged to the *Spaniard*, and *Thurin* to the *French*. These two Towns signifie but one, which is that of *Fossen*, to which to distinguish it from *Marseilles*, he giveth the Epithete of *Thurin*, so much as to say, that he speaketh of *Fossen* a Town of *Piemont*, the chief Town of which is *Thurin*, and not of *Fossen*, which the Author taketh often for *Marseilles*.

Which the Author maketh plain, when he saith in the singular number, that *Fossen, Thurin, chief Ferrare shall run away*, to shew that it is onely one Town of which he speaketh, otherwise if he had intended to speake of two, he would have put it in the plural number, which is more manifest by the History, wherein we learn that *Fossen* belonged to the *Spaniards*, and *Thurin* to the *French*, and consequently, being of contrary parties, they could neither follow, nor fly from a Town which belonged to one of them.

If any one should object, that the sense of the fourth Verse is, that the *Chief Ferrare* shall fly or follow these two Towns, the preceding reason is repugnant to that sense; because a Town that is of one party, cannot be friend to two Towns, one of which is of its party, and the other of the contrary.

The reading of this work shall convince every body, that the Author setteth down sometimes two Towns for one, to distinguish them from others, as he nameth *Paul Mansol*, to distinguish that Town of St. *Paul*, which is three Leagues from the *Rhosne*, over against *Pont* St. *Esprit*, from that St. *Paul* which is in *Provence*.

Now that *Fossen* in *Piemont* shall run from *Cazal* the chief City of *Montserrat*, because that being taken by the *French*, *Fossen* could not expect but perpetual damages from it.

But why? will you say, doth the Author speak rather of *Fossen*, than of other places that held for the *Spaniards*? I answer, because *Fossen* was the strongest place that the *Spaniards* had in *Piemont* and which could not be taken by the *French*, though her neighbour *Saviliane* was, as we shall shew hereafter.

In the Vulgar impression of this Stanza, there is two faults, one is, that in the first Verse it puts *Aquileya*, which is a Town that is not in *Italy*, truth it is, that there is *Aquilee* a little above *Venice*, but this hath no correspondency with *Fossen*, *Thurin*, nor the *Chief of Ferrara*.

In the fourth Verse the impression setteth down *shall follow*, which maketh nonsense, and therefore I put *shall run away*, which is a word in *French* near the other, and maketh a compleat sense, to which agreeth the birth of that Monster in *February*, and the taking of *Cazal* in the Month of *March*. In that year, *John Statius* setteth *Shrove-Tuesday* upon the 16 of *February*, and consequently we must say, that the Town was not taken that year 1554. for the Citadel was taken 12 days after, which should have been the 19 of *February*, and notwithstanding the History marks that it was taken upon the 14 of *March*.

Therefore we must conclude, that it was taken the year following 1555. and to say truth, in that year *Ash-wednesday* was the 27. of *February*; in that day the Town was taken, and two days after the Tower of *Cazal*; after which the Citadel was besieged the second of *March*, and the first *Saturday* of Lent, and was taken twelve days after, which was the 14. of *March*, which convinceth me that *Cazal* was taken in the year 1555. upon the 27. of *February*, and therefore that this Stanza is wholly Prophetical.

LIX.

French.

Les exilez deportez dans les Isles, Au changement d'un plus cruel Monarque, Seront meurtris & mis dans les Scintilles, Qui de parler ne seront este parques. **English.**

They banished that were carried into the Islands, At the change of a more cruel Monarque, Shall be murdered, and put in the sparks of fire, Because they had not been sparing of their tongues.

This is very plain, and signifieth no more, but that some persons that were banished into Islands, and could not hold their tongues; upon the coming of a Monarque, more cruel than his Predecessor, shall be murdered, and burnt.

LX.

French.

Un Empereur naistra pres d'Italie, Qui a l'Empire sera vendu bien cher, Diront avec quels gens il se ralie, Qu'on trouvera moins Prince que Boucher. English.

An Emperour shall be born near *Italy*, Who shall cost dear to the Empire, They shall say, what people he keepeth company! He shall be found less a Prince, than a Butcher.

ANNOT.

This Prophecy is for the future; for since *Nostradamus*'s time till now, such an Emperour was not heard of, that was born near *Italy*, that cost the Empire so dear, and proved more a Butcher, than a Prince.

LXI.

French.

La Republique miserable infelice, Sera vastée du nouveau Magistrat, Leur grand amas de l'exil malefice, Fera Suede ravir leur grand contract. English.

The miserable and unhappy Common-wealth, Shall be wafted by the new Magistrate; Their great gathering from exiled persons, Shall cause *Swedeland* to break her Contract.

ANNOT.

The two first Verses foretell what hath happened to *England* under the Government of a Common-wealth, and how their new Magistrate *Cromwel* made a havock of them. The third and fourth Verses, mention what great sums they exacted from those of the Kings party, and how for that cause *Swedeland* foresook their friendship.

LXII.

French.

La grande perte las que feront les Lettres, Avant le Circle de Latona parfait, Feu, grand Deluge, plus par ignares Sceptres, Que de long siecle ne se verra refait. English.

Alas what a great loss shall learning suffer, Before the Circle of the Moon be accomplished, Fire, great flood, and more by ignorant Scepters, Then can be made good again in a long age.

ANNOT.

Here the Author bemoaneth the loss of one eminent person in Learning, be like of *Julius Scaliger*, who lived in his time, and was once his intimate friend, the two last Verses that great miseries, as Fire and Flood shall happen by the ignorance of Princes.

LXIII.

French.

Les Fleaux passez, diminué le Monde, Long temps la Paix, Terres inhabitées, Seur marchera par le Ciel, Terre, Mer & Onde, Puis de nouveau les Guerres suscitées. English.

The Scourges being past, the World shall be diminished, Peace for a great while, Lands inhabited, Every one safe shall go by Heaven, Land and Sea, And then the Wars shall begin a fresh.

ANNOT.

This foretelleth a great tranquillity every where, and after that, Wars again:

LXIV.

French.

De nuit Soleil penseront avoir veu, Quand le Pourceau demy homme on verra, Bruit, Chant, Bataille au Ciel battre apperceu, Et bestes brutes a parler on orra. English.

They shall think to have seen the Sun in the night, When the Hog half a man shall be seen, Noise, Singing, Battles in Heaven shall be seen to fight, And brute beasts shall be heard to speak.

ANNOT.

This Stanza is full of prodigies that are to happen, and for that in the last Verse, it is no great wonder, for many brute beasts have spoken, speak now a days, and shall speak hereafter.

LXV.

French.

Enfant sans mains, jamais veu si grand Foudre, L'Enfant Royal au jeu d'esteuf blessé, Au puy brisez, fulgures allant moudre, Trois sur les champs par le milieu troussez. English.

A child without hands, so great Lightning never seen, The Royal Child wounded at Tennis, Bruised at the Well, Lightnings, going to grind, Three shall be strucken by the middle.

ANNOT.

The meaning of all this is, that when a child shall be born without hands, there shall be fearful Lightning; a Royal child shall be hurt at *Tennes*, and by that Lightning some shall be bruised by a Well, and in a Mill, and three in the Field shall be killed.

LXVI.

French.

Celuy qui lors portera les nouvelles, Apres un peu il viendra respirer, Viviers, Tournon, Montferrand & Pradelles, Gresle & tempeste les fera souspirer. **English.**

He that then shall carry the news, A little while after shall draw his breath, *Viviers*, *Tournon*, *Montferrant*, and *Pradelles*, Hail and storm shall make them sigh.

ANNOT.

This Stanza hath a connexion with the foregoing, for the two first Verses signifie, that he who shall carry the news of that fearful Lightning, and of the mischief done by it, shall have much ado to recover his breath.

In the last two Verses, the Towns are named which shall suffer most by that storm, and chiefly by the Hail and the Wind.

LXVII.

French.

La grand famine que je vois approcher, Souvent tourner puis estre universelle, Si grande & longue qu'on viendra arracher, Du Bois racine, & l'Enfant de mamelle. **English.**

What a great famine do I see drawing near, To turn one way, then another, and then become universal, So great and long, that they shall come to pluck The root from the Wood, and the child from the breast.

ANNOT.

The words and sense of this are plain, and foretell a great famine, which being first in one Countrey and then in another, shall at last become general, and last so long, that people shall pluck the Roots from the Trees, and the children from the breast to feed upon.

LXVIII.

French.

O quel horrible & malheureux tourment, Trois innocens qu'on viendra a livrer, Poison suspect, mal garde tradiment. Mis en horreur par Bourreaux enyvrez. English.

O to what a horrid and unhappy torment Shall be put three Innocents! Poison shall be suspected, evil Keepers shall betray them, They shall be put to horrour by drunken Executioners.

ANNOT.

This is very plain concerning three innocent persons, who shall be delivered up by their unfaithful keepers, and shall be put to great torments by drunken Executioners, which torments shall be suspected to come by poison.

LXIX.

French.

La grand Montagne ronde de sept Stades, Apres Paix, Guerre, Faim, Inondation, Roulera loing, abisuant grand contrades, Mesmes antiques, & grand Fondation. English.

The great Mount in compass seven Stades, After Peace, War, Famine, and Innundation, Shall tumble a great way, sinking great Countries, Yea ancient Buildings, and great Foundation.

ANNOT.

A Stade cometh from the Greek word σταδιον, ἀπὸ τῆς στασεος, because *Hercules* did overrun so much ground at one breath; but what space of ground the Author meaneth by seven Stades, is unknown to me. The rest of the Prophecy may very well be appropriated to the last fearful eruption of Mount *Ætna*, which sunk so many Towns and Buildings, and the relation of which is so handsomly and truly made by the most honourable the Earl of *Winchelsey*, who was an eye witness to it, in his return from his Embassy at *Constantinople*.

LXX.

French.

Pluye, Faim, Guerre en Perse non cessée, La foy trop grande trahira le Monarque; Par la finie en Gaule commencée, Secret augure pour a un estre parque. English.

The Rain, Famine, War, in *Persia* being not ceased, Too great credulity shall betray the Monarque; Being ended there it shall begin in *France*, A secret Omen to one that he shall die.

ANNOT.

The meaning of the two first Verses, is, that while the Rain, Famine, and War shall be in *Persia*, a Monarque shall be betrayed by his credulity. The third Verse signifieth that this Rain, Famine and War being ended in *Persia*, it shall begin in *France*. And the fourth Verse, that this shall be an Omen to a great Person of his approaching death.

LXXI.

French.

La Tour Marine troisfois prise & reprise, Par Espagnols, Barbares, Ligurins, Marseille & Aix, Arles par ceux de Pise, Vast, feu, fer, pille, Avignon des Thurins. English.

The Sea-tower three times taken and retaken, By *Spaniards*, *Barbarians*, and *Ligurians*, *Marseilles* and *Aix*, *Arles* by those of *Pisa*, Wast, fire, Iron, plunder, *Avignon* of *Thurins*.

ANNOT.

It is hard to guess what this Sea Tower is, which was taken and retaken three times; first by the *Spaniards*, next by the *Barbarians*, and then by the *Ligurians*, that is, either the *Genoeses*, or those of *Ligorne*, unless he meaneth the *Pignon de Velez* in *Africa*, first taken by *Charles* the V. upon the *Barbarians*, then retaken again by them, taken again by the *Spaniards*, by the help of the *Genoeses*. In the third Verse *Marseille*, *Aix*, and *Arles*, are threatned by those of *Pisa*, that is the *Florentines*, of being ruinated by Fire and Sword, and to be plundered, as also *Avignon* by those of *Piemont*.

LXXII.

French.

Du tout Marseille des habitans changee, Course & poursuite jusques pres de Lion, Narbon, Tholoze par Bourdeaux outragée, Tuez, Captifs presque d'un Milion. English.

Marseille shall wholly change her Inhabitants These shall run and be pursued as far as *Lion*, *Narbon*, *Tholoze* shall wrong *Bourdeaux*, There shall be killed and taken prisoner almost a Milion.

ANNOT.

Marseilles is a Sea-Town in *Provence*, *Narbon*, and *Tholoze* are Cities of *Languedoc*, and *Bourdeaux* is the chief Town in *Gascony*, the rest is easie to be understood.

LXXIII.

French.

France a cinq parts par neglect assaillie, Tunis, Argier, esmeus par Persiens, Leon, Seville, Barcelonne faillie, N'aura la chasse par les Venetiens. English.

France by a neglect shall be assaulted on five sides, *Tunis*, *Argier* shall be moved by the *Persians*, *Leon*, *Sevil*, *Barcelone* shall be missed, And not be pursued by the *Venetians*.

ANNOT.

     This Stanza is concerning as many Countreys, as there are Verses: the first is *France*, which by neglect and carelesness of her in Inhabitants, *shall be assaulted on five several sides*. The second is concerning *Tunis* and *Argier*, Cities of *Barbary, which shall be stirred and moved* (I suppose) to rebel. The third regardeth *Leon, Sevil, Barselona*, Cities in *Spain*, and the fourth the *Venetians*.

LXXIV.

French.

Apres sejourné vogueront en Empire, Le grand secours viendra vers Antioche, Le noir poil crespe tendra fort a l'Empire, Barbe d'Airain se rostira en broche. **English.**

After a stay, they shall Sail towards an Empire, The great succours shall come towards *Antioch*, The Black Hair Curled, shall aim much to the Empire, The Brazen Beard shall be roasted on a Spit.

ANNOT.

There is no difficulty in this, but in the last Verse, which I had rather leave to the judgment of the judicious Reader, than to offer any thing that might make me ridiculous.

LXXV.

French.

Le Tyran Sienne occupera Savone, Le fort gaigné tiendra classe Marine, Les deux Armées par la marque d'Ancone, Par effrayeur le chef sen examine. **English.**

The Tyrant *Sienna* shall occupy *Savona*; The Fort being won, shall hold a Fleet, The two Armies shall go in the mark of *Ancona*, By fear the chief shall be examined.

ANNOT.

For the explication of this Stanza, you must understand that *Sienna* is a City in *Italy*, now under the Dominion of the Duke of *Tuscany*, who shall occupy *Savona*, a City now under the Dominion of the Common-wealth of *Genoa*; the rest is plain enough.

LXXVI.

French.

D'un nom farouche tel proferé sera. Que les trois Sœurs auront Fato le nom, Puis grand peuple par langue & fait dira, Plus que nul autre aura bruit & renom. **English.**

By a wild name one shall be called So that the three Sisters shall have the name of *Fato*, Afterwards a great people by Tongue and Deeds, shall say, He shall have fame and renown more than any other.

ANNOT.

By the three Sisters, he meaneth the three Destinies, *viz. Clotho, Lachesis* and *Atropos*, which the Poets have fained to Spin every mans destiny, which he calleth here *Fato*, from the Latin word *Fatum*. The rest may be interpreted as well by the Reader, as by my self.

LXXVII.

French.

Entre deux Mers dressera promontoire, Qui puis mourra par le mors du Cheval, Le fier Neptune pliera Voile noire, Par Calpre, & Classe aupres de Rocheval. English.

Between two Seas shall a Promontory be raised, By him, who shall die by the biting of a Horse, The proud *Neptune* shall fold the black Sail. Through *Calpre*, and a fleet shall be near *Rocheval*.

ANNOT.

I could not find what he meaneth by *Calpre*, nor by *Rocheval*, which I suppose to be the proper names of places, when he saith, that proud *Neptune* shall fold the black Sail; he maketh an allusion to the History of *Theseus*, Son of *Ægeus* King of *Athens*, who being sent with other Children into *Candia*, to become a prey to the *Minotaure*, his Father sent the Ship with black *Sails*, as in a case of Mourning, charging *Theseus*, that if he came back again safe he should put on white Sails, but coming in sight of *Athens*, *Theseus* for joy forgot to put on the white Sails, so that his Father *Ægeus* thinking he had miscarried, cast himself from a Rock into the Sea, so that he saying that *Neptune* shall fold the black Sail, he meaneth, that there shall be joyful news.

LXXVIII.

French.

D'un chef vieillard naistre sens habeté, Degenerant par scavoir & par Armes, Le chef de France par sa Sœur redouté, Champs divisez concedez aux Gensdarmes. English.

An old head shall beget an Idiot, Who shall degenerate in Learning and in Arms, The head of *France* shall be feared by his sister, The fields shall be divided and granted to the Troopers.

ANNOT.

The sense of this is so plain, that any body may make his interpretation of it.

LXXIX.

French.

Bazas, L'Estoure, Condom, Auch, Agine, Esmeus par Loix, querelle & Monopole, Car Bourd, Tholose, Bay, mettra en ruine, Renouveler voulant leur Tauropole. English.

Bazas, L'*Estoure*, *Condom*, *Auch*, *Agen*, Being moved by Laws, quarrels and Monopoly, For they shall put to ruine *Bordeaux*, *Tholose*, *Bayonne*, Going about to renew their *Tauropole*.

This Key of the sense of this Stanza lieth in the last word *Tauropole*, which is compounded of the Latin word *Taurus* a Bull, and of the Greek word πολέω, that is, to sell; so that the meaning of it is, that those Cities mentioned shall rise in Rebellion against the *Monopolites*, and those that shall lay a Tax upon Cattle.

LXXX.

French.

De la sixiesme claire splendeur Celeste, Viendra Tonnerre si fort en la Bourgongne, Puis naistra monstre de treshideuse beste, Mars, Avril, May, Juin, grand charpin & rogne. **English.**

From the sixth bright Cœlestial splendour, Shall come very great Lightning in *Burgundy*, After that shall be born a Monster of a most hideous beast, In *March, April, May, June* shall be great quarelling and muttering.

ANNOT.

The first Verse is of a most dark and abstruse sense, in which I confess my ignorance, unless he meant from the sixth of the seven Planets, the rest is plain enough.

LXXXI.

French.

D'humain troupeau neuf seront mis a part, De Jugement & Conseil separez, Leur sort sera divisé en depart, Kappa, Theta, Lambda, mors, bannis egarez. **English.**

Nine shall be set aside from the human flock, Being divided in Judgement and Counsel Their fortune shall be to be divided, *Kappa, Theta, Lambda*, dead, banished, scattered.

ANNOT.

There is nothing difficult here, but what he meaneth by *Kappa, Theta, Lambda*, which are three Letters of the Greek *Alphabet*.

LXXXII.

French.

Quand les Colomnes de Bois grande tremblée, D'Auster conduite, couverte de rubriche, Tant videra dehors grande assemblée, Tremble Vienne, & le Païs d'Austriche. **English.**

When the wooden Columns shall be much shaken, By *Auster*, and covered with rubbish, Then shall go out a great assembly, And *Vienne*, and the Land of *Austria* shall tremble.

Auster, in Latin is the Southwind. *Vienna* is the chief City of *Austria*, belonging to the Emperour of *Germany*.

LXXXIII.

French.

L'Agent estrange divisera butins, Saturne & Mars son regard furieux, Horrible, estrange, aux Thoscans & Latins, Grees qui seront a frapper curiux. English.

The stranger Agent shall divide booties, *Saturn* in *Mars* shall have his aspect furious, Horrid, and strange to the *Tuscans* and *Latines*, The *Grecians* shall be curious to strike.

ANNOT.

By the *Tuscans* are meant the people under the Dominion of the Duke of *Florence*; and by the *Latines*, those under the *Pope*.

LXXXIV.

French.

Lune obscurie aux profondes tenebres, Son frere passe de couleur ferrugine, Le grand caché long temps soubs les tenebres, Tiedera Fer dans la Pluie sanguine. English.

The Moon shall be darkned in the deepest darkness, Her brother shall pass being of a ferrugineous colour, The great one long hidden under darkness, Shall make his Iron lukewarm in the bloody Rain.

ANNOT.

This signifieth, that when the Moon shall be totally Eclipsed in the night, and that all the next day her Brother the Sun shall be seen of a ferrugineous, (that is an Iron like colour) then shall a great one that was hidden arise, and do great feats of Arms with the death of many men.

LXXXV.

French.

Par la responce de Dame Roy troublé, Ambassadeurs mespriseront leur vie, Le grand ses Freres contrefera doublé, Par deux mourront, hain, ire, & envie. English.

A King shall be troubled by the answer of a Lady, Embassadors shall despise their lives, The great one being double in mind shall counterfeit his Brothers, They shall die by two, anger, hatred, and envy.

There is nothing difficult here, but the last Verse, which yet will be plain enough, if you make these three words anger, hatred, and envy not co-herent with the foremost, but subsisting by themselves; as if one should say, there shall be anger, hatred, and envy.

LXXXVI.

French.

La grande Roine quand se verra vaincue, Fera exces de Masculin courage, Sur le Cheval, Fleuve passera nue, Suite par Fer, a Foy fera outrage. English.

When the great Queen shall see her self vanquished, She shall do a deed of a Masculine courage, Upon a Horse, she shall pass over the River naked, Followed by Iron, she shall do wrong to her Faith.

ANNOT.

It is some great Queen, who seeing her self vanquished, shall swim naked on Horseback over a River, being followed by those that would have either killed or taken her, and after that shall forfeit her faith, but whether it be to her Husband, Friends, or Relations, is not expressed.

LXXXVII.

French.

Ennosigee feu du Centre de Terre Fera trembler autour de Cité Neuve, Deux grands Rochers long temps feront la guerre, Puis Arethuse rougira nouveau fleuve. English.

Ennosigee, fire of the Center of the Earth, Shall make quake about the New City, Two great Rocks shall a great while War one against the other, After that, *Arethusa* shall colour red a new River.

ANNOT.

Ennosigee is a Greek word εννοσίγαιος, in Latin *Terræ quassator*, from ἔνίω *moveo*, and γαῖα *Terra*, and is an Epithete of *Neptune*. The meaning then of this Stanza is, that the Sea shall make the Earth quake, and fire come out of the Earth about *Naples*, which in Greek is called *Neapolis*, that is, a *New City*.

Arethusa is a Fountain in *Sicily*, which a little way from its Spring, groweth into a River. The rest is left to the interpretation of the Reader.

LXXXVIII.

French.

Le Divin mal surprendra un grand Prince, Un peu devant aura femme espousée, Son appuy & credit a un coup viendra mince, Conseil mourra pour la teste rasée. English.

The Divine sickness shall surprise a great Prince, A little while after he hath married a woman, His support and credit shall at once become slender, Council shall die for the shaven head.

ANNOT.

By the Divine sickness, he meaneth the *falling sickness*, called by the Greeks *Epilepsia*, and by the Latines *Morbus Sacer*. By the shaven head, he meaneth some Ecclesiastical person of the *Romish* Religion; the construction of the whole is easie.

LXXXIX.

French.

Tous ceux d'Illerde seront dans la Moselle, Mettant a mort tous ceux de Loire & Seine, Le course Marin viendra pres d'Hautevelle, Quand Espagnols ouvrira toute veine. English.

All those of *Illerde* shall be in the *Mosel*, Putting to death all those of *Loire* and *Seine*, The Sea course shall come near *Hautevelle*, When the *Spaniard* shall open all veins.

ANNOT.

By *Illerde* he meaneth the City of l'*Isle* in *Flanders*, the *Mosel* is a River that runneth through *Lorrain*, the *Loire* and *Seine* are two other Rivers of *France*, the first of which passeth at *Orleans*, and the second at *Paris*; the two last Verses are too hard for me to interpret.

XC.

French.

Bourdeaux, Poitiers, au son de la Campane, A grande classe ira jusqu'a Langon, Contre Gaulois sera leur Tramontane, Quand Monstre hideux naistra pres de Orgon. English.

Bourdeaux, Poitiers, at the sound of the Bell, With a great Navy shall go as far as *Langon*, Against the *French* shall their *Tramontane* be, When an hideous Monster shall be born near *Orgon*.

ANNOT.

Tramontana, in *Italian*, is the North-wind. *Orgon*, is the name of a Town in *Gascony*, the rest of the construction is not difficult.

XCI.

French.

Les dieux feront aux humains apparence, Ce quils seront auteurs de grand conflict, Avant ciel veu serain, Espée & Lance, Que vers main gauche sera plus grande affliction. English.

The Gods shall make it appear to Man-kind, That they are the Authors of a great War; For the Heaven that was Serene, shall shew Sword and Lance, Signifying, that on the left hand the affliction shall be greater.

ANNOT.

He foretelleth here some Prodigies that shall be in the Air, as *Swords* and *Lances* after fair weather, which shall be forerunners of great Wars, and chiefly in those Countries that shall be situated on the left hand of these Prodigies.

XCII.

French.

Soubs un la paix, par tout sera clemence, Mais non long temps, pille & rebellion, Par refus Ville, Terre & Mer entamée, Morts & Captifs le liers d'un Million. English.

Under one shall be peace, and every where clemency, But not a long while, then shall be plundering and Rebellion, By a denyal shall Town, Land and Sea be assaulted, There shall be Dead and taken Prisoners the third part of a Million.

ANNOT.

The words and sense are plain.

XCIII.

French.

Terre Italique des Mons tremblera, Lion & Coq non trop confederez, en lieu & peur l'un l'autre saidera, Seul Catulon & Celtes moderez. English.

The *Italian* Land of the Mountains shall tremble, The *Lion* and the *Cock* shall not agree very well together, Shall for fear help one another, The only *Catulon* and *Celtes* shall be moderate.

ANNOT.

By the *Lion* he understandeth the *English*, because of their Arms, and by the *Cock* the *French*, called in Latin *Gallus*, which signifieth a Cock; *Catulon* is the *Spaniards*, as if he should say *Castilian*; the *Celtes* are the *Dutch* of the Low-Countries.

XCIV.

French.

Au Port Selyn le Tyrant mis a Mort, La liberté non pourtant recouvrée, Le nouveau Mars par vindict & remort, Dame par force de frayeur honorée. English.

In the *Port Selyn* the Tyrant shall be put to death And yet the liberty shall not be recovered, The new *Mars* by vengeance and remorse, Lady by excess of fear honoured.

ANNOT.

By the *Port Selyn*, is meant *Constantinople*, because of several Emperours of the *Turks* that have been of that name, therefore the intention of this Prophecy, is, that one of the Turkish Emperours shall be put to death at *Constantinople*, which for all that, shall not recover her liberty. The *new Mars*, be like he is so called, that shall put him to death *by vengeance without remorse. The Lady by excess of fear honoured*, may be applied to the present great Sultaness, Mother to this present Emperour of the *Turks*, who hath hitherto made her self very considerable by a great party, which she hath raised against her Son, to prevent him from putting his Brothers to death, as is usually practised in that Court.

XCV.

French.

Devant Moustier trouvé enfant besson, D'Heroik sang de Moine & vetustique, Son bruit per Secte, Langue, & puissance Son, Qu'on dira fort eslevé le Vopisque. English.

Before the Minster shall one twin be found, From Heroik blood, of a Monk and Ancient, His fame by Sect, Tongue, and Power shall be sounded, So that they shall say the Vopisk is much raised.

ANNOT.

The meaning of the whole is, that a Twin shall be found before a Church, begot by a Monk, of Illustrious and Ancient Family, and shall become very famous, *So that they shall say the Vopisk is much raised. Vopiscus* in Latin, is, that one of the Twins, which cometh to perfect Birth.

XCVI.

French.

Celuy qu'aura la charge de destruire, Temples & Sectes changez par fantaisie, Plus aux Rochers, qu'aux vivans viendra nuire, Par langue ornée d'oreille rassasie. English.

He that shall have charge to destroy, Churches and Sects, changed by fancy; Shall do more harm to the Rocks, than to the living, By a smooth tongue filling up the Ears.

As the words of this Stanza are plain, so is the sense most obscure, and so to be left to the Readers private Judgement.

XCVII.

French.

Ce que fer, flamme, na sceu parachever, La douce langue au conseil viendra faire, Par respos, songe le Roy fera resuer, Plus l'Ennemy en feu sang militaire. English.

What neither Iron nor Fire could compass, Shall be done by a smooth tongue in the Councel, In sleep a dream shall make the King to think, The more the Enemy in fire and Military blood.

ANNOT.

The sense of this is plain, though the words be somthing untowardly expressed.

XCVIII.

French.

Le Chef qu'aura conduit peuple infiny, Loin de son Ciel: de mœurs & langue estrange, Cinq mille en Crete & Thessalie finy, Le Chef fuiant sauvé en la Marine Grange. English.

The Captain that shall lead an infinite deal of people Far from their Countrey, to one of strange manners and Language, Five thousand in *Candia* and *Thessalia* finished, The Head running away, shall be safe in a Barn by the Sea.

ANNOT.

It is some great Commander that shall lead a multitude of people into a strange Countrey, far from their own; suppose *Candia* and *Thessalia*, where the said Commander shall be compelled to run away, and to save himself in a Barn by the Sea side.

XCIX.

French.

Le grand Monarque qui fera compagnie, Avec deux Rois unis par amitié, O quel souspir fera la grand mesgnie, Enfans, Narbonne alentour, quel pitié! English.

The great Monarch shall keep company, With two Kings united in friendship; O what fights shall be made by their followers! Children, O what pity shall be about *Narbon*.

This Stanza requireth no interpretation more, than what every one will be pleased to give himself.

C.

French.

Long temps au Ciel sera veu gris Oiseau, Aupres de Dole & de Tuscane Terre, Tenant au Bec un verdoiant rameau, Mourra tost Grand, & finira la Guerre. English.

A great while shall be seen in the Air a gray Bird, Near *Dola* and the *Tuscan* Land, Holding in his Bill a green bough; Then shall a great one die, and the War have and end.

ANNOT.

Dola is a Town in *Burgundy.* The *Tuscan* Land, is that which belongeth to the Duke of *Florence.*

Michael Nostradamus.

CENTURY II.

I.

French.

Vers Aquitaine par insults Britanniques, De par eux mesmes grandes incursions, Pluyes, Gelees, feront terroirs iniques, Port Selyn fortes fera invasions. *English.*

Towards *Gascony* by *English* assaults, By the same shall be made great incursions, Rains, Frosts, shall marre the ground. *Port Selyn* shall make strong Invasions.

ANNOT.

Three Prophecies are contained in this Stanza, the first that the *English* shall make an incursion in *Gascony*; the second, that there shall be a great dearth by Rains and Frosts; the third, that the *Turks* shall make great Incursion.

II.

French.

La teste glue sera la teste blanche, Autant de mal que France a fait leur bien, Mort a l'Anthene, grand pendu fus la branche, Quand prins des siens, le Roy dira combien. *English.*

The Glue-head shall do the white head As much harm, as *France* hath done it good, Dead at the Sails yard, a great one hang'd on a Tree, When a King taken by his own, shall say, how much?

ANNOT.

I did never find that word of Glue-head before in any Author, and I believe if *Cotgrave* were alive again, it would puzzle him to give the interpretation thereof.

The third and fourth signifie, that one shall be hanged on the Sails-yard, and another on a Tree, when a King shall be taken by his own Men, and shall say how much? that is, how much money shall I give you to set me free.

III.

French.

Par la chaleur Solaire sur la Mer, De Negrepont, les Poissons demy cuits, Les Habitans les viendront entamer, Quand Rhode & Genes leur faudra le Biscuit. English.

By the heat of the Sun upon the Sea Of *Negrepont*, the Fishes shall be half broiled, The Inhabitants shall come to cut them up, When *Rhodes* and *Genoa* shall want Biscake.

ANNOT.

  Negrepont is an Island of the *Archipelago* near *Morea*, anciently called *Eubœa*. *Rhodes* is another Island, and, *Genoa* a City in *Italy*, by the Seaside. The rest is plain.

IV.

French.

Depuis Monac jusqu'aupres de Sicile, Toute la plage demoura desolée, Il ny aura Fauxbourgs, Cité, ne Ville, Que par Barbares pillée soit & volée. English.

From *Monaco* as far as *Sicily*, All the Sea coast shall be left desolate, There shall not be Suburbs, Cities, nor Towns, Which shall not be pillaged and plundred by *Barbarians*.

ANNOT.

  Monaco is a Town seated by the Sea-side in *Italy*, between *Provence* and *Genoa*. This Prophecy hath been once already fulfilled, when the famous Pyrate *Barbarossa*, being sent by the grand Seignor, to help the *French* King against the Emperour *Charles* the V. in his return home, plundered all that Coast, and carried away an innumerable multitude of people into slavery.

V.

French.

Quand dans Poisson, Fer & Lettre enfermée, Hors sortira qui puis fera la Guerre, Aura par Mer sa classe bien ramée; Aparoissant pres de Latine Terre. English.

When in a Fish, Iron and a Letter shall be shut up, He shall go out that afterwards shall make War, He shall have his Fleet by Sea well provided, Appearing by the *Roman* Land.

ANNOT.

  The words and the sense are plain.

VI.

French.

Aupres des Portes & dedans deux Citez, Seront deux Fleaux & onc n'aperceu un tel, Faim, dedans Peste, de Fer hors gens boutez, Crier secours au grand Dieu immortel. English.

Near the Gates and within two Cities Shall be two Scourges, I never saw the like, Famine, within Plague, people thrust out by the Sword, Shall cry for help to the great God immortal.

ANNOT.

This needeth no Interpretation.

VII.

French.

Entre plusieurs aux Isles deportez, L'un estre nay a deux dens en la gorge, Mourront de Faim, les Arbres esbroutez, Pour eux neuf Roy, nouvel Edict leur forge. English.

Among many that shall be transported into the Islands, One shall be born with two Teeth in his mouth, They shall die of hunger, the Trees shall be eaten, They shall have a new King, who shall make new Laws for them.

ANNOT.

This is so plain, that it needeth no explication.

VIII.

French.

Temples Sacrez, prime facon Romaine, Rejetteront les goffes Fondemens, Prenant leurs Loix premieres & humaines, Chassants non tout, de Saints le cultement. English.

Churches Consecrated, and the ancient *Roman* way, Shall reject the tottering Foundations, Sticking to their first humane Laws, Expelling, but not altogether the worshipping of Saints.

ANNOT.

This Prophecy, is concerning the beginning of the Reformed Religion, when the *Roman* Church rejected it, yet nevertheless, for shame they left off many of their fopperies, for ever since they never appeared so great Worshippers of Saints as before.

IX.

French.

Neuf ans le Regne le maigre en paix tiendra, Puis il cherra en soif si sanguinaire, Pour luy grand peuple sans Foy & Loy mourra, Tué par un beaucoup plus debonaire. **English.**

Nine years shall the lean one keep the Kingdom in Peace, Then he will fall into such a bloody thirst, That a great people shall die without Faith or Law, He shall be killed by one milder than himself.

ANNOT.

It is a lean man that shall keep in Peace the Kingdom, for the space of nine years, and then shall become cruel; so that he shall put to death many people without Law, or regard of his promise.

X.

French.

Avant long temps le tout sera rangé, Nous esperons un siecle bien senestre, L'Estat des masques & des seuls bien changé, Peu trouveront qui a son rang vueille estre. **English.**

Before it be long, all shall be set in order, We look for a sinister Age, The state of the Visards and of *the alone* shall be changed, They shall find few that will keep their ranks.

ANNOT.

All the difficulty of this consisteth in what he meaneth by the *Visard* and *alone*, for my part, I believe he aimeth at the *Popish* Clergy and Monks; the first by reason of their Hypocrisy, the other by reason of their solitariness. The rest is plain.

XI.

French.

Le prochain, fils de l'Aisnier parviendra, Tant eslevé jusqu'au au Regne des fors, Son aspre gloire un chascun la craindra, Mais les enfans du Regne jettez hors. **English.**

The eldest Son of l'*Aisnier* shall prosper, Being raised to the degree of the great ones, Every one shall fear his high glory, But his children shall be cast out.

ANNOT.

This is an Horoscope, for the Interpretation of which we are beholding to, Mr. *Mannessier* of *Amiens*, who saith that the Father of the Lords l'*Aisniers* writ to *Nostradamus* his friend, to know his childrens fortune, who sent him those four Verses for an answer, by which it is evident that the eldest should be an eminent Man, as it fell out, being one of the chiefest men in the Province of

Anjou, and one of the chiefest instruments to make Peace between *Louis* the XIII. and his Mother *Mary* of *Medicis*, after the Battle of *Pont de Cé*.

The fourth Verse saith, that some of his other Children should be expelled the Kingdom, as it happened by reason of a false report raised against one of them, which compelled him to retire into *Portugal* till the truth was known, as it was afterwards to his great repute and honour.

XII.

French.

Yeux clos ouverts d'antique fantaisie, L'habit des seuls sera mis a neant, Le grand Monarque chastiera leur frenesie, Ravir des Temples le Thresor par devant. English.

Eyes shut, shall be open by an antick fancy, The cloths of the alone shall be brought to nothing. The great Monarck shall punish their frenzy, For having ravished the Treasure of the Temple before.

ANNOT.

I can fasten this upon no body, but upon some Monks, which are called here *The alone*, because of their solitary life, who shall be punished by a King, for having robbed the Church.

XIII.

French.

Le corps sans ame plus n'estre en sacrifice, Jour de la mort mis en Nativité. L'Esprit Divin sera l'ame fœlice, Voiant le Verbe en son Eternité. English.

The body without the soul shall be no more admitted in Sacrifice, The day of the death shall be put for the Birth-day, The Divine Spirit shall make the Soul happy, By seeing the Word in its Eternity.

ANNOT.

The first Verse seemed to Prophecy the Reformation of Religion, and the change of opinion concerning the Lords Supper, which should be no more a Sacrifice (as the *Roman* Church calleth the Mass) of a body without a soul, but only a commemoration of the Lords death, as the second Verse confirmeth, saying, *The day of the death shall be put for the Birth-day*, seeing, that by the commemoration of that death, we are renewed into a newness of life, and as it were born again. The last two Verse are easie.

XIV.

French.

A Tours, Gien, Gergeau, seront yeux penetrans, Descouvriront le long de la grande Sereine, Elle & sa Suite au Port seront entrans, Combat poussez Puissance Souveraine. English.

At *Tours, Gien, Gergeau*, shall be piercing eyes, Who shall discover along the great *Syren*, She and her Attendans shall enter into the Port, By a fight shall be thrust out the Soveraign Power.

Tours, Gien, and Gergeau are Cities upon the River of *Loire*, which is called here *the great Syren*, because of the length of its course, the meaning then is, that those Cities shall be watchful, and stand upon their guard, and shall fight against a King, which if it hath already come to pass in the Civil Wars, or shall happen hereafter, I cannot affirm.

XV.

French.

Un peu devant Monarque trucidé, Castor, Pollux, en nef astre crinite, L'Airain public, par Terre & Mer vuidé, Pisa, Ast, Ferrare, Turin Terre interdite. English.

A little before a Monarch be killed *Castor*, and *Pollux* shall appear, and a Comet in the Ship; The publick brass, by Land and Sea shall be emptyed, *Pisa, Ast, Ferrare, Turin*, Countreys forbidden.

ANNOT.

The meaning of this is, that a little before a Monarck be killed, *Castor* and *Pollux* two Meteores so called, as also a Comet in that constellation of the Heavens, called *the ship of Argos*, and *the Publick Brass*, that is, the Canons by Land and Sea shall be emptied, and these Towns of *Italy*, viz. *Pisa, Ast, Ferrare, Turin*, shall be excommunicated by the *Pope*.

XVI.

French.

Naples, Palerme, Sicile, Syracuse, Nouveaux Tyrants, fulgures, feu Cœlestes, Force de Londres, Gand, Bruxelles, & Suse, Grand Hecatombe, Triomphe, faire Festes. English.

Naples, Palermo, Sicily, Syracusa, New Tyrants, Lightnings, Celestial fires, Army from *London, Ghent, Bruxelles*, and *Suse*, A great Hecatomb, Triumphs, and Feasts.

ANNOT.

There is nothing difficult but the word *Hecatomb*, which is a Greek word, signifying a Sacrifice of an hundred Oxen.

XVII.

French.

Le Camp du Temple de la Vierge Vestale, Non esloigné d'Ethene & Monts Pyrenées, Le grand conduit est chassé dans la Male, North gettez Fleuves, & Vignes mastinées. English.

The Camp of the Temple of the Vestal Virgin, Not far from *Ethene* and the *Pyrenean* Mountains, The great Conduit is driven in the Clock-bag, Rivers overflown in the North, and the Vines spoiled.

ANNOT.

There is so many faults in the impression of this, and so hard to be rectified, that I had rather leave it to the liberty of the judicious Reader, then make my self ridiculous in not giving him satisfaction.

XVIII.

French.

Nouvelle Pluie, subite, impetueuse, Empeschera subit deux excercites, Pierre, Ciel, Feux, faire la Mer pierreuse, La mort de sept, Terre & Marin subites. English.

A new Rain, sudden, impetuous, Shall suddenly hinder two Armies, Stone, Heaven, Fire, shall make the Sea stony, The death of seven shall be sudden upon Land and Sea.

ANNOT.

The first two Verses signifie, that a sudden and impetuous Rain shall hinder two Armies from fighting.

The two last Verses foretell several Prodigies, the which happening, seven persons shall suddenly die upon the Sea and Land.

XIX.

French.

Nouveaux venus, lieu basty sans defence, Occuper place pour lors inhabitable, Prez, Maisons, Champs, Villes prendre a plaisance, Faim, Peste, Guerre, arpent long labourable. English.

New comers shall build a place without fence, And shall occupy a place that was not then habitable, They shall at their pleasure take Fields, Houses and Towns. There shall be Famine, Plague, War, and a long arable field.

ANNOT.

This is so plain, that it needeth no Interpretation.

XX.

French.

Freres & Sœurs en divers lieux captifs, Se trouveront passer pres du Monarque, Les contempler ses deux yeux ententifs, Des plaisant vont, Menton, Front, Nez les marques. English.

Brothers and Sisters shall be made slaves in divers places, And shall pass before the Monarck, Who shall look upon them with attentive eyes, They shall go in heaviness, witness their Chin, Forehead and Nose.

This is obvious to the meanest capacity.

XXI.

French.

L'Ambassadeur envoié par Biremes, A my chemin incogneus repoulsez, De Sel renfort viendront quatre triremes, Cordes & Chaines en Negrepont troussez. English.

The Embassadour that was sent in *Biremes*, In the midleway shall be repulsed by unknown Men, From the Salt to his succours shall come four triremes, Ropes and Chains shall be carried to *Negrepont*.

ANNOT.

     Bireme is a Galley that hath two ranges of Oares, *Trireme* is one that hath three ranges. The meaning then of this is, that an Embassadour shall be sent in a Galley with two ranges of Oares, and that he shall be met in his way by unknown men, that is, Pyrates; there shall come to his succours *from the Salt*, that is, from the *French* four *Triremes*, that is four Galleys, every one having three ranges of Oares, but they shall all be carried to *Negrepont*, an Island belonging to the *Turk*.

XXII.

French.

Le Camp Ascop d'Europe partira, Sadioignant proche de l'Isle submergée, D'Arton classe Phalange partira, Nombril du Monde plus grand voix subrogée. English.

The Camp *Ascop* shall go from *Europe*, And shall come near the drowned Island; From *Arton* shall go an Army by Sea and Land, By the Navel of the World a greater vice shall be substituted.

ANNOT.

     The Author hath darkned this Stanza with so many barbarous words, as *Camp Ascop*, *drowned Island*, D'*Arton*, *Navel of the World*, that it is very like either he did not understand himself, or would not be understood by others.

XXIII.

French.

Palaces Oiseaux, par Oiseau dechassé, Bien tost apres le Prince parvenu, Combien qu'hors Fleuve ennemy repoulsé, Dehors saisy, trait d'Oiseau soustenu. English.

Palais Birds, driven away by a Bird, Soon after that, the Prince is come to his own, Although the enemy be driven beyond the River, He shall be seased upon without, by the trick of the Bird.

ANNOT.

The meaning of this is, that many Courtiers (called here *Palace* Birds) shall be justled out of favour by another principal Bird, that is a great Courtier, as soon as the Prince shall come to his own.

The two last Verses seem to foretell that the said principal Courtier shall seize upon the Prince, notwithstanding that some succour shall come to his help, which shall be beaten back beyond the River.

XXIV.

French.

Bestes farouches de faim Fleuves traner, Plus part du Champ encontre Ister sera, En Cage de Fer le grand fera traisner. Quand rien enfant de Germain n'observera. English.

Wild Beasts for hunger shall swim over Rivers, Most part of the field shall be near *Ister,* Into an Iron Cage he shall cause the great one to be drawn, When the Child of *German* shall observe nothing.

ANNOT.

Ister is a River, *German* is a proper name of some considerable person, whose Son shall not observe or take notice when that eminent person mentioned here, shall be drawn into an Iron Cage.

XXV.

French.

La Garde estrange trahira Forteresse, Espoir & umbre de plus haut mariage, Garde deceüe Fort prins dedans la presse, Loire, Saone, Rhosne, Gar, a Mort outrage. English.

The Garrison of strangers shall betray the Fort, Under the hope and shadow of a higher Match, The Garrison shall be deceived, and the Fort taken in the crowd, *Loire, Saone, Rhosne, Gar,* shall do harm to Death.

ANNOT.

There is no difficulty but in the last Verse, where you must observe that *Loire, Saone, Rhosne,* and *Gardon,* which for the Verses sake is contracted into *Gar;* are Rivers of *France,* which are threatned here of overflowing, and causing the death of many people.

XXVI.

Pour la faveur que la Cité fera, Au grand qui tost perdra Camp de Bataille, Le sang d'ans Pau le Thesin versera, De sang feux, mors, noyez de coup de taille. English.

Because of the favour the City shall shew, To the great one, who soon after shall loose the Battle, The *Thesin* shall pour blood into the *Pau*, Of blood, fire, dead, drowned, by Edgeling.

ANNOT.

      This is plain, if you observe that the *Thesin* is a River of *Italy*, and the *Pau* another, into the which the *Thesin* runneth.

XXVII.

French.

Le Divin Verbe sera du ciel frappé, Qui ne pourra proceder plus avant, Du resserrant le secret estoupé, Quon marchera par dessus & devant. English.

The Divine Word shall be struck by Heaven, So that he shall proceed no further, The secret of the close Keeper, shall be so closed up, That people shall tread upon, and before it.

ANNOT.

      By the *Divine Word*, you must not understand the second person of the Trinity, or else all this Stanza would be absurd; but you must understand a Divine or Theologian, called in Greek θεόλογος, which signifieth a *Divine Word*. The meaning therefore of it, is, that a *Theologian shall be struck by Heaven*; that is, shall die, so that he shall proceed no further in his work, which I suppose by the two last Verses, was the Philosophers stone; for in the two last Verses he saith, that the *secret of the close Keeper*, that is, of him that wrought secretly, shall (by his death) be so closed up, *that people shall tread on, and before it.*

XXVIII.

French.

Le penultiesme de Surnom de Prophete, Prendra Diane pour son jour & repos, Loing vaguera par Frenetique teste, Et delivrant un grand peuple d'Impos. English.

The last, but one of the Sirname of the Prophet, Shall take *Diana* for his day and his rest, He shall wander far by reason of his Frenetick head, Delivering a great people from impositions.

ANNOT.

This is concerning a *false Prophet*, which is called here the last but one of that Surname, who shall make *Diana* (that is *Monday* which is dedicated to *Diana*) his *Sunday* or *Sabbath day*, and so wandring to and fro in a *Frenetick* manner, shall perswade many people to pay no Taxes.

XXIX.

French.

L'Oriental sortira de son Siege, Passer les Monts Apennins, voir la Gaule, Transpassera le Ciel, les Eaux & Neige, Et un chacun frappera de sa Gaule. **English.**

The Oriental shall come out of his Seat, Shall pass over the *Apennine* Mountains, and see *France*, Shall go over the Air, the Waters and Snow, And shall strike every one with his Rod.

ANNOT.

It is an Eastern Prince, who leaving his Countrey, shall come over the *Apennine* Mountains, which divide *Italy*, and come as far as *France*, destroying all before him.

XXX.

French.

Un qui les Dieux d'Annibal infernaux, Fera renaistre, effrayeur des Humains, Onc plus d'horreur ne plus dire journaux, Qu'avint viendra par Babel aux Romains. **English.**

One that shall cause the infernal Gods of *Hannibal* To live again, the terror of Mankind, There was never more horror, not to say ill dayes, Did happen, or shall, to the *Romans* by *Babel*.

ANNOT.

This Prophecy was concerning *Charles* V. Emperour, who sacked *Rome*, took the Pope Prisoner, and filled it with more horror and slaughter than *Hannibal* did, though a Heathen.

XXXI.

French.

En Campanie le Cassilin fera tant, Quon ne verra que d'Aux les Champs couvers, Devant apres la pluye de long temps, Hormis les arbres rien lon verra de verts. **English.**

In *Campania* the *Cassilin* shall so behave himself, That nothing shall be seen but Fields covered with Garlick, Before, and after it, shall not Rain for a good while, Except the Trees, no Green shall be seen.

This hath a dependance upon the foregoing Stanza; for *Campania* is the Province wherein *Rome* is seated, and *Cassilin*, called *Campania di Roma*, is the same as *Castillan*, because *Charles* V. was not only Emperour, but also King of *Spain*, the chief Province of which is *Castilia*: therefore the Author describeth here the misery and devastation of *Campania di Roma* by the *Castilian*, who left nothing in the ground, but Garlick, which is their most delicate food, and nothing Green but the Trees.

XXXII.

French.

Lait Sang, Grenovilles, escouldre en Dalmatie, Conflit donné, peste pres de Balene, Cry sera grand par toute Esclavonie, Lors naistra Monstre pres & dedans Ravenne. English.

Milk, Blood, Frogs shall reign in *Dalmatia*, A Battle fought, the Plague near *Balene*, A great cry shall be through all *Sclavonia*, Then shall be born a Monster, near and within *Ravenna*.

ANNOT.

Dalmatia and *Sclavonia*, are Countreys joyning to the *Adriatick* Sea, belonging to the *Venetians*. *Ravenna* is a City in *Italy*, the rest needeth no interpretation.

XXXIII.

French.

Dans le torrent qui descend de Verone, Par lors qu'au Pau guidera son entrée, Un grand Naufrage, & non moins en Garonne, Quand ceux de Genes Marcheront leur contrée. English.

In the torrent which cometh down from *Verona*, About the place where it falleth into the *Pau*, A great Shipwrack, and no less in *Garonna*, When those of *Genoa* shall go into their Countrey.

ANNOT.

Verona is a City in *Italy*, belonging to the *Venetians*, through the middle of which runneth a River called *Adde*, which falleth into the River *Pau*, about which place there shall be a great Shipwrak; as also another in the River of *Garonna*, which passeth at *Bordeaux*, the time that the Author marketh, is when those of *Genoa* shall go into their Countrey, that is to say, when some Ships of *Genoa* shall come to *Bordeaux*.

XXXIV.

L'Ire insensée du Combat furieux, Fera a Table par Freres le Fer luire, Les departir, blessé, curieux, Le fier duel viendra en France nuire. English.

The mad anger of the furious fight, Shall cause by Brothers the Iron to glister at the Table, To part them one wounded, curious, The fierce Duel shall do harm after in *France*.

ANNOT.

It is the short History of two Brothers, who fought at the Table, whereby one that was curious to part them was wounded, they afterwards fought a Duel, in whose imitation many since have been fought, to the great harm of the *French* Gentry.

XXXV.

French.

Dans deux Logis de nuit le feu prendra, Plusieurs dedans estoufez & rostis, Pres de deux Fleuves pour seur il adviendra, Sol, l'Arc, & Caper, tous seront amortis. English.

The fire shall take by night in two Houses, Many shall be stifled and burnt in it; Near two Rivers it shall for certain happen, Sun, Arc, Caper, they shall all be mortified.

ANNOT.

By *Sun, Arc, Caper,* he meaneth the Sun being in the Signs of *Sagitarius* and *Capricornus*.

This Prophecy was fulfilled about 90. years ago in the City of *Lion*, seated upon two Rivers, *viz.* the *Rhosne* and the *Saone*, for about that time several Merchants coming to the Fair, some went to lodge at the Silver Head, in the street *de la Grenete*, where being in an upper room, as they were talking of their businesses, and passing the time merrily, the fire took in the Kitchen where was abundance of Oil, which did burn so suddenly and so violently, that the lower part of the House was presently consumed. Those Merchants that were in the upper room towards the street, begun to look for their Clock-bags, that were lockt up in a Trunk; but while they were busie about opening the Trunk, the Stair-case fell, and the fire got into their Room, then begun they to cry for help through the Windows. They would willingly have thrown themselves down the Windows, but they were barred with Iron, so that they could not save themselves, the House being a fire on all sides; Moreover, the neighbours taking more care of their own Houses, then of those Strangers, did run every one to his own concerns, so that they all miserably perished. *Parradin* in his 3. Book of the History of *Lyon, Chap. 22.*

XXXVI.

French.

Du grand Prophete les Lettres seront prinses, Entre les Mains du Tyran deviendront, Frauder son Roy seront ses entreprinses, Mais ses rapines bien tost le troubleront. English.

The Letters of the great Prophet shall be intercepted, They shall fall into the hands of the Tyrant, His undertakings shall be to deceive his King, But his extortions shall trouble him soon.

ANNOT.

It is some eminent Churchman, whose Letters shall be intercepted, by which he intended to betray his King, therefore his actions shall be called in question, and being found guilty of extortion, he shall suffer for it.

XXXVII.

De ce grand nombre que l'on envoiera, Pour secourir dans le fort assiegez, Peste & Famine tous les devorera, Horsmis septante qui seront profligez. English.

Of that great number which shall be sent, To succour the besieged in the Fort, Plague and Famine shall devour them all, Except seventy that shall be beaten.

ANNOT.

      This is so plain, that it needeth no explication.

XXXVIII.

French.

Des Condamnez sera fait un grand nombre, Quand les Monarques seront conciliez, Mais l'un deux viendra si mal encombre, Que guere ensemble ne seront raliez. English.

There shall be a great number of condemned men, When the Monarchs shall be reconciled, But one of them shall come to such misfortune, That their reconciliation shall not last long.

ANNOT.

      The words and sense of this are easie to be understood.

XXXIX.

French.

Un an devant le conflict Italique, Germains, Gaulois, Espagnols pour le Fort, Cherra l'Escole maison de republique, Ou horsmis peu, seront suffoquez morts. English.

One year before the *Italian* fight, *Germans*, *French*, *Spaniards* for the Fort, The School-house of the Common-wealth shall fall, Where, except few, they shall be suffocated, and dead.

ANNOT.

      It seemeth there should be a Battle between the *Italians*, *Germans*, *French*, *Spaniards* for a Fort, which I suspect to have been that of *Serizoles*, wherein all those Nations were engaged, and that one year before that Battle, the publick house of a *Common-wealth* should fall, and kill abundance of people; But of this I could find nothing in History.

XL.

French.

Un peu apres non point long intervalle, Par Mer & Terre sera fait grand tumulte, Beaucoup plus grande sera pugne Navalle, Feu, Animaux, qui plus feront d'Insulte. English.

A little while after, without any great distance of time, By Sea and Land shall a great tumult be made, The Sea fight shall be much greater, Fire and Beasts which shall make greater insult.

ANNOT.

This hath a Relation to a foregoing Stanza, and likewise is not hard to be understood.

XLI.

French.

La grand Estoile par sept jours bruslera, Nuce fera deux Soleils apparoir, Le gros mastin toute nuit hurlera, Quand grand Pontife changera de terroir. English.

The great Star shall burn for the space of seven days, A Cloud shall make two Suns appear, The big Mastif shall houl all night, When the great Pope shall change his Countrey.

ANNOT.

The meaning of this is, that those three Prodigies, contained in the first three Verses, shall appear when a *Pope* changeth his Countrey.

XLII.

French.

A Coq, Chiens, & Chats de sang seront repeus, Et de la playe du Tyran trouvé Mort, Au lict d'un autre, Jambes & Bras rompus, Qui n'avoit peu mourir de cruel Mort. English.

A Cock, Dogs, and Cats shall be fed with Blood, And with the wound of the Tyrant found dead, In the bed of another, with Legs and Arms broken, Who could not die before by a cruel Death.

ANNOT.

These words signifie, that a great man or Tyrant shall be found dead in another mans Bed, having his *Legs* and *Arms* broken, the body of which shall be devoured by these three kinds of Creatures, a *Cock*, a *Dog*, and a *Cat*. The last Verse signifieth that this Tyrant had escaped a *cruel Death*.

XLIII.

French.

Durant l'estoile cheuelue apparente, Les trois grand Princes seront faits ennemis, Frappez du Ciel, Paix, Terre tremulente, Arne, Tibre, undans Serpent sur le bord mis. English.

During the hairy apparent Star, The three great Princes shall be made Enemies, Struck from Heaven, Peace, quaking Earth, *Arne, Tyber,* full of Surges, Serpent cast upon the Shore.

ANNOT.

In the year 1556. upon the first day of *March* appeared a blazing Star which lasted three Months, and in that year the three great Princes were made Enemies, *viz. Paul* IV. Pope, *Henry* II. King of *France,* and *Philip* II. King of *Spain,* about the breaking of the Truce by *Henry* II.

The Affairs not succeeding according to the Pope's, and the King of *France*'s desire, they made Peace with the *Spaniard* the 14th of *October* 1557. and because it was an effect of Gods Providence, which moved the Pope's, and the Kings hearts; the Author saith, they were *struck from Heaven.*

After this *Peace* the Author mentions an *Earth-quake,* which is very likely considering the overflowing of the *Tyber,* which followed immediately.

The night after, that *Peace* was proclaimed at *Rome,* on a *Tuesday* the *Tyber* did so overflow his Banks, that the inundation was thought the greatest that ever was, yea greater than that which happened in the year 1530. under *Clement* VII.

There were ten or twelve Mills carried away, all the Vine-yards along the *Tyber,* from *Pontemole* to St. *Peters* Church, were buried under the Sands, that the water carried.

Abundance of Houses fell to the ground. In *Rome* many Gardens and houses of pleasure were destroyed, the loss of the Wines, Hay, Wood, and Corn could not be valued.

In *Florence* the River of *Arno* did more mischief than the *Tyber* at *Rome,* the History of the Genealogy of the house of *Medicis,* made by *Peter de Boissat,* mentioneth, that in some places of the City of *Florence,* the water overflowed to the heigth of eight Fathoms, and covered all the valley of *Arne.*

The damage was yet greater at *Empoly,* a Town in *Tuscany,* where, of three thousand people, there escaped but eighteen.

But to return to *Tyber,* its waters being retired into their Channel, left so much mud, where it had overflowed, that no body could walk upon it, and upon that mud near the *Tyber,* was a Serpent seen of a prodigious bigness, which was killed by the Countrey people.

This is the Authors meaning in the last Verse, *Arne, Tyber, full of Surges, Serpent cast upon the Shore.*

In the third Verse he saith, those three Princes were struck or moved from Heaven to make *Peace,* that is, from God; every one considering that this War was only for their mutual distruction.

The Vulgar impression putteth in the fourth Verse, *Pau, Tyber,* in stead of *Arne, Tyber,* which is a visible fault; for the History mentioneth only the inundation of those two Rivers in *Italy,* it may be that the likeness of those words, *Pau* and *Arne,* is the cause of the mistake; as also because the name of *Pau,* which is the biggest River in *Italy,* is more famous in History than that of *Arne,* which is the River that passeth through *Florence.*

XLIV.

French.

L'Aigles poussée entour de Pavillons, Par autre oiseaux d'Entour sera chassé, Quand bruit de Timbres, Tubes, & Sonaillons, Rendront le sens de la Dame insensée. **English.**

The Eagle flying among the Tents, By other Birds shall be driven away, When noise of Cymbals, Trumpets, and Bells, Shall render the sense to the Lady that was without it.

ANNOT.

It is an Eagle driven from the Tents by other Birds, when a mad Lady shall recover her senses by the noise of Cymbals, Trumpets, and Bells.

XLV.

French.

Trop le Ciel pleure l'Androgyn procrée, Pres de Ciel sang humain respandu, Par mort trop tard grand peuple recrée, Tard & tost vient le secours attendu. **English.**

The Heaven bemoaneth too much the *Androgyn* born, Near Heaven humane blood shall be spilt, By death too late a great people shall be refreshed, Late and soon cometh the succours expected.

ANNOT.

Androgyn, is one that is Male and Female, from the Greek word ἀνηρ, which signifieth a Male, and γυνή, which signifieth a Female; the meaning then of the first Verse is, that some great persons, suppose a King and Queen, which he calleth Heaven, by reason of their exaltation above the common sort of people, shall bemoan too long one of their Children, that was, or shall be born Male and Female.

The second Verse is easie to be understood, if you take Heaven in the same sense that we have said. The last two Verses are plain.

XLVI.

French.

Apres grand troche humain, plus grand sapreste, Le grand Moteur les siecles renouvelle, Pluye, Sang, Lait, Famine, Fer & Peste, Au Ciel veu feu courant longue estincelle. **English.**

After a great humane change, another greater is nigh at hand, The great Motor reneweth the Ages, Rain, Blood, Milk, Famine, Sword, Plague, In the Heaven shall be seen a running fire with long sparks.

Troche in Greek is a Pulley, the meaning therefore of the Author, that after a great mutation, God shall renew the Ages, and according to his promise shall create a new Heaven, and a new Earth.

By those prodigies related in the two last Verses, it seemeth the Author intendeth to speak of the last day, and of the fore-runners of it.

XLVII.

French.

L'Ennemy grand viel, deult, meurt de poison, Les Souverains par infinis subjugues, Pierres pleuvoir cache soubs la Toison, Par mort Articles en vain sont alleguez. English.

The great and old Enemy grieveth, dieth by Poison, An infinite number of Soveraign's conquered, It shall rain stones, they shall hide under Rocks, In vain shall death alledge Articles.

ANNOT.

This hath a relation to the foregoing Stanza, and is as it were the second part of it. For as the foremost speaketh of the last day, so doth this of Dooms-day.

First, he saith that *the great and old Enemy grieveth and dieth by Poison*, that's the Devil who shall be cast into a Lake of Fire and Brimstone. The second Verse signifieth, that all the Kings of the Earth shall be subdued by him that is *Lord of Lords and King of Kings*. The third Verse expresseth, the anguish of the reprobate, when they shall cry to the Rocks, hide us, and to the Mountains, fall upon us. And the fourth Verse saith, that Death shall alledge in vain, the Articles she made with the Devil, and his Angels.

XLVIII.

French.

La grand Copie qui passera les Monts, Saturne, Aries, tournant au Poisson Mars, Venins cachez sous testes de Moutons, Leur chef pendu a fil de Polemars. English.

The great Army that shall pass over the Mountains, *Saturn, Aries, Mars*, turning to the Fishes, Poisons hidden in Sheeps heads, Their Captain hang'd with a thred of *Polemars*.

ANNOT.

Paradin relateth in his History, that after the Duke of *Alba* had relieved *Vulpian* with Victuals, which was done from the 22. of *July* to the first of *August*, a Captain of the Emperors Army named *la Trinité*, went out of *Valfrenieres* the same first day of *August*, to plunder the Countrey of *Piemont*.

He had 400 Horses, and 500 Foot: The news being brought to the Marshal of *Brissac*, he sent out a great number of Horses, who did utterly destroy their Foot, so that but thirty escaped, to carry the news to *Valfrenieres*.

The *Spanish* Horse, seeing the *French* in such a fury, ran away, and got some to *Ast*, some to *Alexandria*.

After that, the *Spaniards* seeking to revenge themselves, took a Castle three miles from *Cazal*, called *Frezene*, or *Fracinet du Pau*, where they hanged up the Captain, put to the sword all the *Italians*, and sent all the *French* to the *Galleys*.

This proceeding being not according to the Laws of Arms, we may believe, that the victorious discovered a malitious craft of the vanquished, who had left some Sheeps-heads poisoned, to revenge themselves of the victorious, which obliged the *Spaniards* to serve so the Captain, the *Italians* and the *French*; and because the *French* were not so ill used, as the *Italians*, we may judge that the *Italians* were the chief contrivers of this business.

Therefore the Author foreseeing this, saith, that the great Army of the *French*, which shall go over the Mountains, shall come to this mischief, because of the poison that was hidden in the Sheeps heads.

The Vulgar impression erreth much in putting *Salmons*, for *Muttons*; for every body knoweth that the *Salmons* do not come into the Mountains of *Montserrat*, and that in the Month of *August* it is not a meat fit for Souldiers, therefore in stead of *Salmons*, we have put *Muttons*, or Sheep.

The Captain was hanged with a thread of Polemars, that is, with a Match, of which, I am perswaded, that one certain *Polemars* was the Inventor.

The Author saith in the second Verse, that the time when this accident happened, was, when *Saturn* was in *Aries*, the Vulgar impression putteth *Are* in stead of *Aries*, but that's false, therefore set down *Aries*. *Saturn* was in that Sign in the year 1555. from the 20th of *February*, to the 14th of *July*, where from the 12th degree and four Minutes, he began to retrograde in the same Sign of *Aries*, till the 18th of *November*, so that *Saturn* was almost all that year in *Aries*.

He saith also that *Mars* was going back to *Pisces*; because in that same year, *Mars* that was gone out of the Sign of *Pisces* from the 19 of *March* 1554. was retrograding to come back again into it upon the 20th of *January* 1556.

Thus the Author meaneth, that this accident should happen in the year that *Saturn* should be in *Aries*, and *Mars* should be near the Sign of *Pisces*.

And to say truth, in the Month of *August*, *Mars* was in the Sign of *Scorpio*; upon the 23 of *September*, he entred into that of *Sagitarius*; the third of *November*, into that of *Capricornus*; the 12th of *December* into that of *Aquarius*; and the year following, *viz.* 1556. into that of *Pisces*; so that *Mars* was returning into *Pisces*, which is the end of its particular motion.

By this Astrological and Historical discourse we correct the Vulgar impression, which putteth turning from *Pisces*, *Mars*, in stead of which, we put, turning to *Pisces*, *Mars*, which we do by changing only *from*, into *to*, and sheweth us how careful we ought to be in the explication of these Stanza's, when the time is prefixed to us by Astronomical calculations.

The Authors Phrase doth confirm us in this correction, when he useth this word *turning*, which signifieth the motion that tendeth towards its end, and not the motion that cometh from its end.

XLIX.

French.

Les conseillers du premier Monopole, Les Conquerans seduits par la Melite, Rhodes, Bisance pour leur exposant pole, Terre faudra les pour-suivans de fuite. **English.**

The advisers of the first Monopoly, The Conquerors seduced by the *Melite, Rhodes, Bizance,* for exposing their Pole, The ground shall fail the followers of runaways.

All the difficulty of this lieth in the signification of the word *Pole*, which in Greek signifieth a City. The word *Monopoly* is Vulgar, and signifieth when one or few would engross all the Trade of a Town. The rest is so obscure, that I had rather leave it to the liberty of the Reader, than break my Brains about it, considering chiefly that I am going to bed, the precedent Stanza having exhausted all my Spirits, and so farewell till to morrow.

L.

French.

Quand ceux d'Hainault, de Gand, & de Bruxelles, Verront a Langres le Siege devant mis, Derrier leur flancs seront guerres cruelles, La playe antique sera pis qu'Ennemis. English.

When these of *Hainault*, of *Gand*, and of *Bruxelles*, Shall see the Siege laid before *Langres*, Behind their sides shall be cruel Wars, The old wound shall be worse then Enemies.

ANNOT.

Hainault is a Province of the Low-Countries, and *Gand* the chief Town in *Flanders*, and *Bruxelles* the chief Town of the Dukedome of *Brabant*.

Langres is a City in *France*, in the Province of *Champagne*, which is called the Maiden Town; because it was never besieged. The rest is easie.

LI.

French.

Le sang du juste a Londres fera faute, Bruslez par feu de vingt & trois les Six, La Dame antique cherra de place haute, De mesme secte plusieurs seront occis. English.

The blood of the just shall be wanting in *London*, Burnt by fire of three and twenty, the Six, The antient Dame shall fall from her high place, Of the same Sect many shall be killed.

ANNOT.

Leaving unto the impartial Reader his liberty to judge of this Prophecy, we for our part understand by it the impious and execrable murder, committed upon the person of our last most gracious Sovereign King *Charles* I. of blessed memory, to whose expiation it seemeth our Author attributeth the conflagration of *London*. By that proportion *of three and twenty, the Six*, is to be understood the number of Houses and Buildings that were burnt, which is about the proportion of three in four, and cometh near to the computation, as also by that *three twenties and Six*, may be understood the year 66. *By the antient Dame that shall fall from the high place*, is understood the Cathedral Church of St. *Paul*, which in the time of Paganism was dedicated to *Diana*, meant here by the title of an antient Dame, the *fall from her high place*, hath relation both to the sumptuousness and height of her building, as also to her situation, which is in the most eminent place of the City.

By this Verse, *Of the same Sect many shall be killed*, is signified the great number of other

Churches even the number of 87 (which he intimateth here by the name of the same Sect), that should be involved in the same woful conflagration.

LII.

French.

Dans plusieurs nuits la Terre tremblera, Sur le printemps deux efforts feront suitte, Corinthe, Ephese aux deux Mers nagera, Guerre sesmeut par deux vaillants de Luitte. English.

During many nights the Earth shall quake, About the Spring two great Earth-quakes shall follow one another, *Corinth*, *Ephesus* shall swim in the two Seas, War shall be moved by two great Wrestlers.

ANNOT.

Corinth is a City of *Grecia* and *Ephesus* one of *Asia*; the rest is plain.

LIII.

French.

Le grande Peste de cité maritime, Ne cessera que Mort ne soit vengée, Du juste sang par prix damné sans crime, De la grande Dame par feinte noutragée. English.

The great Plague of the Maritime City, Shall not cease till the death be revenged Of the just blood by price condemned without crime, Of the great Dame not fainedly abused.

ANNOT.

This is a confirmation of the LI. Stanza and foretelleth the great Plague we have had here in the year 1665. which he saith shall not cease till the death of the Just blood, meaning King *Charles* the I. be avenged who was as is here expressed, condemned without crime, and sold for a Price.

By the great Dame unfainedly abused, he meaneth the sumptuous Cathedral of St. *Paul*, which was polluted and made a Stable by those prophane wretches.

LIV.

French.

Par gent estrange & Nation lointaine, Leur grand Cité, apres eau fort troublée, Fille sans trop different de domaine, Prins chef, serreure, navoir esté riblée. English.

By a strange people and remote Nation, The great City near the water shall be much troubled, The Girl without great difference for a portion, Shall take the Captain, the Lock having not been pickt.

ANNOT.

In the explication of this mystical Stanza, I believe every body may be as wise as I.

LV.

Dans le conflit le grand qui peu valoit, A son dernier fera cas merveilleux, Pendant qu'Adrie verra ce qu'il failloit, Dans le Banquet poignarde l'orgueilleux. English.

In the fight the great one who was but little worth, At his last endeavour shall do a wonderful thing. While *Adria* shall see what was wanting, In the Banquet he shall stabb the proud one.

ANNOT.

    This is concerning some eminent person, who having shewed no great valour in a Battle, shall nevertheless in a Banquet be so bold as to stab a person of quality, that was proud.

    This accident must happen somewhere about *Venice*, because he saith that *Adria*, which is taken for *Venice* shall look on.

LVI.

French.

Que Peste & Glaive n'a sceu definer, Mort dans les pluies, sommet du Ciel frappé, L'Abbé mourra quand verra ruiner, Ceux du Naufrage, l'Escueil voulant graper. English.

He whom neither Plague, nor Sword could destroy, Shall die in the Rain being stricken with Thunder, The Abbot shall die when he shall see ruined, Those in the Shipwrack, striving to catch hold of the Rock.

ANNOT.

    There is two accidents contained in this Stanza, the first is in the two first Verses, where he saith that some considerable person, who had escaped the Sword, and the Plague shall be strucken by the Thunder, and die in a great showr of Rain.

    The second is, in the two last Verses, where he saith, an Abbot shall perish by Shipwrack, thinking to save himself by holding the Rock.

LVII.

French.

Avant conflit le grand tombera, Le grand a mort trop subite & plainte, Nay miparfait, la plus part nagera, Aupres du Fleuve, de sang la Terre teinte. English.

Before the Battle the great one shall fall, The great one to death too sudden and bewailed; One shall be born half perfect, the most part shall swim, Near the River the Earth shall be dyed with blood.

ANNOT.

The words are plain enough, but of the sense every one may think what he pleaseth.

LVIII.

French.

Sans pied ne main, dent aigue, & forte. Par Globe au fort de Port & laisne nay, Pres du portail, desloial le transporte, Seline luit, petit grand emmené. English.

Without foot or hand, sharp and strong tooth, By a Globe, in the middle of the Port, and the first born, Near the Gate shall be transported by a Traitor, *Seline* shineth, the little great one carried away.

ANNOT.

The sense of the whole is this, that an Infant begot by some person of quality shall be exposed in the night time, the Moon Shining, which he calleth *Seline*, from the Greek word σεληνη, which signifieth the Moon.

LIX.

French.

Classe Gauloise par appuy de grand Garde, Du grand Neptune & ses tridens Soldats, Ronger Provence pour soustenir grand bande, Plus Mars, Narbon, par Javelots & Dards. English.

The *French* Fleet by the help of the great Guard, Of great *Neptune* and his Tridentary Soldiers Shall gnaw *Provence* by keeping great company, Besides, *Mars* shall plague *Narbon* by Javelins and Darts.

ANNOT.

Here be two things designed in this Stanza one is concerning *Provence*, which shall be eaten up by Soldiers, and the other concerning the City of *Narbon*, which shall be Besieged, or the Citizens fall out among themselves.

LX.

French.

La foy Punique en Orient rompue, Grand Jud. & Rhosne, Loire & Tag changeront, Quand du Mulet la faim sera repeue, Classe espargie, Sang & Corps nageront. English.

The punick faith broken in the East, Great *Jud.* and *Rhosne*, *Loire* and *Tag.* shall be changed, When the Mules hunger shall be satisfied, The Fleet scattered, Blood and Bodies shall swim.

The Punick Faith in Latine *Punica fides*, a false Faith, was so called from the *Carthaginians*, called in Latine *Pœni*, which was an unfaithful Nation.

I do not know what he meaneth by great *Jud.* as for *Rhosne*, *Loire* and *Tag*, they are three Rivers, the two first in *France*, the last is the River of *Lisbone* called in Latine *Tagus*. The rest is easie.

LXI.

French.

Agen, Tonneins, Gironde & la Rochelle, O sang Troien mort au Port de la fleche, Derrier le Fleuve au Fort mise leschelle, Pointes, feu, grand meurtre sur la bresche. English.

Agen, *Tonneins*, *Gironde* and *Rochelle*, O *Trojan* blood death is at the harbour of the Arrow, Beyond the River the Ladder shall be raised against the Fort, Points, fire, great murder upon the breach.

ANNOT.

Agen and *Tonneins* are two Towns in *Gascony*, *Gironde* is a River that passeth in that Countrey, the sense therefore of the whole is, that there shall be great Wars, and fightings in those Towns, as also upon that River, which happened in the time of the civil Wars in *France*, as every body may read in the *Annals*, and also in the Commentaries of the Lord of *Monluck*.

LXII.

French.

Mabus puis tost alors mourra, viendra, Des gens & bestes un horrible desfaite, Puis tout a coup la vengeance on verra, Sang, Main, Soif, Faim, quand courra la Comete. English.

Mabus shall come, and soon after shall die, Of people and beasts shall be an horrible destruction, Then on a sudden the vengeance shall be seen, Blood, Hand, Thirst, Famine, when the Comet shall run.

ANNOT.

Here is nothing hard but who should be this *Mabus*, at last I found by transposition of Letters that he meaneth *Ambus*, which was the name of the Heades man that beheaded the Duke of *Montmorency* at *Thoulouse*, how miraculous therefore appeareth our Author, who did not only foretell general things, but also particular accidents, even the names of the persons that were to be born a hundred years after.

LXIII.

French.

Gaulois, Ausone bien peu subiuguera, Pau, Marne & Seine fera Perme l'Vrie, Qui le grand Mur contre eux dressera, Du moindre au Mur le grand perdra la vie. English.

The *French* shall a little subdue *Ausonne, Pau, Marne,* and *Seine* shall make *Perme l'Urie,* Which shall raise a great Wall against them, From the less to the Wall the great one shall loose his life.

ANNOT.

      Ausonne is always taken by the Author for the City of *Bordeaux,* because *Ausonius* a famous Latine Poet was born there, the rest is so obscure, and the text so corrupted, that I had rather leave it to the liberty of the Reader, then to become ridiculous, by not acknowledging my ignorance.

LXIV.

French.

Seicher de faim, de soif, gent Genevoise, Espoir prochain viendra au defaillir, Sur point tremblant sera Loy Gebenoise, Classe au grand Port ne se peut accueillir. English.

Those of *Geneva* shall be dried up with hunger and thirst, A near hope shall come when they shall be fainting, The *Gebenna* Law shall be upon a quaking point, The Navy shall not be capable to come into the Port.

ANNOT.

      Here you must observe that *Gebenna* in Latine signifieth *Geneva,* and therefore this whole Stanza is concerning the City of *Geneva.*

LXV.

French.

Le park enclin grande calamité, Par l'Hesperie & Insubre sera, Le Feu en Nef, Peste, & Captivité, Mercure en l'Ar, Saturn fenera. English.

The Park enclineth to great calamity, Which shall be through *Hesperia* and *Insubria,* The Fire in the Ship, Plague, and Captivity, *Mercury* in *Aries, Saturn* shall wither.

ANNOT.

      Though the words be plain, nevertheless the sense is very obscure, and chiefly as I suppose by the faults of the impression, all what I can tell you here, is, that *Hesperia* in Latine, is *Spain,* and *Insubria,* is *Savoy.*

LXVI.

French.

Par grand dangers le Captif eschapé, Peu de temps grand a fortune changée, Dans le Palais le peuple est attrapé, Par bonne augure la Cité assiegée. English.

The Prisoner escaped through great danger, A little while after shall become great, his fortune being changed, In the Palace the people shall be caught, And by a good Sign the City shall be besieged.

ANNOT.

All this is plain, both in the words and the Sense.

LXVII.

French.

Le blond au nez forche viendra commettre, Par le Duel & chassera dehors, Les exiles dedans fera remettre, Aux lieux marins commettans les plus forts. English.

The fair one shall fight with the forked Nose, In Duel, and expel him out, He shall re-establish the banished, Putting the stronger of them in Maritine places.

ANNOT.

Both the Sense and the words are plain.

LXVIII.

French.

De l'Aquilon les efforts seront grands, Sur l'Occean sera la Porte ouverte, Le Regne en l'Isle sera re-integrand, Tremblera Londres par voiles descouvertes. **English.**

The endevours of the North shall be great, Upon the Ocean the gate shall be open, The Kingdom in the Island shall be re-established, *London* shall quake, for fear of Sails discovered.

ANNOT.

      This is a very remarkable one, which hath been fulfilled since the happy restauration of his sacred Majesty King *Charles* II. now Reigning: For the endevours of the North, (*viz.* the *Dutch*) have been very great. The *ocean*; like a *gate*, hath been open to all kind of Armies, to play their pranks upon. His Majesty, and Kingdom, have been happily restored.

LXIX.

French.

Le Roy Gaulois par la Celtique dextre, Voiant discorde de la grand Monarchie, Sur les trois parts fera fleurir son Sceptre, Contre la Cappe de la grand Hierarchie. **English.**

The *French* King, by the Low-Countreys right hand, Seeing the discord of the great Monarchy, Upon three parts of it, will make his Scepter to flourish, Against the Cap of the great Hierarchy.

ANNOT.

      This signifieth, that the *French* King, through the discord that is in the *Spanish* Monarchy, shall cause his *Scepter to flourish* upon three parts of the *Netherlands*; notwithstanding the assistance of the King of *Spain*, who is called here *the Cap of the great Hierarchy*; that is, the great defender of the Popedom and Popery.

LXX.

French.

Le Dard du Ciel fera son estendue, Morts en parlant, grande execution, La pierre en larbre la fiere gent rendue, Brait Humain, Monstre purge expiation. **English.**

The Dart of Heaven shall make his circuit, Some die speaking, a great execution, The stone in the tree, the fierce people humbled, Humane noise, a Monster purged by expiation.

ANNOT.

      All this Stanza signifieth nothing but a fearful Thunder and Lightning, called here, *the Dart of Heaven*, that shall do a great deal of mischief; for as he saith, *some shall die speaking*, there shall be *a great execution*, the *Thunderbolt* shall stick in the *Tree, the people that was fierce, shall be humbled, and a Monster purged by expiation*, that some notorious wicked person shall be consumed by that Cœlestial fire.

LXXI.

French.

Les exiles en Sicile viendront, Pour delivrer de faim la gent estrange, Au point du jour les Celtes luy faudront, La vie demeure a raison Roy se range. English.

The banished persons shall come into *Sicily*, To free the forrain Nation from hunger, In the dawning of the day the *Celtes* shall fail them, Their Life shall be preserved, the King shall submit to reason.

ANNOT.

It is hard to judge what he meaneth by that *Forreign Nation*, which shall be relieved in *Sicily*, by the banished, nor what *King* is that which *shall submit to reason*; let it be left to every body's private judgement.

LXXII.

French.

Armée Celtique en Italie vexée, De toutes partes conflit & grande perte, Romains fuis O Gaule repoulsée, Pres du Thesin, Rubicon pugne incerte. English.

The *French* Army shall be vexed in *Italy*, On all sides fighting, and great loss, The *Romans* run away, and thou *France* repulsed, Near the *Thesin*, by *Rubicon* the fight shall be doubtful.

ANNOT.

A *French* Army shall be distressed, if not destroyed in *Italy*. The *Romans*, that is, those under the Pope, that shall take their part, shall be put to flight, and this battle shall be fought by the River *Thesin*. Another shall be fought by the River *Rubicon*, whose event shall be doubtful, that is to say, it shall hardly be known who got the victory.

LXXIII.

French.

Au Lac Fucin de Benacle Rivage, Pres du Leman au port de Lorguion, Nay de trois Bras prædit Bellique Image, Par trois courones au grand Endymion. English.

At the *Fucin* Lake of the *Benacle* Shore, Near the *Leman*, at the Port of *Lorguion*, Born with three Arms, a Warlike Image, By three Crowns to the great *Endimion*.

ANNOT.

There is a Lake in *Italy* called *Lacus Fucinius*; the Lake of *Geneva* is called *Lacus Lemanus*;

the meaning then of this obscure Stanza, is, (if I understand any thing) that a Monster shall be *born with three Arms*, near one of those Lakes, which shall be a sign of great Wars: what he meaneth by the *three Crowns to the great Endymion*, is unknown to me.

LXXIV.

French.

De Sens, d'Autun viendront jusques au Rhosne, Pour passer outre vers les Monts Pyrenée, La gent sortir de la Marque d'Ancone, Par Terre & Mer Suivra a grand trainées. English.

They shall come from *Sens* and *Autun*, as far as the *Rhosne*, To go further to the *Pyrenean* Mountains, The Nation come from the Mark of *Ancona*, By Land and Sea shall follow speedily after.

ANNOT.

Sens and *Autun* are two Cities in *France*, the *Pyrenean* Mountains, are those which divide *France* from *Spain*.

LXXV.

French.

La voix ouie de l'Insolit oiseau, Sur le Canon du respiral estage, Si haut viendra du froment le boisseau, Que l'homme d'homme sera Antropophage. English.

The noise of the unwonted Bird having been heard, Upon the Canon of the highest story, The Bushel of Wheat shall rise so high, That man of man shall be *Antropophage*.

ANNOT.

This is a prediction of a mighty Famine, wherein men shall eat up one another, when an *unwonted Bird* shall be seen and heard to cry, being perched upon one of the biggest pieces of *Ordinance*.

Antropophage is a Greek word, signifying a *Man-eater*, from ἄνθροπος, *homo*, and φαγος, *comedens*, of which sort of men there be too many already.

LXXVI.

French.

Foudre en Bourgongne avec cas portenteux, Que par engin oncques ne pourroit faire, De leur Senat Sacriste fait boiteux, Fera Scavoir aux ennemis l'affaire. English.

Lightning in *Burgundy*, with marvellous accidents, Which could never have been done by art, Of their Senate *Sacriste* being lamed, Shall make known the business to the enemies.

The *Senate* or Parliament of *Burgundy*, sits at *Dijon*, among them there is always a Churchman, that is one of the Judges, to see that nothing be done to the prejudice of the Church. I suspect that it is he, that is called here *Sacriste*, and who shall reveal the business to the *Enemies*. The two first Verses need no explication.

LXXVII.

French.

Par Arcs, Fœux, Poix, & par feux repoussez, Cris hurlemens sur la minuit ouys, Dedans sont mis par les rempars cassez, Par Canicules les Traditeurs fuis. English.

Being repulsed with Bows, Fires, and Pitch, Cries and howlings shall be heard about midnight, They shall get in through the broken Walls, The betrayers shall run away through the Conduits.

ANNOT.

It is a Town Besieged, where after a repulse given to the Besiegers, they shall get in by the Treason of some within, who shall run away through the Conduits or Channels of the Town.

LXXVIII.

French.

Le grand Neptune du profond de la Mer, De sang punique & sang Gaulois meslé, Les Isles a sang pour le tardif ramer, Plus luy nuira que loccult mal celé. English.

The great *Neptune* in the middle of the Sea, Having joyned *African* and *French* blood, The Islands shall be put to the Sword, and the slow rowing Shall do them more prejudice, than the concealed evil.

ANNOT.

To understand this, you must know that Henry the II. King of *France*, having renewed his Alliance with the Grand Seignior *Sultan Solyman*, he asked him succours for to take *Nice*, which he pretended to belong to the Earldom of *Provence*. To that purpose the Marshal of *Brissac* went from Court with the Kings Army in the year 1557. to set upon *Nice*, *Savona*, and *Genoa*, and so to hinder the *Spaniard* from coming by Sea in *Piemont*, and the *Milanese*. The *Turk* sent him a good Fleet, consisting of 105. Galleys, and 14. Galliots.

The *French* Fleet consisted of 26 Galleys, of which the great Prior was Admiral, who went with them from the Castle of *Yf*, the 9. of *June* 1558.

Being at Sea, and not knowing where the *Turkish* Fleet was, he went to and fro to seek it out, at last he found it pillaging and plundering the Island of *Minorica*. The *Turks* had already taken the chief Town, where 800. *Turks* were killed, which so incensed the rest, that they set the Town on fire; then going up and down the Countrey, they took 5000. Prisoners, and if the Lords of *Carces* and *Vence* had not stayed them, they would have ruinated the whole Island.

Then forsaking the Island, they joyned with the *French*, but the perfidious *Bassa* being bribed by the *Genoeses*, and those of *Nice*, went slowly to work, and at last retreated without doing any thing for the *French*. This is the relation of *Cæsar Nostradamus*, in his History of *Provence* under *Henry* the II. and according to this the Author saith, that *the great Neptune in the middle of the Sea, shall joyn French and African blood. Neptune* signifieth the *Mediterranean Sea*.

The Islands shall be put to the Sword, by the taking of *Minorica*, after which the *Turks* being bribed, went slowly to work, and in conclusion did nothing of consequence.

The third and fourth Verse adds, that this *Bassa*'s slow rowing, *shall do them more prejudice then the concealed evil*; that is, shall do more damage to the *French* by his hidden design of the Bassa of not serving the *French*; because this slowness of the Bassa spoiled the *French* activity, lessened their provisions, and at last discouraged them; whereas if the *Turks* had not come, the *French* Galleys alone were able to take *Nice*.

LXXIX.

French.

La Barbe crespe & noire par engin, Subjuguera la gent cruelle & fiere, Le grand Cheyren ostera du longin, Tous les Captifs par Seline Baniere. English.

The frizled and black Beard by fighting, Shall overcome the fierce and cruel Nation, The great *Cheyren* shall free from Bands, All the Captives made by *Selyne* Standard.

ANNOT.

This Prophecy was fulfilled in the year 1571. upon the seventh day of *October*, when that famous Battle of *Lepanto* was fought between the Christians and the Turks, the General of the Christians being *Don Juan of Austria*, whom he calleth here the *frizled and black Beard*.

In this Battle the Christians lost 7566. men, and the Turks about 32000. besides 220. Ships of all sorts, and all the Christian slaves released that were in them. By the *Selyne* Banner is understood that of the great Turk, whose name at that time was *Selyne*. By the great *Cheyren* is understood *Henry* the II. King of *France*, who redeemed many slaves, for *Cheyren* by transposition of Letters is *Henry*.

LXXX.

French.

Apres conflit du læse l'Eloquence, Par peu de temps se trame Saint repos, Point l'on admet les grand a delivrance. Des ennemis sont remis a propos. English.

After the Battle, the eloquency of the wounded man, Within a little while shall procure a holy rest, The great ones shall not be delivered, But shall be left to their Enemies will.

ANNOT.

After the Battle of St. *Laurence*, the Prisoners taken by the *Spaniard* were the Constable of *France*, the Dukes of *Montpensier*, of *Longueville*, the Marshal S. *André*, *Ludovic* Prince of *Mantua*, the *Rhingrave* Colonel of the *Germans*, the Earl of *la Rochefoucaud*, and several other persons of quality.

They were Prisoners from the *10th* of *August* 1557. to the third of *April* 1559. that is, one year and eight Months; during which time the Pope's *Nuncios*, *Christierne* Dutchess Dowager of *Lorraine*, the Constable, and Marshal St. *André* endeavoured to make the peace.

Among them the Constable was chief, and *Philip* the II. King of *Spain* gave him leave to go to and fro upon his Paroll; and of him it is our Author speaketh in the first Verse; *After the Battle the eloquency of the wounded man*, that is after the Battle of *Saint Laurence*, where the Constable of *Monmorency* was wounded in the hip. His eloquency procured the peace, which was concluded in a short time, for had it not been for the death of Queen *Mary* of *England*, that happened upon the 15 of *November* 1558. it should have been concluded three Months after the conference that was begun in the Abbey of *Cercamp* near *Cambray*.

The third Verse saith, that *the great ones shall not be delivered*, because during the Treaty of Peace, *Philip* the II. would not hearken to take any Ransom, but they were kept Prisoners till the Peace. It is the meaning of the fourth Verse, when it saith, *but shall be left to the Enemies will*, viz. the *Spaniards* who gave them liberty after the Peace.

LXXXI.

French.

Par feu du Ciel la Cité presqu'aduste, L'Urne menace encor Deucalion, Vexée Sardaigne par la punique fuste, Apres le Libra lairra son Phaeton. **English.**

By fire from Heaven the City shall be almost burnt, The Waters threatens another *Deucalion*, *Sardaigne* shall be vexed by an *African* Fleet, After that *Libra* shall have left her *Phaeton*.

ANNOT.

All is plain but the last Verse, the sense of which is, that the things before spoken, shall happen when the Sun is newly come out of the sign of *Libra*.

LXXVII.

French.

Par faim la proye fera Loup prisonier, L'Assaillant lors en extresme detresse, Lesnay ayant au devant le dernier, Le grand neschape au milieu de la presse. **English.**

By hunger, the prey shall make the Wolf prisoner, Assaulting him then in a great distress, The eldest having got before the last, The great one doth not escape in the middle of the crowd.

ANNOT.

The two first Verses signifie, that an hungry Wolf seeking for a Prey, shall be caught in some trap, where being almost famished, the Prey shall assault him. The last two Verses being obscure and not material to any thing I have neglected them.

LXXXIII.

French.

Le gros Traffic d'un grand Lion changé, La pluspart tourne en pristine ruine, Proye aux Soldats par playe vendangé, Par Jura Mont, & Sueve bruine. English.

The great Trade of a great Lion alter'd, The most part turneth into its former ruine, Shall become a Prey to Soldiers and reaped by wound, In *Mont-Jura*, and *Suaube* great Foggs.

ANNOT.

  This Prophecy is concerning the City of *Lion* in *France*, which is a Town of an exceeding great Trade, and is threatned to suffer an alteration, and a decay by War.
  The last Verse is concerning a great Mist or Fogg, which shall be upon *Mont-Jura* and in *Suabeland.*

LXXXIV.

French.

Entre Campagne, Sienne, Pise & Ostié, Six mois neuf jours ne pleuvra une goute, L'Estrange Langue en Terre Dalmatie, Courira sus vastant la Terre toute. English.

Between *Campania*, *Sienna*, *Pisa* and *Ostia*, For six Months and nine days there shall be no rain, The strange Language in *Dalmatia*'s Land, Shall overrun, spoiling all the Countrey.

ANNOT.

  All those places mentioned, in the first Verse are seated in *Italy*; the Author saith that in that Countrey it shall not rain for the space of six Months and nine days, which if it be past, or to come, I know not.
  The two last Verses signifie, that a strange Nation shall come into *Dalmatia*, and overrun and spoil all that Countrey.

LXXXV.

French.

Le vieux plein barbe soubs le statut severe, A Lion fait dessus l'Aigle Celtique, Le petit grand trop outre persevere, Bruit d'Arme au Ciel, Mer rouge Ligustique. English.

The old plain beard under the severe Statute, Made at *Lion* upon the *Celtique* Aigle, The little great persevereth too far, Noise of Arms in the Skie, the *Ligustrian* Sea made red.

ANNOT.

  I could scrape no sense out of the first three Verses; the last signifieth, that a noise of Arms shall be heard in the Skies, and that the *Ligustrian* Sea, which is that of *Genoa*, shall be made red with blood, when the former prodigy hath appeared.

LXXXVI.

French.

Naufrage a classe pres d'Onde Adriatique, La Terre tremble emeue sur l'Air en Terre mis Ægypt tremble augment Mahometique, L'Heraut soy rendre a crier est commis. English.

A Fleet shall suffer Shipwrack near the *Adriatick* Sea, The Earth quaketh, a motion of the Air cometh upon the Land, *Ægypt* trembleth for fear of the Mahometan increase. The Herald surrendring shall be appointed to cry.

ANNOT.

In the two first Verses is foretold a great storm by the *Adriatick* Sea, in which a Fleet shall be dispersed, and many suffer Shipwrack.

The two last Verses relate the great fear *Ægypt* was in, when the great Turk *Sultan Selyn* went to conquer it.

The last Verse is concerning a Herald, which was surrendered to the contrary party, and by them was appointed to perform that office in their behalf.

LXXXVII.

French.

Apres viendra des extremes Contrées, Prince Germain dessus Throsne d'Oré, La servitude & les Eaux rencontrées, La Dame serve son temps plus n'adoré. English.

After that shall come out of the remote Countreys, A *German* Prince upon a gilded Throne, The slavery and waters shall meet, The Lady shall serve, her time no more worshipped.

ANNOT.

This Prophecy is concerning *Gustavus Adolphus* King of *Swedeland*, who is called *German* Prince, because his Ancestors came out of *Germany*, he came out of a remote Countrey, that is *Swedeland*, he came upon a gilded Throne, that is a Ship gilded, he shall make slavery and waters meet, because as soon as he was Landed he began to conquer, and to subdue that Lady (*viz.* *Germania*) that was no more worshipped since as she was before.

LXXXVIII.

French.

Le Circuit du grand fait ruineux, Le nom septiesme du cinquiesme sera, D'un tiers plus grand l'estrange belliqueux, De Ram, Lutece, Aix ne garentira. English.

The circumference of the ruinous building, The seventh name shall be that of the fifth, From a third, one greater, a Warlike man, *Aries* shall not preserve *Paris* nor *Aix*.

ANNOT.

The Circumference of that ruinous building, was the *French* league against *Henry* III. and *Henry* IV. which numbers being joyned together, make seven, mentioned in the second Verse.

By the strange Warlike man, in the third Verse, is understood *Henry* IV. because he was not born in *France*, but in *Navarre*, and therefore called a stranger, who subdued both *Paris* and *Aix*, seated under the constellation of *Aries*. If you had not rather, by the name of the *Ram*, or *Aries*, understand the Duke of *Mayenne*, who was head of the league.

LXXXIX.

French.

Un jour seront amis les deux grands Maistres, Leur grand pouvoir se verra augmenté, La Terre neufue sera en ses hauts estres, Au sanguinaire le nombre raconté. English.

One day the two great Masters shall be friends, Their great power shall be increased, The new Land shall be in a flourishing condition, The number shall be told to the bloody person.

ANNOT.

We must suppose here three Kings of *Europe*, two of which shall become friends, and by their agreement, *the new Land*, that is, either the Plantations, or the Trade either in the *East* or *West Indies*, shall flourish, their prosperities shall be related and told to the third King, who shall be a bloody and cruel man.

XC.

French.

Par vie & mort changé Regne d'Hungrie, La loy sera plus aspre que service, Leur grand Cité d'Urlemens plaine & crie, Castor & Pollux ennemis dans la Lice. English.

By Life and Death the Kingdom of *Hungary* shall be changed, The Law shall be more severe than the service, Their great City shall be full of howling and crying, *Castor* and *Pollux* shall be enemies in the List.

ANNOT.

There shall happen a great change in the Kingdom of *Hungary*, caused by the birth of one, and the death of another.

The meaning of the second Verse is, that it will be more tolerable to go to War, than to Law.

The last verse signifieth, that this dissention shall happen between two Brothers; because *Castor* and *Pollux* were such.

XCI.

French.

Soleil levant ungrand feu lon verra, Bruit & clarté vers Aquilon tendans, Dedans le rond mort & cris lon orra, Par Glaive, Feu, Faim, mort les attendans. English.

At the rising of the Sun a great fire shall be seen, Noise and light tending towards the North, Within the round death and cries shall be heard, Death by Sword, Fire, Hunger watching for them.

ANNOT.

These are Prodigies that shall be seen, a little before that a great Calamity shall happen.

XCII.

French.

Feu couleur d'or, du Ciel en terre veu, Frappé du haut nay, fait cas merveilleux, Grand meurtre humain, prinse du grand Neveu, Morts de spectacles, eschapé lorgueilleux. English.

A fire from Heaven of a Golden colour shall be seen, Stricken by the high born, a wonderful case, Great murder of Mankind, the taking of the great Neveu, Some dead looking, the proud one shall escape.

ANNOT.

This is a continuation of the former, relating more Prodigies that are to happen.

XCIII.

French.

Aupres du Tybre bien pres la Lybitine, Un peu devant grand Inondation, Le chef du nef prins, mis a la sentine, Chasteau, Palais en conflagration. English.

Near the *Tyber*, going towards *Lybia*, A little before a great Innundation, The Master of the Ship being taken shall be put into the Sink, And a Castle and Palace shall be burnt.

ANNOT.

This is plain.

XCIV.

Grand Pau, grand mal par Gaulois recevra, Vaine terreur au Maritin Lion, Peuple infiny par la Mer passera, Sans eschaper un quart d'un Million. English.

Great *Pau* shall receive great harm by the *French*, A vain terrour shall seize upon the Maritine Lion, Infinite people shall go beyond Sea, Of which shall not escape a quarter of a Million.

ANNOT.

     The first Verse signifieth that the Countrey about the *Pau*, (which is the greatest River in *Italy*) shall receive great damage by the *French*.

     The second, that the Maritine Lion, *viz.* the *Hollanders* shall fear in vain. The third and fourth are plain.

XCV.

French.

Les lieux peuplez seront inhabitables, Pour Champs avoir grande division, Regnes livrez a prudents incapables, Lors les grands Freres mort & dissension. English.

The populous places shall be deserted, A great division to obtain Fields, Kingdoms given to prudents incapable, When the great Brothers shall die by dissention.

ANNOT.

     This needeth no interpretation.

XCVI.

French.

Flambeau ardant au Ciel soir sera veu, Pres de la fin & principe du Rhosne, Famine, Glaive, tard le secours pourveu, La Perse tourne envahir Macedoine. English.

A burning shall be seen by night in Heaven, Near the end and beginning of the *Rhosne*, Famine, Sword, too late succours shall be provided, *Persia* shall come against *Macedonia*.

ANNOT.

     This is easie.

XCVII.

French.

Romain Pontife garde de taprocher, De la Cité que deux fleuves arrouse, Ton sang viendras aupres de la cracher, Toy & les tiens quand fleurira la Rose. English.

Roman Pontife take heed to come near, To the City watered with two Rivers, Thou shall spit there thy blood, Thou and thine, when the Rose shall blossom.

ANNOT.

Although there may be many Cities watered with two Rivers, yet I know none more famous than *Lions* in *France*, where two famous Rivers, the *Rhosne* and the *Saone* meet together, and I believe this is the place that our Author forewarneth the *Pope* to come to, for fear of his death, and that of his attendants.

XCVIII.

French.

Celuy du sang respersé le visage, De la Victime proche du Sacrifice, Venant en Leo, augure par presage, Mis estre a mort alors pour la fiance. English.

He that shall have his face bloody, With the blood of the Victim near to be sacrificed, The Sun coming into *Leo* shall be an Augury by presage, That then he shall be put to death for his confidence.

ANNOT.

I suppose this to be spoken of a Jewish Priest, who going about to practice the Ceremonial Law, in a Countrey where it is forbidden, shall be put to death for his bold confidence.

XCIX.

French.

Terroir Romain qu'interpretoit Augure, Par gent Gauloise par trop sera vexée, Mais Nation Celtique craindra l'heure, Boreas, classe trop loing l'avoit poussée. English.

The *Roman* Countrey in which the *Augur* did interpret, Shall be too much vexed by the *French* Nation, But the *Celtique* Nation shall fear the hour, The Northwind had driven the Navy in too far.

ANNOT.

Since the Reign of *Henry* the II. King of *France*, the Historians do not mention that the Countrey about *Rome* hath been troubled by the *French* Armies. It was only in the time of *Paul* the

IV. who was assisted by the *French* Troops, under the conduct of the Lord *Strozy*, and Captain *Monluc*, therefore this Stanza belongeth to the time of that Kings Reign.

And indeed what he foretelleth here, came to pass in the year 1556. for the Countrey about *Rome* was vexed by the *French* Nation, who went about then to take the places, which the Duke of *Alba* had taken from the *Pope*, and thereby caused those disorders, which commonly are incident to War.

The second Verse saith, *the Countrey shall be too much vexed*, and not a little, because *Monluc*, whom the Author calleth the *quick Gascon*, did continually torment the Enemies, which could not be done without a great prejudice to the Countrey; Moreover, his Troops being for the most part *Gascons*, and consequently active men; the Soldiers did more harm than ordinary.

In the first Verse he saith, that this Countrey about *Rome* was marked by an *Augury*, to be the place upon which the sad effect of the *Augury* should fall, which proved true; for the first of *March 1556*, appeared a Blazing Star, which did presage to that Countrey of *Rome*, its disaster.

Roman Countrey in which the Augur did interpret, that is to say, which the *Augur* did signifie, and presage should be vexed by the *French* Nation.

Afterwards the Author saith, that the same *French* Nation, or *Celtique*, shall fear the hour when *Boreas* should drive to far the Fleet, that is to say, shall fear much, when the Baron *de la Garde* was so troubled with the storm (as we have said) and in truth it was *Boreas*, or the *Northwind*, that drove him into St. *Florents* road.

C.

French.

Dedans les Isles si horrible tumulte, Rien on n'orra qu'une bellique brigue, Tant grand sera des predareurs l'Insult, Qu'on se viendra ranger a la grand ligue. English.

In the Islands shall be so horrid tumults, That nothing shall be heard but a Warlike surprise, So great shall be the insult of the Robbers, That every one shall shelter himself under the great League.

ANNOT.

This is plain, if by the great League, you understand the soundest and most powerful party.

Michael Nostradamus.

CENTURY III.

I.

French.

Apres Combat & Bataille Navale, Le grand Neptune a son plus haut beffroy, Rouge adversaire de peur de viendra pasle, Mettant le grand Occean en effroy. English.

After the fight and Sea Battle, The great *Neptune* in his highest Steeple, The red adversary shall wax pale for fear, Putting the great *Occean* in a fright.

ANNOT.

I find no mystical sence in this, unless by the red adversary he should understand the *Pope*, because clothed in Scarlet. Therefore I leave the explication to the judgement of every particular Reader.

II.

French.

Le Divin Verbe donra a la substance, Compris Ciel, Terre, or occult au lait mystique, Corps, Ame, Esprit, ayant toute puissance, Tant sous ses pieds comme au Siege Celique. English.

The Divine Word shall give to the substance, Heaven and Earth, and Gold hid in the mystical milk, Body, Soul, Spirit, having all power, As well under his feet, as in the Heavenly Seat.

ANNOT.

I desire the judicious Reader, and chiefly if he be given to the Hermetick Philosophy, to take a special notice of this Stanza, for in it is contained the secret of the *Elixir* or Philosophers Stone, more clearly and plainly then in the *Tabula Smaragdina* of *Hermes*, which to make appearent, we shall expound it Verse by Verse.

The Divine Word shall give to the substance; by the Divine word you must not understand the second person of the Trinity, but a Doctor in Divinity or a Theologian, called in Greek θεόλογος or Divine word, who shall be an *Adeptus*, a Disciple of *Hermes*, and one that shall attain to the secret of the Philosophers stone.

That man shall give to the substance, that is, to Gold; *Heaven and Earth, and gold hid in the mystical Milk*. Heaven and Earth, that is all the Celestial and Terrestrial qualities, lurking in the Gold, which is hid in the mystical milk, that is in the *Azoth*, or *Mercury* of the Philosophers.

Body, Soul, Spirit, having all Power, that is, the three principles, of which the Philosophers say their stone is compounded, *viz. Body, Soul, and Spirit*.

Having *all Power*, that is, having the power to transmute all Mettals into its kind; as also having all the powers from above and below, as *Hermes* saith, *Pater ejus est Sol, Mater vero Luna, & Terra nutrix ejus*.

Which is confirmed by the last Verse, *As well under his feet, as in the Heavenly Seat*.

III.

French.

Mars & Mercure, & Largent joint ensemble, Vers le Midy extreme siccité, Au fond d'Asie on dira Terre tremble, Corinthe, Ephese lors en perplexite. *English.*

Mars and *Mercury*, and Silver joyned together, Towards the South a great drought, In the bottome of *Asia* shall be an Earth-quake, *Corinth* and *Ephesus* shall then be in perplexity.

ANNOT.

After the Author hath in the foregoing Stanza expressed the mistery of the Philosophers stone, he seemeth to give here a receit, though Sophistical, for the relief of the Inquisitors, and as it were a *Viaticum*, for them to subsist till they can attain to the perfection, as *Basilius, Valentinus* hath done since to his disciples.

He saith then, that with *Mars*, that is, Iron, *Mercury* and Silver joyned together, some thing may be done, if you beware of a *drought in the South*; that is, in the middle of the operation; and this is concerning the two first Verses. Those that shall desire to be better and further informed, may come to me, and they shall have all the satisfaction I can afford them.

The two last Verses have no relation to the first two, and foretel onely a great *Earthquake* in *Asia*, by which, those two Towns, *Corinth* and *Ephesus*, shall be in great perplexity.

IV.

French.

Quand seront proches le defaut des Lunaires, De l'un a lautre ne distant grandement, Froid, siccité, dangers vers les frontieres, Mesme ou l'Oracle a pris commencement. *English.*

When the want of the Luminaries shall be near, Not being far distant one from another, Cold, drought, danger towards the Frontiers, Even where the Oracle had his beginning.

ANNOT.

The word *near*, sheweth that the two Eclipses, one of the Sun and the other of the Moon, shall be near one another.

The Ephemerides of *John Stadius*, teach us, that in the year 1556 in the Month of *November*, these two Eclipses did meet. That of the Sun upon the first of *November*, at 17 hours (as the Astrologers reckon) and 53 Minutes. That of the Moon at 12 hours and 43 Scruples; and thus the two last Verses are plain.

Concerning the other two: *Belleforest* teacheth us two things; the first, that the same year was extraordinary dry, in so much that from *April* to *October* it did not rain, but only upon the Eve of St. *John* the Baptist, and that the Vintage was made in *August*, the Wine proving excellent. The second is, that in the Month of *December* began a horrid Frost, which lasted a great while. Thus there was *Cold and drought*.

Concerning the dangers towards the Frontiers, *Belleforest* saith, that towards *Pickardy* the *Spaniard* began to break the truce, making inrodes about *Abbeville*, St. *Spirit* of *Rue*, *la Chapele*, *Rozoy*, *Thierasse*, and *Aubenton*.

When complaints were made of it, they alledged their necessity and want of Victuals; which did oblige the Lord Admiral to permit the Souldiers retaliation; and in this manner, *there was danger towards the Frontiers*.

As for the Town where the *Oracle* (that is, our Author) had his beginning or birth, whether it be that of St. *Remy* or *Salon de Craux*. The dangers that were there, proceeded from the Civil Wars between the Protestants and the *Roman* Catholicks.

V.

French.

Pres le defaut des deux grands luminaires, Qui surviendra entre l'Avril & Mars, O quel cherté! mais deux grands debonnaires, Par Terre & Mer secourront toutes parts. English.

Near the Ecclipses of the two great Luminaries, Which shall happen between *April* and *March*, O what a dearth! but two great ones bountiful, By Land and Sea shall succour them on all sides.

ANNOT.

There shall happen two great Ecclipses between *March* and *April*, one of the Sun, and the other of the Moon; then shall be a great dearth, but the afflicted shall be relieved by the two powerful Princes of a good Nature.

VI.

French.

Dans Temple clos le foudre y entrera. Des Citadins dedans leur fort grevez, Chevaux, Bœufs, Hommes, l'Onde mur touchera, Par faim, soif, soubs les plus foibles armez. English.

Into a close Church the lightning shall fall, The Citizens shall be distressed in their Fort, Horses, Oxen, Men, the Water shall touch the Wall, By hunger, thirst, down shall come the worst provided.

ANNOT.

This is plain.

VII.

French.

Les fugitifs, feu du Ciel sur les Piques, Conflit prochain des Corbeaux sesbatans, De Terre on crie, aide, secours Celiques, Quand pres des murs seront les combatans. **English.**

The runaways, fire of Heaven upon the Pikes, A fight near hand, the Ravens sporting, They cry from the Land, succours O Heavenly powers When near the walls shall be the fighting men.

ANNOT.

The first Verse signifieth, that there shall be some *Fugitives*, upon whose *Pikes* the Lightning shall fall.

The second, that when a multitude of *Ravens shall be sporting*, a great fight shall be near hand.

The third, that there shall be a great exclamation and prayers, when the Souldiers shall come near the wall to give an assault.

VIII.

French.

Les Cimbres joints avecques leurs voisins, Depopuler viendront presque l'Espagne, Gens ramassez, Guienne & Limosins, Seront en ligue & leur feront Compagne. **English.**

The *Cimbres* joyned with their neighbours, Shall come to depopulate almost all *Spain*, People gathered from *Guienna* and *Limosin*, Shall be in league with them, and keep them Company.

ANNOT.

The *Cimbres* and *Teutons* were a Northern people, *viz*: the *Swedes* and *Danes*, who came once out of their Countrey to sack *Rome*, and were overcome by *Marius*, near the Town of *Orenge*, in a place where his Triumphal Arch is seen to this day. The rest is easie.

IX.

French.

Bourdeaux, Rouan & la Rochelle joints, Tiendront autour la grand Mer Occeane, Anglois Bretons, & les Flamans conjoints, Les chasseront jusque aupres de Rouane. **English.**

Bourdeaux, Rouan, and *Rochel* joyned together, Will range about upon the great Ocean, *English Brittans,* and *Flemings* joyned together, Shall drive them away as far as *Rouane.*

By mentioning *Bourdeaux*, *Rouan*, and *Rochel*, the Author understandeth the whole Naval forces of *France*, which (he saith) shall be defeated, by the *English*, *Brittains*, and *Hollanders*, and pursued as far as *Rouane*, which is a Town at the head of the River *Loire*, from whence it runneth down for the space of 500 Miles to *Nantes*, and a while after dischargeth it self into the Ocean.

X.

French.

De sang & faim plus grand calamité, Sept fois sapreste a la Marine plage, Monech de faim, lieu pris, captivité, Le grand mené, Croc, enserré en cage. **English.**

Of blood and famine, what a great calamity! Seven times is ready to come upon the Sea Coast, *Monech* by hunger, the place taken, captivity, The great one carried away, *Croc*, shut up in a Cage.

ANNOT.

Monech or *Monaco* is a Town and Principality belonging to the Family of the *Grimaldi* of *Genua*, and is seated by the Sea side, between *Provence* and *Genoa*; that place is threatned here with many afflictions, as is plain in this Stanza.

XI.

French.

Les Armées battre au Ciel longue saison, L'Arbre au milieu de la Cité tombé, Vermine, Rogne, Glaive en face tison, Lors le Monarque d'Adrie succombé. **English.**

Armies shall fight in the Air a great while, The tree shall fall in the middle of the City, Vermin, Scabs, Sword, fire-brand in the face, When the Monarck of *Adria* shall fall.

ANNOT.

The three first Verses contain several prodigies, that shall happen before the death of the Duke of *Venice*, or rather (because he is no Monarck) before the fall of that Monarchy or Common-wealth.

XII.

French.

Par la tumeur du Heb. Po. Tag. Tibre de Rome, Et par lestang Leman & Aretin, Les deux grands chefs, & Citez de Garonne, Prins, Morts, Noiez. Partir humain butin. **English.**

By the swelling of *Heb. Po. Tag. Tiber* of *Rome*, And by the Lake *Leman* and *Aretin*, The two great Heads, and Cities of *Garonne*, Taken, Dead, Drowned. The human booty shall be divided.

Heb. is the River *Hebrus* in *Thracia*, *Po*, is the great River of *Italy*, *Tag.* is *Tagus*, the River of *Lisbonne*; the rest is plain.

XIII.

French.

Par Foudre en Arche Or & Argent fondu, De deux Captifs l'un l'autre mangera, De la Cité le plus grand estendu, Quand submergée la Classe nagera. English.

By Lightning shall gold and silver be melted in the Arch, Of two Prisoners one shall eat up the other, The greatest of the City shall be laid down, When the Navy that was drowned shall swim.

ANNOT.

The words and the sense are plain.

XIV.

French.

Par le Rameau du vaillant personage, De France infirme, par le Pere infelice, Honeurs, Richesses, travail en son viel Age, Pour avoir creu le conseil d'homme nice. English.

By the Bow of the valliant men, Of weak *France*, by the unfortunate Father, Honours, Riches, labour in his old age, For having believed the councel of a nice man.

ANNOT.

Every body may understand this as well as I do.

XV.

French.

Cœur, vigueur, gloire, le Regne changera, De tous points contre, ayant son adversaire, Lors France enfance par mort subjuguera, Un grand Regent sera lors plus contraire. English.

Heart, vigour, and glory shall change the Kingdom, In all points, having an adversary against it, Then shall *France* overcome Childhood by death, A great Regent shall then be more adversary to it.

The two first Verses seem to have foretold of the late Tyrant *Cromwel*.

The two last Verses may be applied to *France*, when the Infant of *Spain Don Balthazar* died, *&c.*

XVI.

French.

Un Prince Anglois Mars a son cœur du Ciel, Voudra poursuivre sa fortune prospere, Des deux duelles l'un percera le fiel, Hay de luy, bien aymé de sa Mere. English.

An *English* Prince *Mars* hath his heart from Heaven, Will follow his prosperous fortune, Of two Duels one shall pierce the gall, Being hated of him, and beloved of his Mother.

ANNOT.

By this Stanza is promised to *England* a Martial Prince, who shall have his heart from Heaven, and with all endeavours follow his prosperous fortune, which is a remarkable and commendable part in a man.

By the last two Verses, it seemeth that this Prince shall have a Son, who shall fight two duels, for one of which his Father shall be angry and hate him, but his Mother shall love him for it.

XVII.

French.

Mont Aventine brusler nuit sera veu, Le Ciel obscur tout a un coup en Flandres, Quand le Monarque chassera son Neveu, Lors gens d'Eglise commettront les esclandres. English.

Mount *Aventine* shall be seen to burn in the night, The Heaven shall be darkned upon a sudden in *Flanders*, When the Monarch shall expel his Neveu, Then Churchmen shall commit scandals.

ANNOT.

Mount-*Aventine* is one of the seven Mountains in *Rome*. The rest is plain.

XVIII.

French.

Apres la pluye de lait assez longuette, En plusieurs lieux de Rheims le Ciel touché, O quel conflit de sang pres deux lapreste, Pere & Fils Rois, noseront approché. English.

After a pretty long rain of Milk, In many places of *Rhemes* the lightning shall fall, O what a bloody fight is making ready near them, Father and Son, both Kings, shall not dare to come near.

ANNOT.

Rhemes is a City in *France*. The rest is easie.

XIX.

French.

En Lucques sang & lait viendra pleuvoir, Un peu devant changement de Preteur, Grand Peste & Guerre, Faim & soif sera voir, Loin ou mourra leur Prince Recteur. English.

In *Luca* it shall rain Blood and Milk, A little before the change of the Magistrate, A great Plague, War, Hunger and Thirst shall be seen, A great way off, where their Prince Ruler shall die.

ANNOT.

Luca at present is a strong Town, and a little Common-wealth by it self in *Italy*, governed by their own Magistrate: That Town is threatned here to see those prodigies mentioned, a little before the change of their Government, besides a great Plague and dearth; as also the death of their chief Magistrate, who shall die far off that Countrey.

As for the *raining Milk and Blood*, they are Prodigies that have appeared often before, and therefore not incredible, as those that are Versed in History may justifie: and although the reasons may be drawn from natural causes, yet would they be too tedious if I should insert them here.

XX.

French.

Par les Contrées du grand flevue Betique, Loin d'Ibere, au Royaume de Grenade, Croix repoussées par gens Mahometiques, Un de Cordube trahira a la fin Contrade. English.

Through the Countreys of the great River *Betis*, Far from *Iberia*, in the Kingdom of *Granada*, Crosses beaten back by Mahometan people, One of *Corduba* shall at last betray the Countrey.

ANNOT.

The great River, called in Latine *Betis*, and in Spanish *Guadalquivir*, is the River of *Sevilia*, the most famous Town in *Spain* for Trade. This River runneth through most of the *Spanish* Dominions, and dischargeth it self into the Ocean about the mouth of the Straights, over against *Barbary*, upon which Coast of *Spain* lyeth the Kingdom of *Granada*, the chief City of which is *Corduba*, in *Spanish Cordua*. This Kingdom was of time almost immemorial, occupied and inhabited by the *Moores*, till they were expelled and driven back into *Barbary*, by *Ferdinand* and *Isabella*, King and Queen of *Castilia*. The rest is easie.

XXI.

French.

Au Crustamin pres Mer Adriatique. Apparoistra un horrible poisson, De face humaine & de corps aquatique, Qui se prendra dehors de l'Hamecon. **English.**

In the *Crustamin* near the *Adriatick* Sea, An horrid Fish shall appear, Having a mans face, and a fishes body, Which shall be taken without a hook.

ANNOT.

I suppose this *Crustamin* to be some place so called, near the *Adriatick* Sea.

As for Fishes with an humane face, we have several examples of them. *Ambrosius Parœus* relateth divers, and in his works hath inserted the Pictures of them.

1. When *Mena* was Governour of *Ægypt*, and walked by the *Nilus* side, he saw a Sea-man rising out of the River, having an humane shape as far as the Navel, and with a grave look and fair hairs, intermixed with white ones, bony Breast, and distinct Arms, the rest of the body was like a Fish. Three days after in the Morning appeared another Sea-monster like a woman: those two Monsters appeared so long, that every body had time to consider them.

2. *Rondeletius* saith, that in our age was taken a Fish in the Sea of *Norway*, which every body presently called a Monk, because of the resemblance.

3. In the year 1531. was seen a Sea-monster, covered with Scales, which for the resemblance was called a Bishop, *Rondeletius* and *Gesuerus* have the Picture of it.

4. In the year 1523. was seen in *Rome* a Fish about the bigness of a Child of five years old, that had humane shape to the Navel, except the ears: So that all those things related of *Tritons*, *Nereides* and *Sirens* seem not altogether fabulous, and we may conclude with *Pliny*: *Vera est vulgi opinio, quicquià nascatur in parte naturœ ulla, & in Mariesse, prœterque multa quœ nusquam alibi,* lib. 9. cap. 2.

XXII.

French.

Six jours lassaut devant Cité donné, Livrée sera forte & aspre Bataille, Trois la rendront, & a eux pardonné, Le reste a feu & sang trauche taille. **English.**

Six days shall the assault be given to the City, A great and fierce Battle shall be fought, Three shall surrender it and be pardoned, The rest shall be put to fire and sword, cut and slasht.

ANNOT.

Some famous City must be here understood, which the Author hath not named. The same shall be assaulted for six days continually, and in conclusion shall be surrendred or betrayed by three men, who shall be pardoned, and all the rest put to Fire and Sword. Most men that have knowledge in History, interpret this of the City of *Magdebourg* in *Germany*, that was destroyed with Fire and Sword by the Earl of *Tilly*, General for the Emperour against *Gustavus Adolphus*, King of *Swedeland*. For the like devastation and cruelty was never heard of in *Europe*.

XXIII.

French.

Si France passe outre Mer Liquistique, Tu te verras en Isles & Mers enclos, Mahomet contraire plus Mer l'Adriatique, Chevaux & Asnes tu rongeras les os. English.

If *France* goeth beyond the *Ligustick* Sea, Thou shall see thy self inclosed with Islands and Seas, *Mahomet*, against thee besides the *Adriatick* Sea, Of Horses and Asses thou shalt gnaw the bones.

ANNOT.

       This is concerning the miseries which the *French* were to suffer in the Island of *Corsica*, till the peace was concluded in the year 1559. The Author directeth his speech to the *French* Fleet that went to *Corsica* in the year 1555.
       He saith in the first Verse, *If France goeth beyond the Ligustik Sea*; that is, if thou goest to *Corsica*, which is beyond the *Ligustik* Sea towards *Africa*. *Thou shalt see thy self enclosed with Islands and Seas*; that is, thou shalt be constrained to keep within those two Towns which thou hast there, without going out either by Land or Sea; not by Sea for want of Ships, nor by Land the Garrisons being weak, because the King had then so much business that he could not suffice all.
       Moreover the Author addeth that *Mahomet shall be contrary*; not that he was an Enemy to *France*, but because he was then Master of the *Adriatick* Sea; so that the *Venetians*, which were then friends to the *French*, could not succour them.
       And thus the news of the peace being brought, the *French* did eat their Horses and Asses, and there was never a peace so well come as to the *French* that were in *Corsica*.

XXIV.

French.

De l'Entreprise grande confusion, Perte de gens Thresor innumerable, Tu ny doibs faire encore tension, France a mon dire fais que sois recordable. English.

From the undertaking great confusion, Loss of people and innumerable Treasury, Thou oughtest not yet to tend that way, *France* endeavour to remember my saying.

ANNOT.

       This is annexed and hath relation to the precedent, therefore needeth no other interpretation.

XXV.

French.

Qui au Royaume Navarrois parviendra, Quand la Sicile & Naples seront joints, Bigorre & Landes par Foix lors on tiendra, D'Un qui d'Espagne sera par trop conjoint. English.

He that shall obtain the Kingdom of *Navarre*, When *Sicily* and *Naples* shall be joyned, *Bigorre* and *Landes* then by *Foix* shall beheld Of one who shall too much be joyned to *Spain*.

ANNOT.

      Bigorre is a Town in *Gascony*, the *Landes* is a desert Countrey about *Bourdeaux* wherein nothing groweth but *Pine-Trees*, *Foix* is a Country of *Gascony*, called the County, of *Foix*. The rest is easie.

XXVI.

French.

Des Rois & Princes dresseront simulachres, Augures, creux eslevez aruspices: Corne victime dorée, & d'Azur & de Nacre, Intrepretez seront les extispisces. *English.*

Some Kings and Princes shall set up Idols, Divinations and hollow raised Divinators, Victim with gilded Horns, and set with *Azur* and Mother of Pearl The looking into the Entrals shall be interpreted.

ANNOT.

      I can find nothing in this but a description of the Heathens sacrifices in ancient times, where they brought the Victim, that is, the beast that was to be sacrificed, trimmed in a gallant manner, having the Horns gilded, and set with Azure and Mother of Pearl, and after the Entrals were taken out, by the inspection of them they practised their Soothsaying. This inspection of Entrals was called by the Latines *Extispicium*, from the word *Exta* which signifieth Entrals, and *specto* which signifieth to look.

XXVII.

French.

Prince Libique puissant en Occident, Francois d'Arabe viendra tant enflammer, Scavant aux Lettres sera condescendent La Langue Arabe en Francois translater. *English.*

A *Libian* Prince being powerful in the West, The *French* shall love so much the *Arabian* Language, That he being a Learned man shall condescend, To have the *Arabian* tongue translated into *French*.

ANNOT.

      This Prophecy is *de Futuro*, and is concerning a *Libian* Prince (now *Libia* is a Kingdom of *Africa*) who shall be a powerful man in the West, and being a lover of learning shall condescend to have the *Arabian* Language translated into *French*, because the *French* at that time shall be much in love with it.

XXVIII.

French.

De Terre foible & pauvre parentale, Par boute & paix parviendra a l'Empire, Long temps regner une jeune femelle, Qu'oncques en Regne nen survint un si pire. English.

One weak in Lands and of poor Kindred, By thrusting, and peace shall attain to the Empire, Long time shall Reign a young woman, Such as in a Reign was never a worse.

ANNOT.

The words are so plain, that every body may interpret them.

XXIX.

French.

Les deux Neveux en divers lieux nourris, Navale pugne, Terre peres tombez, Viendront si haut eslevez aguerris, Venger l'Injure ennemis succombez. English.

The two Nephews brought up in divers places, A Sea fight, fathers fallen to the Earth, They shall came highly educated, and expert in Arms, To avenge the injury, their enemies shall fall down under them.

ANNOT.

This is concerning two *Nephews*, who shall be educated in divers places, and grow expert in Arms, their Fathers shall be killed, but those *Nephews* shall come, and having fought at Sea, shall revenge the injury done to them, overcoming their enemies.

XXX.

French.

Celuy qu'en luitte & fer au fait Bellique, Aura porte plus grand que luy le prix, De nuit au lit six luy feront la pique, Nud sans harnois subit sera surprins. English.

He who in Wrestling and Martial affairs, Had carried the prize before his better, By night Six shall abuse him in his bed, Being naked, and without harness, he shall suddenly be surprised.

ANNOT.

Many attribute this to the Earl of *Montgomery* in *France*, who having run a tilt against *Henry* II. unfortunately killed him, for which, and for being of the Protestant party, he was afterwards beheaded, though quarter had been given him.

XXXI.

French.

Aux Champs de Mede, d'Arabe, & d'Armenie, Deux grands Copies trois fois sassembleront, Pres du Rivage d'Araxes la mesgnie, Du grand Soliman en Terre tomberont. English.

In the fields of *Media, Arabia,* and *Armenia,* Two great Armies shall meet thrice, Near the Shore of *Araxes,* the people Of great *Solyman* shall fall down.

ANNOT.

       This signifieth no more, but the loss of three famous Battles on the *Turks* side, against the *Persians.*

       The first that I find after the coming out of these Prophesies, is the Battle of *Sancazan,* seven miles from *Tauris,* and hard by the River *Araxes,* where 20000 *Turks* were slain, without any considerable loss of the *Persians;* this was in the time of *Amurath* the III. Emperour of the *Turks,* and son to *Selyman* the second. The other two Battles I could not make good, because I want the supplement of the *Turkish* History, as also because they have not yet happened.

XXXII.

French.

Le grand sepulchre du peuple Aquitanique, S'aprochera aupres de la Toscane, Quand Mars sera pres du coin Germanique, Et au terroir de la gent Mantuane. English.

The great grave of the *Aquitanick* people, Shall come near *Tuscany,* When *Mars* shall be in the *German* corner, And in the Territory of the *Mantuan* people.

ANNOT.

       The Lord of *Thou* saith in his History, that the Cardinal *Caraffa* got by the King of *France*'s permission, out of *Corsica,* several Troops of *Gascons,* and brought some with them, to the number of about 2000 which were quartered about *Rome.* Many of them were among the Troops of the Duke of *Guise,* being allured thither by the reputation of their Countreyman Captain *Monluc.*

       The Author foretelleth, that they shall find their Graves near *Tuscany,* because the Territory of *Rome* joyneth to that Province.

       Then in the 3 and 4 Verse he specifieth the time by two marks; one is, *when Mars shall be near the German corner;* the other, *when he shall be in the Territory of the Mantuan people,* and the War was then in that Territory; for the Duke of *Ferrara* to shew he would not stand still, sent his son *Alphonso d'Este* to make incursions there, and to take some places.

       Moreover the War was then near the *German corner,* which is *Lorrain,* when *Henry* II. besieged *Thionville* in the year 1558. *Paradin* sheweth, that *Mars* was in the *German corner* two years before, sith about the end of the year 1555; the Duke of *Nevers* by an extraordinary endeavour in the middle of the Winter, did relieve *Mariembourg:* and the following years the *French* Garrisons kept the fields to avoid surprises. And in the year 1557. when the Duke of *Guise* fought in *Italy,* the Duke of *Savoy* brought his Army against *Mariembourg;* so it proved true that *Mars, viz.* the War was in the *German corner;* for that Town is in the borders of *Germany,* and was in that corner till the taking of *Thionville*.

XXXIII.

En la Cité ou le loup entrera, Bien pres de la les ennemis seront, Copie estrange grand pais gastera, Aux Monts des Alpes les amis passeront. English.

In the City wherein the Wolf shall go, Near that place the enemies shall be, An Army of strangers shall spoil a great Countrey, The friends shall go over the Mountains of the *Alpes*.

ANNOT.

The two last Verses make me think that this Prophesie was fulfilled in the time of *Henry* II. King of *France*, because the *French* being then friends to the Pope, went over the *Alpes* to serve him.

This Stanza might also be applyed to *Lewis* 13, who caused his Army to go beyond the *Alpes*, but that word *Friends* is more convenient to the time of *Henry* II. because the *French* went then over the *Alpes* in quality of friends to serve the Pope.

According to this conjecture, the *wolf* which signifieth the *Spaniard*, came *anno* 1556. into many Towns, which the Duke of *Alba* took, as we have said in another place, and because among those Towns *Neptune* was one of the most considerable, being seated by the Sea side near *Rome*: I believe that by this word *City* he meaneth that Town which belonged to the *Colonese*.

And to say truth, the *French* were then very near it, to endeavour the relief of it.

Afterwards came the Duke of *Guise*'s Army, which is named by the Author, *an Army of strangers*, because the *French* and *Germans* are strangers to *Italy. This Army shall spoil a great Countrey*; for in that year it went through all *Italy*, and where an Army passeth, nothing but ruine can be expected.

XXXIV.

Quand le defaut du Soleil lors sera, Sur le plein jour le Monstre sera veu, Tout autrement on l'Interpretera, Cherté na garde, nul ny aura pourveu. English.

When the Ecclipse of the Sun shall be At noon day, the Monster shall be seen, It shall be interperted otherways, Then for a dearth, because no body hath provided against it.

ANNOT.

The sense of this is, that when the Sun shall be Eclipsed at noon, a Monster shall be born, which shall presage a dearth, though no body will believe it, because they were unprovided against it.

XXXV.

Du plus profond de l'Occident d'Europe, De pauvre gens un jeune enfant naistra, Qui par sa langue seduira grande troupe, Son bruit au Regne d'Orient plus croistra. English.

Out of the deepest part of the West of *Europe*, From poor people a young child shall be born, Who with his tongue shall seduce many people, His fame shall increase in the Eastern Kingdom.

ANNOT.

This needeth no explication.

XXXVI.

French.

Ensevely non mort Apoplectique, Sera trouvé avoir les mains mangees, Quand la Cité damnera l'Heretique, Qu'avoit leur Loix ce leur sembloit changees. English.

One buried, not dead, but Apoplectical, Shall be found to have eaten up his hands, When the City shall blame the heretical man, Who as they thought had changed their Laws.

ANNOT.

Many persons (according to Histories being only in a fit of Apoplexy) have been buried for dead, and being afterwards taken out of the ground, have been found to have eaten up their hands, as I my self have seen one digged out of Saint *Bartholomews* Church-yard, about the time that the City of *London* began to be weary of *Cromwels* devices and Tyranny, yet I would not here definitively assert, he was the man here pointed at by the Title and Epithete of Heretical man, unless it were in the point of government.

XXXVII.

French.

Avant l'assault l'Oraison pronouncée, Milan prins l'Aigle, par embusche deceus, Muraille antique par Canons enfonsée, Par feu & sang a mercy peu receus. English.

Before the assault the Prayer shall be said, An Eagle shall take a Kite, they shall be deceived by an Embuscado. The ancient wall shall be beaten down with Canons, By fire and blood, few shall have quarter.

ANNOT.

The sense of this is easie.

XXXVIII.

French.

La gent Gauloise & Nation estrange, Outre les Monts, morts pris & profligez, Au mois contraire & proche de vendange, Par les Seigneurs en accord redigez. English.

The *French* Nation, and another Nation, Being over the Mountains, shall die, and be taken, In a month contrary to them, and near the vintage, By the Lords agreed together.

ANNOT.

Two kind of Nations were led into *Italy* by the Duke of *Guise* to succour the Pope, *viz.* *French* and *Germans*, meaning by the *Germans* all those that use the *German* Tongue, as *Switzers*, &c.

The Author saith, these two Nations were led beyond the Mountains, because they went beyond the *Apennine Alpes*, to come down into the Champion Countrey of *Italy*, where some of them died by the Sword, others by famine and sickness; others lost their liberty, being made prisoners of War, others were exposed to the inconveniences that attend a ruined Army. He addeth, that these accidents shall befall them in a Month near the *Vintage*, that Month is *September*: He calleth it *Contrary*, because the Grapes being ripe, the starved Souldiers did eat abundance of them, and so fell into a bloody flux. The *Pope*'s Tenants made use of this Stratagem to ruine that Army.

The *Spaniard* had his revenge the year following, for the Duke of *Guise* having missed his design, and being stept before *Civitella*, and incensed that the *Pope* did not keep his word with him, he resolved to go back again into *France*, and so the *Pope* did by the means of the Common-wealth of *Venice*, and of the Duke of *Florence*, it was concluded and signed with the 23 of *September*.

This is the Authors meaning in the 4 Verse, that all the misfortune which befell the *French*, was by reason of that peace; for the *Pope* disbanded his Troops, consisting most of *French* and *Switzers*, the greatest part of whom fell into the hands of their enemies, and of the Countrey people, others died of sickness. It is true, that the Duke of *Guise* brought his own Army back without much loss, but the Author speaketh here of the *Gascons* and *Switzers*, that were in the *Pope*'s service, under the command of Marshal *Strozzy*, *Monluc*, Cardinal *Caraffa*, and others.

The time of this peace agreeth with the Prophesie, for it was concluded on the 23 of *September*, which is a Month near the *Vintage*.

XXXIX.

French.

Les sept en trois Mois en concorde, Pour subjuger les Alpes Apeninnes, Mais la tempeste & Ligure coüarde, Les profligent en subites ruines. English.

The seven shall agree together within three Months, To conquer the *Apennine Alpes*, But the tempest, and coward *Genoese*, Shall sink them into sudden ruines.

ANNOT.

There shall be seven persons, who shall be three Months in making an agreement to go beyond the *Apennines*, but they shall be hindred by a tempest, and by the cowardliness of the *Genoeses*.

XL.

French.

Le grand Theatre se viendra redresser, Les dez jettez & les rets ia tendus, Trop le premier en glaz viendra lasser, Par arc prostrais de long temps ia fendus. English.

The great Theatre shall be raised up again, The Dice being cast, and the nest spread, The first shall too much in Glass. Beaten down by Bows, who long before were split.

ANNOT.

This must be put among *Insolubilia de Alliaco.*

XLI.

French.

Bossu sera esleu par le Conseil, Plus hideux Monstre en Terre napperceu, Le coup volant luy crevera un œil, Le traistre au Roy pour fidele receu. English.

Crook-back shall be chosen by the Councel, A more hideous Monster I never saw upon Earth. The flying blow shall put out one of his eyes, The Traitor to the King, shall be admited as faithful.

ANNOT.

This needs no explication.

XLII.

French.

L'Enfant naistra a deux dents en la gorge, Purres en Tuscie par pluie tomberont, peu d'ans apres ne sera Bled ny Orge, pour saouler ceux qui de faim failleront. English.

A Child shall be born with two Teeth in his mouth. It shall rain stones in *Tuscany,* A few years after there shall be neither Wheat nor Barley To feed those that shall faint for hunger.

ANNOT.

Those two Prodigies mentioned in the two first Verses, do presage a great Famine that shall ensue a few years after.

XLIII.

French.

Gens d'alentour du Tar, Lot, & Garonne, Gardez les Monts Apennins de passer, Vostre tombeou pres de Rome & d'Ancone, Le noir poil crespe fera Trophée dresser. **English.**

People that live about the *Tar*, *Lot*, and *Garonne*, Take heed to go over the *Apennine* Mountains, Your Grave is near *Rome* and *Ancona*, The black frisled hair shall dress a Trophy of you.

ANNOT.

The *Tar*, the *Lot*, and the *Garone*, are three Rivers of *Gascony*, the Inhabitants of which are forewarned not to go over the *Apennine* Mountains, or else they shall meet with their Graves near *Rome* and *Ancona*. This hath relation to the 38 Stanza, and to the interpretation thereof, therefore *vide*.

XLIV.

French.

Quand l'Animal a l'Homme domestique, Apres grands peines & sauts viendra parler, Le foudre a vierge sera si malefique, De Terre prinse & suspendue en l'Air. **English.**

When the Beast familiar to Mankind, After great labour, and leaping shall come to speak, The Lightning shall be so hurtful to a Virgin, That she shall be taken from the Earth, and suspended in the Air.

ANNOT.

It is a Dog that shall come howling and leaping to his Mistresses friends; because she was killed and suspended in the Air by the Lightning.

XLV.

French.

Les cinq estranges entrez dedans le Temple, Leur sang viendra la Terre prophaner, Aux Thoulousain sera bien dur exemple, D'un qui viendra ses loix exterminer. **English.**

The five strangers having come into the Church, The blood shall prophane the ground, It shall be a hard example to those of *Thoulouse*, Concerning one that came to break their Laws.

ANNOT.

I suppose these *five strangers* to be *five Commissioners*, for the altering something in the Government of *Thoulouse*, who shall be all killed in a Church, and the ground prophaned by their blood, according to the *Romish* opinion.

XLVI.

French.

Le Ciel (de Plancus la Cité) nous presage, Par clercs insignes & par estoiles fixes, Que de son change subit saproche lage, Ne pour son bien, ne pour ses malefices. English.

The Heaven foretelleth concerning the City of *Plancus*, By famous Clerks, and fixed Stars, That the time of her sudden change is near hand, Neither because of her goodness, or wickedness.

ANNOT.

The City of *Plancus* is *Lion*, because he was the Founder of it. That City is threatned here of a sudden change, caused neither by her goodness or wickedness, but by a certain position and aspect of the fixed Stars, which makes it fatal.

XLVII.

French.

Le vieux Monarque dechassé de son Regne, Aux Orients son secours ira querre, Pour peur des Croix ploiera son Enseigne, En Mitylene ira par Mer & par Terre. English.

The old Monarch being expelled out of his Kingdom, Shall go into the East to get succours, For fear of the Crosses he shall fold up his Colours, He shall go into *Mitylene* by Sea and Land.

ANNOT.

Mitylene is an Island of the *Archipelago*, belonging to the Turk.

XLVIII.

French.

Sept cens Captifs attachez rudement, Pour la moitie meurtrir, donné le sort, Le proche espoir viendra si promptement, Mais non si tost qu'une quinziesme mort. English.

Seven hundred prisoners shall be tied together, To murder half of them, the lot being cast, The next hope shall come quickly, And not so quickly, but fifteen shall be dead before.

ANNOT.

By the next hope, he meaneth the reprieve. The rest is clear.

XLIX.

Regne Gaulois tu seras bien changé, En lieu estrange est translaté l'Empire, En autre mœurs & Lois seras rangé, Rouan & Chartres te feront bien du pire. English.

French Kingdom thou shalt be much changed, The Empire is translated in another place, Thou shalt be put into other manners and Laws, *Rouan* and *Chartres* shall do the worse they can to thee.

ANNOT.

Rouan is the chief City of the Province of *Normandie*, and *Chartres* the chief City of that of *Beausse*.

L.

French.

La Republique de la grande Cité, A grand rigueur ne voudra consentir, Roy sortir hors par Trompette Cité, L'Eschelle au Mur la Cité repentir. English.

The Common-wealth of the great City, With great harshness shall not consent, That the King should go out being summoned by a Trumpet, The Ladder shall be put to the Wall, and the City repent.

ANNOT.

It is hard to know what he meaneth by the great City wherein there is a Common-wealth, whether it be *Venice, Genoa, Geneva, Luca,* or some of the Cities of *Switzerland*; but it seemeth that a King shall take shelter in it, who shall be summoned by a Trumpet to come out, but the City will not suffer it, for which the said City shall be scaled, and repent.

LI.

French.

Paris conjure un grand meurtre commettre, Blois le fera sortir en plein effet, Ceux d'Orleans voudront leur Chef remettre, Angers, Troyes, Langres, leur seront un mes fait. English.

Paris conspireth to commit a great murder, *Blois* will cause it to come to pass, Those of *Orleans* will set up their head again, *Angers, Troyes, Langres* will do them a mischief.

ANNOT.

The Prophecy contained in the two first Verses came to pass in the time of *Henry* the III. King of *France*, when the *Parisians* did rebel against him, and made Barricadoes in the streets, thinking to have taken him, who was compelled to run away for his life, and fly to *Chartres*. This rebellion was raised and fomented by *Henry* of *Lorraine* Duke of *Guise*, whom the King afterwards caused to be murdered, with his brother the Cardinal of *Lorraine*, at the Convention of the three Estates kept at *Blois*.

Orleans, *Angers*, *Troyes*, *Langres*, are remarkable Cities in *France*.

LII.

French.

En la Campagne sera si longue pluye, Et en l'Apoville si grande siccité, Coq verra l'Aigle l'aisle mal accomplie, Par Lion mise sera en extremité. English.

In *Campania* shall be so long a rain, And in *Apulia* so great a drought, The Cock shall see the Eagle with his wing disordered, And by the Lion brought to extremity.

ANNOT.

Campania, and *Apulia* are two Provinces of the Kingdom of *Naples*.

The last two Verses of the Prophecy came to pass about the years 1630 and 1631. when *Gustavus Adolphus* King of *Swedeland*, called here the Lion, brought the Empire (signified by the Eagle) to extremity; the King of *France* signified by the Cock, looking upon, and underhand assisting him.

LIII.

French.

Quand le plus grand emportera le prix, De Nuremberg, d'Ausbourg, & ceux de Basle, Par Agripine Chef de Frankfort repris, Traverseront par Flandres jusqu'en Gale. English.

When the great one shall carry the prize, Of *Nuremberg*, *Ausbourg*, and *Basil*, By *Agrippina* the Chief of *Frankfort* shall be taken, They shall go through *Flanders* as far as *France*.

ANNOT.

Nuremberg, *Ausbourg*, and *Basil* are Cities of *Germany*.

By *Agrippine* is understood the City of *Cologne*, called in Latine *Colonia Agrippina*, from the Founderess of it *Agrippina*, Mother of the Emperour *Nero*, or from *M. Agrippa* favourite of *Augustus Cæsar*.

LIV.

French.

L'un des plus grands fuira aux Espagnes, Qu'en longue playe apres viendra seigner, Passant Copies par les hautes Montagnes, Devastant tout, & puis apres regner. English.

One of the greatest shall run away into *Spain*, That shall cause a wound to bleed long, Leading Armies over the high Mountains, Destroying all, and afterwards shall Raign.

This is so plain, that it needeth no interpretation.

LV.

French.

En l'an qu'un œil en France Regnera, La Cour sera en un bien fascheux trouble, Le grand de Blois son amy tuera, Le Regne mis en mal & doubte double. English.

In the year that one eye shall Reign in *France*, The Court shall be in a very hard trouble, The great one of *Blois* shall kill his friend, The Kingdom shall be in an ill case, and double doubt.

ANNOT.

The meaning of the first Verse is, when a King having but one eye shall Reign in *France*. *Blois* is a City in *France* upon the River *Loire*.

LVI.

French.

Montauban, Nismes, Avignon & Besier, Peste, Tonnerre & Gresle a fin de Mars, De Paris Pont, de Lion Mur, Monpelier, Depuis six cens & sept vingt, trois parts. English.

Montauban, *Nismes*, *Avignon* and *Besier*, Plague, Lightning and Hail at the end of *March*, The Bridge of *Paris*, the Wall of *Lion*, and *Monpelier*, shall fall, From six hundred and seven score, three parts.

ANNOT.

Montauban is a Town in *Gascony*, *Nismes* and *Besiers* are Towns in *Languedoc*; *Avignon* is a Town in *France* belonging to the Pope, which shall suffer these damages by Lightning at the end of *March*.

LVII.

French.

Sept fois changer verrez gens Britanique, Teints en sang en deux cens nonante an, France non point par appuy Germanique, Aries double son Pope Bistarnan. English.

Seven times you shall see the *English* to change, Died in blood, in two hundred ninety year, Not *France*, by the *German* support, *Aries* doubleth his *Bastarnan* Pole.

The two first Verses concern *England*; the third *France*; the fourth marketh the time by the motion of the Sign of *Aries*, which shall be favourable to *France*.

We shall leave the two first Verses to be interpreted by the *English* Nation, which is most concerned in it, and come to the last two, which concern *France*.

The third Verse saith that *France* shall not change as *England*, by reason of the help it shall have from *Germany*, which hath been made good already for these hundred years, notwithstanding the Wars between *Henry* II. and the *Spaniard*; the Conspiracy of the Protestant party against *Francis* the II. at *Amboise*; the civil Wars under *Charles* the IX. the League under *Henry* III. and *Henry* IV. the Forrain Wars under *Lewis* XIII. and *Lewis* XIV. now Reigning.

The Authors meaning by these words, *but France not*, is, you shall not see *France* change seven times in two hundred ninety years, as the *Brittish* nation, and then he giveth the reason of it, *by German help*, that is to say, that *France* shall have help from *Germany*.

The fourth Verse saith, that during those two hundred ninety years, *Aries doubleth his Bastarnan Pole*, to understand this, we must suppose first that the Sign of *Aries* ruleth over *France*, *Palestine*, *Bastarnia*, &c.

Secondly, we must learn from *Ptolomy* and other Geographers, that *Bastarnia* containeth the people that are towards *Sarmatia* or *Poland*, which were called by the Ancients, the people of *Admone*, *Sidane*, *Roxolane*, and by others *Peucins*, from the Island *Peuce*, which is in *Istria*.

Thirdly, we must suppose, that the Sign of *Aries* hath two Poles, the first is that of the Æquinoctial Line, and the second, that of the *Eccliptick*, because the Sign of *Aries* beginneth just in the Line of the *Equator*, and afterwards stretcheth towards the North. Now it is so that the place where its extension endeth in the Eccliptical Line of the Sun, is called by the Author the *Bastarnan Pole*.

It is a *Pole* sith in the constellations of Heaven, we call *Poles*, the two ends or extremities of them, and in the constellations of the Zodiack, we call the first Pole that which is next to the Equator, and the second Pole that which stretcheth towards the North, or towards the South in the Eccliptical Line.

In this sense, the first Pole of the Sign of *Aries*, is that which hath its first degree in the Equator; the second is, that which stretcheth towards the North in the Eccliptick, and this last Pole is called *Bastarnan*, because it is Vertical to *Bastarnia*, as the Astrologers set down their Climates, Kingdoms, Provinces and Towns under the twelve Signs.

Fourthly, We must suppose that this word *to double*, may signifie three things. 1. In Seamens tearms; it signifieth to go beyond some place, as to double the Cape of *bona Speranza*, which is called in *Italian*, *Tramontare*; that is, to go beyond. 2. It signifieth to do twice the same thing, as *Jacob* did double his service for *Rachel*, &c. 3. In matter of traveling; it signifieth to go twice as far as is requisite.

To double, in this place cannot be understood in the first sense; because the constellations never stretcht out of their compasses, though the Stars of which they are compounded, have their peculiar motions.

To understand this, we must know that the Stars of the Firmament have their peculiar motions from West to East, upon the Pole of the Eccliptick, and that they go that way a matter of one Degree, in the space of about 100 years, and consequently the Stars do retrograde every year in the Eccliptick from West to East 52 Seconds. *Ptolomeus* holdeth this opinion, but other renowned Astrologers give them more: For my part I am of *Tychobrahe*'s opinion, who allowed them one Degree of retrogradation in 70 years and 7 Months, and consequently 51 Seconds every year.

According to this Doctrine the Star that is in the Horn of *Aries*, was observed by *Tymocharis* in 2d Degree; 150 years after, *Hipparchus* observed it in the first; 265 years after, *Ptolomeus* saw it in the 6 Degree; 740 years after, *Albathognius* observed it in the 18 Degree; 304 years after,

Alphonsus King of *Spain*, found it in the 6 Degree; 265 years after, *Copernicus* did observe it to be in the 27 Degree and two Minutes; 61 years after, *Tychobrahe* saw it in the 27 Degree, and above 37 Minutes; so that in the space of 61 years it had gone 35 Minutes.

By this Doctrine we see that the whole constellations do not go beyond their Poles, though the Stars that Compound them change their Poles every year of 51 Seconds.

To double, then here cannot be taken in the first sense, nor in the third sense, for the first reason, it must then be in the second sense; and thus *Aries doubleth his Bastarnan Pole*; that is, *Aries* maketh twice his Pole, which answereth to *Bastarnia*.

If you ask how it cometh to pass that *Aries* doubleth this Pole, and in what place of Heaven we set this *Bastarnan Pole*. I answer to the first, that *Aries* doubleth his Pole, when one of those 13 Stars cometh to that point, which is a Northern or Western Pole to that sign in the Eccliptick. As to the second: I answer, that the place ought to be its last Degree, *viz.* the end of the 30 Degree.

Why? (will you say) did the Author mark that difference of the Sign of *Aries*, rather than that of *Taurus*, or of another?

I answer, that it was in favour of *France*; because *Aries* doth govern in *France*, and if it hath been favourable to it, when it came first to the *Bastarnan Pole*, it will be so too when it doubleth the same Pole, seeing that it will have the same position and Aspect. Now we see, that in the space of these 100 years, *France* was not overcome, much less shall it be hereafter, seeing that the Stars do promise its exaltation for a long continuance.

If I were a great Astrologer, I should observe exactly by this, that within the space of 290 years, *Aries shall double his Cape Bastarnan*, and consequently *Aries* should come to that Pole just in the year 1845. which is according to that we have said.

LVIII.

French.

Aupres du Rhin des Montagnes Noriques, Naistra un grand de gens trop tard venu, Qui defendra Sarmates & Pannoniques, Qu'on ne scaura quil sera devenu. **English.**

Near the *Rhine*, out of the *Norick* Mountains, Shall be born a great one, though too late come, Who shall defend the *Polonians* and *Hungarians*, So that it shall not be known what is become of him.

ANNOT.

This is plain.

LIX.

French.

Barbare Empire par le tiers usurpé, La plus grand part de son sang mettre amort, Par mort senicle par luy quart frappé, Pour peur que sang par le sang ne soit mort. **English.**

A *Barbarian* Empire shall be usurped by a third person, Who shall put to death the greatest part of his Kindred, By death of old age, the fourth shall be stricken by him, For fear that blood should not die by blood.

The two first Verses are plain, I acknowledge my Ignorance in the last two.

LX.

French.

Par toute Asia grande proscription, Mesme en Mysie, Lydie, & Pamphilie, Sang versera par dissolution, D'un jeune noir remply de felonie. English.

Through all *Asia* shall be a great proscription, Yea in *Mysia*, *Lydia*, and *Pamphilia*, Blood shall be spilled by the debauchness Of a young black man, full of felony.

ANNOT.

Mysia, *Lydia*, and *Pamphilia*, are Countreys of *Asia*.

LXI.

French.

La grande bande & secte Crucigere, Se dressera en Mesopotamie, Du proche Fleuve compagnie legere, Qui telle Loy tiendra pour ennemie. English.

The great troop and sect wearing a Cross, Shall rise up in *Mesopotamia*, Near the next River shall be a light company, Which shall hold that law for enemy.

ANNOT.

It is an Army of Christians (be like *Armenians*) that shall rise in *Mesopotamia* against whom shall an Army of Turkish Horseman come, who did live by the next River.

LXII.

French.

Proche del Duero par Mer Cyrene close, Viendra percer les grands Monts Pyrenees, La main plus courte & sa percée gloses A Carcasonne conduira ses menées. English.

Near the *Duero* closed by the *Cyrenian* Sea, Shall come to pierce the great *Pyrenean* Mountains, The shorter hand and his pierced glose, Shall in *Carcassone* lead his plot.

ANNOT.

The *Cyrenian* Sea, is that Sea which is by the Province of *Cyrene*. The *Pyrenean* Mountains part *Spain* from *France*. *Carcassonne* is a Town in *France* near unto *Spain*. The rest passeth my understanding.

LXIII.

French.

Romain pouvoir sera du tout a bas, Son grand Voisin imiter les vestiges, Occultes haines civiles, & debats, Retarderont aux boufons leur folies. English.

The *Roman* power shall be quite put down, His great Neighbour shall follow his steps, Secret and civil hatreds and quarrels, Shall stop the Buffons folly.

ANNOT.

The first Verse signifieth, that the *Pope*'s Authority shall be put down.

The second, that his great neighbour, that is the Empire shall follow his steps, that is, be put down too. The two last Verses are plain.

LXIV.

Le Chef de Perse remplira grand Olchade, Classe trireme contre gent Mahometique, De Parthe & Mede & piller les Cyclades, Repos long temps au grand Port Jonique. English.

The Head of *Persia* shall fill a great *Olchade*, A Fleet of Galleys against the *Mahometan* Nation, From *Parthia* and *Media* they shall come to plunder the *Cyclades*, A long rest shall be on the *Jonique* Port.

ANNOT.

I could not find what he meaneth by *Olchade*. The second Verse is plain.

Parthia and *Media* are two Kingdoms depending from that of *Persia*. The Islands of *Cyclades* are in the *Ægean* Sea, and are so called because they are like a Garment about the City of *Delos*, for κυκλας in Greek signifieth a round garment of a woman.

The *Jonique* Sea is that Sea in *Grecia*, which is about *Athens* and *Corinth*, &c.

LXV.

French.

Quand le Sepulchre du grand Romain trouvé, Le jour apres sera esleu Pontife, Du Senat gueres il ne sera prouvé, Empoisonné, son sang au Sacre Scyphe. English.

When the Sepulcher of the great *Roman* shall be found, The next day after a Pope shall be elected, Who shall not be much approved by the Senate, Poisoned, his blood in the Sacred *Scyphe*.

ANNOT.

This seemeth to foretel the finding out of the Sepulcher of some famous *Roman*, and that the next day after a *Pope* shall be Elected, who being not well approved of by the Conclave, shall be poisoned in the Chalice, which is the Communion Cup that the Roman Catholicks use at *Mass*, signified here by the Latine word *Scyphus*.

LXVI.

French.

Le grand Baillif d'Orleans mis a mort. Sera par un de sang vindicatif, De mort merite ne mourra, ne par sort, Des pieds & mains mal, le faisoit captif. English.

The great Bailif of *Orleans* shall be put to death, By one of a revengeful blood, He shall not die of a deserved death, nor by chance, But the disease of being tied hand and foot, hath made him prisoner.

ANNOT.

The Bailif of *Orleans* is a great Officer, for he is there Lord Chief Justice, and of all the precincts. It seemeth that this man shall be put to death, by one of a revengeful blood, not that he had deserved it, or come to it by chance, but because he shall be tied hand and foot, and die in prison.

LXVII.

French.

Une nouvelle Secte de Philosophes, Mesprisant mort, or, honneurs & richesses, Des Monts Germains seront fort limitrophes, A les ensuivre auront appuy & presses. English.

A new Sect of Philosophers shall rise, Despising Death, Gold, Honours and Riches, They shall be near the Mountains of *Germany*, They shall have abundance of others to support and follow them.

ANNOT.

This is properly said of the Anabaptists in *Germany*, in the time of *John de Leyden*, and now of the Quakers in *England*, and elsewhere.

LXVIII.

French.

Peuple sans Chef d'Espagne & d'Italie, Morts, profligez dedans le Cheronese, Leur dict trahy par legere folie, Le sang nager per tout a la traverse. English.

A people of *Spain* and *Italy* without a Head, Shall die, being overcome in the *Cheronese*, Their saying shall be betrayed by a light folly, The blood shall swim all over at random.

ANNOT.

Cheronese is a Land or ground unmanured; the rest is plain.

LXIX.

French.

Grand exercite conduit par jouvenceau, Se viendra rendre aux mains des ennemis, Mais le vieillard nay au demy pourceau, Fera Chalon & Mascon estre amis. English.

A great Army led by a young man, Shall yield it self in the hands of the enemies, But the old man born at the sign of the halfe-Hog, Shall cause *Chalon* and *Mascon* to be friends.

ANNOT.

The two first Verses are plain; as for the third Verse, I could not find who that *Old man* should be, that shall be born at the sign of the *half-Hog*.

Chalon and *Mascon* are two Cities in *France*, the first in *Champagne*, the last in *Burgundy*.

LXX.

French.

La grand Bretagne comprise d'Angleterre, Viendra par eaux si haut a inondre, La Ligue nevue d'Ausone fera gerre, Que contre eux ils se viendront bander. English.

Great *Britany* comprehended in *England*, Shall suffer so great an Inundation by Waters, The new League of *Ausone* shall make Wars, So that they shall stand against them.

ANNOT.

This Prophecie is divided in two parts. The first two Verses foretel a great Innundation, that was to happen in *England*.

The last two speak of a league and insurrection, that shall be at *Bordeaux*, which is here called *Ausone*, from a famous Latine Poet, named *Ausonius*, who was born in that City.

As to the first part, after much seeking and enquiry: I found the truth of it in a Latine book, called *Rerum in Gallia, Belgia, Hispania, Anglia, &c. gestarum anno 1607. Tomi septimi Liber secundus conscriptus a Nicolao Gotardo Artus Dantiscano*, where the History is related thus.

About the end of *January* 1607 the Sea broke out so violently in *England*, that after the breaking of Fences and Dikes, it caused very great damages to the Inhabitants. The greatest mischief was done in *Somersetshire*, where the water did overflow, ten Leagues in length, and two in breadth, twelve foot high in the most eminent places. This sudden Innundation brought a fearful alarm to the Countrey people; some of them going to their Plough, were fained to run back to their houses, where they found their enemies at their doors, *viz.* Death and Water, who without distinction swept them away. In a little time, the Towns appeared like Islands, encompassed on all sides, and presently after were swallowed up, so that the tops of the Trees were scarce seen. This new Flood covered so the Towns of *Hansfield*, in the same County, those of *Grantham, Kenhus, Kingston,* and *Briandon,* with several Farms built in the Champion Countrey, that none of the Buildings could be seen. If you add to this the devastation of the places, the quantity of Corn, Fruit, and Grass that was lost, the misery shall be so great, as not to be expressed. During this fearful quarrel between the Water and the Land, an exceeding great number of people died of all Ages, and Sexes, it would avail them nothing to get into the upper Stories and Roofs of houses, nor upon the highest Trees; for the imperious Waters did so swell and rage, that the Foundations of the houses, and roots of the Trees were loosened, so that both fell to the Ground, or rather into the Water. The people seeing no way to escape, resolved to die patiently. No body could without great grief see the Oxen and Sheep drowning; for there was such a numerous quantity of them, that afar off one would have thought them to be Rocks in the Sea, but seeing them swiming, and hearing them bleating and bellowing, one would have thought them to be a storm and hissing of winds. A rich Farmer, and father of seven Children, being involved in the Flood, and much astonished at this accident, nevertheless thinking the danger less then it was, went about to save some of his best Goods; but seeing the Waters to increase, he forsook all, and went to save one of his Children, whom he loved best; but the Waters followed him so close, that all he could do, was to get upon the Roof of his house. Among the Children there was a little one sleeping in a Cradle, which being made of close boards, did swim upon the Waters about three Miles, and was taken up alive, and sound. The Hay-cocks did swim like Ships upon the Waves, the Pigeons and Pigs were upon the Sheaves that the Water carried away. The Coneys being driven out of their holes, had leapt upon the backs of the swiming Sheep. A certain Shepheard being about to gather his Sheep into their Fold, was followed by the Flood, ran for his life, and climbed upon a high Tree, where seeing his Sheep bleating in the water, he began to tear his hair, to smite his breast, to lift up his hands and his eyes to Heaven, and when his Sheep had all perished, and himself endured an extream cold and hunger, he was at last taken up in a Boat that was sent to save the distressed.

But here we must talk of *Bristol*, which is one of the chiefest Cities in *England*, by reason of the Haven, which bringeth thither abundance of Merchants, from several Nations. The same day of that Inundation, the Sea breaking into a great Channel, did presently overflow the Countrey with such quickness and violence, that it covered the Valleys, and the smaller Hills, in so much that nothing but an utter ruine was expected; many whole houses were turned upside down, and carried away with the Flood. The Barns full of Corn, Hay, and Straw, were overthrown, and the Cattle carried away, besides abundance of people of all sorts. The Merchants of *London* and *Bristol*, and the rest of the Inhabitants, besides the loss of Provisions, suffered an inestimable one in their Commodities, which they had provided for the Fair, that was then near hand, the most part of them being carried away by the Flood, and the rest so spoiled, that the owners could not tell what to do with them. A Gentleman dwelling between *Barnstable* and *Bristol*, and two Leagues off from the Sea, being gone abroad in the Morning to oversee his grounds, did look towards the Sea, ran back again to his house, to bring this sad news to his Wife and Servants, while they were endeavouring to pack up the most precious of their Goods, the Water came about the house so fast, that they altered their resolution, and bethought themselves only to save their lives; the servants busied themselves about tying the Goods together, thinking the Water could not have carried them away. As for the Gentleman, he went with his Wife and Children to the top of the house, and got upon the rafters of the Roof. Although nothing appeared to them but the Image of death; nevertheless some hope and desire of escaping, made the Gentleman come down to save a little Trunk, wherein his papers of greatest concernment were. Being come down from the Rafter, he laid hold of the Trunk, and fastened it to a Manger; while he was busie about it, the Waves of the Sea did so beat against that house, that it fell down to the Ground. The Wife, Children, and Servants were swallowed up in the ruine. The Gentleman laid hold on a Rafter, and was carryed away with it above half a League further, to a Mountain, where he set his foot upon dry Ground, being half dead with fear and grief, and bewailing the loss of his Wife, Children, and Servants, he spyed the little Trunk and the Manger, which he drew to Land, and that was all he saved, besides his Life.

Another Gentleman living thereabouts, and newly married, was resolved that day to go to the next Town, and make merry with some friends, whereupon he bid his man make his Horse ready, and himself went to put on his Boots; after he had put on one, and whilst he held the other in his hand, the Waters came so fiercely into that house, that they compelled the half Booted Gentleman to run away for his life, in an upper Chamber, but he was followed so close by that merciless Element, that he was fained to get upon the top of the Roof, to save his life, and to ride upon the upper Rafter, but the house and Roof melting by the violence of the Waves, this new Knight was carried by the violence of them towards the Town where he intended to make merry, and there was saved with much adoe.

It happened at the same time near *Markand*, in the Dutchy of *Norfolk*, that two Thieves, going about to steal some Cattle, while they were driving of them, perceived in the Morning the Justice of God following them; it was the Water, which having overtopped the Dikes, threatned the takers of being taken, and compelled them to save themselves with all speed. From their wickedness did arise a great good; for to the next Town they went, and bid the Sexton to Ring the Bell, and to cry Water, Water: The Inhabitants being for the most part asleep, did not know what to do in such an Alarm: Some climbed into the Church's Steeple; others thinking there were Thieves went about to fence and defend their houses; others hearing of a Flood, laughed at it, and said, that those who brought this News, deserved to be punished; but presently they altered their Languages, and their laughing was turned into a fearful mourning, every one flying to save himself, his Wife, and Children, and whatsoever they could pack up of their most precious Goods. Some thinking to have more wit than others, went about to divert the Current of the Water from their houses; but seeing there was no remedy, they went with their Wives and Children to the tops of their houses, in a lamentable fright.

But when the Water came to seize upon the houses, wherein there were some Playing, some

Drinking, others already Drunken, a great part of them were drowned, others ran to a Hill near the Town, where they spent the rest of that night, and the day following with great lamentations.

The next day they saw their houses half under Water, and many people, who from the windows and Steeples cryed for help; others endeavoured to save themselves upon Boards and Rafters; the Horses tyed to the Manger were all suffocated. The Cattle in the fields, were by this time driven to the Mount called *Truhill*, and for all that, were not out of danger; for the Mountain was encompassed with Water to such a heighth and depth, that without Boats there was no access to it; chiefly because of the Thickets and Bushes. Thus so much Cattle was about to perish, had not some Shepherds brought Boats loaded with provisions for Men and Beasts, till the Waters retired again, and the Dikes were made good.

LXXI.

French.

Ceux dans les Isles de long temps assiegez, Prendront vigueur force contre ennemis, Ceux par dehors morts de faim profligez, En plus grand faim que jamais seront mis. English.

Those in the Islands that have been long besieged, Shall take vigour and force against their enemies, Those without shall die for hunger; being overcome, They shall be put in greater famine then they were before.

ANNOT.

This Prophecy came to pass when the *Spaniards* Besieged *Leyden* in *Holland*, for the *Dutch* broke the Dikes, whereby the water came upon them so fast, that they were more besieged and starved then those of the Town, and their Army wholly destroyed. Read Cardinal *Bentivoglios* his History of the *Low-Countreys*, as also *Strada*.

LXXII.

French.

Le bon Vieillard tout vis Ensevely, Prez du grand Fleuve par faux soupcon, Le nouveaux vieux de richesse ennobly, Prins en chemin tout l'or de la Rancon. English.

The good old man shall be buried alive, Near the great River by a false suspicion, The new old one made noble by his riches, The gold of his ransom shall be taken in the way.

ANNOT.

This Prophecy is divided into two parts: the two first Verses are concerning an old man that shall be buried alive near a great River, upon a false suspition.

The latter two are concerning a young man, who shall assume unto himself the name of a noble Family, and so make himself noble by his riches, but being afterward taken prisoner, the money that was sent for his Ransom, shall be taken in the way.

LXXIII.

Quand dans le Regne parviendra le boiteux, Competiteur aura proche Bastard, Luy & le Regne viendront si fort rogneux, Qu'ains quil guerisse son fait sera bien tard. English.

When the lame man shall attain to the Kingdom, He shall have a Bastard for his near competitor, He, and his Kingdom shall be so scabby, That before he be cured it will be late.

ANNOT.

The words and the sense are plain.

LXXIV.

French.

Naples, Florence, Fayence & Imole, Seront en termes de telle fascherie, Que pour complaire au malheureux de Nole, Plaint d'avoir fait a son Chef moquerie. English.

Naples, Florence, Fayenza, and *Imola,* Shall be put into so much distress, For being complaisant to the unhappy one of *Nola,* Who was complained of for having mocked his Superiour.

ANNOT.

Naples, Florence, Fayenza, Imola and *Nola* are all Cities in *Italy*; the rest is plain.

LXXV.

French.

Pau, Verone, Vicence, Saragousse, De Glaive atteints, Terroirs de sang humides, Peste si grande viendra a la grand gousse, Proche secours & bien long les remedes. English.

Pau, Verona, Vicenza, Saragossa, Shall be hit by the Sword, the Countrey shall be moist with blood, So great a plague and so vehement shall come, That though the succours be near, the remedy shall be far off.

ANNOT.

By *Pau* here are understood the Towns that are seated upon that River.

Verona, Vicenza, are two Cities in *Italy,* belonging to the *Venetians. Saragossa* is a City in *Sicily.*

LXXVI.

French.

En Germanie naistront diverses Sectes, Saprochant sort de l'heureux Paganisme, Le cœur captif & petites receptes, Feront retour a payer le vray disme. English.

In *Germany* shall divers Sects arise, Coming very near the happy *Paganism*, The heart captivated and small receivings, Shall open the gate to pay the true Tithes.

ANNOT.

The first and second Verses have been verified sufficiently.

By the two last Verses, he meaneth that the heart of everyone shall be in fear, so that they shall come to an agreement, which the true Tithes shall be paid, and every one come to his own again.

LXXVII.

French.

Le tiers climat soubs Aries comprins, L'An mil sept cens vingt sept en Octobre, Le Roy de Perse par ceux d'Ægypte prins, Conflict, mort, perte, a la Croix grand opprobre. English.

The third Climat comprehended under *Aries*, In the year 1700. the twenty seven of *October*, The King of *Persia* shall be taken by those of *Ægypt*, Battle, death, loss, a great shame to the Christians.

ANNOT.

Here be three notable things to be observed: one is the plain and punctual specification of the time, in which the Prophecy shall come to pass, *viz.* the 7. of *October* in the year 1700. The second is, that the King of *Persia* shall be taken by those of *Ægypt*. The third is, the shame and confusion that the Christians shall suffer for the same.

LXXVIII.

French.

Le Chef d'Escosse avec six d'Allemagne, Par gents de mer Orientaux captif, Traverseront le Calpre & Espagne, Present en Perse au nouveau Roy craintif. English.

The Chief of *Scotland* with six of *Germany*, Shall be taken prisoners by Seamen of the East, They shall go through the *Calpre* and *Spain*, And shall be made a present in *Persia* to the new fearful King.

ANNOT.

By the *Calpre* is understood the *Capzor* promontory, which is at the mouth of the *Streights*, by and beyond which these Prisoners will be carried into *Persia* for a present to the King, who then shall be some fearful person.

LXXIX.

French.

Le grand criard sans honte audacieux, Sera esleu Governeur le d'Armée, La hardiesse de son contentieux, Le pont rompu, Cité de peur pasmée. **English.**

The great bawler proud without shame, Shall be elected Governour of the Army, The stoutness of his Competitor, The Bridge being broken, the City shall faint for fear.

ANNOT.

Paradin saith, that in the year 1558. the Lord of *Bonnivet* being dead, the King of *France* did chuse *Francis* of *Vendosme*, *Vidame* of *Amiens*, to succeed the said *Bonnivet*, in the Office of Colonel of the *French* Foot. This *Vidame* is noted by all Historians, for a rash proud man, that had a good opinion of himself, and found fault with all the commands of the Marshal of *Brissac*, then General of the Army.

The King in consideration of his Birth, and that he was a good Souldier, gave him the place of the Lord *Bonnivet*, according to what the Author saith, *The great Bawler, &c. shall be elected Governour in the Army.* If you ask in what Army he was elected Governour, the third Verse answereth, *in the Army of his Competitor*, that is, the Marshal of *Brissac*, who did chide him severely for disobeying his commands, and was like once to have killed him.

The fourth Verse proved true at the taking of *Queiras*, where the Bridge, through which the succours came to relieve the Town, being broken, the Town grew so fearful, that it surrendred it self to the Marshal of *Brissac*.

LXXX.

French.

Erins, Antibe, villes auteur de Nice, Seront vastées fort par Mer & par Terre, Les Sauterelles Terre & Mer vent propice, Prins, morts, troussez, pillez, sans loy de guerre. **English.**

Erins, *Antibe*, and the Towns about *Nices*, Shall be destroyed by Sea and Land, The Grashopers shall have the Land, the Sea, and Wind favourable, They shall be taken, killed, thrust up, plundered, without Law of War.

ANNOT.

Erins and *Antibe* are Towns of *Provence*, bordering upon *Nice*, which is a Town of *Piemont*, all that Coast is threatned here to be ruined by the Grashopers, that is, the *Turks*, which fell out about the year 1558. for the King of *France* having called the *Turks* to his succours against *Charles* V. Emperour, they came and took *Nice* in the behalf of the *French*, where they committed unheard cruelties, as also upon all that Coast.

LXXXI.

French.

L'Ordre fatal sempiternal par chaisne, Viendra tourner par ordre consequent, Du Port Phocen sera rompue la chaine, La Cité prinse, l'ennemy quant & quant. English.

The fatal and eternal order by chain, Shall come to turn by consequent order, Of Port *Phocen* the chain shall be broken, The City taken, and the enemy presently after

ANNOT.

This Prophecy regardeth onely the City of *Marseilles*, which is the most famous Port Town that the *French* have upon the *Mediterranean* Sea, and which was anciently a *Greek* Colony, peopled by the *Phocen* Seas. This City is threatned here to have the chain of her Port broken, and to be taken by her enemies, and the said enemies to be a little while after taken in it.

LXXXII.

French.

Du Regne Anglois le digne dechassé, Le Conseiller par ire mis a feu, Ses adherans iront si bas tracer, Que le bastard sera demy receu. English.

From the *English* Kingdom the worthy driven away, The Councellor through anger shall be burnt, His partners shall creep so low, That the bastard shall be half received.

ANNOT.

This is one of those Prophecies that concern the *English* Nation, and which by its event, hath made this Book and the Author thereof famous, for nothing can be more plain to the meanest capacity, then the sense and words of these four Verses.

By the first, is meant the Kings most excellent Majesty *Charles* II. now Reigning, who being the true Heir to the Kingdom, and most worthy to rule, was driven out of the Kingdom by a rebellious rout of his Subjects.

The second Verse expresseth, the punishment inflicted upon the Councellors and Abettors of so hainous a crime, who were most of them hanged, drawn and quartered, their entrals burnt.

The third Verse, signifieth the low estate of the Abettors of that pernicious Councel.

The fourth Verse, is understood that bastard Faction, which was like to supplant *Cromwel*, upon the division of the Army.

LXXXIII.

French.

Les longs cheveux de la Gaule Celtique, Accompagnez d'Estranges Nations, Mettront captif l'Agent Aquitanique, Pour succomber a leurs intentions. English.

The long hairs of the *Celtian France*, Joyned with forrain Nations, Shall put in prison the *Aquitanick* Agent, To make him yield to their intentions.

ANNOT.

The *Celtan France* is that part of *France* included between the River *Loire*, and that of *Scheld* in *Flanders*. they are called here the *long hairs*; because in antient time they used to wear long hairs.

LXXXIV.

French.

La grand Cite sera bien desolée, Des habitans un seul n'y demoura, Mur, Sexe, Temple, & Vierge violée, Par Fer, Feu, Peste, Canon, peuple mourra. English.

The great City shall be made very desolate. Not one of the Inhabitants shall be left in it, Wall, Sex, Church, and Virgin ravished, By Sword, Fire, Plague, Canon, people shall die.

ANNOT.

This is concerning the Town of St. *Quentin*, which was taken by the *Spaniards* in the year 1557. upon the 27 of *August*, and 17 days after the Battle of St. *Laurence*, it was taken by assault, and all the Inhabitants put to the Sword.

LXXXV.

French.

La Cité prinse par tromperie fraude, Par le moyen d'Un bean jeune attrapé, Assaut donné, Raubine pres de Laude, Luy & touts morts pour avoir bien trompé. English.

The City shall be taken by cheat and deceit, By the means of a fair young one caught in it, Assault shall be given, *Raubine* near *Laude*, He, and all shall die, for having deceived.

ANNOT.

It is a City that shall be taken by the cheat and deceit of a young fair man, who himself shall be taken in his craft.

The difficulty lyeth in the third Verse, *viz.* what he meaneth by *Raubine* and *Laude*. I could find nothing by transposition of Letters: therefore I suppose the Author had a mind to reserve the exposition to himself, and to one that should be clearer sighted than I.

LXXXVI.

French.

Un chef d'Ausonne aux Espagnes ira, Par Mer, sera arrest dedans Marseilles, Avant sa mort un long temps languira, Apres sa mort on verra grand merveille. **English.**

A chief man of *Ausone* shall go into *Spain* By Sea, he shall stay at *Marseilles*, He shall languish a great while before his death, After his death great wonders shall be seen.

ANNOT.

Here is nothing obscure but the word *Ausone*, by which is meant the City of *Bordeaux*, so named by the Author every where, for having brought forth that famous Latine Poet, and Counsul of *Rome*, *Ausonius*.

LXXXVII.

French.

Classe Gauloise naproche de Corsegne, Moins de Sardaigne tu ten repentiras, Tretous mourrez frustrez de laide Greigne, Sang nagera, captif ne me croiras. **English.**

French Fleet do not come near unto *Corsica*, Much less to *Sardinia*, thou shalt repent of it, All of you shall die frustrate of the help *Greigne*, Blood shall swim, being Captive thou shalt not believe me.

ANNOT.

The Baron of *la Garde* coming from *Rome*, where he had carryed the Cardinals of *Tournon* and *Lorrain*, received order to go into *Corsica*, to relieve with ammunition the two Towns, that the *French* kept still in possession in that Island, *Glasse* and St. *Boniface*, which after the general peace made at *Cambray*, *anno* 1559. were restored to the Common-wealth of *Genoa*. When he was coming near the Island, there arose such a storm, that they were constrained to go as near land as they could, *viz.* in St. *Florents*, till the storm was over.

At the same time, by reason of the said storm, eleven Ships loaded with six thousand *Spaniards*, going for *Italy*, took shelter in the same place, a good way off from the said Baron.

At the first, the *Spanish* Ships did not spie the *French* Galleys, but the Baron *de la Garde* discovered the *Spaniards*, and bid his Galleys to set upon them. Two of the *Spanish* Ships were taken, in which were 1200. or 1500. *Spaniards*, part of which were drowned, and the rest made slaves.

The Baron chased the rest, but the storm so scattered them, that the nine escaped.

Before this encounter the *Genoese* Captain, *Andrew d'Oria*, took all the Island from the *French*, *Anno* 1553. and kept it ever since, by sending continual supplies. On the other side, the King of *France* sent supplies by the Lord of *Termes*, to those that were retired in the Island of *Glasse*.

One time among the rest, about the latter end of the year 1555. there was sent a notable supplie from the *French*, to which the Author speaketh now in these tearms.

French fleet do not come near unto Corsica, nor *Sardinia*, which is another Island near *Corsica*. The third Verse giveth the Reason of it; *ye shall die, being frustrated of the help Greigne.* *Greigne* is the Provencal Language, which was the Maternal one of our Author, signifieth a Galley: The sense therefore is this, you shall be frustrate of the help of the Galleys, that are under the command of the Baron *de la Garde*, who carryed unto you men, money, and ammunition; because he shall be then in pursute of the *Spanish* fleet, that were scattered by a storm.

In the mean time *Blood shall swim* in the fight of the Baron *de la Garde*, and thou, *poor Prisoner* in that Island, *Thou shalt not believe me*; those slaves were they, which went in the year 1555. And the Author saying, *Thou shalt not believe me*, sheweth, that being very famous in *Provence*, for his Prophecies, the General of the Army had asked him concerning the success of his Journey, and that he did warn him not to undertake it; but having an express command from the King, his Master, he would need go. Therefore he saith, *Poor prisoner thou shalt not believe me.* We find in this work many examples of those, who went to consult with the Author concerning the success of their undertakings, as did the Earl of *Sommerive*, before the besieging of *Bagnole*, to whom he answered, that he should leave the Trees loaded with a new kind of fruit, that is to say, of the Rebels, whom he caused to be hanged on Trees.

LXXXVIII.

French.

De Barcelone par Mer si grande Armée, Toute Marseille de frayeur tremblera, Isles saisies, de Mer aide fermeé, Ton traditeur en Terre nagera. **English.**

There shall come from *Barcelona* by Sea so great a fleet, That *Marseilles* shall quake for fear, The Islands shall be seized, the help by Sea shut up, Thy Traitor shall swim to Land.

ANNOT.

Barcelona is a Town in *Spain*, upon the *Mediterranean* Sea; *Marseilles* is another in *France*, upon the same Sea. The rest is easie.

LXXXIX.

French.

En ce temps la sera frustrée Cypre, De son secours, de ceux de Mer Ægée, Vieux trucidez mais par Mesles & Lipre, Seduit leur Roy, Roine plus outragée. **English.**

At that time *Cyprus* shall be frustrated Of its succours, of those of the *Ægean* Sea, Old ones shall be killed, but by *Mesles* and *Lipre*, Their King shall be seduced, and the Queen more wronged.

ANNOT.

The two first Verses are plain, the two last have need of an *Oedipus*.

XC.

Le grand Satyre & Tygre d'Hircanie, Don presenté a ceux de l'Occean, Un chef de Classe istra de Carmanie, Qui prendra Terre au Thyrren Phocean. English.

The great *Satyr* and *Tyger* of *Hircania*, Shall be a gift presented to those of the Ocean, An Admiral of a fleet shall come out of *Carmania*, Who shall Land in the *Thyrren Phocean*.

ANNOT.

By the great Satyr and Tyger of Hircania, is meant, the King of *Persia*, who is also King of *Hircania*, abounding with *Tygers*.

That King of *Persia* shall be made a gift to those of the Ocean; that is, shall be either drowned in it, or do some wonderful things upon it.

Carmania is a Province in *Asia*, belonging to the *Turk*.

The *Thyrren Phocean* is the City of *Marseilles* in *France*, so called by the Author in this Book; because it was a Colony of the *Phocenses* in *Greece*; it is also called *Thyrren*, because it is seated upon the *Tyrrhenean* Sea, as *Virgil* saith,

————*Thyrrenum navigat Æquor.*

XCI.

French.

L'Arbre qu'estoit par long temps mort seiché, Dans une nuit viendra a reverdir, Son Roy malade, Prince pied attaché, Craint d'ennemis fera Voiles bondir. English.

The Tree that had been long dead and withered, In one night shall grow green again, His King shall be sick, his Prince shall have his foot tied, Being feared by his enemies, he shall make his Sails to rebound.

ANNOT.

The two first Verses are Metaphorical, and are to be understood of a considerable person, who having been for a long time despised and under a cloud, shall on a sudden rise again and be in repute. The two last Verses are intelligible enough.

XCII.

French.

Le monde proche du dernier periode, Saturn encor sera tard de retour, Translat Empire devers Nations brode, L'œil arraché a Narbon par Autour. English.

The world being near its last period, *Saturn* shall come yet late to his return, The Empire shall be translated into *brode* Nations, *Narbon* shall have her eye pickt out by a Hawk.

The meaning of the first and second Verses is, that the world shall be at an end, before *Saturn* hath performed his whole course, which (if I do not mistake) is thought by the Astronomers to be of 36000. years.

The third Verse signifieth, that before the end of the world, the Empire shall be translated or possessed by a black Nation, for *brode* in old *French* signifieth black, whence it cometh that to this day they call a handsom black woman, *une belle Brode*, that is a fair black woman.

Narbon is a famous City in *Languedoc*, and the seat of an Archbishop.

XCIII.

French.

Dans Avignon tout le Chef de l'Empire, Fera arrest, pour Paris desole, Tricast tiendra l'Annibalique ire, Lion par change sera mal consolé. English.

In *Avignon* all the Chief of the Empire, Shall stay, by reason of *Paris* being desolate, *Tricast* shall stop the *Annibalik* anger, *Lion* by change shall be ill comforted.

ANNOT.

The first and second Verse signifie, that the Pope once more shall keep his seat in *Avignon*, which is a Town in *France* belonging to the Pope, and where formerly they kept their See, for the space of above an hundred years. As for the word *Tricast*, there must be a foul errour in the impression or else; I must confess I understand it not. By the *Annibilik* anger, is meant those of *Barbary*, where *Annibal* was born. *Lion* is a famous Town in *France*, where is kept the greatest trading for Bills of Exchange.

XCIV.

French.

De cinq cens ans plus compte l'on tiendra, Celuy qu'estoit l'ornement de son temps, Puis a un coup grande clarté donra, Que pour ce Siecle les rendra tres-contens. English.

For five hundred years no account shall be made, Of him who was the ornament of his time: Then on a sudden he shall give so great a light, That for that age he shall make them to be most contented.

ANNOT.

The words and the sense are plain.

XCV.

French.

Lu Loy Morique on verra defaillir, Apres un autre beaucoup plus seductive, Boristhenes premier viendra faillir, Par dons & langue une plus attractive. English.

We shall see the *Morish* Law to decline, After which, another more seducing shall arise, *Boristhenes* shall be the first that shall fall, By gifts and tongue that Law shall be most seducing.

ANNOT.

This foretelleth the declining of the *Mahometan* Religion, after which another Religion shall be set up worse then the *Mahometan*. The first decay of it shall begin in *Scythia*, a Kingdom belonging to the King of *Persia*, through which runneth the River *Boristhenes*.

XCVI.

French.

Chef de Fossan aura gorge coupée, Par le Ducteur du Limier & L'curier, Le fait patré par ceux du Mont Tarpée, Saturne en Leo 13. de February. English.

The Chief of *Fossan* shall have his throat cut, By the Leader of the Hunt and Greyhond, The fact committed by those of the *Tarpeian* Mountain, *Saturn* being in *Leo* the 13. of *February*.

ANNOT.

Fossan is a City in *Piemont*, belonging to the Duke of *Savoy*, the Chief man or Governour of which is threatned here to have his throat cut by some Souldiers, either of *Rome*, or belonging to *Rome*, signified here by the *Tarpeian* Mountain, upon which the Capitol was built, and this fact to be committed by one that shall be a famous Huntsman; upon the 13 of *February*, *Saturn* being then in the Sign of *Leo*.

XCVII.

French.

Nouvelle Loy, Terre neuve occuper, Vers la Syrie, Judée & Palestine, Le grand Empire, Barbare corruer, Avant que Phebe son Siecle determine. English.

A new Law shall occupy a new Countrey, Towards *Syria*, *Judea* and *Palestina*, The great *Barbarian* Empire shall fall down, Before *Phœbe* maketh an end of her course.

ANNOT.

The words and sense are plain.

XCVIII.

Deux Royal Freres si fort guerroieront, Qu'entreux sera la guerre si mortelle, Qu'un chacun places fortes occuperont, De Regne & vie sera leur grand querelle. English.

Two Royal Brothers shall War so much one against the other, That the War between them shall be mortal, Each of them shall seize upon strong places, Their quarrel shall be concerning Kingdom and Life.

ANNOT.

      This needeth no interpretation.

XCIX.

French.

Aux Champs Herbus d'Alein & du Varneigre, Du Mont Lebron proche de la Durance, Camps des deux parts conflict sera si aigre, Mesopotamie defaillira en France. English.

In the Meadow Fields of *Alein* and *Varneigre*, Of the Mountain *Lebron* near the *Durance*, Armies on both sides, the fight shall be so sharp, That *Mesopotamia* shall be wanting in *France*.

ANNOT.

      Alain and *Varnaigre* are two small Towns in *France*, seated by the Mountain *Lebron*, near the River called *Durance*, where the Author saith there shall be such a sharp fight, that *Mesopotamia* shall be wanting in *France*, to understand this you must know, that *Mesopotamia* is a Countrey between two Rivers from the Greek words μεσος, which signifieth middle, and ποταμὸς which signifieth a River, the meaning then of the Author is, that the Battle so sharp, the ground shall be wanting to bury the dead.

C.

French.

Entre Gaulois le dernier honoré, D'homme ennemy sera victorieux, Force & terreur en moment exploré, D'Un coup de trait quand mourra l'envieux. English.

He that is the least honoured among the *French*, Shall be Conqueror of the man that was his Enemy, Strength and terrour shall in a moment be tried, When the envious shall be killed with an Arrow.

ANNOT.

      This is plain.

Michael Nostradamus.

CENTURY IV.

I.

French.

Sera du reste de sang non espandu, Venice quiert secours estre donné, Apres avoir bien lon temps attendu, Cité livrée au premier Cor sonné. English.

There shall be a remnant of blood unspilt, *Venice* shall seek for succours, After having long waited for it, The City shall be surrendred at the first sound of the Trumpet.

ANNOT.

This to my judgement is concerning the Siege of *Candia*, in which the *Venetians* for the space of about twenty years desired and expected succours from the Christian Princes, which came so slowly, that the City was fained to surrender upon honorable terms, which is the meaning of the first Verse, *There shall be a remnant of blood unspilt.*

II.

French.

Par mort la France prendra voiage a faire, Classe par Mer, marcher Monts Pyrenées, Espagne en trouble marcher gent militaire, Des plus grands Dames en France emmenées. English.

By reason of a death, *France* shall undertake a Journey, They shall have a Fleet at Sea, and march towards the *Pyrenes*, *Spain* shall be in trouble by an Army, Some of the greatest Ladies in *France* carried away

ANNOT.

The whole sense of this is, that by reason of some bodies death, *France* shall make war against *Spain* by Sea and Land, and put *Spain* in great trouble.

The fourth Verse saith, that some of the greatest Ladies in *France* shall be carried away, but the question is, whether by the *Spaniards*, or (which is more probable) by their own Husbands going to war against *Spain*.

III.

French.

D'Arras & Bourges de Brodes grands enseignes, Un plus grand nombre de Gascons battre a pied, Ceux long du Rhosne saigneront les Espagnes, Proche du Mont ou Sagunte sassied. English.

From *Arras* and *Bourges* many colours of black men shall come, A greater number of *Gascons* shall go on foot, Those along the *Rhosne* shall let *Spain* blood, Near the Mountain where *Saguntus* is seated.

ANNOT.

      Arras and *Bourges* are Cities of *France*. As for *brodes*, we have said before that it signifie brown men, such as are the *Gascoins*, inhabiting the Province of *Aquitania* near *Spain*.
      Saguntus is a City in *Spain*, that was destroyed by the *Romans*.

IV.

French.

L'Important Prince fasché, plaint & querelle, De rapts & pillé par Coqs & par Libiques, Grand & par Terre, par Mer infinis Voiles, Seule Italie sera chassant Celtiques. English.

The considerable Prince vexed, complaineth and quarelleth, Concerning rapes and plunderings done by the Cocks and Libiques Great trouble by Land, by Sea infinite Sails, *Italy* alone shall drive away the *French*.

ANNOT.

      This considerable Prince was *Philip* the II. King of *Spain*, who was vexed to see the Cocks, that is the *French*, and Libiques that is the *Turks* joyned together, under *Barbarossa* to commit so many Rapes and violences upon his Subjects.

V.

French.

Croix Paix, soubs un accomply Divin Verbe, L'Espagne & Gaules seront unis ensemble, Grand clade proche & combat tresacerbe, Cœur si hardy ne sera qui ne tremble. English.

The Cross shall have peace, under an accomplished Divine Word, *Spain* and *France* shall be united together, A great Battle near hand, and a most sharp fight, No heart so stout but shall tremble.

ANNOT.

      We have said before that by *Divine Word*, we must not understand the second person of the Trinity, but a Divine or Theologian, called in Greek θεόλογος, which also signifieth *Divine Word*.

Therefore the meaning of the first Verse is, that under the Goverment of some eminent Divine, (be like a good Pope) the Cross shall have peace, that is, the Christian Religion shall be in Peace, and persecution shall cease. The last three Verses are plain.

VI.

French.

D'Habits nouveaux apres faite la treuve, Malice, trame, & machination, Premier mourra qui en fera la preuve, Couleur Venise, insidiation. English.

After the new Cloaths shall be found out, There shall be malice, plotting and machination, He shall die the first that shall make trial of it, Under colour of *Venice*, shall be a conspiracy.

ANNOT.

Everybody may be as wise as I in the interpretation of this.

VII.

French.

Le fils mineur du grand & hay Prince, De Lepre aura a vingt ans grande tache, De dueil mourra triste & mince, Et il mourra la ou tombe chair lache. English.

The younger Son of the great and hated Prince, Being twenty years, old shall have a great touch of Leprosie, His mother shall die for grief, very sad and lean, And he shall die of the disease loose flesh.

ANNOT.

This is easie to be understood, if we remember that *Charles* IX. King of *France*, younger son to *Henry* II. died of a foul disease, and his Mother *Catharine* of *Medicis* died of grief.

VIII.

French.

La grand Cité dassaut prompt repentin Surpris de nuit, gardes interrompus, Les Excubies & veilles Saint Quentin, Trucidez gardes, & les Portails rompus. English.

The great City shall be taken by a sudden assault, Being surprised by night, the Watch being beaten, The Court of Guard and Watch of Saint *Quentin* Shall be killed, and the Gates broken.

ANNOT.

This great City was the City of St. *Quentin* in *Picardy*, taken by assault by *Philip* the II. *Anno* 1557.

IX.

Le Chef du Camp au milieu de la presse, D'un coup de flesche sera blessé aux cuisses, Lors que Geneve en larmes & destresse, Sera trahie par Lozanne & Souisses. English.

The Chief of the Camp in the middle of the crowd, Shall be wounded with an Arrow through both his thighs, When *Geneva* being in tears and distress, Shall be betrayed by *Lozane* and the *Switzers*.

ANNOT.

The words and sense are plain.

X.

French.

Le jeune Prince accusé faucement, Mettra le camp en trouble & en querelles, Meurtry le chef par le souslevement, Sceptre appaiser, puis guerir escroüelles. English.

The young Prince being falsely accused, Shall put the Camp in trouble, and in quarrele, The chief shall be murdered by the tumult, The Scepter shall be appeased, and after cure the Kings-evil.

ANNOT.

This Prophecie must needs be concerning *England* or *France*; for there is but those two Kings that challenge the cure of the Kings-evil.

XI.

French.

Celuy quaura couvert de la grand Cappe, Sera induit a quelque cas patrer, Les douze rouges viendront soüiller la nappe, Soubs meurtre, meurtre se viendra perpetrer. English.

He that shall be covered with a great Cloak, Shall be induced to commit some great fact, The twelve red ones shall Soil the Table-cloth, Under murder, murder shall be committed.

ANNOT.

Every one may interpret this as well as I, provided that by the *twelve red ones*, he understandeth twelve Cardinals.

XII.

Le Camp plus grand de route mis ensuite, Gueres plus outre ne sera pourchassé, Ost recampé & legion reduite, Puis hors, des Gaules du tout sera chassé. English.

The greatest Camp being in disorder, shall be routed, And shall be pursued not much after, The Army shall incamp again, and the Troops set in order, Then afterwards, they shall be wholly driven out of *France*.

ANNOT.

This Prophecie is concerning an out-landish Army that shall invade *France*, and though numerous, yet shall be put to flight, and shall not be much pursued: therefore it shall incamp again, and collect and gather again its Troops, and afterwards shall be wholly driven out of *France*.

I am much mistaken if this Prophecie came not to pass, when the Duke of *Parma* at the head of a *Spanish* numerous Army came into *France* in favour of the League; for *Henry* IV. met him at the siege of *Roven*, beat him off, and suffered him to retire quietly, and as the common saying is, made him a Golden Bridge, to retreat into the Low-Countries again.

XIII.

French.

De plus grand perte nouvelles rapportées, Le rapport fait le camp festonnera, Bandes unies encontre revoltées, Double Phalange, grand abandonnera. English.

News being brought of a great loss, The report divulged, the Camp shall be astonished, Troops being united and revolted, The double *Phalange* shall forsake the great one.

ANNOT.

This hath a connexion with the precedent; for while the Prince of *Parma* was busied in *France*, news was brought to his Camp, that the *Hollanders* had taken *Antwerp*, which discouraged his whole Host, and made him retire with all speed.

The Word *Phalange* signifieth a Battailion or part of an Army, which being expressed here by the word *double Phalange*, signifieth, that both Horse and Foot deserted the Duke of *Parma* upon the hearing of this news.

XIV.

French.

La mort subite du premier personage, Aura changé & mis un autre au Regne, Tost, tard venu a si haut & basage, Que Terre & mer faudra que lon le craigne. English.

The sudden death of the chief man, Shall cause a change, and put another in the Raign, Soon, late come to so high a degree, in a low age, So that by Land and Sea he must be feared.

ANNOT.

The two first Verses are plain.

The two last signifie, that a youth shall come to the Kingdom, *soon*, that is, by reason of the sudden death of the *chief man*, and *late*; because being but young, he shall Reign so long, that he shall be famous, and feared by Sea and Land.

XV.

French.

D'ou pensera faire venir famine, De la viendra le rassasiement, L'œil de la Mer par avare canine, Pour de l'un lautre donra Huile, Froment. **English.**

Whence one thought to make famine to come, Thence shall come the fulness, The eye of the Sea through a doggish covetousness, Shall give to both Oyl and Wheat.

ANNOT.

This Prophecie was fulfilled at the famous Siege of *Ostend*, which lasted three years and three Months; for the *Hollanders* that brought relief to the Town, did for covetousness sell the ammunition to the *Spaniards* that besieged it, for which complaint being made by the States to the Prince of *Orenge, Maurice* of *Nassaw*, as also that they did the like to *Newport*, which he had besieged; he replyed smartly, do you not know that your Countrey men would Sail into Hell, were it not for fear to have their Sails burnt.

XVI.

French.

La Cité franche de liberté fait serue, Des profligés & resueurs fait azyle, Le Roy changé a eux non si proterue, De cent seront devenus plus de Mille. **English.**

The free City from a free one shall become slave, And of the banished and dreamers shall be a retreat, The King changed in mind, shall not be so froward to them. Of one hundred they shall become more than a thousand.

ANNOT.

Here you must observe that the Author being a Papist, speaketh this concerning the City of *Geneva*, which he saith from a free City became a slave, when it shook off the Duke of *Savoy*'s domination, and became a retreat to the Protestants, whom he called the *banished* and *dreamers*.

In the third Verse, by *the King changed in his mind that shall not be so froward to them*, he meaneth, *Henry* IV. who having changed the Protestant Religion, to be a *Roman* Catholick, did undertake their protection against the Duke of *Savoy* their Prince.

Hence followeth the explication of the fourth Verse, when he saith, that *of one hundred they shall become more than a thousand*; for in few years the Protestants became so numerous, that they drove the *Roman* Catholicks wholly out of the Town, and so have remained to this day Masters of it.

XVII.

French.

Changer a Beaune, Nuis, Chalons, & Dijon, Le Duc voulant amender la barrée, Marchant pres Fleuve, Poisson, bec de plongeon, Verra la queüe: Porte sera serrée. English.

There shall be a change at *Beaune, Nuis, Chalons, Dijon*, The Duke going about to raise Taxes, The Merchant near the River shall see the tail Of a Fish, having the Bill of a Cormorant: the door shall be shut.

ANNOT.

      Beaune, Chalons, and *Dijon*, are Cities in *France, Nuis* is a Town in *Germany* near the *Rhyne*, three or four Leagues below *Colen*.
      For the rest, every one may make his own interpretation, for it is hard to guess who this Duke should be, or that Fish either, that shall have a Cormorants Bill after whom the door shall be shut.

XVIII.

French.

Les plus Lettrez dessus les faits Cœlestes, Seront par Princes ignorans reprouvez, Punis d'Edict, chassez comme scelestes, Et mis a mort la ou seront trouvez. English.

The most Learned in the Celestial sciences, Shall be found fault with, by ignorant Princes. Punished by proclamation, chased away as wicked, And put to death where they shall be found.

ANNOT.

      This is plain, and signifieth no more then a persecution against the Professors of Heavenly sciences, such as are Astrologers, Astronomers, *&c.*

XIX.

French.

Devant Rouan d'Insubres mis le Siege, Par Terre & Mer enfermez les passages, D'Hainaut, de Flandres de Gand & ceux de Liege, Par leurs levées raviront les Rivages. English.

Before *Rouan* a Siege shall be laid by the *Insubrians*. By Sea and Land the passages shall be shut up, Those of *Hainaut, Flanders, Ghent*, and *Liege*, With their Troops shall plunder the Sea-shore.

This is still concerning the Duke of *Parma*'s Army, when he came into *France* against *Henry* the IV. in favour of the League, for his Army wherewith he Besieged *Rouen*, was compounded of all those Nations; the greatest part of which were *Italians*, called here *Insubrians*, from the Latin word *Insubria*, which signifieth the Countreys of *Savoy* and *Piemont*.

XX.

French.

Paix uberté long temps on ne loüera, Part tout son Regne desert la fleur de Lis, Corps mort d'Eau, Terre on apportera, Sperants vain heur d'estre la ensevelis. **English.**

Peace and plenty shall not be long praised, All the time of his Reign the Flower de Luce shall be deserted, Bodies shall die by water, Earth shall be brought, Hoping vainly to be there Buried.

ANNOT.

This only foretelleth a great Famine and Inundation in *France*, signified here by the *Flower de Luce*.

XXI.

French.

Le changement sera fort difficile, Cité Province au change gain fera, Cœur haut, prudent mis, chassé l'Inhabile, Mer, Terre, Peuple, son estat changera. **English.**

The change shall be very hard, The City and Countrey shall gain by the change, A high prudent heart shall be put in, the unworthy expelled, Sea, Land, People shall change its condition.

ANNOT.

This needeth no Interpretation.

XXII.

French.

La grand Copie qui sera dechassée, Dans un moment fera besoing au Roy, La Foy promise de loing sera faucée, Nud se verra en piteux defarroy. **English.**

The great Army that shall be rejected, In a moment shall be wanted by the King. The faith promised a far off shall be broken, So that he shall be left naked in a pitiful case.

ANNOT.

This is plain.

XXIII.

French.

La Legion dans la Marine classe, Calcine Magnes, Souphre & Poix bruslera, Le long repos de l'asseurée place, Port Selin chercher, feu les consumera. English.

The Legion in the Maritine Fleet, *Calcineth Magnes*, shall burn Brimstone and Pitch, The long rest of the secure place, They shall seek *Port Selyn*, but fire shall consume them.

ANNOT.

Here we must observe four things, the first is, that *Calais* is called by the Author, *The long rest of the secure place*. Because then *viz.* in the year 1555. it was yet in the power of the King of *England*, and had been quietly before, for the space of 287. years, that is, from the year 1347. till the year 1555. and was so still, till the year 1557. when the Duke of *Guise* took it, whence we gather that it was a secure place that had enjoyed so long a rest.

The second is, that those of *Diepe* did watch for the *Spaniards*, in the passage between *Dover* and *Calais*, therefore the Author saith, *They shall seek Port Selyn, Selyn* Port or Harbour is always taken by the Author for an Harbour in the *Ocean*.

The third is, that the great fight between the *French* and the *Spaniards* was by fire, so that most part of the Ships on each side were burnt, and the *Spanish* and *French* Souldiers did cast themselves into the Sea, to save their lives in their enemies Ships, where they were slain.

The fourth is, that those of *Diepe* being extraordinary skilful in Sea-fights had made great quantity of artificial fires, to cast into the *Spanish* Ships, but the Ships grapling one with another, they were burnt on both sides.

Upon those four circumstances the two first Verses say, that *the Legion in the Fleet Calcineth magnes*, that is Loadstone burnt, and shall *burn Pitch and Brimstone*, to make Artificial fires.

The third and fourth Verse say, that this *Sea Legion* shall seek an Harbour in the Ocean, which shall be *a secure place, by a long rest*, that is *Calais*. She will seek that *Selyn* Harbour to shelter her self, because *Calais* did then belong to the *English*, but by reason of the narrowness of the *Sea*, the *French* watched for the *Spaniards* there, and to shew that they sought onely for *Calais* to meet the *Spaniards*, they carried the *Spanish* Ships which they took into *Diepe*, and not into *Calais*.

The *French* Impression hath a fault here, putting *Port Hercle* instead of *Port Selyn*, which is a manifest error, for the taking of *Port Hercle* by the *Florentines* the 14. of *June* 1555. was by a Land Army, besides, that *Port Selyn* is always taken by the Author for a Port in the Ocean.

XXIV.

French.

Ouy soubs Terre Sainte Dame voix feinte, Humaine flamme pour Divine voir luire, Fera des sœurs de leur sang Terre tainte, Et les Saints Temples par les impurs destruire. English.

Under ground shall be heard the fained voice of a Holy Dame, An humane flame to see a Divine one, Shall cause the ground to be died with the sisters blood, And the Holy Temples to be destroyed by the wicked.

ANNOT.

Every one may understand this as well as I.

XXV.

French.

Corps sublimes sans fin a l'œil visibles, Obnubiler viendront par ces raisons, Corps, front compris, sens & chef invisibles, Diminuant les Sacrées Oraisons. English.

The Celestial bodies that are always visible to the eye, Shall be darkened for these reasons, The body with the forehead sense and head invincible. Diminishing the Sacred Prayers.

ANNOT.

This is of the same nature as the foregoing.

XXVI.

French.

Lou grand Cyssame se levera d'abelhos, Que non lauran don te siegen venguddos, Denuech lenbousq, lun gach dessous las treilhos, Ciutad trahido per cinq lengos non nudos. English.

The great swarm of Bees shall rise, And it shall not be known whence they come, Towards the Ambush so the Jay shall be under a Vine, A City shall be betray'd by five tongues not naked.

ANNOT.

The Author having made this Stanza in the *Provencal* Language, that was his Mother Tongue, which hath very little relation to the rest of the *French* tongue, hath put me to some trouble to understand it; at last I found the meaning to be this, that when a great swarm of Bees shall light on some place, and it shall not be known whence they came, then shall be seen a Jay under a Vine, and a City shall be betrayed by five several Nations.

XXVII.

French.

Salon, Mansol, Tarascon, de Sex, Larc, Ou est debout encor la Pyramide, Viendront livrer le Prince Denemark, Rachat honny au Temple d'Artemide. English.

Salon, Mansol, Tarascon, Desex, the arche, Where to this day standeth the *Pyramis*, Shall come to deliver the Prince of *Denmark*, A shameful ransom shall be paid in the Temple of *Artemis*.

ANNOT.

Salon, Mansol, Tarascon, Desex, are Towns in *Provence* and *Languedo*.

By the *Arch*, here is meant the Triumphal Arch of *Caius Marius*, which he erected after the defeat of the *Cimbres* and *Teutons*, and remaineth to this day in that Province, within two or three Leagues off the Town of *Orenge*.

Artemis is an Epethete of *Diana*, so called 'πο τοῦ ἀερὰ τεμνειν, *a secando aerem*.

XXVIII.

French.

Lors que Venus du Sol sera couvert, Soubs la splendeur sera la forme occulte, Mercure au feu les aura descouvert, Par bruit Bellique sera mis a l'Insulte. English.

When *Venus* shall be covered by the Sun, Under the splendor of it shall be an occult form, *Mercury* in the fire shall discover them, And by a Warlike rumor shall be provoked.

ANNOT.

If this Book cometh ever into the hands of *Hermes*'s Disciples, I shall desire they would consider diligently this Stanza, and the three following; for they are all concerning the *Elixir* of the Philosophers, or the making of the Philosophers stone. To begin with this:

When Venus shall be covered by the Sun.

This is the Astral point, so much sought after by the Philosophers, for the beginning of their work, without the knowledge of which they cannot begin their work, or come to any good.

Under the splendor of it shall be an occult form, that is, under that conjunction lyeth a great mystery.

Mercury in the fire shall discover them, viz. Mercury of the Philosophers, made by Cœlestial fire.

And by a Warlike rumor shall be provoked; that is, the Planet of *Mercury* shall be provoked to mix his variable and changable disposition with theirs, by his Aspects, Oppositions, Conjunctions, &c. It is not possible to speak more plainly.

XXIX.

Le Sol caché, eclipsé par Mercure, Ne sera mis que pour le Ciel second, De Vulcan Hermes sera faite Pasture, Sol sera veu pur, rutilant & blond. English.

The Sun shall be hid and eclipsed by *Mercury*, And shall not be set but for the second Heaven, *Hermes* shall be made a prey to *Vulcan*, And after that the Sun shall be seen pure, shining and yellow.

ANNOT.

Here I must lead the Reader with *Ariadnes* Thread, that he may extrecate himself out of this Labyrinth.

The Sun shall be hid and Eclipsed by Mercury; that is, Gold shall be Eclipsed and dissolved by the Philosophers Mercury, which is the Key and foundation of all the work.

And shall not be set but for the second Heaven; that is, shall not be used till you come to the second part of the work, which is that of the Furnace.

Hermes shall be made a prey to Vulcan; that is, the matter and composition of the *Elixir*, shall be put upon the fire in a Furnace.

And after that the Sun shall be seen pure, shining, yellow; that is, in conclusion after projection made, thou shalt see pure, shining, and Yellow Gold.

XXX.

Plus d'unze fois Luna Sol ne voudra, Tous augmentes & baissez de degre, Et si bas mis que peu d'Or on coudra, Qu'apres faim, peste, descouvert le secret. English.

The Moon will not have the Sun above eleven times, Then both shall be encreased and lessened in degree, And put so low, that a little Gold shall be sowed up, So that after hunger and plague, the secret shall be discovered.

ANNOT.

The Moon will not have the Sun above eleven times; that is, the Moon of the Philosophers will not imbibe their Sun above Eleven times.

Then both shall be encreased and lessened in degree; that is, both shall be encreased in quality, and lessened in quantity.

And put so low that a little Gold shall be sowed up; that is, the powder of projection, or Philosophers stone shall be so small in Bulk, that one may sow it about him, and hide it in his Cloths.

After famine and plague the secret shall be discovered; that is, somebody shall die, with famine or plague, about which the secret shall be found and discovered.

XXXI.

La Lune au plain de nuit sur le haut Mont, Le nouveau Sophe d'Un seul cerveau la veu, Par ses Disciples estre immortel semond, Yeux au Midy, enfin, mains corps au feu. English.

The Moon at full by night upon the high Mount, The new *Sophe* with one onely Brain hath seen it, Invited by his Disciples to become immortal, His eyes to the South, conclusion, his hands and body to the fire.

ANNOT.

      Sophe in Greek signifieth a wise man or Philosopher, who shall find the Philosophers stone, when the Moon shall come to the full in the night upon a high Mount. His Disciples shall perswade him to make himself immortal, they being perswaded that the *Elixir* cureth all diseases.

      The last Verse saith, *His eyes to the South, his hands and body to the fire*; that is, this Chymist or *Adeptus*, shall retire into some Southern Countrey to work.

      I cannot omit here that a conceited Chymist in *Paris*, whose name was *Haumont*, in *English*, *Highmount*, could not be disswaded but our Author spake of him in this Stanza, and that he could not die till he had got the Philosophers stone, but to other matters.

XXXII.

Es lieux & temps chair au poisson donra lieu, La loy commune sera faite au contraire, Vieux tiendra fort puis osté du milieu, Le Panta, Choina, Philon mis fort arriere. English.

In places and times, flesh shall give place to fish, The common Law shall be made against it, The old man shall stand fast, then being taken away The *Panta, Choina, Philon*, shall be set aside.

ANNOT.

      Panta, Choina, Philon, are three Greek words, παντὰ χοινα φιλῶν, which signifie in Latine, *omnia inter amicos communia*, and in *English*, all things are common among friends. The rest is easie.

XXXIII.

Jupiter joint plus Venus qu'a la Lune, Apparoissant de plenitude blanche, Venus cachée soubs la blancheur Neptune, De Mars frappée par la gravée branche. English.

Jupiter being more joyned to *Venus* then to the Moon, Appearing in a full whiteness, *Venus* being hid under the whiteness of *Neptune*, Stricken by *Mars* through the ingraved branch.

These terms being *Astronomical* and *Astrological*, it is hard to guess at the Authors mind.

XXXIV.

Le grand mené captif d'estrange Terre; Dor enchainé au Roy Cheyren offert, Qui dans Ausonne, Milan perdra la Guerre, Et tout son Ost mis a Feu & a Fer. English.

The great one brought Prisoner from a far Countrey, And chained with Gold, shall be presented to the King *Chyren*, Being then at *Ausone*. *Milan* shall loose the War. And all its Host shall be put to fire and sword.

ANNOT.

The meaning of this is, that when a great one from a far Countrey, shall be brought Prisoner chained with gold, and presented to a King called *Henry* (for *Cheyren* by transposition of letters is *Henry*) who then shall beat *Bordeaux*; *Milan* shall loose a great Army.

XXXV.

French.

Le feu esteint, les vierges trahiront, La plus grand part de la bande nouvelle, Pouldre a feu les seuls Rois garderont, Hetrusque & Corse, de nuit, gorge alumelle. English.

The fire being put out, the Virgins shall betray, The greatest part of the new troup, Gunpowder, Lance, shall keep only the Kings, In *Hetruria* and *Corsica* by night throats shall be cut.

ANNOT.

Hetruria is the Country *Tuscany* now under the Duke of *Florence*, and *Corsica* is an Island in the *Mediterranean* Sea belonging to the *Genoese*. The rest is plain.

XXXVI.

French.

Les jeux nouveaux en Gaule redressez, Apres Victoire de l'Insubre Campagne, Monts d'Hesperie, les grands liez troussez, De peur trembler la Romagne & l'Espagne. English.

The new plays shall be set up again in *France*, After the Victory obtained in *Piemont*, Mountains of *Spain*, the great ones tied, carried away, *Romania* and *Spain* shall quake for fear.

ANNOT.

This is a Prognostication of the rejoycing that should be in *France*, after the winning of that famous battle *Serizoles* in *Piemont*, against the Armies of the Emperour and the King of *Spain*.

XXXVII.

French.

Gaulois par saults Monts viendra penetrer, Occupera le grand Mont de l'Insubre, Au plus profond son Ost sera entrer, Genes, Monech pousseront classe rubre. **English.**

The *French* by leaping shall go over the Mountains, And shall seize upon the great Mount of the *Savoyard*, He shall cause his Army to go to the furthermost, *Genoa*, and *Monaco* shall set out their red Fleet.

ANNOT.

This Prophecy is concerning *Henry* the IV. King of *France*, who went over the *Alpes* and conquered the Duke of *Savoy*'s Countrey, because he would not restore the Markdom of *Salvees*. *Genoa* and *Monaco* are Cities near *Savoy*.

XXXVIII.

French.

Pendant que Duc, Roy, Roine occupera, Chef Bizantin captif en Samothrace, Avant lassault l'un l'autre mangera, Rebours ferré suivra du sang la trace. **English.**

While the Duke shall busie the King and the Queen, A great man of *Constantinople* shall be prisoner in *Samothracia*, Before the assault one shall eat up the other, *Rebours* shod shall trace one by the blood.

ANNOT.

The three first Verses are plain, as for the fourth, either it is falsly Printed, or I must confess I understand it not.

XXXIX.

French.

Les Rhodiens demanderont secours, Par le neglect de ses hoirs delaissée, L'Empire Arabe ravalera son cours, Par Hesperie la cause redressée. **English.**

The *Rhodiens* shall ask for succours, Being forsaken by the neglect of her Heirs, The *Arrabian* Empire shall slack his course, By the means of *Spain* the case shall be mended.

ANNOT.

By the *Rhodians* are understood the Knights of *Maltha*, because they dwelt first at *Rhodes*. By the second Verse it is said, it was *the neglect of her Heirs*, that is of the Heirs of *Rhodes* the Knights of *Maltha*, who being careless of themselves, were besieged by *Solyman*, which constrained them to ask succours of all the Christian Princes, which came very slowly, at last *Dom Garcia* Viceroy of *Sicily* relieved them, and drove away the Turks that had suffered great loss, therefore the Author saith in the third Verse, *The Arabian Empire shall slack his course.*

XL.

French.

Les Forteresses des Assiegez serrez, Par poudre a feu profondez en abysme, Les proditeurs seront tous vifs serrez, Onc aux Sacristes navint si piteux schisme. English.

The strong places of the Besieged shall be straightned, By Gunpowder they shall be plonged into a pit, The Traytors shall be shut up alive, Never did happen so pitiful schisme to the *Sacristes*.

ANNOT.

By the *Sacristes*, he understandeth the Clergy of the Roman Religion.

XLI.

French.

Gynique Sexe captive par Hostage, Viendra de nuit custodes decevoir, Le Chef du Camp deceu par son language, Lairra la gente, sera piteux a voir. English.

Gynical sexe being captive by Hostage, Shall come by night to deceive her keepers, The Chief of the Camp being deceived by her Language, Shall leave her folks, a thing pitiful to behold.

ANNOT.

Gynical Sex is a woman from the Greek word γυνὴ, which signifieth a woman.

The meaning then of this Stanza is, that a woman being given in Hostage, and made prisoner, shall deceive her keepers, and among the rest, the chief Captain who shall forsake his Troops and run away with her.

XLII.

French.

Geneve & Langres par ceux de Chartre & Dole, Et par Grenoble captif au Montlimar, Seysset, Lausane, par fraudulente dole, Les trahiront pour Or soixante mark. English.

Geneve and *Langres* by those of *Chartres* and *Dole*, And by one of *Grenoble* captive at *Montlimar*, *Seisset, Lozanne* by a fraudulent deceit, Shall betray them for thirty pounds weight of Gold.

ANNOT.

All those Towns are in *France*, the sense is plain.

XLIII.

French.

Seont ouis au Ciel les Armes battre, Celuy an mesme les Divins ennemis, Voudront Loix Saintes injustement debatre, Par Foudre & guerre bien croians a mort mis. English.

There shall be heard in the Air noise of Weapons, And in that same year the Divines shall be enemies, They shall unjustly put down the Holy Laws, And by the Thunder and the War true believers shall die.

ANNOT.

There is no obscurity in this.

XLIV.

French.

Deux gros de Mende, de Rhodez, & Millaud, Cahors, Limoges, Castre, malo sepmano, De nuech l'intrado, de Bourdeaux an cailhau, Par Perigort au toc de la Campano. English.

Two great ones of *Mende*, of *Rhodez* and *Milliaud*, *Cahors*, *Limoges*, *Castres* an evil week, By night the entry shall be from *Bourdeaux* one cailhau, Through *Perigort* at the ringing of the Bell.

ANNOT.

This Stanza is half *French* and half *Provencal* language.

All the Cities named here, *Mende, Rhodez, Milliaud, Cahors, Limoges, Castres, Bourdeaux, Perigort*, are Cities of *France*, bordering upon *Provence*, which is the Countrey wherein our Author was born.

The meaning of it is, that all those Cities shall rise against the Collectors of the Kings Taxes, and shall set upon them by the sound of the Bell, which is already come to pass, and may come to pass yet.

XLV.

French.

Par conflict, Roy Regne abandonera, Le plus grand Chef faillira au besoing, Morts, profligez peu en rechapera, Tous destrenchez un en sera tesmoin. English.

By a Battle the King shall forsake his Kingdom, The greatest Commander, shall fail in time of need, They shall be killed and routed, few shall escape, They shall be cut off, one only shall be left for a witness.

ANNOT.

This is a Prognostication of a great Battle, by the loss of which a King shall forsake his Kingdom, his chief Commander having deserted him in time of need. The slaughter shall be so great, that none shall be left but one for a witness.
XLVI.

French.

Bien defendu le fait par excellence, Garde toy Tours de ta proche ruine, Londres & Nantes par Rheims fera defence, Ne passes outre au temps de la bruine. **English.**

The fact shall be defended excellently well *Tours* beware of thy approaching ruine, *London* and *Nantes* by *Rhemes* shall stand upon their defence, Do not go further in foggy weather.

ANNOT.

Tours is the chief City of a Province in *France*, called *Touraine*, which is commended here for having resisted excellently well; but is forewarned to look to her self after that, and to beware of her approaching ruine.
XLVII.

French.

Le noir farouche quand aura essayé, Sa main sanguine par feu, fer, arcs tendus, Trestout le peuple sera tant effrayé, Voir les plus grands par col & pieds pendus. **English.**

The wild black one, after he shall have tryed, His bloody hand by fire, Sword, bended Bows, All the people shall be so frighted, To see the greatest hanged by the neck and feet.

ANNOT.

It is a description of a Tyrant, who after he shall have tryed his bloody hand by Fire, Sword, and bent Bows, shall cause his chief men to be hanged by the neck and feet. Since the Author did write there had been such a Tyrant in the world, namely, *John Basilides*, great Duke of *Russia*, in the year 1572. Read *Paul Osburne* in his Life.
XLVIII.

French.

Planure Ausone fertile spacieuse, Produira taons, & tant de sauterelles, Clarte solairé deviendra nubilense, Ronger le rout, grand peste venir delles. **English.**

The Plain about *Bourdeaux* fruitful and spacious, Shall produce so many Hornets and so many Grashopers, That the light of the Sun shall be darkened, They shall crap all, a great plague shall come from them.

I cannot find in History that this hath yet happened, since the writing of these Prophecies, therefore I reckon it *de futuro*.

XLIX.

French.

Devant le peuple sang sera respandu, Qui du haut Ciel ne viendra esloigner, Mais d'un long temps ne sera entendu, L'Esprit d'un seul le viendra tesmoigner. English.

Before the people blood shall be spilt, Who Shall not come far from the high Heaven, But it shall not be heard of for a great while, The Spirit of one shall come to witness it.

ANNOT.

This Prophecie is concerning some just person, that shall be murdered openly: His blood shall cry to Heaven, but shall not be heard for a good while, till at last it shall be discovered by some body.

L.

French.

Libra verra regner les Hesperies, De Ciel & Terre tenir la Monarchie, D'Asie forces nul ne verra peries, Que sept ne tiennent par rang la Hierarchie. English.

Libra shall see *Spain* to Reign, And have the Monarchy of Heaven and Earth, No body shall see the forces of *Asia* to perish, Till seven have kept the Hierarchy successively.

ANNOT.

Libra is one of the twelve signs of the *Zodiack*, which is favourable to *Spain*, so that the meaning of this is, that *Libra shall see Spain to Reign*.

And besides that, *to have the Monarchy of Heaven and Earth*; that is, to have the command of the Pope, and of the best part of *Europe*. So that no *Asian* or *Turkish* forces shall receive damage by the Christians, till seven Popes of the *Spanish* faction have Reigned successively, and one after another.

LI.

Un Duc cupide son ennemy poursuivre, Dans entrera empeschant la Phalange, Hastez a pied si pres viendront poursuivre, Que la journée conflite aupres du Gange. English.

A Duke being earnest in the pursute of his enemy Shall come in, hindering the Phalange, Hastened on foot shall follow them so close, That the day of the Battle shall be near *Ganges.*

ANNOT.

A *Phalange*, in Latine *Phalanx*, is a Squadron of Souldiers, which word was anciently proper only to the *Macedonians. Ganges* is a River in *India.*

LII.

French.

En Cité obsesse aux murs hommes & femmes, Ennemis hors, le chef prest a soy rendre, Vent sera fort encontre les gens darmes, Chassez seront par chaux, poussiere & cendre. English.

In a besieged City, men and women being upon the walls, The enemies without, the Governour ready to surrender, The Wind shall be strong against the Souldiers, They shall be driven away by lime, dust, and ashes.

ANNOT.

This is a peculiar and remarkable accident, wherein the besiegers of a City shall be driven away from their enterprise, by Lime, Dust, and Ashes, scattered and dispersed against them by a mighty wind.

LIII.

French.

Les fugitifs & bannis revoqués, Peres & Fils garnissant les hauts puits, Le cruel pere & les tiens suffoquez, Son Fils plus pire submergé dans le puits. English.

The runnaways and banished men being recalled, Fathers and Sons garnishing the high wells, The cruel father and his retinue shall be suffocated, His Son being worse, shall be drowned in the Well.

ANNOT.

The words are plain, out of which every one may make his own sense.

LIV.

Du nom qui on ne fut au Roy Gaulois, Jamais ne fut un Foudre si craintif, Tremblant l'Italie, l'Espagne, & les Anglois, De femmes estrangeres grandement attentif. English.

Of the name that a *French* King never was, There was never a Lightning so much feared, *Italy* shall tremble, *Spain* and the *English*, He shall be much taken with women strangers.

ANNOT.

This foretelleth that when a *French* King shall have a name that never any of his Predecessors had, he shall be so much feared as that *Italy*, *Spain*, and *England* shall tremble, and that besides he shall be much given to women.

LV.

French.

Quand la Corneille sur Tour de Brique jointe, Durant sept heures ne fera que crier, Mort presagée, de sang Statue teinte, Tyran meurdry, aux Dieux peuple prier. English.

When the Crow upon a Tower made of Brick, For seven hours shall do nothing but cry, Death shall be foretold, and the Statue died with blood, Tyrant shall be murdered, and the people pray to the Gods.

ANNOT.

This extraordinary Prodigy of a Crow crying for seven hours together upon a Brick Tower, foretelleth that some notorious Tyrant shall be put to death, and his statue sprinkled with blood, and withall, that the people either for joy or fear shall be much given to prayer.

LVI.

French.

Apres Victoire de rabieuse Langue, L'Esprit tempté, en tranquil & repos, Victeur sauguin par conflict, fait Harangue, Roustir la Langue, & la Chair & les Os. English.

After the Victory got over a raging tongue, The mind that was tempted, shall be in tranquility and rest, The bloody Conqueror by Battle shall make a Speech, And roast the tongue, the flesh, and the bones.

ANNOT.

It is a Conquerour who having been much railed at by his enemies, shall in conclusion after he hath overcome them, take a severe vengeance of them.

LVII.

French.

Ignare envie au grand Roy supportée, Tiendra propos deffendre les escrits, Sa femme non femme par un autre tentée, Plus double deux ira au fort de cris. English.

Ignorant envy being supported by the great King, Shall talk of prohibiting the writtings, His wife no wife, being tempted by another, Shall more then they two prevail by crying.

ANNOT.

Some ignorant envious person being in favour with the King, shall go about to suppress learning, but the Kings wife no wife, that is his Concubine, shall persuade him to the contrary, and shall prevail.

LVIII.

French.

Soleil ardent dans la gosier couler, De sang humain arrouser Terre Etrusque, Chef seille d'eau, mener son fils filer, Captive Dame conduite Terre Turque. English.

Burning Sun shall be poured into the throat, This human blood shall wet the *Hetrurian* ground, The chief pale of water, shall lead his son to Spin, A captive Lady shall be carried into the *Turkish* Countrey.

ANNOT.

By burning Sun must be understood melted gold, which shall be poured into ones throat, in the *Hetrurian* ground, that is in *Tuscany*.

By the chief Pale of water is to be understood, some Water-bearer, who shall make his son an Eunuch to make benefit on't. The fourth Verse is plain.

LIX.

French.

Deux assiegez en ardante ferveur, De soif estaints pour deux plaines Tasses; Le fort limé & un vieillard resueur, Au Genois, de Nizza monstrera trace. English.

Two besieged, being in a burning heat, Shall die for thirst, want of two Bowls full, The Fort being filed, an old doting man, Shall show to the *Genoese* the way to *Nizza*.

ANNOT.

The two first Verses are plain. The two last Verses signifie that an old doting man shall shew to the *Genoeses* the way how to take *Nizza*, a Town hard by them, by filing some Iron Grates, by which they shall get into the Town.

LX.

French.

Les sept enfans en Hostage laissez, Le tiers viendra son enfant trucider, Deux par son fils seront d'estoc percez, Genes, Florence les viendra seconder. English.

The seven Children being left in Hostage, The third shall come to kill his child, Two by their sons shall be run through, *Genoa* and *Florence* shall second them.

ANNOT.

The words being so plain, every body may give as good an interpretation as I.

LXI.

French.

Le vieux mocqué & privé de sa place, Par l'Estranger qui le subornera, Mais de son filz mangé devant sa face, Le Frere a Chartres. Orl. Rouen trahira. English.

The old man shall be baffled and deprived of his place, By the stranger that shall suborn him, But of his son shall be eaten before his face, The Brother at *Chartres. Orl.* shall betray *Rouen.*

ANNOT.

This Stanza is divided into two parts. The first part runneth from the first Verse to the middle of the fourth. The meaning is, that an old man shall be baffled and deprived of his place by a stranger that shall suborn him, but that strangers sons brother shall be eaten up before his face in the Town of *Chartres*; what he meaneth by eaten up, is hard to guess, whether it be by poverty, sutes at Law, Envy, Lice, &c.

The Hemisthikion of the last Verse, *Orl. shall betray Rouen*, signifieth, that *Orleans* shall betray *Rouen.*

LXII.

French.

Un Coronel machine ambition, Se saisira de la plus grande Armée, Contre son Prince feinte invention, Et descouvert sera soubs sa ramée. English.

A Colonel deviseth a plot by his ambition, He shall seize upon the best part of the Army, Against his Prince he shall have a fained invention, And shall be discovered under the Harbour of the Vine.

I never saw the last Tyrant *Cromwel* better painted to the life, then in the three first Verses.

As for the fourth, it is certain that his intention among his Camerades was first discovered by him unto them at the *Star Tavern in Coleman-street*, which is the place that the Author calleth the *Harbour of the Vine.*

LXIII.

French.

L'Armée Celtique contre les Montagnars, Qui seront sus & pris a la pipée, Paisants irez pulseront tost faugnars, Precipitez tous au fil de l'Espée. English.

The *Celtique* Army shall go against the *Highlanders*, Who shall stand upon their guard, and be taken with Bird-lime twigs, The Peasant being angry, shall roll down the stones, They shall be all put to the edge of the sword.

ANNOT.

This is a description of the attempt made by the *French* upon *Savoy*, which Countrey lieth in the Mountains of the *Alpes*, therefore called here *Highlanders*; where the Peasants being incensed for the loss of their goods and the ruine of their Countrey, rolled stones from the top of the Mountains against the *French* Army, which could not hinder them from being destroyed; this came to pass under *Henry* the IV. King of *France*, in the year 1662.

LXIV.

French.

Le defaillant en habit de Bourgeois, Viendra le Roy tenter de son offence, Quinze Soldats la pluspart Villageois, Vie derniere & chef de sa chevance. English.

The guilty, in a Citizens habit, Shall come to tempt the King concerning his offence, Fifteen Soldiers the most part Countrey men, The last shall be his life, and the best part of his Estate.

ANNOT.

This signifieth that a great man having committed an offence against the King, shall come to him in a mean habit, to sue for his Pardon, and shall be carried away by fifteen Souldiers, the most part Countrey fellows; and in conclusion he shall have his life saved, and the best part of his Estate.

LXV.

French.

Au deserteur de la grand Forteresse, Apres qu'aura son lieu abandonné, Son adversaire fera si grand provesse, L'Empereur tost mort sera condamné. English.

After that the desertor of the great Fort, Shall have forsaken his place, His adversary shall do so great feats, That the Emperor, shall soon be condemned to death.

ANNOT.

This is plain.

LXVI.

French.

Soubs couleur feinte de sept testes rasées, Seront formez divers explorateurs, Puits & Fontains de poison arrousées, Au Fort de Genes humains devorateurs. English.

Under the fained colour of seven shaven heads, Shall divers spies be framed, Wells and Fountains shall be sprinkled with poison, In the Fort of *Genoa* shall be humane devourers.

ANNOT.

The three first Verses belong to the same sense; *viz.* that seven men shall be spies, under pretence to be Priests or Monks, (which is the meaning of the shaven heads) and shall poison the Wells and Springs.

The last Verse signifieth that in the Fort of *Genoa*, their shall be devourers of men, that is, Usurers and Extortioners, which is no new thing in that Nation.

LXVII.

French.

L'An que Saturne & Mars esgaux combust, L'Air fort seiché, longue trajection, Par feux secrets d'ardeur grands lieux adust, Peu pluye, Vent chauds, Guerres, Incursions. English.

In the year that *Saturn* and *Mars* shall be fiery, The Air shall be very dry, in many Countreys, By secret fires, many places shall be burnt with heat, There shall be scarcity of Rain, hot Winds, Wars, in-roads.

ANNOT.

This is the Prognostication of a mighty dry season, and other accidents that shall happen when *Saturn* and *Mars* shall be in a fiery disposition, which whether it be by Opposition,

Conjunction, Aspect, &c. Let the Astrologers judge.

LXVIII.

French.

En l'an bien proche non esloigné de Venus, Les deux plus grands de l'Asie & d'Affrique, Du Rhine & Ister qu'on dira sont venus, Cris, pleurs a Malthe, & coste Ligustique. English.

In a year that is to come shortly, and not far from *Venus*, The two greatest ones of *Asia* and *Affrica*, Shall be said to come from the *Rhine* and *Ister*, Crying, and tears shall be at *Maltha* and in the *Ligurian* shore.

ANNOT.

The *Rhine* is a River in *Germany, Ister* is another in the Countrey of *Istria*, belonging to the *Venetians*.

By the first Verse, I conclude that this Prophecy came to pass a little while after the Author wrote this Book, when the grand Segnor *Solyman* besieged *Maltha*, and put in fear all the *Ligurian* Coast, which is that of *Genoa*.

LXIX.

French.

La Cité grande les exilez tiendront, Les Citadins morts, meurtris & chassez, Ceux d'Aquilee a Parme promettront, Monstrer l'entrée par les lieux non tracez. English.

The banished shall keep the great City, The Citizens being dead, murdered and expelled, Those of *Aquileia* shall promise to *Parma*, To shew the entrance by unknown paths.

ANNOT.

Aquileia and *Parma* are two Cities in *Italy*. The rest is easie.

LXX.

French.

Bien contigu des grands Monts Pyrenées, Un contre l'Aigle grand copie, adresser, Ouvertes veines, forces exterminées, Que jusqu'au Pau le chief viendra chasser. English.

Near the great *Pyrenean* Mountains, One shall raise a great Army against the Eagle, Veins shall be opened, forces driven out, So that the chief shall be driven as far as the *Pau*.

ANNOT.

By the Eagle here is understood the Empire; because his Ensign is an Eagle.

LXXI.

En lieu d'Espouse les Filles trucidées, Meurtre a grand faute, ne sera superstite, Dedans le puis vestues inondées, L'Espouse esteinte par haut d'Aconite. English.

Instead of the Bride, the Maid shall be killed, The murder shall be a great fault, none shall be surviving, In the Well they shall be drowned with their Cloaths, The Bride shall be extinguished by an high Aconite.

ANNOT.

This is a Prophecie of a Tragical Nuptial, where all the Maids shall be drowned with their Cloaths in a Well, insomuch that none shall survive, and the Bride shall be poisoned, and die by *Aconite*, which is one of the most poisonous herbs that is, witness *Juvinal: Lurida terribiles miscent asonita novercæ.*

LXXII.

Les Artomiques par Agen & Lectoure, A saint Felix feront leur Parliament, Ceux de Bazas viendront a la malhoure, Saisir Condon & Marsan promptement. **English.**

The *Artomiques* through *Agen* and *Lectoure*, Shall keep their Parliament at Saint *Fœlix*, These of *Bazas* shall come in an unhappy hour, To seize upon *Condon* and *Marsan* speedily.

ANNOT.

By the *Artomiques* he meaneth the Protestants; because they take the Communion with leavened Bread, which in Greek is called *Artos.*

Agen, Lectoure, saint *Fœlix, Bazas, Condon* and *Marzan,* are Cities of *Gascony.* The rest is plain.

LXXIII.

French.

Le neveu grand par force prouvera, Le peche fait de Cœur pusillanime, Ferrare & Ast le Duc esprouvera, Par lors qu'au soir sera le Pantomime. **English.**

The great nephew by force shall provoke, The sin committed by the pusillanimous heart, *Ferrara* and *Ast* shall make tryal of the Duke, When the *Pantomime* shall be in the evening.

ANNOT.

To understand the whole sense of this, we must first know what is meant by the particular terms.

The great Nephew is the Brother or Sisters son of some great person, who by force shall discover the Treason or Cowardise, committed by some pusillanimous or fearful man.

Ferrara and *Ast* are two towns in *Italy,* shall make tryal of a Duke, by being either taken or assaulted.

When the Pantomime shall be in the evening; that is, when the Comedy shall be acted; for *Pantomime* in Greek signifieth a Comedian.

LXXIV.

French.

Du lac Leman & ceux des Brannonices, Tous assemblez contre ceux d'Aquitaine, Germans beaucoup encores plus Sovisses, Seronts des faits avec ceux du Maine. **English.**

From lake *Leman,* and from the *Brannonues,* They shall be gathered against those of *Aquitania,* Great many *Germans,* and many more *Switzers,* Shall be routed together with those of *Maine.*

ANNOT.

Lake *Leman,* is the Lake of *Geneva.* The *Brannonices* are those of *Sens,* so called; because they took *Rome* under the Conduct of their Captain *Brennus*, and afterwards built *Brenona*, a Town belonging since to the *Venetians*, who calls it *Verona*.

Aquitania is that Province of *France*, called now *Gascony*. *Maine* is a Province in *France*. The rest needeth no explication.

LXXV.

French.

***Prest a combattre fera defection, Chef adversaire obtiendra la victoire, Larriere garde fera defension, Les defaillans morts au blanc terretoire.* English.**

One being ready to fight, shall faint, The chief of the adverse party shall obtain the victory, The rearegard, shall withstand it out, Those that fall away shall die in the white Terretory.

ANNOT.

There is nothing difficult here, but what he meaneth by the white Terretory, whether it be positive, or Allegorical, I leave the judgement of it to the Reader.

LXXVI.

French.

***Les Nictobriges par ceux de Perigort, Seront vexez tenants jusques au Rhosne, L'Associé de Gascons & Bigorre, Trahir le Temple le prestre estant au Prosne.* English.**

The *Nictobriges* by those of *Perigort*, Shall be vexed as far as the *Rhosne*, The associate of the *Gascons* and *Bigorre*, Shall betray the Church while the Priest is in his Pulpit.

ANNOT.

Nictobriges in Greek signifieth a people living in a dark and moist Countrey. *Perigort* and *Bigorre* are two Towns in *France*. The rest is plain.

LXXVII.

French.

***Selyn Monarque, l'Italie pacifique, Regnes unis, Roy Chrestien du monde, Mourant voudra coucher en Terre Blesique, Apres Pyrates avoir chassé de L'onde.* English.**

Selyn being Monarch, *Italy* shall be in peace, Kingdoms shall be united, a Christian King of the world, Dying, shall desire to be buried in the Countrey of *Blois*, After he shall have driven the Pyrates from the Sea.

ANNOT.

Selyn is the name of a *Turkish* Emperour, the meaning therefore of this, is, that under the Reign of one *Selyn* a *Turkish* Emperour, *Italy* shall be in peace, and all the Christian Princes united.

LXXVIII.

French.

La grand Armée de la pugne civile, Pour de nuit Parme a l'Estranger trouvée, Septante neuf meurtris dedans la Ville, Les estrangers passez tous a l'Espée. English.

The great Army belonging to the Civil War, Having found by night *Parma* possessed by Strangers, Shall kill seventy nine in the Town, And put all the Strangers to the Sword.

ANNOT.

Parma is a City in *Italy.* The rest is plain.

LXXIX.

French.

Sang Royal fuis, Monheurt, Mars. Aiguillon, Remplis seront de Bourdelois les Landes. Navarre, Bigorre, pointes & Aiguillons, Profonds de faim, vorer de Liege, Glandes. English.

Royal blood run away from *Monheurt, Marsan, Aiguillon,* The *Landes* shall be full of *Bourdeloir, Navarre, Bigorre,* shall have points and Pricks. Being deep in hunger, they shall devour the Cork and Akorns.

ANNOT.

Monheurt, Marsan, Aiguillon, are Towns in *Gascony.*

Landes is a desert Countrey, wherein nothing groweth but Pine-trees, *Bourdelois* are those of *Bourdeaux.*

Navarre is a Kingdom, and *Begorre* a Province joyning to those *Landes,* or Pine-trees Countrey.

LXXX.

French.

Pres du grand Fleuve, grand fosse, terre egeste, En quinze parts l'eau sera divisée, La Cité prinse, feu, sang, cris, conflict mettre, Et la plus part concerne au collisée. English.

Near the great River, a great pit, Earth digged out, In fifteen parts the Water shall be divided, The City taken, fire, blood, cries, fighting, And the greatest part concerneth the Collisés.

This Prophecy was fulfilled, when *Rome* was taken and sacked by *Charles* Duke of *Bourbon*, and *Philibert* of *Chalon* Prince of *Orenge*, Generals of the Emperour *Charles* the V. with such cruelties, as never was committed by the bloody *Goths* and *Vandales*, and to shew that the Author intended *Rome*, is apparant by two instances. The first is by *the great River*, which is the *Tyber*, which though not very great in its Channel and depth, yet is very great, yea, the greatest in *Europe* by its fame. The other is the word *Colisée*, which is that famous Arch of *Traian* in *Rome*, remaining yet to this day.

LXXXI.

French.

Pont on fera promptement de nacelles, Passer l'Armée du grand Prince Belgique, Dans profondres, & non loing de Bruxelles, Outrepassez detrenchez sept a picque. English.

A Bridge of Boats shall suddenly be made, To pass over the Army of the great *Belgick* Prince, In deep places, and not far from *Bruxelles*, Being gone over, there shall be seven cut with a Pike.

ANNOT.

This is concerning the Siege of *Antwerp* by the Prince of *Parma*, Governour of the *Low-Countreys* for the King of *Spain*, who having besieged, caused a Bridge of Boats to be made upon the River *Scheld*, to hinder the succours of the *Hollanders*, who by that means were constrained to surrender it.

LXXXII.

French.

Amas sapproche venant d'Esclavonie, L'Olestant vieux Cité ruinera, Fort desolée verra sa Romanie, Puis la grand flamme estaindre ne scaura. English.

A great troop gathered, shall come from *Sclavonia*, The old Olestant shall ruine a City, He shall see his *Romania* very desolate, And after that, shall not be able to quench that great flame.

ANNOT.

That great troop from *Sclavonia* shall be the *Venetians*, because they possess most part of that Countrey. *The old Olestant* is their Duke, because he is not chosen unless he be very old, by *Romania* is understood what the *Venetians* possess in that Countrey.

LXXXIII.

French.

Combat nocturne le vaillant Capitaine, Vaincu fuira, peu de gens profligé, Son peuple esmeu, sedition non vain, Son propre fils le tiendra assiegé. English.

In a fight by night, the valliant Captain, Being vanquished shall run away, overcome by few, His people being moved, shall make no small mutiny, His own son shall besiege him.

ANNOT.

This needeth no interpretation.

LXXXIV.

French.

Un grand d'Auxerre mourra bien miserable, Chassé de ceux qui soubs luy ont esté. Serré de chaines, apres d'un rude cable, En l'an que Mars, Venus & Sol mis en Esté. English.

A great man of *Auxerre* shall die very miserably, Being expelled by those that have been under him, Bound with Chains, and after that with a strong Cable, In the year that *Mars, Venus,* and *Sol* shall be in a conjunction in the Summer.

ANNOT.

Auxerre is a City of *France,* distant from *Paris* 40. leagues to the *Southward.*

LXXXV.

French.

Le Charbon blanc du noir sera chassé, Prisonier fait, mené au Tombereau, More Chameau sus pieds entrelassez, Lors le puisné fillera l'Aubereau. English.

The white Coal shall be expelled by the black one, He shall be made Prisoner, carried in a Dung-cart, His feet twisted upon a black Camel, Then the youngest, shall suffer the Hobby to have more thread.

ANNOT.

The first Verse is altogether Allegorical and Metaphorical, therefore I leave it to the judgement of every Reader. I shall only deliver my opinion upon the whole: I take it to be some white Prince, that shall be overcome by a black one, put in a Dungcart, after that, tied upon a black Camel, and then the younger son of that black Prince shall give the prisonner a little more liberty.

LXXXVI.

French.

L'An que Saturne en eau sera conjoint, Avecques Sol le Roy fort & puissant, A Rheims & Aix sera receu & oingt, Apres Conquestes meurtrira innocens. **English.**

In the year that *Saturn* in *Aquarius* shall be in conjunction With *Sol*, the King being strong and powerful, Shall be received and Anointed at *Rheines* and *Aix*, After Conquest he shall murder innocent persons.

ANNOT.

This Prophecy is remarkable for the things that it foretelleth, *viz.* that in the year that *Saturn* shall be in conjunction with *Sol* in the Sign of *Aquarius*, a King of *France* shall be annointed both at *Rhemes* and *Aix*, for *Rhemes* is a City in *France*, where the Kings use to be Annointed and Crowned, and *Aix* is another in *Germany*, where the Emperours use to be so. But the last Verse is ominous, where he saith, that after his Conquests he shall murder innocent persons.

LXXXVII.

French.

Un fils de Roy tant de Langues apprins, A son Aisné au Regne different, Son Pere beau au plus grand fils comprins, Fera perir principal adherent. **English.**

A son of a King having learned divers Languages, Shall fall out with his elder Brother for the Kingdom, His father in Law being more concerned with his elder son, Shall cause the principal adherent to perish.

ANNOT.

One King shall have two Sons, the eldest shall succeed him in the Kingdom, the youngest having been well brought up and educated, shall raise troubles, against the King his Brother; but he shall be destroyed by the means of his own Father in Law.

LXXXVIII.

French.

La grand Antoine du nom de fait sordide, De Phtyriase a son dernier rongé, Un qui de plomb voudra este cupide, Passant le port d'Esleu sera plongé. **English.**

The great *Antony* by name, but in effect sordid, Of *Phtyriasis* shall at last be eaten up, One that shall be covetous of Lead, Going upon Port d'*Esleu* shall fall into the Water.

Phtyriasis in Greek is the disease called by the Latines *Morbus pedicularis*, when one is devoured by Lice, as were *Herodes*, *Sylla*, *Pherecydes*, and *Philip* II. King of *Spain*, &c.

As for Port d'*Esleu*, the question is, whether it be the proper name of a place, or the name of a man, that shall throw another in the water.

LXXXIX.

French.

Trente de Londres secret conjureront, Contre Leur Roy, sur le pont l'Entreprise, Les Satellites la mort desgouteront, Un Roy esleu blond & natif de Frize. English.

Thirty of *London* shall secretly conspire, Against their King, upon the Bridge the Plot shall be made, These *Satellites* shall taste of death, A King shall be elected, fair, and born in *Friezeland*.

ANNOT.

Here may be alleadged that passage of Scripture, *There is nothing so secret but shall be revealed*; for here is plainly told the number of those wicked persons, who conspired against their lawful Sovereign King *Charles* I. of blessed memory, as also the place where the Plot was first laid; for it is well known that they used to assemble at the *Bear* at the Bridge foot.

XC.

French.

Les deux copies au murs ne pourront joindre, Dans cet instant trembler Milan, Thesin, Faim soif, doutance si fort les viendront prendre, Chair, pain, ne vivres nauront un seul boucin. English.

The two Armies shall not be able to joyn by the Walls, At that instant *Milan* and *Thesin* shall tremble, Hunger, thirst, and fear shall so seize upon them, They shall not have a bit of meat, bread, nor victuals.

ANNOT.

Milan is a City in *Italy*, and *Thesin* is the River that passeth by it.

XCI.

French.

Au Duc Gaulois contraint battre au Duelle, La nef de Mole, Monech naprochera, Tort accuse, prison perpetuelle, Son Fils regner avant mort taschera. English.

A *French* Duke compelled to fight a Duel, The Ship of Mole shall not come near *Monaco*, Wrongfully accused shall have a perpetual Prison, His son shall endeavour to Reign before his death.

To understand this Stanza, we must suppose four Histories, *Paradin* relateth the first, which is, that the *French* and *Spanish* Armies having their Winter quarters in the Dukedome of *Milan*, *Anno* 1555.

The Marquess of *Pescaire*, sent word to the Duke of *Nemours*, by a *French* Gentleman, that he and three more desired to break a Lance with him upon the borders of *Ast*.

The Duke accepted the challenge, without giving notice to the Marquess of *Brissac*, then General of the *French* Army, who was very angry at it, nevertheless he advised the Duke to go, but not with a Guilt and light Armour, but with a wrong one, such as became a Cavaliero, which he did not do, nor the other three that went with him: whence it came, that the Lord *Classe* a *French* man, running against *Malespine*, was wounded to death in the shoulder; nevertheless one of the seconds to the Duke of *Nemours*, the Lord *Moncha* killed upon the place *Carassa*, Nephew to pope *Marcel* II. and the Lord *Manoa*, one of the Duke of *Nemours* party, falling from his Horse a little wounded, broke his neck.

As for the Duke of *Nemours*, he ran twice against the said Marquess, without hitting one another, but at the third time they both brake their Lances, without doing any harm. Thus, *the French Duke was compelled to fight a Duel*.

We have the second History from *Turpin*, and many others, which is, that the Marquess of *Masseran*, having put himself into the King of *France*'s service, in hopes to have the Government of *Bielais*; and proving a Traitor, the Marshal of *Brissac*, who had discovered his perfidiousness, resolved to take him in his house of *Gaillany*, which he had fortified to secure his retreat after his Treason.

The Lord *de Termes* was commanded to do it, which he did so dexterously, that he took him into his house after dinner, and then compelled him presently to surrender the Castle of *Jamaglia*, the Marquess obeying, sent thither presently his son *Claudius*, to put it into the hands of the Lords *de la Mante*, and of *Villars*.

These two viewing the Castle, to observe the places that might be fortified, and going from room to room, heard a lamentable voice, crying. *Have mercy upon me.* They caused presently the Prison doors to be opened, and found a poor Gentleman of *Vercelle*, whom the Marquess had detained there 18 years, for endeavouring to serve an execution against him, in the Duke of *Savoy*'s behalf.

And it is remarkable that his Imprisonment was all this while concealed, so that no body ever heard of it, in so much that his friends suspecting he had been killed by one of his enemies, they prosecuted him so hard, that after much tortering, he confessed what he had not done, and was consequently put to death in the presence of the said Marquess of *Masseran*, who knew the Countrey. Thus we see *one wrongfully accused* that was executed, and this Gentlemans Imprisonment, which was to be perpetual.

After this, they carryed the poor Gentleman almost all naked, and being nothing but skin and bones, to the Lord of *Termes*, who caused him to be clothed, and gave him Money to go back to his friends.

The third History is, that the Duke of *Nemours* Son was one of the chief ring-leaders of the League against *Henry* IV. and did what he could before he dyed to get the Kingdom of *France*, endeavouring first to make himself Sovereign Prince of *Lion, Forrest*, and *Beaucolois*.

The fourth History is, that at the latter end of the year 1555. the Lord *la Mole* carrying to *Rome* the Cardinals of *Tournon* and *Lorrain*, went directly to the Island of *Corsica*, whence he drew some Forces, which he joyned to his, and to those of *Monluc*, and would not Land at *Monaco* for some reasons, but went directly to *Civita Vecchia*. By this we understand that Verse of the Stanza. *The Ship of the Mole shall not come near Monaco.*

XCII.

French.

Teste trenchée du vaillant Capitaine, Sera jettée devant son adversaire, Son corps pendu de la Classe a l'Antenne, Confus fuira par rames avent contraire. **English.**

The head cut off the valliant Captain Shall be thrown down before his adversary, His body hanged at the Sails Yard, Confused, they shall fly with Oars against the Wind.

ANNOT.

These words are plain enough, though no body can tell whether the thing is past already, or shall come to pass hereafter.

XCIII.

French.

Un Serpent veu proche du lict Royal, Sera par Dame nuict chien n'abageronts Lors nastre en France un Prince tant Royal, Du Ciel venu tous les Princes verront. **English.**

A Serpent shall be seen near the Royal bed, By a Lady in the night, the Dogs shall not bark, Then shall be born in *France* a Prince so Royal, Come from Heaven all the Princes shall see it.

ANNOT.

This seemeth to be an allusion to the Birth of *Alexander* the great; for it is said, that when his mother *Olympia* proved with Child of him, there was seen in her Bed, and about her Bed a great Serpent, which was the presage of his future greatness: therefore our Author also will have, that when such a Prodigie shall appear in *France*, that then shall be born such a Prince as he mentioneth here: the circumstances are, that this Serpent shall be seen by a Lady in the night time, and that the Dogs of the house shall not bark at him.

XCIV.

French.

Deux grand, freres seront chassez d'Espagne, Laisné vaincu soubs les Monts Pyrænæes, Rougis Mer, Rhosne, sang Leman, d'Alemagne, Narbon, Blyterre, d'Agath contaminées. **English.**

Two great Brothers shall be driven from *Spain*, The elder of them shall be overcome under the *Pyrenean* Mountains Bloody Sea, *Rhosne*, Blood *Leman* of *Germany*, *Narbon*, *Bliterre* of *Agath* polluted.

ANNOT.

The two first Verses are easily understood by those that know the *Pyrenean* Mountains, to be those that part *Spain* from *France*. The two last Verses signifie there shall be bloody Wars in those places; the *Rhosne* is a swift River of *France*, that passeth through the City of *Lyons*; *Leman* is the Lake of *Geneva*, and *Narbon* is a City of *Languedock*.

XCV.

French.

Le Regne a deux laissé bien peu tiendront, Trois ans sept mois passez feront la guerre, Les deux vestales contre rebelleront, Victor puisnay en Armorique Terre. **English.**

The Kingdom being left to two, they shall keep it but a little while, Three years and seven months being past, they shall make War, The two Vestals shall rebel against them, The youngest shall be Conquerour in the *Armorick* Countrey.

ANNOT.

This signifies, that a Kingdom shall be left to two, who shall keep it but a little while, about the space before mentioned.

By the two Vestals that shall rebel, are to be understood two Nuns, who having Interest in the state by their nearness of blood, shall challenge a title in the Kingdom. The last Verse signifies, that the youngest that contended for the Kingdom, shall overcome the eldest, in the Province of *Gascony*.

XCVI.

French.

La sœur aisnée de l'Isle Britannique, Quinze ans devant le frere aura naissance, Par son promis moyenant verifique, Succedera au Regne de Balance. **English.**

The eldest Sister of the *Brittain* Island, Shall be born fifteen years before her Brother, By what is promised her, and help of the truth, She shall succeed in the Kingdom of *Libra*.

ANNOT.

This signifies, that the Princess born so long after her Brother, shall be married to a King of *France*, which is understood here by the Kingdom of *Libra*; therefore the last King *Lewis* the XIII. was called *the Just*, because born under the Sign of *Libra*.

XCVII.

French.

L'An que Mercure, Mars, Venus retrograde, Du grand Monarque la ligne ne faillit, Esleu du peuple Lusitant pres de Pactole, Qu'en Paix & Regne viendra fort enveillir. English.

When *Mercury, Mars* and *Venus* shall retrograde, The Line of the great Monarch shall be wanting, He shall be elected by the *Lusitanians* near *Pactole*, And shall Reign in Peace a good while.

ANNOT.

This signifies the late change of state in *Portugal*, when they threw off the *Spanish* yoke, and chose a King amongst themselves, *John* the IV. Duke of *Branganza*, Father to the present Queen of *England*; for by the *Lusitanians* are meant the *Portugals*, so called from their Countreys name *Lusitania*; *Pactoles* is the River that runs by *Lisbonne*, otherwise called *Tagus*, in Greek χροσοροος from the Sands.

XCVIII.

French.

Les Albanois passeront dedans Rome, Moyennant Langres demipiler affubles, Marquis & Duc ne pardonnes a l'homme, Feu, sang, morbilles point d'eau, faillir les blés. English.

The *Albanians* shall pass through *Rome*, By the means of *Langres* covered with half Helmets, Marquess and Duke shall spare no man, Fire, blood, small Pox, Water shall fail us, also Corn.

ANNOT.

The meaning is, that when the people of *Albania* lying between the *Venetian* Territories, and *Grecia*, shall come to *Rome*, by the means of a Bishop of *Langres*, who is a Duke and Peer of *France*; being *covered with half Helmets*, a kind of a Cap that they wear in War; then shall be *fire, blood, small Pox, and want of Corn.*

XCIX.

French.

L'Aisné vaillant de la fille du Roy, Repoussera si profond les Celtiques, Qu'il mettra Foudres, combien en tel arroy, Peu & loing puis profond es Hesperiques. English.

The valliant eldest son of the daughter of the King, Shall beat back so far those of *Flanders*, That he will cast Lightnings, O how many in such orders Little and far, after shall go deep in *Spain*.

ANNOT.

This is scarce to be understood of any body, but the present King of *France Lewis* the XIV.

who was the elder son, and born of Queen *Ann*, Daughter to the King of *Spain*, who by his valour and fortune made last year such progress in the Conquest of *Flanders*, that it hath caused admiration in every body; insomuch that is he do the like this year, it may be probably suspected, he will afterwards go deep into *Spain* according to the contents of this Prophecy.

C.

French.

Du feu Celeste au Royal edifice, Quand la lumiere de Mars defaillira, Sept mois grand Guerre, mort gent de malefice, Rouen, Eureux au Roy ne faillira. **English.**

Fire shall fall from the skies on the Kings Palace, When *Mars*'s light shall be Ecclipsed, A great War shall be for seven months, people shall die by witchcraft. *Rouen*, and *Eureux* shall not be wanting to the King.

ANNOT.

The meaning is, that when *Mars* is Ecclipsed, the Lightning shall fall on some of the King of *Frances* Palaces, then shall be a great War, for the space of seven Months, and many shall die by witchcraft; and *Rouen* the chief City of *Normandy*, and *Eureux* another of the same province, shall stick fast to the Kings Interest.

This is of the same nature as the foregoing, therefore I leave it to the same expositors.

XXVI.

French.

La gent esclave par un heur Martial, Viendra en haut degré tant eslevée, Changeront Prince, naistra un Provincial, Passer la Mer, copie aux Monts levée. English.

The Slavish Nation shall by a Martial luck Be raised to so high a degree, That they shall change their Prince, and elect one among themselves, They shall cross the Sea with an Army raised in the Mountains.

ANNOT.

This is so plain, that it needeth no interpretation.

XXVII.

French.

Par feu & armes non loin de la Mar negro, Viendra de Perse occuper Trebisonde, Trembler Pharos, Metelin, Sol alegro, De sang Arabe d'Adrie couvert l'Onde. English.

By Fire and Sword not far from the black Sea, They shall come from *Persia* to seize upon *Trebisonde*, *Pharos* and *Methelin* shall quake, Sun be merry, The Sea of *Adria* shall be covered with *Arabian* blood.

ANNOT.

This Prophecy foretelleth clearly and plainly, that the *Persians* shall come to invade the Turkish dominions, a part of which is the Empire of *Trebisond*, and that *Pharos* and *Methelin* two Islands in the *Mediterranean* Sea, shall quake for fear.

As also that the *Adriatick* Sea, which is that Sea that belongeth to the *Venetians* shall be covered with Turkish blood, at which the Author is so jocund, as with an exclamation he inviteth the Sun to be merry, and rejoyce at it.

XXVIII.

French.

Le bras pendu & la jambe liée, Visage pasle, au sein poignard caché, Trois qui seront jurez de la meslée, Au grand de Genes sera le Fer lasché. English.

The arm hanging, and the leg bound, With a pale face, a Dagger in the bosom, Three that shall be sworn to the fray, To the great one of *Genoa* the Iron shall be darted.

This manifestly foretelleth a conspiracy of three men against the Duke of *Genoa*, one of which three men, under the shew of a sore Arm, and an impotent Leg, shall carry a Dagger in his bosom, with which he shall stabb the said Duke.

XXIX.

French.

La liberté ne sera recouvrée, L'Occupera noir, fier, vilain inique; Quand la matiere du Pont sera ouvrée, D'Hister, Venise faschée la Republique. English.

The liberty shall not be recovered, It shall be occupied, by a black, fierce, and wicked villain; When the work of the *Hister*-Bridge shall be ended, The *Venetian* Common-wealth shall be vexed.

ANNOT.

This Stanza is divided into two parts, the first of which is comprehended in the two first Verses, *viz.* that the liberty of some politick body (he nameth not which) shall not be recovered, but shall be seized upon, by a black, fierce, and wicked villain.

The second part is contained in the two last Verses, wherein he saith, that the Common-wealth of *Venice* shall be in trouble, when the Bridge made over the River *Hister* shall be finished.

XXX.

French.

Tout a l'entour de la grande Cité, Seront Soldats logez par Champs & Villes, Donner l'assaut Paris, Rome incité, Sur le Pont sera faite grand pille. English.

Round about the great City, Soldiers shall lye in the Fields and Towns, Paris shall give the Assault, *Rome* shall be attached; Then upon the Bridge shall be great plundering.

ANNOT.

This is concerning the taking and sacking of *Rome*, by the Duke of *Bourbon*, General of *Charles* V. Forces, therefore he saith that *Paris* shall give the Assault, because the said Duke of *Bourbon* was a *Frenchman*.

XXXI.

French.

Par Terre Attique chef de la sapience, Qui de present est la Rose du Monde, Pont ruiné & sa grand preeminence, Sera subdite & naufrage des Ondes. English.

In the Countrey of *Attica* which is the head of wisdom, And now is the Rose of the World, A Bridge shall be ruinated with its great preeminence, It shall be subdued, and made a wrack by the Waves.

ANNOT.

He foretelleth the destruction of a famous Bridge in the Countrey of *Attica*, of which *Athens* is the chief City, and because it was always famous for learning, he calleth it here the head of Wisdom; and that Wisdom, the Rose of the World.

XXXII.

French.

Ou tout bon est, tout bien Soleil & Lune, Est abondant, sa ruine s'approche, Le Ciel s'advance a changer ta fortune, En mesme estat que la septiesme Roche. **English.**

Where all well is, all good O Sun and Moon, Is existent, his ruine draweth near, The Heaven is making hast to change thy fortune, Into the same case as the seventh Rock is.

ANNOT.

By this dark Stanza, the Author seemeth to foretell the woful condition of a Countrey that was happy before, but shall fall to ruine, I suspect he intended *France*, because being a *Frenchman* he did not name it, for I think there was never such a change in the world as was in that Kingdom, in the time of the Civil Wars between the Roman Catholicks, and the Protestants.

XXXIII.

French.

Des principaux de Cité rebellée, Qui tiendront fort pour liberté r'avoir, Detrencher masles, infœlice meslée! Cris, hurlemens a Nantes pitieux voir. **English.**

Of the chief men in a rebelled City, Who shall stand out to recover their liberty, The Males shall be cut in pieces, O unhappy quarrel! Cries and houlings, it shall be pity to see at *Nantes*.

ANNOT.

The Author applyeth this Prophecie to the City of *Nantes* in *Britany*, but want of Books that treat of the History of that Countrey; I could neither satisfie my self, nor the Reader, if this hath come to pass already or not.

XXXIV.

French.

Du plus profond de l'occident Anglois, Ou est le chef de l'Isle Britanique, Entrera classe en Garonne par Blois, Par Vin & Sel faux cachez aux barriques. English.

From the deepest Westerly part of *England*, Where the chief of the *Britain* Island is, A Fleet shall come into the *Garonne* by *Blaye*, By Wine and Salt fire shall be hidden in Barrels.

ANNOT.

There is a notable and sensible error in the *French* Copy, and without reforming it, the sense is not only obscure, but also impossible; for instead of *Blois*, which the Author hath put here, I suppose to make the rime good, it must be written *Blaye*, which is a Sea Town of the mouth of the River *Garonne*, and *Blois* is a mid-Land Town, upon the River *Loire*, about a hundred Leagues distant from the other.

The rest signifieth no more, but that there shall be some Warlike Stratagem made use of by the *French* (understood here by the names of *Wine and Salt*) in puting fire into Barrels.

XXXV.

French.

Par Cité franche de la grand Mer Seline, Qui porte encor l'estomach la pierre, Angloise classe viendra soubs la bruine, Prendre un rameau de grand ouverte guerre. English.

By a free City of the *Selyne* Sea, Which carrieth yet the stone in the Stomach, An *English* Fleet shall come under a fog, To take a branch of great open War.

ANNOT.

What should the Author mean by the free City of the great *Seline* Sea that carryeth yet the stone in the Stomach, is hard to guess; for my part I believe it to be *Venice*. First, because by the *Seline* Sea, he always understands the *Mediterranean*; because the great *Turks* name in our Authors time was *Selyn*, who was Master of the greatest part of it. Secondly, there is no other free City so considerable as this. Thirdly, by the stone in the Stomach, may be understood, the Pillars that are in the *Piazza* of St. *Mark*, and as it were in the Centre of *Venice*, as the Stomach is in the Body. The sense therefore is this, as I take it, that a considerable *Fleet* shall come to *Venice*, or rather to *Molamocco*, which is the Harbour, and there take a branch of great open War, that is, to be either against the *Venetians*, or against the *Turk* in their behalf.

XXXVI.

French.

De Sœur le frere par simulte feintise, Viendra mesler rosee en Mineral, Sur la placente donne a vieille tardive, Meurt le goustant, sera simple rural. **English.**

The Brother of the Sister, with a fained dissimulation, Shall mix Dew with Mineral, In a Cake given to a slow old woman, She dieth tasting of, the deed shall be simple, and Countrey like.

ANNOT.

This foretelleth a notable poisoning that shall be done by a Brother upon his Sister, which, because she died not fast enough, according to his mind: and therefore called her *slow*, he would set her forward with a poisoned Cake, the Poison was *Mineral*, and therefore *Arsenick* or *Sublimate*, mixed with *Manna*, called here *Dew*; because *Manna* is nothing but a *Dew*, condensed upon the Bark of a certain Tree; the Conclusion is, that the woman shall die eating of it, though the meat seemed to be simple and rural.

XXXVII.

Trois sens seront d'un vouloir & accord, Qui pour venir au bout de leur attainte, Vingt mois apres tous eux & leurs records, Leur Roy trahy simulant haine, feinte. **English.**

Three hundred shall be of one mind and agreement, That they may compass their ends, twenty months after by all them and their partners, Their King shall be betrayed, by dissembling a fained hatred.

ANNOT.

The difficulty of meeting in any Countrey three hundred men of one mind, hath perswaded me that our Author writ this for *England*; but by reason there hath been since a general pardon, I will keep my mind to my self.

XXXVIII.

French.

Ce grand Monarque qu'au mort succedera, Donnera vie illicite & lubrique, Par nonchalance a tous concedera, Qua la parfin faudra la loy Salique. **English.**

The great Monarch that shall succeed to the great one, Shall lead a Life unlawfull, and lecherous, By carelesness he shall give to all, So that in Conclusion the *Salique* Law shall fail.

ANNOT.

This hath a Relation to the precedent Stanza, therefore, *&c.*

XXXIX.

French.

Du vray rameau de fleur de Lis issu, Mis & loge heritier d'Hetrurie, Son sang antique de longue main tissu, Fera Florence florir en l'Armoirie. **English.**

Issued out of the true branch of the City, He shall be set for Heir of *Hetruria*, His ancient blood waved by a long while, Shall cause *Florence* to flourish in the Scutcheon.

ANNOT.

This is only in commendation of the Family of the *Medicis*, and of their Alliance with the Crown of *France*; for *Catharine* of *Medicis*, wife to *Henry* II. was Queen of *France* when our Author lived.

XL.

French.

Le sang Roial sera si tresmeslé, Contraints seront Gaulois de l'Hesperie, On attendra que terme soit coulé, Et que memoire de la voix soit perie. English.

The Royal blood shall be so much mixed, The *French* shall be constrained by the *Spaniards*, They shall stay till the term be past, And the remembrance of the voice be over.

ANNOT.

This only signifieth a strict Union between the *French* and the *Spaniards*, by several Alliances.

XLI.

French.

Nay soubs les ombres & journée nocturne, Séra en Regne & bonté Souveraine, Fera renaistre son sang de l'antique Urne, Renouvelant siecle d'Or pour l'airain. English.

Being born in the shadows and nocturnal time, He shall be a Soveraign in Kingdom and bounty, He shall cause his blood to come again from the ancient *Urn*, Renewing a golden Age instead of a brazen one.

ANNOT.

This foretelleth the greatness and goodness of a Prince that shall be born in the beginning of the night.

XLII.

French.

Mars eslevé en son plus haut befroy, Fera retraire les Allobrox de France, La gent Lombarde fera si grand effroy, A ceux de l'Aigle comprins soubs la Balance. English.

Mars being elevated in its higher Steeple, Shall cause the *Allobrox* to retreat from *France*, The people of *Lombardy* shall be in so great fear, Of those of the Eagle comprehended under *Libra*.

ANNOT.

The *Allobrox* are the people of *Savoy*. Those of the Eagle comprehended under *Libra*, are the subjects of the Empire that use the *French* tongue.

XLIII.

French.

Le grand ruine des Sacrez ne sesloigne, Provence, Naples, Sicile, Seez & Ponce, En Germanie au Rhin & la Coloigne, Vexez a mort par tous ceux de Mogunce. English.

The great ruine of the sacred things is not far off, *Provence, Naples, Sicily, Sez* and *Ponce*, In *Germany* towards the *Rhyne* and *Colen*, They shall be vexed to death by those of *Moguntia*.

ANNOT.

He foretelleth the troubles that were to be shortly in those Countreys for Religion.

XLIV.

French.

Par Mer le rouge sera prins the Pyrates, La paix sera par son moyen troublée, L'une & l'auare commettra par faincte acte, Au grand Pontife fera l'Armée d'oublée. English.

By Sea the red one shall be taken by Pyrates, The peace by that means shall be troubled, He shall commit anger and coveteousness by a feigned action, The High Priest shall have a double Army.

ANNOT.

By the red one is understood some Cardinal that shall be taken by Pyrates, for which the peace shall be in danger to be broken, the same Cardinal shall by a feigned action be guilty of choler and covetousness, and for his recovery and the defending the Rites of the Church, the Pope shall have a double Army granted to him.

XLV.

French.

Le grand Empire fera tost desolé, Et translate pres d'Arduenne silve, Les deux batards par l'aisné decollé, Et Regnera Ænodarbnez de milve. English.

The great Empire shall soon be made desolate, And shall be translated near the Forrest of *Arden*, The two Bastards shall have their heads cut off by the eldest son, And he that shall reign, shall be *Ænodarbnez* nosed.

ANNOT.

By the great Empire is meant that of *Germany*, which he says shall be translated near the Forrest of *Ardens*, which is near the borders of *France*. Two Bastards shall be beheaded by command of the elder Brother of the House, and he that shall Reign shall have a reddish beard, and a Hawks nose.

XLVI.

French.

Par Chapeaux rouges querelles & nouveaux schismes, Quand on aura esleu le Sabinois, On produira contre luy grands sophismes, Et sera Rome lessée par Albanois. English.

By red Hats, quarrels and new schismes, When the *Sabin* shall be Elected, Great sophismes shall be produced against him, And *Rome* shall be endamaged by the *Albanois.*

ANNOT.

By red Hats are understood Cardinals of *Rome*, who shall raise great quarrels and schismes, when a Pope of the Countrey of the *Sabins* (which is near *Rome*) shall be Elected, against whom many things shall be objected, and that *Rome* shall be endamaged by the *Albanians*, which are a Warlike people, and for the most part subject to the Common-wealth of *Venice.*

XLVII.

French.

Le grand Arabe marchera bien avant, Trahy sora par le Bisantinois: L'Antique Rhodes luy viendra au devant, Et plus grand mal par Austre Pannonois. English.

The great *Arabian* shall proceed a great way, He shall be betrayed by the *Bisantines*, The ancient *Rhodes* shall come to meet him, And a greater evil by a South wind from *Hungary.*

ANNOT.

By *Bisantine* is understood the great Turk, Master of *Constantinople*, formerly called *Bysantium.*

XLVIII.

French.

Apres la grande affliction du Sceptre, Deux ennemis par eux seront defaicts: Classes d'Affrique aux Pannons viendra naistre, Par Mer & Terre seront horribles Faicts. English.

After the great afflictions of the Scepter, Two enemies shall be overcome by themselves, A Fleet of *Affrica* shall be born to the *Hungarians*. By Sea and Land shall be horrid facts.

ANNOT.

The words of this Stanza are plain, though the sense be something obscure.

XLIX.

French.

Nul de l'Espagne, mais de l'antique France, Sera esleu pour le tremblant nacelle, A l'ennemy sera faicte fiance, Qui dans son Regne sera peste cruelle. English.

None out of *Spain*, but of the ancient *France*, Shall be Elected to govern the tottering Ship. The enemy shall be trusted, Who to his Kingdom shall be a cruel plague.

ANNOT.

       The two first Verses foretell a schisme in the Church of *Rome*, understood by a tottering Ship, and that a *French-man* shall be Elected Pope to remedy it.
       The two last Verses are easie to be understood.

L.

French.

L'An que les Freres du Lys seront an Aage, L'Un d'euz tiendra la grand Romanie: Trembler les Monts ouvert Latin passage, Bache marcher contre Fort d'Armenie. English.

In the year that the Brethren of the Lillies shall be at Age, One of them shall hold the great *Romanie*: The Mountains shall tremble, the *Latine* passage shall be opened, A *Bassha* shall march against the Fort of *Armenia*.

ANNOT.

       By the Brethren of the Lillies are meant the Heirs of the Crown of *France*; the rest is plain.

LI.

French.

La gent de Dace, d'Angleterre, & Polone, Et de Boësme feront nouvelle ligue, Pour passer outre d'Hercules la Colonne, Barcins, Thyrrans dresser cruelle brigue. English.

The people of *Dacia*, *England*, and *Poland*, And of *Bohemia* shall make a new League, To go beyond *Hercules* Pillars, *Barcins* and *Thyrrens* shall make a cruel plot.

ANNOT.

       By *Barcins* he means those of *Carthage*, which is now *Tunis*, and by the *Thyrrens*, those that live near that Sea.

LII.

French.

Un Roy sera qui donra l'opposite, Les exilez eslevez sur le Regne, De sang nager la gent caste hyppolite, Et florira long-temps sous telle enseigne. English.

A King shall be, who shall be opponent To the banished persons raised upon the Kingdom, The chast *Hippolite* Nation shall swim in blood, And shall flourish a great while under such an Ensign.

ANNOT.

Here is *Demorritus*'s Well where the truth may be, but I cannot find it.

LIII.

French.

La Loy du Sol, & Venus contendans, Appropriant l'Esprit de Prephetie: Ne l'un ne l'autre ne seront entendus, Par Sol tiendra la Loy du grand Messie. English.

The Law of the *Sun* and *Venus* contending, Appropriating the spirit of Prophecy, Neither one nor the other shall be heard, By *Sol* the Law of the great *Messias* shall subsist.

ANNOT.

This is of the same obscurity with the foregoing one.

LIV.

French.

Du pont Euxine, & la grand Tartarie, Un Roy sera qui viendra voir la Gaule, Transpercera Alane & l'Armenie, Et dans Bisance Lairra sanglante Gaule. English.

From the *Euxin* Sea, and great *Tartaria*, A King shall come to see *France*, He shall go through *Alanea* and *Armenia*, And shall leave a bloody rod in *Constantinople*.

ANNOT.

This is so plain, that it needeth no interpretation.

LV.

French.

De la felice Arabie contrade, Maistra puissant de la loy Mahometique, Vexer l'Espagne, conquestre la Grenade, Et plus par Mera la gent Ligustique. English.

Out of the Countrey of *Arabia* the happy, Shall be born a powerful man of the Mahometan Law, Who shall vex *Spain* and conquer *Grenada*, And by Sea shall come to the *Ligurian* Nation.

ANNOT.

The *Ligurian* Nation are those of *Genoa*.

LVI.

French.

Par le traspas du tres-vieillard Pontife, Sera esleu Romain de bon aage, Qui sera dit que le siege debiffe, Et long tiendra & de picquant courage. English.

By the death of the very old high-Priest, Shall be a *Roman* elected of good age, Of whom it shall be said, that he dishonoureth the Seat, And shall live long, and be of a fierce courage.

ANNOT.

The sense and the words are plain.

LVII.

French.

Istra du Mont Gaulsier & Aventine, Qui par le trou advertira l'Armée, Entre deux Rocs sera prins le butin, De Sext. Mansol faillir la renommée. English.

One shall go out of the Mountains *Gaulsier* and *Aventine*, Who through a hole shall give notice to the Army, Between two Rocks the booty shall be taken, Of *Sext. Mansol* shall loose his renown.

ANNOT.

The Mountains of *Gaulsier* and *Aventine* are two of the seven Mountains of *Rome*, out of which, it seems, one shall go out to give notice to the Army without, and the Booty of the *Pope*, called *Sextus*, shall be taken.

But what he meaneth by *Mansol*, I am ignorant.

LVIII.

French.

De l'Aqueduct d'Uticense, Gardoing, Par le Forest & Mont inaccessible, Emmy du pont sera taché ou poing, La chef Nemans qui tant sera terrible. English.

From the Conduit of *Uticense* and *Gardoing*, Through the Forrest and unaccessible Mountain, In the middle of the Bridge shall be tyed by the Wrist, The chief *Nemans*, that shall be so terrible.

ANNOT.

By the Conduit of *Gardoing*, he means that of the River *Gardon*, that passeth by *Nismes*, where there is a famous Conduit.

But what he meaneth by the chief *Nemans*, I cannot find.

LIX.

French.

Au chef Anglois a Nismes trop sejour, Devers l'Espagne au secours Ænobarbe, Plusieurs mouront par Mars ouvert ce jour, Quand en Artois faillir estoile en Barbe. English.

The chief *English* shall stay too long at *Nismes*, A red haird man shall go to the succours of *Spain*, Many shall die by open War that day, When in *Artois* the Star shall fail in the Beard.

ANNOT.

All the difficulty lyeth in the last Verse: for my part I believe he meaneth by it a bearded Comet, such as the Latines call *Cometa barbatus*.

LX.

French.

Par teste rase viendra bien mal eslire, Plus que sa charge ne porte passera, Si grand fureur & rage fera dire, Qua feu & sang tout Sexe tranchera. English.

By a shaven head shall be made an ill choice, That shall go beyond his commission, He shall proceed with so great fury and rage, That he shall put both Sexes to fire and Sword.

ANNOT.

By a shaven head must be understood a Priest of the *Romish* Religion; because they all have their heads shaven.

LXI.

French.

L'Enfant du grand nestant a sa naissance, Subjugera les hauts Monts Apennins, Fera trembler tous ceux de la balance, Depuis Monts Feurs jusques a Mont Senis. English.

The Child of the great man that was not at his birth, Shall subdue the high *Apennine* Mountains, Shall make all those under *Libra* to quake, From Mount *Feurs*, as far as Mount *Senis*.

ANNOT.

The *Apennine* Mountains, are those that divide *Italy* in two parts.

Those under the Sign of *Libra* are the people of *France*. *Feurs* is a City in *France*, in the Province of *Forrest*. Mount *Senis* is a high Mountain in Savoy.

LXII.

French.

Sur les Rochers sang on verra pleuvoir, Sol Orient, Saturne Occidental, Pres d'Orgon Guerre, a Rome grand mal voir, Nefs parfondrées, & prins le Tridental. English.

It shall rain blood upon the Rocks, The Sun being in the East, and *Saturn* in the West, War shall be near *Orgon*, and great evil at *Rome*, Ships shall be cast away, and the Trident be taken.

ANNOT.

I could not find what he meaneth by *Orgon*. As by *the Trident being taken*, I suppose he meaneth a Ship called *Neptune*, because *Neptune* is always painted with a Trident.

LXIII.

French.

De vaine emprise l'honneur indue plainte, Galliots errants par Latins froid, faim vagues, Non loin du Tybre de sang la Terre teinte, Et sur humains seront diverses plagues. English.

Honour bringeth a complaint against a vain undertaking, Galleys shall wander through the *Latin* Seas, cold, hunger, Waves, Not far from *Tyber* the Earth shall be died with blood, And upon Mankind shall be several plagues.

ANNOT.

Tyber is the River of *Rome*, the rest are several prodigies that shall come to pass.

LXIV.

French.

Les assembles par repos du grand nombre, Par Terre & Mer conseil contremandé, Pres de l'Autonne, Genes, Nue, de lombre, Par Champs & Villes le Chef contrebandé. English.

The gathered by the rest of the great numbers, By Land and Sea shall recall their Councel, Near *Autonne*, *Genes*, and *Nue* of the shadow, In Fields and Towns the Chief shall be one against another.

ANNOT.

This passeth my understanding.

LXV.

French.

Subit venu l'effrayeur sera grande, Des principaux de l'affaire cachés: Et Dame Embraise plus ne sera en veuë, Et peu a peu seront le grands fachés. English.

One coming upon a suddain shall cause a great fear, To the Chief men that were hidden and concerned in the business, And the Lady *Ambraise* shall be seen no more, And by little and little the great one shall be angry.

ANNOT.

What he meaneth by the lady *Ambraise*, I cannot find, the rest is easie.

LXVI.

French.

Sous les antiques edifices Vestaux, Non esloignez d'Aqueduct ruiné, De Sol & Lune sont les luissans metaux, Ardente Lampe Trajan d'or buriné. English.

Under the ancient edifices of the *Vestals*, Not far from an *Aqueduct* ruinated, Are the bright mettals of Sun and Moon, A burning Lamp of *Trajan* of ingraven gold.

ANNOT.

Monsieur *Catel* in his second Book of *Languedoc* Chap. V. saith, that there was a famous *Aqueduct*, which the *Romans* builded from the River *Gar* to the Town of *Nismes*, which at present is ruinated.

Secondly, Near the Town there was a famous Temple dedicated to *Diana*, where there is a Spring of water so great, that it seemeth rather a Lake then a Fountain.

Thirdly, I find that the Emperour *Adrian* caused a Temple to be built in the honour of

Plotina Trajan's wife.

Fourthly, He relateth that *Jean Poldo* found in the Town of *Aix* a Marble with this inscription: *Plotina Trajanis uxor, summa honestate & integritate fulgens, sterilitatis defectu sine prole fecit conjugem, qui ejus opera Adrianum adoptatum in Imperio Successorem habuit, a quo in beneficii memoriam Nemausi æde sacra maximo Sumptu, sublimique structura, ac Hymnorum cantu decorata, post mortem donata est*: That is to say, *Plotina, Trajans* wife, famous for her honesty and integrity, was barren and left no Children to her Husband, which she perceiving, intreated the Emperour to adopt *Adrian* for his Son, and to make him his Successor in the Empire, which being come to pass, the new Emperour in acknowledgement of such a benefit, did build her a Temple of a magnificent Structure, and caused it to be Consecrated with Musick after her death.

Fifthly, The said Author saith, that this Marble was taken out of that Temple, when the River of *Gardon* did so overflow, as we have said.

By all this we see, that there was a Temple of *Vestals* at *Nismes*, *Diana* the Maid being their chief Patroness, which is made now a Nunnery, called *la Fontaine*. There is also to be seen the Temple of *Plotina, Trajans* wife, built by *Adrian* his Successor. And as it was the manner of the Ancients to put some of those inextinguishable Lamps in their Graves; it is very likely, there was one of them in this Temple, and because it should be known whose Grave it was, he caused *Trajans* name to be Engraven in the foot of the said Lamp.

Let us explain now the Stanza: *Under the Ancient Vestal buildings of the Temple of Diana, not far from the ruined Aqueduct*, which carrieth the water from the River *Gar* to *Nismes, shall be found shining mettals of Sol and Luna*, that is, Meddals of gold and silver, with *a burning Lamp of gold*, wherein the name of *Trajan* was Engraven. Histories make mention of several burning Lamps in this manner, that have been found still burning in the ground, and not consumed, though they had been there above 500 years; certainly the Oil of it must have been incombustible, and could be extracted out of nothing but gold, *quia nil dat quod non habet*.

LXVII.

Quand Chef Perouse n'osera sa Tunique, Sens au convert tout nud s'expolier: Seront prins sept faict Aristocratique, Le Pere & Fils morts par poine te au collier. English.

When the Chief of *Perouse* shall not dare without a Tunick, To expose himself naked in the dark, Seven shall be taken for setting up Aristocracy, The Father and the Son shall die by pricks in the Collar.

ANNOT.

Perouse is a City in *Italy*; the rest is plain.

LXVIII.

French.

Dans le Danube & le Rhine viendra boire, Le grand Chameau, ne sen repentira: Trembler le Rhosne & plus fort ceux de Loire, Et pres des Alpes Coq le ruinera. English.

In *Danubius* and the *Rhine* shall come to drink, The great Camel, and shall not repent; The *Rhosne* shall tremble, and more those of *Loire*, And near the *Alpes* the Cock shall ruine him.

This foretelleth a great incursion of the *Turks* into *Germany*, insomuch that they shall water their Camels in the Rivers of *Danubius*, and of the *Rhyne*, to the great terrour of *France*, wherein those Rivers of *Rhosne* and *Loire* are.

But the last Verse, saith the Cock; that is, the *French*, shall overcome and ruine the *Turks*, near the Mountains of the *Alpes*.

LXIX.

French.

Plus ne sera le grand en saux sommeil, L'Inquietude viendra prendre repos, Dresser Phalange d'Or, Azur, & vermeil, Subjuguer Affrique & ronger jusqu'aux os. English.

The great one shall be no more in a false sleep, The restlessness shall take rest, He shall raise an Army of Gold and Azure, He shall conquer *Affrica* and gnaw it to the bones.

ANNOT.

This is concerning some great Prince, who shall raise a powerful Army, and conquer *Affrica* with it.

LXX.

French.

Les Regions subietes a la Balance, Feront trembler les Monts par grande Guerre, Captifs tout sexe, avec toute Bizance, Qu'on criera a l'Aube Terre a Terre. English.

The Regions under the sign of *Libra*, Shall make the Mountains quake with great War, Slaves of all sexes, with all *Bizance*, So that in the dawning of the day, they shall cry to Land to Land.

ANNOT.

This foretelleth the destruction of *Constantinople*, anciently called *Byzantium*, by those that live under the Sign of *Libra*, that is, the *Europeans*, and chiefly the *French*.

LXXI.

French.

Par la fureur d'un qui attendra l'eau, Par la grand rage tout l'exercite esmeu, Charge des Nobles a dixsept Bateaux, Au long du Rhosne tard Messager venud. English.

By the fury of one staying for the Water, By his great rage the whole Army shall be troubled, There shall be seventeen Boats full of Noblemen Along the *Rhosne*, the Messenger shall come too late.

The words and sense are plain.

LXXII.

French.

Pour le plaisir d'Edict voluptueux, On meslera la poison dans la Loy, Venus sera en cours si vertueux, Qu'obfusquera du Soleil tout alloy. English.

By the pleasure of a voluptuous proclamation, The poison shall be mixed in the Law, *Venus* shall be in so great request, That it shall darken all the allay of the Sun.

ANNOT.

By a Proclamation, favouring or promoting Licentiousness, poison shall be mixed in the Law, and leachery so much countenanced, as it shall obscurate the allay of the Sun, that is, piety so much commended in the Gospel, to all those that will fight under Christs Banner.

LXXIII.

French.

Persecutée sera de dien l'Eglise, Et les Saints Temples seront expoliez, L'Enfant la mere mettra nud en chemise, Seront Arabes au Polous ralliez. English.

The Church of God shall be persecuted, And the holy Temples shall be spoiled, The Child shall turn out his Mother in her Smock, *Arrabians* shall agree with the *Polonians*.

ANNOT.

The Author could not be mistaken in this Prophecie; for the Church of God shall always be persecuted, the Apostle confirmeth it, when he saith, *that all those that will live piously in Christ, must suffer persecution*: As for the spoiling of Churches, and other barbarous actions, it hath been seen so often in *France*, in the time of the Civil Wars for Religion, that it needeth no confirmation.

The last Verse concerning a peace between the *Turks* and the *Polonians*, was fulfilled in the year 1623. when *Sigismundus* King of *Poland*, by his Embassador the Duke *Šbarasky*, and by the mediation of the *English* Embassador, concluded a Peace with the great Turk *Mustapha*, the Articles of which you may read at large in the *Turkish* History.

LXXIV.

De sang Trojen naistra cœur Germanique, Qui deviendra en si haute puissance, Hors chassera gent estrange Arabique, Tournant l'Eglise en pristine préeminence. **English.**

Of *Trojan* blood shall be born a *German* heart, Who shall attain to so high a power, That he shall drive away the strange *Arrabian* Nation, Restoring the Church to her former splendor.

ANNOT.

It seemeth to signifie, that by Alliance made between a *German* Emperour, and a Daughter of *France*, which derive their Pedigree from the *Trojans*, a Prince shall be born of so stout and valiant a heart, as shall drive away all the *Turkish* power out of *Germany*, and shall restore the Church to her former splendor.

LXXV.

French.

Montera haut sur le bien plus a dextre, Demourra assis sur la pierre carrée, Vers le midy posé a la senestre, Baston tortu en main, bouche ferrée. **English.**

He shall go up upon the good more on the right hand, He shall stay sitting upon the square stone, Towards the South; being set, on the left hand, A crooked stick in his hand, and his mouth shut.

ANNOT.

I do acknowledge my Ignorance in this.

LXXVI.

French.

En lieu libere tendra son Pavillon, Et ne voudra en Citez prendre place, Aix, Carpentras, Lisle, Volce, Mont Cavaillon, Par tous ces lieux abolira sa trace. **English.**

He shall pitch his Tent in the open air, Refusing to lodge in the City, *Aix, Carpentras, Lisle, Volce, Mont Cavaillon*, In all those places, he shall abolish his trace.

ANNOT.

Aix, Carpentras, Lisle Volce, Mont Cavaillon, are Cities of *Provence*.

LXXVII.

French.

Tous les degres d'honneur Ecclesiastique, Seront changez en Dial Quirinal, En Martial, quirinal, Flaminique, Puis un Roy de France le rendra Vulcanal. English.

All the degrees of Ecclesiastical honour, Shall be changed into a Dial Quirinal, Into Martial, Quirinal, Flaminick; After that, a King of *France* shall make it Vulcanal.

ANNOT.

All what I can say upon this, is, that *Dialis* in Latine is a Priest of *Jupiter*, and *Quirinal* is a Priest of *Romulus*, *Martial Flamen* is a Priest of *Mars*, *Vulcanal* is a Priest of *Vulcan*, let the ingenious Reader make of all these the best construction he can.

LXXVIII.

French.

Les deux unis ne tiendront longuement, Et dans treize ans au Barbare Satrape, Aux deux costez feront tel perdement, Qu'un benira la Barque & sa cappe. English.

The two united shall not hold long, Within thirteen years to the Barbarian *Satrape*, They shall cause such loss on both sides, That one shall bless the Boat and its covering.

ANNOT.

The word *Satrape* is a *Persian* word, signifying one of the Grandees at Court. By the last Verse is meant, one that shall save his life and make his escape, by the means of a covered Boat or Barge.

LXXIX.

French.

La sacree Pompe viendra baisser les aisles, Par la venue de grand Legislateur, Humble haussera, vexera les rebelles, Naistra sur Terre aucun Æmulateur. English.

The sacred Pomp shall bow down her wings, At the coming of the great Lawgiver, He shall raise the humble and vex the rebellious, No Emulator of his shall be born.

ANNOT.

This seemeth to have a relation to the birth of Christ, or Christmas-day.

LXXX.

L'Ogmion grande Bizance approchera, Chassée sera la Barbarique ligue, Des deux Loix l'une unique lachera, Barbare & France en perpetuelle brigue. English.

The *Ogmion* shall come near great *Bizance*, And shall expel the Barbarian League, Of the two Laws, the wicked one shall yeild, The *Barbarian*, and the *French* shall be in perpetual jar.

ANNOT.

By the word *Ogmion*, every where in his Book, the Author meaneth the King of *France*, who according to his words shall come near *Constantinople*, and shall break the Barbarian League, and of the two Laws, that is, the Christian and the Mahometan, the Mahometan shall yield to the other.

LXXXI.

French.

L'Oyseau Royal sur la Cité solaire, Sept mois devant fera nocturne augure: Mur d'Orient cherra Tonnerre esclaire, Sept jours aux Portes les ennemies a l'heure. English.

The Royal Bird upon the solar City, Seven Months together shall make a nocturn augury, The Eastern Wall shall fall, the Lightning shall shine, Then the enemies shall be at the Gate for seven days.

ANNOT.

By the Royal Bird is meant an Eagle, which for seven days together shall be observed upon some Eastern City, and shall be taken for a presage, that the Eastern Wall of that City shall fall by Lightning, at which time the enemies shall be at the Gate for seven days together.

LXXXII.

French.

Au conclud pache hors de la Forteresse, Ne sortira celuy en desespoir mis: Quand ceux d'Arbois, de Langres, contre Bresse, Auront mis Dolle bouscade d'ennemis. English.

Upon the agreement made, out of the Fort, Shall not come he that was in despair, When those of *Arbois*, of *Langres*, against *Bresse*, Shall have put in *Dolle* an Ambuscado of foes.

ANNOT.

The sense is, that according to the Articles or agreement made between the Besieger of a

Fort, and the Governour of it, the said Governour by despair will not come out, and this shall happen, when those of *Arbois* and *Langres*, shall be against those of *Bressia*, and shall have put an Ambuscado in the City of *Dolle*.

LXXXIII.

French.

Ceux qui auront entreprins subvertir, Nompareil Regne, puissant & invincible, Feront par fraude, nuicts trois advertir, Quand le plus grand a Table lira Bible. English.

Those that shall have undertaken to subvert The Kingdom that hath no equal in power and victories, Shall cause by fraud, notice to be given for three nights together, When the greatest shall be reading a Bible at the Table.

ANNOT.

What place is meant by the unparalell'd Kingdom, the Author hath hid as well from me as the Reader.

LXXXIV.

French.

Naistre du Gouphre & Cité immesurée, Nay de parens obscurs & tenebreux: Qui la puissance du grand Roy reverée, Voudra destruire par Rouen & Eureux. English.

One shall be born out of the Gulf and the unmeasurable City, Born of Parents obscure and dark, Who by the means of *Rouen* and *Eureux*, Will go about to destroy the power of the great King.

ANNOT.

Without doubt by this Gulf and unmeasured City the Author means *Paris*, by reason of its greatness, and the multitude of its Inhabitants.

LXXXV.

French.

Par les Sueves & lieux circonvoisins, Seront en guerre pour cause des nuées: Gammares, locustes & cousins, Du Leman fautes seront bien desnuées. English.

Through *Swedeland* and the Neighbouring places, By reason of the Clouds shall fall to War, The Lobstars, Grass-hoppers and Gnats, The faults of *Leman* shall appear very naked.

ANNOT.

By *Leman* is meant the City of *Geneva*, the rest needeth no further interpretation.

LXXXVI.

Par les deux testes, & trois bras separez, La grand Cité sera par eaux vexée; Des Grands d'entre eux par esgarez, Par teste Perse Byzance fort pressée. **English.**

Divided in two heads and parted into three arms, The great City shall be troubled with Waters, Some great ones among them scattered by banishment, By a *Persian* head *Byzance* shall be sore oppressed.

ANNOT.

This Prophecy containeth three things, the first is an Inundation by which *Paris* is threatened, for without doubt he meaneth here that City, at the head of which the River *Seine* is divided in two heads, and makes an Island where the Cathedral Church and the Palace are situated, and then parted into three branches, one of which runneth by the Church of the *Augustines*, the other by the *Quay* of *la Megisserie*, and the third passeth under the great Hospital; this City then is threatned here of an Inundation, to which it is very subject, by reason of the lowness of her situation, and the confluence of several Rivers that meet at the head of it. The second part of the Prophecy hinteth that at that time, some great ones of that City shall be banished; and the third, that *Constantinople*, which was anciently called *Byzantium*; or rather the great Turk by a figure of Rhetorick, called *Synecdoche*, shall be much oppressed by the *Persians*.

LXXXVII.

French.

L'An que Saturne hors de servage, Au franc terroir sera d'eau inondé, De sang Troien sera son mariage, Et sera seur d'Espagnols circondé. **English.**

In the year that *Saturn* out of slavery, In the free Countrey shall be drowned by water, With *Troian* blood his marriage shall be, And for certain he shall be hedged about with *Spaniards*.

ANNOT.

By *Troian* blood is understood the *French* Nation, the meaning therefore is, that in the year that a great Inundation shall be in *France*, then shall a notable marriage be made, by which the *French* shall be hedged about, or fenced by *Spaniards*.

LXXXVIII.

French.

Sur le Sablon par un hideux Deluge, Des autres Mers trouvé Monstre Marin, Proche de lieu sera fait un refuge, Tenant Savone esclave de Turin. **English.**

Upon the sand through an hideous Deluge Of other Seas, shall be found a Sea Monster, Near to that place shall be made a Sanctuary, Which shall make *Savone* a slave to *Turin*.

ANNOT.

When by the overflowing of the Neighbouring Seas, a Sea Monster shall be cast upon the Sand, near to that Place shall be built a Fort, that shall make *Savona* a slave to *Turin*.

Savona is a Town by the Sea side, belonging to the *Genoese*, *Turin* is the chief City of *Piemont*, belonging to the Duke of *Savoy*.

LXXXIX.

French.

Dedans Hongrie par Boheme, Navarre, Et par Banieres feintes seditious, Par fleurs de Lis paix portant la barre, Contre Orleans fera esmotions. English.

In *Hungaria*, through *Bohemia* and *Navarre*, And by banners fained seditions, Through flower de Luce the Countrey that wears the Bar, Against *Orleans* shall make commotions.

ANNOT.

This Stanza is divided into two parts; the two first Verses foretell the troubles that were to happen in *Hungaria*, *Bohemia*, and *Navarre* for Religion sake. The two last ones were fulfilled, when the Prince of *Condé*, who in his Arms wears the flower de Luce with the Bar, did seize upon *Orleans* for the Protestant party.

XC.

French.

Dans les Cyclades, en Corinthe, & Larisse, Dedans Sparte tout le Peloponese, Si grand famine peste far faux conisse, Neuf mois tiendra & tout le Cherronesse. English.

In the *Cyclades*, in *Corinthe*, and *Larisse*, In *Sparta*, and all *Peloponesus*, There shall be so great a famine and plague by false arts, That shall last nine months in *Chersonesus*.

ANNOT.

Cyclades are the Islands in the *Ægean* Sea; *Corinth*, *Larissa*, *Sparta*, *Peloponesus*, and *Chersonesus*, are Countreys of *Grecia*.

XCI.

French.

Au grand marché qu'on dit des mensongers, De tout Torrent & Champ Athenien, Seront surpris par les Chevaux legers, Des Albanois, Mars, Leo, Sat. au Versien. English.

In the great Market called of the Liars, Which is all *Torrent* and *Athenian* Field, They shall be surprised by the light Horse, Of the *Albanese*, *Mars* in *Leo*, *Saturn* in *Aquarius*.

ANNOT.

   When *Mars* shall be in the sign of *Leo*, and *Saturn* in that of *Aquarius*, then the Countrey of *Athens* shall be over-run by light Horsemen of *Albania*.

XCII.

French.

Apres le siege tenu dixsept ans Cinq changeront en tel revolu terme, Puis sera l'un esleu de mesme temps, Qui des Romains ne sera trop conforme. English.

After the seat possessed seventeen years, Five shall change in such a space of time; After that, one shall be elected at the same time, Who shall not be very conformable to the *Romans*.

ANNOT.

   The meaning is, that when a Pope shall have sat in the Chair, for the space of 17 years, within the same space of 17 years, five others shall be elected; and after them another, that shall not be well approved of by the *Roman* Clergy, and Nobility. If my memory doth not fail me, this is come to pass already; but wanting the Popes Chronology, I could not make it good.

XCIII.

French.

Soubs le terroir du rond Globe Lunaire, Lors que sera dominateur Mercure, L'Isle d'Escosse fera un Lumenaire, Que les Anglois mettra a desconfiture. English.

Under the Territory of the round Lunary Globe, When *Mercury* shall be Lord of the ascendant; The Island of *Scotland* shall make a Luminary, That shall put the *English* to an overthrow.

ANNOT.

   This Prophecie must of necessity be past; for since the union of both Kingdom under one King, such a thing hath not happened, nor is it likely it should be hereafter.

XCIV.

French.

Translatera en la grand Germanie, Brabant & Flanders, Gand, Bruges & Bologne, La trefue fainte le grand Duc d'Armenie, Assailera Vienne & la Coloigne. English.

He shall translate into the great *Germany*, *Brabant*, *Flanders*, *Gand*, *Bruges*, and *Bullen*, The truce fained, the great Duke of *Armenia*, Shall assault *Vienna* and *Colen*.

It is concerning an Emperour that shall add all those Countreys to the Empire of *Germany.*

XCV.

French.

Nautique rame invitera les umbres, Du grand Empire lors viendra conciter, La mer Ægee des lignes des Encombres, Empeschant londe Tirrhene de fletter. English.

The Sea Oare shall invite the shades, Of the great Empire, then shall it come to stir, The *Ægean* Sea, with lines of Encumbers, Hindering the *Tirrhene* Sea to roll.

ANNOT.

This is either Mistical or Metaphorical, or I understand it not.

XCVI.

French.

Sur le milieu du grand monde la Rose, Pour nouveaux faits sang public espandu, A dire uray on aura bouche close, Lors au besoing viendra tard lattendu. English.

The Rose shall be in the middle of the great world, Blood shall be publickly spilt for new deeds; To say the truth, every one shall stop his mouth, Then at the time of need shall come long looked for.

ANNOT.

The words are plain, out of which every one may make what construction he pleaseth.

XCVII.

French.

Le na difforme par horreur suffoqué, Dans la Cité du grand Roy habitable, L'edit severy des captifs revoqué, Gresle & Tonnerre, Condon inestimable. English.

The deformed born shall through horror be suffocated, In the habitable City of the great King, The severe Proclamation against banished shall be recalled, Hail and Thunder shall do inestimable harm at *Condon.*

ANNOT.

Condon is a Town in *France*; the rest is plain.

XCVIII.

French.

A quarante huit degré Climacterique, A fin de Cancer si grande secheresse, Poisson en Mer, Fleuve, Lac cuit hectique, Bearn, Bigorre, par feu Ciel en detresse. **English.**

At the Climacterical degree of eight and fourty, At the end of *Cancer*, shall be such a drought, That Fish in the Sea, River, and Lake shall be boiled to a consumption, *Bearn* and *Bigorre* by Heavenly fire shall be in distress.

ANNOT.

Bearn and *Bigorre* are two Provinces of *France*; the rest is plain.

XCIX.

French.

Milan, Ferrare, Turin & Aquilee, Capne, Brundis vexez par gent Celtique, Par le Lion & Phalange Aquilee, Quand Rome aura le chef vieux Britannique. **English.**

Milan, *Ferrara*, *Turin*, and *Aquileia*, *Capne*, *Brundis*, shall be vexed by the *French*, By the Lion and troop of *Aquileia*, When *Rome* shall have an old *Brittanick* Head.

ANNOT.

The Cities here mentioned are all in *Italy*.

C.

French.

Le boutefeu par son feu attrapé, Du feu du Ciel a Tartas & Comminge, Foix, Aux, Mazere, haut vieillard escapé, Par ceux de Hess, de Saxe & de Turinge. **English.**

The incendiary shall be overtaken by his own fire, Heavenly fire shall fall at *Tartas* and *Cominge*, *Foix*, *Auch*, *Mazerre*, a tall old man shall escape, By the means of those of *Hessia*, *Saxony*, and *Turinge*.

ANNOT.

Tartas, *Cominge*, *Foix*, *Auch*, *Mazere* are Towns in *France*. *Hessia*, *Saxony*, and *Turinge* are Provinces of *Germany*.

Michael Nostradamus.

CENTURY VI.

I.

French.

Autour des Monts Pyrenees grand amas, De gent estrange secourir Roy nouveau, Pres de Garonne du grand Temple du Mas, Un Romain Chef le craindra dedans l'Eau. English.

About the *Pyrenean* Mountains there shall be a great gathering Of strange Nations to succour a new King; Near *Garonne* and the great Temple of *Mas*, A *Roman* Captain shall fear him in the Water.

ANNOT.

The *Pyrenean* Mountains are those that part *Spain* from *France*; *Garonne* is the River that runneth at *Bourdeaux*, it seemeth then, that upon that River a *Roman* Captain shall stand in much fear of the new King before mentioned.

II.

French.

En la cinq cens octante plus & moins, On attendra le siecle bien estrange, En l'an sept cens & trois (cieux en tesmoins), Regnes plusieurs un a cinq feront change. English.

In the year five hundred fourscore more or less, There shall be a strange Age, In the year seven hundred and three (witness Heaven), Many Kingdoms, one to five shall be changed.

ANNOT.

What strange age it was in the year 1580. every one may satisfie himself by History. As for the year 1703. our Author saith there will be great wonders, chiefly there shall many changes be in Kingdoms, insomuch, that one shall be divided into five.

III.

Fleuve qu'esproune le nouveau nay Celtique, Sera en grande de l'Empire discorde: Le jeune Prince par gent Ecclesiastique, Le Sceptre osté Corone de concorde. **English.**

The River that makes tryal of the new born *Celtick,* Shall be at great variance with the Empire, The young Prince shall be an Ecclesiastical person, And have his Scepter taken off, and the Crown of concord.

ANNOT.

This River is the River of *Rhyne,* because the ancient *French* when they had a King newly born, they used to put him upon a Target, to make him swim upon that River, to try whether by his swimming he was lawfully begotten or no; the meaning therefore is, that this new born *Celtique* or *French* King shall be at variance with the Empire, and that in his young years the Clergy shall take his Scepter and Crown from him.

IV.

French.

Fleuve Celtique changera de Rivage, Plus ne tiendra la Cité d'Agripine, Tout transmué horsmis le viel Language, Saturn, Leo, Mars, Cancer en rapine. **English.**

The River of the Low-Countreys shall change her Shoare, It shall touch no more the City of *Agrippina,* All shall be transformed, except the old Language, *Saturn, Leo, Mars, Cancer* in *Rapine.*

ANNOT.

This is a strange prediction, if it should prove true, that the *Rhine* should change its course, and should touch no more the City of *Colen,* which is here called *Agrippina;* because its name in Latine is *Colonia Agrippina,* being a Colony of the *Romans,* built by *M. Agrippa,* son in Law to *Augustus;* others say by *Agrippina,* Mother to the Emperour *Nero.*

The last Verse signifieth no more than an unfortunate position and Aspect of the two Planets, *Saturn* and *Mars,* and of the two Signs, *Leo* and *Cancer.*

V.

French.

Si grand famine par une pestifere, Par pluye longue le long du Pole Artique. Samarobryn cent lieux de l'Hemisphere, Vivront sans loy exempt de politique. **English.**

So great a famine with a plague, Through a long Rain shall come along the *Artick* Pole, *Samarobryn* a hundred Leagues from the Hemisphere, Shall live without Law, exempt from pollicy.

The two last Verses foretel a great Plague and Famine that shall come from the North, by the means of the long Rain.

Samarobryn he calls a people, that shall be a hundred Leagues from our Hemisphere, and shall live without Law and Policy.

VI.

French.

Apparoistra vers le septentrion, Non loing de Cancer l'estoille cheveluë, Suze, Sienne, Boëce, Eretrion, Mourra de Rome grand, la nuict disperuë. English.

Towards the North shall appear, Not far from *Cancer* a blazing Star, *Suza, Sienna, Boëce, Eretrion*, There shall die at *Rome* a great man, the night being past.

ANNOT.

Here he foretelleth the apparition of a Commet that shall be vertical to the Cities here named, and not far from the Sign of *Cancer*, at which time a great person shall die at *Rome*, about the dawning of the day.

VII.

French.

Norvege & Dace, & l'Isle Britannique, Par les unes freres seront vexées, Le chef Romain issu du sang Gallique, Et les copies aux forests repousées. English.

Norvegia, and *Dacia*, and the *Brittish* Island, Shall be vexed by the Brothers united. The *Roman* Captain issued from *French* blood, His Forces shall be beaten back to the Forrest.

ANNOT.

The difficulty lyes in the word *Brothers*, which I suppose to be the United Provinces. The rest is plain.

VIII.

French.

Ceux qui estoient en regne pour scavoir, Au Royal change deviendront a pauvris, Uns exilez sans appuy, Or navoir, Lettréz & lettres ne seront a grand pris. English.

Those that were in esteem for their learning, Upon the change of a King shall become poor, Some banished, without help, having no Gold, Learned and learning shall not be much valued.

This Prophecie is clear enough, and here the Author hath said nothing, but what doth commonly happen.

IX.

French.

Aux Temples Saints seront faits grands scandales, Comptez seront peur honneurs & louanges, D'un que l'on grave d'Argent, d'Or les Medals, La fin sera en tourmens bien estranges. **English.**

To the holy Temples shall be done great scandals, That shall be accounted for honours and praises, By one, whose medals are graven in Gold and Silver, The end of it shall be in very strange torments.

ANNOT.

Here the Reader must understand that the Author was a *Roman* Catholick, and therefore calleth Holy Temples, the Churches of the *Romish* Religion, which in the beginning of the Civil Wars in *France*, were much abased by those of the Protestant Religion, then called *Huguenots*, whose chief was *Henry* King of *Navarre*, who was the only man amongst the Protestant party, that could have Money and Medals coined to his stamp, as being King of *Navarre*. But the last Verse of this Prophecie proved too true, when upon St. *Bartholomews* day, the 24 of *August*, in the year 1572. the general Massacre of the Protestants was made through *France*.

X.

French.

Un peu du temps les Temples des Couleurs, De blanc & noir des deux entremislée, Rouges & jaunes leur embleront les leurs, Sang, terre, peste, faim, feu, eau affollée. **English.**

Within a little while the Temples of the Colours, White and Black shall be intermixt, Red and Yellow shall take away their Colours, Blood, earth, plague, famine, fire, water shall destroy them.

ANNOT.

By the Temples of the Colours White and Black, I suppose he means that of Peace, and of War; by the Red and Yellow, may be meant the Empire of the *Sweads*, who shall be at variance together; and by their long War shall bring the Plagues here mentioned, as it came to pass in the Wars of *Germany*, between the Emperour and *Gustavus Adolphus*, King of the *Sweads*.

XI.

Les sept rameaux a trois seront reduits, Les plus aisnez seront surprins par morts, Fratricider les deux seront seduits, Les Conjures en dormant seront morts. English.

The seven branches shall be reduced to three, The eldest shall be surprised by death, Two shall be said to kill their Brothers, The Conspirators shall be killed, being asleep.

ANNOT.

It is apparent, that he speaks of seven Brethren, that shall be reduced to three, whereof the eldest son shall be surprised by death, and two of the rest shall be said to have murdered their Brother, the Conspirators shall afterwards be killed in their sleep.

XII.

French.

Dresser Copie pour monter a l'Empire, Du Vatican le sang Royal tiendra, Flamens, Anglois, Espagne aspire, Contre l'Italie & France contendra. English.

To raise an Army, for to ascend unto the Empire, Of the *Vatican*, the Royal blood shall endeavour, *Flemings*, *English*, *Spain* shall aspire, And shall contend against *Italy* and *France*.

ANNOT.

This prediction signifies no more, but that there shall be a great commotion among the Nations, of *Europe*, concerning the election of a Pope, which is called here the Empire of the *Vatican*; because the *Vatican* is the Popes Palace in *Rome*.

XIII.

French.

Un dubieux ne viendra loing du regne, La plus grand part le voudra soustenir, Un Capitole ne voudra point quil regne, Sa grande Chaire ne pourra maintenir. English.

A doubtful man shall not come far from the Reign, The greatest part will uphold him, A Capitol will not consent that he should Reign, His great Chair he shall not be able to maintain.

ANNOT.

What should that doubtful man be, whom our Author doth mention here, is not easie to be understood; but it seemeth that it shall be some body pretending to the Popedom, who shall have a great party for himself, and yet for all that shall be excluded, and not able to keep his Seat; so that this Prophecie is but the second part of the foregoing; for they have both a relation together. The Capitol anciently was the Citadel of *Rome*, and now is the place where the Courts of Judicature meet, called *Campidoglio*.

XIV.

French.

Loing de sa Terre Roy perdra la Bataille, Prompt, eschapé poursuivy, suivant pris, Ignare pris soubs la dorée maille, Soubs feint habit, & l'Ennemy surpris. **English.**

Far from his Countrey the King shall loose a Battle, Nimble, escaped, followed, following, taken, Ignorantly taken under the gilded Coat of Mail, Under a feigned habit the enemy taken.

ANNOT.

This Prophecy was fulfilled in the year 1578. when *Don Sebastian* King of *Portugal*, went into *Affrica*, to help and succour *Muley Hamet*, against *Muley Maluc*, that had expelled him out of the Kingdom of *Fez* and *Morocco*, and there fought that famous Battle of *Alcasserquibir*, wherein his whole Army was routed, and himself slain by the *Moores*, and his body afterwards sold to the King of *Spain* for a 100000. Crowns.

XV.

French.

Dessous la Tombe sera trouvé le Prince, Qu'aura le pris par dessus Nuremberg: L'Espagnol Roy en Capricorne mince, Feinct & trahy par le grand Vutitemberg. **English.**

Under the Tomb shall be found the Prince, That shall have a price above *Nuremberg*, That *Spanish* King in *Capricorn* shall be thine, Deceived and betrayed by the great *Vutitemberg*.

ANNOT.

We hear of no Prince that had that advantage upon *Nuremberg*, but only *Gustavus Adolphus* King of *Sweden*, who took it. The last two Verses signifie no more, then that the King of *Spain* shall be wasted at the time when the Sun is in *Capricorn*.

XVI.

French.

Ce que ravy sera du jeune Milve, Par les Normans de France & Picardy, Les noirs du Temple du lieu de Negrisilve, Feront aux Berge & feu de Lombardie. **English.**

That which shall be taken from the young Kite, By the *Normans* of *France* and *Picardie*, The black ones of the Temple of the place called black Forrest. Shall make a Rendezvouz, and a fire in *Lombardie*.

The meaning is, that what the *Normans* and those of *Picardie* shall save from the hand of a young conquering Prince, the same shall be imployed in building a Temple in the black Forrest, which is that part of the Forrest of *Arden*, that lies near *Bohemia*, and another part of it to build a House in *Lombardie*.

XVII.

French.

Apres les livres bruslez les Asiniers, Contraints seront changer d'habits divers: Les Saturnins bruslez par les meusniers, Hors la pluspart qui ne sera convers. **English.**

After the Books shall be burnt, the Asses, Shall be compelled several times to change their Cloaths, The *Saturnins* shall be burnt by the Millers, Except the greater part, that shall not be discovered.

ANNOT.

This seems to foretell a persecution of ignorant men against the learned, after which shall happen a confusion amongst the ignorant persons, who shall be forced to disguise themselves.

The last two Verses seem to be of the same sense, for by the *Saturnins* I understand studious people, and by the *Millers* rude and unlearned persons.

XVIII.

French.

Par les Physiques le grand Roy delaissé, Par sort non art de l'Ebrieu est en vie, Luy & son Genre au Regne hault pousé, Grace donnée a gent qui Christ envie. **English.**

The great King being forsaken by Physicians, Shall be kept alive by the Magick and not by the art of a Jew, He, and his kindred shall be set at the top of the Kingdom, Grace shall be given to a Nation that envieth Christ.

ANNOT.

This in plain words signifieth no more, but that a King shall be desparately sick and forsaken by his *Physicians*, and shall recover by the help of a Jew, for which fact those of that Nation shall be reestablished in his Countrey.

XIX.

French.

La vraye flamme engloutira la Dame, Que voudra mettre les Innocens a feu, Pres de l'aussaut l'exercite s'enflamme, Quand dans Seville monstre en Bœuf sera veu. English.

The true flame shall swallow up the Lady, That went about to burn the guiltless, Before the Assault the Army shall be incouraged, When in *Seville*, a Monster like an Ox shall be seen.

ANNOT.

Seville is the chiefest City of *Andalusia* a Province in *Spain*; the rest is plain.

XXI.

French.

L'Union feinte sera peu de durée, Les uns changes reformez la plus part: Dans les Vaisseaux sera gent endurée, Lors aura Rome un nouveau Leopart. English.

The feigned union shall not last long, Some shall be changed, others for the most part reformed, In the Ships people shall be pen'd up, Then shall *Rome* have a new Leopard.

ANNOT.

When the things contained in the three first Verses shall come to pass, then *Rome* shall have a new Pope, expressed here by the word Leopard from the variousness, that is, in his Pontifical Garments.

XXI.

French.

Quand ceux du Pole Artique unis ensemble, En Orient grand effrayeur & crainte, Esleu nouveau soustenu le grand tremble, Rodes, Bisance de sang Barbare taincte. English.

When those of the *Artick* Pole shall be united together, There shall be in the East a great fear and trembling, One shall be newly Elected, that shall bear the brunt, *Rodes*, *Bisance*, shall be dy'd with *Barbarian* blood.

ANNOT.

This foretelleth an union between the *Europeans*, or Nations of the North against the Eastern people, or Turks, and that the Christians shall make choice of such a General, that shall make the East quake, and get such Victories, whereby *Rhodes* and *Constantinople* shall be dyed with Turkish blood.

XXII.

French.

Dedans la Terre du grand Temple Celique, Neveu a Londres par paix feinte meurtry, La Barque alors deviendra Schismatique, Liberté feinte sera au corne & cry. English.

Within the ground of the great Cœlestial Temple, A Nephew at *London* by a fained peace shall be murdered, The Boat at that time shall become Schismatical, A fained liberty shall be with *Hue and Cry.*

ANNOT.

       I think that by the *great Cœlestial Temple*, he meaneth that of St. *Paul*, in which, or in the ground about it, shall be murdered a Nephew by his Uncle, which shall cause great divisions and dissensions in the City, compared here to a Boat, and that a dissembled or fained liberty shall be proclaimed.

XXIII.

French.

Despit de Roy, numismes descriez, Peuples seront esmeus contre leur Roy, Paix fait nouveau, Saintes Loix empirées, Rapis onc fut en si piteux arroy. English.

The despight of a King, and Coin being brought lower People shall rise against their King, Peace newly made, Holy Laws being made worse, *Rapis* was never in such a great disorder.

ANNOT.

       The first thing here to be observed, is the word *Rapis*, which is the *Anagramme* of *Paris*, which he saith was never in such a trouble before, as it shall be when the people shall rebel against the King for hatred, and because he shall have put low the price and intrinsical value of Coin and Money; he foretelleth also that there shall be a new Peace made, and that the Holy Laws shall be much impaired.

XXIV.

French.

Mars & le Sceptre se trouvera conjoint, Dessoubs Cancer calamiteuse guerre, Un peu apres sera nouveau Roy oingt. Qui par long temps pacifiera la Terre. English.

Mars and the Scepter, being conjoyned together, Under *Cancer* shall be a calamitous War, A little while after a new King shall be anointed, Who for a long time shall pacifie the Earth.

The meaning of this is, that when the Planet of *Mars* shall be in conjunction with the constellation he calleth here the *Scepter*, that then shall be a very calamitous War. The two last Verses are plain enough of themselves.

XXV.

French.

Par Mars contraire sera la Monarchie, Du grand Pescheur en trouble ruineux, Jeune, noir, rouge prendra la Hierarchie, Les proditeurs iront jour bruineux. English.

By *Mars* contrary shall the Monarchy Of the great Fisherman, be brought into ruinous trouble, A young, black, red shall possess himself of the Hierarchy, The Traitors shall undertake it on a misty day.

ANNOT.

This Prophecie is concerning a certain Pope, signified here by the word of great *Fisherman*; because in his Seal is graven a Fisherman, and therefore in all his Bulls and Expeditions, it is always written, *Datum Romæ sub sigillo piscatoris*: this Pope then it seemeth, shall be brought to ruine, and another it seemeth shall succeed him, having here three Epithetes, *viz. Young, Black*, and *Red*, which signifieth, that against the common election of Popes, he shall be elected young, and shall be Black in his complexion, and Red in Cloaths, *viz.* a Cardinal. *Hierarchy* is a Greek word, signifying Dominion over the Church. The last Verse needeth no explication, being plain enough of it self.

XXVI.

French.

Quattre ans le siege quelque peu bien tiendra, Un surviendra libidineux de vie, Ravenna, & Pise, Verone soustiendront, Pour eslever la Croix de Pape envie. English.

Four years he shall keep the Papal seat pretty well, Then shall succeed one of a libidinous life, *Ravenna, Pisa*, shall take *Verona*'s part, To raise up the Popes Cross to Life.

ANNOT.

This Prediction seemeth to have not only a relation to the foregoing, but also a connexion; for the Author still handleth the matter of the Popedome, and saith, that after that Pope shall have Reigned four years, there shall succeed one that shall be notorious for debauchedness and lechery, and that those Towns he mentioneth here (which are all in *Italy*) shall take the Popes part.

XXVII.

Dedans les Isles de cinq fleuves a un, Par le croissant du grand Chyren Selin, Par les bruynes de l'air fureur de l'un, Six eschapez, chachez fardeaux de lin. English.

In the Islands from five Rivers to one, By the increase of great *Chyren Selin*, By the Frost of the Air one shall under furious, Six shall escape, hidden within bundles of Flax.

ANNOT.

     Chyren by transposition is taken for *Henry*, and *Selin* for a King called so; because it is the name of a *Turkish* Emperour: So that by this Stanza I suppose he means *Henry* II. his Master, King of *France*. The rest is plain.

XXVIII.

French.

Le grand Celtique entrera dedans Rome, Menant amas d'exilez & bannis, Le grand Pasteur mettra a mort tout homme, Qui pour le Coq estoient aux Alpes unis. English.

The great *Celtique* shall enter into *Rome*, Leading with him a great number of banished men, The great Shepheard shall put to death every man, That was united for the Cock near the *Alpes*.

ANNOT.

     Because this word *Celtique* is often repeated in this Book, it would not be amiss to satisfie the Reader of the meaning of it; it is properly the Nation of the *Flemings*, and some others of the Low-Countreys as far as the *Mase* and the *Rhyne*, which anciently were called *Galli Celtæ*. By *the great Shepheard*, is meant the Pope, and by the *Cock* is meant the *French* Nation. The rest is easie.

XXIX.

French.

La Veufve Sainte entendant les nouvelles, De ses rameaux mis en perplex & trouble, Qui sera duit appaiser les querelles, Par son pourchas des Razes sera comble. English.

The holy Widow hearing the News Of her Branches put in perplexity or trouble, That shall be skilfull in appeasing of quarrels, By his purchase shall make a heap of shaven heads.

ANNOT.

     By the *holy Widow*, is meant the City of *Rome*, which is called in *Italian*, *Roma la santa*, because of the blood of so many Martyrs that hath been shed there, for the maintenance of the Christian Religion, he calleth it a *Widow*; because at that time there will be no Pope elected, and

there shall be a kind of *interregnum*, as it always happens when a Pope is dead, until the new one be elected. What he calleth here Branches, are the Clergy men, and the shaven heads the Priests.
XXX.

French.

Par l'apparence de feinte Saincteté, Sera trahy aux ennemis le siege, Nuit qu'on croioid dormir en seureté, Pres de Brabant marcheront ceux de Liege. English.

 By the appearance of a feigned holiness, The siege shall be betrayed to the enemies, In a night that every one thought to be secure, Near *Brabant* shall march those of *Liege*.

ANNOT.

Brabant is one of the seventeen Provinces, and *Liege* is a great City upon the River of *Maze*. The rest is not difficult.
XXXI.

French.

Roy trouvera ce quil desiroit tant, Quand le Prelat sera repris a tort, Response au Duc le rendra mal content, Qui dans Milan mettra plusieurs a mort. English.

A King shall find what he so much longed for, When a Prelate shall be censured wrongfully, An answer to the Duke will make him discontented, Who in *Milan* shall put many to death.

ANNOT.

This Prophecie is too indefinite, to admit of a particular sense; for there be so many Prelates, so many Kings, so many Dukes, that it is not easie to fix upon any particular one, and therefore we must leave this Stanza in *Democritus*'s Well.

XXXII.

French.

Par trahison de verges a mort battu, Puis surmonté sera par son desordre, Conseil frivole au grand captif sentu, Nez par fureur quand Berich viendra mordre. English.

 By Treason one shall be beaten with rods to death, Then the Traitor shall be overcome by his disorder, The great Prisoner shall try a frivilous Counsel, When *Berich* shall bite anothers nose through anger.

ANNOT.

The words are so plain, that every one may make his own interpretation of them.

XXXIII.

French.

Sa main derniere par Alus sanguinaire, Ne le pourra par la Mer garentir, Entre deux fleuves craindra main militaire, Le noir l'Ireux le fera repentir. **English.**

His last hand bloody through *Alus*, Shall not save him by Sea, Between two Rivers he shall fear the military hand, The black and Cholerick one shall make him repent.

ANNOT.

This seemeth to be concerning a bloody man, that had killed one *Alus*, and sought to save himself by Sea; but was taken between two Rivers, and put to death by the command of one that was a black and Cholerick man.

XXXIV.

French.

De feu volant la machination, Viendra troubler le Chef des Assiegez, Dedans sera telle sedition, Qu'en desespoir seront les profligez. **English.**

The device of flying fire Shall trouble so much the Captain of the Besieged, And within shall be such mutiny, That the Besieged shall be in despair.

ANNOT.

It is a Fort or Town besieged by an Enemy, who shall torment the besieged so much with Bombs and Granadoes, and other flying fire, that they shall despair to escape.

XXXV.

French.

Pres de Rion & proche Blanchelaine, Aries, Taurus, Cancer, Leo, La Vierge, Mars, Jupiter, le Sol ardra grand plaine, Bois & Citez, Lettres cachez au Cierge. **English.**

Near *Rion* going to *Blanchelaine, Aries, Taurus, Cancer, Leo, Virgo, Mars, Jupiter, Sol* shall burn a great Plain, Woods and Cities, Letters hidden in a wax Candle.

ANNOT.

The meaning of it is, that when by the virtues and meetings of the said Constellations, a great plain shall be burnt by *Rion* (which is a City in *Auvergne*) that then Letters shall be found hidden in a wax Candle.

XXXVI.

French.

Ne bien ne mal par bataille terrestre, Ne parviendra au confins de perouse, Rebeller pise, Florence voir mal estre, Roy nuit blessé sur mulet a noire house. **English.**

Neither good nor evil by a Land-fight, Shall reach to the Borders of *Perusa*, *Pisa* shall rebel, *Florence* shall be in an ill case, A King being upon his Mule shall be wounded in the night time.

ANNOT.

   Perusa, *Pisa*, and *Florence* are Cities in Italy; the rest is plain.

XXXVII.

French.

L'œuvre ancienne se parachevera, Du toit cherra sur le grand mal ruine, Innocent fait, mort on accusera, Nocent caché taillis a bruine. **English.**

The ancient work shall be finished, From the tiling shall fall upon the great one an evil ruine, The innocent declared to be so, shall be accused after his death, The guilty shall be hidden in a wood in a misty weather.

ANNOT.

By the first Verse is understood an ancient building, which shall be finished and brought to perfection, I suppose it to be the *Louvere*, which hath been a building in the Reign of seven Kings. But before it be throughly finished, some ruine shall fall upon a great man and kill him; one declared innocent of the fact shall be accused of it after his death, and he that shall be guilty of it shall escape by hiding himself in a Wood in misty weather.

XXXVIII.

French.

Aux profligez de Paix les ennemis, Apres avoir l'Italie superée, Noir sanguinaire, rouge sera commis, Feu, sang verser, eau de sang colorée. **English.**

To the vanquished the enemies of peace, After they shall have overcome *Italy*, A bloody black one shall be committed, Fire and blood shall be powerd, and water coloured with blood.

ANNOT.

A bloody black man shall be put into the hands of the vanquished, by those that were enemies to peace, after they have conquered *Italy*, whence shall proceed fire and blood, and water coloured with blood.

XXXIX.

French.

L'Enfant du Regne par Paternelle prinse, Expolier sera pour delivrer, Aupres du Lac Trasym en la Tour prinse, La troupe hostage pour trop fort s'enyvrer. **English.**

The Child of the Kingdom, through his Fathers imprisonement, Shall be deprived of his Kingdom for the delivering of his father, Near the Lake *Trasymene* shall be taken in a Tower, The troop that was in Hostage, being drunk.

ANNOT.

The Lake *Trasymene* in *Italy*, is that near which *Annibal* got that famous Battle upon the *Romans*. The rest is as plain as the words can bear.

XL.

Grand de Mogonce pour grande soif esteindre, Sera privé de sa grand dignité, Ceux de Cologne si fort le viendront plaindre, Que le grand Groppe au Rhin sera jetté. English.

The great one of *Ments* for to quench a great thirst, Shall be deprived of his high dignity, Those of *Colen* shall bemoan him so much. That the great *Groppe* shall be thrown into the *Rhine.*

ANNOT.

      This foretelleth the fall of an Archbishop of *Ments*, in Latine *Moguntia*, who is the first Ecclesiastical Elector, and shall be deprived of his dignity by a covetous and powerful Prince to satisfie his covetousness, at which those of *Colen* his neighbours shall be so incensed, that they shall throw that covetous person into the *Rhine.*

XLI.

Les second Chef du Regne Dannemark, Par ceux de Frize & l'Isle Britannique, Fera despendre plus de cent mille mark, Vain exploiter voiage en Italique. English.

The second head of the Kingdom of *Dannemark*, By those of *Friezeland*, and the *Brittish* Island, Shall cause to be spent above 100000. Mark, Vainly endeavouring a journey into *Italy.*

ANNOT.

      This signifieth onely a conjunction of the *Dutch*, *Danish*, and *English* Forces, to attempt something in *Italy*, which shall prove fruitless, and cost a great deal of Money.

XLII.

A l'Ogmion sera laissé le Regne, Du grand Selin, qui plus fera de fait, Par l'Italie estendra son enseigne, Regira par prudent contrefait. English.

Unto l'*Ogmion* shall be left the Kingdom, Of great *Selyn*, who shall do more then the rest, Through *Italy* he shall spread his Ensigns, He shall govern by a prudent dissimulation.

ANNOT.

      We have said before, that when ever the Author speaks of *Ognion*, he meaneth the King of *France*, the meaning therefore of this whole Stanza is, that *Henry* the II. Son to *Francis* the I. whom he calls here great *Selin*, shall do more in *Italy* then his Predecessors had done, which proved true, and he governed his Kingdom with a prudent dissimulation.

XLIII.

French.

Long temps sera sans estre habitée, Ou Siene & Marne autour vient arrouser, De la Thamise & Martiaux tentée, Deceus les gardes en evidant repousser. English.

A great while shall be unhabited, Where *Seine*, and *Marne* comes to water about, Being attempted by the *Thames* and Martial people, The Guards deceived in thinking to resist.

ANNOT.

By the two first Verses, he meaneth without doubt the City of *Paris*, for it is watered by those two Rivers the *Seine* and *Marne*, that joyn together at the head of it, but how this City should become unhabited is the great question, and chiefly by the means here alledged, *viz.* of the *English* signified by the *Thames*, and other Martial people, *the Guards deceived in thinking to repulse* the enemy.

XLIV.

French.

De nuict par Nantes l'Iris apparoistra, Des Arcs Marins susciteront la pluye: Arabique Goulfre grand classe parfondra, Un Monstre en Saxe naistre d'Ours & Truye. English.

By night in *Nantes* the Rain-bow shall appear, Sea Rain-bows shall cause Rain; The *Arabian* Gulf shall drownd a great Fleet, A Monster shall be in *Saxony* from a Bear and a Sow.

ANNOT.

Nantes is a City in *France*, *Iris* is the Rainbow, *Saxony* is a Province in *Germany*; the rest is plain.

XLV.

French.

Le Governeur du Regne bien scavent, Ne consentir voulant au faict Royal: Medite classe par le contraire vent, Le remettra a son plus desloyal. English.

The Governour of the Kingdom being learned, Shall not consent to the Kings will: He shall intend to set out a Fleet by a contrary Wind, Which he shall put into the hands of the most disloyal.

ANNOT.

This signifies that the Governour or Vice-Roy of a Kingdom shall refuse to consent to his

Kings Deeds; the rest needeth no interpretation.
XLVI.

French.

Unjuste sera en exil Anvoyé, Par pestilance aux confins de non seggle, Response au rouge le fera desvoye, Roy retirant a la Rane & a l'Aigle. English.

A just person shall be banished, By plague to the Borders of Non seggle, The answer to the red one shall make him deviate, Retiring himself to the Frog and the Eagle.

ANNOT.

I cannot find what he meaneth by *Non-seggle*; by the Eagle he meaneth the Emperour, and by the Frog the King of *France*, for before he took the Flower de Luce, the *French* bore three Frogs.
XLVII.

French.

Entre deux Monts les deux grands Assemblez, De laisseront leur simulte secrete, Bruxelle & Dolle par Langres accablez, Pour a Maline executer leur peste. English.

Between two Mountains the two great ones shall meet, They shall forsake their secret enmity, *Brusselle* and *Dolle* shall be crushed by *Langres*, To put their plague in Execution at *Maline*.

ANNOT.

Brussel is a Town of *Brabant*, and so is *Maline*; *Dolle* is one of *Burgundy*; and *Langres* another of *France*.
XLVIII.

French.

La saincteté trop faincte & seductive, Accompagne d'une langue diserte, La Cité vieille, & Parme trop nastive, Florence & Sienne rendront plus desertes. English.

The fained and seducing holiness, Accompanied with a fluent tongue, Shall cause the old City, and too hasty *Parma*, *Florence* and *Sienna* to be more desert.

ANNOT.

I know not what he means by the old City, unless it be *Rome*, by reason of its antiquity.

XLIX.

French.

De la partie de Mammer grand Pontife, Subjuguera les confins du Danube, Chasser les croix, par fer raffe ne riffe, Captifs, Or, bagues, plus de cent mille Rubles. English.

From the party of *Mammer* high Priest, They shall subdue the borders of *Danubius*, They shall expel crosses, by Sword topse-turvy, Slaves, Gold, Jewels, more than 100000. Rubles.

ANNOT.

     Some parties of the Popes side, shall subdue those bordering upon *Danubius*, and drive away the Priests, turn all things topse-turvy, make slaves, and take a booty above the value of 100000. Rubles. A Ruble is a piece of Gold of the great *Mogul*, worth two or three pound sterling.

L.

French.

Dedans le puis seront trouvez les os, Se l'inceste commis par la Marastre, L'estat changé, en fera bruit des os, Et aura Mars ascendant pour son astre. English.

In the Well shall be found the bones, Incest shall be committed by the Stepmother, The case being altered, there shall be great stir about the bones, And she shall have *Mars* for her ascending Planet.

ANNOT.

     It is the strange wickedness of a woman, that shall incestuously be got with Child by her Son in Law, and when she is delivered, shall kill her Child, and throw him into a Well; a while after the water beginning to corrupt, a search shall be made of the cause, and then the Childs Bones shall be found, which shall cause a great stir, and for to know this wicked woman, he saith, that the Planet of *Mars* shall be the ascendant in her Horoscope.

LI.

French.

Peuple assemble voir nouveau spectacle, Princes & Roys par plusieurs assistans, Piliers faillir, murs, mais comme miracle, Le Roy fauve & trente des instans. English.

People assembled to see a new show, Princes and Kings, with many assistants, Pillars shall fail, walls also, but as a miracle, The King saved, and thirty of the standers by.

ANNOT.

     The words of this prediction are plain and easie, and signifie no more than what often happeneth, and may happen yet, *viz.* that where a concourse of people shall be to see a new show, the Pillars and walls of the Building shall fall, and people perish by the ruine, (as if it were by a Miracle) the King and thirty of the spectators shall be preserved.

LII.

French.

En lieu du grand qui sera condamné, De prison hors, son amy en sa place, L'espoir Troyen en six mois joinct, mort né, Le Sol a l'Vurne seront prins fleuves en glace. English.

Instead of the great one that shall be condemned And put out of Prison, his friend being in his place, The *Trojan* hope in six months joyn, still born, The *Sun* in *Aquarius*, then Rivers shall be frozen.

ANNOT.

By the *Trojan* hope, is meant a King of *France*, who after he hath been marryed six Months, shall have a Child still born.

LIII.

French.

Le grand Prelat Celtique a Roy suspect, De nuict par cours sortira hors du Regne, Par Duc fertile a son grand Roy Bretagne, Bisance a Cypres, & Tunis insuspect. English.

The great *Celtique* Prelate suspected by his King, Shall in hast by night go out of the Kingdom By the means of a Duke the fruitful *Britanie*, *Bisance* by *Cyprus*, and *Tunis* shall be unsuspected.

ANNOT.

The great *Celtique* Prelate, was the Cardinal of *Lorrain*, Brother to the Duke of *Guizse*, who being suspected by the King, went away by night to *Rome*.

By fruitfull *Brittain*, is understood the province of that name in *France*, which by the means of the Duke of *Mercure*, her Governour shall be unsuspected by the King.

LIV.

French.

Au point du jours au second chant du Coq, Ceux de Tunes, de Fez, & de Bugie, Par les Arabes captif le Roy Maroq, L'an mil six cens & sept, de Liturgie. English.

At the break of day, at the second crowing of the Cock, Those of *Tunis*, and *Fez*, and *Bugia*, By means of the *Arabians*, shall take Prisoner the King of *Morocco*, In the year 1607. by Liturgie.

By *Liturgie*, I suppose he meaneth under pretext of Religion. The rest is easie to be understood.

LV.

French.

Au Chelme Duc, en arrachant l'esponce, Voile Arabesque voir, subit descouverte: Tripolis, Chio, & ceux de Trapesonce, Duc prins, Marnegro, & la Cité deserte. English.

The *Chelme* Duke, in pulling a spunge, Shall see *Arabian* Sails suddenly discovered: *Tripolis*, *Chios*, and those of *Trapesan*, The Duke shall be taken, *Marnegro* and the City shall be desert.

ANNOT.

Chelme is a *German* word, that signifies a Rogue. By *Marnegro*, is meant the Black Sea, or *Nigropont*. By pulling a Spunge, I suppose the great quantity of Spunges that stick to the Rocks in that Sea.

Tripolis, *Chios*, and *Trapezon*, are places in the *Turkish* Dominions.

LVI.

French.

La crainte Armée de l'ennemy Narbon, Effroyera si fort les Hesperiques, Parpignan vuide par l'aveugle d'Arbon, Lors Barcelon par Mer donra les piques. English.

The feared Army of the enemy *Narbon*, Shall so much terrifie the *Spaniards*, That *Parpignan* shall be left empty by the blind d'*Arbon*, Then *Barcelon* by Sea shall give the Chase.

ANNOT.

A great Army gathered about *Narbon*, shall so much terrifie the *Spaniards*, that *Parpignan* a Town of theirs shall be desolate, and left empty by the Governour, here called *the blind d'Arbon*, then *Barcelon*, which is a Sea-Town in *Catalonio*, belonging to the *Spaniards* shall come to its succours, and chase the enemy by Sea.

LVII.

French.

Celuy qu'estoit bien avant dans le Regne, Ayant Chef rouge proche a la Hierarchie, Aspre & cruel, & se fera tant craindre, Succedera a sacrée Monarchie. English.

He that was a great way in the Kingdom, Having a red head and near the Hierarchy, Harsh and cruel, shall make himself so dreadful, That he shall succeed to the Sacred Monarchy.

This is a person of great quality, and near of blood to a King, who being a Cardinal, cruel and dreadful, shall be Elected Pope, I suppose *Clement* the VII.

LVIII.

French.

Entre les deux Monarques esloignez, Lors que le Sol par Selin clair perdue: Simulté grande entre deux indignez, Qu'aux Isles & Sienne la liberté renduë. English.

Between the two Monarchs that live far one from the other, When the Sun shall be Ecclipsed by *Selene,* Great enmity shall be between them two, So that liberty shall be restored to the Isles and *Sienne.*

ANNOT.

Here is nothing difficult but the word *Selene,* which is the Moon from the Greek σεληνη.
The meaning is, that at such a time when the Sun is Ecclipsed by the Moon, *Sienna* and the Islands about it shall be at liberty.

LIX.

French.

Dame en fureur par rage d'adultere, Viendra a son Prince conjurer non dire, Mais bref cogneu sera le vitupere, Que seront mis dixsept a Martyre. English.

A Lady in fury by rage of an Adultery, Shall come to her Prince and conjure him to say nothing, But shortly shall the shameful thing be known, So that seventeen shall be put to death.

ANNOT.

The sense of this Stanza and the words are plain.

LX.

French.

Le Prince hors de son Terroir Celtique, Sera trahy, deceu par interprete, Rouen, Rochelle, par ceux de l'Armorique, Au Port de Blavet deceux par Moin & Prestre. English.

That Prince being out of his *Celtick* Countrey, Shall be betrayed and deceived by an Interpreter, *Rouen, Rochel,* by those of *Gascony,* At the Port of *Blavet* shall be deceived by Monk and Priest.

We have said many times before, what is meant by the word *Celtique*. The Port of *Blavet* is that of the River of *Bordeaux*.

LXI.

French.

***Le grand Tapis plié ne monstrera, Fors qu'a demy la pluspart de l'Histoire, Chassé du Regne aspre loin paroistra, Au fait Bellique chacun le viendra croire.* English.**

The great Carpet folded shall not shew, But by half the greatest part of the History, The driven out of the Kingdom shall appear sharp afar off, In Warlike matters every one shall believe him.

ANNOT.

This needeth no interpretation.

LXII.

French.

***Trop tard tous deux les fleurs seront perdües, Contre lay loy Serpent ne voudra faire, Des ligueurs forces par gallops confondues, Savone, Albingue, par Monech grand martyre.* English.**

Both the flowers shall be lost too late, Against the Law the Serpent will do nothing, The forces of the Leaguers by gallops shall be confounded, *Savone, Albingue,* by *Monech* shall suffer great pain.

ANNOT.

The two first verses are too mistical for me; the third signifieth, that by gallops; that is, by Troops of Horses, the Leaguers, *viz.* those that held the party of the League, shall be routed by the Kings Cavalry. The fourth, that *Savone* and *Albingue*, two Towns of the *Genoeses*, shall be put to much trouble by those of *Monech* and *Monaco*, another Town near them, belonging to the Prince of *Monaco*, a *Genoese* of the house of *Grimald*.

LXIII.

French.

***La Dame seule au Regne demurée, L'unique esteint premier au lict d'honneur, Sept ans sera de douleur epleurée, Puis longue vie au regne par bonheur.* English.**

The Lady shall be left to reign alone, The only one being extinguished, first in the Bed of Honour, Seven years she shall weep for grief, After that she shall live long in the Reign by good luck.

ANNOT.

The second and fourth Verses perswade me, that this Stanza came to pass in the time of *Catharine* of *Medicis*, wife to *Henry* II. because she lived long, and the King died in the bed of Honour, and thus he saith, *that she was left to Reign alone*; because her four Sons were all little ones, so that she alone was Regent in *France*.

The second Verse saith, *The holy one being extinguished, first, in the Bed of Honour.*

By this word *the only one*, the Author meaneth not the only Son, but the only one living, such as *Henry* II. was to her, *who was extinguished in the Bed of Honour*, and died of the wound he received at Tilting.

The third Verse saith, that after his death, her mourning lasted seven years, that is, from the first of *August* 1559. to the first of *August* 1566. because that all those 16 Months that *Francis* II. she had nothing but continual sorrow, by the conspiracy of *Amboise*, the secret practises of the King of *Navarre*, and Prince of *Condé* his Brother, by the insurrection of the Protestants, when *Charles* IX. visited his Kingdom, *Anno* 1556. after which she put off her mourning.

The fourth Verse signifieth, that she should be long lived; for she lived above 60 years, He saith also, that she was Regent by great luck, that is, great luck for her self, but not for the Kingdom, for it was most unhappy in her time.

LXIV.

French.

On ne tiendra pache aucun arresté, Tous recevants iront par tromperie, De trefue & paix, Terre & Mer protesté, Par Barcelone classe prins d'industrie. English.

No agreement shall be kept, All those that shall admit of it deal falsly, There shall be protestations made by Land and Sea, *Barcelone* shall take a Fleet by craft.

ANNOT.

This is a description of the sad and calamitous estate of *France*, in the time of the Civil wars, when no agreement could be kept on the *Roman* Catholicks side, witness the several Peaces that were made and broken, the Massacre of *Vassa*, and that infamous perfidy committed by them on St. *Bartholomews* day, being the 24 of *August, Anno* 1572.

LXV.

French.

Gris & bureau demy ouverte guerre, De nuit seront assaillis & pillez, Le bureau prins passera par la serre, Son Temple ouvert, deux au plastre grillez. English.

Between the Gray and sad Gray shall be half open War, By night they shall be assaulted and plundered, The sad Gray being taken, shall be put in Custody, His Temple shall be open, two shall be put in the Grate.

ANNOT.

This Stanza affordeth us a commical History, which is, that about the year 1601. when there sprang up in *France* a Kind of Friers, who bosted themselves to be the true observers of the Rule of St. *Francis*, and that the Cordeliers and Capushines did not keep it so exactly, but they had need of a great reformation; the King *Henry* IV. granted them a Convent at *Beaufort*, and upon his example many other places desired them, they went to possess themselves of the house of *la Blamet*, near *Angiers*; but the Cordeliers being loath to be dispossessed by these new comers, called *Recollets*, did besiege them by main force, broke open the Gates, scaled the Walls, the besieged did not defend themselves by words or exorcismes, but with good Stones and Flints, so that if the people had not come, the fray would not have ended without murder, some of them were put in Prison, others kept in Custody: this is the meaning of the Author, when he saith, *There will be half an open War between the Gray and the sad Gray*; for the Cordeliers have a Gray habit, and the Recollets a sad Gray.

LXVI.

French.

Au fondement de nouvelle secte, Seront les os du grand Romain trouvez, Sepulchre en Marbre, apparoistra converte, Terre trembler en Auril mal enfeüvez. **English.**

At the foundation of a new sect, The Bones of the great *Roman* shall be found, The Sepulchre shall appear covered with Marble, The Earth shall quake in *April*, they shall be ill buried.

ANNOT.

The meaning is, that when they shall go about to make a foundation of a house, for a new Sect of Friers; they shall find the bones of a famous *Roman* in a Marble Sepulchre, and that in *April* the Earth shall quake, whereby many shall be swallowed up.

LXVII.

French.

Au grand Empire par viendra tout un autres, Bonté distant plees de felicité, Rege par un issu non loing du peautre, Corruer Regnes grande infelicité. **English.**

To the great Empire quite another shall come, Being farther from goodness and happiness, Governed by one of base parentage, The Kingdom shall fall, a great unhappiness.

ANNOT.

This needeth no Interpretation.

LXVIII.

French.

Lors que Soldats fureur seditieuse, Contre leur Chef seront denuit fer livre, Ennemy d'Albe doibt par main furieuse, Lors vexer Rome & principaux seduire. English.

When the seditious fury of the Souldiers, Against their Chief shall make the Iron shine by night, The enemy d'*Albe* shall by a furious hand, Then vex *Rome*, and seduce the principal one.

ANNOT.

The Lord *de Thou* doth judiciously observe, that the Pope being unacquainted with things belonging to War, as to Money, Victuals, and Ammunition, was easily persuaded by Cardinal *Caraffa* to make war against *Spain*, for without being provided of all these things, he put his Armies into the Field, *nec satis perpendens quám a pecuniâ, milite ac cæteris rebus ad bellum necessariis imparatus intempestive arma sumeret.*

In the 15. Book of his History: the Duke of *Vrbin* had commission to raise 6000. Foot and 300. Horses in the Dukedom of *Spoleto*, and in *Mark* of *Ancona*. *John Caraffe* the Popes Nephew was made General of the Army, and being but Earl of *Mortor*, was Created Duke of *Palliano*, by the confiscation of the goods of *Mark Antony Colonna*. *Camillo Ursini* was made General of the Forces in *Rome*, and in the Territory thereof; *Blasius* of *Monluc*, the *Mars* of his time, and by birth a *Gascon*, was sent by the King to help (with his advice and courage) the *Romans*, who are always fitter for the Breviary, then for the Sword.

Besides these Forces raised within the Church Dominions, *Charles Caraffa* gathered all the Banditts of *Naples* and *Florence*, and raised some Regiments of *Switzers* that came to succour the Pope.

With these Troops the Pope seized upon the most important places and persons belonging to the *Spanish* party, as the *Coloneses* and the *Vitelly*.

These asked succours of the Emperour *Charles* the V. who presently commanded *Ferdinand* of *Toledo* Duke of *Alba* to succour them. He was then tasked in the *Piemont* and *Milanes*, to resist the *French* that were then under the conduct of the Marshal of *Brissac*.

To conclude his design the better, he wrote many Letters to the Pope and the Colledge of Cardinals, full of respect and submission, desiring them to moderate their passion against the *Spanish* party, but the Pope being angry by several reports, answered him, complaining of many things, which made the Duke resolve to the war, and to be there in person.

He took his occasion as a prudent Captain, when the news was brought to him that the Popes Forces were in mutiny against their General for want of pay, and made a great tumult in the night, hearing that he was approaching with a great train of Artillery. *Bzovius* saith, that the Earl of *Montor* regarded more his profit then the Popes Interest, and kept back a great part of the money that was to pay the Souldiers, whence proceeded this tumult, which helped much the Duke of *Alva*'s business.

This is the explanation of the two first Verses of this Stanza, concerning the mutiny of the Souldiers that were in the Popes service, during which mutiny the enemy d'*Alba* did not fail to vex *Rome*; this word the enemy d'*Alba* doth not signifie the enemy of the Duke of *Alba*, as if one should say in Latine *Hostis Albanus*. He did then vex *Rome*; for in a short time he took *Ponte Corvino, Frusino Anagnia, Marino, Lavaci, Præneste, Tivoli, Ostia, Neptuno, Alba Vico-Varro, Monte Fortino*, and almost all the places of the *Roman* Territory.

This did streighten *Rome* so much, that the General *Camillo Ursini* made several Trenches within the Walls of *Rome*, instead of preserving the outworks, as *Montluc* would have persuaded him to do; the alarums were so great at *Rome*, that *Montluc* was fain to encourage the *Romans*, and to make a Warlike Speech to them, which is inserted in his Works.

Moreover, the same Duke began to seduce the Principals of *Rome* by his friends that he had in it, but particularly by the cheat that he put upon the Pope; for his design being to prevent the *French* Forces, and to surprize the Pope, he resolved to go streight to *Rome*, and to bring his design the better to pass, he sent *Pyrrhus Coffrede* to the Pope, to see if there was any way of agreement, to the end that upon this proposition the Pope should mistrust nothing. In the mean time the Duke of *Alba* was coming near *Rome*, at which the Pope was so angry, that he put this Embassadour in Prison, where he was kept till the conclusion of the Peace; in this sort were the principal men of *Rome* seduced, having no thought of the *Spaniards* approaches, this is the relation of the Lord *de Thou, Lib.* 16.

LXIX.

French.

La grand pitie sera sans long tarder, Ceux qui donnoient seront contraints de prendre Nuds affamez, de froid, soif, soy bander, Passer les Monts en faisant grand esclandre. *English.*

What a great pitty will it be e're-long, Those that did give shall be constrained to receive, Naked, famished with cold, thirst, to mutiny, To go over the Mountains making great disorders.

ANNOT.

The words of the first Verse, *before it be long*, is the Key of the Stanza, because we infer from thence it was shortly to happen, as in truth it did at the latter end of the year 1556. when the Duke of *Guise* came into *Piemont* to joyn with the Marshal of *Brissac*. Then the troops of the *Marshal* seeing those of the Duke better paid then they were, forsook the Marshal, the History saith there was above 1500. of them, and that the Marshal paid the Souldiers of his own money to stay them.

The great pitty was, when he had no more to give, he was compelled by the Kings order it self, and against his own inclination to raise some moneys upon the Countreys. Secondly, to take some Towns and give the plunder to the Souldiers. Thirdly, to permit the Souldiers to pillage the Countrey.

The Author was willing to foretell this, because there was never a man more strict in keeping the Martial discipline, then this General was.

The Marshal of *Brissac* being thus abused, some of his troops forsook him to follow the Duke of *Guise*, being for the most part naked and starved with cold, hunger and thirst, which makes the Author to specifie *hunger, cold and thirst*; want having compelled them to disband, they went over the Mountains, not of *Piemont*, but the *Apennines* of *Montserrat*, and whatsoever thing they found was a Fish for their Net.

LXX.

French.

Un Chef du Monde le grand Cheiren sera, Plus outre, apres aime, craint, redouté, Son bruit & los les Cieux surpassera, Et du seul titre Victeur sort contente. English.

A Chief of the World the great *Cheiren* shall be, Moreover, beloved afterwards, feared, dreaded, His fame and praise shall go beyond the Heavens, And shall be contented with the only title of Victor.

ANNOT.

We have said already before, that the Author by the word *Cheyren* meaneth *Henry* the II. his Master, by transposition of Letters, who as he saith was contented with the bare title of Victorieux, when he had undertaken the protection of the *German* Princes against the Emperour *Charles* the V.

LXXI.

French.

Quand on viendra le grand Roy parenter, Avant quil ait du tout l'Ame rendue, On le verra bien tost apparenter, D'Aigles, Lions, Croix, Courone de Rüe. English.

When they shall come to celebrate the obsequies of the great King, A day before he be quite dead, He shall be seen presently to be allyed With Eagles, Lions, Crosses, Crowns of Rüe.

ANNOT.

In the general Peace made *Anno* 1559. two Marriages were concluded, one of *Elizabeth* of *France*, daughter to *Henry* II. King of *France*, with *Philip* II. King of *Spain*, which was Celebrated at *Paris* with an extraordinary magnificence, in the presence of the Duke of *Alba*, the Prince of *Orenge*, and the Earl of *Egmont*, who came to fetch the Princess.

In the Celebrating of these Nuptials happened the unfortunate death of *Henry* II. This brought such a sadness to the Court, that the second match which was between *Margaret* of *France*, Daughter to *Francis* I. and the Duke of *Savoy* was Celebrated without solemnity.

We must add to this, that the Duke weareth in his Coat of Arms some Eagles, some Lions, some Crosses, and a Crown of Rue; by this, we understand this Stanza, which saith, that the King being mortally wounded, every one was preparing himself to render him the last duties, which the Author calleth to *Parante*, from the Latine word *Parentare*, which signifieth to Celebrate the Funeral duties of a man. Thus the second Verse saith, *before the day that he yieldeth up his Soul*, in hast was the Marriage Celebrated, between the Lady *Margaret* of *France*, and the Duke of *Savoy*, who beareth for his Arms some Eagles, some Lions, some Crosses, and a Crown of Rue.

LXXII.

French.

Par fureur feinte devotion Divine, Sera la femme du grand fort violée, Judges voulants damner telle Doctrine, Victime au peuple ignorant immolée. English.

By a faigned fury of Divine inspiration, The wife of the great one shall be ravished, Judges willing to condemn such a Doctrine, A Victimo shall be sacrificed to the ignorant people.

ANNOT.

Of this fact and others as bad, have been seen strange examples, formerly done by those called *Enthousiastes*, who have committed horrible villanies, under pretence of divine inspiration, some commiting Incests, others rapes, others murders, as may be seen at large in the History of *John de Leiden*, and other desperate Anabaptists, too tedious to be inserted here; I shall only relate here a little remarkable History, in confirmation of this, to discover the Wiles of the spirits of error, transformed into an Angel of Light.

The 7 day of *February* 1526. two Brothers, *Thomas* and *Leonard Schyker*, living near the Town of St. *Gal* in *Switzerland*, did assemble together with some other Anabaptists, in their fathers house, where they passed the most part of the night in discourses, making of faces, and relating of Visions, which every one said he had seen. The next day, upon break of day; *Thomas* did lay hold on his Brother *Leonard*, and dragged him in the middle of the company, bid him kneel in the presence of his Father and Mother, and of all the rest there present, and as all the rest of the Company bid him take heed to do any thing amiss; he answered, that there was no need to fear, and that in this business, nothing could be done against the Will of the Father; thereupon he drew his Sword, and cut off the head of his Brother, who was on his knees, all besotted before this murderer. All the rest being astonished, and besides their wits for this furious blow, and lamenting the dead, *Thomas* ran towards the Town with a fearful Countinance, as a Phanatick besides himself, without Shooes; and having no Cloaths but his Shirt and Breeches. At that time the Burg-master of St. *Gal* was *Joachim Vadian*, a wise and learned person, before whom the said *Thomas* stood, crying aloud with a fearful Countenance, that the day of Judgment was near; saying besides, that strange things had come to pass, (without telling what) that the will of his Father was done for his part. The Burg-master after he had reprehended him very much for his madness, and insolent carriage, commanded a Cloak to be put upon him, and to lead him home softly back again. But in the mean time, news was brought of his detestable murder, whereupon he was apprehended, examined, convicted, and executed. The like hath been done many times for Rapes and Incests: What is particular here, is, that our Author saith, that the Judges being willing to punish such Villanies, yet that unhappy accident shall fall, that an innocent person shall be put to death (belike) instead of the guilty, to please the people.

LXXIII.

French.

En Cité grande en moyne & artisan, Pres de la porte logez & aux murailles, Contre modene secret, Cave disant, Trahis pour faire sous couleur d'espousailles. English.

In a great City a Monk and an Artificer, Dwelling near the Gate, and the Walls, Near an old woman, 'tis a secret saying Cave, A Treason shall be plotted under pretence of a Marriage.

ANNOT.

Paradin maketh mention, that in the year 1552. a Monk deceived the Marshal of *Brissac*, making him believe that he would put him in possession of the Town of *Quizres*, if he would give him so much for reward. The Marshal used all the Caution possible, not to be deceived by that Imposter, who took Money on both sides, *viz.* the *French* and the *Spaniards*; nevertheless the Monk plaid the Knave with him, and the undertakings proved prejudicial to the *French*, though not considerably by reason of the precaution of the said Marshal.

      The same Author writes, that in the year 1555. the 17 of *August*, the *Spaniard* had designed to retake *Cazal*, the same way that the *French* had surprised it. First, they had got a Widow in the Town, who received the undertakers in her house, which was near the Gate, and the Wall. Secondly there was a Marriage to be made between two persons of quality, where great Cheer and rejoycings were to be. Thirdly they got a woman that carryed Herbs to sell in the Town, and under the Herbs the Letters were hidden. The Author says likewise, that there was a Monk and a Tradesman, that lodged at this Widows house, those two actors in this business, *viz.* the Monk said Tradesman, ane secretly to the woman that sold Herbs, *Cave*, which signifies take heed, they said these words *secretly near Matrone*, that is, they whisperd in her ear *Cave*. Their design was to betray the Town, under pretence of a Marriage, but it did not succeed; because the Letters in the womans Basket were intercepted, the Vulgar impression hath a fault in the third Verse, where there is Modene instead of Matrone, and another in the fourth Verse, when instead of Treason, they have put for betrayed. The History obligeth us to correct it, as we have done.

LXXIV.

French.

Le dechassé au regne tournera, Ses ennemis trouvez des conjurez, Plus que jamais son temps triomphera, Trois & septante a mort trop asseurez. **English.**

The expelled shall come again to the Kingdom, Her enemies shall be found to be the Conspirators, More than ever his time shall triumph, Three and seventy appointed for death.

ANNOT.

      This is a clear and express prediction of the happy restauration of his sacred Majesty, and our dread Sovereign *Charles* II. now Reigning, who after a long exile is come again to enjoy his own Kingdom, and to flourish more than ever he did before, by these seventy appointed to death, are meant the Judges and murderers of his Father, who with some few others of the same gang made about that number, and some of which have payed their shot by the hand of publick Justice, others have prevented their shame by dying before hand, others have been their own Executioners, and those that remain, lead a life worse then death it self; so true it is that vengeance dances the round.

LXXV.

French.

Le grand Pilot sera par Roy mandé, Laisser la classe pour plus haut lieu atteindre, Sept ans apres sera contrebandé, Barbare Armée viendra Venise craindre. **English.**

The great Pilot shall be sent for by the King, To leave the Fleet, and be preferred to a higher place, Seven years after he shall be countermanded, A *Barbarian* Army shall put *Venice* to a fright.

ANNOT.

      This needeth no further explanation.

LXXVI.

La Cité antique d'Antenorée forge, Plus ne pouvant le Tyran supporter, Le manche feint au Temple couper gorge, Les siens le peuple a mort viendra bouter. English.

The ancient City founded by *Antenor*, Being not able to bear the Tyrant any longer, With a fained haft, in the Church cut a throat, The people will come to put his servants to death.

ANNOT.

The City founded by *Antenor* (who was Companion and came into *Italy* with *Æneas*) is *Padua*, a University of the *Venetians*, of which it is said here, that being no longer able to bear a Tyrant, the said Tyrant shall be murdered in the Church with a knife hidden in a haft, and all his Men and Servants killed by the people of the Town.

LXXVII.

French.

Par la victoire du deceu fraudulente, Deux classes une, la revolte Germaine, La Chef meurtry & son fils dans la Tente, Florence, Imole pourchassez dans Romaine. English.

By the deceitful victory of the deceived, One of the two Fleets shall revolt to the *Germans*, The Chief and his Son murdered in their Tent, *Florence, Imole* persecuted in *Romania*.

ANNOT.

The three first Verses are plain. *Florence* and *Imole* are two Cities of *Italy*, seated in the Province of *Romania*.

LXXVIII.

French.

Crier victoire du grand Selin croissant, Par les Romains sera l'Aigle clamé, Ticin, Milan, & Gennesny consent Puis par eux mesmes Basil grand reclamé. English.

They shall cry up the victory of the great *Selins* half Moon, By the *Romans* the Eagle shall be claimed, *Ticin, Milan* and *Genoa*, consent not, Then by themselves the great *Basil* shall be claimed.

ANNOT.

The first Verse foretelleth some conquests of the *Turks*, whose Arms is the half Moon. The second Verse signifies, the *Romans* shall move the Emperour to succour them, which is the Eagle. *Ticin, Milan* and *Genoa* shall refuse to give help, and afterwards they shall call the great *Basil* (which in Greek signifies the great King, from βασίλευς) to their help.

LXXIX.

French.

Pres de Tesin les habitants de Logre, Garonne & Saone, Seine, Tar, & Gironde: Outre les Monts dresseront promonitoire, Conflict donné, Pau franchi, submerge onde. English.

Near the *Tesin* the Inhabitants of *Logre, Garonne* and *Saone, Seine, Tar* and *Gironde,* Shall erect a promontory beyond the Mountains, A Battle shall be fought, the *Po* shall be passed over, some shall be drowned in it.

ANNOT.

Tesin is the River that passeth by *Milan. Garonne, Saone, Seine, Tar,* and *Gironde* are Rivers of *France. Po* is the greatest River of *Italy.*

LXXX.

French.

De Fez le Regne parviendra a ceux d'Europe, Feu leur Cité, & Lame tranchera, Le grand d'Asie Terre & Mer a grand troupe, Que bleux, pars, Croix a mort dechassera. English.

The Kingdom of *Fez* shall come to those of *Europe,* Fire and Sword shall destroy their City, The great one of *Asia* by Land and Sea with a great troop, So that blews, greens, Crosses to death he shall drive.

ANNOT.

This is strange Prophecy if it prove true, *viz.* that the Kingdom of *Fez* (which is in *Africa*) shall be taken by those of *Europe,* and the Town put to Fire and Sword, after which the great one of *Asia* (meaning the great Turk) shall come by Land and by Sea with an innumerable Army, and shall drive and destroy all before him.

LXXXI.

French.

Pleurs, cris & plaincts, heurlemens, effrayeur, Cœur inhumain, cruel, noir & transy: Leman, les Isles de Gennes les majeurs, Sang espancher, tochsain, a nul mercy. English.

Tears, cryes and complaints, howlings, fear, An inhumane heart, cruel, black, astonished, *Leman,* the Islands the great ones of *Genoa,* Shall spill blood, the Bell shall ring out, no mercy shall be given.

ANNOT.

This foretels bloody Wars only, and needs no interpretation.

LXXXII.

French.

Par les Deserts de lieu libre & farouche, Viendra errer Neveu du grand Pontife, Assomme a sept avec lourde souche, Par ceux qu'apres occuperont le Scyphe. English.

Through the Deserts of a free and ragged place, The Nephew of the Pope shall come to wander, Knockt in the head by seven with a heavy Club, By those who after shall obtain the *Scyphe*.

ANNOT.

This signifies that the Nephew of a Pope shall be driven away, and shall wander in a desert place, where he shall be knockt in the head by seven men, one of which shall afterwards enjoy the Papacy; for *Scyphe* is a Latine word, signifying a Cup or Chalue, such as the *Romish* Priests say Mass with, and take the Sacrament.

LXXXIII.

French.

Celuy qu'aura tant d'honneurs & caresses, A son entrée en la Gaule Belgique, Un temps apres sera tant de rudesses, Et sera contre a la fleur tant bellique. English.

He that shall have had so many honours and welcoms, At his going into *Flanders*, A while after shall commit so many rudenesses, And shall be against the warlike flower.

ANNOT.

This is positively concerning the Duke of *Alencon*, Brother to *Henry* III. King of *France*, who having been sent for by the States of the Low-Countreys, and received with much honour to be their General and Governour against the *Spaniard*, did most unworthily break his trust, and being come to *Antwerp*, he was so ravished with the beauty and riches of the Town, that he seized upon it for himself, but was beaten out by the Citizens, and most of his men killed.

The fourth Verse saith. *He shall be against the warlike flower*; that is, his action shall be against Military Honour, and common practice of Honourable Souldiers.

LXXXIV.

Celuy qu'en Sparte Claude ne veut regner, Il fera tant par voye seductive, Que du court, long, le sera arraigner, Que contre Roy fera sa perspective. English.

He that *Claudius* will not have to reign in *Sparta*, The same shall do so much by a deceitful way, That he shall cause him to be arraigned short and long, As if he had made his prospect upon the King.

ANNOT.

     I believe the words of *Claudius* and *Sparta* here are Metaphorical, and the Author was unwilling they should be known.

     The sense is, one shall be hindred from Reigning by another, whom he shall accuse of Treason against the King.

LXXXV.

French.

La grand Cité de Tharse par Gaulois, Sera d'estriute captifs tous a Turban, Secours par Mer du grand Portugalois, Premier d'esté le jour du sacre Vrban. English.

The great City of *Tharsis* shall be taken by the *French*, All those that were at *Turban* shall be made slaves, Succours by Sea from the great *Portugals*, The first day of the Summer, and of the installation of *Urban.*

ANNOT.

     Here are two difficulties in this Stanza; the first is, what the Author means by the great City *Tharsis*; the second is in the last Verse, what he meaneth by the Installation of *Vrban*, I believe he meaneth no more then the election of a Pope, whose name shall be *Urban.*

LXXXVI.

French.

Le grand Prelat un jour apres son songe, Interprete au rebours de son sens, De la Gascogne luy surviendra un Monge, Qui fera eslire le grand Prelat de Sens. English.

The great Prelate the next day after his dream, Interpreted contrary to his sense, From *Gascony* shall come to him a Monge, That shall cause the great Prelate of *Sens* to be elected.

Monge is a Barbarous word, that hath no relation to any Language in the world, (that I know) unless it signifies a Monk. *Sens* is a fine City, about threescore Miles beyond *Paris*, towards the South, and the Seat of an Arch-Bishop, who it seemeth shall be elected into some eminent place, the next day after he that was in it shall dream a dream, that shall be interpreted contrary to the sense and meaning of it.

LXXXVII.

French.

L'election faicte dans Francfort, N'aura nul lieu, Milan s'opposera, Le sien plus proche semblera si grand fort, Qu'oute le Rhin Marais les chassera.* English.

The election made at *Francford*, Shall be void, *Milan* shall oppose it, He of the *Milan* party shall be so strong, As to drive the other beyond the Marshes of the *Rhine*.

ANNOT.

The Election of *Francford* is concerning an Emperour; for there they are elected, Crowned. The rest is plain.

LXXXVIII.

French.

Un Regne grand demourra desolé, Aupres de l'Hebro se seront assemblées, Monts Pyrenees le rendront consolé, Lors que dans May seront Terres tremblées.* English.

A great Kingdom shall be left desolate, Near the River *Hebrus* an assembly shall be made, The *Pyrenean* Mountains shall comfort him, When in *May* shall be an Earth-quake.

ANNOT.

This needeth no interpretation, but what any one may give that knoweth where the River *Hebrus* is.

LXXXIX.

French.

Entre deux cymbes pieds & mains attachez, De miel face oingt & de laict substante, Guespes & mouches feront amour fachez, Poccilateurs faucer, Scyphe tente.* English.

Between two Boats one shall be tyed hand and foot, His face annointed with Honey, and he nourished with Milk, Wasps and Bees shall make much of him in anger, For being treacherous Cup-bearers, and poisoning the Cup.

This is a description of the punishment which the *Persians* use to afflict upon poisoners; for they were put between two Troughs, which are here called Boats, from their likeness to them, with their face only uncovered, which was daubed with Honey, that the Wasps and Bees might be drawn to it and torment them, they were fed with Milk, which if they refused to do, and had rather dye than be so tormented, then did the Tormenter prick their Eyes with Needles to force them to their diet, and so were they left, till the Vermin eat them up. We have an example of this in the Life of *Artaxerxes* King of *Persia*.

XC.

French.

L'honnessement puant abominable, Apres la faict sera felicité, Grand excusé, pour n'estre favorable, Qu'a paix Neptune ne sera incité. English.

The stinking and abominable defiling After the secret shall succeed well, The great one shall be excused for not being favourable, That *Neptune* might be perswaded to peace.

ANNOT.

By the two first Verses it seemeth that some abominable action, after its effect shall succeed well; the two last signifie, that a great person shall be excused for not permitting the Fleet to be at peace.

XCI.

French.

Le conducteur de la guerre Navale, Rouge effrené, severe horrible grippe, Captif eschapé de l'aisné dans la baste, Quand il naistra du grand un Fils Agrippe. English.

The leader of the naval forces, Red, rash, severe, horrible extortioner, Being slave, shall escape, hidden amongst the Harnesses, When a Son named *Agrippa*, shall be born to the great one.

ANNOT.

This needeth no Interpretation, the words being so plain.

XCII.

French.

Princesse de beauté tant venuste, Au chef menée, le second faict trahy, La Cité au Glaive poudre face aduste, Par trop grand meurtre le chef du Roy hay. English.

A Princess of an exquisite beauty, Shall be brought to the General, the second time the fact shall be betrayed, The City shall be given to the Sword and fire, By two great a murder the chief Person about the King shall be hated.

ANNOT.

The only difficulty lyes in what City he doth mean.

XCIII.

French.

Prelat avare, d'ambition trompé, Rien ne fera que trop cuider viendra, Ses Messagers, & luy bien attrapé, Tout au rebours voir qui les bois fendra. **English.**

A covetous Prelate, deceived by ambition, Shall do nothing but covet too much, His messengers and he shall be trapt, When they shall see one cleave the Wood the contrary way.

ANNOT.

This needeth no Annotation.

XCIV.

French.

Un Roy iré sera aux sedifragues, Quand interdicts seront harnois de guerre, La poison taincte au succre par les fragues, Par eaux meurtris, morts, disant, serre, serre. **English.**

A King shall be angry against the Covenant-breakers, When the Warlike Armour shall be forbidden, The Poison with Sugar shall be put in the Strawberries, They shall be murdered and die, saying, close, close.

ANNOT.

The words are plain.

XCV.

French.

Par detracteur calomnié puis nay, Quand istront faicts enormes & martiaux, La moindre part dubieuse a l'aisné, Et tost au Regne seront faicts partiaux. **English.**

The youngest Son shall be calumniated by a slanderer, When enormous and Martial deeds shall be done, The least part shall be left doubtfull to the Eldest, and soon after they shall be both equal in the Kingdom.

ANNOT.

This lacketh no interpretation.

XCVI.

French.

Grand Cité a Soldats abandonnée, Onc ny eut mortel tumult si proche, O quelle hideuse calamités approche, Fors une offence n'y sera pardonnée. English.

A great City shall be given up to the Souldiers, There was never a mortal tumult so near, Oh! what a hideous calamity draws near, Except one offence nothing shall be spared.

ANNOT.

This is concerning the taking of the Town of St. *Quentin* in 1557. because the Author saith, no tumult was like this, so near the year 1555. when our Author writ.

He calleth it great City; because it is one of the most considerable in *France*, therefore it was besieged by the King of *Spain* with 37000. men, and 12000. Horses and 8000. *English*. The plunder was given to the Souldiers; for it was taken by assault.

There was never a mortal tumult so near; for the Souldiers taking revenge upon the Inhabitants, and Garrison, put all to the Sword; the Admiral having much ado to save himself.

In consequence of this our Prophet cryeth, *O what a fearfull calamity*; because the taking of this Town joyned with the loss of St. *Laurence* did almost ruine *France*. He addeth, *except one offence nothing shall be forgiven*; that is, the Town should be afflicted in all respects, except that it should not be burnt. The taking of this Town was upon the 27 of *August*, 17 days after the Battle of St. *Laurence*.

The loss was so great to *France*, that the King was fained to call the Duke of *Guise* back from *Italy*, and *Charles* V. hearing this news, asked presently if his Son *Philip* was not in *Paris*, as much as to say, it was a thing he ought to have done.

But God permitted that the King of *Spain* went another way, and in the mean time, the King of *France* strengthned himself, and the Duke of *Guise* took from the *English*, *Calais*, *Guines*, and the County of d'*Oye*. The *Spanish* History saith, that *Philip* had forbidden to touch any old people, Children and Ecclesiastical persons; but above all St. *Quentins* reliques.

XCVII.

French.

Cinq & quarante degrez ciel bruslera, Feu approcher de la grand Cité neuve, Instant grand flamme esparse sautera, Quand on voudra des Normans faire preuve. English.

The Heaven shall burn at five and forty degrees, The fire shall come near the great new City, In an instant a great flame dispersed shall burst out, When they shall make a trial of the *Normans*.

This signifies some extraordinary lightning under five and forty degrees, which is about the Southern part of *France*.

It is not easie to guess what he meaneth by the great new City, unless it be one in the Authors Countrey, called *Villa Nova*.

The last Verse seemeth to intimate, that this shall happen when an Army of *Normandie* shall be raised.

XCVIII.

French.

Ruyne aux Volsques de peur si fort terribles, Leur grand Cité taincte, faict pestilent: Piller Sol, Lune, & violer leur Temples, Et les deux Fleuves rougir de sang coulant. English.

A ruine shall happen to the *Volsques* that are so terrible, Their great City shall be dyed, a pestilent deed: They shall plunder Sun and Moon, and violate their Temples, And the two Rivers shall be red with running blood.

ANNOT.

The *Volsi* were a warlike people of *Italy* joyning to *Rome*, which makes me believe that by the great City he meaneth *Rome*, which was plundered and sackt by the Duke of *Burgondy* and the Prince of *Orange*, Generals of the Emperour *Charles* V.

XCIX.

French.

L'Ennemy docte se tournera confus, Grand Camp malade, & de faict par embusches Monts Pyrenees luy seront faicts refus. Roche du Fleuve descouvrant antique ruches. English.

The learned enemy shall go back confounded, A great Camp shall be sick, and in effect through ambush, The *Pyrenean* Mountains shall refuse him. Near the River discovering the ancient Hives.

ANNOT.

The words are plain, though the sense be too obscure, and I shall not endeavour to give an interpretation, when every one may make one himself.

C.

French.

Fill de Laure, asyle du mal sain, Ou jusqu'au Ciel se void l'Amphitheatre: Prodige veu, ton mal est fort prochain, Seras captive, & des fois plus de quatre. **English.**

Daughter of *Laura*, Sanctuary of the sick, Where to the Heavens is seen the *Amphitheatre*, A prodigy being seen, the danger is near, Thou shalt be taken captive above four times.

ANNOT.

This is an ingenious Stanza, concerning the City of *Nismes* in *Languedoc*, famous for its *Amphitheatre* built by the *Romans*, and remaining to this day, which Town he calleth Daughter of *Laura*, because the Lady *Laura*, Mistress to the famous Poet *Petrarche* was born thereabout; he also calleth it Sanctuary of the sick, for the salubrity of the air.

The meaning of the two last Verses is, that when a prodigy shall be seen, *viz.* Civil War in *France*, it shall be taken above four times, as it hath happened by one party or other.

Legis cautio contra ineptos Criticos.

Qui legent hos versus, maturè censunto: Prophanum vulgus & inscium ne attrectato: Omnesque Astrologi, Blenni, Barbari procul sunto, Qui aliter faxit, is rite sacer esto.

Michael Nostradamus.

CENTURY VII.

I.

French.

L'Arc du Thresor par Achilles deceu, Aux procrées sceu le Quadrangulaire, Au fait Roial le comment sera sceu, Corps veu pendu au Sceu du populaire. English.

The bow of the Treasure by *Achilles* deceived, Shall shew to posterity the Quadrangulary, In the Royal deed the Comment shall be known, The body shall be seen hanged in the knowledge of the people.

ANNOT.

By the bow of the Treasure, is understood the Marshal d'*Ancre*, Favorite to the Queen Regent of *France Mary* of *Medicis*, who was first complained of, for his maleversations by *Achilles de Harlay* President of *Paris*, whence followed his death being Pistolled in the Quadrangle of the *Louvre*, by the command of *Lewis* XIII. and his body afterwards dragged through the streets, and hanged publickly by the people upon the new Bridge.

II.

French.

Par Mars ouvert Arles ne donra guerre, De nuit seront les Soldats estonnez, Noir, blanc, a l'Inde dissimulez en terre. Soubs la feinte ombre traistre verrez sonnez. English.

Arles shall not proceed by open War, By night the Souldiers shall be astonished, Black, white, and blew, dissembled upon the ground. Under the fained shadow you shall see them proclaimed Traitors.

ANNOT.

Arles is a considerable City in *France*; the rest is plain.

III.

French.

Apres de France la victoire Navale, Les Barchinons, Salinons, les Phocens, Lierre d'or, l'Enclume serré dans balle, Ceux de Toulon au fraud seront consents. English.

After the Naval victory of the *French*, Upon those of *Tunis*, *Sally*, and the *Phocens*, A golden Juy the Anvil shut up in a pack, Those of *Toulon* to the fraud shall consent.

ANNOT.

This foretelleth a Naval victory to the *French* against the *Turks*, by the means of a Granado, called *Anvil*, that shall be shut up in a Barrel by a plot, to which those of *Toulon* shall be privy.

IV.

French.

Le Duc de Langres assiegé dedans Dole, Accompagné d'Authun & Lionnois, Geneve, Auspourg, ceux de la Mirandole, Passer les Monts contre les Anconois. English.

The Duke of *Langres* shall be besieged in *Dole*, Being in company with those of *Autun* and *Lion*, *Geneva*, *Auspourg*, those of *Mirandola*, Shall go over the Mountains against those of *Ancona*.

ANNOT.

Langres is a City in *France*, whose Bishop is a Duke and a Peer of the Kingdom; *Dole* is a City in *Burgundy*, so is *Autun* and *Lion*, *Geneva* is a City by *Savoy*, *Auspourg*, another in *Germany*, *Mirandola* is a Countrey in Italy, so is *Ancona*.

V.

French.

Vin sur la Table en sera respandu, Le tiers naura celle quil pretendoit, Deux fois du noir de Parme descendu, Perouse & Pise fera ce quil cuidoit. English.

Wine shall be spilt upon the Table, By reason that a third man shall not have her whom he intended, Twice the black one descended from *Parma*, Shall do to *Perusa* and *Pisa* what he intended.

ANNOT.

Perusa, *Pisa*, and *Parma*, are three Cities in *Italy*.

VI.

Naples, Palerme, & toute la Sicile, Par main Barbare sera inhabitée, Corsique, Salerne & de Sardaigne l'Isle, Faim, peste, guerre, fin de maux intemptée. English.

Naples, *Palermo*, and all *Sicily*, By barbarous hands shall be depopulated, *Corsica, Salerno*, and the Island of *Sardinia*, In them shall be famine, plague, war, and endless evils.

ANNOT.

Naples is a City in *Italy*, *Palermo* is a City in the Island of *Sicily*. *Corsica*, an Island in the *Mediterranean Sea*, belonging to the *Genoese*; *Salerno* is a Town in *Italy*; *Sardinia* an Island in the *Mediterranean*. The Reader may easily make an interpretation of the rest.

VII.

French.

Sur le combat des grands chevaux legers, On criera le grand croissant confond, De nuit tuer Moutons, Brebis, Bergers, Abysmes rouges dans le fossé profond. English.

At the fight of the great light Horsmen, They shall cry out, confound the great half Moon, By night they shall kill Sheep, Ewes, and Shepherds, Red pits shall be in the deep ditch.

ANNOT.

By the great half Moon, is understood the *Turk*.

VIII.

French.

Flora fuis, fuis le plus proche Romain, Au Fesulan sera conflict donné, Sang espandu les plus grands pris en main, Temple ne Sexe ne sera pardonné. English.

Flora fly, fly from the next *Roman*, In the *Fesulan* shall be the fight, Blood shall be spilt, the greatest shall be taken, Temple nor Sex shall be spared.

ANNOT.

Fesulan is a Countrey in *Italy*. *Flora* is the Goddess of Flowers, the rest is easie.

IX.

French.

Dame en l'absence de son grand Capitaine, Sera priée d'amour du Viceroy, Feinte promesse & malheureuse estreine, Entre les mains du grand Prince Barroy. English.

A Lady in the absence of her great Captain, Shall be intreated of love by the Viceroy, A fained promise, and unhappy new years gift, In the hand of the great Prince of *Bar*.

ANNOT.

      Bar is a principality joyning to *Lorrain*, which *Henry* IV. King of *France* gave for a Portion to his Sister *Catharine*, when she married the Duke of *Lorrains* Son. The rest is plain.

X.

French.

Par le grand Prince limitrophe du Mans, Preux & vaillant chef de grand exercite, Par Mer & Terre de Galois & Normans, Cap passer Barcelonne pillé l'Isle. English.

The great Prince dwelling near the *Mans*, Stout and valiant, General of a great Army, Of *Welchmen* and *Normans* by Sea and Land, Shall pass the Cape *Barcelone*, and plunder the Island.

ANNOT.

      Mans is a City in *France*, chief of the Province called *le Main*. The rest is plain.

XI.

French.

L'Enfant Roial contemnera la Mere, Oeil, pieds blessez, rude inobeissant, Nouvelle a Dame estrange & bien amere, Seront tuez des siens plus de cinq cens. English.

The Royal Child shall despise his Mother, Eye, feet wounded, rude disobedient, News to a Lady very strange and bitter, There shall be killed of hers above five hundred.

ANNOT.

      This was fulfilled about the year 1615. when *Lewis* XIII. King of *France*, being then about 15 years of age, by the perswasion of some Grandees about him, made War against his own Mother *Mary* of *Medicis*, then Regent of the Kingdom, whereupon was fought between them the Battle *du pont de say*, where above five hundred on the Queens side were slain, whereupon it was a good Jest of the Prince of *Guimena*, who being required by the Queen *Anna* of *Austria*, to lay his hand upon her side; and to feel her Child (now *Lewis* XIV.) stirring, after he had felt; now I know, said he, he is a true Son of *Bourbon*; for he beginneth to kick his Mother.

XII.

French.

Le grand puisnay fera fin de la guerre, En deux lieux assemble les excusez, Cahors, Moissac, iront loing de la serre, Rufec, Lectoure, les Agenois rasez. English.

The great younger Brother shall make an end of the War, In two places he shall gather the excused, *Cahors*, *Moissac*, shall go out of his clutches, *Ruffec*, *Lectoure*, and those of *Agen* shall be cut off.

ANNOT.

Cahors, *Moissac*, *Ruffec*, *Lectoure*, *Agen*, are all Cities of the Province of *Guyenne* in *France*.

XIII.

French.

De la Cité Marine & tributaire, La teste rase prendra la Satrapie, Chasser sordide qui puis sera contraire, Par quatorze and tiendra la Tyrannie. English.

Of the City Maritine and tributary, The shaven head shall take the Government, He shall turn out a base man who shall be against him, During fourteen years he will keep the tyranny.

ANNOT.

This is positive concerning the Cardinal of *Richelieu*, who made himself Governor of *Havre de Grace*, called here the Maritine City, and there kept his Treasure, and tyrannised for the space of about fourteen years.

XIV.

French.

Faux exposer viendra Topographie, Seront les Urnes des Monuments ouvertes, Pulluler Sectes, sainte Philosophie, Pour blanches noires, & pour antiques vertes. English.

They shall expound Topography falsly, The Urnes of the Monuments shall be open, Sects shall multiply, and holy Philosophy Shall give black for white, and green for old.

ANNOT.

This is a perfect description of our late miserable estate in *England*, when there was such multiplicity of Sects, and such a Prophanation of sacred things.

XV.

French.

Devant Cité de l'Insubre Countrée, Sept ans sera le Siege devant mis, Le tres-grand Roy fera son entrée, Cité puis libre hors de ses ennemis. English.

Before a City of *Piemont*, Seven years the Siege shall be laid, The most great King shall make his entry into it, Then the City shall be free being out of the enemies hand.

ANNOT.

This needeth no interpretation.

XVI.

French.

Entrée profonde par la grande Roine faite, Rendra le lieu puissant inaccessible, L'Armée de trois Lions sera défaite, Faisant dedans cas hideux & terrible. English.

The deep entry made by the Queen, Shall make the place powerful and inaccessible, The Army of the three Lions shall be routed, Doing within an hideous and terrible thing.

ANNOT.

A Queen shall cause such a deep Trench to be made before a Town, that it shall be impregnable, and the Army of Lions, that is either Generals, or of a Prince that shall bear three Lions in his Arms, shall be routed.

XVII.

French.

Le Prince rare en pitié & clemence, Apres avoir la paix aux siens baillé, Viendra changer par mort grand cognoissance, Apres grand repos le regne travaillé. English.

The Prince rare in pity and Clemency, After he shall have given peace to his Subjects, Shall by death change his great knowledge, After great rest the Kingdom shall be troubled.

ANNOT.

This positively concerneth *Henry* the IV. King of *France*; who after he had by many Battles and dangers given peace to his Kingdom, was by a Murderer snatched away, and the Kingdom put into new troubles, by the war that the Princes had among themselves.

XVIII.

French.

Les Assiegez couloureront leurs paches, Sept jours apres feront cruelle issüe, Dans repoulsez, feu, sang, sept mis a l'hache, Dame captive qu'avoit la paix issüe. English.

The Besieged shall dawb their Articles, Seven days after they shall make a cruel event, They shall be beaten back, fire, blood, seven put to death, The Lady shall be Prisoner who endeavoured to make peace.

ANNOT.

This needeth no interpretation.

XIX.

French.

Le Fort Nicene ne sera combatu, Vaincu sera par rutilant metal, Son fait sera un long temps debatu, Aux Citadins estrange espouvental. English.

The Fort *Nicene* shall not be fought against, By shining metal it shall be overcome, The doing of it shall be long and debating, It shall be a strange fearful thing to the Citizens.

ANNOT.

Nice is a Town in *Piemont*, situated by the Sea side, now whether this Prophecy came to pass in the time of the Wars between *France* and *Savoy*, or shall come to pass hereafter, it is more then I can tell. As for winning of it by glistering Metal, it is no new thing or practice, witness *Philippus* of *Macedon*, who said no City was impregnable, wherein might enter an Ass loaded with gold.

XX.

French.

Ambassadeurs de la Toscane langue, Avril & May Alpes & Mer passer, Celuy de Veau exposera l'harangue, Vie Gauloise en voulant effacer. English.

The Embassadors of the *Tuscan* tongue, In *April* and *May*, shall go over the *Alpes* and the Sea, One like a Calf shall make a speech: Attempting to defame the *French* customes.

ANNOT.

The sense and the words are plain.

XXI.

French.

Par pestilente inimitie Volsicque, Dissimulée chassera le Tyran, Au Pont de Sorgues se fera la trafique, De mettre a mort luy & son adherent. English.

By a pestilent *Italian* enmity, The dissembler shall expel the Tyrant, The bargain shall be made at *Sorgues* Bridge, To put him and his adherent to death.

ANNOT.

There is no difficulty in this.

XXII.

French.

Les Citoiens de Mesopotamie, Irez encontre amis de Tarragone, Jeux, Ris, Banquets toute gent endormie, Vicaire au Prone, pris Cité, ceux d'Ausone. English.

The Citizens of *Mesopotamia*, Being angry with the friends of *Tarragone*, Playes, laughter, feasts, every body being asleep, The Vicar being in the Pulpit, City taken by those of *Ausone*.

ANNOT.

By the Citizens of *Mesopotamia*, is understood a people that live between two Rivers, from the Greek words μέσος and ποταμὸς, the rest is easie. We have said before, that by *Ausone* the Author understands the City of *Bourdeaux*, which he called *Ausone*, from the Poet and Consul of *Rome Ausonius* who was born there.

XXIII.

French.

Le Roial Sceptre sera contraint de prendre, Ce que ses Predecesseurs voient engagé, Puis a Laigneau on fera mal entendre, Lors qu'on viendra le Palais saccager. English.

The Royal Scepter shall be constrained to take What his Predecessors had morgaged; After that, they shall mis-inform the Lamb, When they shall come to plunder the Palace.

ANNOT.

This is obvious to every body's capacity.

XXIV.

French.

L'Ensevely sortira du tombeau, Fera de chaisnes lier le fort du pont, Empoisoné avec œufs de Barbeau, Grand de Lorrain par le Marquis du pont. English.

The buried shall come out of his Grave, He shall cause the fort of the Bridge to be tied with Chains, Poisoned with Barbels hard Row, Shall a great one of *Lorrain* be by the Marques du pont.

ANNOT.

This Prophecie is divided in two parts. The first two Verses talk of a man that shall be taken out of his Grave alive. The two last speak, that a great man of *Lorrain* shall be poisoned by the Marques *de pont*, in the Row of a Barbel, which according to Physitians, is a dangerous meat of it self, and chiefly if it be Stewed, the Poisoner himself seemeth to be no other than a Duke of *Lorrain*, or one of his Sons, for he stileth himself *N.* Duke of *Lorrain*, Prince of *Bar*, and Marques *du Pont*.

XXV.

French.

Par guerre longue tout l'exercite espuiser, Que pour Soldats ne trouveront pecune, Lieu d'Or, d'Argent cair on viendra cuser, Gaulois Ærain, signe croissant de Lune. English.

By a long War, all the Army drained dry, So that to raise Souldiers they shall find no Money, Instead of Gold and Silver, they shall stamp Leather, The *French* Copper, the mark of the stamp the new Moon.

ANNOT.

This maketh me remember the miserable condition of many Kingdoms, before the *west-Indies* were discovered; for in *Spain* Lead was stamped for Money, and so in *France* in the time of King *Dagobert*, and it seemeth by this Stanza, that the like is to come again, by reason of a long and tedious War.

XXVI.

French.

Fustes Galées autour de sept Navires, Sera livrée une mortelle guerre, Chef de Madrid recevra coups de vires, Deux eschapées & cinq menez a Terre. English.

Fly-boats and Galleys round about seven Ships, A mortal War there shall be, The chief of *Madrid* shall receive blows of Oars, Two shall escape, and five carried to Land.

Paradin saith in his History, that in the year 1555. towards the end of *August*, those of *Diepe* had permission from the King to fight a Fleet of the *Spaniards*, which was coming into *Flanders*, and brought Men, Money, and several Merchandises. They went to Sea, and after much searching, they discovered the Fleet, wherein were 22 great Ships.

The *Diepois* had but 19 men of War, and five or six Pinnaces, with which they set upon them between *Calais* and *Dover*. The fight was very bloody, almost all the Ships grapled one with another, and being so close together, represented a Land fight.

The *French* at last did their utmost endeavour against the Admiral, which was succoured by six other Ships, of which two were taken with the Admiral, and carryed to *Diepe*; this is the Authors meaning, when he saith, *Fly-boats and Galleys about seven Ships*. He nameth the Admiral *Chief of Madrid*; that is, chief *Spaniard*, which received blows of Oars, whose Ship was taken, and four more of his Company, which were brought to *Diepe*. In this agree the Historians on both sides.

XXVII.

French.

Au coin de Vast la grand Cavalerie, Proche a Ferrare empeschée au Bagage, Pompe a Turin front telle volerie, Que dans le fort raviront leur hostage. **English.**

In the corner of *Vast* the great Troop of Horse, Near *Ferrara*, shall be busied about the baggage, *Pompe* at *Turin*, they shall make such a robbery, That in the Fort they shall ravish their hostage.

I could not find what he meaneth by this place *Vast*, which being the Key of all the rest, I could proceed no further, but am constrained to go to bed, and leave this for to night, among *Insolubilia de Alliaco*.

XXVIII.

French.

Le Capitaine conduira grande proye, Sur la Montagne des ennemis plus proche, Environné par feu fera telle voye, Tous eschapez, or trente mis en broche. **English.**

The Captain shall lead a great Prey Upon the Mountain, that shall be nearest to the Enemies, Being encompassed with fire, he shall make such a way, That all shall escape, but thirty that shall be spitted.

The two first Verses are plain.

The meaning of the last two is, that the said Captain being encompassed with Fire, shall make himself such a way, that all his men shall escape, but thirty that shall be spitted by the enemies.

XXIX.

French.

Le grand Duc d'Albe se viendra rebeller, A ses grands peres fera le tradiment, Le grand de Guise le viendra debeller, Captif mené & dresse monument. English.

The great Duke of *Alba* shall rebel, To his Grandfathers he shall make the Plot, The great *Guise* shall vanquish him, Led Prisoner, and a Monument erected.

ANNOT.

     Ferdinand of *Toledo*, Duke of *Alba* in *Spain*, a faithfull servant of *Charles* V. and *Philip* II. his Son, after he had made several proofs of his Valour, and prudence in the affairs of *Piemont* and *Milanese*, was commanded to go to *Naples* and *Rome*, to succour the *Colonesse*, and others of the *Spanish* party; to obey this command, the Author saith, *He went about to rebel*, not against his Prince, but his *Grandfathers*, *viz.* the Pope and the Cardinals, upon which the Senate of *Venice* wrote to him, desiring that he would not trouble the Pope, seeing that all his Predecessors had fought for him, as the Lord of *Thou* saith in his sixteenth Book; but he answered, that it was the Pope himself that was the cause of it, and that he was bound to oppose him.

     During that rebellion to his great fathers, as the Author calleth it, the great *de Guise*, came with his Troops, and compelled him to a diversion, and to let alone Marshal *Strozzy*, the Cardinal *Caraffa*, Captain *Montluc*, *Camillo Ursini*, Captain *Charry*, and others; so that all the Countrey about *Rome* was freed, and thus the Author saith, *the great de Guise shall come to quell him.*

     The fourth Verse addeth two things, that a Prisoner was carryed away, and that a Monument was erected. History makes no mention of the Prisoner, unless it were that Captain *Montluc*, having taken by assault the Town of *Pianea* or *Corsmian*, by a sink which he broke; the Captain *Gougues* a *Gascon* being a Prisoner of War in the Town, with many others, and hearing the cries of *France, France*, perswaded his Comrades to fall upon their Keepers, and to kill them with their own weapons and this Prisoner that was taken at *Montisel*, was brought back again into *France*, as well for his known Valour, as for his Warlike deliverance, and since that made himself famous in *Florida*.

     As for the Monument erected, makes me think he meaneth the Constable of *France*, who was taken Prisoner at the Battle of St. *Quentin*, and by the Monument, he meaneth the *Escurial*, which *Philip* the II. caused to be built in memory of that Victory, which obliged *Henry* the II. to call back again in all hast the Duke of *Guise* with all his Forces, or else *France* had been in danger to be lost.

XXX.

French.

Le sac sapproche, feu, grand sang espandu, Pau grand Fleuve, aux Bouviers l'entreprise, De Genes, Nice apres long temps attendu, Fossan, Thurin, a Savillan la prise. English.

The plundering draws near, fire, abundance of blood spilt, *Pau* a great River, an enterprise by Herdsmen, Of *Genes*, *Nice* after they shall have staid long, *Fossan*, *Thurin*, the prize shall be at *Savillan*.

The plundering draweth near, here the Author speaketh of things that should happen in his days. He writ this the first of *March* 1555. and History mentioneth that from the first of *March* 1555. till the beginning of 1559. the plundering of *Piemont* in *Italy* was very great, since the taking of *Cazal* by the *French*, for there was nothing but continual fightings, taking and retaking Towns, Skirmishes and Battles, and most of them by the River *Pau*, the greatest of *Italy*. The rest of the second Verse, and the beginning of the third saith, that the undertaking of *Genoa* shall be by the Herdsmen, by whom he meaneth the *Turks*, who being called by the *French* to help them in the taking of *Nice*, made an action fit for Herdsmen and villanous Traitors, doing nothing, because they had been bribed by the *Genoeses*.

This was done after the *French* had stay'd long for this infidel, who endeavoured to delude the *French*, and take all for himself; and this is the meaning of, *After Nice had stayed long*. In the mean time the *Spaniards* increased their Victories, as the fourth Verse witnesseth to the taking of *Fossan*, *Thurin*, and *Savillan*.

Fossan is a Town of *Piemont*, which that it might be distinguished from *Marseilles*, which the Author often calleth *Fossen* or *Phocen*, he putteth in the Epithete of *Thurin*, to signifie he meaneth *Fossan* in *Piemont*.

He saith that *Fossan* of *Piemont* shall have the taking towards *Savillan*, that is, this *Fossan* which belongeth to the *Spaniards*, will take some Towns near *Sivillan*.

XXXI.

French.

De Languedoc, & Guienna plus de dix Mille, voudront les Alpes repasser. Grans Allobroges marcher contre Brundis, Aquin & Bresse les viendront recasser. English.

From *Languedoc*, and *Guienna* more then 10000. Would be glad to come back over the *Alpes*. Great *Allobroges* shall march against *Brundis*, *Aquin* and *Bresse* shall beat them back.

Languedoc and *Guienne* are two Provinces in *France*, from whence many Souldiers shall be raised to go into *Italy*, but being distressed, shall wish to come back again over the *Alpes*. By the great *Allobroges*, I understand those of *Savoy* and *Piemont*, who shall go against *Brundis*, in Latine *Brundusium*, but shall be beaten back by *Aquin* and *Bresses*, Cities belonging to the *Venetians*.

XXXII.

French.

Du Mont Royal naistra d'une Casane, Qui Duc, & Compte viendra tyranniser, Dresser Copie de la marche Millane, Favence, Florence d'or & gens espuiser. English.

Out of the Royal Mount shall be born in a Cottage, One that shall tyranise over Duke and Earl, He shall raise an Army in the Land of *Millan*, He shall exhaust *Favence* and *Florence* of their gold.

This needeth no Interpretation.

XXXIII.

French.

Par fraude Regne, forces expolier, La classe obsesse, passages a l'espie, Deux faincts amis se viendront r'allier, Esueiller haine de long temps assoupie. English.

By fraud a Kingdom and an Army shall be spoilt, The Fleet shall be put to a strait, passages shall be made to the spies, Two feigned friends shall agree together, They shall raise up a hatred that had been long dormant.

ANNOT.

The words are plain.

XXXIV.

French.

En grand regret sera la gent Gauloise, Cœur vain, leger croira temerité, Pain, sel, ne vin eau venin ne cervoise, Plus grand captif, faim, froid, necessité. English.

In great regret shall the *French* Nation be. Their vain and light heart shall believe rashly. They shall have neither Bread, Salt, Wine, nor Beer, Moreover they shall be Prisoners, and shall suffer hunger, cold, and need.

ANNOT.

The words are plain, and the onely question is whither this distress threatned here to *France* is past or to come.

XXXV.

French.

La grand poche viendra plaindre pleurer, D'avoir esleu, trompez seront en l'Aage, Guiere avec eux ne voudra demeurer, Deceu sera par ceux de son langage. English.

The great Pocket shall bewaile and bemoan, For having Elected one, they shall be deceived in his Age, He shall not stay long with them, He shall be deceived by those of his own language.

ANNOT.

The great Pocket which is the Key of this Stanza being obscure, forceth me to leave the rest

unperfect.
XXXVI.

Dieu, le Ciel tout le Divin Verbe a l'Onde, Porté par rouges sept razes a Bizance, Contre les oingts trois cens de Trebisonde, Deux Loix mettront, & horreur, puis credence. English.

God, Heaven, all the Divine Word in water, Carryed by red ones, seven shaved heads at *Bisantium*, Against the anointed three hundred of *Trebisond*, They shall put two Laws, and horror, and afterwards believe.

ANNOT.

This seemeth to foretel that the Sacrament according to the *Roman* Church, shall be carried by Cardinals and seven Priests to *Constantinople*, against which three hundred of *Trebison* shall dispute, who shall compare the two Laws with horror, and afterwards believe.

XXXVII.

French.

Dix envoyez, chef de nef mettre a mort, D'un adverty, en classe guerre ouverte, Confusion chef, l'un se picque & mord, Leryn, Stecades nefs, cap dedans la nerte. English.

Ten shall be sent to put the Captain of the Ship to death, He shall have notice by one, the Fleet shall be in open War, A confusion shall be amongst the Chief, one pricks and bites, *Leryn, Stecades* nefs, caps dedans la nerte.

ANNOT.

The three first Verses are plain; as for the fourth I believe it to be the Language of the *Antipodes*, for I think no man can understand it.

XXXVIII.

French.

L'Aisné Roial sur coursier voltigeant, Picquer viendra si rudement courir, Gueule lipée, pied dans l'Estrein pleignant, Traine, tiré, horriblement mourir. English.

The eldest Royal prancing upon a Horse, Shall spur, and run very fiercely Open mouth, the foot in the Stirrup, complaining, Drawn, pulled, die horribly.

ANNOT.

This foretelleth of the eldest Son of a King, who prancing upon his Horse, shall Spur and run so fiercely, that his foot being intangled in the Stirrup he shall be dragged and pulled, and die a fearful death.

In the year 1555. upon the 25 of *May*, this came to pass in the person of *Henry* of *Albret*, the second of that name, King of *Navarre*.

This Prince *Henry* II. the eldest Royal riding upon a horse did spur him so hard, that he ran away with him, so that he perceiving the danger he was in, pulled the Bridle so hard that the horse's mouth was broken; the pain did not stop the horse, but contrariwise, he grew the more untoward, that *Henry* fell down, and in falling one of his feet hung in the stirrup, so that he was drawn, and died a horrid death. This I found in the History of *Naples*.

XXXIX.

French.

Le conducteur de l'Armée Francoise, Cuidant perdre le principal Phalange, Par sus pavé de l'Avaigne & Ardoise, Soy parfondra par Gennes gent estrange. **English.**

The leader of the *French* Army, Thinking to rout the chiefest Phalange, Upon the Pavement of *Avaigne*, and Slate, Shall sink in the ground by *Gennes*, a strange Nation.

ANNOT.

It seemeth that a *French* General, thinking to rout and overcome the chiefest strength of his enemy, and going upon a brittle Pavement, made of Slate, shall sink in the ground not far from *Genoa*, which he calleth a strange Nation to the *French*.

XL.

French.

Dedans tonneaux hors oingts d'huile & graisse, Seront vingt un devant le port fermez, Au second guet feront par mort prouesses, Gaigner les portes & du quet assommez. **English.**

With Pipes annointed without with Oyl and Grease, Before the harbour, one and twenty shall be shut, At the second Watch, by death, they shall do great feats of Arms, To win the Gates, and be killed by the Watch.

ANNOT.

The words and sense of this Stanza are plain.

XLI.

French.

Les os des pieds, & des mains enferrez, Par bruit maison long temps inhabitée, Seront par songes concavant deterrez, Maison salubre & sans bruit habitée. **English.**

The bones of the feet and of the hands in shackles, By a noise a house shall be a long time deserted, By a dream the buried shall be taken out of the ground, The house shall be healthful, and inhabited without noise.

I have found the truth of this Stanza upon the place, in my going to *Lion*, it was my fortune to lye at a Town four Leagues on this side of it, called *Lapacodier*, where this Story was told me to have happened few days before.

It chanced that a Company of Foot was to lie in the Town, and distressed for quarter, they enquired why such a house was empty, and were told it was not inhabited by reason of a noise heard there every night. The Captain of the Troop resolved, since he feared not the living, not to fear the dead, and thereupon lay in the house that night, where Beds were provided for him, and about half a Dozen of his stoutest Souldiers; so they laid down their weapons on the Table, and began to be merry at Cards and Dice, expecting the event. The door being fast locked, about twelve and one they heard as though some body knockt at the door, one of the Souldiers by the Captains command, with a Pistol in his hand, and a Candle, opened the door, then appeared to them a Phantasm, in the shape of an old man, loaded with Chains, that made a great noise, this Phantasm beckened to the Captain at the Table to come to him, the Captain also rising, beckened to the Phantasm to come to him, this lasted for a while, till the Captain resolved to go to him, and so taking a Candle in one hand, and a Pistol in the other, bid his Souldiers follow him hand in hand with their Arms, then taking the Phantasm by the hand, which was exceeding cold, he led them into the Cellar, and through many turnings, till at last the Phantasm vanished, and the Candles went out, then were they constrained to remain there till day light, when perceiving where they were, and having taken notice of the Place where the Phantasm left them, they went out, and related the story to the Townsmen; so afterwards they digged in that place, where they found a kind of a Trunk, and the bones of a man in it shackled, they buryed the body in a Church-yard, and no noise was heard afterwards in that house, this came to pass about 1624.

XLII.

French.

Quand Innocent tiendra le lieu de Pierre, Le Nizaram Sicilian se verra, En grands honneurs, mais apres il cherra, Dans le bourbier d'une Civile guerre. English.

When *Innocent* shall hold the place of *Peter*, The *Sicilian Nizaram* shall see himself In great honours, but after that he shall fall Into the dirt of a Civil war.

Nothing can be more plain and true than this Prophecie, and those that deny it, may also deny the light of the Sun, but to make it more evident, we will examine it Verse by Verse.

When Innocent shall hold the place of Peter; that is, when one named *Innocent* shall be Pope, as he was that preceded the last.

The Sicilian Nizaram shall see himself in great honours; that is, the *Sicilian Nizarim*, for *Nizaram*, is the Annagramme of *Mazarin*, letter for letter, who was born in *Sicily*, shall see himself in great honours, as he did; for he was then in his greatest splendor.

But after that he shall fall into the dirt of a Civil war; As every one knows he did, having put in Prison the Prince of *Condé*, the Prince of *Conty*, and the Duke of *Congueiulle*, can any thing be more plain, and yet when I read this forty years ago, I took it to be ridiculous.

XLIII.

French.

Lutece en Mars, Senateurs en credit, Par une nuict Gaule sera troublée, Du grand Cræsus l'Horoscope predit, Par Saturnus, sa puissance exillée. English.

Lutetia in *Mars*, Senators shall be in credit. In a night *France* shall be troubled, The Horoscope of the great *Cræsus* foretelleth, That by *Saturn* his power shall be put down.

ANNOT.

       Lutetia in Latine is the City of *Paris*, after the death of *Henry* IV. the Parliament of *Paris* began to prick up their ears, and to go about to call the great ones to account, amongst whom was the Marquess d'*Ancre*, favourite of the Queen Regent, that had gathered great riches, and therefore is called here *Cræsus*, our Author saith, that his power shall be put down by *Saturnus*, which must here be understood mistically, which proved true, for by the Kings command, then *Lewis* XIII. he was shot with three Pistols in the *Louvre.*

XLIV.

French.

Deux de poison saisis nouveaux Venus Dans la cuisine du grand Prince verser, Par le souillard tous deux au fait cogneus, Prins qui cuidoit de mort l'aisné vexer. English.

Two newly come being provided with poison, To pour in the Kitchin of the great Prince, By the Cooks Boy the fact shall be known, And he taken, that thought by death to vex the elder.

ANNOT.

       This came to pass in the time of *Henry* IV. who was poisoned at *Melan*, by two unknown men, who were discovered by the Cooks Boy in the doing of it, and were both taken, the History is at large in *Peter Matthew* his Historiographer, which I could not insert here for the satisfaction of the Reader; because I could not get the Book, the Reader may satisfie himself upon the place.

Other Stanzas, taken out of twelve, under the seventh Century, out of which eight have been rejected, because they were found in the foregoing Centuries.

LXXIII.

French.

Renfort de Sieges manubis & maniples, Changez le sacre & passe sur le pronsne, Prins & captifs n'arreste les prez triples, Plus par fonds mis elevé, mis au Trosne. English.

Recruit of Sieges, spoils and prizes, *Corpus Christi* day shall be changed, and the pronsne slighted,

They shall be taken and made Prisoners, do not stay in the threefold Field, Moreover, one put in the bottom shall be raised to the Throne.

LXXX.

French.

L'Occident libre les Isles Britanniques, Le recogneu passer le bas, puis haut, Ne content triste Rebel corss. Escotiques, Puis rebeller par plui & par nuict chaut. English.

The West shall be free, and the *Brittish* Islands, The discovered shall pass low, then high, *Scottish* Pirates shall be, who shall rebel, In a rainy and hot night.

LXXXII.

French.

La stratageme simulte sera rare, La Mort en voye rebelle par contrée, Par le retour du voyage Barbare, Exalteront la potestante entrée. English.

The stratagem and grudge shall be scarce, Death shall be in a rebellious way through the Countrey, By the return from a *Barbarian* travel, They shall exalt the Protestant entrance.

LXXXIII.

French.

Vent chaut, conseil, pleurs, timidité, De nuict au lict assailly sans les Armes: D'oppression grand calamité, L'Epithalame converty pleurs & larmes. English.

Hot wind, councel, tears, fearfulness, He shall be assaulted in his bed by night without Arms, From that oppression shall be raised a great calamity, The *Epithalamium* shall be converted into tears.

ANNOT.

The reason why I have put no Annotations to these, as I have done to the rest, is, because according to my judgement, and that of the most Learned, they are spurious.

Friendly Reader,

Before you Read the following Epistle, I would have you be warned of a few things: One is, that according to my opinion, it is very obscure and intelligible in most places, being without any just connection, and besides the obscurity of the sense, the crabbedness of the expression is such, that had not the importunity of the Bookseller prevailed, I would have left it out, but considering the respect due to Antiquity, the satisfaction we owe to curious persons, who would perhaps have thought the Book imperfect without it, we let it go, trusting to your Candor and Ingenuity.

Farewell.

Michael Nostradamus.

CENTURY VIII. IX. & X.

That had not been Printed before, and are in the same Edition of 1568.

TO THE

Most Invincible, most High, and most Christian King of France HENRY the Second;
Michael Nostradamus his most obedient Servant and Subject, wisheth Victory and Happiness.

By reason of that singular observation, I had O most Christian and Victorious King, since my Face, who had been cloudy a great while, did present it self before your immeasurable Majesty. I have been ever since perpetually dazled, continually honouring and worshipping that day, in which I presented my self before it, as before a singular humane Majesty; now seeking after some occasion, whereby I might make appear the goodness and sincerity of my heart, and extend my acquaintance towards your most Excellent Majesty; and seeing that it was impossible for me to declare it by effects, as well because of the darkness and obscurity of my mind, as for the enlightning it did receive from the face of the greatest Monarch in the World; I was a great while before I could resolve to whom I should Dedicate these three last Centuries of my Prophecies, which make the compleat thousand, and after I had a long time considered, I have with a great temerity made my address to your Majesty, being no ways dainted by it, as the grave Author *Plutarch* related in the Life of *Lycurgus*, that seeing the offerings and gifts that were Sacrificed in the Temples of their Heathen Gods, durst not come thither no more, least the people should wonder at the costs and charges. Notwithstanding, seeing your Royal Splendour joyned with an incomparable Humanity, I have made my address to it, not as to the Kings of *Persia*, of whom to come near, it was forbidden, but to a most Prudent and Wise Prince I have Dedicated my Nocturnal and Prophetical Supputations, written rather by a natural instinct, and Poetical furour, then by any rules of Poetry; and most part of it written and agreeing with the Years, Months and Weeks, of the Regions, Countreys and most part of the Towns and Cities in *Europe*; touching also some thing of *Africa*, and of a part of *Asia*, by the change of Regions that come near to those Climats, and compounded of natural faction. But some body may answer (who hath need to blow his Nose) the Rime to be as easie to be understood, as the intelligence of the sence is hard and difficult, and therefore O most humane King, most of the Prophetical Stanza's are so difficult, that there is no way to be found for the Interpretation of them; nevertheless being in hope of setting down the Towns, Cities, and Regions, wherein most of those shall happen, especially in the year 1585. and in the year 1606. beginning from this present time, which is the 14. of *March* 1557. and going further to the fulfilling of those things, which shall be in the beginning of the seventh Millenary, according as my Astronomical Calculation, and other Learning could reach, at which time the adversaries of Christ and of his Church shall begin to multiply; all hath been composed and calculated in days and hours of Election, and well disposed, and all as accurately as was possible for me to do. And the whole *Minerva libera & non invita*, Calculating almost as much of the time that is come, as of that which is past, comprehending it in the present time, and what by the course of the said time shall be known to happen in all Regions punctually as it is here written, adding nothing superfluous to it, although it be said; *Quod de futuris contingentibus, non est determinata omnino veritas*. It is very true Sir, that by my natural instinct given me by my Progenitors, I did think I could foretel any thing; but having made an agreement between this said instinct of mine, and a long Calculation of Art, and by a great tranquility and repose of mind, emptied my Soul of all care and carefulness, I have foretold most part of these *ex tripode æneo*, though there be many who attribute to me some things that are no more mine, then what is nothing at all. The only Eternal God, who is the searcher of men's hearts, being pious, just, and merciful, is the true Judge of it, whom I beseech to defend me from the calumny of the wicked men, who would as willing calumniously inquire for what reason all your ancient Progenitors Kings of *France* have healed the disease called the *Kings-evil*, and some other Nations have cured the biting of venomous Beasts; others have had a certain instinct to foretell things that are to come, and of several others, too tedious to be here inserted; notwithstanding those in whom the malignancy of the wicked spirit shall not be suppressed by length of time; after my decease my work shall be in more esteem, then when I was alive; nevertheless if I should fail in the supputation of times, or could not please some, may it please your most Imperial Majesty to forgive me, protesting before God and his Saints, that I do not intend to insert any thing by writing in this present Epistle, that may be contrary to the true Catholick Faith, in conferring the Astronomical Calculation, according to my learning; for the space of times of our Fathers that have been before us, are such, submitting my self to the correction of the most Learned, that the first man *Adam* was before *Noah*, about one thousand two hundred forty two years, not computing the time according to the supputation of the *Gentiles*, as *Varro* did, but onely according to the Sacred Scriptures, and the weakness of my wit in my Astronomical Calculations. After *Noah* and the universal Flood about a thousand and fourscore years came *Abraham*, who was a supreme Astrologer, according to most mens opinion, and did first invent the *Chaldæan* Letters; after that came *Moses*, *viz.* some five hundred and fifteen or sixteen years after, and between the time of *David* and *Moses* have passed about 570. years. After which between the time of *David* and that of our Saviour and Redeemer Jesus Christ, born of the Virgin *Mary*, have passed (according to some Chronographers) a thousand three hundred and fifty years. Some body may object, that this supputation is not true; because it differeth from that of *Eusebius*. And from the time of humane redemption, to that of the execrable seduction of the *Saracens*, have passed six hundred and four and twenty years, or thereabouts. From that time hitherto, it is easie to collect what times are past, if my supputation be not good among all Nations; because all hath been calculated by the course of the Cœlestial bodies, joyned with motion, infused in me at certain loose hours, by the motion of my ancient Progenitors; but the injury of the time (most excellent King) requireth, that such secret events should not be manifested, but by an enigmatical Sentence, having the only sense, and one only intelligence, without having mixed with it any ambiguous or amphibological calculation, but rather under a Cloudy obscurity, through a natural infusion, coming near to the Sentence of one of the Thousand and two Prophets, that have been since the Creation of the World, according to the supputation and punical Chronick of *Joel. Effundam spiritum meum super omnem, & carnem & prophetabunt filii vestri & filiæ vestræ*: But such a Prophecy did proceed from the mouth of the Holy Ghost, who was the Supreme and eternal Power, which being come with that of the Cœlestial bodies, hath caused some of them to foretel great and wonderful things; as for my part I challenge no such thing in this place, God forbid, I confess truly, that all cometh from God, for which I give him thanks, honour, and praise, without having mixed any thing of that divination, which proceedeth *a Fato*, but only of that which proceedeth *a Deo & Natura*, and most of it joyned with the motion and course of the Cœlestial Bodies; insomuch that seeing as in a burning Glass, and through a Cloudy Vision, the great and sad events, the prodigious and calamitous accidents, that shall befall the Worshippers, first of God, and secondly, those that are Earthly propped up, with a thousand other calamitous accidents, which shall be known in course of time; for God will take notice of the long barrenness of the great Dame, who afterwards shall conceive two principal Children: But being in danger, she that shall be added to her by the temerity of age, running a danger in the 18, and not able to go beyond the 36, shall leave behind her three females, and he shall have two that never had any of the same father, the differences between the three Brothers shall be such, and then shall they be united and agreed, insomuch that the three and four parts of

Europe shall quake: by the lesser in years shall the Christian Monarchy be upheld and augmented, Sects shall rise, and presently be put down again, the *Arabians* shall be put back, Kingdoms shall be united, and new Laws made. Concerning the other Children; the first shall possess the furious Crowned Lions, holding their Paws upon the Escutcheons. The second, well attended, will go so deep among the Lions, that the second way shall be open, all trembling and furious going down, to get upon the *Pyrenæan* Mountains. The ancient Monarchy shall not be transferred, the third innundation of humane blood shall happen, and for a good while *Mars* shall not be in Lent. And the Daughter shall be given for the preservation of the Church, the Dominator of it falling into the *Pagan* Forces of the new unbelievers, she shall have two Children, one from faithfulness, and the other from unfaithfulness, for the confirmation of the Catholick Church; and the other, who to his confusion and late repentance, shall go about to ruine her. There shall be three Regions by the extreme differences of the leagues, *viz.* the *Roman*, the *German*, and the *Spanish*, who by a Military hand shall make divers Sects, forsaking the 50 and 52 degrees of altitude, and all those of remote Regions shall do homage to the Regions of *Europe*, and of the North of 40 Degrees Altitude, who by a vain fright shall quake, after that those of the West, South, and East shall quake because of their power, insomuch that what shall be done, cannot be undone by Warlike power. They shall be equal in Nature, but much different in Faith. After this, the barren Dame of a greater power then the second, shall be admitted by two people, by the first obstinate that had power over the others; by the second, and by the third, that shall extend his Circuit of the East of *Europe*, as far as the *Hungarians*, vanquished and overcome, and by a Maritine Sail, shall make his excursions into the *Trinarrian* and *Adriatick* Sea, by his *Mirmidons*, and *Germany* shall fall, and the *Barbarian* Sect shall be wholly driven from among the Latines. Then the great Empire of Antichrist shall begin in the *Attila*, and *Xerxes* to come down with an innumerable multitude of people, insomuch that the coming of the Holy Ghost, proceeding from the 48 Degree, shall transmigrate, driving away the abomination of the Antichrist, who made War against the Royal, who shall be the great Vicar of *I. C.* and against his Church, and his Kingdom, *per tempus, & in occasione temporis*, and before this shall precede a Solar Eclipse, the most dark and obscure that was since the Creation of the World, till the death and passion of *I. C.* and from him till then, and it shall be in the Month of *October*, when such a great Translation shall be made, that every body will think that the weight of the Earth, shall have lost its natural motion, and be swallowed up in perpetual darkness. In the Spring before and after this, shall happen extraordinary changes, mutations of Kingdoms, and great Earth-quakes, with pullulation of the new *Babylons* miserable daughter, increased by the abomination of the first Holocaust, and shall last only 73 years and 7 Months, then from that Stock she that had been long time barren, proceeding from the fifth Degree, who shall renew all the Christian Church, and then shall be a great Peace, Union and Concord, between one of the Children of the wandring and seperated foreheads by divers Kingdoms, and such Peace shall be made, that the Instigator and Promoter of Military function, by diversity of Religions, shall be tied to the bottom of the deep, and the Kingdom of the *Rabious*, who shall counterfeit the wise, shall be united. And the Countreys, Towns, Cities and Provinces, that had deserted their first ways to free themselves, captivating themselves more deeply, shall be secretly angry at their liberty and Religion lost, and shall begin to strike from the left, to turn to the right, restoring the holiness beaten down long before with their former writing; so that after the great Dog, shall come forth the biggest Mastif, who shall destroy all that was done formerly, then Churches shall be built up again as before, the Clergy shall be restored to its former state, and shall begin to Whore, and Luxuriate, and to commit a Thousand Crimes. And being near unto another desolation, when she shall be in her higher and more sublime dignity, there shall rise powers and Military hands, who shall take away from her the two Swords, and leave her only the Ensigns, from which by the means of the crookedness that draweth them, the people causing it to go straight, and not willing to submit unto them by the end opposite to the sharp hand that toucheth the Ground, they shall provoke till that a branch shall proceed from the barren, which shall deliver the people of the World from that meek and voluntary slavery, putting themselves under the protection of *Mars*, depriving *Jupiter* of all his honours and dignities, for the free City established and seated in another little *Mesopotamia*. And the chief Governour shall be thrust out of the middle, and set in the high place of the Air, being ignorant of the conspiracy of the Conspirators, with the second *Thrasibulus*, who long before did manage this thing, then shall the impurities and abominations be objected with great shame, and made manifest to the darknes of the darkened light, and shall cease towards the end of the change of his Kingdom, the chief men of the Church shall be put back from the love of God, and many of them shall apostatise from the true faith, and from the true Sects, the middlemost of which by her worshippers, be a little put into ruine; the first, wholly in all *Europe*, and most part of *Africa* undone by the third, by the means of the poor in Spirit, who by madness elevated, shall through libidinous luxury, commit adultery. The people will rise and maintain it, and shall drive away those that did adhere to the Legislators, and shall seem by the Kingdoms spoiled by the Eastern men, that God the Creator hath loosed Satan from his Infernal Prison, to cause to be born the great *Dog* and *Doham*, who shall make so great and abominable a fraction in the Churches, that the Red nor the White, without Eyes and without Hands, shall not judge of it, and their power shall be taken away from them. Then shall be a greater persecution against the Church than ever was, and in the mean time shall be so great a Plague, that two parts of three in the world shall fail, insomuch that no body shall be able to know the true owners of fields and houses, and there shall happen a total desolation unto the Clergy, and the Martial men shall usurpe what shall come back from the City of the Sun, and from *Molita*, and the *Stœchades* Islands, and the great Chain of that Port shall be open, which taketh its denomination from a Sea Oxe, and a new incursion shall be made through the Sea Coasts, willing to deliver the *Castulan* Leap from the first Mahometan taking, and the assaulting shall not altogether be in vain, and that place where the habitation of *Abraham* was, shall be assaulted by those, who shall have a respect for the Jovials. And that City of *Achem*, shall be encompassed and assaulted on all sides, by a great power of Armed men; their Sea Forces shall be weakened by the Western men, and to that Kingdom shall happen great desolation, and the great Cities shall be depopulated, and those that shall come in, shall be comprehended within the vengeance of the wrath of God, and the Sepulchre held in so great veneration, shall remain a great while open to the universal Aspect of the Heavens, Sun and Moon, and the sacred place shall be converted into a Stable for small and great Cattle, and put to prophane uses. O what a calamitous affliction shall be then for women with Child, and chiefly by the principal Easterly head, being for the most part moved by the Northern and Westerly men, vanquished and put to death, beaten, and all the rest put to flight, and the Children he had by many women, put in Prison, then shall be fulfilled the Prophecy of the Kingly Prophet. *Ut audiret gemitus compeditorum, ut solveret filios interemptorum*, what great oppression shall be made then upon the Princes and Governours of Kingdoms, and especially of those that shall live Eastward and near the Sea, and their Languages inter-mixed very sociably. The Language of the *Arabians* and Latines by the *African* communication, and all the Eastern Kings shall be driven away, beaten and brought to nothing, not altogether by the means of the strength of the Kings of the North, and by the drawing near of our age, by the means of three secretly united, seeking for death by ambushes one against another. And the renewing of the Triumvirate shall last seven years, while the fame of such a sect shall be spread all the world over, and the Sacrifice of the Holy and immaculate Host shall be upheld: And then shall the Lords be two in number victorious in the North against the Eastern ones, and there shall be such a great noise and Warlike tumult, that all the East shall quake for fear of those two Brothers, not Northern Brothers. And because, Sir, by this discourse, I put all things confusedly in these predictions, as well concerning the event of them, as for the account of the time which followeth, which is not at all, or very little conformable to that I have done before, as well by Astronomical way, as other of the sacred Scriptures which cannot erre, I could have set down to every quatrain the time in which they shall happen, but it would not please every body, much less the interpretation of them, till, Sir, your Majesty hath granted me full power so to do, that my Calumniators may have nothing to say against me. Nevertheless reckoning the years since the Creation of the World to the Birth of *Noah* have passed 1506. years, and from the Birth of *Noah* to the perfect building of the Ark near the universal Flood have passed 600. years, whither solary, or lunary, or mixed, for my part according to the Scriptures, I hold that they were solary. And at the end of those 600. years *Noah* entered into the Ark, to save himself from the Flood, which Flood was universal upon the Earth, and lasted a year and two months; and from the end of the Flood, to the birth of *Abraham* did pass the number of 295. years; and from the birth of *Abraham* to that of *Isaac* did pass 100. years, and from *Isaac* to *Jacob* 60. years; and from the time that he went into *Ægypt* till he came out of it, did pass 130. years; and from the time that *Jacob* went into *Ægypt* till his posterity came out of it did pass 430. years; and from the coming out of *Ægypt* to the building of *Salomon*'s Temple in the fourth year of his Reign did pass 480. years; and from the building of the Temple till Jesus Christ, according to the supputation of the Chronographers, did pass 490. years; and so by this supputation, which I have gathered out of the Holy Scriptures, the whole cometh to about 4173. years, eight Months more or less. But since the time of I. C. hitherto, I leave it because of the diversity of Opinions. And having calculated these present Prophecies according to the order of the Chain, which containeth the revolution, and all by Astronomical Doctrine, and according to my natural instinct, and after some time, and in it comprehending since the time that *Saturn* shall turn to come in on the 7 of the Month of *April*, till the 25 of *August*; *Jupiter* from the 14 of *June* to the 7 of *October*; *Mars* from the 27 of *April* till 22 of *June*; *Venus* from the 9 of *April* to the 22 of *May*; *Mercury* from the 3 of *February* till the 24 of the same; afterwards from the 1 of *June* till the 24 of the same; and from the 25 of *September* till the 16 of *October, Saturn* in *Capricorn, Jupiter* in *Aquarius, Mars* in *Scorpio, Venus* in *Pisces, Mercury* within a Month in *Capricorn, Aquarius* in *Pisces, Luna* in *Aquarius*, the *Dragons head* in *Libra*, the Tail opposite to her sign according to a Conjunction of *Jupiter* and *Mercury*, with a quadrin Aspect of *Mars* to *Mercury*, and the head of the *Dragon* shall be with a Conjunction of *Sol* and *Jupiter*: the year shall be peacefull without Eclipse, and in the beginning of that year shall be a greater persecution against the Christian Church than ever was in *Affrica*, and it shall last till the year 1792. at which time every body will think it a renovation of Age. After that the *Roman* people shall begin to stand upright again, and to put away some obscure darknesses, receiving some of its former light, but not without great divisions, and continual changes. *Venice* after that with great strength and power shall lift up her Wings so high, that she will not be much inferiour to the strength of the old *Rome*, and in that time great *Bizantine* Sails, joyned with the *Ligustiques*, by the Northern help and power shall give some hinderance, whereby those of *Crete* shall not keep their faith, the Arches built by the antient Martial men, will keep company together with *Neptun*'s Waves. In the *Adriatick* shall be a great discord, what was united shall be parted asunder, and what was before, and is a great City, will go near to becom a house, including the *Pempotan*, and the *Mesopotamia* of *Europe* to 45, and others to 41, 42, and 37. And in that time, and Countrey, the Infernal power shall rise against the Church of I. C. with the power of the Enemies to his Law, which shall be the second Antechrist, who shall persecute the said Church and its Vicar by the means of the power of Temporal Kings, who through their Ignorance shall be seduced by Tongues more sharp than any Sword in the hands of a mad man. The said Reign of Antichrist shall not last but till the ending of him, born by Age, and of the other in the City of *Plancus*, accompanied by the Elect of *Modone, Fulcy* by *Ferrara*, maintained by *Adriatick, Liguriens*, and the proximity of the great *Trinacria*, and after that shall pass over the Mount *Jovis*. The *Gallique Ogmyon* followed with such a number, that even from afar off the Empire of the great Law, shall be presented to him, and then, and after shall be profusedly spilled the blood of the Innocent by the Nocent, raised on high; then by great Floods the memory of those things contained by such Instruments, shall receive an innumerable loss, as also shall learning towards the North by the Divine Will, Satan bound once more, and an universal Peace shall be among men, and the Church of I. C. shall be free from all tribulation, although the *Azosrains* would fain mix among it the Honey of their pestilent seduction, and this shall happen about the seventh Millinary; so that the Sanctuary of I. C. shall be no more trodden down by the unbelievers that shall come from the North, the world being near to some conflagration, although by my supputations in my Prophecies, the course of the time goeth much further. In the Epistle that within the late years I have dedicated to my Son *Cæsar Nostradamus*, I have openly enough declared some things, without prognosticating. But here (Sir) are comprehended many great and wonderful events, which those that come after us shall see. And during the said Astrological supputation, conferred with the sacred Scripture, the persecution of the Clergy shall have its beginning from the power of Northern Kings, joyned with the Eastern ones; that persecution shall last Eleven years and a little less, at which time the chief Northern King shall fail, which years being ended, shall come in his united Southern one, who shall yet more violently persecute the Clergy by the Apostatical seduction of one that shall have the absolute power over the Militant Church of God: And the Holy people of God and keeper of his Law, and all order of Religion shall be grievously persecuted and afflicted, insomuch that the blood of the true Ecclesiastical men shall float all over, and unto one of those horrid Kings this praise shall be given by his followers to have spilt more humane blood of the Innocent Clergymen, than any body can do Wine, and the said King shall commit incredible crimes against the Church; humane blood shall run through publick streets and Churches, as water coming from an impetuous Rain, and the next Rivers shall be red with blood, and by another Sea fight the Sea shall be red, insomuch that one King shall say to another, *Bellis rubuit navalibus æquor.* After that in the same year, & those that follow, shall happen the most horrid Plague, caused by the precedent famine, and so great tribulations as ever did happen since the first foundation of the Christian Church through all the Latine Regions; some marks of it remaining in some Countreys of *Spain.* At that time the Northern King hearing the complaint of the people of his principal title, shall raise up so great an Army, and shall go through the straights of his last Ancestors and Progenitors, that he will set up all again in their first state, and the great Vicar of the Cope, shall be restored in his former estate, but desolate and altogether forsaken, and then shall the *Sancta sanctorum* be destroyed by Paganism, and the old and New Testament be thrust out and burnt, after that shall Antechrist be the infernal Prince, and once more for the last all the Kingdoms of Christendom and also of the unbelievers shall quake for the space of 25 years, and there shall be more grievous Wars and Battles, and Towns, Cities, Castles and other buildings shall be burnt, desolate, and destroyed with a great effusion of Vestal blood, Married Women and Widows ravished, sucking Children dashed against the Walls of the Towns, and so many evils shall be committed by the means of the Infernal prince Satan, that almost the universal world shall be undone and desolate, and before these events many unusual Birds shall cry through the Air, *Huy, Huy,* and a little while after shall vanish away: And after that time shall have lasted a good while, there shall be renewed a Kingdom of *Saturn* and Golden Age. God the Creator shall say, hearing the affliction of his people, Satan shall be put, and tied in the bottom of the deep, and there shall begin an universal peace between God and men, and the Ecclesiastical power shall be in its greater force, and Satan shall be left bound for the space of a thousand years, and then shall be loosed again. All these Figures are justly fitted by the sacred Scripture, to the visible Cœlestial things, *viz. Saturn, Jupiter,* and *Mars,* and others joyned with them, as more at large may be seen in some of my Stanza's. I would have calculated it more deeply, and compared one with the other, but seeing (most excellent King) that some stand ready to censure me, I shall withdraw my Pen to its Nocturnal repose. *Multa etiam O Rex potentissime præclara, & sane in brevi ventura, sed omnia in hac tua Epistola innectere non possumus, nec volumus, sed ad intelligenda quedam facta, horrida fata pauca libanda sunt, quamvis tanta sit in omnes tua amplitudo & humanitas homines, deosque pietas, ut solus amplissimo & Christianissimo regis nomine, & ad quem summa totius Religionis authoritas deferatur, dignus esse videare.* But only I shall beseech you O most Merciful King, through your singular and prudent goodness, to understand rather the desire of my Heart, and the earnest desire I have to obey your most excellent Majesty, since my Eyes were so near your Royal Splendor, than the greatness of my work can deserve or require.

 From Selin this 27 June, 1558.

 Faciebat   *Michael*   *Nostradamus,*
Salonæ Petreæ, Provinciæ.

Michael Nostradamus.

CENTURY VIII.

I.

French.

Pau, Nay, Loron, plus feu qu'a sang sera, Laude nager, fuir grands aux Surrez, Les Agassas entrée refusera, Pampon, Durance, les tiendront enserrez. English.

Pau, *Nay*, *Loron*, more in fire then blood shall be, *Lauda* to swim, great ones run to the *Surrez*, The *Agassas* shall refuse the entry, *Pampon*, *Durance* shall keep them enclosed.

ANNOT.

The Prophecies of this, and of the remaining Centuries being for the most part so obscure, as no man is able to make any sense of them, the judicious Reader must not expect from me, what no man else can do; let him suffice if I give him as much light as I can, and leave the rest to his own judgement and industry.

Pau is the chief Town of the Province of *Bearn*, in the Kingdom of *Navarre*, where *Henry* the IV. King of *France* and *Navarre* was born. *Nay* and *Loron* are barbarous words, so are *Surrez*, *Agassas* and *Pampon*. *Durance* is a River of *France*.

II.

French.

Condon & Aux, & autour de Mirande, Je voy du Ciel feu qui les environne, Sol, Mars, conjoint au Lion, puis Marmande, Foudre, grand guerre, mur tomber dans Garonne. English.

Condon and *Aux*, and about *Mirande*, I see a fire from Heaven that encompasseth them, *Sol*, *Mars*, in conjunction with the Lion, and then *Marmande*, Lightning, great War, Wall falls into the *Garonne*.

ANNOT.

Condon, *Aux*, *Mirande*, and *Marmande* are Towns in the Province of *Guyenne* and *Languedoc*, *Garonne* is the River of *Bourdeaux*.

III.

Au fort Chasteau de Vigilanne & Resviers, Sera serré les puisnay de Nancy, Dedans Turin seront ards les premiers, Lors que de dueil Lyon sera transy. English.

In the strong Castle of *Vigilanne* and *Resviers*, Shall be kept close the youngest son of *Nancy*, Within *Turin* the first shall be burnt up, When *Lyon* shall be overwhelmed with sorrow.

ANNOT.

    Vigilanne and *Resviere* being falsly written here, it must be set down *Veillane* and *Riuiere*, which are two strong Castles, the first being seated in *Piemont*, and the last in *Burgundy*.
    Nancy is the chief Town of *Lorrain*, and *Turin* of *Piemont*, *Lyon* is a famous City in *France*, so that the sense of this Prophecy seemeth to be, that the youngest Son of *Nancy*, (that is of *Lorrain*) shall be kept close Prisoner in those two Castles of *Veillane* and *Riuiera*, and that the chief men of *Turin* shall be burnt, when the City of *Lyon* shall be oppressed with sorrow.

IV.

Dedans Monech le Coq sera receu, Le Cardinal de France apparoistra, Par Logarion Romain sera deceu, Foiblesse a l'Aigle, & force au Coq croistra. English.

Within *Monech* the Cock shall be admitted, The Cardinal of *France* shall appear, By *Logarion*, *Roman* shall be deceived, Weakness to the Eagle, and strength to the Cock shall grow.

ANNOT.

    Monech is false written here, it must be *Monaco*, which is a Principality and Town in *Italy* by *Genoa*, belonging to the House of the *Grimaldi*, wherein the *French* were admitted by the policy of Cardinal *Richelieu*, during the Wars between *France* and *Spain*.
    Logarion is a Barbarous name, by which he meaneth some body unknown to us.
    By the Eagle is meant the Emperour, who was very low at that time, and by the Cock, the King of *France*, who was very powerful, where it is to be observed, that by the Eagle the Emperour is always understood, because it is his Arms, and by the Cock is meant the King of *France*, because a *Frenchman* is called in Latine *Galius*, which also signifieth a Cock.

V.

Apparoistra Temple luisant orné, La Lampe & Cierge a Borne & Bretueil, Pour la Lucerne le Canton destourné, Quand on verra le grand Coq au Cercueil. English.

A shining adorned Temple shall appear, The Lamp and wax Candle at *Borne* and *Bretueil*, For *Lucerne* the Canton turned of, When the great Cock shall be seen in his Coffin.

Borne and *Bretueil* are two particular places, the first is one of the four Baronies of the River *Mase*, *viz. Petersem, Steen, Horne, Borne*, the other is a little Town in *Britany*.

Lucerne is one of the Cantons of *Switzerland*. We have said before what is meant by the great Cock, *viz.* the King of *France*. Let the Reader make up the rest, according to his fancy.

VI.

French.

Charté fulgure a Lyon apparente, Luysant, print Malte, subit sera estainte, Sardon, Mauris traitera decevante, Geneve a Londres, a Coq trahison feinte. English.

A thundering light at *Lyons* appearing, Bright, took *Maltha*, instantly shall be put out, Sardon shall treat *Mauris* deceitfully, To *Geneva*, *London*, and the Cock a fained treason.

ANNOT.

Maltha is an Island in the *Mediterranean* Sea, famous for the Knights that inhabit it, and take their name from thence. *Sardon* and *Mauris* are barbarous words.

VII.

French.

Verceil, Milan donra intelligence, Dedans Tycin sera faite la paye, Courir par Seine eau, sang, feu par Florence, Unique choir d'hault en bas faisant maye. English.

Verceil, Milan shall give intelligence, In the *Tycin* shall the Peace be made, Run through *Seine* water, blood, fire through *Florence*, The only one shall fall from top to bottom making maye.

ANNOT.

Verceil and *Milan* are two Cities in *Italy*, the *Tycin*, or rather *Thesin* is a River of the same Countrey; *Seine* is the River that runneth at *Paris*. *Florence* is a famous City in *Italy*, and *maye* a barbarous word, foisted up to patch up his Rime.

VIII.

French.

Pres de Linterne dans des tonnes fermez, Chivas fera pour l'Aigle la menée, L'Esleu cassé, luy ses ges enfermez, Dedans Turin rapt espouse emmenée. English.

Near *Linterne*, enclosed within Tuns, *Chivas* shall drive the plot for the Eagle, The Elect cashiered, he and his men shut up, Within *Turin*, a rape, and Bride carried away.

Linterne is a small Town in *Italy*; by *Tuns* are meant woodden Vessels, such as they put Rhenish wines and others in.

Chivas is a Town in *Piemont*, and *Turin* the chief Town of the said Countrey.

IX.

French.

Pendant que l'Aigle & le Coq a Savone, Seront unis, Mer, Levant & Hongrie, L'Armée a Naples, Palerme, Marque d'Ancone, Rome, Venise, par barbe horrible crie. English.

Whilst the Eagle and the Cock at *Savona*, Shall be united, Sea, *Levant*, and *Hungary*, Army at *Naples*, *Palermo*, Mark of *Ancona*, *Rome*, *Venice*, cry because of a horrid beard.

ANNOT.

By the Eagle is meant the Emperour, and by the Cock the King of *France*; the rest is easie.

X.

French.

Puanteur grande sortira de Lausane, Qu'on ne scaura l'origine du fait, L'on mettra hors toute la gent loingtaine, Feu veu au Ciel peuple estranger deffait. English.

A great stink shall come forth out of *Lausane*, So that no body shall know the ofspring of it, They shall put out all the Forreiners, Fire seen in Heaven, a strange people defeated.

ANNOT.

Lausane is a City situated in *Savoy*, by the Lake of *Geneva*, but now as I take it in the possession of the *Switzers*.

XI.

French.

Peuple infiny paroistre a Vicence, Sans force feu brusler la Basilique, Pres de Lunage des fait grand de Valence, Lors que Venise par morte prendre pique. English.

Infinite deal of people shall appear at *Vicence*, Without force, fire shall burn in the *Basilick*, Near *Lunage* the great one of *Valence* shall be defeated, When *Venice* by death shall take the pique.

Vicenza is a Town in *Italy*, under the dominion of the *Venetians*. *Basilick* is the name of the biggest sort of Canons or pieces of Ordinance. As for *Valence* there is three Cities of that name, one in *Spain*, the second in *France*, and the third in *Italy*; instead of *Lunage*, it must be *Lignago* which is a Town in *Italy*.

XII.

French.

Apparoistra aupres du Bufalore, L'haut & procere entré dedans Milan, L'Abbé de Foix avec ceux de Saint Maure, Feront la fourbe habillez en vilain. **English.**

Near the *Bufalore* shall appear, The high and tall, come into *Milan*, The Abbot of *Foix* with those of Saint *Maure*, Shall make the trumpery being cloathed like rogues.

ANNOT.

Bufalore is a barbarous word; *Foix* is a Countrey in *France*, and St. *Maure* a little Town in the said Countrey.

XIII.

French.

Le croisé Frere par amour effrenée, Fera par Praytus Bellerophon mourir, Classe a mil ans, la femme forcenée, Beu le breueage, tous deux apres perir. **English.**

The crossed Brother through unbridled love, Shall cause *Bellerophon* to be killed by *Praytus*, Fleet to thousand years, the woman out of her wit, The drink being drunk, both after that, perish.

ANNOT.

Bellerophon and *Praytus* are two supposed and fictitious names.

XIV.

French.

Le grand credit, d'or, d'argent l'abundance, Aveuglera par Libide l'honneur, Cogneu sera d'adultere l'offence, Qui parviendra a son grand deshonneur. **English.**

The great credit, the abundance of Gold and Silver Shall blind honour by lust, The offence of the Adulterer shall be known, Which shall come to his great dishonour.

ANNOT.

This is easie to be understood; for it is frequently seen, that Honour is made blind by lust, and chiefly if that lust be propped up with credit; and abundance of Gold and Silver.

XV.

French.

Vers Aquilon grands efforts par hommasse, Presque l'Europe, l'Univers vexer, Les deux Eclipses mettra en telle chassé, Et aux Pannons vie & mort renforcer. English.

Towards the North great endeavours by a manly woman, To trouble *Europe*, and almost all the world, She shall put to flight the two Eclipses, And shall re-inforce life and death to the *Pannons*.

ANNOT.

By the *Pannons* is meant the *Hungarians*. The rest is easie.

XVI.

French.

Au lieu que Hieson fit sa nef fabriquer, Si grand Deluge sera & si subite, Qu'on n'aura lieu ne Terre sattaquer, L'onde monter Fesulan Olympique. English.

In the place where *Jason* caused his Ship to be built, So great a Flood shall be, and so sudden, That there shall be neither place nor Land to save themselves, The Waves shall climb upon the *Olympick Fesulan*.

ANNOT.

Jason was Son to King *Æson*, who built a Ship called *Argos*, in which he went to *Colchos*, to Conquer the Golden Fleece.

Fesulan here is to be understood of some high and eminent place, which therefore he calleth *Olympick*, from *Olympus* a high Mountain in *Grecia*. The place where *Jason* builded his Ship.

XVII.

French.

Les bien aisez subit seront desmis, Le monde mis par les trois freres en trouble, Cité Marine saisiront ennemis, Faim, feu, sang, peste, & de tous maux le double. English.

Those that were at ease shall be put down, The world shall be put in trouble by three Brothers, The Maritine City shall be seized by its enemies, Hunger, fire, blood, plague, and the double of all evils.

It is not easie to tell what them three Brothers have been, or shall be, nor that Maritine or Sea City, therefore we leave it to the liberty of every ones judgement, the words being plain enough.

XVIII.

French.

De Flore issue de sa mort sera cause, Un temps devant par jeusne & vieille bueyre, Car les trois lis luy feront telle pause, Par son fruit sauve comme chair crüe mueyre. **English.**

Issued from *Flora* shall be the cause of her own death, One time before, through fasting and old drink, For the three Lillies shall make her such a pause, Saved by her fruit, as raw flesh dead.

ANNOT.

This is one of those, wherein the Author would not be understood, and may be did not understand himself.

XVIX.

French.

A soustenir la grand cappe troublée, Pour l'esclaireir les rouges marcheront, De mort famille sera presqu'accablée, Les rouges rouges, le rouge assommeront. **English.**

To maintain up the great troubled Cloak, The red ones shall march for to clear it, A family shall be almost crushed to death, The red, the red, shall knock down the red one.

ANNOT.

This seemeth to carry no other sense than a conspiracy of the Cardinals, called here by the name of the *Red*, the *Red* against the Pope, who is called the *Red one*.

XX.

French.

Le faux message par election feinte, Courir par Urbem rompue pache arreste, Voix acheptées de sang chappelle teinte, Et a un autre qui l'Empire conteste. **English.**

The contract broken, stoppeth the message, From going about the Town, by a fained election, Voices shall be bought, and a Chappel died with blood, By another, who challengeth the Empire.

ANNOT.

This was so falsely printed, and so preposterously set in order, that I had much ado to pick out this little sense of it, which amounteth to no more, than that by reason of an agreement broken, the Messenger, that went to publish a faigned election (it seemeth of the Empire) shall be hindred, and that one of the Competitors to the said Empire, shall be killed in or near a Chappel, that shall be soiled by his Blood.

XXI.

French.

Au port de Agde trois fustes entreront, Portant infection avec soy, pestilence, Passant le pont mil milles embleront, Et le pont rompre a tierce resistance. English.

Three Galleys shall come into the harbour of *Agde*, Carrying with them infection and Pestilence, Going beyond the Bridge, they shall carry away thousands, At the third resistance the Bridge shall be broken.

ANNOT.

Agde is a Sea Town in *France* upon the *Mediterranean* Sea, which is threatned here of three Galleys, that shall come into the Harbour of it, and shall bring with them infection and Plague; and besides carry away thousands of Captives, by which it seemeth, that these should be *Turkish* Galleys, till at last upon the third resistance of the Townsmen the Bridge shall be broken.

XXII.

French.

Gorsan, Narbonne, par le Sel advertir, Tucham, la Grace Perpignan trahie, La ville rouge ny voudra consentir, Par haute Voldrap, Gris vie faillie. English.

Gorsan, Narbonne, by the Salt shall give notice, To *Tucham,* the Grace *Perpignan* betrayed, The red Town will not give consent to it, By high *Woldrap,* Gray, life ended.

ANNOT.

This is another, wherein my best skill faileth me; for take away *Narbonne,* which is a City of *France,* in the Province of *Languedoc,* and *Perpignan,* which is another in the County of *Roussilon* near *Spain.* The rest are either barbarous words or nonsensical to me.

XXIII.

Lettres trouvées de la Reyne les Coffres, Point de subscrit, sans aucun nom d'Autheur, Par la police seront cachez les offres, Qu'on ne scaura qui sera lamateur. English.

Letters found in the Queens Coffers, No superscription, no name of the Author, By policy shall be concealed the offers, So that no body shall know who shall be the lover.

ANNOT.

This needeth no great explication, being pretty plain, and foretelleth only that a Queens Trunks shall be opened, wherein many love Letters shall be found without subscription, with many great offers, which by policy being suppressed, or no notice taken of. The lover was never known.

XXIV.

French.

Le Lieutenant a l'entrée l'huis, Assommera le grand de Perpignan, En se cuidant sauver a Montpertuis, Sera deceu Bastard de Lusignan. English.

The Lieutenant shall at the doors entry. Knock down the great one of *Perpignan*: And the Bastard of *Lusignan* shall be deceived, Thinking to save himself at *Montpertuis*.

ANNOT.

The words and the sense are clear, though the meaning is hard to be understood.

XXV.

French.

Cœur de l'Amant ouvert d'amour furtive, Dans le ruisseau sera ravir la Dame, Le demy mal contrefaira lascive, Le Pere a deux privera corps de l'Ame. English.

The Lovers heart being by a stoln love, Shall cause the Dame to be ravished in the Brook, The lascivious shall counterfeit half a discontent, The Father shall deprive the bodies of both of their souls.

ANNOT.

This signifieth nothing but a Lover, who meeting in or by a Brook, his Mistress shall enjoy her, for which she shall fain a little discontent, as if she had been ravished against her will, but her jealous Father not contented therewith, shall kill them both, which is an ordinary *Italian* trick.

XXVI.

French.

De Carones trouvez en Barcelonne, Mys descouvers, lieu terrouers & ruine, Le grand qui tient ne voudra Pampelone, Par l'Abbaye de Montferrat bruine. English.

The *Carones* fond in *Barcelona*, Put discovered, place soil and ruine, The great that hold will not *Pampelona*, By the Abbaye of *Montferrat*, mist.

ANNOT.

Barcelona is a Town of a Province in *Spain*, called *Catalonia. Pampelona* is the chief Town of the Kingdom of *Navarre. Montferrat* is an Abbaye in the Mountains of *Catalonia*; the rest is insignificant.

XXVII.

French.

La voye Auxelle l'un sur l'autre fornix, Du muy de fer hors mis brave & genest, L'Escrit d'Empereur la Phœnix, Veu en celuy ce qu'a nul autre nest. English.

The way *Auxelle*, one Arch upon another, Being brave and gallant put out of the Iron vessel, The writing of the Emperour the Phœnix, In it shall be seen, what no where else is.

ANNOT.

I can find nothing in this worth interpretation.

XXVIII.

French.

Les Simulachres d'or & d'argent enflez, Qu'apres le rapt, Lac au feu furent jettez, Au descouvert estaints tous & troublez, Au Marbre escripts, prescripts interjettez. English.

The Images sweld with Gold and Silver, Which after the rape were thrown into the Lake and fire, Being discovered after the putting out of the fire, Shall be written in Marble, prescripts being intermixed.

ANNOT.

It seemeth that this gold and silver Idols having been stoln, were afterwards thrown into a Lake and a fire, which fire being put out, those Idols were found, and the memorial engraven in Marble.

XXIX.

Au quart pilier ou l'on sacre a Saturne, Par tremblant Terre & Deluge fendu, Soubs l'edifice Saturnin trouvée Urne, D'or Capion, ravy puis tost rendu. English.

At the fourth Pillar where they sacrifice to *Saturn,* Cloven by an Earth-quake and a Flood, An Urne shall be found under that *Saturnian* building, Full of *Capion* gold stoln, and then restored.

ANNOT.

      This foretelleth, that at the fourth Pillar of a Temple that was dedicated to *Saturn,* which Pillar shall be split by an Earth-quake and a Flood, there shall be found an Urne, (which is an Earthen Vessel, wherein the ancient *Romans* used to keep the ashes of their dead friends) full of gold, that shall be carried away, and then restored.

XXX.

French.

Dedans Tholose non loin de Beluzer, Faisant un puis loing Palais d'espectacle, Thresor trouvé un chacun ira vexer, Et en deux locs tout aupres des Vesacle. English.

Within *Tholose* not far from *Beluzer,* Digging a Well, for the Pallace of spectacle, A treasure found that shall vex every one, In two parcels, in, and near the *Basacle.*

ANNOT.

      Tholose is the chief City of *Languedoc, Beluzer* is a private place within its precinct, Spectacle is insignificant, and is onely foisted in, to Rime with *Basacle,* which is a place in *Tholose,* where there is aboundance of Water-mills, that make a hideous and fearful noise.

XXXI.

French.

Premier grand fruit le Prince de Pesquiere, Mais puis viendra bien & cruel malin, Dedans Venise perdra sa gloire fiere, Et mis a mal par plus joyve Celin. English.

The first great fruit the Prince of *Pesquiere,* But he shall become very cruel and malicious, He shall loose his fierce pride in *Venice,* And shall be put to evil by the younger *Celin.*

ANNOT.

      Pescaire is a Town in the Kingdom of *Naples,* belonging to the noble *Spanish* Family of *Avalos,* of which it seemeth one shall prove cruel and malicious; but he shall be killed in *Venice* by one young *Celin*, by which formerly, and in other places the Author understandeth the *Turk*.

XXXII.

French.

Garde toy Roy Gaulois de ton Nepveu, Qui fera tant que ton unique filz, Sera meurtry a Venus faisant vœu, Accompagné de nuit que trois & six. English.

Take heed O *French* King of thy Nephew, Who shall cause that thine only Son Shall be murdered making a vow to *Venus*, Accompanied with three and six.

ANNOT.

This is a plain warning to a *French* King to beware of his Nephew, who accompanied with nine others, shall cause his Son to be murdered when he went about some venereal employment.

XXXIII.

French.

Le grand naistra de Verone & Vicence, Qui portera un surnom bien indigne, Qui a Venise voudra faire vengeance, Luy mesme prins homme du guet & signe. English.

The great one of *Verona* and *Vicenza* shall be born, Who shall bear a very unworthy surname, Who shall endeavour at *Venice* to avenge himself, But he shall be taken by a Watch-man.

ANNOT.

Verona and *Vicenza* are two famous Cities in *Italy*, under the dominion of the *Venetians*; the rest is easie.

XXXIV.

French.

Apres victoire du Lion au Lion, Sur la Montagne de Jura Secatombe, Delues, & Brodes septiesme milion, Lyon Ulme a Mausol mort & tombe. English.

After the Victory of the Lion against the Lion, Upon the Mountain *Jura Secatomb*, *Delues*, and *Brodes* the seventh Million, *Lyons*, Ulme fall dead at *Mausol*.

ANNOT.

The Mount *Jura* is in *Switzerland*; *Lyon* is a great City in *France*; and *Ulme* another in *Germany*; the rest is either barbarous or insignificant.

XXXV.

Dedans l'entree de Garonne & Blaye, Et la Forest non loing de Damazan, De Marsaves gelées, puis gresle & Bize, Dordonois gelé par erreur de Mezan. **English.**

Within the entrance of *Garonne* and *Blaye*, And the Forrest not far from *Damazan*, Of *Marsaves* frosts, then Hail and North wind, *Dordonois* frozen by the error of *Mezan*.

ANNOT.

     Garonne is the River that runneth at *Bourdeaux*, and *Blaye* is the Port Town that lieth at the mouth of it; I should think that instead of *Dordonois*, it should be Printed *Dordone*, which is another River thereabouts, and is here threatned to be frozen.

XXXVI.

French.

Sera commis contre Oinde a Duché De Saulne, & Saint Aubin, & Belœuvre, Paver de Marbre, de tours loing pluche, Non Bleteran resister & chef d'œuvre. **English.**

A Dukedom shall be committed against *Oinde*, Of *Saulne*, and Saint *Aubin*, and *Belœuvre*, To pave with Marble, and of Towers well pickt, Not *Bleteran* to resist, and master-piece.

ANNOT.

     I confess my Ignorance, and should be glad that a better *Oedipus* than I would undertake this.

XXXVII.

French.

La forteresse aupres de la Thamise, Cherra par lors, le Roy dedans serré, Aupres du pont sera veu en chemise, Un devant mort, puis dans le fort barré. **English.**

The strong Fort near the *Thames* Shall fall then, the King that was kept within, Shall be seen near the Bridge in his Shirt, One dead before, then in the Fort kept close.

ANNOT.

     The Dream be to them that hate thee, and the Interpretation thereof to thine Enemies, Dan. 4, v. 10.

XXXVIII.

Le Roy de Blois dans Avignon regner, Un autrefois le peuple emonopole, Dedans le Rhosne par murs fera baigner, Jusques a cinq, le dernier pres de Nole. English.

The King of *Blois* in *Avignon* shall Reign Another time the people do murmur, He shall cause in the *Rhosne* to be bathed through the Walls, As many as five, the last shall be near *Nole*.

ANNOT.

       This foretelleth that a King of *France* shall take *Avignon*, which is a City in *France* belonging to the Pope. And that some of the people beginning to murmur and mutiny, he shall cause five of them to be thrown over the Walls into the *Rhosne*, which is a swift River that passeth by. *Nole* must be some place thereabouts.

XXXIX.

Qu'aura esté par Prince Bizantin, Sera tollu par Prince de Tholose, La foy de Foix, par le chef Tholentin, Luy faillira ne refusant l'espouse. English.

What shall have been by a *Bizantin* Prince, Shall be taken away by the Prince of *Tholose*, The faith of *Foix* by the chief *Tholentin*, Shall fail him, not refusing the Spouse.

ANNOT.

       I can understand nothing else by Prince *Bizantin*, but some Prince of the house of *Gonzague*, who derive their pedigree from that of the *Palæologues*, formerly Emperours of *Constantinople*, called in ancient time *Bizantium*. As for the Prince of *Tholose*, there having been none this two or three hundred years since that Country was devolved to the Crown of *France*; but the King himself, I suppose he must be understood here; so that the sense of this Prophecie, (if any be) is, that the King of *France* shall take something from the Duke of *Mantua*, who is the head of the *Gonzagues*, as he hath done formerly several times.

       By the faith of *Foix*, is understood the late Duke of *Rohan*, who descended from the house of *Foix*, and who did war against the said Duke of *Mantua* at that time, when the King of *France*, *Lewis* XIII. would not suffer his Brother the Duke of *Orleans* to Marry the Princess *Mary*, Daughter of the Duke of *Nevers*, of the house of *Gonzague*, and lately Queen of *Poland*.

XL.

Le sang du juste par Taur & la Dorade, Pour se vanger contre les Saturnins, Au nouveau Lac plongeront la Mainade, Puis marcheront contre les Albanins. English.

The blood of the just by *Taur* and *Dorade*, To avenge themselves against the *Saturnins*, In the new Lake shall sink the *Mainade*, Then shall go forth against the *Albanins*.

ANNOT.

Here the Author hath kept his mind to himself, as for my part, being ignorant of his barbarous words, I had rather leave the sense of this to the judgment of the Reader, than by an incongruous and far fetched interpretation make my self ridiculous.
XLI.

French.

Esleu sera Renard ne sonnant mot, Faisant le Saint public, vivant pain d'orge, Tyranniser apres tant a un cop, Mettant le pied des plus grands sur la gorge. English.

A Fox shall be elected that said nothing, Making a publick Saint, living with Barley bread, Shall tyrannise after upon a sudden, And put his foot upon the Throat of the greatest.

ANNOT.

This Prophecy seemeth to regard particularly the Pope, who having played the Hypocrite before his Election, eating nothing but Barley bread, that he might be reputed a Spaint, shall after his Election shall tyrannise upon a sudden, and trample upon the Throat of the greatest Monarchs, as they have done formerly, and would do yet if they could.
XLII.

French.

Par avarice, par force & violence, Viendra vexer les siens chefs d'Orleans, Prez Saint Memire assaut & resistance, Mort dans sa Tente, diront quil dort leans. English.

By avarice, by force and violence, Shall come to vex his own chief of *Orleans*, Near Saint *Memire* assault and resistance, Dead in his Tent, they'l say he sleepeth there.

ANNOT.

The construction of this must be thus made. The Chiefs of *Orleans*, (which is a famous Town in *France*) shall come to vex their own (I suppose) Citizens. And near that place called Saint *Memire*, shall be a fight, where one of those chief ones shall be killed, or die in his Tent, and shall be denyed under pretence of being asleep.
XLIII.

French.

Par le decide de deux choses Bastars, Nepveu du sang occupera le Regne, Dedans Lectoure seront les coups de dards, Nepveu par peur pleira l'Enseigne. English.

By the decision of two things, Bastards, Nephew of the Blood shall occupy the Kingdom, Within *Lectoure* shall be strokes of Darts, Nephew through fear shall fold up his Ensign.

I think that instead of decision it should be division, and then the sense is easily made up, thus; that through the division of two Bastards, the Nephew of the Blood shall occupy the Kingdom, which Nephew afterwards in a fight at *Lectoure*, (which is a strong Town in *Gascony*) shall be put to the worst, and compelled to fold up his Ensigns.

XLIV.

French.

Le procrée naturel d'Ogmion, De sept a neuf du chemin destourner, A Roy de longue & amy au my hom, Doit a Navarre fort de Pau prosterner. English.

The natural begotten of *Ogmyon*, From seven to nine shall put out of the way, To King of long, and friend to the half man, Ought to *Navarre* prostrate the fort of *Pau*.

ANNOT.

A man needeth a good pair of Spectacles to see through all this, what I understand in it is that this Bastard of *Ogmyon*, by whom he meaneth the King of *France*, ought to submit the Fort of *Pau* to *Navarre*, and good reason too; for *Navarre* is the Kingdom, and *Pau* only the chief Town of one Province of it, called *Bearn*.

XLV.

French.

La main escharpe & la jambe bandée, Louis puisné de Palais partira, Au mot du guet la mort sera tardée, Puis dans le Temple a Pasques seignera. English.

The hand on a Scarf, and the leg swadled, The younger *Lewis* shall go from *Palais*, At the Watch word his death shall be protracted, Then afterwards at *Easter* he shall bleed in the Temple.

ANNOT.

The Prince of *Condé*, whose name was *Lewis*, and the youngest of the Children of *Charles* of *Bourbon*, the first Duke of *Vendosme*, father to *Anthony* of *Bourbon*, King of *Navarre*, went away from the Court in the time of *Francis* the second King of *France*, and came into *Bearn* to the King his Brother. He was summoned many times by *Francis* II. to come to Court; but finding his name to be amongst those that intended to surprise *Lion*, he durst not venture.

Nevertheless he was perswaded by his Uncle the Cardinal of *Bourbon*, and came to the Court at *Orleans*. It is easie to believe that he fained himself to be hurt by a fall from his Horse, or that really he was so; *having his Arm in a Scarf, and his Leg swadled up*, in which posture he came to testifie his obedience to the Kings commands.

In this posture of a wounded man, whether really and fictitiously he came from *Palais*, which by mistake is printed *Calais*; the Printer being ignorant, that in *Bearn*, where the Prince had sheltered himself, there is a Castle called *Palais*, which was the place that the Prince used to live in.

Being come to Court he was presently arrested, arraigned and condemned to death. Nevertheless the Kings sickness proving mortal, the execution was suspended, and his life saved. After that the Prince sought all occasions to revenge himself, and began about *Easter* in *April* following. It was not by an open Rebellion against the King, but under pretence to maintain the Protestant Religion: therefore the Author saith, *that this life saved shall bleed in the Temple*; because the Princes pretext was the Temple and the Church; that is Religion. Hence the fourth Verse is clearly understood. Resteth the third Verse, which saith, that his life was differred till the *Watch word*; because the Queen seeing the King her Son upon his death bed, caused secretly the execution of the Sentence to be differred, that she might make use of the King of *Navarre*, and of the Prince his Brothers favour, against the house of *Guise*, for the obtaining of the Regency.

Moreover I observe, that in the year 1562. the Prince of *Condé* began openly to rebel, surprising the City of *Orleans* the 29 of *March*, which was *Easter day* that year, which sheweth the truth of the fourth Verse.

XLVI.

French.

Pol Mensolée mourra trois lieues du Rhosne, Fuis les deux prochains Tarare destrois, Car Mars sera le plus horrible Throsne, De Coq & d'Aigle, de France frere trois. English.

Paul Mensolée Shall die three Leagues from the *Rhosne*, Avoid the two straights near the *Tarare*; For *Mars* shall keep such a horrible throsne, Of Cock and Eagle, of *France* three Brothers.

ANNOT.

By this *Pol Mensolée*, he meaneth some proper name. *Tarare* is a great Mountain near the City of *Lions*, that hath two principal ways to go through, which here he calleth Straights; for indeed they are very dangerous for Thieves and Murderers. The rest is but a threating of War between the Emperour and *France*, when there shall be three Brothers in *France*.

XLVII.

French.

Lac Trasmenien portera tesmoignage, Des conjurez ferrez dedans Perouse, Un Despolle contrefera le sage, Tuant Tedesque de Sterne & Minuse. English.

Trasmenian Lake shall bear witness Of the Conspirators shut up in *Perugia*, A *Despolle* shall counterfeit the wise, Killing *Tedesque* of *Sterne* and *Minuse*.

ANNOT.

I think that the Impression is false here; for instead of *Despolle*, which is a barbarous word, and signifieth nothing, I would have it in *French Despoville*, in *English* robbed of all; so that *Trasmenian* Lake is that Lake in *Italy* not far from the Town of *Perugia*, where *Hannibal* gave that notable overthrow to the *Romans*, and killed above 20000. of them, with their consul *Flaminius*.

That man whom he calleth here robbed of all, shall kill some *Germans*; for *Tudesco* in

Italian, is a *German*, the two last words are barbarous.

XLVIII.

French.

Saturne en Cancer, Jupiter avec Mars, Dedans Fevrier Caldondon, Salvaterre, Sault, Castalan, assailly des trois parts, Pres de Verbiesque, conflict mortelle guerre. English.

Saturn in *Cancer*, *Jupiter* with *Mars*, In *February Caldondon*, *Salvaterre*, *Sault*, *Castalon*, assaulted on three sides, Near *Verbiesque*, fight and mortal War.

ANNOT.

The multiplicity of barbarous and insignificant words, makes this incapable of any construction, if any body will exercise his wit thereupon, I shall willingly lend him my ear.

XLIX.

French.

Satur au Bœuf, Jove en l'Eau, Mars en fleche, Six de Fevrier mortalité donra, Ceux de Tardaigne a Bruges si grand breche Qu'a Ponterose chef Barbarin mourra. English.

Satur in Ox, *Jupiter* in water, *Mars* in arrow, The sixth of *February* shall give mortality, Those of *Tardaigne* shall make in *Bruges* so great a breach, That the chief *Barbarin* shall die at *Pontrose*.

ANNOT.

Satur in Ox; that is, *Saturn* in *Taurus*, *Jupiter in Water*; that is, *Jupiter* in *Aquarius*; *Mars in arrow*, is *Mars* in *Sagitarius*; when these things shall happen. *The sixth day of February shall bring a great mortality*. *Tardaigne* is a fictitious name, unless he intended *Sardaigne*. *Bruges* is a Town in *Flander*, *Ponterose* is some place, where he saith, that the chief *Barbarin* shall die, the chief Barbare was the Pope *Urban* the eighth; but because I do not know the particularities of his death, and the place of it, I cannot make the rest good.

L.

French.

La Pestilence lentour de Capadille, Un autre faim pres de Sagunt sapreste, La Chevalier Bastard de bon senille, Au grand de Thunes fera trancher la teste. English.

The Plague shall be round about *Capadille*, Another famine cometh near to that of *Sagunce*, The Knight Bastard of the good old man, Shall cause the great one of *Tunis* to be beheaded.

The difficulty here, is what is meant by that word *Cappadille*, for my part I think he meaneth *Italy*, for some times the *Italians* use by way of admiration to say *Capoli*, or *Capadillo*. *Sagunce* is a Town in *Spain*, which for the love of the *Carthaginians* withstood the *Romans* a great while, till they were brought to an extremity of famine, and then set fire in their Town.

LI.

French.

Le Bizantin faisant oblation, Apres avoir Cordube a soy reprinse, Son chemin long, repos, pamplation, Mer passant proye par la Cologne a prinse. English.

The *Bizantin*, making an offering, After he hath taken *Cordua* to himself again, His way long, rest, contemplation, Crossing the Sea hath taken a prey by *Cologne*.

ANNOT.

This is an express delineation of *Charles* the V. Empire, who at the latter end of his days retired into a Monastery, reserving unto himself for his subsistance the revenue of the Kingdom of *Castille*, expressed here by *Cordua*, which is a City of *Spain*.

LII.

French.

Le Roy de Blois dans Avignon Regner, D'Amboise & Seme viendra le long de Lindre. Ongle a Poitiers Saintes aisles ruiner, Devant Bony. English.

The King of *Blois* shall Reign in *Avignon*, He shall come from *Amboise* and *Seme*, along the *Linder*, A Nail at *Poitiers* shall ruine the Holy Wings, Before *Bony*.

ANNOT.

The first Verse and the interpretation is easie.
Amboise is a Town in *France* upon the River of *Loire*.
The two last Verses being inperfect, admits of no interpretation, onely to let the Reader know that *Poitiers* is a very great City in *France*, and Capital of the Province of *Poitou*.

LIII.

French.

Dedans Boulogne voudra laver ses fautes, Il ne poura au Temple du Soleil, Il volera faisant choses si hautes, En Hierarchie n'en fut onc un pareil. English.

He shall desire to wash his faultes in *Bulloin*, In the Church of the Sun, but he shall not be able, He shall fly doing so high things, That the like was never in *Hierarchy.*

ANNOT.

There is two Towns called *Bolloin*, one is in *Italy*, the other in *France*, the last is that which is meant here; for Cardinal *Richelieu* who is the man that did so high things, and the like of which was never in *Hierarchy* (that is in the Clergy) a little afore his death had vowed if he recovered his health to go in Pilgrimage to *Bulloin*, where there is a famous Temple for Miracles, (as they say) dedicated to our Lady, which is called here the Sun, by an allusion to that passage of the Revelation: *And there appeared a Woman cloathed with the Sun*; but the said Cardinal was prevented by death.

LIV.

French.

Soubs la couleur du traité mariage, Fait magnanime par grand Chiren Selin, Quintin, Arras, recouvrez au voiage, D'Espagnols fait second banc Macelin. English.

Under pretence of a Treaty of Marriage, A Magnanimous act shall be done by the great *Cheiren Selin, Quintin, Arras* recovered in the journey, Of *Spaniards* shall be made a second *Macelin* Bench.

ANNOT.

This is a Prognostication concerning a King of *France*, meant here by the great *Cheiren Selin*, who under pretence of a Treaty of Marriage, shall recover in his journey these two Towns Saint *Quintin* and *Arras*, for the Shambles are called in Latine *Macellum. Quod ibi mactentur pectora quæ mercatoribus venundantur.*

LV.

French.

Entre deux Fleuves se verra enserré, Tonneaux & caques unis a passer outre, Huit Pont rompus chef a tant enferré, Enfans parfaits sont jugulez en coultre. English.

Between two Rivers he shall find himself shut up, Tuns and Barrels put together to pass over, Eight Bridges broken, the chief at last in Prison, Compleat children shall have their throat cut.

ANNOT.

It is an accident that hath often happened to a Commander of an Army, to find himself either by his own oversight, or by the policy of his enemies, shut up between two Rivers, having upon neither of them a Bridge at his command; as it did happen once to the Prince of *Condé*, the Grandfather of this, in the time of the Civil war for Religion, who was forced by it to dissolve his Army, and bid every one shift for himself, so that they almost all escaped by several small parties, some going one way some another, at such time it is an ordinary shift to make use of empty Vessels and Caskes to make a Bridge, as our Author doth mention here.

LVI.

French.

La bande foible la Terre occupera, Ceux du haut lieu feront horribles cris, Le gros troupeau d'estre coin troublera, Tombe pres D. nebro descouvert les escrits. English.

The weak party shall occupy the ground, Those of the high places shall make fearful cries, It shall trouble the great flock in the right corner, He falleth near *D. nebro* discovereth the writings.

ANNOT.

I dare not comment upon this, for fear it should be said of me, what was said of the Glose of *Accurtius*; *obscura per obscurius*.

LVII.

French.

De Soldat simple parviendra en Empire, De Robe courte parviendra a la longue, Vaillant aux Armes, en Eglise ou plus pire, Vexer les Prestres comme l'eau fait l'espouge. English.

From a simple Souldier he shall come to have the supreme command, From a short Gown he shall come to the long one, Vaillant in Arms, no worse man in the Church, He shall vex the Priests, as water doth a Spunge.

ANNOT.

I never knew nor heard of any body to whom this Stanza might be better applied, then to the late Usurper *Cromwel*, for from a simple Souldier, he became to be Lord Protector, and from a Student in the University he became a graduate in *Oxford*, he was valliant in Arms, and the worse Churchman that could be found; as for vexing the Priests, I mean the Prelatical Clergy, I believe none went beyond him.

LVIII.

French.

Regne en querelle aux freres divisé, Prendre les Armes & les nom Britannique, Tiltre Anglican sera tard advisé, Surprins de nuit, mener a l'air Gallique. English.

A Kingdom in dispute, and divided between the Brothers, To take the Arms and the *Britannick* name, And the *English* title, he shall advise himself late, Surprised in the night and carried into the *French* air.

ANNOT.

This prognosticateth a great division in *England* between Brothers, about the Title and

Kingdom of *England*, insomuch, that in conclusion one shall be surprised by night, and carried away into *France*.

LIX.

French.

Par deux fois haut, par deux fois mis a bas, L'Orient aussi l'Occident foiblira, Son adversaire apres plusieurs combats, Par Mer chassé au besoin faillira. **English.**

Twice set up high, and twice brought down, The East also the West shall weaken, His adversary after many fights, Expelled by Sea, shall fail in need.

ANNOT.

This foretelleth of some considerable person, who shall be twice set up, and brought down again. The second Verse is pronounced after the manner of the old Oracles, as
Aio te Æacida Romanos vincere posse,

For no body can tell here whither the East shall weaken the West, or otherways. The last two Verses are easie.

LX.

French.

Premier en Gaule, premier en Romanie, Par Mer & Terre aux Anglois & Paris, Merveilleux faits par cette grand mesgnie, Violant, Terax perdra le Norlaris. **English.**

The first in *France*, the first in *Romania*, By Sea and Land to the *English* and *Paris*, Wonderful deeds by that great company, By ravishing, *Terax* shall spoil the *Norlaris*.

ANNOT.

The first in *France* is the King, the first in *Romania* is the *Pope*, who it seemeth shall joyn together by Sea and Land, and come against *Paris*, who shall call the *English* to its help, insomuch, that strange deeds shall be done by that great company. As for *Terax*, it seemeth to be the proper name of some man, who by ravishing a woman called here the *Norlaris*, shall spoil her and cause sad consequences. *Norlaris* by transposition of Letters is *Lorrain*.

LXI.

French.

Jamais par le decouvrement du jour, Ne parviendra au signe Sceptrifere, Que tous Sieges ne soient en sejour, Portant au Coq don du Tag a misere. **English.**

Never by the discovering of the day, He shall attain to the Sceptriferous sign, Till all his seats be settled, Carrying to the Cock a gift from the *Tag* to misery.

ANNOT.

This signifieth that one pretending to a Kingdom, shall never attain to it by often removing his place, until all his seats be settled, that is, untill his wandring be ceased. And a gift brought by him to the King of *France* from *Portugal*, signified here by the *Tag*, which is the River of *Lisbon* the Capital City of it, from which gift shall proceed misery.

LXII.

French.

Lors qu'on verra expiler le Saint Temple, Plus grand du Rhosne, & sacres prophaner: Par eux naistra pestilence si grande, Roy fait injuste ne sera condamner. English.

When one shall see spoiled the Holy Temple, The greatest of the *Rhosne*, and sacred things prophaned, from them shall come so great a pestilence, That the King being unjust shall not condemn them.

ANNOT.

The greatest Temple of the *Rhosne*, is that of the City of *Lion*, which is seated upon that River of *Rhosne*, which when it shall be robbed and spoiled, then shall come a horrid Pestilence, which our Author attributeth to the injustice of the King then Reigning, who shall neglect to punish those Sacriledges.

LXIII.

French.

Quand l'adultere blessé sans coup aura, Meurdry la femme & le fils par depit, Femme assomée l'Enfant estranglera, Huit captifs prins sestoufer sans respit. English.

When the Adulterer wounded without a blow, Shall have murdered the wife and son by spight, The woman knocked down, shall strangle the child, Eight taken prisoners, and stifled without tarrying.

ANNOT.

This is the description of a sad Tragedy, which to understand, you must joyn all the Verses together, and make it one sense. The Adulterer wounded without a blow, is one that shall get a disease, (suppose the *Pox*) his wife finding fault with it, he shall murder her, and her Son; she not being quite dead shall strangle another Child (which it seemeth she had by this Adulterer) and for this fact eight shall be taken prisoners and immediately hanged, by which you must suppose the fact to be done in *France*, for there they Judge and Hang immediately, whereby in *England* they must stay till Sessions-time.

LXIV.

Dedans les Isles les enfans transportez, Les deux de sept seront en desespoir, Ceux de terrouer en seront supportez, Nompelle prins, des ligues fuy l'espoir. English.

In the Islands the Children shall be transported, The two of seven shall be in despair, Those of the Countrey shall be supported by, *Nompelle* taken, avoid the hope of the League.

ANNOT.

This seemeth to have a great relation to our late unhappy troubles in *England*, when the Princess *Elizabeth* and the Duke of *Glocester* were transported into the Isle of *Wight*, which are the two of the seven, (for the Queen hath had seven children) and the Kings Majesty and his Highness the Duke of *York*, were driven into the *Low-Countreis*, being in a manner in dispair of ever coming again, and those Countreys were much the better for the harbouring of them; in the last Verse by *Nompelle* I understand Anagrammatically *Monpelier*, which being taken, there is no more hope in the League, as it did happen in the time of *Henry* the IV. King of *France*, who never saw the League or Covenant quite routed, till that Town was taken; for it is familiar enough to those kind of Prophets to make an ὕστερον πρώτερον, and joyn things past, to those that are to come, to darken the Readers understanding, and as the Scripture saith, *Ut videntes non videant*.

LXV.

French.

Le vieux frustré du principal espoir, Il parviendra au chef de son Empire, Vingt mois tiendra le Regne a grand pouvoir, Tyran, cruel en delaissant un pire. English.

The old man frustrated of his chief hope, He shall attain to the head of his Empire, Twenty months he shall keep the Kingdom with great power, Tyrant, cruel, and having a worse one.

ANNOT.

The words of this Prophecy are plain enough, and because I cannot learn in History that such things have come to pass yet, therefore I reckon it among those *de futuro*.

LXVI.

French.

Quand l'Escriture D. M. trouvée, Et Cave antique a Lampe descouverte, Loy, Roy, & Prince Vlpian esprouvée, Pavillon, Royne & Duc soubs la couverte. English.

When the writing D. M. shall be found, And an ancient Cave discovered with a Lamp, Law, King, and Prince *Ulpian* tried, Tent, Queen and Duke under the rugge.

In the year 1555. *Ferdinand Alvaro* of *Toledo* Duke of *Alba*, being sent by *Charles* the V. into *Italy* to resist the *French*, arrived in *June* at *Milan*, and having gathered together, all his Forces, Besieged the Town St. *Jago*, but *Henry* II. King of *France* sending some succours by the Duke of *Aumale*, he raised up his siege, and put his Army into Garrisons. The Duke of *Alba* leaving the Field in this manner, the Duke of *Aumale* besieged *Vulpian*, wherein were 1000. souldiers in Garrison, under the command of *Cæsar* of *Naples*, besides the Inhabitants. Never was a place so furiously assaulted, and so manfully defended, so that the *French* were many times beaten back; but at last after 24. days siege the Duke of *Aumale* did gloriously take it.

The Author foretelling the time of this victory, said it was when the writing D. M. in big letters was found, that is to say, about the 11. of *September* after the Equinox, because in the Ephemerides, the Meridional descension of the Planets, and chiefly of *Sol, Venus*, and *Mercury* is marked with these two Letters D. M. which descension cometh to pass after the Equinox of *Autumn* towards the end of *September*. At the same time was discovered an ancient Cave, wherein was found one of those Lamps, that cannot be put out, and burns continually without any addition of Oil, by an invention that is lost. Such another was found in the time of *Alexander* the VI. and *Adrian* the VI.

The Town of *Vulpian* was at that time tried by a King and a Prince, *viz. Henry* the II. and the Duke of *Aumale* Prince of *Lorrain*, and Brother to the Cardinal of *Lorrain*, and to the Duke of *Guise*.

The Author addeth, that besides these three things, *viz.* the finding of the letters D. M. The Cave discovered the siege of *Vulpian*; there happened a fourth one, *viz.* that a Queen and a Duke should consult together in a Summer-house, about the important affairs of the Kingdom. To understand this, we must suppose that Pope *Paul* the IV. willing to secure his own person and the Ecclesiastical State against the *Spanish* faction, and that of the *Colonese*, did seize upon many places belonging to the said *Colonese*, and knowing besides that the *Spaniards* being of the *Coloneses* party, would not fail to come upon him, he disposed the King of *France* to come to his succours, so that the Queen having a particular confidence in the Duke of *Guise*, did consult with him about this business in some Summer-house, which the *French* call a *Pavillon*.

LXVII.

French.

Par. Car. nersaf, a ruine grand discorde, Ne l'un ne l'autre n'aura election, Nersaf du peuple aura amour & concorde, Ferrare, Collonne grande protection. English.

Par. Car. Nersaf, to ruine great discord, Neither one nor the other shall be Elected, *Nersaf*, shall have of the people love and concord, *Ferrare, Colonna*, great protection.

ANNOT.

It is very hard to say what the Author meaneth by these disjunctives *Par. Car. Nersaf*, all what can be gathered by what follows, is, that there shall be a great variance and strife about an Election, (I suppose of a Pope as it useth to be) and that *Nersaf* shall have the good will of the people, and yet none of them shall be Elected.

As for the fourth Verse, it is to be noted first that *Ferrara* is a strong Town in *Italy* belonging to the Pope, and *Colonna* is the name of the chief Family in *Rome*, now whether *Ferrara* shall be a protection to *Colonna*, or *Colonna* to *Ferrara*, we leave it to the Reader to judge, because the Verse hath a double sense.

LXVIII.

Vieux Cardinal par le jeune deceu, Hors de sa charge se verra desarmé, Arles ne monstres double fort apperceu, Et l'Aqueduct & le Prince embaumé. English.

An old Cardinal shall be cheated by a young one, And shall see himself out of his imployment, *Arles* do not show, a double fort perceived, And the *Aqueduct*, and the embalmed Prince.

ANNOT.

   The two first Verses are very plain, the two last not so; therefore observe that *Arles* is a City in *France*, in the Countrey of *Dauphine* or *Provence*, famous for antiquity, which is forwarned here not to shew its Fords, nor its Aqueducts, (which are buildings to convey water), nor its embalmed Prince, which it seemeth lyeth thereabout buried. The Author hath deprived here the Author of the reasons for why.

LXIX.

French.

Aupres du jeune se vieux Ange baiser, Et le viendra surmonter a la fin, Dix ans esgaux aux plus vieux rabaisser, De trois deux l'un huitiesme Seraphin. English.

Near the young one the old Angel shall bowe, And shall at last overcome him, Ten years equal, to make the old one stoop, Of three, two, one, the eighth a *Seraphin*.

ANNOT.

   This is the description of a grand Cheat, when an old man called here Angel, shall stoop before a young one, whom he shall overcome at last, after they have been ten years equal. The last Verse is Mistical, for there is four numbers, three, two, one, which make six; and eight, which he calleth *Seraphin*, whether by allusion to that Quire of Angels, which some call the eight, or whether to the Order of St. *Francis*, who calleth it self *Seraphical*, is not easie to determine.

LXX.

French.

Il entrera vilain, meschant, infame, Tyrannisant la Mesopotamie, Tous amis fait d'Adulterine Dame, Tetre horrible noir de Physiognomie. English.

He shall come in villaen, wicked, infamous, To tyranise *Mesopotamia*, He maketh all friends by an adulteress Lady, Foul, horrid, black in his *Physiognomie*.

ANNOT.

   Mesopotamia is a Greek word, signifying a Countrey between two Rivers; and though there be many Countreys so seated, yet to this day, it properly belongeth to that Countrey, that lyeth between the two famous Rivers *Tigris* and *Euphrates* near *Babylon*; the rest is easie.

LXXI.

French.

Croistra le nombre si grand des Astronomes, Chassez bannis & livres censureq, L'An mil six cens & sept par sacrez glomes, Que nul au sacres ne seront asseurez. English.

The number of Astronomers shall grow so great, Driven away, bannished, Books censured, The year one thousand six hundred and seven by sacred glomes, That none shall be secure in the sacred places.

ANNOT.

The sense of this is clear, *viz.* that about the year 1607. the number of Astronomers shall grow very great, of which some shall be expelled and banished, and their Books censured and suppressed: the rest is insignificant to me.

LXXII.

French.

Champ Perusin O l'Enorme deffaite, Et le conflict tout aupres de Ravenne, Passage sacra lors qu'on fera la feste, Vaincueur vaincu, Cheval mange L'avenne. English.

Perugian Field, O the excessive rout, And the fight about *Ravenna*, Sacred passage when the Feast shall be celebrated, The victorious vanquished, the Horse to eat up his Oats.

ANNOT.

Perugia is a City in *Italy*, and so is *Ravenna*, by which it seemeth there shall be a notable Battle fought, as was once before in the time at *Lewis* the XII. King of *France* between *Gaston de Foix* his Nephew, and *Don Raimond de Cardonne* Vice-roy of *Naples*, for there the *French* got the Battle; in conclusion of which, the said *Gaston de Foix* pursuing a Troop of *Spaniards* that were retiring, was unfortunately kill'd, and so the victorious were vanquished.

LXXIII.

French.

Soldat Barbare le grand Roy frapera, Injustement non esloigné de mort, L'Avare Mere du fait cause sera, Conjurateur & Regne en grand remort. English.

A Barbarous Souldier shall strike the King, Unjustly, not far from death, The covetous Mother shall be the cause of it, The Conspirator and Kingdom in great remorse.

These words are so plain that they need no interpretation.

LXXIV.

French.

En Terre neuve bien avant Roy entré, Pendant subjects luy viendront faire accueil, Sa parfidie aura tel rencontré, Qu'aux Citadins lieu de feste & recueil. English.

A King being entered far into a new Countrey, Whilst his Subjects shall come to welcom him, His perfidiousness shall find such an encounter, That to the Citizens it shall be instead of feast and welcom.

ANNOT.

The sense of this seemeth to be, that a certain King being far got into a new conquered Countrey, where he shall deal perfidiously with his Subjects, that then he shall meet with such an accident, as to his Citizens shall be instead of feast & welcom.

LXXV.

French.

Le Pere & fils seront meurtris ensemble, Le Prefecteur dedans son Pavillon, La Mere a Tours du fils ventre aura enfle, Cache verdure de fueilles papillon. English.

The Father and Son shall be murdered together, The Governour shall be so in his Tent, At *Tours* the Mother shall be got with child by her son, Hide the greenness with leaves Butter-flye.

ANNOT.

There is nothing hard here but the last Verse, whereby it is signified, that after such an incest of the Mother with the Son in the City of *Tours* (which is a Town in *France*) the fruit of it shall be secretly buryed, and green Turfs laid upon the place, and Leaves upon them, to take away the knowledge of it.

LXXVI.

French.

Plus Macelin que Roy en Angleterre, Lieu obscur ne par force aura l'Empire, Lasche, sans foy, sans loy, seignera Terre, Son temps s'aproche si presque je souspire. English.

More *Macelin* then King in *England*, Born in obscure place, by force shall reign, Of loose disposition, without faith, without Law, the ground shall bleed, His time is drawing so near that I sigh for it.

ANNOT.

Macelin, is a Butcher or cruel man, from the Latine word *Macellum*, which signifieth the Shambles, it is without contradiction that by this Prophecy is plain concerning the late tyrant *Cromwel*, and his unlawful Government.

LXXVII.

French.

L'Antechrist bien tost trois annichilez, Vingt & sept ans durera sa guerre, Les Heretiques morts; captifs exilez, Sang corps humain eau rougie, gresler Terre. English.

By Antichrist three shall shortly be brought to nothing, His War shall last seven and twenty years, The Hereticks dead, Prisoners banished, Blood, humane body, water made red, Earth hailed.

ANNOT.

What he meaneth here by Antichrist is not easie to determine, for he cannot mean the Pope, himself being a Papist, nor the great Antichrist, whose Reign, according to the Scripture, shall last but three years and a half, it is more likely then that this Stanza hath coherence with the precedent, and that by it he meaneth *Henry* the VIII. who for the space of about 27 years before he dyed, did handle something roughly the Clergy and Clergy-men.

LXXVIII.

French.

Un Bragamas avec la langue torte, Viendra des dieux rompre le Sanctuaire, Aux Heretiques il ouvrira la porte, En suscitant l'Eglise Militaire. English.

A *Bragamas* with his crooked Tongue, Shall come and break the Gods Sanctuary, He shall open the Gates unto Hereticks, By raising the Militant Church.

ANNOT.

Bragamas is the same thing that we call now *Bragadocio*. By the Gods Sanctuary, he meaneth the Temples of the *Romish* Religion, who are reputed Sanctuaries, and are full of Images, which they worship as Gods, praying and offering Incense to them.

LXXIX.

French.

Qui par fer pere perdra, nay de Nonnaire, De Gorgon sur la fin sera sang perferant, En Terre estrange fera si tout de taire, Qu'il bruslera luy mesme & son entant. English.

He that by Iron shall destroy his Father, born in *Nonnaire*, Shall in the end carry the blood of

Gorgon, Shall in a strange Countrey make all so silent, That he shall burn himself and his intent.

ANNOT.

Nonnaire and *Gorgon* are two barbarous words, as for the sense of that and the rest, he that shall be able to read the words, shall be as wise as my self.

LXXX.

French.

Des innocens le sang de Vefue & Vierge, Tant de maux faits par moiens ce grand Roge, Saints simulachres trempez en ardant cierge, De frayeur crainte ne verra nul que boge. English.

The blood of the innocent Widow and Virgin, So many evils committed by the means of that great Rogue, Holy Images, dipt in burning wax Candles, For fear no body shall be seen to stir.

ANNOT.

What he meaneth by the great Rogue is not obvious, but the main drift of this Stanza seemeth to be, to foretel the abuses that should be offered to the Popish Images by the Protestant party, as it was done in the time of the Civil Wars of *France*, and a little while after our Author had written his Prophecies.

By the great Rogue, he meaneth some chief Commander of the Protestant party, that were in those days, as the Prince of *Condé*, the Admiral of *Castilon*, or his Brother *Dandelot*.

LXXXI.

French.

Le neuf Empire en desolation, Sera changé du Pole Aquilonaire, De la Sicile viendra l'emotion, Troubler l'Emprise a Philip tributaire. English.

The new Empire in desolation, Shall be changed from the Northern Pole, The commotion shall come from *Sicily*, To trouble the undertaking, tributary to *Philip*.

ANNOT.

This threatneth the Empire that now is in *Germany*, of a great desolation, and to be removed from its place, and threatneth also the Island of *Sicily* of a fearful commotion, which shall trouble the undertakings of *Philip*, that is, King of *Spain*, because they usually are called by that name.

LXXXII.

French.

Ronge long, sec, faisant du bon valet, A la par fin n'aura que son congie, Poignant poison & Lettres au colet, Sera saisy, eschapé, en dangié. English.

Long gnawer, dry, cringing and fawning, In conclusion shall have nothing but leave to be gone, Piercing poison and Letters in his Collar, Shall be seised, escape, and in danger.

ANNOT.

The words of this are easie to be understood, but not who should be that man to whom he giveth these four famous Epithetes of *Long-gnawer, dry, cringing* and *fawning*.

LXXXIII.

French.

Le plus grand voile hors du port de Zara, Pres de Bizance fera son entreprise, D'Ennemy perte & l'amy ne séra, Le tiers a deux fera grand pille & prise. English.

The greatest Sail out of the Port of *Zara*, Near *Bizance* shall make his undertaking, There shall be no loss of foes or friends, The third shall make a great pillage upon the two.

ANNOT.

By *Zara* I suppose that the *Venetians* are meant, who have a very strong Town of that name, situated in *Dalmatia*. *Bizance* is *Constantinople*, as we have said before; now whether this Prophecy was fulfilled when the *Venetians* took the Island of *Tenedos*, some 20 years ago, which is not far from *Constantinople*, or whether it is to come, I dare not assert.

LXXXIV.

French.

Paterne aura de la Sicile crie, Tous les aprests du Gouphre de Trieste, Qui s'entendra jusques a la Trinacrie, De tant de voiles, fuy, fuy, l'horrible peste. English.

Paterne shall have out of *Sicily* a cry, All the preparations of the Gulph of *Trieste*, That shall be heard as far as *Trinacry*, Of so many Sails, fly, fly, the horrid plague.

ANNOT.

It hath been impossible for me to make any sense of this, and therefore I believe that it is falsely printed, and that instead of *Paterne*, it should be *Palerme*, which is the chief Town in *Sicily*. *Trinacry* is *Sicily* it self, so called, *quod tria habeat, ἄκρα seu promontoria*.

LXXXV.

French.

Entre Bayonne & a Sainct Jean de Lux, Sera posé de Mars la promottoire, Aux Hanix d'Aquilon, Nanar hostera Lux, Puis suffoque au lit sans adjoutoire. English.

Between *Bayonne* and Saint *John de Lux*, Shall be put down the promoting of *Mars*, From the *Hunix* of the North, *Nanar* shall take away *Lux*, Then shall be suffocated in his bed without help.

ANNOT.

     Bayonne is a Town in *France*, upon the frontiers of *Spain*, and Saint *John de Lux* is the utmost frontiere of *France*, that way, (that being supposed) he saith, that about Saint *John de Lux*, the promoting of the war shall be set down; that is, that peace shall be made, as it was about seven or eight years ago between *France* and *Spain*, and the Marriage concluded between the King and the *Infanta*. The two last Verses are nonsensical, and only set down to make up the rhime.

LXXXVI.

French.

Par Arnani, Tholose, & Villefranque, Bande infinie par le Mont Adrian, Passe Riviere, hutin par pont la planque, Bayonne entrer tous Bichoro criant. English.

By *Arnani, Tholose*, and *Villefranche*, An infinite deal of people by the *Aprian*, Cross Rivers, noise upon the Bridge and plank, Come all into *Bayonne* crying *Bichoro*.

ANNOT.

     Arnani, Tholose, and *Villefranche* are Towns of a Province in *France* called *Languedoc*. Mont *Adrian* is a Mountain thereabout, and *Hutin* is an old *French* word, signifying noise and strife, the sense then of this Prophecy is, that by those Towns and Mountains, shall pass an infinite multitude of people, with a great noise and strife, and shall come and enter into *Bayonne*, every one crying in that Countrey Language *Bichoro*, which is as much as to say, *Victory*.

LXXXVII.

French.

Mort conspirée viendra en plein effet, Charge donnée & voyage de mort, Esleu, crée, receus, par siens desfait, Sang d'innocence devant soy par remort. English.

A conspired death shall come to an effect, Charge given, and a journey of death, Elected, created, received, by his own defeated, Blood of Innocency before him by remorse.

There is no mistical sense in this, and the words are plain, although of a crabbid construction.

LXXXVIII.

French.

Dans la Sardaigne un noble Roy viendra, Qui ne tiendra que trois ans le Royaume, Plusieurs couleurs avec soy conjoindra, Luy mesme apres soin sommeil Matrirscome. English.

A noble King shall come into *Sardinia*, Who shall hold the Kingdom only three years, He shall joyn many Colours to his own, Himself afterwards, care, sleep matrirscome.

ANNOT.

Sardinia is an Island in the *Mediterranean* Sea, now in the possession of the *Spaniard*, since he took the Kingdom of *Naples*, the three first Verses are something intelligible, the last is altogether impossible and barbarous.

LXXXIX.

French.

Pour ne tomber entre mains de son oncle, Qui ses enfans par regner trucidez, Orant au peuple mettant pied sur Peloncle, Mort & traisné entre Chevaux bardez. English.

That he might not fall into the hands of his Uncle, That had murdered his Children for to rule, Taking away from the people, and putting his foot upon *Peloncle*, Dead and drawn among armed Horses.

ANNOT.

This signifieth that an Uncle shall murder his Nephews Children, that he may Reign, and that the said Nephew shall withdraw, and save himself from the said Uncle. The rest is altogether obscure, if not absurd.

XC.

French.

Quand des croisez un trouvé de sens trouble, En lieu du sacre verra un Bœuf cornu, Par vierge porc son lieu lors sera double, Par Roy plus ordre ne sera soustenu. English.

When of the crossed, one of a troubled mind, In a sacred place shall see a horny Oxe, By Virgin Pork then shall his place be double, By King no henceforth, order shall be maintained.

ANNOT.

By the crossed is understood some order of Knight-hood, who for the most part wear that Badge, one of which being mad, and seeing in a Church a Horny Oxe come, by a Virgin Hog shall be kept from harm, or rescued by a Hog or Sow that was a Virgin, and it seems crossed the said Oxe, that he should not gore the Knight, that then such order of Knighthood shall be no more maintained nor upheld by the King of that Countrey, wherein such thing shall happen.

XCI.

French.

Parmy les Champs des Rhodanes entrées, Ou les croisez seront presques unis, Les deux Brassiers en Pisces rencontrées, Et un grand nombre par Deluge punis. English.

Through the Fields of the *Rhodanes* comings in, Where the crossed shall be almost united, The two *Brassiers* met in *Pisces*, And a great number punished by a Flood.

ANNOT.

Rhodanus in Latine is the River of *Rhosne*, which cometh from *Switzerland*, and passing through the Lake of *Geneva*, runneth to *Lyon*, it seemeth then that in those Fields that are about that River there, will be a fearful inundation, when the *Brassiers* (or rather *Croziers*, which is a constellation so called) shall meet in *Pisces*, which is one of the twelve Signs of the *Zodiack*.

XCII.

French.

Loin hors du Regne mis en hazard voiage, Grand Ost duyra, pour soy l'occupera, Le Roy tiendra les siens captif, ostage, A son retour tout Pais pillera. English.

Far from the Kingdom a hazardous journey undertaken, He shall lead a great Army, which he shall make his own, The King shall keep his prisoners, and pledges, At his return he shall plunder all the Countrey.

ANNOT.

These obscure words signifie no more but that a King shall send a great Army far from his Kingdom, the Commander of which Army shall make the Army his own, which the King hearing, shall seize upon the Commanders Relations, and keep them Prisoners and Hostages, for which the said General being angry, shall at his return spoil the Countrey.

XCIII.

French.

Sept mois sans plus obtiendra prelature, Par son decez grand schisme fera naistre, Sept mois tiendra un autre la Preture, Pres de Venise paix union renaistre. English.

Seven months and no more, he shall obtain the Prelacy, By his decease he shall cause a great Schisme, Another shall be seven months chief Justice, Near *Venice* peace and union shall grow again.

ANNOT.

By this Prophecy three things are foretold, the first is of a Pope that shall sit but seven months, at whose death there will be a great Schisme; the second is of a great Governour or Chief Justice, such as were called by the ancient *Romans Prætores*, shall be in authority also but seven months; and the third, that hard by *Venice* all these differences shall be composed, and peace made again.

XCIV.

French.

Devant la Lac ou plus cher fut getté, De sept mois & son Ost desconfit, Seront Hispans par Albanois gastez, Par delay perte en donnant le conflict. English.

Before the Lake wherein most dear was thrown, Of seven months, and his Army overthrown, *Spaniards* shall be spoiled by *Albaneses*, By delaying; loss in giving the Battle.

ANNOT.

It is very difficult, if not impossible to tell what our Author meaneth by the Lake, wherein the most dear was thrown, and lost his Army. The *Albaneses* are a Nation between the *Venetians* and *Greece*, now for the most part subject to the said *Venetians*.

XCV.

French.

Le Seducteur sera mis dans la Fosse, Et estaché jusques a quelque temps, Le Clerc uny, le Chef avec sa Crosse, Pycante droite attraira les contems. English.

The Deceiver shall be put into the Dungeon, And bound fast for a while, The Clerk united, the head with his Crosierstaf, Pricking upright, shall draw in the contented.

ANNOT.

The two first Verses are plain, the two last Verses not so, which seemeth to foretell of a great union among the Clergy, which shall draw to them those that were peaceably affected.

XCVI.

French.

La Synagogue sterile sans nul fruit, Sera receue entre les Infideles, De Babylon la fille du poursuit, Misere & triste luy trenchera les Aisles. English.

The Synagogue barren, without fruit, Shall be received among the Infidels, In *Babylon*, the daughter of the persecuted, Miserable and sad shall cut her wings.

ANNOT.

A Synagogue is a place where the Jews assemble for Divine Worship, as the Christians do in Churches or Temples, the said Jews Synagogue is threatned here to be unfruitful and barren, and chiefly in *Babylon*, by the means of a woman, daughter of one persecuted; belike of some of their own tribe, whom the rest did persecute.

XCVII.

French.

Au fins du Var changer le Pompotans, Pres du Rivage, les trois beaux enfans naistre, Ruine au peuple par Aage competans, Regne au Pais changer plus voir croistre. English.

At the ends of the *Var* to change the *Pompotans*, Near the Shore shall three fair Children be born, Ruine to the people by competent Age, To change that Countreys Kingdom, and see it grow no more.

ANNOT.

The first Verse being made of insignificant words, as *Var* and *Pompotans* cannot be understood; the other three doth foretel of three handsom Children, that shall be born near the Shore, which when they have attained a competent Age, shall change the Kingdom of that Countrey, and suppress it.

XCVIII.

French.

Des gens d'Eglise sang sera espanché, Comme de l'eau en si grande abundance, Et de long temps ne sera retranché, Veüe au Clerc ruine & doleance. English.

The blood of Churchmen shall be spilt, As water in such abundance, And for a good while shall not be stayed, Ruine and grievance shall be seen to the Clerk.

ANNOT.

This is easie to be understood, which foretelleth a very great persecution to the Clergy-men, *viz.* Papists, of which Religion our Author was, if this be not already past in the Civil Wars of *France*, that were made for Religion, in the beginning of Reformation, where abundance of Clergy-men did perish on both sides.

XCIX.

French.

Par la puissance des trois Rois temporels, En autre lieu sera mis la Saint Siege, Ou la substance de l'Esprit corporel, Sera remis & receu pour vray Siege. English.

By the power of three Temporal Kings, The Holy See shall be put in another place, Where the substance of the Corporeal Spirit, Shall be restored and admitted for a true seat.

ANNOT.

This Stanza is very remarkable, for the thing it foretelleth, *viz.* a translation of the See of *Rome*, that is, the Popedom into another place by three Temporal Kings, and not onely that, but it seemeth by the sense of the last two Verses, that these will keep the Ecclesiastical authority to themselves.

C.

French.

Pour l'abundance de l'Armée respandue, Du haut en bas, par le bas au plus haut, Trop grande foy par jeu vie perdue, De soif mourir par abondant defaut. English.

Through the abundance of the Army scattered, High and low, low and high, Too great a belief a life lost in jesting, To die by thirst, through abundance of want.

ANNOT.

The sense of this is, that by reason of a great Army that shall be much scattered, and occupy a great deal of room, water will be so scarce, that some shall die for thirst, it is that he calleth here, *To die by thirst, through abundance of want*.

Other Stanza's heretofore Printed, under the VIII. CENTURY.

I.

French.

Seront confus plusieurs de leur attente, Aux habitans ne sera pardonné, Qui bien pensoint perseverer l'attente, Mais grand loisir ne leur sera donné. English.

Many shall be confounded in their expectation, The Citizens shall not be forgiven, Who thought to persevere in their resolution, But there shall not be given them a great leisure for it.

ANNOT.

This is plain, and needeth no interpretation.

II.

French.

Plusieurs viendront & parleront de Paix, Entre Monarques & Seigneurs bien puissans, Mais ne sera accordé de si pres, Que ne se rendent plus qu'autres obeissans. English.

Many shall come and shall talk of Peace, Between Monarchs and Lords very powerful, But it shall not be agreed to it so soon, If they do not shew themselves more obedient then others.

ANNOT.

We are just now at the Eve of this Prophecy, when so many Princes and Potentates do busie themselves about a Mediation between the two Crowns of *France* and *Spain*, &c.

III.

French.

Las quelle fureur, helas quelle pitie, Il y aura entre beaucoup de gens, On ne vit onc une tell amitié, Qu'auront les Loups a courir diligens. English.

Ha! what fury, alas what pitty, There shall be betwixt many people, There was never seen such a friendship, As the Wolfs shall have in being diligent to run.

ANNOT.

It is indeed a great fury and pity to see how wicked people, and chiefly Usurers and false dealers, (understood here by the name of Wolfs) are diligent in doing mischief, and to make good the old Proverb, *Homo homini Lupus*, there being no other Creature but the Wolf that devours those of his own kind.

IV.

French.

Beaucoup de gens viendront parlementer, Aux grand Seigneurs qui leur feront la guerre, On ne voudra en rien les escouter, Helas! si Dieu n'envoie Paix en Terre. English.

Many folks shall come to speak, To great Lords that shall make War against them, They shall not be admitted to a hearing, Alas! if God doth not send Peace upon Earth.

ANNOT.

This carrieth its sense with it, and is plain.

V.

French.

Plusieurs secours viendront de tous costez, De gens lointains qui voudront resister, Ils seront tout a coup bien hastez, Mais ne pourront pour cette heure assister. English.

Many helps shall come on all sides, Of people far off, that would fain to resist, They shall be upon a sudden all very hasty, But for the present they shall not be able to assist.

ANNOT.

This seemeth to point at this present conjuncture of affairs, where there is so many buisying themselves about the relief of *Flanders*, of which I see no great likelihood.

VI.

French.

Las quel plaisir ont Princes estrangers, Garde toy bien qu'en ton Pais ne Vienne, Il y auroit de terribles dangers, Et en maintes Contrées, mesme en la Vienne. English.

Ha! what pleasure take Forrain Princes? Take heed least any should come into thy Countrey, There should be terrible dangers, In several Countreys, and chiefly in *Vienna*.

ANNOT.

There is two Towns called *Vienna*'s, one is in *Germany*, in the Province of *Austria*, and is the Emperours Seat, the other in *France*, a metter of twenty miles beyond *Lion*, the rest is easie.

Michael Nostradamus.

CENTURY IX.

I.

French.

Dans la maison du Traducteur de Boure, Seront les lettres trouvées sur la Table, Borgne, roux blanc, chenu, tiendra de cours, Qui changera au nouveau Connestable. *English.*

In the house of the Translator of *Boure*, The Letters shall be found upon the Table, Blind of one eye, red, white, hoary, shall keep its course, Which shall change at the coming of the new Constable.

ANNOT.

It is not easie to understand what he meaneth by the Translator of *Boure*, unless it be some mean and pittiful fellow, that lived by Translating things from one language into another, because the *French* use to call a man that is inconsiderable, *un homme du boure*, that is a man of Flocks; and so much the more I am of this opinion, because of the scurvy Epithetes, he attributeth to the same person, by which he might easily be known as *blind of one eye, red, white, hoary,* &c.

II.

French.

Du haut du Mont Aventin voix ouye, Vuidez, vuidez de tous les deux costez, Du sang des rouges sera l'Ire assouvie, D'Arimin, Prato, Columna debotez. *English.*

From the top of Mount *Aventin*, a voice was heard, Get you gone, get you gone on all sides, The Choler shall be fed with the blood of the red ones, From *Arimini* and *Prato*, the Colonnas shall be driven away.

ANNOT.

Mount *Aventine* is one of the seven Mountains of *Rome*, from the top of which our Author saith that a voice was heard crying and repeating, *get you gone*, and the reason is, because choler and anger shall feed upon the blood of the Cardinals, understood here by the name of *red ones*.

Arimini and *Prato* are two cities in *Italy*.

The *Colonna* is the chiefest and ancientest family of *Rome*.

III.

Le magna vaqua a Ravenne grand trouble, Conduits par quinze enserrez a Fornase, A Rome naistra deux Monstres a teste double, Sang, feu, deluge, les plus grands a l'espase. English.

The *Magna vaqua* great trouble at *Ravenna*, Conducted by fifteen, shut up at *Fornase*, At *Rome* shall be born two Monsters with a double head, Blood, fire, Flood, the greater ones astonished.

ANNOT.

This word of *Magna vaqua* is either falsly printed, or altogether barbarous and insignificant, and so is that of *Fornase*, which maketh the two first Verses incapable of translation; the other are easie.

IV.

French.

L'An ensuivant descouverts par Deluge, Deux chefs esleus, le premier ne tiendra, De fuyr ombre a l'un deux le refuge, Saccagée case qui premier maintiendra. English.

The year following being discovered by a Flood, Two Chiefs elected, the first shall not hold, To fly from shade, to one shall be a refuge, That house shall be plundered which shall maintain the first.

ANNOT.

Our Author meaneth, that the year after the former Prophecy is come to pass, this shall also be fulfilled, whereby two Chief Commanders shall be chosen, the first of which shall not stand, but shall be compelled to run away, and to seek his security in the open Fields, and that house that did uphold the first shall be plundered.

V.

French.

Tiers doigt du pied au premier semblera, A un nouveau Monarque de bas haut, Qui Pise & Luiques tyran occupera, Du precedent corriger le defaut. English.

The third toe of the foot shall be like the first, To a new high Monarch come from low estate, Who being a Tyrant shall cease upon *Pise* and *Luica*, To correct the faults of him that preceded him.

ANNOT.

The meaning of this is, that some body pretending to mend the Government of those two places that are in Italy, shall tyrannically make himself Master of them.

VI.

French.

Par la Guyenne infinité d'Anglois, Occuperont par nom d'Angle Aquitaine, Du Languedoc. I. palme Bourdelois, Quils nommeront apres Barboxitaine. English.

There shall be in *Guyenna* an infinite number of *English*, Who shall occupy it by the name of *Angle Aquitaine*, Of *Languedoc*, *I* by the Land of *Bourdeaux*, Which afterwards they shall call *Barboxitaine*.

ANNOT.

Here is foretold a famous invasion, that shall be made by the *English* upon that part of *France* called *Guyenne*, and in Latine *Aquitania*, of which *Bourdeaux* is the chief City, insomuch, that the *English* afterwards shall call that Countrey *Angl' Aquitaine*.

VII.

French.

Qui ouvrira le Monument trouvé, Et ne viendra le serrer promptement, Mal luy viendra & ne poura prouvé, Si mieux doibt estre Roy Breton ou Normand. English.

He that shall open the Sepulchre found, And shall not close it up again presently, Evil will befall him, and he shall not be able to prove Whether is best a *Britain* or *Norman* King.

ANNOT.

The sense of this is perspicuous.

VIII.

French.

Puisnay Roy fait son pere mettre a mort, Apres conflict de mort tres in honeste, Escrit trouvé soupcon, donra, remort, Quand loup chassé pose sur la couchete. English.

A younger King causeth his father to be put To a dishonest death, after a Battle, Writing shall be found, that shall give suspicion and remorse, When a hunted Wolf shall rest upon a truckle bed.

ANNOT.

The words and sense are plain.

IX.

Quand Lampe ardente de feu inextinguible, Sera trouvée au Temple des Vestales, Enfant trouvée, feu, eau passant par crible, Nismes eau perir, Tholouse cheoir les Halles. English.

When a Lamp burning with unquenchable fire, Shall be found in the Temple of the Vestals, A Child shall be found, Water running through a Sieve, *Nismes* to perish by Water, the Market-hall shall fall at *Tholouse*.

ANNOT.

The ancient *Vestals*, were a Kind of Religious Virgins in the ancient *Romans* time, who if they did forfeit their honour, were buried alive in a Cave, with a little Bread and Water, and a Lamp burning, our Author would have, that when a Lamp shall be found lighted with an unquenchable fire, in that place where then their Temple was, that then *Nismes* (which is a City of *Languedoc*), shall perish by Water, and the Market-hall of *Tholouse* shall fall, whether such a Lamp may be contrived as to burn with an unquenchable fire, is too long and tedious a discourse to be disputed here.

X.

French.

Moine, Moinesse d'Enfant mort exposé, Mourir par Ourse & ravy par verrier, Par Foix & Panniers le Camp sera posé, Contre Tholose, Carcas, dresser forrier. English.

Monk and Nun having exposed a dead Child, To be killed by a she Bear, and snatcht away by a Glazier, The Camp shall be set by *Foix* and *Panniers*, And against *Tholouse*, *Carcas* shall raise a Harbinger.

ANNOT.

Foix and *Panniers* are two Towns in *Languedoc*, and so are *Tholouse* and *Carcassonne*, called here *Carcas*, for the abbreviation of the Verse, the sense then of this prophecy is, that when the two first Verses shall come to pass, that then an Army shall lie about those Towns, and *Carcassonne* shall be against *Thoulouse*.

XI.

French.

Le juste a tort a mort l'on viendra mettre, Publiquement, & du milieu estaint, Si grande Peste en ce lieu viendra naistre, Que les Jugeans fouyr seront contraints. English.

The just shall be put to death wrongfully, Publickly, and being taken out of the midst, So great a Plague shall break into that place, That the Judges shall be compelled to run away.

ANNOT.

Many understand this of the late King, and last Plague.

XII.

French.

Le tant d'argent de Diane & Mercure, Les simulachres au Lac seront trouvez, Le Figulier cherchant argille neuve, Luy & les siens, d'or seront abreuvez. English.

The so much Silver of *Diana* and *Mercury*, The Statues shall be found in the Lake, The Potter seeking for new clay, He and his shall be filled with Gold.

ANNOT.

This Prophecy is concerning a *Potter*, who seeking and digging for new Clay, shall find in a drained Lake the Statues of *Diana* and *Mercury* all of silver, besides other great riches; seeing this Prophecy is not come to pass yet (that I know) it will not be amiss, for the divertisement of the Reader, to relate here a notable and authentical History of a Potter that hath much ressemblance with this, and will be a convincing Argument, that Mines grow in the Earth as Turfs do, and as *Virgil* sayeth of the golden branch:
   Uno avulso non deficit alter.

It is written by Doctor *de Rochas*, Physitian to the present Chancellor or *France*, who was upon the place, and an eye witness of the circumstances of it, having also an interest in it, in the behalf of his Father, who was overseer of the Mines in that Province, therefore I shall relate it in his own words, as they are in his Book of *Mineral Waters.*
A notable History.   In *Provence* near *Thoulon*, is a Mountain called *Carquairené*, at the foot of which and near the brim of the Sea, there dwelled a Potter with all his tools about him; It chanced that on a day as he went to fetch Wood in that Mountain, to bake his wares, he heard a voice of a little Kid, which some Shepherd had left behind them unawares, and was fallen in a little hole that answered to natural, great and deep Caves; this man seeing no Shepherds about him, thought presently it was a strayed Kid, therefore he followed the cry with his ear so directly, that he came by the orifice of that hole, where he heard and saw the Kid, which he resolved to carry away with his Wood, therefore he took the Cords that were at his Mules Saddle, and that he used to bind his Load with, and with the help of them, and of some big pieces of Wood he got down, where, he did observe round about him many other Caves, contiguous and separated from this, which his curiosity caused him to view, and found in the chief of these Caves a great quantity of stones heaped upon one another, & of a substance and colour of Brass, and among the rest there was one that came forth out of the Rock, about the bigness, shape, and length of a mans arm, when it is stretched out; he did apparently judge that the weight and brittleness of that matter had caused those stones to fall down, and that the same that he saw come out of the Rock in this manner, was already loose and like to fall; this man finding himself among such an abundance of rich Lingots, which fortune did offer him, did not know the value of them, but did like the Cock of *Æsop* which left the precious Pearl to take the Corn of Wheat; thus this *Jason* took very little of this Golden Fleece, and only a small piece, which he broke from a bigger with one of his Tools, and imployed all his industry to carry away his Kid, which at last with much ado he got out, and carried upon his Mule, believing certainly that this provision would be more profitable to him and his Family, then the yellow stone which he had in his pocket, weighing about five pounds, and which he intended to give to a Tinker

of *Thoulon*, his Gossip and good friend, in hope that for the same he might be presented with a bottle of Wine, to keep company to his Kid; and accordingly the next morning by break of day he went to *Thoulon* and stayed in the Shop of his friend, who did look with admiration upon so resplendent Brass; a Gold-smith who lodged over the way, and observed the splendor of that Divine mettal, drew near, and presently would have bargained for it, with a great deal of transportation and alteration. The Potter asked him only twenty pence, which the Gold-Smith would have given him presently, but the Tinker making sign to him to retract his words, he put his lingot in his pocket again, with protestation that he would not part with it, unless he had something that were worth the pains of going where he had it; in conclusion, after many contestations and disputes, the Potter who did suspect that it might be gold, would not sell nor deliver it under the sum of thirty Crowns, which the Gold-Smith paid him presently, and which he carried away with more joy, then if he had been possessor of greater riches; the Gold-smith on the other side, who thought that his profit would be above a hundred pounds sterlings, did refine this stone, that was about five pound weight, out of which he drew four pound weight, of very good and pure gold, the rest was a kind of dross, that made it thus brittle; one ought not to think that the Mine is all of the same perfection, but it purifieth it self, according as nature thrusteth it out of the Rock, as we see that Rubies and Emeralds are purer, then the Rock from whence they come. This Gold-Smith having found such fortune, and being resolved to make the best use of it, went to the Lord *Scaravaque*, then Governour of the Town, and imparted unto him this new discovery, that he might have his assistance and favour in it, and that under his power and authority he might follow and wait upon this precious business without being disturbed by any body, to which the Governour did so much the easier consent, that this Tradesman did oblidge himself to give him the best part of the profit that should arise from thence, and that should exceed any Travels into the *Indies* or *Peru*.

In the mean time the Potter was not asleep, the Gold-smiths money had stirred his appetite, and the charm of this witchcraft that worketh generally upon all spirits, did put him upon new hopes. He went into the Mountain with his wife, and with the help of a rope Ladder, which he had provided, and some Iron tools, wherewith he had loaded his Mule, he went down into the Caves, and with much endeavour did at last break that piece, that came out of the Rock like a mans arm, because all the other that were tumbled upon the ground, were so big and heavy that he could not remove them, when he had broken it down, though it were about fourscore and two pounds weight, nevertheless with the help of his wife and of his Ropes and Ladder he got out again, and stopt the hole with a large stone, and some Earth, upon which he planted some small Bushes so ingeniously, that this hole could never be found out again.

The Lord *Scaravaque* who was most impatient, to conquer like another *Jason* this Golden Fleece, and who was set on by the persuasions of the Gold-smith, sent for the Potter, under pretence to employ him in the making and furnishing of some Tiles and other small commodities that depended on his art. The Potter obeyed presently, drawn by the hopes to sell his wares well, and mistrusting nothing at all what they would ask him. As soon as he came, the Governour asked him and perswaded him with the best and most flattering words he could, to tell where he had the yellow stone that he sold to the Gold-smith. The Potter who more and more began to know the value of this rare Treasure, invented presently a lie, to free himself of the importunity of them that would have deceived him; therefore with an ingenuity, as simple as artificial he answered, he had found it upon the brim of the Sea, where may be some Ship had been cast away, or the Waves had cast it upon the shore.

The Governour answered that this could not be, and therefore threatned him of violence, and to send for all that he had in his House, which put the fellow into a great perplexity, because of the other stone that should be found there, therefore he chose rather to give it them out of his good will, then to put himself in danger of loosing all, and perchance of being abused to boot, without any more ado, he ingenuously confessed he had another piece of the same stuff as the former in his House, which he had likewise found in the same place, which he was ready to put into their hands, provided he might have his share of it, and be suffered to get his livelihood peaceably. The Lord *Scaravaque* did promise him all what he desired, and gave him some men to keep him company, with command to bring him back again, and to take special care he should not make an escape. At last this poor man came back again with that piece, which did more inflame the passion that the Governour had to know the place whence came that rich treasure; but neither for prayers, promises, or threats he would never reveal it, which did oblige the Governour to shut him up close in a Chamber, where nevertheless they gave him Victuals and made ready a Bed, but he refused both, and by an extraordinary sadness, gave shew that some notorious mischance was waiting on him, which proved true, for he was found dead in the Morning; which did put the Lord *Scaravaque* in a grief unexpressible, to see himself deprived by this accident, of the fruit that his hopes had made him conceive. He had recourse to the Potters wife for this discovery, but she could never attain to it, whatsoever exact searches she could make: yea, and after she was married again with a young man, who had spent in that search most of his time. The Lord *Scaravaque* and other persons of quality have employed all their skills and endeavours, but all their industry and charges have been without effect, as well as of many others, who attempted the same; about that time my Father who was overseer of the Mines in *Provence*, having received the news of a business of such consequence, that did concern his place, went presently unto that Mountain, to see if he could discover those wonders, I was then in his company, as also that woman, *viz.* the Potters wife, who carried us in several places for many days, without any success at all, although she gave notice that she could here the Waves of the Sea, when she was in the Cave with her first Husband, so that all our endeavours proved fruitless and unprofitable, because my Father fell sick, which made us forsake our quest, which is of such a consequence as not to be neglected.

During the time of our painful visiting that Mountain, I did consider the particularities of that rich Mountain, and observed that the top of it was almost all Azur, which tokens are the beams of that golden Sun and are the hairs of that fair goodness, under whose feet all things submit; in a word, are the true and infallible signs that underneath are Mines of Gold and Silver. And as I have directed all my thoughts many times to find out the means to compass so excellent a work, whose profit would surpass all what the *Indies* furnish unto strangers, and that with so much less charges and danger, that there is no heed of Ships or Fleet to cross over the Sea, from one Pole to the other, nor fight against any enemies: at last I have attained to a certain knowledge, which putteth me in hope, and makes me promise and engage my word, that at least I shall find a thred of that golden Mine, which may chance to lead us to the Centre of all these Treasures, but the Royal Authority being necessary to prop up this design, it belongeth to his Majesty to take what course he thinketh best for this, and to me to obey, execute his will. This digression which is an assured experiment, (that is a certain truth), is not come into this discourse, but only to prove that Mines grow by augmentation, in converting into their own nature the more subtle parts of the Neighbouring Earth. Thus far Doctor *de Rochas*.

XIII.

French.

Les Exilez autour de la Sologne, Conduits de nuict pour marcher en l'Auxois, Deux de Modene truculent de Bologne, Mis discouverts par feu de Burancois. English.

The banished about *Sologne*, Being conducted by night to go into *Auxois*, Two of *Modena*, the cruel of *Bolonia*, Shall be discovered by the fire of *Burancois*.

ANNOT.

Sologne is a Province in *France*, between the *Perche* and the *Main*. *Auxois* is a Countrey in the South of *France*, so called of its chief Town called *Auch*, the seat of an Archbishop. *Modena* is a

Town in *Italy*, and *Bolonia* another not far from it. *Burancois* is a part of the Province of *Dauphiné*. The meaning then of this Prophecy is, this being known, the Reader may easily find out the rest of the sense.

XIV.

French.

Mis en planure chauderon d'Infecteurs, Vin miel en huile & bastis sur Fourneaux, Seront plongez sans mal dit malfacteurs, Sept. fum. extaint au Canon des Borneaux. English.

A Dyers Kettle being put an a Plein, With Wine, Honey and Oil, and built upon Furnace, Shall be dipt, without evil, called Malefactors, Seven. fum. put out at the Canon of *Borneaux*.

ANNOT.

This hath a relation to the punishment, which in some parts of *France* and *Flanders* is inflicted upon false Coiners, which are commonly boiled in Oil, in a great Kettle, such as our Author here saith belong to Dyers. The Author then will have that the time shall come, when seven of that gang shall be so punished together in a Plain, where a great Kettle shall be set for that purpose upon a Furnace.

XV.

French.

Pres de Parpan les rouges detenus, Ceux du milieu parfondrez menez loing, Trois mis en pieces, & cinq mal soustenus, Pour le Seigneur & Prelat de Bourgoing. English.

Near unto *Parpan* the red ones detained, Those of the middle sunk and carried far off, Three cut in pieces, and five ill backed, For the Lord and Prelate of *Burgoing*.

ANNOT.

Parpan is either a barbarous or fained name, by the *red ones*, he hath hitherto understood some Cardinals, the Reader may expound the rest according to his fancy.

XVI.

French.

De Castel Franco sortira l'assemblée, L'Ambassadeur non plaisant fera Schisme, Ceux de Riviere seront en la meslée, Et au grand Goulphre desnieront l'entrée. English.

Out of *Castel Franco* shall come the Assembly, The Embassador not pleased, shall make a Schisme, Those of *Riviere* shall be in the medley, And shall deny the entry of the great Gulf.

Castel Franco is a Town in *Piemont*; *Riviere* is a strong Castle in *Burgundy*, but what he meaneth by the great Gulfe, is more then I can tell.

XVII.

French.

Le tiers premier, pis que ne fit Neron, Vuidez vaillant que sang humain respandre, Redifier fera le Forneron, Siecle d'or mort, nouveau Roy grand esclandre. English.

The third first, worse than ever did *Nero*, Go out valliant, he shall spill much humane blood, He shall cause the Forneron to be builded again, Golden Age dead, new King great troubles.

ANNOT.

This Prophecy pointeth directly at our Authors Master *Charles* the IX. King of *France*, whom he calleth he *the third first*, because he was the third son to *Henry* II. and came to be King, using more cruelties then ever *Nero* did, for he was the cause of the Massacre of the Protestants in *France* in the year 1572. where above a hundred thousand people were murdered. *Forneron* is a barbarous word, put here to make a Verse, and to rhime with *Neron*. At that time he saith the *Golden Age was dead*, and upon the coming of a new King, who was *Henry* III. great tumults did happen, and great Wars, as is to be seen in the *French* History.

XVIII.

French.

Le Lys Dauffois portera dans Nancy, Jusques en Flanders Electeur de l'Empire, Neusve obturée au grand Montmorency, Hors lieux pronez delivre a clere peyne. English.

Dauffois shall carry the Lillie into *Nancy*, As far as *Flanders* the Elector of the Empire, New hinderance to great *Montmorency*, Out of proved places, delivered to a clear pain.

ANNOT.

Although the words and sense of this Prophecy be most obscure, nevertheless we shall endeavour as much as we can to render them something intelligible to the Reader.

By the first Verse is to be understood that *Dauffois*, or rather *Dauphinois*, which is the Title of the Kings of *France* eldest Son shall carry the Lillie, which is the Arms of *France* into *Nancy*, the chief Town in *Lorrain*, which came to pass in the time of the last King *Lewis* the XIII.

By the second Verse is understood the Elector of *Triers*, who was taken by the *Spaniards* in his own Town, and carried prisoner to *Bruxelles*.

By the third and fourth is expressed the ill luck of the Duke of *Montmorency*, who having taken part with the Duke of *Lorrain*, and the Duke of *Orleans* the Kings Brother, was routed in a Battle, taken prisoner, and afterwards beheaded at *Thoulouse*.

XIX.

French.

Dans le milieu de la Forest Mayenne, Sol au Lion la Foudre tombera, Le grand Bastard issu du grand du Maine, Ce jour Fougeres pointe en sang entrera. English.

In the middle of the Forrest of *Mayenne*, *Sol* being in *Leo* the Lightning shall fall, The great Bastard begot by the great *du Main*, That day *Fougeres* shall enter its point into blood.

ANNOT.

  Fougeres is either the name of a Town in little *Britanny*, or that of a Noble House, the words are very plain, therefore I leave the sense to every ones capacity.

XX.

French.

De nuit viendra par la Forest de Rennes, Deux parts Voltorte Herne, la pierre blanche, Le Moine noir en gris dedans Varennes, Esleu Cap. cause tempeste, feu, sang tranche. English.

By night shall come through the Forrest of *Rennis*, Two parts *Voltorte Herne*, the white stone, The black Monk in gray within *Varennes*, Elected Cap. causeth tempest, fire, blood cutteth.

ANNOT.

  Rennes is the chief Town of little *Britanny*; the second Verse being made of barbarous words, is impossible to be understood. The third and fourth Verse signifieth, that when a black Monk in that Town of *Varennes* shall put on a gray sute, he shall be elected Captain, and cause a great tempest or broils by fire and blood.

XXI.

French.

Au Temple hault de Blois sacre Salonne, Nuict Pont de Loire, Prelat, Roy pernicant, Cuiseur victoire aux marests de la Lone, D'ou Prelature de blancs abormeant? English.

At the high Temple of *Blois* sacred *Salonne*, In the night the Bridge of *Loire*, Prelat, King mischievous, A smarting Victory in the Marsh of *Lone*, Whence Prelature of white ones shall be abortive.

ANNOT.

  There is a mistake in the first Verse, for instead of *Salonne*, it must be written *Soulaire*, which is a *Priory* and Church at the top of *Blois*, all the rest signifieth that in one night these shall happen, *viz.* that the Bridge, the Prelat, and a pernicious King with a smart victory shall perish, whence the Prelature, that is the place of Command upon the white ones, *viz.* Canons and Prebends in their Surplices, shall be void and empty.

XXII.

French.

Roy & sa Cour au lieu de la langue halbe, Dedans le Temple vis a vis du Palais, Dans le Jardin Duc de Montor & d'Albe, Albe & Mantor, poignard, langue, en Palais. English.

King and his Court in the place of *langue halbe*, Within the Church over against the *Pallace*, In the Garden Duke of *Montor* and *Albe*, *Albe* and *Mantor*, dagger, tongue and Pallate.

ANNOT.

This Stanza is very obscure, for, first no body can tell what he meaneth by *langue halbe*, which is the foundation of all the rest of the sense; Secondly, what this Duke of *Montor* and *Mantor* should be, which has been unknown in the Histories hitherto; and thirdly, what construction and sense can be made of these disjunctives: *Albe, Mantor, Dagger, Tongue, Palate.* Therefore i'le leave it free to every bodies opinion to make his construction.

XXIII.

French.

Puisnay jouant au fresch dessous la tonne, Le haut du toit du milieu sur la teste, Le Pere Roy au Temple Saint Solonne, Sacrifiant sacrera sum de feste. English.

The youngest Son playing under the tun, The top of the House shall fall upon his head, The King his Father in the Temple of Saint *Soulaine*, Sacrificing shall make festival smoak.

ANNOT.

By this is meant, that the youngest Son of a King, shall be knocked in the head, while he is a playing under a tun; his Father being at the same time in the Temple of Saint *Soulaine* at Mass.

XXIV.

French.

Sur le Palais au Rocher des Fenestres, Seront ravis les deux petits Roiaux, Passer Aurelle, Lutece, Denis cloistres, Nonnain, Mollods avaler verts noiaux. English.

Upon the Pallace at the Rock of the Windows; Shall be carried the two little Royal ones, To pass *Aurele, Lutece, Denis* Cloisters, *Nonnain, Mollods* to swallow green stones of fruit.

ANNOT.

These two or three last Stanzas have been concerning the City of *Blois*, to which it seemeth that this hath also relation, for he saith that two little Royal Children shall be carried at the top of the Castle, and shall be conveyed beyond *Aurelle* (which is *Orleans* in Latine *Aurelianum*) *Lutece*, which is *Paris*; S. *Denis* Cloisters, which is beyond *Paris*, and a Nunnery besides, where it is like they shall be left to eat green stones of fruit, which is not easie to be understood, no more then the word *Mollods*.

XXV.

French.

Passant les Ponts, venir prez de Roziers, Tard arrivé plustost quil cuidera, Viendront les noves Espagnols a Beziers, Qui icelle chasse emprinse cassera. **English.**

Going over the Bridge to come near the Rose-trees, Come late, and sooner then he thought, The new *Spaniards* shall come to *Beziers*, Who shall cashiere this new undertaken hunting.

ANNOT.

Beziers is a City in *Languedoc*; the rest may be construed by the meanest capacity.

XXVI.

French.

Nise sortie sur nom des Lettres aspres, La grande Cappe fera present non sien, Proche de Vultry aux murs des vertes capres, Apres Plombin le vent a bon escient. **English.**

A silly going out, caused by sharp Letters The great Cap shall give what is not his, Near *Vultry* by the Walls of green Capers, About *Piombino* the wind shall be in good earnest.

ANNOT.

This signifieth that there shall be a silly surrendring of a Town, caused by sharp and threatning Letters that shall be sent into it. By the great *Cap* he useth to understand the *Pope*, who he saith shall give what is not it, as he hath done many times; *Vultry*, in Latine *Velitrum*, and *Piombino* are two Cities in *Italy*, which are threatned here with mighty winds.

XXVII.

French.

De bois la garde vent clos ront Pont sera, Haut le receu frappera le Dauphin, Le vieux Teccon bois unis passera, Passant plus outre du Duc le droit confin. **English.**

The Fence being of Wood, close Wind, Bridge shall be broken, He that's received high, shall strike at the *Dolphin*, The old *Teccon* shall pass over smooth Wood, Going over the right confines of the Duke.

The first Verse signifieth that a woodden Bridge shall be broken by a close wind, as did happen to the Millers Bridge, and the Birds Bridge in *Paris*.

The second Verse seemeth to foretel the conspiracy of the Mareshal of *Biron*, against *Henry* IV. his Dolphin and Estate.

The third and fourth, the Wars and Conquest which the said King (whom he called old *Teccon*), made upon the Duke of *Savoy*, who had corrupted the said Marshal of *Biron*.

XXVIII.

Voile Symacle, Port Massiliolique, Dans Venise Port marcher aux Pannons, Partir du Goulfre & sinus Illirique, Vast a Sicile, Ligurs coups de Canon. English.

Symaclian Sail, *Massilian* Port, In *Venice* to march towards the *Hungarians*, To go away from the Gulf and *Illirick* Sea, Toward *Sicily*, the *Genoeses* with Cannon shots.

ANNOT.

      What he meaneth by *Symaclian Sail*, is not easie to determine; *Massilian Port* is that of *Marseilles* in *France*, called in Latine *Massilia*, the sense of this Prophecy then if any be, is, that a great Fleet shall go from thence to *Venice*, to carry succours to the *Hungarians*, who it seemeth shall be much distressed at that time by the *Turks*, and that *Sicily* and *Genoa* shall add to this Fleet a considerable succour of Men, and Warlike Munition.

XXIX.

Lors que celuy qu'a nul ne donne lieu, Abandonner voudra lieu prins non pris, Feu, Nef, par faignes, bitument a Charlieu, Seront Quintin, Bales repris. English.

When he that giveth place to no body, Shall forsake the place taken, and not taken, Fire, Ship, by bleeding bituminous at *Charlieu*, Then *Quintin* and *Bales* shall be taken again.

ANNOT.

      He that giveth place to no body is the Pope; as for the last Verse, I had rather read St. *Quintin* and *Gales*, which are two considerable Towns in *France*, then otherwise.

      That place taken, not taken was the City of *Noyon* in *Picardy*, which was taken by the *Spanish* Cavalry, cloathed after the *French* Mode, which stratagem deceived the Citizens and Soldiers that defended it: so he saith taken, because it fell into the hands of the *Spaniards*, and *not taken*, because it was by a stratagem or deceit.

XXX.

Au Port de Puola & de St. Nicolas, Perir Normande au Gouffre Phanatique, Cap de Bizance rues crier Helas! Secours de Gaddes & du grand Philippique. English.

At the Harbour of *Puola* and of St. *Nicolas*, A *Norman* Ship shall perish in the Phanatick Gulf, At the Cape of *Byzantium* the streets shall cry Alas! Succours from *Cadis* and from the great *Philippe*.

ANNOT.

      Puola is for *Paulo* here, and by it is understood the port of *Malta*, which being Besieged by the *Turks*, *Philip* the II. King of *Spain*, sent an Army to relieve it, which made those of *Byzantium* (which is *Constantinople*) cry alas, &c.

XXXI.

French.

Le tremblement de Terre a Mortara, Cassich, St. George a demy perfondrez, Paix assoupie la guerre esuaillera, Dans Temple a Pasques abysmes enfondrez. English.

There shall be an Earthquake at *Mortara, Cassich*, St. *George* shall be half swallowed up, The War shall awake the sleeping pace, Upon Easterday shall be a great hole sunk in the Church.

ANNOT.

   Mortara is a Town in *Italy*, by *Cassich* and St. *George* he meaneth two other places.

XXXII.

French.

De fin Porphire profond Collon trouvée Dessoubs la laze escrits Capitolin, Os, poil retors, Romain force prouvée, Classe agiter au Port de Methelin. English.

A deep Column of fine *Porphyry* shall be found, Under whose Basis shall be *Roman* writings, Bones, haires twisted, *Roman* force tried, A Fleet a gathering about the Port of *Methelin*.

ANNOT.

   Porphiry is a kind of hard red Marble speckled with white spots, which is very scarce, and chiefly in great pieces; our Author then saieth that a great Colomn of that stuff shall be found, and about the Basis of it some words in Roman Characters, and that about that time a great Fleet shall be a gathering at the Port of *Methelin*, which is an Island in the *Archipelago*, belonging now to the *Turks*, as for the third Verse, I cannot tell what to make of it.

XXXIII.

French.

Hercules Roy de Rome & Dannemark, De Gaule trois Gayon surnommé, Trembler l'Itale & l'un de Saint Marc, Premier sur tous Monarque renommée. English.

Hercules King of *Rome*, and *Denmark*, Of *France* three *Guyon* surnamed, Shall cause *Italy* to quake and one of St. *Marck*, He shall be above all a famous Monarch.

ANNOT.

   All these intricated words and sense foretell that, when a King of *Danmarck* named *Hercules* shall be made King of the *Romans*, that then *Italy* and *Venice* it self shall stand in great fear of him; and that he shall be as great a Prince or Monarch as ever was in *Europe*; and that very likely, for by his dignity of King of the *Romans* he consequently shall attain to the Empire.

XXXIV.

French.

Le part solus Mary sera Mitré; Retour conflict passera sur la tuille, Par cinq cens un trahir sera tultré, Narbon & Saulce par coutaux avons d'huile. English.

The separated Husband shall wear a Miter, Returning, Battle he shall go over the Tyle, By five hundred one dignified shall be betrayed, *Narbon* and *Salces* shall have Oil by the Quintal.

ANNOT.

The first Verse signifieth, that some certain man who was married, shall be parted from his wife, and shall attain to some great Ecclesiastical Dignity.

The second Verse is, that in coming back from some place or entreprise, he shall be met and fought with, and compelled to escape over the Tyles of a House.

The third Verse is, that a man of great account shall be betrayed by five hundred of his men.

And the last, that when these things shall come te pass, *Narbon* and *Salces*, which are two Cities of *Languedoc*, shall reap and make a great deal of Oil.

XXXV.

French.

Et Ferdinand blonde sera descorte, Quitter la fleur suivre le Macedon, Au grand besoing defaillira sa routte, Et marchera contre le Myrmidon. English.

And *Ferdinand*, having a Troop of faire men, Shall leave the flower to follow the *Macedonian*, At his great need his way shall fail him, And he shall go against the *Myrmidon*.

ANNOT.

This Prophecy ought to be understood of an Emperour of *Germany*, whose name shall be *Ferdinand*, who being accompanied with many *Germans*, that for the most part are faire haired people shall come and War against *Græcia*, which is expressed here by the names of *Macedon* and *Myrmidon*, the first of which is a Countrey, and the last a Nation, both in *Græcia*.

XXXVI.

French.

Un grand Roy prins entre les mains d'un jeune, Non loin de Palques confusion, coup cultre: Perpet. cattif temps que foudre en la Hune, Trois Freres lors se blesseront & meurtre. English.

A great King taken in the hands of a young one, Not far from Easter, confusion, stroke of a knife, Shall commit, pittiful time, the fire at the top of the Mast, Three Brothers then shall wound one another, and murder done.

This Prophecy was fulfilled in the year 1560. when *Antony* of *Bourbon* King of *Navarre*, and his Brother *Lewis* of *Bourbon* Prince of *Condé*, coming to King *Francis* II. at *Orleans*, upon the 29. of *October*, the Prince of *Condé* was put in prison, and the King of *Navarre* arrested. The Lord *Andrew Fauyn* in his History of *Navarre*, saith, that the opinion of the Councel was, that the Prince of *Condé* should be beheaded, for having been the chief of the conspiracy at *Amboise*, and the King of *Navarre* should be stabbed in the Kings Chamber by the King himself, assisted by others for that purpose. The Lady of *Montpensier* gave notice of it to the King of *Navarre*, who being sent for by the King, charged expresly *Cattin* his waiting man and an old servant of his Father take a care and preserve his bloody shirt after his death till his son came to Age, to revenge it upon the murderers. God be thanked this came not to pass, for the King having called him, and going about to provoke him with foul words, he answered so meekly and humbly, that the Kings anger was appeased, where upon the Duke of *Guise* going out of the room said, *O what a cowardly Prince is this*. These things are expressed in the first and second Verse, when he saith that a great King should be put in Prison by a young one, because *Antony* of *Bourbon*, though he was not a great King in Lands, yet he was a great one in courage and prudence. And it was *not far from Easter*, sith it was but five months before, *viz.* from the beginning of *November*, to the sixth of *April* 1591 which was Easterday; the Author putteth in this circumstance, because the next Easter after, the King of *Navarre* was made General of *France* under the Queen Regent.

He addeth *the blow of a Knife*, as we have shewed; he also saith *a lasting bad time*, which proved very true; moreover, he saith, *what lightning in the Hunt* or Topmast, because King *Francis* died presently after. In the fourth Verse he saith, *that three Brothers shall be hurt and killed*, those three Brothers were *Antony* of *Bourbon* King of *Navarre*, killed at the Siege at *Rouen*, the Cardinal of *Bourbon*, and *Lewis* of *Bourbon* Prince of *Condé*, killed at the Battle of *Jarnac*.

XXXVII.

French.

Pont & Molins en December versez, En si haut lieu montera la Garonne: Murs, Edifice, Thoulouse renversez, Qu'on ne scaura son lieu coutant matrone. **English.**

Bridges and Mills in *December* overturned, In so high a place the *Garonne* shall come, Walls, Building, *Thoulose* overturned, So that none shall know its place, so much Matrone.

ANNOT.

Here is foretold a prodigious inundation of the River *Garonne*, in the month of *December*, by which the Walls, Building, and the City of *Thoulouse* is threatned to be overturned. The last word of all is barbarous, and added to make up the rhime.

XXXVIII.

French.

L'Entrée de Blaye par Rochelle & l'Anglios, Passera outre le grand Æmathien: Non loing d'Agen attendra le Gaulois, Secours Narbonne deceu par entretien. English.

The coming in at *Blaye* by *Rochel* and the *English*, Shall go beyond the great *Æmathien*, Not far from *Agen* shall expect the *French*, Help from *Narbonne* deceived by entertainment.

ANNOT.

For the better understanding of this, the hard words must first be made plain; *Blaye* is a City upon the River *Garonne*, and the Port-Town to *Bourdeaux*; *Rochel* is a City upon the same Coast; *Agen* is a City in *Gascony* not far from *Bourdeaux*, and *Narbonne* is a City in *Languedoc*, by the Mediterranean Sea; *Æmathian* was formerly the Countrey of *Macedonia*, wherein *Julius Cæsar* and *C. Pompeius* fought their last Battle in the *Pharsalian* Fields, and therefore saith the Latine Poet *Lucanus*:
  Bella per Æmathios plusquam civilia campos.

These things being considered the sense is, that there shall be an Invasion made by the *English*, to whom those of *Rochel* shall joyn, upon the Town of *Blaye*, which shall proceed as far as *Agen*, and that thereabout will be a bloody Encounter between the *English* and *French*, beyond that which was fought in the *Æmathian* Fields, and that the succours that should come from *Narbonne* to the *French*, shall be deluded and hindered by the speech and discourse of some.

XXXIX.

French.

En Arbissella, Vezema & Crevari, De nuit conduits pour Savonne atraper, Le vif Gascon, Giury, & la Charry, Derrier Mur vieux & neuf Palais grapper. English.

In *Arbissella*, *Vezema* and *Crevari*, Being conducted by night to take *Savona*, The quick *Gascon*, *Giury* and the *Charry*, Behind old Walls and new Pallace to graple.

ANNOT.

Arbissella is a Town situated by the Sea-side above *Savona*, going towards *Genoa*. *Vezema* and *Crevari* are in the Inland Countrey, and a little further remoted from the Sea then *Arbissella*. *The quick Gascon* was *Blasius* of *Monluc*, one of the Valliantest men of his time, who came from a single Souldier to be Marshal of *France*. *Guiry* and *la Charry* were two of his Companions. This Stanza doth Prophetically foretell two things, one is, the design that the Marshal of *Brissac*, then Governour of *Piemont* had upon *Savona*: the other, the taking of *Pianca* by *Blasius* of *Monluc*, as to the first, the Lord of *Villars* writeth in his Memorials, that the Lord *Damzay* sent advice to the King, that the taking of *Savona* was more probable then any other design, which signifieth that the Marshal of *Brissac* had of a long time eyed that Town, and therefore he sent by night some Troops into those three little Towns, to see if they could surprise *Savona*, but the design did not succeed.

The Histories only mention that the Marshal of *Brissac* went from Court in the year 1557. with a design to take *Savona*; but this stanza speaketh of the same design 1556.

At the same time in the year 1556. the 29. of *June Blasius* of *Monluc*, as he relateth in his Commentaries, did surprise the Town and Fort of *Piance*, called in Latine *Corsinianum*, he had with him the Captain *la Charry*, the Captain *Bartholomew* of *Pezero*, and the son of Captain *Luzzan*. At first the *French* were beaten back, but the valliant *Monluc* did encourage them again by his example, going the first in, and saying only, *follow your Captain.*

Which having said, he thrust himself under the Gate, where three or four men might stand sheltered by the planks of the Fort, and having his Sword in the left hand, and his dagger in the right, he began to break and cut the Brick and made a hole, which opening by degrees, he thrust his arm through, and pulled the gap so strongly, that he caused all the Wall to fall down upon himself, without being hurt by it. This is the meaning of the Author in the fourth Verse; when he saith, *the quick Gascon was behind the Wall*; In prosecution of this, the Switzers did beat down the rest of the Wall, and all came into the Town crying, *France, France. Monluc* ran presently to the Fort, and with the help of his men took it, that is the meaning of the Author, when he saith, *old and new Pallace to graple*. The old Pallace was adjoining to the Market-place of the Town, in which the *French* were prisoners with the Captain *Gourgues*, to the number of fifty or sixty tied two and two, and so kept by twenty Souldiers, whom they did kill as we have said. The new Pallace was the Fort. The Author used that ancient word *grapper*, which in the *Provencal* languague signifieth, to pull down with ones hands, and in the contrary sense, to shut and plaister so well some thing, that there will be a necessity of the help of the hands to open what was shut up.

XL.

French.

Pres de Quentin dans la Forest Bourlis, Dans l'Abbaye seront Flamands tranchez, Les deux puisnez de coups my estourdis, Suitte appressée & gardes tous hachez. English.

Near *Quentin* in the Forrest *Bourlis*, In the Abby the *Flemmings* shall be slashed, The two younger sons half astonished with blows, The followers oppressed, and the Guards all cut in pieces.

ANNOT.

This is a peculiar accident that happened before the taking of the Town of Saint *Quentin* by the *Spaniard* in the year 1557. and fell out thus. News being come to the King of *France*, that the powerful Army of the *Spaniard* was gone to Besiege St. *Quentin*, he made all imaginable diligence to succour it; the *Spaniards* to hinder the relief had seized upon an ancient Abby of the *Vermandois*, which is in the next Forrest, that was anciently called the Forrest *Bourlis*, and is at present called the Forrest of the *Abbay Vermandois*, called in Latine *Augusta Veromanduorum*, builded by an ancient *Hungarian* Captain called *Vermandig*. In process of time it was all ruinated, and only one Abby left, wherein was the Episcopal See, which afterwards was transferred into the City of *Noyon*. After the ruine of this Town, that of St. *Quentin* next to it became the chief City of *Vermandois*; It was named St. *Quentin*, because the Emperor *Dioclesian* having sent St. *Quentin* a *Roman* Senator to be Governour of it, he did convert the Inhabitants to the Christian Faith, and after he himself did suffer there Martyrdom.

In that Abby a great many *Flemmings* had intranched themselves, but the *French* going to relieve the Town, did force their Trenches and Fortifications, and in the heat of the fight the two younger Sons of the Captain being armed *Cap a pée*, though they were not killed, yet were astonished with blows they did receive upon their heads, their followers and Guards being all cut in

pieces.
XLI.

Le grand Chyren soy saisir d'Avignon, De Rome Lettres en miel plein d'amertume, Lettre, Ambassade partir de Chanignon, Carpentras pris par Duke noir, rouge plume. English.

The great *Cheyren* shall seize upon *Avignon*, Letters from *Rome* shall come full of bitterness, Letters and Embassies shall go from *Chanignon*, *Carpentras* taken by a black Duke with a red Feather.

ANNOT.

This did happen lately, *viz.* some five or six years ago, when the Duke of *Crequy* Embassadour at *Rome* was affronted by the *Corses*, which are the Popes Guard: for which the King of *France* demanded reparation, and seized upon *Avignon*, till the Pope granted him that all the said *Corses* should be banished, and a Pyramis erected in *Rome* to the perpetual infamy of that Nation.
XLII.

French.

De Barcelonne, de Gennes & Venise, De la Sicile pres Monaco unis, Contre Barbare classe prendront la vise, Barbar poulsé bien loing jusqu'a Thunis. English.

From *Barcelona*, from *Genoa* and *Venice*, From *Sicily* near *Manaco* united, Against the Barbarian the fleet shall take her aim, The Barbarian shall be driven back as far as *Thunis*.

ANNOT.

The sense of these words is very plain and signifieth onely, that there will be an union and League between these Towns, *viz. Barcelona, Genoa, Vinice*, and the Kingdom of *Sicily* against the Turks, whom they shall encounter near *Monaco*, and put them to flight, and follow them as far as *Tunis*.
XLIII.

French.

Proche a descendre l'Armée Crucigere, Sera guettée par les Ismaelites, De tous costez battus par nef Raviere, Prompt assailies de dix Galeres d'eslite. English.

The *Crucigere* Army being about to Land, Shall be watched by the *Ismaelites*, Being beaten on all sides by the Ship *Raviere*, Presently assaulted by ten chosen Galleys.

ANNOT.

By the *Crucigere* Army is understood the Christian Army, because the word *Crucigere* signifieth one that beareth a Cross, from the two Latine words *Crux* and *gero*; the *Ismaelites* are the *Turks*, who boast themselves to be descended from *Ismael*, the son of *Abraham* and *Agar*, the meaning of this is, that the Christians going about to attempt some landing place, the Turks shall watch them, and set upon them by Land and Sea, in which Sea fight he mentioneth only ten choice Galleys, and a notable Ship called *Raviere*, (if it be not false printed) I am much of an opinion that this came to pass when *Philip* the II. King of *Spain* made an attempt upon *Algiers*, by his Admiral *André d'Oria*, who had to do with the *Moores* upon the Land, ready to receive him, and some part of their fleet that watched him, but cross and contrary winds caused him to return *re infecta*.

XLIV.

French.

Migrez, migrez de Geneve tretous, Saturne d'Or en Fer se changera, Le contre Raypoz exterminera tous, Avant l'advent le Ciel signes sera. English.

Go forth, go forth out of *Geneva* all, *Saturn* of gold, shall be changed into Iron, They against *Raypos* shall extermine them all, Before it happeneth, the Heavens will shew signs.

ANNOT.

Called here against Raypos. This is a Prophecy concerning *Geneva*, out of which he warneth every one to come; his reason is, that the golden Age of that Town shall be changed into an Iron one; and that there shall be one against *Raypos*, that shall extermine them all, before which there shall appear some signs in Heaven. Now the Author being a rank Papist, it is to be supposed that he warneth out of *Geneva* all those of his Faith, because of the coming of *Calvin*, whom he foresaw was to come into that Town, and to change the Government thereof, and to *extermine them all*, which is to be understood, in point of Religion, as for what prodigies did precede that change; I had no time to consult Authors upon it, the judicious Reader may chance to find them in those that have written of this matter.

XLV.

French.

Ne sera soul jamais de demander, Grand Mendosus obtiendra son Empire, Loing de la Cour fera contremander, Piemont, Picard, Paris, Tyrhen le pire. English.

He shall never be weary of asking, Great *Mendosus* shall obtain his dominion, Far from the Court he shall cause him to be countermanded, *Piemont, Picardy, Paris, Tyrhen* the worse.

ANNOT.

By *Mendosus*, is Anagrammatically to be understood *Vendosme*; but who is that shall never be weary of asking, or whose Dominion *Vendosme* shall have, or what is meant by the last two

Verses, passeth my understanding.

XLVI.

French.

Vuidez fuyez de Thoulouse les rouges, Du Sacrifice faire expiation, Le Chef du mal dessoubs l'ombre des courges, Mort estrangler carne omination. English.

Get you gone, run away from *Thoulouse* ye red ones, There shall expiation be made of the Sacrifice, The chief cause of the evil under the shade of gourdes, Shall be strangled, a presage of the destruction of much flesh.

ANNOT.

This Prophecy doth onely and properly belong to the City of *Thoulouse*; and by it are warned all the red ones, that is, all those that usually wear Red or Scarlet Gowns, as those of the Parliament and the Capitols to come out of it, because saith he, *There shall an expiation be made of the Sacrifice*, meaning that there shall be a great slaughter among the Citizens, as it did happen at several times, the first *Anno* 1563. another time when the first President *Durauti*, and several other of the red Gowns were put to death, *&c.* The two last Verses signifie, that the chief contriver of this uproar shall be strangled, and many others besides him.

XLVII.

French.

Les soubsignez d'indigne deliverance, Et de la multe auront contre advis, Change Monarque mis en perrille pence, Serrez en cage se verront vis a vis. English.

The underwritten to an unworthy deliverance, Shall have from the multitude a contrary advice, They shall change their Monarch and put him in peril, They shall see themselves shut up in a Cage over against.

ANNOT.

This is plainly to be understood of those Traytors, the delivered and signed the death of King *Charles* the I. of blessed Memory, against the sense and advise of at least three parts of four of the Nation, and who afterward saw themselves for the most part shut in Prison for this fact and brought to a shameful end.

XLVIII.

French.

La grand Cité d'Occean Maritime, Environnée de Marests en Crystal, Dans le Solstice hyemal & la prime, Sera tentée de vent espouvental. English.

The great Maritime City of the Ocean, Encompassed with Chrystaline Fens, In the Winter *Solstice* and in the spring, Shall be tempted with fearful wind.

By *the great Maritime City of the Ocean, Encompassed with Crystaline Fens*, is to be understood the City of *London*, for as for that of *Venice*, it is situated upon the *Mediterranean* or rather *Adriatick* Sea: *London* then is threatned here of a fearful wind, which whether the Author meaneth for the time that is past now, and that shall come hereafter I know not, sure I am, that I have within this fifteen years seen two such winds in *London*, as I never saw the like any where else; the first was that day that *Olivier* the Usurpator died, the other was about six or seven years ago, caused by the lightning that fell in *Hereford-shire*, and did mix with a Western wind and came as far as *London*, carrying the tops of houses, and doing then for above 10000. pounds dammage.

XLIX.

French.

Gand & Bruxelles marcheront contre Anvers, Senat de Londres mettront a mort leur Roy, Le Sel & Vin luy seront a l'envers, Pour eux avoir le Regne or desarroy. English.

Gand and *Bruxelles* shall go against *Antwerp*, The Senat of *London* shall put their King to death, The Salt and Wine shall not be able to do him good, That they may have the Kingdom into ruine.

ANNOT.

This Prophecy taken with all its circumstances, and the subject it treateth of, is the most remarkable of all those that ever *Nostradamus* was Author of, for here we see a concatenation of circumstances linked together, to make it true to any bodies eyes, for first the number of this Stanza being 49, signifieth the year wherein the King died, for although by the *English* account, who begin their year at the 25. of *March*, it may be said it was in 48, because it did happen upon the 30*th.* of *January*, yet according to the general account of the most part of the World, the year begin upon the first day of *January*, so that the King dying on the 30*th.* of *January*, it may be said it was in the year 1649.

The first Verse signifieth, that at that time there was no good intelligence between the Cities of *Flanders* and *Brabant*, as I remember very well that there was not, but upon what score, I have forgotten.

The second Verse is plain to any body that can either read or hear it.

The third Verse by *the Salt and Wine*, understandeth *France*, who was then in War with the *Spaniard*, and in some divisions among themselves, so that they could not take the Kings part as to relieve and free him by force, but sent Embassadours to mediate a composure of the difference.

The fourth Verse intimateth that by reason of the said Wars that were in *France*, the said murdering Parliament had liberty to do what they listed for the bringing the Kingdom into ruine.

L.

French.

Mensodus tost viendra a son haut Regne, Mettant arriere un peu le Norlaris, Le rouge blesme, le masle a l'interregne, Le jeune crainte & frayeur Barbaris. English.

Mensodus shall soon come to his high Government, Putting a little aside the *Norlaris*, The red, pale, the Male at the interreigne, The young fear, and dread barbarisme.

ANNOT.

     Mensodus is the Anagramme of *Vendosme*, by which is meant *Antony* of *Bourbon* Duke of *Vendosme*, brother to the then Prince of *Condé*, and father to *Henry* IV. *Norlaris* is the Anagram of *Lorrain*; now any body that understandeth any thing in History, knoweth what dissention and feud there was between the House of *Bourbon*, and that of *Lorrain* in the time of *Francis* the II. for the House of *Bourbon*, though next to the Royal blood, was the least in favour, and those of the House of *Lorrain* did Govern all, and had so far prevailed as to have got the Prince of *Condé* into their hands, and had him condemned to have his head cut of, which would have been executed, had not the King that very day fallen sick of the disease he died of. Now this being understood our Author will have that *Mensodus*, which is *Vendosme* shall lay aside the *Norlaris*, that is *Lorrein*. By *the red pale* is meant the Cardinal of *Lorrain*, brother to the Duke of *Guise*, who grew pale at this. By *the male at the interreigne* is so obscure, that we leave it to the judgement of the Reader.

LI.

French.

Contre les rouges Sectes se banderont, Feu, eau, fer, corde, par paix se minera, Au point mourir ceux qui machineront, Fors un que monde sur tout ruinera. English.

Against the red, Sects shall gather themselves, Fire, water, iron, rope, by peace it shall de destroyed, Those that shall conspire shall not be put to death, Except one, who above all shall undo the World.

ANNOT.

     The name of *red Sects*, may very well be applied to the Protestants of *France*, against whom in those days it seemed that fire, Water, Iron and Rope had conspired, for they were put to death by each one of those fatal instruments for their Religion sake. This is a lively expression of the unhappy Massacre of the Protestants in *France* upon St. *Bartholomews* day 1572.

     The two last Verses signifie, that all the Contrivers of that Councel, were of opinion at first to proceed some other way, but only the Duke of *Guise*, who was the principal actor in it, and whom our Author saith, did undo the world; for he was the cause of mischief, not only then but ofterwards.

LII.

French.

La paix sapproche d'un cosié & la guerre, Oncques ne fut la poursuite fi grande, Plaindre homme & femmene sang Innocent par Terre, Et ce sera de France a toute bande. English.

Peace is coming on one side and War on the other, There was never so great a pursuing, Man, Woman shall bemoan, Innocent blood shall be spilt, It shall be in *France* on all sides.

ANNOT.

This Prophecy was fulfilled in the Reign of *Charles* the IX. in the year 1558. when the peace was treated of, and concluded the year after 1559. the War on the other side begun to appear by the raising of the Protestants, who begun publickly their opinion in the time of *Francis* the II. and *Charles* the IX.

There was never seen such a prosecution of War and of Peace together; for there was never an estate more embroiled in Wars than that of *Charles* the IX. was, nor where Peace was more sought after; for there was nothing but Wars and treaties of Peace, Men and Women did complain on all sides, for the wrong and dammages they received from both parties, the Protestants believing to do God a good service in destroying Images, and killing Priests and Monks. And the Papists on the other side thinking to make a sweet Sacrifice unto God, in practising the same cruelties upon the Protestants, and so in all corners of *France* every one did set himself to do evil.

LIII.

French.

Le Neron jeune dans les trois Cheminées, Sera de Pages vifs pour ardoir ietter, Heureux qui loin sera de tels menées, Trois de son sang le feront mort guetter. English.

The young *Nero* in the three Chimneys. Shall cause Pages to be thrown to be burnt alive, Happy shall he be who shall be far from this doing, Three of his own blood shall cause him to be put to death.

ANNOT.

A young Tyrant called here *Nero*, shall cause some Pages to be burnt alive in three Chimneys, and afterwards himself shall be put to death by three of his own blood, this fact savoureth so much of bestial cruelty, that I cannot belive any Christian Prince can ever be guilty of it.

LIV.

French.

Arrivera au port de Corsibonne, Pres de Ravenne, qui pillera la Dame, En Mer profonde legat de Ulisbone, Soubs Roc cachez raviront septante ames. English.

There shall come into the Port of *Corsibonne*, Near *Ravenna*, those that shall plunder the Lady, In the deep Sea shall be the Embassador of *Lisbonne*, The hidden under the Rock, shall carry away seventy Souls.

ANNOT.

      The Port of *Corsibonne*, must of necessity be that of *Ancona*; first because there is no Port of the former name near the City of *Ravenna*. Secondly, because *Ancona* is near *Ravenna*.

      By the Lady is meant the Chappel or Church of our Lady of *Loretto*, which is threatned here to be plundred by some *Turks* or Pyrates, inticed thereunto by the manifold riches that are said to be therein.

      The third Verse speaketh of a *Portugues* Embassador, who it seemeth shall be drowned or buried in the main Sea.

      The fourth Verse giveth warning of some Robbers and Pyrates, very like to be *Turks*, who being in Ambuscado, and shrouded among the Rocks by the Sea side, shall carry away seventy Souls.

LV.

French.

L'Horrible guerre qu'en Occident s'appreste, L'An ensuivant viendra la Pestilence, Si fort terrible, que jeune, viel, ne beste, Sang, feu, Mercu. Mars, Jupiter en France. English.

An horrid War is a preparing in the West, The next year shall come the Plague, So strangly terrible, that neither young nor old, nor beast shall escape Blood, fire, *Mercu. Mars*, *Jupiter* in *France*.

ANNOT.

      That word *a preparing* in the first Verse, signifieth that he speaketh of a time, wherein War was a making ready, when he was a writing.

      The *West*, of which our Author speaketh, is not formerly the West which is *Spain*, but is the West respectively to his Countrey of *Provence*, which is *Picardy, Lorrain*, and the Countrey of *Mets*, in all these Places that are Westerly from *Provence*, there was great Wars in the year 1557 in *Picardy* in the year 1558. at *Calais* and *Thionville*, and at last from the middle of that year to the end of it, were seen two great Armies of both Kings, which threatned a horrid slaughter, had not God Almighty provided against it by the treaty of Peace of the *3d.* of *April* 1559 the year following, which was 1559. there did happen what he foretelleth, *viz.*, the Plague so strangely terrible to Young, Old, and Beasts *&c.*

      And in those quarters there was nothing but Fire and Blood; that is, Massacres and ruines of all sorts, then did Rule in *France*, the three Planets of *Jupiter, Mars* and *Mercury, Jupiter* and *Mercury*, for the peace that was then concluded, and *Mars* for the War that was then on foot.

      The History of *Provence* mentioneth, that that Pestilence was called by the Physitians, *Febris erratica*, by which within the space of five or six Months, died almost an infinite number of

people.
LVI.

French.

Camp prés de Noudam pasiera Goussanville, Et a Maiotes laissera son enseigne, Convertira en instant plus de mille, Cherchant le deux remettre en chaine & legne. English.

A Camp shall by *Noudam* go beyond *Goussanville*, And shall leave its Ensign at *Maiotes*, And shall in an instant convert above a thousand, Seeking to put the two parties in good understanding together.

ANNOT.

These three words of *Noudam*, *Goussanville*, and *Maiotes* are three little inconsiderable Countrey Towns, situated near one another; the meaning then of it is, that an Army near *Noudam*, shall go through *Goussanville*, and shall in an instant convert, that is, draw to his party above a thousand of the contrary party, the business being about the procuring of a good understanding and amity between two great ones.

LVII.

French.

Au lieu de Drux un Roy reposera, Et cherchera Loy changeant d'Anatheme, Pendant le Ciel si tresfort Tonnera, Portée neufve Roy tuera soy mesme. English.

In the place of *Drux* a King shall rest himself, And shall seek Law changing Anatheme, In the mean while the Heaven shall Thunder so strongly, That a new gate shall kill the King him self.

ANNOT.

Drux is a City in *Normandy*, near which *Henry* the IV. got a memorable victory.

It is said that in that place a King shall rest himself, and shall endeavour to change Religion, but at that time it shall Thunder and Lighten so much, that by the fall of a new gate, the King himself shall be killed.

LVIII.

French.

Au costé gauche a lendroit de Vitry, Seront guettez les trois rouges de France, Tous assommez rouge, noir non meurdry, Par les Bretons remis en asseurance. English.

On the left hand over against *Vitry*, The three red ones of *France* shall be watched for, All the red shall be knockt dead, the black not murdered, By the *Britains* set up again in security.

What is meant here by the three red ones of *France* is hard to decide, whether they be Cardinals or Judges; because both wear commonly Scarlet Gowns, or some Noblemen cloathed in Scarlet, but it seemeth by this that there shall be a lying in wait for four men, three of which shall be cloathed in Red, and one in Black, those in Red shall be knockt down dead, but he in Black shall not, and this is to be done on the left hand, over against *Vitry*, which is a City in *Champagne*.

LIX.

French.

A la Ferté prendra la Vidame, Nicol tenu rouge quavoit produit la vie, La grand Loyse naistra qui fera clame, Donnant Bourgongne a Bretons par envie. English.

In the *Ferté* the *Vidame* shall take *Nicol*, reputed red, whom life hath produced, The great *Lewis* shall be born, who shall lay claim, Giving *Burgundy* to the *Britains*, through envy.

ANNOT.

This Stanza wanting both quantity in the Cadence of the Verse, and Connexion in the sense, sheweth that it is either falsly printed, or else the Author had no mind it should be understood; we shall only say, the *Ferté* is a Town in *Champagne*. *Vidame* is a Lords Title in *France*, of which there are but four of that sort, and are called in Civil Law *Vicedominus*, who by his first Institution, was temporal Judge of the Bishop; the first of those *Vidames* or *Vicedomini* in *France*, is that of *Amiens*, the second of *Chartres*, the third of *Rhemes*, and the fourth of *Gerberon*.

LX.

French.

Conflict Barbare en la Cornere noire, Sang espandu trembler la Dalmatie, Grand Ismael mettra son promontoire, Ranes trembler, secours Lusitanie. English.

A *Barbarian* fight in the black Corner, Blood shall be spilt, *Dalmatia* shall tremble for fear, Great *Ismael* shall set up his promontory, Frogs shall tremble, *Portugal* shall bring succour.

ANNOT.

This Prophecie foretelleth divers accidents in several places, without determination of any precise time; as for example, I understand by that *Barbarian conflict, near the black Corner*, to be some famous Battle among the Infidels themselves, some where about the Black Sea; then he saith, *that abundance of Blood shall be spilt, and Dalmatia shall tremble*, which is a Province belonging to the *Venetians*, and bordering upon *Græcia*; by great *Ismael* he understandeth the great Sophy of *Persia*, whose name hath been often so. By the Frogs it is not easie to know whether he meaneth *France* or *Spain*, for both abound in that kind of Insects.

LXI.

French.

La pille faite a la Coste Marine, Incita nova & parens amenez, Plusieurs de Malthe par le fait de Messine, Estroit serrez seront mal guerdonnez. **English.**

The plunder made upon the Sea Coast, *Incita nova* and friends brought up, Many of *Maltha*, for the fact of *Messina*, Being close kept, shall be ill rewarded.

ANNOT.

It seemeth that this Plunder made upon the Sea Coast, shall be about *Messina*, by the *Maltheses*, who afterwards shall rue for it, being taken Prisoners, and severely punished.

As for the expression *Incita nova*, it is a barbarous derivation of the Latine, to signifie the stirring of new troubles.

LXII.

French.

Au grand de Cheramonagora, Seront croisez par rangs tous attachez, Le Pertinax Oppi, & Mandragora, Raugon d'Octobre le tiers seront laschez. **English.**

To the great one of *Cheramonagora*, Shall be crossed by Ranges, all tyed up, the *Pertinax Oppi*, and *Mandragora, Raugon* the third of *October* shall be set loose.

ANNOT.

The word *Cheramonagora*, is either altogether barbarous and insignificant, or must be derived from these three Greek words, χεὶρ, *manus*, μόνος, *folus*, and ἄγω, *duco*, and so it may signifie one than leadeth along by the hand, in which sense may be understood the King of *France*, who alone leadeth his people by the hand, without any help of Councel.

The second Verse signifieth the Oppositions he shall meet with among his Neighbours, combined together to hinder him.

By *Oppi*, he meaneth here *Opium*, the Juice of Poppies, which he calleth here *Pertinax*; because of its pertinacious quality in procuring sleep, as also *Mandragora*.

By *Raugon*, he meaneth some other soporiferous Herb; so that it seemeth that those three things shall be given upon the third of *October* to some body, it seemeth to that *Cheramonagora*, by whom some understand the King of *France*, others *Oliver* the last usurpator.

LXIII.

French.

Plaintes, & pleurs, cris, & grands hurlemens, Pres de Narbonne, a Bayonne & en Foix, O quels horribles, calamitez, changemens, Avant que Mars revolu quelquefois. English.

Complaints and tears, cries, and great howlings, Near *Narbonne, Bayonne* and in *Foix*, O what horrid calamities and changes, Before *Mars* hath made sometimes his revolution.

ANNOT.

      Narbonne, Bayonne, and *Foix* are Towns of *Languedoc*, a Province in *France*; the rest is easie.

LXIV.

French.

L'Æmathian passer Monts Pyrenées, En Mars Narbon ne fera resistance, Par Mer & Terre sera si grand menée, Cap. n'ayant Terre seure pour demeurance. English.

The *Æmathian* shall pass by the *Pyrenean* Mountains, In *March Narbon* shall make no resistance, By Sea and Land he shall make so much ado, Cap. shall not have safe ground to live in.

ANNOT.

      The *Æmathian* properly should be the *Macedonian*, but by it is understood here the *Spaniard*, whose Countrey is on one side fenced by the *Pyrenean* Mountains; the rest is plain.

LXV.

French.

Dedans le coing de Luna viendra rendre, Ou sera prins & mis en Terre estrange, Les fruits immeurs seront a grand esclandre, Grand vitupere, a l'un grande loüange. English.

He shall come into the corner of *Luna*, Where he shall be taken and put in a strange Land, The green fruits shall be in great disorder, A great shame, to one shall be great praise.

ANNOT.

      This Stanza hath relation and connexion to the precedent, and by it ought to be understood, that the said *Æmathian* or *Spaniard* shall come as far as the corner of *Luna*, wherein he shall be taken and sent into a strange Countrey, at which time the green Fruits and Grass shall be much damaged, for which one of the parties shall receive great shame, and the other great praise. But what he meaneth by the Corner of *Luna*, I must leave the judgement of it to the Reader, for I do ingeniously confess that I neither know City nor Countrey of that name.

XLVI.

French.

Paix, union, sera & changement, Estats, Offices, bas hault, & hault bien bas, Dresser voiages, le fruit premier, torment, Guerre cesser, civils proces, debats. English.

Peace, union, shall be, and mutation, States, and Offices, low high, and high low, A journey shall be prepared for, the first fruit, pains, War shall cease, as also, civil suits, and strifes.

ANNOT.

This is easie to be understood, many interpret it of the downfall of *Rome*, at which time all quarrels both of Religion and States would be laid aside, if the world were all of one mind.

LXVII.

French.

Du haut des Monts a lentour de Dizere, Port a la Roche Valent, cent assemblez, De Chasteau-Neuf, Pierrelate, en Douzere, Contre le Crest, Romans soy assemblez. English.

From the top of the Mountains about *Dizere* Gate at the Rock *Valence*, a hundred gathered together, From *Chasteau-Neuf, Pierrelate*, in *Douzere* Against the *Crest, Romans*, shall be gathered.

ANNOT.

This is a peculiar Prophecy for the Provinces of *Dauphiné* and *Languedoc*, in which all the Towns and Rivers here mentioned are situated.

LXVIII.

French.

Du Mont Aymar sera noble obscurcie, Le mal viendra au joint de Saone & Rhosne, Dans bois cachez Soldats jour de Lucie, Qui ne fut onc un si horrible Throsne. English.

From Mount *Aymar* shall proceed a Noble obscurity, The evil shall come to the joyning of the *Saone* and *Rhosne*, Soldiers shall be hid in the Wood on St. *Lucy*'s day, So that there was never such an horrid Throne.

ANNOT.

There is a notable fault in the impression of the first Verse of this Stanza, for instead of Mount *Aymar*, it must be *Montlimar*, which is a Town in *Provence* or *Languedoc*, situated by the River *Rhosne*, the sense therefore of this, is, that from *Montlimar* shall proceed some notable and obscure design, and that shall reach as far as *Lyons*, which is the City where the *Saone* and *Rhosne* meet, and that for that purpose, there shall be hidden a great many Souldiers in a Wood on St. *Lucy*'s day, which is the *13th.* of *December*.

LXIX.

French.

Sur le Mont de Bailly & la Bresse, Seront cachez de Grenoble les fiers, Outre Lyon, Vien. cula si grand gresle, Langoult en Terre n'en cessara un tiers. English.

Upon the Mount of *Bailly*, and the Countrey of *Bresse*, Shall be hidden the fierce ones of *Grenoble*, Beyond *Lyons*, *Vienna*, upon them shall fall such a hail, That languishing upon the ground, the third part shall not be left.

ANNOT.

The Mount *Bailly*, and the Countrey of *Bressia*, are by *Savoy*, in which place (our Author saith) the fierce ones; that is, the stout men of *Grenoble*, the chief Town of *Dauphiné*, shall be hidden, and that such a Hail shall fall upon them, as not one third part shall be left.

LXX.

French.

Harnois trenchans dans les flambeaux cachez, Dedans Lyon le jour du Sacrement, Ceux de Vienne seront tretous hachez, Par les Cantons Latins, Mascon eront. English.

Sharp Weapons shall be hidden in burning Torches, In *Lyons* the day of the Sacrament, Those of *Vienna* shall be all cut to pieces, By the Latin *Cantons*, after the example of *Mascon*.

ANNOT.

This foretelleth a notable Treason that shall be acted at *Lyons*, upon the Sacraments day, otherwise called *Corpus Christi* day, upon which the *Roman* Catholicks are wont to make a Procession with the Sacrament about the Town, with abundance of burning Torches, of fearful bigness, insomuch that some (as at *Angeirs*) require 20 or 24 men to carry them, in those Torches (our Author saith) shall Weapons be hidden, by means of which the fact shall be committed. The rest is easie.

LXXI.

French.

Au lieux Sacrés, animaux veus a Trixe, Avec celuy qui nosera le jour, A Carcassonne pour disgrace propice, Sera posé pour plus ample sejonr. English.

In the Sacred places, Animals shall be seen at *Trixe*, With him that shall not dare in the day, In *Carcassonne* for a favourable disgrace, He shall be set to make a longer stay.

Whether the Author did understand himself here I know not, I am sure I do not; *Carcassonne* is a City of *Languedoc*, and *Trixe* is a barbarous word.

LXXII.

French.

Encor seront les Saints Temples pollus, Et expilez par Senat Tholosain, Saturne deux trois Siecles revolus, Dans Auril, May, gens de nouveau Levain. English.

Once more shall the Holy Temples be polluted, And depredated by the Senate of *Thoulouze, Saturn* two three Ages finished, In *April, May*, people of a new Leaven.

ANNOT.

This is, when the Planet *Saturn* hath finished twice three Ages; that is, 600 years from the time that this Prophecy was written, then the Senates of *Thoulouze*, being men of a new Leaven (meaning being Protestants) shall cause the *Romish* Churches to be polluted and depredated in the Months of *April* and *May*.

LXXIII.

French.

Dans Foix entrez Roy Cerulée Turban, Et regnera moins evolu Saturne, Roy Turban Blanc, Bizance cœur ban, Sol, Mars, Mercure, pres la Hurne. English.

In *Foix* shall come a King with a Blew Turbant, And shall Reign before *Saturn* is revolved, Then a King with a White Turbant shall make *Bizance* to quake, *Sol, Mars, Mercury*, being near the top of the Mast.

ANNOT.

Foix is a Countrey of *France*, near *Gascony*, where the Author saith, a King with a Blew Turbant shall come, and shall govern less then an Age, that is 100 years, after which another King with a White Turbant shall come, and shall Conquer *Bizance* (which in Latine is *Constantinople*) the Blew or Green Turbant is attributed to the great *Turk*, and the White one to the King of *France*, by whom the *Turks* have a Prophecie, their Monarchy shall be subverted.

LXXIV.

French.

Dans la Cité de Fertsod homicide, Fait & fait multe Bœuf arant ne macter, Retour encore aux honneurs d'Artemide, Et a Vulcan corps morts sepulturer. English.

In the City of *Fertsod* one murdered, Causeth a Fine to be laid for killing a plowing Oxe, There shall be a return of the honours due to *Artemide*, And *Vulcan* shall bury dead bodies.

ANNOT.

What is that City of *Fertsod*, is hard to guess, there being none of this name in *Europe* that I know. The rest of the words are plain, though the sense be abstruce enough, therefore we shall leave them to the liberty of the Reader.

LXXV.

French.

De l'Ambraxie & du pais de Thrace, Peuple par Mer, Mal, & secours Gaulois, Perpetuelle en Provence la Trace, Avec vestiges de leur Coustumes & Loix. English.

From *Ambraxia*, and from the Countrey of *Thracia*, People by Sea, Evil, and *French* succours, The Trace of it shall be perpetual in *Provence*, The footsteps of their Customs and Laws remaining.

ANNOT.

What Countrey this *Ambraxia* should be, is yet unknown, for my part I take it to be a forged word, as for *Thracia* it is a Countrey between *Hungary* and *Greece*.

Observe here that Evil is not an Epithete, to either People or Sea, but a word of admiration by it self, as *malum* in Latine, which is called *vox admirantis*.

LXXVI.

French.

Avec le noir Rapax & sanguinaire, Yssu du peaultre de l'inhumain Neron, Emmy deux Fleuves main gauche Militaire, Sera meurtry par Joyn Chaulveron. English.

With the Black and bloody *Rapax*, Descended from the paultry of the inhumane *Nero*, Between two Rivers, on the left Military hand, He shall be murdered by *Joyne Caulveron*.

ANNOT.

This Prophecie portendeth the death of a black, bloody, and ravenous man (which in Latine is *Rapax*) who shall be murdered between two Rivers, by one whose proper name shall be *Joyne Chaulveron*.

LXXVII.

French.

Le Regne prins le Roy conviera, La Dame prinse a mort jurez a sort, La vie a Royne Fils on desniera, Et la pellix au fort de la consort. English.

The Kingdom being taken, the King shall invite, The Lady taken to death, The Life shall be denyed unto the Queens Son, And the Pellix shall be at the height of the Consort.

ANNOT.

You must observe, that there is a word false printed, which is *Pellix*, instead of which should be *Pellex*, which in Latine signifieth a Whore or Concubine.

The sense therefore of this is, that a certain King having taken another Kingdom, shall put the Queen of it to death, as also her own Son, after which, he shall make his Concubine Queen.

LXXVIII.

French.

La Dame Grecque de Beauté laydique, Heureuse faite de proces innumerable, Hors translatée au Regne Hispanique, Captive prinse mourir mort miserable. English.

The *Græcian* Lady of exquisite Beauty, Made happy from innumerable quarrels, Being translated into the *Spanish* Kingdom, Shall be made a Prisoner, and die a miserable death.

ANNOT.

This Stanza is concerning the Lady *Elizabeth* of *France*, Daughter to *Henry* the II. and Sister to *Charles* the IX. who being promised first to *Don Carlo Infante* of *Spain*, was afterwards Married to his Father *Philip* the II. at which the young man being vexed and discontented, began to raise combustions in the State, for which, and his too much familiarity with his Mother in Law, he was strangled by his Fathers command, and she poisoned.

LXXIX.

French.

Le Chef de Classe par fraude, stratageme, Fera timides sortir de leurs Galeres, Sortis meurdris chef renieux de Cresme, Puis par l'Embusche luy rendront les salaires. English.

The Commander of a Fleet by fraud and stratagem, Shall cause the fearful ones to come forth of their Galleys, Come out murdered, chief renouncer of Baptism, After that by an Ambuscado they'l give him again his salary.

The two first Verses are plain, the third signifieth, that these fearful ones being come out of their Galleys, part of them shall be murdered, and among them the Captain, a renouncer of his Baptism, or Renegado, and the rest afterwards by an Ambuscado, shall requite in the same Coin those that had used them so.

LXXX.

French.

Le Duc voudra les siens exterminer, Envoyera les plus forts, lieux estranges, Par tyrannie Bize & Luc ruiner, Puis les Barbares sans Vin feront Vendanges. English.

The Duke shall endeavour to exterminate his own, And shall send away the strongest of them into remote places, He shall also ruinate *Bize* and *Luc*, The *Barbarians* shall make Vintage without Wine.

ANNOT.

There is a great fault in the impression of the *French* Copy in this Stanza, which maketh the sense altogether inexplicable, it must then in stead of *Bize* and *Luc*, be written *Pise* and *Lucques*, which are two Towns in *Italy*, near the Duke of *Florence*'s Dominions; one of these Towns, *viz. Pisa* he hath taken already, and from a Common-Wealth made it subject to himself; the other though several times attempted by him, hath preserved its liberty to this day. The last Verse signifieth, that after this is come to pass, the *Barbarians*, that is, the *Florentins shall make Vintage without Wine*; that is, shall plunder and spoil at their pleasure.

LXXXI.

French.

LeRoy rusé entendra ses Embusches, De trois quartiers Ennemis assaillir, Un nombre estrange Larmes de coqueluches, Viendra Lamprin du traducteur faillir. English.

The crafty King shall hear of his Ambuscadoes, And shall assail his Enemies on three sides, A strange number of Friers, mens Tears, Shall cause *Lamprin* to desert the Traitor.

ANNOT.

The only difficulty here is to know who that *Lamprin* should be, who shall be diverted from following a Traitor (which he meaneth here by the *French* word *Traducteur*) and shall be diverted from it by the Tears of Fryers, which are meant here by the ancient *French* word *Coqueluches*, which signifieth a Fryers Cool or Capuchon.

LXXXII.

Par le Deluge & pestilence forte, La Cité grande de long temps Assiegée, La Sentinelle & Garde de main morte, Subite prinse mais de nul outragée. English.

The great City having been long Besieged, By an Innundation and violent Plague, The Sentinal and Watch being surprised, Shall be taken on a sudden, but hurt by no body.

ANNOT.

This is very plain, if by the great City you understand *Paris*, who is subject to frequent Innundations and Plagues.

LXXXIII.

French.

Sol Vingt de Taurus, si fort terre tremblera, Le grand Theatre remply ruinera, L'Air, Ciel, & Terre, obscurcir & troubler, Lors l'Infidele Dieu, & Saints voguera. English.

The Sun being in the *20th* of *Taurus*, the Earth shall so quake, That it shall fill and ruinate the great Theater The Air, the Heaven, & the Earth shall be so darkened, and troubled, That the unbelievers shall call upon God, and his Saints.

ANNOT.

This famous Earth-quake having not yet happened in *Europe*, it is like to happen within few years, for our Authors Prophecies (by his own confession) do not extend further than the year 1700.

LXXXIV.

French.

Roy exposé parfaira l'Hecatombe, Apres avoir trouve son Origine, Torrent ouvrir de Marbre & Plomb la Tombe, D'un grand Romain d'Enseigne Medusin. English.

The King exposed shall fulfill the Hecatombe, After he hath found out his Offspring, A Torrent shall open the Sepulcher, made of Marble and Lead, Of a great *Roman*, with a *Medusean* Ensign.

ANNOT.

This Prophecie is divided into two parts, The first two Verses are concerning a King, who shall perform the Funeral Rites and Ceremonies to his Parents, when he is come to the knowledge of them, having been exposed for lost before.

The two last Verses are concerning an ancient Sepulcher of a *Roman*, that shall be digged up and found out by a Torrent, and the Arms of the said *Roman* shall be something like the head of *Medusa*, whose Hairs were Serpents, and was so fearful to behold, that by seeing of it, the beholders were turned into stones.

LXXXV.

French.

Passer Guenne, Languedoc, & le Rhosne, D'Agen tenants, de Marmande & la Reole, D'Ouvrir par foy parroy, Phocen tiendra son Throne, Conflict aupres Saint Pol de Manseole. English.

They shall pass over *Gascony, Languedoc*, and the *Rhosne*, From *Agen* keeping *Marmande*, and the *Reole*, To open the Wall by Faith, *Phocen* shall keep his Throne, A Battle shall be by St. *Paul* of *Manseole*.

ANNOT.

The whole of this Prophecie signifieth no more, but that an Army shall pass through all these places, and that at last there will be a Battle fought by that place, called St. *Paul de Manseole*.

LXXXVI.

French.

Du Bourg la Reyne parviendront droit a Chartres, Et feront pres du Pont Antony pose, Sept pour la paix cauteleux comme Martres, Feront entrée d'Armée a Paris clause. English.

From *Bourg la Reyne* they shall come straight to *Chartres*, And shall make a stand near *Pont Antony*, Seven for Peace as crafty as *Martres*, They shall enter in *Paris* besieged with an Army.

ANNOT.

Bourg la Reyne is a little town within six Miles of *Paris*, *Chartres* is the chief City of the Province *Beausse*, *Pont Antony* is a little Town between them both, so that the sense of the whole is this, that seven men, crafty like *Martres* (which are those *Russia* Foxes that afford the richest Furres, called *Martres Zibellines*) shall go from *Bourg la Reyne* to *Chartres*, making a little stay at *Pont Antony*, and then shall come with an Army into *Paris*, which shall be besieged at that time, I believe this Prophecy is come to pass already in the time of the Civil Wars of *France*; but for want of the History I could not quote the time.

LXXXVII.

French.

Par la Forest du Touphon essartée Par Hermitage sera posé le Temple, Le Duc d'Estampes par sa ruse inventée, Du Montlehery Prelat donra exemple. English.

By the Forrest *Touphon* cut off, By the Hermitage shall the Temple be set, The Duke of *Estampes* by his invented trick, Shall give example to the Prelat of *Montlehery.*

ANNOT.

Here is a fault in the Impression, for instead of *Touphon*, it must be written *Torfou*, which is a Forrest some 30 Miles from *Paris* towards *Beausse*, near which is seated the Town of *Montlehery*, in the said Forrest is seated an Hermitage, and not far from thence the City of *Estampes*, which carryeth the Title of Dutchy; so that the sense of it is this, that this Forrest being cut off (as it is now for the most part) in the place where that Hermitage was, shall be built a Church or Convent, as it is now *Cælestins friars*, called *Marcoussy*, and that the said Hermitage shall be taken from the jurisdiction of the Town of *Montlehery*, under which it was before.

LXXXVIII.

French.

Calais, Arras, secours a Theroanne, Paix & semblant simulera l'escoute, Soulde d'Allobrox descendra par Roane, Destornay peuple qui defera la routte. English.

Calais, Arras, shall give succours to *Theroanne*, Peace or the like, shall dissemble the hearing, Souldiers of *Allobrox* shall descend by *Roane*, People perswaded, shall spoil the March.

ANNOT.

This Prophecy did happen in the time of *Henry* the II. King of *France*, about the year 1559.

The last Verse saith, that those two Towns *Calais* and *Arras* gave succours to *Theroanne*, that is to the Countrey where *Therouenne* was seated, which was destroyed by *Charles* the V. Emperour. This Countrey was called *Ponthieu*, of which *Therouenne* was the chief Town.

The second Verse doth determine the time whereabout this came to pass, when he saith, *peace or the like shall dissemble the hearing*; because in the year 1556. in the beginning of *February* there was a Truce for five years between the two Crowns of *France* and *Spain*, concerning the Low Countreys, and this Truce signified not much, nor was well cemented, so that the Author saith, *Peace or the like shall dissemble the hearing*; that is, shall fain not to hear that the Cardinal *Caraffa* did endeavour in *France* to have the Truce broken.

The third Verse is obscure, because of a fault in the Impression, wherein they have put *Ronane* instead of *Noanne*, that is *Hannone* by transposition of letters, but that being corrected, the Verse is clear, supposing that *Philibertus Emanuel* Duke of *Savoy* was General of the Army, against *France* in the *Low-Countreis*, and wandering about to do some notable exploit, he came down through the Province of *Hainault*, called in Latine *Hannonia*, and came to *Mariembourg*, as if he would have Besieged it, but after some light skirmishes he laid Siege to *Rocroy*, and this is the meaning of the third Verse, when he saith, *Souldiers of Allobrox shall descend by Noanne*, that is, Souldiers in the Army of the Duke of *Savoy*, which in Latine is *Allobrox*, came down to *Mariembourg*, and turned back again to *Rocroy.*

The fourth Verse mentioneth what did happen at the Siege of *Rocroy*; that place being not yet very well fortified; the King was unwilling to put any of his best Souldiers therein, but the Duke of *Nevers* undertook the defence of it, which he did really and gloriously perform, in so much, that the Duke of *Savoy* was compelled to raise up the Siege, and going back towards St. *Quentin*, he took *Vervins* by storm, and gave the booty of it to his Souldiers, who took heart upon it, having been much discouraged before by the resistance of the Duke of *Nevers*. This is the sense of the fourth Verse, *People persuaded shall spoil the march*; that is, the people of *Rocroy* persuaded to hold out by the courage and presence of the Duke of *Nevers*, spoiled the march that the Duke of *Savoy* had propounded to himself, insomuch, that raising the Siege he went to *Vervins*, and from thence to St. *Quentin*.

LXXXIX.

French.

Sept ans Philip fortune prospere, Rabaissera des Barbares l'effort, Puis son midy perplex rebours affaire, Jeune Ogmion abysmera son fort. English.

Philip shall have seven years of prosperous fortune, Shall beat down the attempt of the *Barbarians*, Then in his Noon he shall be perplexed and have untoward business, Young *Ogmion* shall pull down his strength.

ANNOT.

This Stanza was made concerning *Philip* the II. King of *Spain*, who for the first seven years that he came to his Crown, had prosperous fortune, did brave exploits against the *Barbarians*, and chiefly in the person of his Brother *Don Juan* of *Austria*, who got the memorable Battle of *Lapantho* against the *Turks*, but in the middle of *his Noon*, that is of his Age, fell into great perplexities and cross businesses, being constrained to put his onely son *Don Carla* to death, and to poison his wife and after that never prospered, when young *Ogmion* (that is *Henry* IV. King of *France*) came to the Crown.

XC.

French.

Un Capitaine de la grand Germanie, Se viendra rendre par simulé secours, Au Roy des Roys, aide de Pannonie, Que sa revoke fera de sang grand cours. English.

A Captain of the great *Germany*, Shall come to yield himself with a fained help, Unto the King of Kings, help of *Hungary*, So that his revolt shall cause a great bloodshed.

ANNOT.

Pannonia in Latine is *Hungary*, there is nothing hard in this, unless it be what he meaneth by the King of Kings, whether it be the great Turk or the Emperour.

XCI.

French.

L'Horrible peste Perynthe & Nicopole, Le Chersonese tiendra & Marceloine, La Thessalie naistera l'Amphipole, Mal incogneu & le refus d'Antoine. English.

The horrid pestilence shall seize upon *Perynthe* and *Nicopolis*, The *Chersonese* and *Marceloine*, It shall waste *Thessalia* and *Amphipolis*, An unknown evil and the refusal of *Antony.*

ANNOT.

There is several faults in the impression here, for instead of *Perynthe*, it must be *Corinth.* For *Marceloine*, it must be *Macedoine*: the substance of the whole is, that there shall be a great plague in all these Countries of *Asia.* The refusal of *Antony* is foisted here to make up the rime with *Macedony.*

XCII.

French.

Le Roy voudra dans Cité neufve entrer, Par ennemis expugner l'on viendra, Captif libere, faulx dire & perpetrer, Roy dehors estre, loin d'ennemis tiendra. English.

The King shall desire to enter into the new City, With foes they shall come to overcome it, The Prisoner being free, shall speak and act falsly, The King being gotten out, shall keep far from enemies.

ANNOT.

The sense of all these words so ill jointed, is no more but that a certain King shall desire to enter into a new City, and there they shall come and Besiege him, where he shall both act and speak deceitfully to get his liberty, which having obtained, shall keep far from his foes.

XCIII.

French.

Les ennemis du Fort bien esloignez, Par Chariots conduits le Bastion, Par sur les Murs de Bourges esgrongnez, Quand Hercules battra l'Hæmathion. English.

The enemies being a good way from the Fort, Shall upon Wagons be conducted to the Bulwark, From the top of *Bourges* Walls they shall be cut less, When *Hercules* shall beat the *Hæmathion.*

ANNOT.

Bourges is the chief City of a Province in *France* called *Berry.*

There is nothing difficult in this, but onely what he meaneth by *Hercules beating the Æmathion*, unless by *Hercules* he meaneth the *French*, and by *Æmathion* the *Spaniard*.
XCIV.

French.

Foibles Galeres seront unis ensemble, Ennemis faux, le plus fort en rempart, Foible assailies Wratislavie tremble; Lubeck & Mysne tiendront Barbare part. English.

Weak Galleys shall be united together, False enemies, the strongest shall be fortified, Weak assaults, and yet *Breslaw* quaketh for fear, *Lubeck* and *Misne* shall take the part of the *Barbarians*.

ANNOT.

Breslaw, *Lubeck* and *Misne*, are three Cities of *Germany*; the rest is plain.
XCV.

French.

Le nouveau fait conduira l'exercite, Proche apamé jusque aupres du Rivage, Tendant secours de Melanoise eslite, Duc yeux privé, a Milan fer de Cage. English.

The new man shall lead up the Army, Near *Apamé*, till near the Bank, Carrying succours of choice Forces from *Milan*, The Duke deprived of his eyes, and an Iron Cage at *Milan*.

ANNOT.

Apamé is a barbarous word, at least I cannot tell what language it is, the rest is plain enough, and signifieth that a Duke shall be deprived of his eyes, and shall be put in an Iron Cage at *Milan*.
XCVI.

French.

Dans Cité entrer exercite desniée, Duc entrera par persuasion, Aux foibles portes clam Armée amenée, Mettront feu, mort, de sang effusion. English.

The Army being denied the entrance of the City, The Duke shall enter by persuasion, To the weak Gates, *clam* the Army being brought, Shall put all to fire and sword.

ANNOT.

Clam here is in Latine *præposition*, signifying secretly; the rest is easie.

XCVII.

De Mer Copies en trois parts divisées, A la seconde les Vivres failliront, Desesperez cherchant Champs Elisées, Premiers en breche entrez victoire auront. English.

A Fleet being divided into three parts, The victuals will fail the second part, Being in despaire they'l seek the *Elysian* Fields, And entring the breach first, shall obtain victory.

ANNOT.

A Fleet being divided into three parts, the second division shall fall into want of victuals, for which being desperate, they shall attempt the Town of the enemy, and shall enter it by the breach, and get the victory.

XCVIII.

French.

Les affligez par faute d'un seul taint, Contremenant a partie opposite, Aux Lygonois mandera que contraint, Seront de rendre le grand chef de Molite. English.

The afflicted want of one only died, Carrying against the opposite part, Shall send word to those of *Lyon*, they shall be compelled, To surrender the great chief of *Molite*.

ANNOT.

This is the most nonsensical thing that is in all the Book, for neither the words nor the connexion is intelligible, therefore it being so much out of the common road of our Author, I am apt to believe that it was at first very falsly printed, and that those that came after, were loth to alter it for the respect of antiquity.

XCIX.

French.

Vent Aquilon fera partir le Siege, Par murs jetter cendres, chaulx, & poussiere, Par pluye apres qui leur sera bien piege, Dernier secours encontre leur Frontiere. English.

The North wind shall cause the Siege to be raised, They shall throw ashes, lime, and dust, By a rain after that shall be a trap to them, It shall be the last succours against their Frontiere.

ANNOT.

Here is described a notable stratagem of a Besieged Town, who against rainy weather cast so much ashes, lime and dust, that the rain coming thereupon, it made such a mire, as the Besiegers were not able to assault it.

C.

Navale pugne nuict sera superée, Le feu, aux Naves a l'Occident ruine, Rubriche neuve, la grand néf colorée, Ire a vaincu, & victoire en bruine. **English.**

In a Sea-fight, night shall be overcome, By fire, to the Ships of the West ruine shall happen, A new stratagem, the great Ship coloured, Anger to the vanquished, and victory in a Mist.

ANNOT.

He foretelleth of a Sea-fight in the night, wherein by the light of the burning Ships night shall be overcome, the Ships that came from the West shall be worsted, and by a stratagem of a great Ship painted in colours, anger shall remain to the vanquished, and the victory shall be got in a Mist.

Michael Nostradamus.

CENTURY X.

I.

French.

A l'Ennemy, l'ennemy foy promise, Ne se tiendra, les captifs retenus, Prins preme mort & le reste en chemise, Donnant le reste pour estre secourus. English.

To the enemy, the enemy faith promised, Shall not be kept, the prisoners shall be detained, The first taken, put to death, and the rest stripped, Giving the remnant that they may be succoured.

ANNOT.

These words are plain, though the sense be a little intricated, and the contents being of small concernments, deserve no further explanation.

II.

French.

Voile Gallere Voile nef Cachera, La grand Classe viendra sortir la moindre, Dix Naves proches le tourneront poulser, Grand vaincüe, unies a soy joindre. English.

The Galley and the Ship shall hide their Sails, The great Fleet shall make the little one to come out, Ten Ships near hand, shall turn and push at it, The great being vanquished, they shall unite together.

ANNOT.

These are some particularities of a Sea fight between a great Fleet and a small one, wherein he saith, that some had hid their Sails, belike they were unwilling to come out of the Harbour and to fight; but he saith, that the great Fleet will compel the little one to come out; but ten great Ships will come to help the little Fleet, and after the great one hath been overcome, will joyn themselves to the little Fleet.

III.

French.

En apres cinq troupeau ne mettra hors, Un fuitif pour Penelon laschera, Faux murmurer secours venir par lors, Le Chef le Siege lors abandonnera. English.

After that, five shall not put out his flock, He'l let loose a runaway for *Penelon*, There shall be a false rumour, succours shall come then, The Commander shall forsake the Siege.

ANNOT.

      This Stanza is either nonsensical or falsely printed, and what he meaneth by *Penelon*, is utterly unknown.

IV.

French.

Sur la minuit conducteur de l'Armée, Se sauvera subit esvanovy, Sept ans apres la fame non blasmée, A son retour ne dira oncq ouy. English.

About midnight the leader of the Army, Shall save himself, vanishing suddenly, Seven years after his fame shall not be blamed And at his return he shall never say yea.

ANNOT.

      This is plain of a General of an Army, who shall forsake his Army, and save himself, and yet seven years after when he cometh back, his reputation shall be as clear, as if he never had committed such an errour.

V.

French.

Albi & Castres feront nouvelle ligue, Neuf Arriens, Lisbonne, & Portuguez, Carcas. Thoulouze, consumeront leur brigue Quand chef neuf monstre de Lauraguez. English.

Albi and *Castres* shall make a new league, Nine *Arriens*, *Lisbonne*, and *Portuguez*, *Carcas. Thoulouse*, shall make an end of their confederacy; When the new chief shall come from *Lauragais*.

ANNOT.

      Albi, *Castres*, *Carcassonne*, and *Thoulouse*, are Cities of *Languedock*, which our Author saith, will enter into a confederacy among themselves, and joyn with *Lisbon* and the *Portuguez*, and this shall happen when the general of the Army, shall be one born in *Lauragais*, which is another of the same Province.

VI.

French.

Gardon a Nismes eaux si haut desborderont, Qu'on cuidera Deucalion renaistre, Dans le Colosse la pluspart fuiront, Vesta Sepulchre feu esteint apparoistre. English.

Gardon at *Nismes*, waters shall overflow so high, That they'l think that *Deucalion* is born again, Most of them will run into the *Colossus*, And a Sepulchre, and fire extinguished, shall appear.

ANNOT.

Near *Nismes* there is the River called *Gardon*, which cometh from St. *Romans*, and dischargeth it self into the *Rhosne* at *Beaucaire*, there is to be seen in that City abundance of *Antiquitez*, which the *Goths* had built 1150. years before; there is also many *Roman* Antiquities, as an *Amphitheater*, so well builded that neither the *Goths* nor the *Saracens*, nor *Attila*, nor *Charles Martel*, with all their power, could not utterly demolish it. The Author nameth it *Colossus*, because its building appeared like a *Colossus* for solidity.

There is also an ancient Temple which is called the *Fountain*, builded as a Quadrangle, and supported by two rows of great Pillars, which at present is a Church of Nuns.

This being supposed, the River of *Gardon* did overflow so much, that its Waters joyning with that of a Flood that happened there the ninth of *September* 1557. every one thought that *Deucalion* had been born again. The Author saith this; because in the fables of the ancients. *Deucalion* is thought to be the Author of the Flood which *Ovid* mentioneth. During this Flood which was like to overflow the Town, as well as the Countrey, many did retire themselves into that Amphitheater.

And in that ancient Temple of the *Fountain*, the Waters overthrowing a great many old buildings did discover abundance of Antiquities, and amongst the rest one of those Lamps that burneth always, in the Sepulchre of a *Vestal*, which went out as soon as it felt the fresh Air.

In confirmation of this, the History of *Provence* saith, that the storm began about five of the Clock in the Morning, and lasted till Eight of the Clock at night, and that these waters did uncover abundance of Antiquities that were hidden 1100. years before, as Pillars, Portico's, Medals, Jasper-stones, and serpentine-stones, pieces of broken Vessels, Epitaphs, lodging Rooms, and Caves, and all other things that use to be found in the ruines of a Palace.

There was also heard in the Air Dogs barking, Pillars of fire, Armed men fighting, and were seen two Suns in the Clouds of the Colour of Blood, all which were the sad presages of the Civil Wars of *France* presently after, and chiefly that of *Provence*.

The ninth Century in the ninth Stanza, speaketh almost the same, and sheweth that *Nismes* shall perish by Water.

VII.

French.

Le grand conflict qu'on appreste a Nancy, L'Æmathien dira tout je soubmets, L'Isle Britane par Vin Sel en solcy, Hem. mi. deux Phi. long temps ne tiendra Mets. English.

A great War is preparing at *Nancy*, The *Æmathien* shall say I submit to all, The *British* Island shall be put in care by Salt and Wine, *Hem. mi.* two *Phi.* shall not keep *Mets* long.

      Nancy is the chief City of *Lorrain*, and by the *Æmathien* is understood the *French*, the *British* Isle is *England*, which is said here, shall come into great distress by Salt and Wine, because the Countrey aboundeth in those two Commodities. The last Verse I do not understand, save that *Mets* is a great City in *Lorrain*.

VIII.

French.

Index & Poulse parfondera le front De Senegalia le Comte a son Fils propre, La Myrnamée par plusieurs de plain front, Trois dans sept jours blessez mort. English.

    Index and *Poulse* shall break the forehead, Of the Son of the Earl of *Senegalia*, The *Myrnamée* by many at a full bout, Three within seven days shall be wounded to death.

ANNOT.

      Senegalia is a Town in *Italy*, all what can be gathered out of the obscurity of this Stanza, is, that the son of the Earl of that Town shall have his forehead broken, and within seven days after, three more shall be wounded to death.

IX.

French.

De Castilon figuieres jour de brune, De femme infame naistra Souverain Prince, Surnum de chausses per hume luy posthume, Onc Roy ne fut si pire en sa Province. English.

    Out of *Castilon figuieres* upon a misty day, From an infamous woman shall be born a Soveraign Prince, His surname shall be from *Breeches*, himself a posthume, Never a King was worse in his Province.

ANNOT.

      Castilon figuieres is a petty Town in *Provence*, in which he saith that a Soveraign Prince shall be born of an infamous Woman, and shall be a posthume, which in Latine signifieth one that is born after his Fathers death; he saith also that his name shall be derived from *Breeches* and that never a King was worse in his Countrey, whether by worse, he meaneth in manners or fortune, I know not.

X.

Tasche de murdre, enormes Adulteres, Grand ennemy de tout le genre humain, Que sera pire qu'ayeulx, Oncles ne Pere, En fer, feu, eau, sanguin & inhumain. English.

Endeavour of Murder, enormous Adulteries, A great enemy of all mankind, That shall be worse then Grand-father, Uncle, or Father, In Iron, fire, water, bloody and inhumane.

ANNOT.

This Stanza as well as the next hath relation to the precedent, making mention what a wicked person shall that Posthume be of which he spoke before.

XI.

French.

Dessoubs Jonchere du dangereux passage, Fera passer le posthume sa bande, Les Monts Pyrens passer hors son bagage, De Parpignan courira Duc a Tende. English.

Below *Joncheres* dangerous passage, The posthume shall cause his Army to go over, And his Baggage to go over the *Pyrenean* Mountains, A Duke shalt run from *Perpignan* to *Tende.*

ANNOT.

This is still concerning the same posthume or Bastard, who shall cause his Army to pass at *Jonchere,* and his Bagage to go over the *Pyrenean* Mountains, which parts *Spain* from *France,* and that upon the fear of him a Duke shall run from *Perpignan,* which is the chief City of *Roussillon* to *Tende,* which is a little Town in *Provence.*

XII.

French.

Esleu en Pape, d'Esleu sera mocqué, Subit soudain, esmeu prompt & timide, Par trop bon doux a mourir provoqué, Crainte estainte la nuit de sa mort guide. English.

Elected for a Pope, from Elected shall be baffled, Upon a sudden, moved quick and fearful, By too much sweetness provooked to die, His fear being out in the night shall be Leader to his death.

ANNOT.

This Prophecy was fulfilled in the person of the Cardinal *Santa Severina,* who in the Conclave of Cardinals after the death of Pope *Innocent* IX. was Elected Pope, and presently after was baffled by the same Cardinals, and *Clement* the VIII. chosen in his place, for which the other a little while after died for grief.

XIII.

French.

Soubs la pasture d'animaux ruminans, Par eux conduits au ventre Herbi-polique, Soldats cachez, les armes bruit menants, Non loin tentez de Cité Antipolique. English.

Under the pasture of Beasts chewing the cud, Conducted by them to the *Herbi-polique* belly, Souldiers hidden, the Weapons making a noise, Shall be attempted not far from *Antipolick* City.

ANNOT.

The sense of this is, that some Souldiers disguised like Herds-men, shall lead Oxen into a place where were hidden before Weapons in the Grass, but the Weapons making a noise by their clashing they shall be discovered, not far from a place that he calleth here *Antipolique*, purposely to rime with *Herbipolique* in *French*, which word *Herbipolique* signifieth a Town of Pasture.

XIV.

French.

Urnel, Vaucile, sans conseil de soy mesmes, Hardy, timide par crainte prins vaincu, Accompagné de plusieurs putains, blesme, A Barcelonne aux Chartreux convaincu. English.

Urnel, Vaucile, without advice of his own, Stout and fearful, by fear taken and overcome, Pale, and in company of many Whores, Shall be convicted at *Barcelone* by the Charterhouse.

ANNOT.

This Stanza is an Horoscope, which the Author made upon that Gentleman named *Urnel Vaucille*, and signifieth that the said man should find himself in such perplexity that he could not be able to take advice what to do, and that fear should make him hide himself, to be apprehended, in a place where he should be taken.

When he was taken, he was presently convicted of those crimes that he was accused of: therefore the Officers of Justice did conduct him to the Charter-house of *Barcelone*, which is four miles from the said Town, in a place called *Campo alegre*, for the beauty and situation of it, to that place many Whores did accompany him to receive the punishment they had deserved, therefore the Author saith that he went thither pale, as foreseeing the terrour of the punishment he was to undergo.

XV.

French.

Pere Duc vieux d'ans & de soif chargé, Au jour extreme fils desniant l'esguiere, Dedans le puis vif, mort viendra plongé, Senat au fils la mort longue & legere. English.

A Father Duke, aged and very thirsty, In his extremity, his son denying him the Ewer, Alive into a

Well, where he shall be drowned, For which the Senate shall give the son a long and easie death.

ANNOT.

It is a Duke very aged who shall die of a Dropsie, or of some other burning disease, which will make him very thirsty, the Physitians shall forbid any water to be given him, therefore this Duke shall press his son very much to give him the Ewer, that he may drink his fill, but his son refusing, the Father shall fall into such a rage, that being alone he will go and throw himself into a Well, where he shall be drowned.

This unhappy death will be the cause of much murmuring, and the Senate or Parliament of that place will make enquiry after it, by which enquiry the son will be found guilty, therefore for his punishment, he shall be condemned to a long and easie death, as to live all his days in some Monastery.

XVI.

French.

Heureux au Regne de France heureux de vie, Ignorant sang, mort, fureur, rapine, Par non flatteurs seras mis en envie, Roy desrobé, trop de foy en cuisine. English.

Happy in the Kingdom of *France*, happy in his Life, Ignorant of blood, death, fury, of taking by force, By no flatterers shall be envied, King robbed, too much faith in Kitchin.

ANNOT.

This is a Prognostication of a King of *France*, who though happy in his Reign and Life, and being given to no great vices, as blood, fury, or taking by force, yet shall be much envied and robbed by his Subjects, and chiefly by those he trusteth about his Kitchin.

XVII.

French.

La Reyne Ergaste voiant sa fille blesme, Par un regret dans l'estomach enclos, Cris lamentables seront lors d'Angolesme, Et au germain mariage forclos. English.

Queen *Ergaste* seeing her Daughter pale, By a regret contained in her Breast, Then shall great cries come out of *Angolesme*, And the Marriage shall be denyed to the Cousin German.

ANNOT.

It is unknown what Queen he meaneth by the name of *Ergaste*; the rest is easie. *Angolesme* is a City of *Gascony* or *Languedoc*.

XVIII.

French.

Le rang Lorrain fera place a Vendosme, Le haut mis bas, & le bas mis en haut, Le fils d'Hamon sera esleu dans Rome, Et les deux grands seront mis en defaut. English.

The House of *Lorrain* shall give place to *Vendosme* The high pulled down, the low raised up, The son of *Hamon* shall be Elected into *Rome*, And the two great ones shall not appear.

ANNOT.

      The two first Verses of this Prophecy were fulfilled in the time of *Henry* the third King of *France*, in whose time the Duke of *Guise*, and House of *Lorrain* were grown so powerful in *France*, that they drove the King from *Paris*, and assumed themselves a rank and authority over the Princes of the Blood, so that the King was forced to cause them to be slain, after which *Henry* IV. who was King of *Navarre* and Duke of *Vendosme* took his place again as first Prince of the Blood.

      The two last Verses are too obscure to be interpreted, and I believe were onely forced by our Author to make up his Rime, as he hath done in several other places.

XIX.

French.

Jour que sera pour Roine saluée, Le jour apres le salut, la Priere, Le compte fait raison & valbuée, Par avant humble oncques ne fut si fiere. English.

The day that she shall be saluted Queen, The next day after the Evening Prayer, All accompts being summoned and cast up, She that was humble before, never was one so proud.

ANNOT.

      It is a woman (be like of a small Fortune) who coming to be a Queen by her humility, the next day after Evening Prayer she shall appear so proud, as the like was never seen.

XX.

French.

Tous les amis qu'auront tenu party, Pour rude en lettres mis mort & saccage, Biens publiez par fixe, grand neanty, Onc Romain peuple ne fut tant outrage. English.

All the friends that shall have taken the part Of the Unlearned, put to death and robbed, Goods sold publickly by proclamation, a great man seized of them, Never *Roman* people was so much abused.

The sense of this is, that a great man that took part with all those that were unlearned shall be put to death, and their goods praised and sold publickly, upon which goods another great man shall seize, and this is to be done in *Rome*.

There is fault in the Impression of the third *French* Verse, for instead of *fixe* it must be *fisc* and instead of *Neanty* it must be *Nancy*.

XXI.

French.

Par le despit du Roy soustenant moindre, Sera meurdry luy presentant les bagues, Le Pere & Fils voulant Noblesse poindre, Fait comme a Perse jadis firent les Magues. English.

To spite the King, who took the part of the weaker, He shall be murdered, presenting to him Jewels, The Father and the Son going to vex the Nobility, It shall be done to them as the *Magi* did in *Persia*.

ANNOT.

This is a King who with his son taking the peoples part against the Nobility shall be killed, in presenting to him Jewels, and he and his son shall be dealt with all as the *Magi*, that is the Grandees of *Persia* used to do with their Kings, whom they were wont to murder, or depose.

XXII.

French.

Pour ne vouloir consentir au divorce, Qui puis apres sera cogneu indigne, Le Roy des Isles sera chassé par force, Mis a son lien qui de Roy n'aura signe. English.

For not consenting to the divorce, Which afterwards shall be acknowledged unworthy, The King of the Island shall be expelled by force, And another subrogated, who shall have no mark of a King.

ANNOT.

This is plain concerning *England* and the late calamities thereof, when our gracious King for not consenting to the wicked factions of the Parliament then, and that have been acknowledged so since, was expelled by force, and an Usurpator that had not the least sign of a King sat in his place.

XXIII.

French.

Au peuple ingrat faites les remonstrances, Par lors l'Armée se saisira d'Antibe, Dans larc Monech feront les doleances, Et a Freius l'un l'autre prendra ribe. English.

The remonstrances being made to the ungrateful people, At that time the Army shall seize upon

Antibe, In the River of *Monaco* they shall make their complaints, And at *Freius* both of them shall take their share.

ANNOT.

This signifieth that at the same time that the remonstrances shall be made to an ungrateful people; the Army shall seize upon the Town of *Antibe*, which is a Sea Town between *France* and *Italy*, and that there shall be great complaints at *Monaco*, which is another Sea Town near it, and at the place called *Freius*, both parties shall either agree, or divide their shares.

XXIV.

French.

Le captif Prince aux Itales vaincu, Passera Gennes par Mer jusque a Marseille, Par grand effort des forens survaincu, Sauf coup de feu, barril liqueur d'Abeille. English.

The captive Prince vanquished in *Italy*, Shall pass by Sea through *Genoa* to *Marseilles*, By great endeavours of forrain forces overcome, But that a Barrel of Honey shall save him from the fire.

ANNOT.

A Prince vanquished in *Italy*, and taken Prisoner shall come through *Genoa* to *Marseilles*, where he shall be once more overcome by strangers, but that a Barrel of Honey shall save him from being burnt. This is the sense of the words as near as I can judge, the judicious Reader may make what construction he pleaseth upon them.

XXV.

French.

Par Nebro ouvrir de Brisanne passage, Bien esloignez el tago fara muestra, Dans Pelligouxe sera commis l'outrage, De la grand Dame assise sur l'Orchestra. English.

By *Nebro* to open the passage of *Brisanne*, A great way off, *el tago fara muestra*, In *Pelligouxe* the wrong shall be done Of the great Lady sitting in the *Orchestra*.

ANNOT.

Here once more I lost my Spectacles, and could not see through, therefore I had rather be silent then coin lies, I shall only tell you, that *orchestra* in Latine is the seat wherein noble Personages sit at the beholding of Stage-plays.

XXVI.

Le successeur vengera son Beau frere, Occuper Regne soubs ombre de vengeance, Occis obstacle son sang mort vitupere, Long temps Bretagne tiendra avec la France. English.

The Successour shall avenge his Brother in Law, Shall hold by force the Kingdom, upon pretence of revenge, That hinderance shall be killed, his dead blood ashamed, A long time shall *Brittany* hold with *France*.

ANNOT.

This is plain enough of it self, without any interpretation.

XXVII.

French.

Charle cinquiesme & un grand Hercules, Viendront le Temple ouvrir de main bellique, Une Colonne, Jules & Ascan reculez, L'E'pagne, clef, Aigle neurent onc si grand pique. English.

Charles the Fifth, and one great *Hercules*, Shall open the Temple with a Warlike hand, One Colonne, *Julius* and *Ascan* put back, *Spain*, the Key, Eagle were never at such variance.

ANNOT.

Charles the V. was the Emperour, and that great *Hercules* was *Henry* the II. King of *France*, whom he calleth *Hercules*, because he was King of *France*, and the Author nameth often in his Stanzas the Kings of *France Hercules* or *Ogmions*, because that great Captain of the Antiquity left his name glorious in the *Gaules*, whence the ancient Historians have given him the name of *Hercules Gallicus*. *Henry* the II. also was not only an *Hercules* by being King of *France*, but also a great *Hercules*, because of his Warlike humour, and for his great feats in Arms.

To open the Temple, signifieth to make War, because the *Romans* in ancient time were wont to shut the Temple of *Janus* in time of Peace, and kept it open during the War. *Cæsar Augustus* did shut that Temple once in his time, which was never done before but twice, the first under *Numa Pompilius*, the second after the overcoming of *Charthage*.

XXVIII.

French.

Second & tiers qui font prime Musique, Sera par Roy en honneur sublimée, Par grasse & maigre presque a deny etique; Rapport de Venus faux rendra deprimée. English.

Second and third that make prime Musick, Shall by the King be exalted to honour, By a fat one, and a lean one, one in consumption, A false report of *Venus* shall pull her down.

ANNOT.

Notwithstanding the obscurity of this sense, and the bad connexion of the words, we may perceive that by this Stanza is meant, that a King having two Mistresses shall exalt them in great honour, till by a report made by a fat woman and a lean one, that is in a consumption, that the said Ladies prove unfaithful to the King, he will depress them as low as they were before.

XXIX.

French.

De Pol Mansol dans Caverne caprine, Caché & pris extrait hors par la barbe, Captif mené comme beste mastine, Par Begourdans amenée pres de Tarbe. English.

From *Pol Mansol* in a Goats Den, Hidden and taken, drawn out by the beard Prisoner, led as a Mastiff, By *Begourdans* shall be brought near to *Tarbe*.

ANNOT.

Here and in some other places of this work is to be observed, that the Author doth sometimes put two Towns instead of one, that he may distinguish it from others of the same name, as here he calleth *Pol Mansol* to distinguish the Town of St. *Paul*, which is three Leagues from the *Rhosne*, over against the Town of *Pont St. Esprit*, from that which is in the lower parts of *Provence*.

The sense therefore of this Stanza is, that this *Begourdans* (a proper name of a man) shall pull out another by the beard, that was hidden in a Goats Den, and shall lead him captive as far as *Tarbe*, which is another Town of *Provence*.

XXX.

French.

Nepveu & sang du St. nouveau venu, Par le surnom soustient arcs & couvert, Seront chassez mis a mort chassez nu, En rouge & noir convertiront leur vert. English.

Nephew and blood of the Saint newly come, By the surname upholdeth Vaults and Covering, They shall be driven, put to death, and driven out naked. They shall change their red and black into green.

ANNOT.

Here I confess to be at a loss, as may be a wiser man then I.

XXXI.

French.

Le Sainct Empire viendra en Germanie, Ismaelites trouveront lieux ouverts, Asnes viendront aussy de la Caramanie, Les soustenans de Terre tous couverts. English.

The Holy Empire shall come into *Germany*, The *Ismaelites* shall find open places, Asses shall also come out of *Caramania*, Taking their part, and covering the Earth.

ANNOT.

By the *Ismaelites* he meaneth the *Turks*, who brag to be descended from *Ismael*.
Caramania is a Province of *Turky*, so that the sense of this Stanza is, that there shall be a great Invasion of the *Turks* into *Germany*, and that those of *Caramania* with their Asses shall come to their help, and shall be in such numbers, as that the Earth shall be covered with them.

XXXII.

French.

Le grand Empire chascun en devoit estre, Un sur les autres le viendra obtenir, Mais peu de temps sera son Regne & estre, Deux ans aux Naves se pourra soustenir. English.

The great Empire, every one would be of it, One above the rest shall obtain it, But his time and his Reign shall last little, He may maintain himself two years in his Shipping.

ANNOT.

This is plain enough without interpretation.

XXXIII.

French.

La faction cruelle a Robe longue, Viendra cacher soubs les pointus Poignards, Saisir Florence, le Duc & le Diphlongue, Sa discouverte par Immeurs & Flagnards. English.

The cruel faction of long Robe, Shall come and hide under the sharp Daggers, Seize upon *Florence*, the Duke and the *Diphlongue*, The discovery of it shall be by Countrey fellows.

ANNOT.

This is the Prognostication of a conspiracy against the Duke and City of *Florence*, by those of the long Gown, which shall be discovered by Countrey fellows, that live in places without Walls.

XXXIV.

Gaulois qu'Empire par Guerre occupera, Par son Beau-frere mineur sera trahi, Par Cheval rude voltigeant trainera, Du fait le frere long temps sera hay. English.

A *Frenchman* who shall occupy an Empire by War, Shall be betrayed by his Brother in Law a Pupil, He shall be drawn by a rude prancing Horse, For which fact his brother shall be long hated.

ANNOT.

  This foretelleth of a *Frenchman*, who shall by War obtain an Empire or Kingdom, and shall be betrayed by his Brother in Law a Pupil, whom afterwards he shall treacherously cause to mount a fierce prancing Horse, who shall throw him down and drag him, for which the said King shall be hated long after.

XXXV.

French.

Puisné Roial flagrant d'ardant libide, Pour se jouir de cousine Germaine, Habit de femme au Temple d'Artemide, Allant murdry par incogneu du Marne. English.

The Kingly youngest son heated with burning lust, For to enjoy his Cosen German, Shall in womans apparrel go to the Temple of *Artemis*; Going, shall be murdered by unknown *du Marne*.

ANNOT.

  This is concerning the younger son of a King, who being extreamly in love with his Cosen German, shall disguise himself in a womans apparel, and shall go so disguised to the Temple of *Artemide* (that is of some Church Dedicated to the Virgin *Mary*) to meet her, but in going, shall be murdered by an unknown man named *du Marne*.

XXXVI.

French.

Apres le Roy du Sud guerres parlant, L'Isle Harmotique le tiendra a mespris, Quelques ans bons rongeant un & pillant, Par tyrannie a l'Isle changeant pris. English.

After that the King of the South shall have talked of Wars, The *Harmotick* Island shall despise him, Some good years gnawing one and plundering, And by tyranny shall change the price of the Island.

ANNOT.

  The two first Verses are concerning *Philip* the II. King of *Spain*, who is called here the King of the *South*, whom after his vain and frustrated Invasion of 88. the *Harmotique* Island (that is *England*) shall deride, and he after that shall have some good years, that is of Peace, still pillaging and plundering his Subjects, and shall change the price of *England*, that is, make it of a higher value, and more flourishing then ever it was before, as it did prove in Queen *Elizabeth*'s time.

XXXVII.

French.

Grande assemblée pres du Lac du Borget, Se rallieront pres de Montmelian, Passants plus outre pensifs feront projet, Chambray, Morienne, combat Saint Julian. English.

A great assembly of people near the Lake of *Borget*, Will go and gather themselves about *Montmelian*, Going beyond, they shall make an enterprize, Upon *Chambery*, *Moriene*, and shall fight at St. *Julian*.

ANNOT.

This Lake of *Borget* is in *Savoy*, as also *Montmelian*, *Chambery*, *Moriene*, and St. *Julian*; the meaning of it then is, that a great Army shall be gathered about that Lake, which shall go through *Chambery*, *Moriene*, and *Montmelian*, and shall fight at St. *Julian*.

XXXVIII.

French.

Amour alegre non loin pose le Siege, Au Saint Barbar seront les Garnisons, Ursins, Hadrie pour Gaulois feront plaige. Pour peur rendus de l'Armée, aux Grisons. English.

Cheerful love doth lay Siege not far, The Garrisons shall be at Saint *Barbar*, *Ursini*, *Hadria* shall be sureties for the *French*, And many for fear shall go from the Army to the *Grisons*.

ANNOT.

The first two Verses are inexplicable; the two last signifie that there shall be an Army of *Frens*, with whom *Hadria* (that is *Venice*) and the *Ursini* the noblest Family in *Italy* shall take part, insomuch, that many of the contrary party shall run for fear to the *Grisons*, which is a Nation dwelling in the *Valteline* and other Countreis there about, between the *Venetians* and the *Switzers*.

XXXIX.

French.

Premier fils veusve malheureux mariage, Sans nuls enfans deux Isles en discord, Avant dixhuit incompetant Aage, De l'autre pres plus bas sera l'accord. English.

Of the first son a widow, an unhappy match, Without any Children, two Islands at variance, Before eighteen an incompetant Age, Of the other lower shall be the agreement.

ANNOT.

Although the words be intricate, nevertheless the sense is plain, concerning *Francis* the II.

King of *France*, who being married young, and before he was 18. years of Age, to *Mary Stuart* Queen of *Scotland*, died presently after, and left her a widow, and also *England* and *Scotland* (which he calleth here two Islands) at variance among themselves; of the last Verse the sense is very obscure, and hath relation to what did happen afterwards to the said *Mary* Queen of *Scots* and Dowager of *France*.

XL.

French.

Le jeune nay au Regne Britannique, Qu'aura le Pere mourant recommandé, Iceluy mort Londre donra topique, Et a son fils le Regne demandé. *English.*

The young man born to the Kingdom of *Britanny*, Whom his Father dying shall have recommended, After his death *London* shall give him a topick, And shall ask the Kingdom from his son.

ANNOT.

This Prophecy is plain, concerning his Majesty King *Charles* II. now Reigning, who having been recommended by his dying Father to his Subjects, presently after his death they turned tail, and took the Kingdom from him for a good while.

XLI.

French.

En la frontiere de Caussade & Charlus, Non gueres loing du fond de la valée, De Ville Franche Musique a son de Luths, Environnez Combouls & grand myrtée. *English.*

Upon the Frontiere of *Caussade* and *Charlus*, Not far from the bottom of the Valley, Of *Ville Franche* there shall be Musick of Lutes, Great dancing and great company of people met together.

ANNOT.

Caussade, Charlus, and *Villefranche* are little Towns in *Provence*, not far one from another; the rest is easie.

XLII.

French.

Le Regne humain d'Angelique geniture, Fera son Regne, paix, union tenir, Captive guerre demy de sa closture, Long temps la paix leur fera maintenir. *English.*

The humane Reign of an Angelical brood, Shall cause his Reign to be in peace and union, Shall make War, captive shutting it half up, He shall cause them to keep peace a great while.

This is only a foretelling of some Gallant Prince, who shall maintain his Subjects in great peace and tranquility.

XLIII.

French.

Le trop bon temps, trop de bonté Roiale, Faits & desfaits prompt, subit, negligence, Leger croira faux, despouse loiale, Luy mis a mort par sa benevolence. English.

The time too good, too much of Royal bounty, Made and unmade, nimble, quick, negligence, Fickle shall believe false o' his loyal Spouse, He shall be put to death for his good will.

ANNOT.

This is concerning another King, who through his too much goodness, simplicity and negligence, shall make and unmake those about him, and being fickle, shall believe false reports, made concerning his own wife; and at last by his to much goodness, shall be put to death.

XLIV.

French.

Par lors qu'un Roy sera contre les siens; Natif de Blois subjuguera Ligueres, Mammel, Cordube, & les Dalmatiens, Des sept puis l'ombre a Roy estrennes & Lemures. English.

At that time that a King shall be against his own, One born at Blois shall subdue the *Ligures, Mammel, Cordua* and the *Dalmatians,* After that the shadow of the seven shall be to the King a new-years gift and Hoggoblins.

ANNOT.

Blois is a City in *France*; *Ligures* are the *Genoeses,* in Latine called *Ligures*; as for *Mammel* I cannot tell what to make of it; *Cordua* is a City of *Spain,* and the *Dalmatians* is a Nation near the *Adriatick* Sea, and under the *Venetians*; I leave the interpretation of the last Verse to the ingenious Reader.

XLV.

French.

Lombre du Regne de Navarre non vray, Fera la vie de sort illegitime, La vers promis incertain de Cambray, Roy d'Orleans donra mur legitime English.

The shadow of the Reign of *Navarre* not true, Shall make the life of illegitimate chance, The uncertain allowance from *Cambray,* King of *Orleans* shall give a lawfull Wall.

The *Reign* or Kingdom of *Navarre* is called *not true*, because the King of *Spain* doth possess it, and not the King of *France*, who is the lawful King thereof, as also in regard of the Kings of *France*, and before of *Jane* of *Albret*, and *Antony* of *Bourbon*.

This Kingdom being *not true* in regard of the said ones, the title and quality is called here *shadow*. The Author saith that the quality of the King of *Navarre shall make the life of illigitimate chance*, because after the death of *Francis* the II *Catherine* of *Medicis* being not opposed in the Regence by *Antony* of *Bourbon* King of *Navarre*, she was willing to gratifie him in what she could.

And because his Brother *Lewis* Prince of *Condé* had been condemned to death, and not executed, it was a fair occasion for her to shew the King of *Navarre* how much she did defer to him. Therefore twelve days after the death of King *Francis*, he was freed out of Prison, and was admitted to justifie himself under the King of *Navarre*'s Bail.

Thus the *shadow of the Kingdom of Navarre not true*, did cause the life of a Prince to be saved, but that life was illegitimate, *and that Kingdom not true by chance*, that is, by accident, because of the death of King *Francis*.

Leaving off the third Verse to be explained after the fourth; *King* (saith the Author) *shall give* Orleans *for legitimate*, because *Charles* the IX. who during the life of *Francis* the II. did bear the title of Duke of *Orleans*, did succeed his Brother; thus the Verse saith that *Orleans shall give a King for legitimate*.

Now for the third Verse, you must suppose that by the Treaty at *Madrid* 1526. and after this by that of *Cambray*, the King *Francis* the I. did part with the Sovereignty of *Flanders*, and of all the *Low Countreis* in favour of *Charles* the V. Emperour, it is of that *uncertain allowance* of Cambray, of which the Author talketh here, and saith, that in that time *viz.* of the death of *Francis* the II. that *allowance shall be uncertain*, because *Francis* the I. having no power of himself to renounce the rights and dependance of the Crown of *France*, the Parliament that was assembled then, would have made void that *allowance* without breaking the Peace, declaring that the Kings of *France* ought to preserve the right they had upon the *Low-Countreis*, and to require them again upon any occasion, and upon that *France* did not refuse the Election which the *Low-Countreis* made of the Duke of *Alencon* for their Sovereign Prince and Duke of *Brabant*.

XLVI.

French.

Vif sort mort de l'or vilain indigne, Sera de Saxe non nouveau Electeur, De Brunswick mandra d'amour signe, Faux le rendant au peuple seducteur. **English.**

The living receives his death from Gold, infamous slut! Shall be of *Saxony* not the new Elector, From *Brunswick* shall come a sign of love, Falsly persuading the people that he is a seductor.

This Prophecy is concerning an old Elector of *Saxony*, who being in health before, shall die suddenly, being poisoned in a golden Cup by a woman, whom he calleth here *infamous slut*.

And that from *Brunswick* (a Countrey adjacent to *Saxony*) shall come a Messenger, upon pretence of Love, who shall persuade the people that the said Elector was a Seducer.

XLVII.

De Bourze Ville a la Dame Guyrlande, L'on mettra sus par la trahison faite, Le grand Prelat de Leon par Formande, Faux Pellerins & Rauisseurs deffaite. English.

From *Bourze* City belonging to the Lady *Garlant*, They shall impose by a set treason, The great Prelate of *Leon* by *Formande*, False Pilgrims and Ravishers destroyed.

ANNOT.

      I believe that there is a fault here in the impression, and that instead of *Bourze* it must be *Bourges*, which is a famous City in *France*, and Capitol of the Province of *Berry*, for I do not know any Town in *Europe* called *Bourze*. What he meaneth by the Lady *Garlant* is unknown. I believe also that instead of *Leon* it should be *Lyon*, which is another famous City, and the first Archbishoprick of the said Kingdom. *Formande* is a barbarous word, and I believe put in only to make up the Rime, as he hath done in several other places, as much then as can be gathered out of the sense is this, that from that City *Bourges*, which usually is a Dowry for a Queen of *France*, which is called here *Garlant*, shall a treason be hatched against the Archbishop of *Lion*, which I suppose came to pass in the time of *Henry* the III. when *Peter* of *Pinac* Archbishop of the said *Lion*, being accused by the Deputies of *Bourges* for siding with the League, escaped narrowly to be killed, when the Duke of *Guise* and the Cardinal his brother were. Queen *Catherine* of *Medicis* the Kings Mother having then the said Province and Town of *Bourges* for her jointure.

      The last Verse hath no relation to the three foremost, and hath its interpretation by it self, which is plain enough.

XLVIII.

Du plus profond de l'Espagne ancienne, Sortants du bout & des fins de l'Europe, Trouble passant aupres du Pont de Laigne, Sera deffaits par bande sa grand troppe. English.

From the utmost part of old *Spain*, Going out of the extremities of *Europe*, He that troubled the travellers by the Bridge of *Laigne*, Shall have his great Troop defeated by another.

ANNOT.

      Every Traveller knoweth that *Castille* (which is taken here for *Spain*) is divided into two parts *viz. Castilia la Vecchia*, and *Castilia la Nuova*, our Author then saith that out of *Castilia la Vecchia*, which is situated at the further end of *Europe* on that side, shall come a band of men, who shall destroy the Thieves that robbed and vexed the Travellers by the Bridge of *Laigne*, which it seemeth was an infamous place for robbing.

XLIX.

Jardin du Monde aupres de Cité neufve, Dans le chemin des Montagnes cavées, Sera saisi & plongé dans la Cuve, Beuvant par force eaux Soulphre envenimées. English.

Garden of the World, near the new City, In the way of the digged Mountains, Shall be seized on, and thrown into the Tub, Being forced to drink Sulphurous poisoned waters.

ANNOT.

This word *Garden of the World*, doth signifie a particular person, seeing that this *Garden of the World* was seized on and poisoned in a Tub of Sulphurous water, in which he was thrown.

The History may be this, that *Nostradamus* passing for a Prophet and a great Astrologer in his time, abundance of people came to him to know their Fortunes, and chiefly the Fathers to know that of their Children, as did Mr. *Lafnier*, and Mr. *Cotton*, Father of that renowned Jesuit of the same name, very like then that Mr. *du Jardin* having a son did ask *Nostradamus* what should become of him, and because his son was named *Cosmus*, which in Greek signifieth the World, he answered him with these four Verses.

Garden of the World, for *Cosmus of the Garden*, In his travels shall be taken hard by the New City, in a way that hath been digged between the Mountains, and there shall be thrown in to a Tub of poisoned Sulphurous water to cause him to die, being forced to drink that water which those rogues had prepared for him.

Those that have learned the truth of this History, may observe it here. This ought to have come to pass in the last Age, seeing that the party mentioned was then born when this Stanza was written, and this unhappy man being dead of a violent death, there is great likelyhood, that he was not above forty years old.

There is another difficulty, to know which is that new City, there being many of that name in *Europe*, nevertheless the more probable is, that there being many Knights of *Maltha* born in *Provence* (the native Countrey of our Author) it may be believed that by the new City he meaneth the new City of *Maltha* called *la Valete*, hard by which there is paths and ways digged in the Mountains, which Mountains are as if it were a Fence and a Barricado against the Sea, or else this *Cosmus* might have been taken by Pyrats of *Algiers*, and there in the new City of the *Goulette* be put to death in the manner aforesaid.

L.

La Meuse au jour Terre de Luxembourg, Descouvrira Saturne & trois en Lurne, Montaigne & plaine, Ville, Cité & Bourg, Lorrain Deluge, trahison par grand hurne. English.

The *Maes* by day in the Land of *Luxembourg*, Shall discover *Saturn*, and three in the *Lurne*, Mountain and plain, Town, City, and Countrey Town, A *Lorrain* flood, treason by a great *hurne*.

ANNOT.

The *Maes* is a River that runneth through a part of *Lorrain* and *Luxembourg*; as for the words *Lurne* and *hurne* I do not understand them, neither do I think they are to be found in all the *French* Language, both obsolete and modern; all what I can gather out of this, is, that a great overflowing of the River *Maes*, shall be both in *Luxembourg* and *Lorrain*, insomuch that three Leaden Mines (which is meant here by *Saturn*) shall be discovered, and after that, a great Treason shall happen in the said *Lorrain*.

LI.

French.

Des lieux plus bas du Pais de *Lorraine*, Seront des basses *Allemagnes* unis, Par ceux du Siege *Picards*, *Normans*, du *Maine*, Et aux Cantons se seront reunis.

Transcriber's Note: An English version was omitted from this printing, but the annotation below is an accurate enough (if not very poetic) translation.
ANNOT.

The sense of this is, that the lower *Lorrain* and *Germany* being united together, shall have War with the other three Nations, of *Picards*, *Normans*, and *Manceaux*, which having Besieged a Town, shall constrain the *Lorrainers* and *Low-germans*, to unite themselves with the Cantons of *Switzerland*.

LII.

French.

Au lieu ou Laye & Scelde se marient, Seront les Nopces de long temps mamée, Au lieu d'Anvers ou la grappe charient, Jeune vieillesse conforte intammée. English.

In the place where *Laye* and *Scelde* are united, Shall the Nuptials be, that were long a doing. In the place of *Antwerp* where they draw the grape, The young unspotted will comfort the old Age.

ANNOT.

There is fault in the Impression, for instead of *Laye* it must be *Lis*, which is a River that runneth through *Flanders*, and dischargeth it self into the *Scelde*, which is the River that passeth at *Antwerp*, the sense therefore of this Prophecy is, that in the place where the River of *Lis* joyneth with the *Scelde*, there shall the Nuptials be consummated that were long a doing, and the place of *Antwerp*, where they unload the Wines, there shall a young unspotted Lady Marry, and comfort an old man.

LIII.

French.

Les trois Pellices de loing s'entrebattront, La plus grand moindre demeurera a l'ecoute, Le grand Selin n'en sera plus patron, Le nommera feu, pelte, blanche, route. English.

The three Concubines shall fight one with another a far off, The greatest less shall remain watching, The great *Selin* shall be no more their Patron, And shall call it fire, pelte, white, route.

ANNOT.

This Prophecy is concerning the *Turkish* Empire, where three of the great *Turks* Concubines, which in Latine are called *Pellices*, shall make War one against another, the great *Turk* himself favouring neither party.

LIV.

French.

Née en ce Monde par Concubine furtive, A deux hault mise par les tristes nouvelles, Entre Ennemis sera prinse Captive, Et amenée a Malines & Bruxelles. English.

Born in this world from a stolen Concubine, Set up at two heights by the sad news, Shall be taken Prisoner among the Enemies, And brought to *Malines* and *Bruxelles*.

ANNOT.

This is concerning some Lady of quality, born of a Concubine, who shall be set up by reason of some sad news that shall be brought, and afterwards shall be taken Prisoner, and carryed to *Malines* and *Bruxelles*, two Cities of the Low-Countreys.

LV.

French.

Les malheureuses Nopces celebreront, En grande joye mais la fin malheureuse, Mary & Mere Nore desdaigneront, Le Phibe mort, & Nore plus piteuse. English.

The unhappy Nuptials shall be celebrated, With great joy, but the end shall be unhappy, Husband and Mother shall scorn *Nore*, The *Phybe* dead, and *Nore* more pitifull.

ANNOT.

If by *Phybe* we understand the Admiral of *Chastillon*, and by *Nore*, Queen *Margaret* of *Valois*, the rest will be easie. For in the year 1572. a Match was made between *Henry* the IV. then King of *Navarre*, chief of the Protestant party, and *Margaret* of *Valois*, Sister to *Charles* the IX. to this Wedding were the chief of the Protestant party invited, who were there Massacred, and among the rest *Gaspard* of *Coligny*, Lord of *Chastillon*, and Admiral of *France*, whom he calleth here *Phybe*. And when he saith, that *Husband and Mother shall scorn Nore*, he sheweth the slight Opinion and regard that the Queen Mother had for her Daughter, and *Henry* the IV. for his Wife, whom he after repudiated.

LVI.

French.

Prelat Roial soy baissant trop tiré, Grand Flux de Sang sortira par sa bouche, Le Regne Anglicque par Regne respiré, Long temps mort vif en Tunis comme souche. English.

Royal Prelate bowing himself too much, A great flood of Blood shall come out of his mouth, The *English* Reign by Reign respited, A great while dead, alive in *Tunis* like a Log.

ANNOT.

A Prelate, is a man of eminent dignity in the Church, the Royal prelate must be a Churchman of the Royal Blood, who bowing himself too much, shall fall into an Hæmorhagie or Flux of Blood at his Mouth. The third Verse signifieth, that the Kingdom of *England* shall be relieved from some distress by another Kingdom or Prince that had been a Slave a great while at *Tunis*, and lyen there, *dead alive like a Log of Wood.*

LVII.

French.

Le sublevé ne cognoistra son Sceptre, Les enfans jeunes des plus grands honnira, Oncques ne fut un plus ord cruel estre, Pour leur Espouses a mort noir bannera. English.

The exalted shall not know his Scepter He shall put to shame the young Children of the greatest, Never was one more dirty and cruel, He shall banish to Black death their Spouses.

ANNOT.

This is concerning a great Tyrant, who being exalted to the dignity of a King, shall not know how to govern; but shall slight and put to shame the Children of the greatest Nobility, and shall banish their Wives out of the Land; this hath a relation to the late Tyrant *Cromwell*.

LVIII.

French.

Au temps du dueil que le Selin Monarque, Guerroiera le jeune Æmathien, Gaule bransler, pericliter la barque, Tenter Phocens au ponant entretien. English.

In the time of mourning, when the Monarch *Selin*, Shall make War against the young *Æmathien*, *France* shall quake, the Ship shall be in danger, *Phocens* shall be attempted, the business shall be in the West.

ANNOT.

You must observe here, that by *Æmathien* the Author meaneth the King of *France*, as he doth in many other places; and by *Selin*, he meaneth the great *Turk*, because such was the name of him that lived in his time, this being presupposed the meaning of this is, that the great *Turk* shall fight against the King of *France*, and shall attempt *Phocens*, which is *Marseilles*, as being a Colony of the old *Phocenses* in *Græcia*, which shall cause all *France* to quake, and the Ship to be in danger, which is *Paris*, who beareth a Ship for its Arms.

LIX.

French.

Dedans Lion vingt & cinq d'une haleine, Cinq Citoyens Germains, Bressans, Latines, Par dessous Noble conduiront longue traine, Et descouvers par abboy de Mastins. English.

In *Lyons* five and twenty of a breadth Five Citizens *Germans*, *Bressans*, *Latines*, Under Noblemen shall conduct a long Train, And shall be discovered by the barking of Mastiffs.

ANNOT.

The Marshal of St. *André*, Governour of *Lyon* being absent, the Protestants undertook the taking of it, at the solicitation of some principal Lords at Court, among whom were named the Prince of *Condé*, and the Vidame of *Chartres*, *Francis* of *Vendosme*, Knight of the Order. The Abbot of *Savigny*, who did supply the place of the Governour, and was named *Antony* of *Albon*, since that Archbishop of *Arles*, having discovered this Conspiracy, went to surprise the undertakers, but as he was going upon the night of the 5 of *September*, he met with some of the confederates upon the Bridge of *Saone*, which made him retreat with some loss.

The next day having gathered more Forces, he took three of them that were strangers and young, the rest escaping, those three were hanged the next *Saturday*, which was the 7 of that Month.

The Marshal being come to Town, there was Execution made upon some of the Inhabitants, to the number of 4 that were hanged.

After that there were informations made concerning the Authors and Abettors of the said conspiracy, and many other Citizens and strangers were put to Prison, and besides them the Vidame of *Chartres*, who was carryed to *Paris*, and put into the *Bastille*, and after that in the *Tournelles*, where he died before his process was ended, the *23 December 1560*.

It is what our Author saith in this stanza; in the first Verse he saith, that there were *five and twenty of a breadth*, of whose five and twenty there was *five Citizens of the Town*, and the rest were *Germans, Bressans and Italians*, of these Citizens 4 were hanged, and three of the strangers.

Those 25 undertakers, of which the Author saith, that *under Noblemen they shall conduct a long Train*; that is, that under the support and favour of many Noblemen, they would undertake a thing that should not end so soon as it proved afterwards; for although this enterprise did fail, yet was the beginning of horrid combustions that followed afterwards.

This enterprise it seemeth was discovered by barking of Mastiffs.

The Apology for the City of *Lyon* treateth at large of this, and nameth all those conspirators, who for the most part were of *Germany* and *Geneva*.

LX.

French.

Je pleure Nice, Monaco, Pise, Genes, Savone, Sienne, Capoue, Modene, Malthe, Le dessus sang & glaive par estrenes, Feu, trembler Terre, eau, malheureuse nolte. English.

I bewail *Nice, Monaco, Pisa, Genoa, Savona, Sienna, Capoua, Modena, Maltha,* Upon them blood and sword for a new years-gift, Fire, Earth-quake, water, unhappy *nolte.*

ANNOT.

All these Cities are situated by the *Mediterranean* Sea, and most of them upon that part of it, which is called the River of *Genoa,* and are threatned here by all the plagues above mentioned; as for the word *nolte* it is a barbarous one, forced here to make up the Rime in *French.*

LXI.

French.

Betta, Vienne, Comorre, Sacarbance, Voudront livrer aux Barbares Pannone, Par picque et feu, enorme violence, Les conjurez d'escouverts par Matrone. English.

Betta, Vienna, Comorre, Sacarbance, Shall endeavour to deliver *Pannone* to the Barbarians, By Pike, and fire, extraordinary violence! The conspirators discovered by a Matron.

ANNOT.

It seemeth that there will be a conspiracy of some men out of all the above mentioned Cities, to surrender *Hungary* (which in Latine is called *Pannonia*) to the great Turk, but that conspiracy shall be discovered by a Matron, that is, a grave ancient Woman.

LXII.

French.

Pres de Sorbin pour assaillir Hongrie, L'Heraut de Bude le viendra advertir, Chef Bizantin, Sallon de Sclavonie, A Loy d'Arabes les viendra convertir. English.

Near *Sorbin,* to invade *Hungary,* The Herald of *Buda* shall come to give them notice of it, Chief *Bizantin, Sallon* of *Sclavonia,* Shall come to turn them to the *Arabian* Religion.

ANNOT.

This seemeth to have a relation to the precedent, and that near that place he calleth *Sorbin,* preparations shall be made to Invade *Hungary,* but they shall have notice of it by some body of *Buda.*

He that is called here *Chief Bizantin*, is the great Turk or his grand Vizir, who hath his abode in *Constantinople*, anciently called *Bizantium*.

LXIII.

Cydron, Ragusa, la Cité au Sainct Hieron, Reverdira le medicant secours, Mort fils de Roy part mort de deux Heron, L'Arabe, Hongrie, feront un mesme cours. English.

Cydron, *Raguse*, the City of Saint *Hieron*, Shall make green again the Physical help, The Kings Son dead, by the death of two *Herons*, *Arabia* and *Hungary* shall go the same way.

ANNOT.

      The meaning of this is, that when those three Cities named in the first Verse shall have need of succours, and that a Kings Son shall die in flying two *Herons*, then shall *Arabia* and *Hungary* be under the same Master.

LXIV.

French.

Pleure Milan, pleure Lucques, Florence, Que ton grand Duc sur le Char montera, Changer le Siege pres de Venise s'advance, Lors que Colonne a Rome changera. English.

Weep *Milan*, weep *Lucques*, and *Florence*, When the great Duke shall go upon the Chariot, To change the Siege near *Venice* he goeth about, When *Colonne* shall change at *Rome*.

ANNOT.

      This Prophecy seemeth to portend the change of the See of *Rome* in some place near to *Venice*, and this is to happen when the great Duke of *Tuscany* shall ascend upon a Triumphant Chariot, and that the House of *Colonne* (which is the more powerfull in *Rome*) shall take his part.

LXV.

French.

O vaste Rome ta ruine s'aproche, Non de tes Murs, de ton sang, & substance, L'aspre par lettres fera si horrible coche, Fer pointu mis a tous jusques au manche. English.

O great *Rome* thy ruine draweth near, Not of thy Walls, of thy blood and substance, The sharp by Letters shall make so horrid a notch, Sharp Iron thrust in all to the haft.

ANNOT.

      This is a confirmation of the foregoing Prophecy, by which it is said that the destruction of *Rome* shall not be in *her Walls, blood or substance*, but onely by Letters or Doctrine that shall put quite down the *Roman* Religion.

LXVI.

French.

Le Chef de Londres par Regne l'Americh, L'Isle d'Escosse tempiera par gelée, Roy, Reb. auront un si faux Antechrist, Que les mettra tretous dans la meslée. English.

The Chief of *London* by Reign of *America*, The Island of *Scotland* shall catch thee by a frost, King and Reb. shall have so false an Antichrist, As will put them altogether by the ears.

ANNOT.

I conceive this Prophecy can be appropriated to no body better then *Oli. Cromwel*, who is called here *the Chief of London by Reign of America*, that is, by Reign of confusion, whose projects and treasons were all brought to nought, by the victorious *Mars* of the ever renowned General *Monck*, who came with his Army from *Scotland* to *London* in the Winter time, he is called also a false Antichrist, because he was an enemy to King and Reb. that is *Respublica* or Common-wealth.

LXVII.

French.

Le tremblement si fort au mois de May, Saturne, Caper, Jupiter, Mercure au Bœuf, Venus aussy, Cancer, Mars en Nonnay, Tombera gresle lors gresse qu'un œuf. English.

The Earth-quake shall be so great in the month of *May, Saturn, Caper, Jupiter, Mercury* in the Bull, *Venus* also, *Cancer, Mars* in *Nonnay*, Then shall fall Hail bigger then an Egge.

ANNOT.

The meaning is, that when all these Cœlestial bodies shall be so disposed, that there will be a fearful Earth-quake and Hail.

LXVIII.

French.

L'Armée de Mer devant Cité tiendra, Puis partira sans faire longue allée, Citoyens grande proye en Terre prendra, Retourner classe reprendre grand emblée. English.

The Fleet shall stand before the City, Then shall go away for a little while, And then shall take a great troop of Citizens on Land, Fleet shall come back and recover a great deal.

ANNOT.

It seemeth here he speaketh of two Fleets, one of which shall stand a little while before a Town, and carry a great many Citizens away, but that the other Fleet shall come in the mean time, and redeem them.

LXIX.

French.

Le fait luysant de neuf vieux eslevé, Seront si grands par Midy Aquilon, De sa sœur propre grandes alles levé, Fuyant meurdry au buisson d'Ambellon. English.

The bright actions of new old exalted, Shall be so great through the South and North, By his own Sister great forces shall be raised, Running away he shall be murdered near the bush of *Ambellon*.

ANNOT.

The question here is, whether this *neuf vieux* in *French* or *new old* in *English* be the proper name of a man, or be a Metaphor, to express a young man of an ancient Family, when the Reader hath satisfied himself upon that, the rest is easie enough.

LXX.

French.

L'œil par objet fera telle excroissance, Tant & ardente que tombera la Neige, Champ arrousé viendra en decroissance, Que le Primat succombera a Rhege. English.

The eye by the object shall make such an excressency, Because so much, and so burning shall fall the Snow, The Field watered shall come to decay Insomuch that the *Primat* shall fall down at *Rhege*.

ANNOT.

All this is nothing but an extraordinary great Snow that shall fall about *Rhegio* a City of *Italy*, whereby the Fields shall be drowned and fall to decay; insomuch, that the chief men, called here *Primate* shall fall to poverty.

LXXI.

French.

La Terre & l'Air geleront si grand eau, Lors qu'on viendra pour Jeudy venerer, Ce qui sera jamais ne fut si beau, Des quattre parts le viendront honorer. English.

The Earth and the Air shall freeze with so much water, When they shall come to worship *Thursday*, That which shall be never, was so fair, From the four parts they shall come to honour him.

ANNOT.

This signifieth an exceeding great frost, which shall happen on a Holy *Thursday*, where the ground and sky shall be so clear, that men may come from the four parts (*viz.* of the Earth) without trouble for to worship.

LXXII.

French.

L'an mil neuf cent nonante neuf, sept mois, Du Ciel viendra un grand Roy d'effrayeur, Resusciter le grand Roy d'Angoumois, Avant apres, Mars Regner par bonheur. English.

In the year a thousand nine hundred ninety nine, and seven months, From Heaven a great terrible King, To raise again the great King of *Angoulesme*, Before and after, *Mars* shall Reign luckily.

ANNOT.

He that is called here King of *Angoulesme* was *Francis* the I. as gallant a Prince as ever *France* had, who before he was King went by the title of Duke of *Angoulesme*; the rest is easie.

LXXIII.

French.

Le temps present avecque le passé, Sera jugé par grand Jovialiste, Le Monde tard de luy sera lassé, Et desloial par le Clergé juriste. English.

The time present, together with the past, Shall be judged by a great *Jovialiste*, The World shall at last be weary of him, And he shall be thought unfaithful by the Canon-Law Clergy.

ANNOT.

This Prophecy concerneth meerly *Francis Rabelais*, who was the greatest *Jovialist*, that is, Merry-man that ever was, and did so lash and censure the abuses of every profession, and chiefly of the Clergy, that to this very day he goeth among them for an Atheist, and a Prophaner of Sacred and Civil things.

LXXIV.

French.

An revolu du grand nombre septiesme, Apparoistra au temps jeux d'Hecatombe, Non esloignez du grand age milliesme, Que les entrez sortiront de leur Tombe. English.

The year of the great number seven being past, Shall be seen at that time the sports of *Hecatombe*, Not far from the great age thousand, That the Buried shall come out of their Graves.

ANNOT.

Hecatombe signifieth a Sacrifice, wherein a hundred beasts were killed.
The sense therefore is this, that when the year a thousand seven hundred is past, that such

sport of *Hecatombe* shall be seen again, not far from the sixth Millenary, when the day shall rise, for it is a common opinion among the Learned, that as God Created the World in six days, and rested the seventh, so when the World hath lasted six thousand years, for a thousand years before God are as one day, there shall be an Eternal Sabbath and a Resurrection, both of the just and unjust.

LXXV.

French.

Tant attendu ne reviendra jamais, Dedans l'Europe, en Asia apparoistra, Un de la ligne yssu du grand Hermes, Et sur tous Rois de Orient croistra. English.

So long expected shall never come Into *Europe*, in *Asia* shall appear, One come forth of the line of the great *Hermes*, And shall grow above all the Kings in the East.

ANNOT.

All is plain, but only this, whether he taketh *Hermes* as a King of *Ægypt*, or as the Father of the Hermetick Philosophers.

LXXVI.

French.

Le grand Senat decernera la Pompe, A un qu'apres sera vaincu chassé, Des adhærans seront a son de trompe, Biens publiez, ennemy dechassé. English.

The great Senate will decree a Pomp, To one who after shall be vanquished and expelled, The goods of his partners shall be Publickly sold, and the enemy shall be driven away.

ANNOT.

What Senate and particular man he meaneth, is the only difficulty in this.

LXXVII.

French.

Trente adhærans de l'Ordre des Quirettes, Bannis, leurs biens donnez ses adversaires, Tous leurs bienfaits seront pour demerites, Classe espargie, delivrez aux corsaires. English.

Thirty associated of the Order of *Quirettes*, Banished, their goods shall be given to their adversaries, All their good deeds shall be imputed to them as crimes, The Fleet scattered, they shall fall into the hands of Pyrates.

ANNOT.

I could not find any man or Author that knew what is meant here by *Quirettes*, which is only the difficulty of this Stanza.

LXXVIII.

French.

Subite joye en subite tristesse, Sera a Rome aux graces embrassées, Dueil, cris, pleurs, larm, sang, excellent liesse, Contraires bandes surprises & troulsées. English.

Sudden joy shall turn into a sudden sadness, At *Rome* to the embraced graces, Mourning, cries, weeping, tears, blood, excellent joy, Contrary Troops surprized and carryed away.

ANNOT.

There is nothing difficult here, but what he meaneth by *Embraced graces*, for my part I believe them some new married Couples, who in the middle of their jollity shall fall into these disasters.

LXXIX.

French.

Les vieux chemins seront tous embellis, L'on passera a Memphis somentrées, Le grand Mercure d'Hercule fleur de lys, Faisant trembler Terre, Mer, & Contrées. English.

The old ways shall be made all fair, There shall be a passage to *Memphis Somentrées*, The great *Mercury* of *Hercules* Flower de luce, Making the Earth, the Sea, and the Countreys to quake.

ANNOT.

This word *Somentrees*, being altogether barbarous, is the reason that neither sense nor construction can be made of all these words.

LXXX.

French.

Au Regne grand, du grand Regne Regnant, Par force d'armes les grands Portes d'airain, Fera ouvrir le Roy & Duc joignant, Port demoly, nef a fonds jour serain. English.

In the great Reign, of the great Reign Reigning, By force of Arms the great Brass Gates, He shall cause to be open, the King being joyned with the Duke, Haven demolish'd, Ship sunk on a fair day.

ANNOT.

The words and the sense are plain, though the parties be unknown.

LXXXI.

French.

Mis Tresor Temple, Citadins Hesperiques, Dans iceluy retire en secret lieu, Le Temple ouvrir, les liens fameliques, Repris, ravis proye horrible au milieu. English.

A Treasure put in a Temple by *Hesperian* Citizens, In the same hid in a secret place, The hungry bonds shall cause the Temple to be open, And take again and ravish, a fearful prey in the middle.

ANNOT.

This is concerning a Treasure hid by *Spaniards* (called here *Hesperian Citizens*) in a Church, which the people of a Town being poor, and almost starved, caused to be open, and did ransack it, but in the middle of it they found a strange prey, but what it was God knows.

LXXXII.

French.

Cris, pleurs, larmes viendront avec couteaux, Semblant faux donront dernier assaut, L'entour parques planter profons plateaux, Vifs repoussez & meurdris de plain saut. English.

Cries, weeping, tears, shall come with daggers, With a false seeming they shall give the last assault, Set round about they shall plant deep, Beaten back alive, and murdered upon a sudden.

ANNOT.

This seemeth to have a relation to the Scalado of *Geneva*, of which you shall have a full account in the 69 Stanza, of the twelfth Century.

LXXXIII.

French.

De batailler ne sera donné signe, Du Parc seront contraints de sortir hors, De Gasp l'entour sera cogneu l'enseigne, Qui fera mettre de tous les siens a mort. English.

There shall no sign of battle be given, They shall be compelled to come out of the Park, Round about *Gasp* shall be known the Ensign, That shall cause all his own to be put to death.

ANNOT.

This Prophecie was fulfilled in the year 1556. by the Marshal of *Brissac* in *Piemont*, when he took the Town of *Vignal* by assault, where 1200. *Neapolitans* were put to the Sword, who were called the braves of *Naples*; because they were all very gallantly habited, and the Governour being wounded, cast himself desperately into a Well, whence the Marshal caused him to be taken up, and to be cured of his wounds.

In this conflict *there was no sign of Battle given*; because it was done by the rashness of a Souldier, Bastard of a Bastard of the house of *Boissy*, who without expecting the command of the General, went alone upon the breche, and after he had [Transcriber's Note: the text is illegible here with 1-2 words missing] against the Enemies, drew his Sword, and did fight a great while hand to hand without being wounded.

Some of his Companions seeing his valour, did follow him, and others came to their help, and these carryed along with them all those that were appointed to give the assault; insomuch that by a kind of Warlike emulation, all did carry themselves so valliantly, that after a long and stout resistance, they routed the Enemies, and put all the Garrisons to the Sword.

It is what the Author saith in the first and second Verse, seeing that those that were appointed to give Battle, every one in his Regiment or Squadron, were compelled by emulation to come out of their *Park*; that is, from the Precinct of place wherein they were. The third Verse addeth, that *round about the Ensign of Gasp. shall be known*; that is, in the assault the Captain of that place, named *Gaspar Pagan*, was remarked to fight valliantly every where the *French* did assault, which the Marshal of *Brissac* seeing, as also the forwardness of his men commanded the general assault to be given. The Captain seeing the Town taken, though he had above twenty wounds, for marks of his Valour, yet by that despair threw himself into a Well, near which the Marshal passing, heard his voice, and caused him to be drawn out, and cured of his wounds.

This Captain being resolved to perish in this assault, *did cause all his own to be put to death*, as the fourth Verse saith. The History of this Town was famous, for which the Marshal of *Brissac* did present Gifts to the most Valiant, and among the rest to this Bastard, after he had put him in jeopardy of his life, for having violated the Military Orders in a matter of such concernment. That Town of *Vignal* is situated upon a Mountain of the Countrey of *Montserrat*, of a difficult access, where no pieces of Ordinance can be brought up, but by the help of Mens Arms; after the taking of it, the Marshal did cause it to be raised even to the ground, because it could not be useful to the *French*, that had many other places to keep, and might have been very beneficial to the *Spaniard*.

LXXXIV.

French.

Le Naturel a si haut, haut non bas, Le tard retour sera marris contens. Le Recloing ne sera sans debats, En emploiant & perdant tout son temps. English.

The Natural to so high, high not low, The late return shall make the sad contented, The *Recloing* shall not be without strife, In employing and loosing all his time.

ANNOT.

The *Recloing*, being a forged word, without signification, and being the Key of all this Stanza, no body can tell what to make of it.

LXXXV.

French.

Le vieil Tribun au point de la Trehemide, Sera presse Captif ne delivrer, Le vueil non vueil, le mal parlant timide. Par legitime a ses amis livrer. English.

The old *Tribun*, at the point of the *Trehemide*, Shall be much intreated not to deliver the Captain,

They will not will, the ill speaking fearful, By legitimate shall deliver to his friends.

The old *Treban* is an old Captain or Governour of a Town, who shall be much entreated not to deliver at the end of the *Trehemede* (that is, three Months) one that he kept prisoner, but will they or not, he shall lawfully deliver him to his friends.

LXXXVI.

French.

Comme un Gryphon viendra le Roy d'Europe, Accompagne de ceux d'Aquilon, De rouges & blancs conduira grande Troupe, Et Iront contre le Roy de Babylon. English.

As a Griffin shall come the King of *Europe*, Accompanied with those of the North, Of red and white shall conduct a great Troop, And they shall go against the King of *Babylon*.

ANNOT.

This is concerning the King of *Swedeland, Gustavus Adolphus*, who is called here the King of *Europe*; because he lived in a part of it, and because he was one, if not the most gallant Prince of his time, who with a great Army of his Subjects, named here those of *Aquilon*, invaded *Germany*, and made War against the Emperour, whom he calleth here the King of *Babylon*, either because he is a great favourer of the *Roman* Church, or because the Empire, by reason of so many sovereign Princes in it is like a *Babel* and confusion.

The great Troop of Red and White, were his own Souldiers, whom he distinguished by their several habits. Clothing them with several Colours, to breed an emulation among them, there being the Red Regiment, the White, the Blew, the Yellow, the Green, &c.

LXXXVII.

French.

Grand Roy viendra prendre port pres de Nice, Le grand Empire de la mort si en fera Aux Antipodes posera son genisse, Par Mer la Pille tout esvanouira. English.

A great King shall land by *Nice*, The great Empire of death shall interpose with it. He shall put his Mare in the *Antipodes*, By Sea all the Pillage shall vanish.

ANNOT.

A great King shall land hard by *Nice*, which is a Sea Town in *Savoy*, but he shall have a great loss of his men by death, and the Sea shall swallow all his plunder.

LXXXVIII.

Pieds & Cheval a la seconde veille, Feront entrée vastiant tout par Mer, Dedans le Port entrera de Marseille, Pleurs, cris & sang, onc nul temps si amer. English.

Foot and Horse upon the second Watch, Shall come in destroying all by Sea, They shall come into the Harbour of *Marseilles*, Tears, cryes and blood, never was so bitter a time.

ANNOT.

This is so clear that it needeth no interpretation.

LXXXIX.

French.

De Bricque en Marbre seront les Murs reduits, Sept & cinquante années pacifiques, Joye aux humains renevé l'aqueduct, Santé, grands fruits, joye & temps mellifique. English.

The Walls shall be turned from Brick into Marble, There shall be peace for seven and fifty years, Joy to mankind, the Aqueduct shall be built again, Health, abundance of fruit, joy and mellifluous time.

ANNOT.

After so many calamities Prognosticated by the Author, he promiseth here seven and fifty year of a golden Age, but when? he maketh no mention.

XC.

French.

Cent fois mourra le Tyran inhumain, Mis a son lieu scavant & debonnaire, Tout le Senat sera dessoubs sa main; Fasche sera par malin temeraire. English.

The inhumane tyrant shall die a hundred times, In his place shall be put a Learned and mild man, All the Senate shall be at his command, He shall be made angry by a rash malicious person.

ANNOT.

This Prognostication is easie to be understood, only it is indeterminate, and specifieth neither time nor persons.

XCI.

French.

Clergé Romain l'an mil six cens & neuf, Au chef de l'an fera Election, D'un gris & noir de la Campagne yssu, Qui oncques ne fut si malin. English.

The *Roman* Clergy in the year a thousand six hundred and nine, In the beginning of the year shall make choice Of a gray and black, come out of the Countrey, Such a one as never a worse was.

ANNOT.

Wanting the Chronology of the Popes, I have not set down who that Pope was, then whom our Author saith there never was a worse, but the time being so punctually prefixed, it will be an easie matter for the Reader to find out satisfaction in this point.

XCII.

French.

Devant le Pere l'Enfant sera tué, Le Pere apres entre cordes de jonc, Genevois peuple sera esvertué, Gisant le Chef au milieu comme un tronc. English.

The Child shall be killed before the Fathers eyes, The Father after shall enter into ropes of rushes, The people of *Geneva* shall notably stir themselves, The Chief lying in the middle like a log.

ANNOT.

This Prophecy is twofold, the two first Verses foretel of a man that shall have his Son killed before his eyes, and himself afterward shall be strangled by a rope made of Rushes.

The two last Verses are concerning the people of *Geneva*, who (as he saith) shall lustily bestir themselves, while their Captain, Chief, or Commander shall carelesly lie like a log.

XCIII.

French.

La Barque neuve recevra les Voiages, La & aupres transfereront l'Empire, Beaucaire, Arles, retiendront les Hostages, Pres deux Colomnes trouvées de Porphyre. English.

The new Ship shall make journeys Into the place, and thereby where they shall translate the Empire, *Beaucaire, Arles*, shall keep the Hostages, Near them shall be found two Columns of *Porphyry*.

ANNOT.

This Prophecy is concerning three things, the first is of a considerable new Ship, that shall sail several times into a place where the Empire shall be translated.

The second is concerning two Towns of *Languedoc*, *Beaucaire*, and *Arles*, who shall not surrender the Hostages that they had.

The third is concerning two Columns of *Porphiry* that shall be found there about.

XCIV.

French.

De Nismes, d'Arles, & Vienne contemner, Nobeyront a ledict Hesperique, Au Labouriez pour le grand condamner, Six eschapez en habit Seraphique. *English.*

From *Nismes*, d'*Arles* and *Vienna* contempt, They shall not obey the *Spanish* Proclamation, To the *Labouriez* for to condemn the great one, Six escaped in a *Seraphical* habit.

ANNOT.

It seemeth that those three aforenamed Towns will refuse to obey a *Spanish* Proclamation, that would compel them to condemn a great man; as for *Labouriez* it is a barbarous and non-sensical word.

The last Verse signifieth, that six shall escape, cloathed in *Franciscan* habits, called here *Seraphical*, because the Franciscans believe that a *Seraphin* did appear to St. *Francis* their Patron, from whence their Order is called by many the *Seraphical* Order.

XCV.

French.

Dans les Espagnes viendra Roy trespuissant, Par Mer & Terre subjugant au Midy, Ce mal sera rabaissant le croissant, Baisser les aisles a ceux de Vendredy. *English.*

A most potent King shall come into *Spain*, Who by Sea and Land shall make great Conquests towards the South, This evil shall beat down the horns of the new Moon, And slack the Wings of those of *Friday*.

ANNOT.

A great and potent King shall come out of Spain, who by Sea and Land shall make great Conquest towards the South, that is *Barbary*, which shall be a great prejudice to the *Turkish* Empire, who hath for his Arms a new Moon; *And slack the wings of those of Friday*, that is, of the Turks, because they keep the *Friday* for their *Sabbath*. This Prophecy was fulfilled by *Philip* the II. King of *Spain*, who drove away all the *Moores* out of the South part of it, and took a great many places in the Coasts of *Barbary*.

XCVI.

French.

Religion du nom des Mers viendra, Contre la Secte fils Adaluncatif, Secte obstinée deplorée craindra, Des deux blessez par Aleph & Aleph. English.

Religion of the name of the Seas shall come, Against the Sect son *Adaluncatif*, Obstinate Sect deplorate shall be afraid, Of the two wounded by *Aleph* and *Aleph*.

ANNOT.

I confess my ignorance in the intelligence of this Stanza.

XCVII.

French.

Triremes pleines tout aage captifs, Temps bon a mal, le doux pour amertume, Proye a Barbare trop tost seront hastifs, Cupide de voir plaindre au vent la plume. English.

Triremes full of Captives of all Age. Time good for evil, the sweet for bitter, Pray to the *Barbarian*, they shall be too hasty, Desirous to see the feather complain in the wind.

ANNOT.

Triremes are Galleys with three benches of Oares, the rest is much of the nature of the former.

XCVIII.

French.

La splendeur clairëa Pucelle joieuse, Ne luira plus, long temps sera sans Sel, Avec Marchans, Ruffiens, Loups, odieuse, Tous pesle mesle monstre universel. English.

The clear splendour of the merry Maid, Shall shine no more, she shall be a great while without Salt, With Merchants, Ruffans, Wolves, odious, All promiscuously, she shall be an universal Monster.

ANNOT.

This is concerning a famous beauty, who in her latter age shall prostitute her self to all comers.

XCIX.

*A la fin le Loup, le Lion, Bœuf & l'Asne, Timide dama seront avec Mastins, Plus ne cherra a eux la douce Manne, Plus vigilance & custode aux Mastins. **English.***

At last the Wolf, the Lion, Oxe and Asse, Fearful Doe, shall be with the Mastiffs, The sweet Manna shall no more fall to them, There shall be no more watching and keeping of Mastiffs.

ANNOT.

     This is a Prognostication of a general peace all *Europe* over.
     The sweet Manna shall no more fall to them, signifieth that the *Europeans* shall be fed no more with Manna, as the Jews were in the Desert, but shall pass to the Land of Promise, that is of peace and quietness.

C.

French.

*Le grand Empire sera par l'Angleterre, Le Pempotan des ans plus de trois cens, Grandes Copies passer par Mer & Terre, Les Lusitains n'en seront pas contens. **English.***

The great Empire shall be in *England*, The *Pempotan* for more then three hundred years, Great Armies shall pass through Sea and Land, The *Portugueses* shall not be contented therewith.

ANNOT.

     This is a favourable one for *England*, for by it the Empire, or the greatest Dominion of *Europe* is promised to it, for the space of above three hundred years, at which the *Portugueses* or *Spaniards* shall much repine.

Michael Nostradamus.

CENTURY XI.

IX.

French.

Meysinier, Manthi, & le tiers qui viendra, Peste & nouveau insult, enclos troubler. Aix & les lieux fureur dedans mordra, Puis les Phocens viendront leur mal doubler. English.

Meysinier, *Manthi*, and the third that shall come, Plague and new attempt shall trouble them enclosed, The fury of it shall bite in *Aix* and the places there about, Then they of *Phocens* shall come and double their misery.

ANNOT.

These are names of particular persons that are here threatned of the Plague, as also the City of *Aix* Capital of *Provence*, and the Countrey about it, and after that the City of *Marseilles* named here *Phocens*, because they are a Colony of the old *Phocenses* in *Greece*.

XCVII.

French.

Par Ville Franche, Mascon en desarroy, Dans les Fagots seront Soldats cachez, Changer de temps en prime pour le Roy, Par de Chalon & Moulins tous hachez. English.

By *Ville Franche, Mascon* shall be put in disorder, In the Faggots shall Souldiers be hidden, The time shall change in prime for the King, By *Chalon* and *Moulins* they shall be all hewed to pieces.

ANNOT.

Ville Franche is a Town five Leagues from *Lion*; and *Mascon* another about the same distance from *Ville Franche*, and *Chalon* from *Mascon*, and *Moulins* from *Chalon*.

The meaning of it is this, that there shall be an attempt from *Ville Franche* upon *Mascon*, by Souldiers hidden in Faggots, that shall be cut off by the succours of those *Chalons* and *Moulins*; which like did happen in the time of the Civil Wars in *France*, between the King and the League, when the Towns stood one against another, but because I can find nothing of it in the History, I suspend my further judgement therein.

Michael Nostradamus.

CENTURY XII.

V.

French.

Feu, flamme, faim, furt, farouche fumée, Fera faillir, froissant fort, soy faucher, Fils de Deité! toute Provence humée, Chasse de Regne, enragé sans crocher. English.

Fire, flame, hunger, theft, wild smoak, Shall cause to fail, brusing hard, to move Faith, Son of God! all *Provence* swallowed up? Driven from the Kingdom, raging mad without spitting.

ANNOT.

The curiosity of the Author in striving to begin all his words, in the two first Verses hath made the tense of this Stanza so obscure, that I believe no body ever did or shall truely understand it, all what can be gathered out of it, is great threatning of several calamities, that were to happen upon *Provence* his native Countrey, as it did a little while after his death, by the Civil Wars for Religion.

XXIV.

French.

Le grand secours venu de la Guyenne, S'arrestera tout aupres de Poitiers, Lion rendu par Montluel en Vienne, Et saccagez par tous gens de Mestiers. English.

The great succours that came from *Gascony*, Shall stop hard by *Poitiers*, *Lion* surrendred by *Montluel* and *Vienna*, And ransacked by all kinds of Tradesmen.

ANNOT.

The words and sense of this are plain.

XXXVI.

French.

Assault farouche en Cypre se prepare, La larme a l'œil de ta ruine proche, Bizance Classe Morisque si grand tare, Deux differens le grand vast par la Roche. **English.**

A cruel assault is preparing in *Cyprus*, Tears in my eye, thou art near thy ruine, The Fleet of *Constantinople* and the *Morick* so great damage. Two differents the great wast shall be by the Rock.

ANNOT.

A cruel assault is preparing, signifies the shortness of the time in which it was to happen, for our Author Prophecied 1555. and *Cyprus* was taken by the *Turks* in the Month of *August* 1571. *Selymus* the II. fifth Emperour of the *Turks*, where the perfidiousness of the Bassa *Mustapha* that Besieged it is remarkable, for having the Town delivered him upon Articles; First, that the Inhabitants of the City yet alive should enjoy their lives, liberty, and goods, with free exercise of Christian Religion, that the Governour *Bragadinus* with the rest of the Captains and Souldiers might in safty depart with Bag and Baggage, and at their departure take with them five pieces of Ordinance, and three Horses, which soever it should please them to make choise of, and that the *Turks* should safely conduct them into *Crete*, finding them both Victual and Shipping; yet all these matters agreed upon, and commenced into Writting, as also by solemn Oaths on both side confirmed; the perfidious Bassa nevertheless caused *Bragadinus* to have his Ears cut off, then caused him to be set in a Chair, and his skin to be flain off from him quick, his head to be cut from his dead body, and upon the point of a Spear to be set upon a high place, his skin also stuffed with Chaff, he caused to be hanged up at the Yards Arm, and so to be carried about.

IV.

French.

Deux corps un chef, champs divisez en deux, Et puis respondre a quattre non ouys, Petits pour grands a pertius mal pour eux, Tour d'Aigues foudre, pire pour Eussovis. **English.**

Two bodies, one head, fields divided into two, And then answer to four unheard ones, Small for great ones, open evil for them, The Tower of *Aigues* beaten by Lightning, worse for *Eussovis*.

ANNOT.

Out of this crabbid Stanza we shall pick what we can, and leave the rest to the judgment of the judicious Reader. First,

The two bodies, one head may be understood either a Monster that was so, as it did happen once in *Italy*, as *Pareus* witnesseth; or of the union of the two Kingdoms of *France* and *Navarre*, under *Henry* the IV. or of *England* and *Scotland* under King *James*.

The Tower of Aiguemortes was strucken with the Lightning, a while after our Author had put out his Prophecies.

V.

Tristes Conseils, desloiaux, cauteleux, Aduis meschant, la loy sera trahie, Le peuple esmeu, farouche, querelleux, Tant Bourg que Ville toute le paix haie. English.

Sad Councels, unfaithful, malicious, Ill advice the Law shall be betrayed, The people shall be moved, wild & quarrelsome, Both in Countrey and City the peace shall be hated.

ANNOT.

This is plain.

VI.

French.

Roy contre Roy, & le Duc contre Prince, Haine entre iceux dissension, horrible, Rage & fureur sera toute Province, France grand guerre & changement terrible. English.

King against King, and Duke against a Prince, Hatred between them, horrid dissension, Rage and fury shall be in every Province, Great War in *France*, and horrid changes.

ANNOT.

This is a true picture of the miseries of the Civil Wars in *France*, when *Charles* the IX. King of *France*, was against *Henry* King of *Navarre*, and the Duke of *Guise* against the Prince of *Condé*.

VII.

French.

L'accord & pache sera du tout rompue, Les amitiez pollues par discorde, L'haine euvieille, toute foy corrompue, Et l'esperance, Marseilles sans concorde. English.

The agreement and contract shall be broken in pieces, The friendships polluted by discord, The hatred shall be old, all faith corrupted, And hope also, *Marseilles* without concord.

ANNOT.

This is a second part of the foregoing.

VIII.

French.

Guerre & debats, a Blois guerre & tumulte, Divers aguets, adveux inopinables, Entrer dedans Chasteau Trompette, insulte, Chasteau du Ha qui en seront coulpables. English.

War and strifes, at *Blois* war and tumult, Several lying in wait, acknowledgment unexpected, They shall get into the *Chasteau Trompette* by assault, And into the *Chasteau du Ha*, who shall be guilty of it.

ANNOT.

This Prophecy is concerning the Civil Wars of *France* between the King and the League.

He saith, *at Blois war and tumult*; because the Duke of *Guise*, and the Cardinal his Brother were both killed there, at the convention of Estates by the Kings command, which he calleth here *acknowledgment unexpected*, because the Kingdom did own the fact.

The last two Verses are concerning the two Castles or Fortresses of *Bourdeaux*, who in those days were sometimes by one party, and sometimes by another.

LXV.

French.

A tenir fort par fureur contraindra, Tout cœur trembler, Langon advent terrible, Le coup de pied mille pieds te rendra, Girond. Garon. ne furent plus horribles. English.

He shall by fury compel them to hold out, Every heart shall tremble, *Langon* shall have a terrible event, The kick shall return to thee a thousand kicks, *Girond. Garon.* are no more horrid.

ANNOT.

The two last Verses seem to have a relation to the foregoing Stanza, and to import, that the Governour of *Bourdeaux* shall compel them to hold out, and because *Langon*, a Town 20 or 30 Miles distant from *Bourdeaux*, was of the contrary party, and did annoy sometimes those of *Bourdeaux*, it is threatned here to have a thousand kicks for one.

Gironde and *Garonne* are the two Rivers of *Bourdeaux*.

LXIX.

French.

Eiovas proche, esloigner Lac Leman, Fort grand apprests, retour confusion, Loin des Nepueux, du feu grand Supelman, Tous de leur suyte. English.

Eiovas near, yet seemeth to be far from the Lake *Leman*, Very great preparatives, return confusion, Far from the *Neveux* of the late great *Supelman*, All of their train.

This is a notable one, directly foretelling the Enterprise or Scalado made by the Duke of *Savoy*, upon *Geneva*: for the better Intelligence of which, we shall first give the sense word for word, and then set down the whole History as a piece of Cabinet, that the Reader after so much tedious and crabbid reading, may have some field to spatiate and recruit it self.

Eiovas near, Eiovas by Anagram is *Savoy*, or the Duke of it, who at that time was near *Geneva*; *yet seemeth far from the Lake Leman*, which is the Lake that passeth through *Geneva*, called in Latine *Lacus Lemannus. Very great preparatives*; because at that time he made great preparations to Scale the Walls of *Geneva. Return*; because he was forced to retire. *Confusion*; because he was confounded in his undertaking. *Far from the Neveux of the great Supelman*; that is, an action much unworthy the Kindred of *Henry* the IV. called here great *Supelman*, to whom he was Allied. *All of their Train*; that is, all that were with him in that undertaking, did partake of his return and confusion. Now the History is thus.

About the latter end of the year 1600. the Duke of *Savoy* having done before all his endeavours to take the City of *Geneva* by force, did resolve at last to have it by craft, and stratagem. He did frame a design full of Courage, Understanding, and Conduct, as well as of misfortune; it was long a hatching without being discovered, and although it was known that he caused Ladders to be made, and that he bought every where men of courage and resolution, and had a great number of them already at *Chambery*, well payed and maintained, waiting for the ripeness of the design, though Ignorant of it. No body could believe that it was against those of *Geneva*; because at that time he did treat with them of the manner of living friendly, and of the liberty of Trade, having sent to them for this purpose a few days before the President *Rochette*, to treat and advise of a manner of living friendly together, for the ease of the people. They did so much hearten and relish his propositions and promises, that although Cities of such condition, do not lightly believe them that have been their Enemies, nevertheless they trusted to that, and grew careless of their own preservation, thinking that there was nothing more powerfull for their security than the treaties of peace between *France, Spain*, and *Savoy*, in which they thought themselves included, under the name of the confederate with the Cantons of *Switzerland*; insomuch that the Dukes subjects went thither so familiarly, that the day before this Execution some Gentlemen that knew something of the design, being come into the Town to buy some Horses, said they would come again the next day to conclude the Bargain, and others had kept she same Language for other Wares, so fully perswaded were they of a success, though Heaven, who laugheth at the thoughts of the proud, had resolved to humble and abase them.

The Governour of *Lion* had presently notice that the Duke of *Savoy* was coming on the side of the Mountain, and carryed with him scaling Ladders, of which he sent notice to the King, and provided what was necessary for the defence of *Lion*, although the same Advice said it was not for *France*; yet all this could not hinder the Execution which was in the mean time a doing. D'*Albigny* Lieutenant General of the Duke in those Countreys he had on this side of the Mountains, had made the Troops to pass, and for that purpose had assigned them of their Quarters in the Towns of *Geneva*, in several places, that they might not be so soon discovered. The Randezvous was at a place called *Chambery*, the time of the Execution was reserved to the prudence of the Leader. The time was not according to the precept of the *Parthians*, who ever fought by night, nor of the *Lacedemonians*, who undertook nothing but in the time of the full Moon; for it was one of the darkest and longest nights of all the year, the Troops began their March about six of the Clock. *Brignoles* Governour of *Bonnes*, a small Town in *Fossigny*, distant three Leagues from *Geneva*, was the man that had contributed most of his own for the performance of this design, whom he thought so certain, that he said he would die to the world, if he did not live in *Geneva*. D'*Albigny* had set up Watches upon all the passes, to stop all Travellers, for fear notice should be given of their coming; and of that of the Duke of *Savoy*, to whom the Execution had been represented so sure and certain, in that he should be there himself to reap the Honour and profit of it, and to end the Triumph that his Grandfather had begun. He came over the Mountains with five Gentlemen only in his Company, and the same day came to *Tremblures*, a Village distant from *Geneva* about three Miles; and for all that they could not hinder, but an unknown Trooper did ride as far as the New-gate, and asked to speak to him that commanded there, bidding him look to themselves, because the duke of *Savoy*, wished them no good, and so retreated galloping. This News was brought to *Blondel*, the fourth Syndic of the Town, and who had the charge of the Guard that year; he answerd, he would provide for that. Another came afterwards, and told him that the Dukes Forces were about the Town, but knew not upon what design, and that himself was at *Bonne*; he answered, that they were not Birds, and could not fly. Mistrust is not always be commended; but too much confidence in such business, is exceedingly dangerous.

Those that were to do the Execution, and to get up first upon the Ladders, went along by the River of *Albe*, that the noise of the Waters might hinder the Sentinals to hear them. Two things did happen, that were an ill Omen for them, they saw in the Skies unusual fires, a Hare did many times cross their way, and gave them a false Alarm, and as many things being considered in the night time, do trouble the imagination, and that fear maketh one think that Bushes are Squadrons, and Thistles Pikes, as it did happen once at the Siege of *Paris* by the *Burgundians*. They did discover about Eleven of the Clock some Posts, to whom the Cloth-workers of *Geneva* use to nail their Stuffs to dry them. Those that went formost would have Charged them, thinking they had been an Ambuscado; from thence they went all along the *Rhosne* to the Meadow of *Plain Palais*. *Brignolet*, and those that were ordained for the Scalado followed d'*Albigny*, who led them down into the Town-Ditch, on the side of the *Corraterie*, without being discovered by the Sentinals, although the Ducks that were in the Ditch, did (for to awake those of *Geneva*) what the Geese did at *Rome* against the *French*. They went over the Ditch upon Hurdles for fear to sink in the Mire, and did set up three Ladders of a wonderful invention; because they could be easily carried upon Mules, and they could be folded into so many pieces, that they could reach the highest wall that is; and besides that, so strong and firm, that no Ladder of one piece could be more; they had besides that provided Hatchets, Hammers, Pincers, and other such Tools, to cut Iron Chains, break Locks, draw Nails and Bars, they had besides several Petardoes and Petardo-Masters. Fortune, who hath a great power in such undertakings, did fail them in their need, after she had brought them to the middle of the City, and made them masters of the streets for above two hours.

By one of those Ladders went up about two hundred men, *Brignolet* was the first, followed by d'*Attignac* and *Sonas*, and did carry himself more valliantly and prudently; having got over the Wall, he surprized the Sentinal, and drew from him the Watch-word, and his Life, then threw him over into the Ditch, and stood in his place to stay for the Round, that he might do as much to him, as he did when it came near him to give him the Watch-word. D'*Albigny*, and one Father *Alexander* a *Scotchman*, and a Jesuite, were at the Ladders foot, incouraging those that went up. The Boy that carryed the Lanthorn saved himself, and gave notice to the *Court de Garde* of what had befallen his Master, at which the *Court de Garde* was not much moved. This was a doing between One and Two of the Clock, expecting that of four, at the which they had proposed to make their greater attempt, and in the mean while to give time to the succour to draw near, and to the day to break, because all Warlike Executions done by night, carry always some confusion with them. No body had gone to bed in the Town with a thought to be awakened so soon, they rested upon the assurance of the Peace. The undertakers had a whole hours time to get up, and as much before they met with any opposition. If d'*Albigny* had been Within to husband that time better than did *Sonas*, *Brignolet*, and d'*Attignac*, they might have cried, the Town is won. About half an hour past two of the Clock, a Sentinal that was in the Mints Tower, having heard some noise in the Ditch, shot off his Gun to give the Alarm, which compelled *Brignolet* to discover himself, charging all that was in the *Court de Garde* of the New-gate, that he might Plant the Petard, and make way for the main Body that was in *Plain Palais*. They got very well the *Court de Garde*, but against the Rule of War, which commandeth to kill all, they let one escape that had so much wit as to get up, and to let down the Port-Cullis, to frustrate the effect of the Petard. The Town was at that time full of Cries and horrid Houlings, of which the *Savoiards* should have made their profit, and increased their courage, as it did weaken that of the Townsmen, that knew not where to run, some crying one way, some another. The undertakers lost themselves in the appearance of so happy a success, those that were without should have given the Alarm at some other Gate, to divide the Forces of the Town, those that were within made no use of their Hatchets, Hammers and Pincers, they forgot to set some Houses on fire; the spirit of astonishment seized upon them, having in their thoughts the Sack and Plunder of the Town, more than the perfection of their Conquest; they made only use of a certain croaking like Frogs, as the *Turks* use the *Bret, Bret,* to animate and rally themselves. *Brignolet* being compelled to discover himself, marched towards the New Gate, distant from that place about 200. Paces, and there was wounded, and died a little after; the Fight began in the dark, and the *Court de Garde* was dispersed, one Souldier hearing them call for the Petard, got upon the Gate, and cut the Rope that held the Port-Culis, and shut up the Petard between the Port-Culis, and the Gate which they went about to break open, with their Hatchets and Hammers, at the first resistance the Petards Master was killed. The Order is such at *Geneva,* that in all extraordinary accidents, every Citizen knoweth the place of his Randezvous, and there goeth with his Arms, and the Town House is never destitute of Souldiers.

In the mean time the Magistrate cryeth, He that loveth me let him follow me. Some Countrey Fellows of the Neighbouring Towns, who kept their watch by turns, being led by some Captains and Citizens, did present themselves at the New Gate, where they were stoutly received, and beaten back, and yet the first shot of theirs killed the Petard-Master, who was much troubled with his Tools. This first Charge would not have driven them back, if the body of the Citizens had not come, and Charged them so furiously, that they lost all their Courage; Necessity which strengthens even those that want Courage, did so animate the Citizens to their defence, that the undertakers were fained to give back. The more nimble went again to their Ladders, which proved useless; because the Canon that was Planted in the Fort of *Loye,* near the Ditch, had broken them; so that they left four and fifty dead upon the place, and upon the Curtain of the *Corraterie,* and thirteen that were taken alive. If the Town had had Souldiers in readiness to make a Sally in that Andabatism, the night being sometimes favourable to such expeditions, those that were at *Plain Palais,* would not have retreated in so good an Order.

There were thirteen taken alive, among whom were the Baron of *Attignac,* the Lord *Sonas,* the Lord *Chaffardon,* upon promise of their Lives, and to be Prisoners of War, or else they had preserved an Honourable death to all the promises, to be spared in laying down their Arms; among them was d'*Attignac,* who fought valiantly, and gave his order of St. *Maurice* to his man, bidding him save himself, being resolved to die with his Sword in his hand.

The Lords of *Geneva* would not use them as Prisoners of War; but as Thieves and Robbers come into the City over the Walls. They said that the Duke was too generous a Prince for so wicked and perfidious an action: there was several Opinions concerning their Sentence of Death, the more moderate would have them be put to Ransom, others would have them be kept Prisoners, that they might serve for exchange, if some of the Town were taken in the continuation of the War; but the more violent did stir the people, in representing unto them the loss of their Religion, the ravishing of their Wives and Maids, the Massacre, the Sack and Plunder of the Town, and their perpetual slavery, and the complaints of the Widows and Children of those that had been killed, were so much considered, that the more moderate Opinions did not appear injust, but in how much they tended to Death. They were Condemned to be Hanged, which is thought the most Ignominious Death: they desired to have their Heads cut off as Gentlemen, which was granted, but it was after they were Hanged. Fifty nine were found killed and wounded, who had all their Heads cut off. In the Ditch there were some Arms found, thirty dead, and four wounded, all their Heads were cut off, and set with the rest upon the Gallows. Of the Citizens of the Town there were seventeen found dead, most of them killed by their Companions in the dark. Their Names were *John Canal,* one of the Lords of the Councel, *Lewis Baudiere, John Vandel, Lewis Galatin, Peter Cabriol, Mark Cambiagua, Nicolas Baugueret, James Mercier, Abraham de Baptista, Daniel Humbert, Martin de Bolo, Michael Monard, Philip Potter, Francis Bouzesel, John Buignet, James Petit, Gerrard Muzy,* and about twenty wounded. The Sunday after Dinner, about two of the Clock, 67 Heads, as well of those that were killed, as of those that were Hanged, were fastened upon the Gallows, and the Bodies thrown into the *Rhosne*. The next *Tuesday* there was a solemn Fasting day kept, and they began to publish every where the wonders of this Deliverance.

Here followeth the Copy of their Letter, to the Governour of *Lion*.

My Lord,

You have known before this by many of your Letters, how his Highness of Savoy, notwithstanding he knew, and had confessed that we were included in the Peace made in the year 1600. between his Royal Majesty of France, and him; hath nevertheless divers times oppressed us, by detaining our Rents, prohibiting of Trade, other violences and extortions, refusing to hearken to the just and pressing remonstrances, which his Majesty hath made him several times in our behalf; but hath also contrived many designs to surprise us in time of Peace. Now it is so, that for the encompassing his pernicious design, the Lord d'Albigny, Saturday last, the Eleventh of this Month, did bring before our Town, on the side of Plain Palais, about two Thousand men, Horse and Foot, all choice men, and hath caused to pass about 200. of them over our Ditch, by the Corraterie, and having set up Ladders one within another, hath caused them to come into our Town, about three of the Clock in the Morning, upon Sunday the Twelfth of this Month, encouraging them himself, being in the Ditch; so that being come down into the Town, some went towards our New Gate to force it open, and give entrance to their Companions, who were in the plain of Plain Palais, others went towards the Mint Gate, that they might by this means come into the middle of the Town. But it hath pleased God to look upon us with his favourable Eye, and to give such a Heart to the Citizens, that they beat them back, and killed the best part of them taken upon the place, the rest hath been taken, and since that Hanged by our Order, the rest threw themselves down from the wall; so that we hear, many of them are either dead or grievously wounded. It is a wonderfull deliverance of our God, for which we are particularly bound to Praise him. But as it is probable, that the said Lord d'Albigny will continue his ill designs, by so much the more that we hear his Highness is not far from us, we do intreat and request by all our affection, that you would be pleased to consider what prejudice the taking of this place would be to his Majesty, and to continue us your favour, and assist us with your wise and prudent advise, &c.

Many did judge of the success of this enterprise by the beginning, and were more forward to write, than to perform well. The King had notice that the Duke was Master of the Town, and the manner of doing was represented with so much felicity and facility, that there was less reason to doubt of it, than believe it. The Truth was not known, but by the advise of the Governour of Lion, which came before any discourse that the Town did publish after its deliverance:

The Duke went Post back again over the Mountains, and left his Troops within three miles of Geneva in three places, at Tournon, Fossigny, and Ternier, he caused his Embassadours to say to the Lord of Berne, that he had not made that enterprise to trouble the Peace of the Cantons; but to prevent l'Esdiguieres to seize upon it for the King of of France, who should have been so powerfull a Neighbour, as would have given them great occasion of fears and jealousies.

The success of this undertaking made it appear, that God will not have those Treaties to the assurance of which his name hath been called for a Witness, to be violated, whatsoever appearance or pretext of Religion there be.

Thus Gentle Reader thou seest by all these Circumstances the Truth of our Authors Prognostication.

LXXI.

French.

Fleuves, Rivieres, de mal seront obstacles, La vielle flame d'ire non appaisée, Courir en France, cecy come d'Oracles, Maisons, Manoirs, Palais, secte rasée. English.

Brooks and Rivers shall be a stopping to evil, The old flame of anger being not yet ceased, Shall run through *France*, take this as an Oracle, Houses, Mannors, Palaces, Sect shall be raced.

ANNOT.

This hath a perfect relation to the miseries that followed the general Massacre of the Protestants in *France* in the year 1572. when the Rivers were a stop to the cruelty of the Persecutors, and when so many Houses, Mannors and Palaces belonging to those of the reformed Religion were demolished, and to signifie the certainty thereof, he saith in the third Verse, *take this as an Oracle*.

Gentle Reader,

Thou shalt take notice, that in this place the covetousness of Booksellers and Printers, hath in the modern Copies vented new Prophecies, which they call Prognostications, drawn out of those of Michael Nostradamus, which are so absurd and nonsensical, that they have been rejected, both by his Son, and the best Wits of this age; therefore I would not soil the Paper with them, for fear to put such a course List upon so fine a Cloth, but shall proceed on to give you the rest of those Prophecies, which truly and undoubtedly belong to our Author.

and that he should never have more of him then he had at his first coming; the Earl of *Soissons*, seeing his obstinacy, left him.

The next day early the King walking in the little Garden, sent for the Duke of *Biron*, and spoke to him a great while, thinking to overcome his obstinacy, and to give him means to escape the danger he was running into; he was seen a great while with his Hat off, his eyes lifted up to Heaven, smiting his breast, and making great protestations to uphold his innocency; there appeared then in the Kings face a great deal of anger, and in that of the Duke of *Biron* a great deal of fire and violence, all his words were nothing but threatnings, lightnings, ruines, and Hell against those that had spoken ill of him; from thence he went to dinner, and met with a man who brought him a Letter, to advise him to look to himself, he shewed it to the Captain of his Guards, and made slight of it, and said, he would be beholding to his valor for his life, and not to a flight; all the afternoon the King stayed in the Gallery, and spoke four hours to the Lord of *la Curée*, the Queen being present and speaking never a word; the King was in a great perplexity of mind, before he could resolve himself. The Lords of *Vileroy, Sillery* and *Geure* were seen often to go to and fro, which made some suspect, that it was to begin by the execution in so great a crime; but the King was against that, such proceedings had been blamed in his Predecessor, he would have every body to know that he had authority and power enough to exterminate his enemies, according to the Laws.

The resolution was taken to have him arrested, and also the Earl of *Auvergne*, the King would not have them to be taken in the Castle, but in their own Lodgings; the Duke of *Biron*, who was in some suspicion of it, and had prepared himself to what he could, neither prevent nor hinder, did imagine that there was no fear of any thing in the Kings Chamber, and that all the danger should be at the going out, and therefore by time had provided himself with a short Sword, with which he promised to make himself room through all dangers. They represented to the King, that if he were Arrested any where but in the Castle, it could not be done without bloodshed, and that it was no matter where the Lyon was taken, so that profit might arise of his prize.

It was perceived that in the same Gallery the King sent for *Vitry* and *Pralin*, two Captains of his Guards, and gave them the order he would have to be observed for the execution of his commands, and then called for his Supper. The Duke of *Biron* was at supper in the Lord *Montignys* Lodging, where he spoke more highly and bravely then ever of his Deserts, and of the friends he had made lately in *Switzerland*; then began to fall upon the praises of the late King of *Spain*, extolling his Piety, Justice and liberality; *Montigny* stopt him, saying, that the greatest commendation that could be given to his memory, was, that he had put his own Son to death, for endeavouring to trouble his Estate; this word stopt those of the Duke of *Biron*, who answered only with his eyes, and thought upon it with some amazement. After supper the Earl of *Auvergne* and the Duke of *Biron* came to the King, who was walking in the Garden, the King making an end of his walk did invite the Duke of *Biron* to play at Cards, they went into the Queens Cnamber, the Earl of *Auvergne* passing by the Duke of *Biron* told him softly, *we are undone*; the Game begun at the *primara*, the Queen was one of the Gamsters, the Duke of *Biron* another, and two more. The King went into his Closet, divided between two contrary passions; the love he had formerly for the Duke of *Biron*, the knowledge he had of his valour, and the remembrance of his services, excluded all thoughts of his Justice; on the other side, the fear of troubles in his Estate, the horrid effects of so unnatural a conspiracy did accuse his Clemency of cruelty, if he went about to prefer the particular good to the publick, he prayed to God to assist him with his Holy Spirit, to appease the troubles of his soul, and to strengthen him with a Holy resolution, that he might do what was for the good of his people, upon whom he Reigned by his only Grace; his prayer being ended, all the difficulties that troubled his soul vanished away, there remained only a firm resolution, to put the Duke into the hands of Justice, if he could not draw the truth out of him; the Game went on still, the King took sometimes the Queens Cards, expecting the appointed time. The Earl of *Auvergne* was gone to his Lodging, the King sent for him, and walked in the Chamber, while the Duke thought upon nothing but his play. *De Varennes* Lieutenant of his Troop faining to take up his Cloak, whispered him softly that he was undone; this word did trouble him so much, that he neglected his play, and oversaw himself, the Queen gave him notice of it; the King did bid them to give over playing, and commanded every one to retire, he went into his Closet, and took the Dake of *Biron* with him, whose good and bad fortune depended from an answer pleasing his Majesty, who bid him once for all to tell what he had done with the Duke of *Savoy* and the Earl of *Fuentes*, assuring him, that his clemency should be greater than his fault. The Duke of *Biron* answered the King more proudly than ever, that it was to press an honest man too much, that he never had any other design, but what he had told him already. *Would to God it were so*, said the King. You will not tell me: Farewell, good night.

As he went out of the Closet, and had passed the Chamber door, he met *Vitry*, who with his right hand seized upon the Hilt of his Sword, and with his left upon his right Arm, saying, *The King hath commanded me to give him an account of your Person, give up your Sword. You jeer*, said the Duke. *No my Lord, he hath so commanded me.* The Duke of *Biron* answered, *I pray thee let me speak to the King.* No my Lord, the King is gone to Bed. He saw the Duke of *Monbazon*, and desired him to intreat the King, that he might surrender it into his own Hands. The King sent word to *Vitry* to obey his commands. The Duke was fained to suffer his Sword to be taken from him; saying, *My Sword that hath done so many good services!* Yes my Lord, give me your Sword, said *Vitry*. To me, said the Duke, that have served the King so well, that my Sword should be taken from me, my Sword that hath made an end of the War, and given Peace to *France*, that my Sword, which could not be taken by my Enemies, should be taken away by my Friends. All these complaints availed nothing; he ungirted his Sword with his left hand, and gave it to *Vitry*, looking about if he could seize upon any other, but care was taken for that.

When he saw all the Guards in order in the Gallery, he thought he should have been Massacred upon the place, and cryed to them, fellow Souldiers give me a little time to pray to God, and let me have some Firebrand or Candlestick in my hand, that I may have the Honour to die defending my self. He was answered, that no Body would offend him, that his best defence was to obey the King, who commanded to lead him to Bed, you see said he, how the good Catholicks are used. He was carried into the Arms Closet, where he neither slept nor lay down, but past the night in blasphemies against God, and reviling words against the King.

Pralin was staying for the Earl of *Auvergne* at the Castle Gate, and when he offered to go out to his lodging; stay my Lord, you are the Kings Prisoner. The Earl astonished, answered I, I? and *Pralin* answered, yes my Lord, you, I Arrest you by the King, and make you his Prisoner, give up your Sword, take it said the Earl it never killed any thing but Boars, if you had given me notice of this, I should have been in Bed and asleep two hours ago.

The next day about dinner time the Duke of *Biron* sent word to the King, that if he did not take care of the Province of *Burgundy*, it would be lost, because the Baron of *Lux* would let in the *Spaniards* as soon as he should have notice of his detention. The King was very much offended at this message, and said, see the impudence and boldness of the Duke of *Biron*, who sendeth me word that *Burgundy* is lost, if I do not look to it. His obstinacy hath undone him, if he would have confessed the truth of a thing that I have under his hand, he should not be where he is. I wish I had paid 200000. Crowns, and he had given me the means to forgive him. I never loved any man so much, I would have trusted him with my Son and my Kingdom. 'Tis true, he hath served me well, but he cannot deny but that I have saved his life three times; I rescued him once from the hands of the Enemy at *Fontain Francoise*, so wounded and astonished with blows, that as I plaid the part of a Souldier to save him, I was also fained to make that of a Captain to make the retreat; for he told me he was not in a case to do it.

The *Saturday* next the prisoners were carried to *Paris* by water, and put into the *Bastille* in several Chambers. The Duke of *Biron* was put into that, called of the Saints famous, for the Prison of the Constable of Saint *Paul*, executed in the time of *Lewis* the XI. and the Earl in the Chamber above him.

The care, the order and vigilancy, with which he was guarded, did put him in some amazement; for his Guards waited on him without Arms, and served him with a Knife without a point, which made him say, that it was the way to the Grave (the place of Execution.) But when he knew that the Hangman of *Paris* was a *Burgundian*, he remembred that *La Brosse* an Astrologer had foretold him sometimes, seeing his Horoscope, which he fained to be that of one of his friends, that he should be beheaded, and *Cæsar* a Magician, that a blow of a *Burgundian* given behind; should hinder him to attain the Kingdom.

The Arch-Bishop of *Bourges* went to see him, and endeavoured to settle his Conscience, and to disswade him from some Atheistical opinions that he had: *Villeroy* and *Sillery* went also to see him, and by the Kings Command, and at his request.

Few days after, the King being at St. *Mourder, Fossez,* the *Lords la Force,* the Earl of *Roussy,* Brother in Law to the Duke of *Biron,* Saint *Blancard* his Brother, *Chasteau-neuf, Themines, Salignac,* St. *Angel, Longuac,* Friends and Kinsmen of the Duke of *Biron,* went and cast themselves at the Kings feet, to implore his Mercy, and that he would be pleased to moderate the severity of his Justice, requesting that the same clemency which he had shewed to many others that had as grievously offended him, would at least save his life, and confine him into such a place, where he might do no harm, that their whole Kindred might not be branded with Infamy, and have a regard to his Fathers service and his, which though they were not equal to his offence, yet at least to consider, that he was only guilty for his intention.

The King bid them rise, and told them, that their requests were not displeasing to him. That he would not be like his Predecessors, who would not suffer any body to intercede for those that were guilty of high Treason. The King *Francis* II. would never give a hearing to the Wife of the Prince of *Condé* my Uncle. Concerning the clemency you would have me shew to the Duke of *Biron*; it should not be clemency but cruelty, if it were only my particular Interest, I would forgive him, as I do now with all my heart; but my Kingdom and my Children, to whom I owe much, are concerned in it; or they might reproach me hence forwards, that I have tollerated an evil which I might have prevented; my Life, that of my Children, and the preservation of my Kingdom, are concerned in it. I will leave it to the course of Justice, you shall see what Judgement shall be given: I will contribute what I can to his Innocency, I give you leave to do the same till he be found guilty of high Treason; for then the Father cannot intercede for the Son, nor the Son for the Father; the Wife for the Husband, nor the Brother for the Brother. Do not become odious to me for the love you bear him: As for the note of Infamy, there is none but himself. Have the Constable of St. *Paul,* from whom I derive my Pedigree, and the Duke of *Nemours,* of who I am Heir (both beheaded) left any note of Infamy upon their Posterity, should not the Prince of *Condé* my Uncle have been beheaded the next day, if King *Francis* the II. had not dyed? Therefore ye that are Kinsmen to the Duke of *Biron,* cannot be noted with Infamy, if you continue in your faithfulness, as (I assure my self) you will. And I am so far from depriving you of your Offices, that if any new one should fall, I would bestow them upon you: I am more sorry for his fault than you can be; but to conspire against me that am his King and Benefactor, is a crime that I cannot forgive, without losing my self, my Wife, my Son, and my Estate, I know you to be so good *French* men, that you would not have the last, and shall take Patience for the first. Thus the King dismissed him, and sent his Commission to the Court of Parliament, to decide the business. The Process was framed in the *Bastille,* by the Lords of *Achilles de Harlay,* first President in the Court of Parliament of *Paris, Nicolas Potier* second President, *Stephen Fleury,* and *Philibert* of *Thurin,* Councellors in the same Court. They asked him if he did not write in Cyphers, he denyed it, then were shewed unto him several Letters, written and sealed with his own hand, which did witness his Intelligences with the *Spaniard* and the Duke of *Savoy,* and contained advices that he gave of the wants that were in the Kings Army; How little Money he had to maintain the War, and to satisfie the *Suitzers* of the discontent of the *French* Nobility, and how several *French* Troops might easily be defeated, and that to divert the Kings forces it was necessary to invade *Provence,* and did much press upon the 50000. Crowns, and the 4000 men promised or else said, all is lost. Some of these things he confessed, and did so intangle and contradict himself, that the Commissioners had pity on his indiscretion.

He was asked what opinion he had of *La Fin,* he said he took him for an honest Gentleman, his Friend and Kinsman, his Evidences being read to him, and himself brought face to face, he did with the most horrid Imprecations and Blasphemies in the World deny them, and charged *La Fin* with the most horrid Crimes that can be Imagined, calling still God for a Witness of his Innocency;

La Fin stood firm in the confirming of his Evidence, and did more particularly declare the whole conspiracy. The Duke answered, that if *Renazé* were there he would tell the contrary, *Renazé*, who had a little while before escaped his Prison in *Piemont*, was brought before him, and confirmed all what *La Fin* had said.

Next to that was brought one of the Kings waiting men, who witnessed, that having lyen in his Chamber by the Kings command, the first night of his Imprisonment he had adjured him, by several offers and promises of rewards, to give notice to his Secretaries to be out of the way for some days, and to tell the Earl of *Roussy* his Brother in Law, that he should send presently to *Dijon*, to give the same advice to those that were left there, and above all that if they were examined; they should all constantly deny that ever he did write in Cyphers.

Thus the business having been thorowly examined, it remained only to proceed unto Judgment; but the Prisoner being a Peer of *France*, (the King having erected the Barony of *Biron* into a Dukedom) by the Laws the Prisoner could not be judged, but by his Peers, which being summoned, and not appearing, the Court of Parliament being authorised by the Kings Commission, proceeded to Judgement.

The 23 of *July* 1602. the Chancellor, with the *Maisses* and *Pontcarré*, Privy Councellors, went to the Parliament, where all the Chambers were assembled together. There he made known the Kings intention, in a business, wherein the good of the Kingdom was so much concerned, and represented on one part the quality of a Person, commendable for his services; but on the other, the foulness of the Crime, for the Judgement of which the King did rely upon the integrity and prudence of the Court. The Kings Attorney, and Soliciter, having represented to the Court, that the Peers summoned, gave no appearance, and that the Prisoners petition (who asked for Councel), was not to be received. The Court proceeded to examine the Evidences, whereupon they sat three times, after which the Prisoner was brought from the *Bastille*, by *Montigny* Governour of *Paris*, and *Vitry*, Captain of the Kings Guards, in a close Barge, covered with Tapistry, and followed by two other Barges full of Souldiers, and *Switzers*. He entred into the Palace, through the Garden of the first President, and rested himself in one of the Chambers, where he was offered a Breakfast.

The time being come, he was to be heard, the Recorder went and called him into the Guild-hall, where when he saw one Hundred and twelve Judges before his face, he was some thing daunted, and was made to sit within the Bar upon a joint stool; where he sat in such a posture, as stretching forth his right foot, and having his Cloak under his arm, and his left hand upon his side, he kept the right one free, either to stretch it forth to Heaven, or to smite his brest, when occasion served. The Chancellor did so frame his discourse, that he never named him by his name, nor that of his qualities.

Of many evidences there was five chiefly urged against him.

The first to have been conversant with one *Picotée*, born in *Orleans*, and refugied in *Flanders*, to keep intelligence with the Arch-duke, and to have give him 150. Crowns for two journeys to that end.

The second to have treated with the Duke of *Savoy*, three days after his arrival to *Paris* without the Kings leave, and to have offered him all assistance and service against any person whatsoever, upon the hope or promiss of marrying his third daughter.

The third to have kept intelligence with the said Duke in taking of the City of *Bourg* and other places, giving him advice how he might defeat the Kings Army, and destroy his person, with many other circumstances to that purpose.

The fourth to have sent by *Renazée* a note to the Governour of the Fort of Saint *Catherine*, promising to bring the King before the said Fort, so near that he might be either killed or taken, telling what cloths he himself would wear, and what Horse he would ride, that he might be distinguished.

To have sent several times *la Fin* to treat with the Duke of *Savoy*, and the Earl of *Fuentes* against the Kings service.

These are the first confessions and acknowledgements that the Prisoner made before the Commissioners in the Bastille, but now he thinketh, he may as lightly deny them, as he had unadvisedly before confessed them.

Upon the first Article he answered, that *Picoté* being once his Prisoner, had offered his service for the reduction of the Town of *Seurre* in *Burgundy*, and that the King had approved of it, that it is true he had given him the said sum, but it was as a reward for his pains and charges in this negotiation, which sum he hath charged upon the Kings account, with some other small ones, laid out by him for the King; that since the reduction of the said Town he had not seen *Picoté* but in *Flanders*, when he went thither Embassadour for the confirmation of the Peace, where the said *Picotée* came to him with many others, intreating him he would be pleased to mediate with the King, for the liberty of returning into their Countrey, and enjoying their Estates, and that he did wish them to go to the Lords *Belieure* and *Sillery*, who would prescribe them what orders they were to follow in this business, and never had any other conversation with *Picoté*.

Upon the second, That he could not have treated with the Duke of *Savoy* three days after his arrival at *Paris*, seeing that himself did not come there but a fortnigh-after, and that *la Fin* came but after him, that all his discourses with him were in publick and before witnesses, and therefore could not be suspected; that *Roncas* had sometimes mentioned to him the Marriage of the third daughter of the Duke, and that he did impart it to the King; that his Majesty having sent him word by *la Force* his Brother in Law, that he did not approve of it, he never thought of it since; that the intelligence he is accused to have kept with the Duke of *Savoy*, is confuted enough by what he did, for when the King had commanded him to wait and keep company to the Duke in his return from *France*, and to shew him the strongest places upon the Frontiers of *Burgundy*, he did humbly excuse himself to the King of it, saying, that he foresaw well enough that the Duke would not keep the Treaty of Peace, and that it would be a great grief to him to make War against a Prince, with whom he should have kept company, and made good cheer; and that he did advise the Baron of *Lux* to let him see only the weaker places, that he might not know the strength of the Countrey.

Upon the third, That if he had kept correspondence with the Duke of *Savoy*, he would not have undertaken the taking of *Bourg*, almost against the Kings will, without any other help then of those that were ordinarily with him; that of fourty Convoys that were brought to relieve the Town, he had routed thirty seven, and the other three entered in his absence; that the King knoweth very well he was offered 200000. Crowns to let the succours enter into the Citadel of *Bourg*; that although his Majesty had commanded him in the time of a Truce made with the Duke of *Savoy*, to let those of the Citadel of *Bourg* have every day 400. Loafs of Bread, 50. bottles of Wine, half an Oxe, and six Sheep, he did only let them have fifty bottles of Wine and one Sheep, by which means the Town was surrendred within the time promised; that if he had had any evil design against the King and Kingdom, he would not so freely and willingly put the Town into the hands of him that is now Governour of it; that the Governours of Places that were in the Duke's service, and are now in that of the King, can witness whether he shewed them any favour; that for his giving advice to the Duke to defeat the Regiment of *Chambauld*, he will prove that *Chambauld* did not come into the Army, but one Month after the time mentioned in his Calumny; besides that, this advice was without appearance of reason, for from *Chambauld*'s quarters to his, there was at least six days journey, and as much to go to the Duke, and as much to come back, besides the time required for the marching of the Forces; therefore all that was a meer invention of *la Fin*.

Upon the fourth, That he intreated his Majesty to call to memory, that he was the onely man who dissuaded him to go and view the Fort, representing unto him that there was in it extraordinary good Gunners, and that he could not view it without great danger, and upon that he offered the King to bring him the next day the Plat-form of it, and to take it with 500. Musquettiers, and that himself would be in the Head of them.

Upon the fifth, That it was true all the evil he had done was in two Months time that *la Fin* had been with him, during which, he did hearken and write more then he ought: but that with the same he had written, he had so long served the King, that it was enough to prove the sincerity of his intentions; that the refusal of the Citadel of *Bourg*, which he thought the King had promised him, had put him into such a discontent, that he found himself in a capacity to hearken to any thing, and to do any thing, that if he had been a Protestant, it may be the place should have been refused him no more then it was to *de Boaisse*, who was such an one, as he told the King himself at *Lyon*; that *la Fin* had also once told him, that the King speaking of him, and of his Father, said, that God had done well for to take him out of this world when he was killed, for he was a very chargeable and unprofitable servant; and for the Son, it was not all Gold that shined; that these words had so much incensed him, that he could have found in his heart to be all covered with blood. Upon that the Chancellor asked him of what blood he meaned? he answered, of my own: desiring not to live any longer, after he had heard such reproches, as blemished the services of his Father and his own; that nevertheless his anger and discontent went never so far, as to attempt upon the King; that his fault was only in words, and it may be little in Writting; that his Majesty seeing with how much ingenuity he did acknowledge his fault, had forgiven him all what was past, in the presence of the Lords *Villeroy* and *Sillery*, and that if since that time he was found to have done any thing amiss, he would blame his Judges of Injustice, if they did not condemn him to death, that if he had done nothing amiss since, he thought the Kings pardon to be sufficient for what was, and if there was need to ask for it again, his knees were as supple and plyable as ever.

But a Letter, which he had written to *la Fin* since the pardon of *Lyon*, and the Birth of the Dolphin, did spoil all, for it was a manifest evidence of the continuation of his ill designs, and the Chancellor having produced it, he answered, he would never deny his hand, but that *Imbert* and *Renazée* Domestick Servants to *la Fin* could counterfeit it; that though he might have some ill thoughts, he had always well done; that although the King would not forgive him this fault, it was not in the power of men to condemn him justly for single words, which were contradicted by the effects; that his consolation was in his misfortune, his Judges were not ignorant of the services he had done to the Kingdom, which he had Sealed with five and thirty wounds; that his body whose life and death was in the disposition of their Justice, had not a vain but had bleeded for their service, and to restore them into their places, from whence the League had driven them; that the hand which had written the Letters produced against him, was the same that had done contrary to what it did write; that he had written and spoke more then he ought, but that it could not be proved he had ever ill done; that there was no Law that punished with death the lightness of a single word or motion of the thoughts; that anger and discontent had made him capable of saying and doing any thing, but that his reason had not given leave to say or to do, ought but what deserveth to be commended; which words were as carefully considered, as he repeated them often with several Oaths and Imprecations.

Upon that the Chancellor having asked him why then he did not open himself more to the King, who desired him with great affection to do it at *Fountain-bleau*, seeing he knew in his conscience to have done nothing against his duty since his pardon. There he cut himself in his answer, and said he thought *la Fin* had revealed nothing of what was between them, and that he had lately assured him so with Oaths and fearful imprecations, that he would never have thought *la Fin* had been such a damnable man, as to reveal that which with so many deep Oaths and Imprecations they had promised to keep secret between themselves; that having propounded the question to a Monk of the Order of *Minimes* at *Lyon*, whether he might with a safe conscience reveal what was between them, and what he had promised with Oath to *la Fin* to keep secret, because he suspected that *la Fin* would deceive him, and tell all to the King, and so ruine him. The *Minime* had answered, that seeing they had no more intention to put in execution the things they had projected, he was not to reveal them, and if *la Fin* did it, he should go to Hell, and himself to Heaven; that he did so firmly believe this, that although the Archbishop of *Bourges* had visited him in Prison, and alledged many reasons to the contrary, yet his soul was so settled in that belief, that he thought it was only the part of an Atheist to swear with intention to deceive.

Upon this he begin to accuse *la Fin* of the most execrable crimes that a man is capable of, saying that he made use of *Renazée* for *Sodomy* that he was a Witch, and had ordinary communication with the Devils, that he had so be witched him with enchanted Waters and Wax Images, that spoke, that he was constrained to submit himself to all his will; that he never spoke to him but whispering, and in unknown words, and after he had kissed him in the left eye, and he could not deny but he had shewed him a Wax Image, speaking and saying, *Rex impie morieris, thou shalt die ungodly King*, and called him continually his Master, Lord, Prince and King; that he was a false Coiner, and had persuaded him many times to attempt upon the King, but that he would never hearken to it, that the quality of the Accusators was to be considered, who not only were partners, but instigators of the Fact; that certainly the Duke of *Savoy* was his mortal enemy, for having since his pardon left of all his intelligences with him, and seeing that after a long detention he had released *Renazée*, to come and to be a witness against him; that the King had forgiven him at *Lyon* and that upon his acknowledging many times to the King, that the refusal of the Citadel of *Bourg* had very much incensed him, his Majesty did comfort him with these words. Marshal never remember *Bourg*, and I will never remember what is past, that in 22 Months after he had not offended, that if he had continued his ill designs, he might have done it easily in *England* and *Switzerland*. That above 100. Gentlemen shall be Witnesses of his first Embassy, and for the second, he desireth no other Witnesses than the Kings Embassadors themselves, that if they would be pleased to consider how he was come, and in what case he had left the Province of *Burgundy*, it was impossible to have an ill opinion of his designs; for there was not one Souldier in all the Countrey, and at his going away he gave no other charge to the Commanders and Captains, than to serve the King faithfully, that every one disswaded him to come to Court, and in the way he received many Letters to that purpose, that he was come upon the Kings word, trusting upon his own Conscience and Innocency. If the King be not pleased to consider my services (said he to the Court) and those assurances he hath given me of his Mercy, I acknowledge my self guilty of Death, and do not expect my life from his Justice, but from yours, (my Lords) who will remember better than he what dangers I have undergone for his service. I confess I had a mind to do ill, but I never proceeded to effects: It would be a hard matter if I should be the first in whom thoughts should be punished; Great offences require great clemency. I do implore that of the King, and nevertheless I am the onely one in *France*, that is made an example of his severity, and that can have no hope in his clemency, which he never denyed to those that had done worse: However I trust more in you my Lords, than I do in the King, who having heretofore looked upon me with his Eyes of love, looketh upon me now with those of his anger, and thinketh it a Vertue to be cruel unto me, and a Vice to excercise upon me the act of clemency.

Thus pleaded the Prisoner, with so much eloquency and boldness, that if his Judges had not seen evidently the truth of the fact, under his own Hand and Seal, the respect of his first condition might have perswaded them to believe his Innocency, and to take compassion of his ruined fortune.

The Court did hear him as long as he would speak, with so much patience, that never a man had the like audience. The Prisoner spoke so much, that his last reasons were found contrary to his first, his allegations did not shew his Innocency; for the Embassadors themselves which he took for Witnesses of his carryage in *Switzerland*, did report many words of his, which shewed his anger and passion. Besides the King had not given his word, that he might come in Safety, and those Letters which he alleadged for his justification, did prove the continuation of his treacherous designs, seeing that he had sent *la Fin* and *Hebert*, to *Turin* and *Milan*, since the pardon, He could not then expect but Justice, in a case where neither passion nor favour could alter Judgment: Nevertheless he shewed himself much satisfied with his answers, and therefore being come back again to the *Bastille*, he passed the rest of that day, and the two next, to relate unto his Guards the questions of the Court and his answers therereunto, counterfeiting the gesture and the words which he Imagined the Chancellor had spoken after his going away, though that grave and venerable old man neither said nor did any thing, but what was becoming to his Age and quality, having shewed himself as full of compassion, as the prisoner was of his vanity; for when he was nearer to death he thought less upon it, and thinking himself the only man capable of commanding an Army, he found some fault in those that were thought capable of it, saying, that one was unhappy in his undertakings, the other was not respected by the Souldiers, such a one was a brave man, but he wanted experience, and another that hath both was a Protestant. To conclude, he did so please himself with his own praise and deserts, that he thought no body could come near him, and that he was so useful to the Kingdom, that it would be a great Crime to think to undo him.

He had spoken so long the 27 of the Month, that there was no time left to gather the Voices: The Chancellor therefore went into the Palace the 29 following to gather the Voices of the Judges. *Fleury* the reporter of the Proces, did conform his opinion to the conclusions of the Kings Attorney, all the rest agreed to it, either by Words or by Signs, and all the proofs necessary for the verification of a Crime meeting in this case, as his Answers, Confessions, Writings, Letters, Instructions, and Evidence of Witnesses not reproached; It was found, that the unnatural Conspiracy against the State, the detestable attempt upon the Kings Person, makes him guilty of high Treason in the first and second degree.

He confesseth he had evil intentions, it is enough, the Laws do punish the Councels, the resolutions, and the effects; for if the Traitor be not prevented, time may give him the opportunity to accomplish his Design and Will, and the Will of a Subject in point of State, doth depend immediately upon that of the Prince. He sayeth moreover, that without the Kings Mercy he is undone, and that if he would have put in Execution the ill designs that were propounded to him against his Majesty, he should have been gone long ago: Did he ever give notice of them to the King or to any body else. If the Prisoner had brought to pass his intent, we might have said, farewell State, farewell Justice, it is too late to believe the Conspiracy against Princes, when they are murdered by the Conspirators.

He hath well Served the King, it is true; but his Offices and Dignities did call him to that Duty, he hath had notable rewards for it, and from the time that he hath shewed himself so unfaithfull, he hath diminished the lustre of his deserts. His deserts had made him capable of the first dignities of the Kingdom, but the merit of them is vanished away, by the greatness of his Crime.

And what is the State beholding to him, if after he hath contributed so much for its restauration, he goeth about to turn up side down the Foundation of it, and to betray it to the Enemies. It is nothing to begin well unless you end well, the actions are judged by the end: Those that have deserved best of the States, are the most severely punished when they fall into Sedition and Rebellion. There is many sheets of Paper in the Hands of the Court, containing in them one hundred advices given to the Enemy, the least of which is capable to make him guilty.

The Prisoners quality is not considerable in this case; Justice is blind to all distinctions, and rather considereth the offence according to the quality of the offender; Crimes of high Treason are not considered by things past, but by things present and that are to come; we must not put in an account what he hath done, but what he had a mind to do. The quality of a Duke and Peer of *France*, of Knight of the Kings Order, of Marshal, doth not exempt him from the Law, and from being judged as an Enemy to the State, and to the Majesty of the Prince, seeing he would have troubled the State, and attempted upon the Kings person. Who in *France* besides is more obliged to the King? the greater then is the Obligation, the greater the ingratitude. God forbid that the respect of the quality should stop the course of Justice: a Limb must be cut off to save all the body.

But his offence hath been forgiven: The pardon cannot extend but to the things that are confessed; but he acknowledgeth himself that he hath not told all, therefore he hath confessed as little as he could, his own confessions Witness, he only asked forgiveness, that he might continue his Crimes with more security: Besides, he would not acknowledge his fault to the King, for all the King promised to forgive him, and lately he told the Court, he did not believe that *la Fin* had revealed what was secret between them; and thought he would have kept his word, which he had confirmed with so many Oaths, and that if he had doubted of it, he would have cast himself at his Majesties Feet as readily as he, and asked him forgiveness. It followeth then that there was some thing left behind that was not confessed: Thus he accuseth himself, thinking to excuse his fault; besides, he mistaketh himself thinking to persuade the Court, that since the pardon he hath done nothing amiss, for the Pardon was in *January* 1600. and here be Letters of *September* last, by which he recalleth *la Fin*, telleth him, he will think no more upon the Vanities that were past since, God was pleased to have given the King a Dolphin. It is apparent then that he hath employed *la Fin* at least since the Pardon, till the birth of the Dolphin, and *la Fin* maintaineth that there was a note quite to the contrary, and that they did continue their intelligences and practises unknown to the King. That the Duke did recal him, fearing he should discover the Conspiracy, when a man continues in his faults and abuseth his Pardon, the last fault payeth for all.

Besides, the Court hath not seen that Pardon, he oughted to have produced it in writing under the Kings Hand and Seal, and to forgive him once more, would put him into such a condition, as to contrive always Treasons against the State; the remedy of a present evil is not to be neglected upon the hope of an uncertain good; he is in a case to be no more useful; nothing can be expected from his courage but revenge; he that can bring no profit by his virtue and faithfulness, must do it by being made an exemple.

Such were for the most part the reasons of the Court, according to which, and to the conclusions of the Attorney General, the Chancellor did pronounce Sentence of death against the Prisoner; some were of opinion that *la Fin* should be arrested, as one that could not justifie himself, for having concealed such a damnable Conspiracy, till he saw that the *Spanish* affairs went to wrack. The Chancellor did moderate these opinions, representing that the Conspiracy was not yet wholly discovered, and that such things would hinder the rest of those that knew some thing of it to reveal it; that a man that saveth the Kings Person and his Estate, ought rather to be rewarded then punished. And in confirmation of this, the King sent Letters to *la Fin*, by which he assured him, that such a service done to him and his Kingdom, should never prove his ruine.

The Court stayed onely for the Kings intention upon the execution of the Sentence, which *Sillery* had carried to St. *Germain*. The Scaffold was ready to be set up in the place of *Greve*, but the execution might have proved dangerous, in the middle of so much people of different humors and tempers; and already there was a rumour, as if some body should throw him a Sword, with which he should make himself a passage, or else have died with a blow less shameful then that of the Hangman; upon his friends intreaty the execution was ordered to be done in the *Bastille*.

The next day about noon, the people knowing that the Sentence was past, went some to the *Greve*, thinking that the execution should be done there, others to St. *Antony* street, to see the Prisoner pass by; he saw from his Chamber that multitude, and guessed that he was to be the Spectacle of those Spectators; here the anguish of the Grave began to beset him, and drawing a consequence from the shadow of death, that the body was not far of; he sent *Baranton* a *Scotish* Gentleman to intreat the Marquess of *Rhosny* to come to see him, or if he could not come, to sue for his Pardon to the King. He sent him answer, he could do neither, and that he was extreamly sorry for his misfortune, that if he had believed him at his coming to Court, he should have confessed what the King did desire to know of him, for by concealing of it, he did hinder the King to give him his life, and all his friends to sue for it.

The next day last of *July* 1602. the Chancellor, the first President, *Sillery*, three Masters of Requests, some Officers of the Chancery, *Rapin* Lieutenant of the short Gown, his Lieutenant, *Daniel Voisin* Register of the Court of Parliament, six Sergeants, and seven or eight more went to the Bastille, about ten of the Clock in the morning, as soon as they were come in the Chancellor commanded that the Prisoners Dinner should be carryed, without giving him notice of his coming, and in the mean time he and the first President made a List of those whom they would have to be present in that action: Some Presidents, three Masters of Requests, three Auditors, six Serjeants of the Parliament, the Lieutenant Civil, the Kings Attorney at the *Chastelet*, *Rapin* and his Lieutenant, the Knight of the Watch, the Prevost of the Merchants, four Aldermen, four Councellors of the City, and some few others, to the number of fifty.

About noon the Prisoner looking through the Grates of his Chamber Windows, perceived the Wife of *Rumigny*, Captain of the Castle, weeping with her hands up and guessed that those Tears were drawn by the compassion of his Fortune. He was confirmed in his opinion, when he saw the Chancellor followed by the Serjeants, *Rapin* and his Lieutenant, and some others go through the *Bastilles* Yard into the Chappel, then he began to cry aloud, O my God I am a dead man, ah, what injustice it is to put an Innocent Person to death, thereupon he intreated *Rumigny* to tell his Brothers, Sisters and Kindred, that they should not be ashamed of his death, because he was Innocent of that he was accused.

The Chancellor commanded he should be brought down into the Chappel, where as soon as he saw the Chancellor, are you come, said he, to pronounce me my death: The Chancellor saluted him, then put on his Hat, the Prisoner stood bare headed, and began to speak first. Ah my Lord

Chancellor, is there no pardon? is there no Mercy? such and such (whom he did name one after another) have committed such offences and yet have been pardoned. What? you that look like an honest man, have you suffered that I should be so miserably condemned? ah! my Lord, if you had not told the Court that the King would have me to die, they would not have condemned me so. My Lord, my Lord, you could have hindred that evil, and you have not done it, you shall answer for that injustice before all the rest of the Judges that have condemned me, and saying so, he stroke the Chancellor upon the Arm. Ah! what a great service the King doth this day to the King of *Spain*, to rid him of such an Enemy as I was, might I not have been kept within four Walls, till some occasion had offered where I might have been useful? Ah my Lord, have you forgot my fathers love to you so much, as not to give notice to the King of what I say, and what dammage he suffereth in loosing me: I am yet as willing as ever to do Service to the Kingdom, you could let him know so much, he hath so good an opinion of you, I am sure he would believe you: A Messenger could quickly go thither and back again; what shall a thousand Gentlemen my Kinsmen say? doth he think that after my death they can do him any service? and what if I had been guilty, would I have come upon those false assurances that President *Janin* that great Cheat gave me, when he told me, that businesses were so ill mannaged in *France*, that it was fit I should see the King and tell him of it, who at my perswasion would settle them in better order: I have neglected all the advices of my friends to hearken unto his perswasions. I have trusted to that cursed Traitor *la Fin*, who writ to me that I could come in all safety, and that he had told the King nothing but of the Marriage that was propounded to me with a daughter of *Savoy*, that the King would receive me with all kindness. What then? the goings to and fro of many, the reasons of those who advised me to come, and the Kings Letters, were they all baits to catch me: I am well served to have trusted to much upon his Word, I could have sought and got other securities, if I had not trusted to my Innocency; I am come upon the confidence of my integrity since his pardon. Ah! doth he not know that he hath forgiven me; I have lied some evil designs, I have hearkened, I have written, I have spoken, I confessed them all at *Lyon*, he did assure me never to remember it, and did exhort me that from hence forwards I should commit nothing that might compel me to have recourse to his clemency: Nevertheless I am now accused of things that are blotted out by his pardon; I have not offended him since, unless it be in that I desired War rather than Peace, because my humour is not peaceable, had not the King at that time reason to approve of it? if this Crime deserveth death I fly to his clemency, I implore his Mercy. The Queen of *England* told me, that if the Earl of *Essex* would have humbled himself, and asked forgiveness, he should have obtained it: I do, being Innocent, what he would not do being guilty. Ah! Shall all Mercy be put out for me; those that have done worse have found Grace and Mercy: I perceive what it is, I am not the more guilty but the most unhappy, and the King, who hath been so sparing of his Subjects lives, hath a mind to be prodigal of mine.

To conclude, he forgot nothing of what might be said by a soul pierced with grief spite, anger, and violent threatning, in exclamations and revilings against the King and his Parliament, in reproaches against the Chancellor, that he had more contributed to his condemnation than to his absolution, in words that are not fit to be spoken nor related.

His words ran so fast that the Chancellor could not stop them: Nevertheless he took occasion to tell him, his passion suggested him many things without appearance of reason, and against his own judgment, that no body had known his defects better than he, and that he could have wished his faults had been as unknown as dissembled, that the knowledge of them had been so visible and apparent, that his Judges had more ado to moderate his punishment than to inflict it. That Sentence was given upon the proofs of several attemps he had made against the Kings Person and his Estate, and for having kept intelligence and correspondency with the Enemies of the Kingdom, of which he had been found guilty, that if he had concealed the truth in the answers to his accusations, he should now reveal it being so near to his end, and that for these causes the King did ask his Order of Knighthood, and his staff of Marshal of *France*, with which he had formerly honoured him: He pulled the Order out of his Pocket and put it into the Chancellors hands, Protesting and Swearing upon the Salvation of his Soul, that he never had broken the Oath he made in receiving it, that (it is true) he had desired War more than Peace; because he could not preserve in Peace, the reputation he had got in War, as for the Staff, he never carryed it: Nevertheless by the Oath that the Knights of the Holy Ghost take, they are bound to take no Pension, Wages nor Money from forrain Princes, and to engage themselves in no bodies service but the Kings, and faithfully to reveal what they shall know to be for or against the Kings service.

After that the Chancellor exhorted him to lift up his thoughts from Earth to Heaven, to call upon God, and to hear patiently his Sentence.

My Lord (said he) I beseech you do not use me as other men; I know what my Sentence beareth, my accusations are false, I wonder the Court would Condemn me upon the Evidence of the most wicked and detestable man that is alive; he never came near me without Witchcraft, nor never went from me till he had bewitched me, he did bite my left ear off, and made me drink inchanted waters, and when he said, that the King had a mind to rid himself of me, he called me his King, his Benefactor, his Prince, his Lord, he hath communication with the Devils, and hath shewed me a Wax Image, speaking these words in Latine, *Rex impie morieris*, ungodly King thou shalt die. If he hath had so much power by his Magick, as to make an inanimate body to speak, it is no wonder that he should make my Will conformable to his.

Here the Chancellor stopt him, and told him, that the Court had well considered his answers, and his Letters, that he ought not to find fault with his Sentence, that it had done him the same justice as a Father should do to his son, if he had offended in the like manner. He had scarce spoken these words when the other answered, what Judgment? I have been heard but once, and had no time to tell the fiftieth part of my justification; if I had been heard at large, I could have made it clearly appear that *la Fin* is such a one as I say; what Judgment upon the Evidence of a Bougerer? of a Rogue that hath forsaken his Wife, of a treacherous and perfidious man, that had Sworn so many times upon the Holy Sacrament, never to reveal what was between us, of a Knave that hath so often counterfeited my Hand and Seal: It is true, I have written some of those Letters that were shewed me, but I never intended to put them in Execution: and the rest are falsified: Is there not many that can counterfeit so well the Hand and Seal of others, that themselves can scarce distinguish them. It is well known that the Lady *Marchioness* of *Vernevil* hath lately acknowledged that to be her own hand, which she had never written. My Heart and my Actions have sufficiently countervailed the faults of my Hand, and of my Tongue. Besides, the King hath forgiven me, I do implore his Memory for a Witness. You say I have been found guilty to have attempted upon the Kings Person; that is false, that never came into my mind, and I knew nothing of it till that *la Fin* did propose it to me before St. *Katherines* Fort, six or seven days after the Siege, if I had been thus minded, I could have easily brought it to pass; I was the only man that hindred the King to go before the Fort: If my services had been taken into consideration, I should not have been thus condemned: I believe that if you had not been present, the Parliament would not have judged me so rigorously; I wonder that you, whom I thought to be prudent and wise, have used me so cruelly; it would have been more honourable for your quality and old age to implore for me the Kings Mercy, than his Justice. There is Dungeons here where I might have been kept bound hand and foot; I should have at last that comfort to pray for those who should have got me that favour from the King. If I had been but a single Souldier, I should have been sent to the Galleys; but because I am a Marshal of *France*, I am thought to be as dangerous a man to the State, as I have been useful heretofore. My life is sought after, I see there is no Mercy for me; the King hath often forgiven those, who not only intended to do evil, but had done it; this Vertue is now forgotten, he giveth occasion now to the World to believe, that he never used clemency or forgiveness, but when he was afraid. I was of opinion, that if I had killed one of his Children he would have forgiven me. Is it not pity that my Father should have run so many dangers, and at last died in the field to keep the Crown upon his Head, and that now he should take my head off my Shoulders, is it possible he should forget the services I have done him? doth he not remember the conspiracy of *Mantes*, and the dangers he should have been in if I had taken the Conspirators part? Hath he forgotten the Siege of *Amiens*, where I have been so often among the fire and Bullets, neglecting my own life to preserve his, I have not a Vein but hath been open to preserve his own Blood, I have received five and thirty wounds to save his life; he sheweth now that he never loved me but when he had need of me, he taketh away my head, but let him beware that the Justice of God doth not fall upon his. My Blood shall cry for revenge for the wrong that is done me to day, I call the King of *Spain* and the Duke of *Savoy* to Witness, if I know any thing what is laid to my charge. *La Fin* himself did shew me sometimes a Catholick List of about fourscore Gentlemen, who received Pension from the King of *Spain*, I had never so much curiosity as to read it; let him be put to the rack he shall tell many particularities of it; the King within a little while shall perceive what he getteth by my death; I shall at last die a good Catholick, and constant in my Religion, I believe that's the cause of my death.

The Chancellor seeing that all his discourses were full of passion, vanity and repetitions, and void of reason, and were like an impetuous Torrent that cannot be stopt, and that all his words were nothing but reproaches against the King and the Court of Parliament, blasphemies against God, and execrations against his Accusers; said that his business called him away, and that in his absence he would leave him two Divines to comfort him, and to dispose his soul to leave quietly this World, for the enjoying of a better.

As the Chancellor was going out, the Prisoner begged of him that he might have the liberty to make his Will, because he did owe much, and much was owing to him, and he desired to satisfie every body. The Chancellor answered, that the Recorder *Voisin* should stay with him to write his Will under the Kings good pleasure. And as the Chancellor spoke to *Voisin*, the Prisoner turning to *Roissy*, Master of Requests, asked him if he were, one of those that had condemned him: my Father hath loved you so much, that though you were one, yet should I forgive you. *Roissy* answered, my Lord, I pray God Almighty to comfort you.

They went out, and he with a quiet mind and free from passion, did dictate his Will in what form he would, with the same *Garbe*, as if he had been making a Speech at the head of an Army; he remembered his friends and servants, and did not forget the Baron of *Lux*, whom he loved above all the rest. He lest eight hundred Livers a year to a Bastard of his, whom he begot of a woman that he left with Child of another, to which child he left a Mannor near *Dijon* that had cost him six thousand Crowns, he disposed all the rest of his Debts, and answered modestly, and without confusion to all the Notes and Bills that were brought him about his affairs. Took three Rings off his fingers, and intreated *Baranton* to give them to his Sisters, two to the Countess of *Roussy*, and the other to that of Saint *Blancard*, desiring they would wear them for his sake; he distributed in Alms about 200. Crowns that he had in his Pocket, fifty to the *Capuchines*, fifty to the *Fueillants*, fifty to the *Minimes*, and the rest to several poor people.

The Will being made, the Recorder put him in mind how my Lord Chancellor had told him he was condemned to death, and that according to the ordinary forms of the Law, he must have his Sentence read to him; that this action required humility, therefore willed him to kneel before the Altar, leaving off hence forth all thoughts of this World, to think upon the Father of Mercies; he kneeled with the right knee upon the first step of the Altar, and heard it read as followeth:

Seen by the Court, the Chambers being assembled together, the Process extraordinarily made by the Presidents and Councellors, appointed by the King under his Letters Patents, dated the 18 and 19 of June, at the request of the Kings Sollicitor General, against the Lord Charles of Gontault of Biron, Knight of both Orders, Duke of Biron, Peer and Marshal of France, Governour of Burgundy, Prisoner in the Castle of Bastille, accused of high Treason, Informations, Interrogations, Confessions and denials, Confrontations, and Witnesses, Letters, Advices, and Instructions given to the Enemies, and acknowledged by him, and all what the Solliciter General hath produced. Sentence of the 22 of this Month, by which it was ordered, that in the absence of the Peers of France summoned, it should be further proceeded to Judgment Conclusions of the Kings Sollicitor, the accuser being heard and interrogated, all things being duly considered, hath been concluded, that the said Court hath declared, and declareth the said Duke of Biron, attainted and convicted of high Treason, for the conspiracies by him made against the Kings Person and Estates, Proditions and Treaties with his Enemies, when he was Marshal of the Army of the said King, for reparation of which Crime, the said Court hath deprived and depriveth him of all his Estates, Honours and Dignities, and hath condemned and condemneth him to be beheaded upon a Scaffold, which for that purpose shall be erected in the place of Greve, hath declared, and declareth, all and every one of his Goods, moveable or unmoveable, in whatsoever places scituated and seated, to be acquired and confiscated to the King, the Mannor of Biron, deprived for ever of the Title and Dukedom and Peerage, and altogether all his other Goods, immediately holden from the King, reunited to the Crown again. Done in Parliament the last day of July 1602. Signed in the Original by de Belieure, Chancellor of France, Councillor in the Court, Reporter of the Process.

He was not moved at these words, *attainted and convicted of high Treason*, but at these, *against the Person of the King*, he fell into a rage, and Swearing as he had done many times before, and shall do hereafter with great Oaths and Imprecations, there is no such thing, said he to the Recorder, it is false, blot out that; he was also very angry, hearing that he was to be executed in the place of *Greve*, thinking that for several respects he was to be distinguished from the common sort of people, and Swore again, that he would not go thither, and that he had rather to be torn in pieces by wild Horses, and that it was not in the power of all those that stood by to carry him thither, then he was a little appeased, when *Voisin* told him, that the King had done him that favour to change the place of Execution, and that it was to be done in the *Bastille*. The confiscation of his Goods, and the revenues of the Dukedom of *Biron* to the Crown, was the last point of the Sentence that vexed him. What? said he, doth the King intend to grow rich out of my poverty? The Lordship of *Biron* cannot be confiscated, I only possessed it by substitution of my Brethren, what shall my Brethren do, the King ought to have been satisfied with the loss of my life.

The Sentence being pronounced, *Voisin* did exhort him again to renounce all the vanities of the world, to take no other care but of the Salvation of his Soul, which was to be first by reconciling himself to God Almighty, and that there was two Divines for that purpose, and that according to the usual forms of Executions, he would be pleased to suffer himself to be bound. That word of Execution did seem so horrid to him, that he fell into a new rage, Swearing, that he would never permit so infamous a person to touch him, otherwise than with the Sword, and that he had rather be hewen in pieces. To keep him from falling into a further despair, *Voisin* left him, with his Divines, viz. *Garnier Almonec*, and Confessor to the King, and after that Bishop of *Montpelier*, and *Magnan*, Curate of St. *Nicolas* in the fields at *Paris*, who began to talk boldly to him of his death, and to disvest himself of all his thoughts, as he had done of his Goods, and to take no other care than that of his Soul, whereupon he fell into a passion again, Let me alone (said he) it is I that must think upon my Soul, you have nothing to do with it, I had no need of you, you shall not be troubled to hear my confession; what I speak aloud is my confession, I have been these eight days a confessing my self, and the last night, me thought I saw the Heavens opened, and that God lent me his Hand; my Keepers heard me laugh for joy in my sleep. The Divines did not loose Courage for all that, but more and more intreated him to consider, that he was no more what he had been before, that within one or two hours he should be no more, that he must change to be for evermore, that his Soul was ready to appear before the fearfull Throne of the living God, to be rewarded with a more happy life than that he had hitherto passed; or be condemned to an Eternal pain and that in comparison of that which he was to suffer now, it was no more than the slight pricking of a Pin, and having in some measure appeased him, they left him to examine his Conscience, while *Voisin* went to give notice of his refusing to be bound; the Chancellor doubted whether he should be compelled to it; the first President said, that it was dangerous to let him loose; *Sillery* having learned of *Voisin* that the Prisoner was at that time very quiet, said, that if they went about to bind him, he would break all the bonds of Patience, and should never be brought to Execution but in a rage and dispair; according to that opinion he was left free in his body, that he might be the more free in his thoughts.

Which were more to the World, and to the setling of his affairs, than to the saving of his Soul, which he had neglected all his life time, and shewed himself utterly ignorant of the principles of his Religion, for which he said a little before, he was put to death, and those that were present related, that his Prayers made him appear more a Souldier than a Christian; he prayed in commanding, and commanded in praying.

His Confession being ended, he walked in the Chappel with one hand upon his side, and with the other holding the strings of his Shirt, did unbutton and button again his Doublet. *Voisin* being come back told him, that the Chancellor and the first President were very glad to hear of his Patience, and of his constant resolution to die. He talked much of the Money he had at *Dijon*, of the worth of his Jewels, and of what was owing to him, and what himself did owe, he desired that some Sums of Money should be paid to certain Gentlemen, that had no Obligation for it: But still he broke forth into exclamations concerning his Innocency, and execrations against *la Fin*, asking if it should not be lawfull for his Brothers to prosecute him, and to cause him to be burnt.

Upon this, those that kept him during his Imprisonment, came to take their leave of him, every one having his left hand upon the handle of his Sword, and Tears in his Eyes, he moved them to compassion by the sight of his present condition, and exhorted them to serve the King faithfully, against whom he had said he had done nothing amiss, and complained that he could find no Mercy at his Hands, intreated them to pray to God for him, and to oblige them to that, distributed among them all his Cloaths and linnen, and Watches; he desired also the Knight of the Watch to tell the King, that his Servants knew nothing of his Affairs, that the Earl of *Auvergne* was not to be questioned upon that account: He intreated much one exempt of the Guards to go to the said Earl, and tell him he had laid nothing to his charge, and that he went to die without any grief, but of the loss of his friendship, and that the shortness of his life would not give him leave to shew in effect how much he was his servant. The Earl sent him word, that he did accept of his farewell, as of an intimate friend; and that he remained behind to lament all the days of his life the loss he suffered in him, intreated him to leave him his Bastard Son, to have him brought up with his own Children. After this the Prisoner saw a Gentleman belonging to the Duke of *Mayene*, and entreated him to tell his Master, that if ever in his life he had given him some occasion not to love him, that he prayed to believe that he would die his servant, as also of the Duke of *Aiguillon*, and Earl of *Sommerive* his Children; he likewise intreated *Arnaut*, Secretary to the Marquess of *Rhosny*, to remember his last commendations to his Master, and desire him to remember not so much him that went to die, as his Brethren whom he left behind, that he had him in opinion of a good and usefull servant to the King, and repented much he had not believed his Councel.

About three of the Clock the Chancellor and the first President went up again into the Chappel, and finding him in a good disposition, did fortifie his resolution by their discourses, and desiring to know more particularities from his own mouth, sent all the standers by away, except the Divines and the Recorder: They did exhort him to consider, that the days of man are limited, that the end of his days depended from the Providence of the Almighty, who would take him out of this world before some great and long misery should make him weary of it. He answered, no, no my Lords, do not trouble you about comforting me and strengthning me against the fear of death, I have not been afraid of it these 20 years; you have given me 40 days to study it, but I could not believe that having not been in the power of my Enemies to take away my life, I should be so miserable as to loose it by the consent of my friends; having said this they left him, and took their leaves of him with Tears in their Eyes, he would not suffer them to depart till they had received a new Protestation of his, that he never had attempted any thing against the King, Swearing, that if he would have done it, the King should not have been alive three years ago.

As they were going out of the *Bastille* with *Sillery*, he sent the Knight of the Watch to intreat the Chancellor, that his Body might be buried at *Biron*, in the Sepulchre of his Ancestors, and that he would desire the King to give to his younger Brother some Office in the house of the *Dolphin*, and shewing by his Countenance, Carryage, and Words, to care as little for death as one that is a great way from it gave cause to suspect, that he was not out of hope to obtain his pardon from the King, or to escape by some extraordinary means.

The Divines did exhort him to keep nothing back of what might serve for the discharging of his Conscience, and to consider, that they could give him absolution for no more than what he did confess. Although, said he, the King causeth me to die unjustly, nevertheless I have served him with so much affection and obedience, and I have near my death so much good will and affection for him, that if I knew any thing against his Person or State, I would tell it freely, and upon that whispered some things to his Confessors, which *Voisin* did presently write.

Being about five of the Clock, *Baranton* was sent to tell him it was time to go; let us go said he, seeing I must die, and desired he would charge his Brothers from him, to remain faithful to the King, and not to go to Court, till time had blotted, or at least lessened the shame of his death. He kneeled before the Altar, and having ended his Prayer, he desired the Company to pray for him.

Coming out of the Chappel, he met the Executioner, who offered to follow him, and he thinking it was to bind him; keep off, (said he) and do not touch me till it be time; I shall go willingly to die without troubling any body; but it shall never be said that I am dead like a Slave, or a Thief, and swore by God that if he came near him he would strangle him. The Divines exhorted him going down the stairs to resist those impaciencies and temptations of the Devil, who striveth most to deviate the Soul from her Salvation, when as he hath most need of the Divine assistance to withstand his assaults, remonstrating also unto him, that all his violences and passions could not hinder the Soul to depart from a place where she was but a Tenant at Will. He hearkened to them, and saying three times ah, ah, ah, raising his voice at every one, he said, is there no Mercy in the world, I see to day, that all the world hath forsaken me.

He came into the Yard, and seeing the Lieutenant of the City, in whose house the King had put *la Fin*, to secure him from all attempts, My Lord Lieutenant (said he) I am very much your friend, take heed to have any thing to do with that Witch and Magician that lyeth at your house, if you meddle with him he will undo you.

The Scaffold was set up in the corner of the Yard, over against the Garden gate, six foot high, and seven long, without any Ornament or distinction. He kneeled upon the first step, lifted up his Eyes to Heaven and made a short Prayer, like a Souldier, and went up as couragiously as if he had gone to an assault, clad in a Gray Taffety Suit, with a black Hat on his Head, but as soon as he saw the Executioner, he looked furiously upon him, and bid him stand aside till he were ready to receive the last stroke: He threw his Hat, his Handkarchief, and Doublet to the first that would take it, nevertheless one of the Executioners men was nimbler than all the rest, and looking upon the Souldiers that kept the Gate armed, with Musquets and Fire-locks. Ah! said he, must I die? is there no pardon? if at least some of those good fellows would shut me (opening his Breast) he should oblige my very much, what pity is it to die so miserably, and of so shameful a blow, then directing his speech to the Spectators, he said, I have put my Soul into such a state as she ought to be to appear before the face of Almighty God, but I pity that of the King, who causeth me to die unjustly: I have erred I confess, but I never attempted anything against the Kings Person, he should have been dead ten years ago if I would have believed the evil Councel that was given me concerning that the trouble and distress of his Soul was so great, that a little while before he said three years, and now he says ten; the Divines having setled him a little once more, he received their absolution.

The Executioner then presented unto him a Frontlet, but it proved to him a new wound, an increase of grief, and swore if he toucht him any other way than with the Sword he would strangle him, & thereupon he asked again for his own Handkarchief to make use of it, his hollow and gastly Eyes shewed he was not in his right mind. *Voisin* intreated him to be patient, and to raise his thoughts to the place where his Soul was to go, and to be attentive to the reading of his Sentence. He was unwilling to hear the repetition of his Crimes, and to have occasion to exclaim again against the Iniquitie, of those that had condemned him, against the Kings cruelty, as he called it, that would not grant him his pardon, and that this was to make him feel death before death. *Voisin* answered, that it could not be done otherwise. He answered that every body knew for what reason he was there and then as if it were by confession, he said, *well, read*, and thereupon held his Peace till *Voisin* came to these words, *for having attempted against the Kings Person*; for then he fell into a passion again, as he had done before, and said, that it was false, that this never came into his mind, that as God was his Judge, he would be for ever deprived of his Grace if it were true, that since two and twenty Months he had done nothing against the Kings service, that it is true he had written some Letters, but that the King had forgiven him, protesting and calling the Spectators to Witness, that it was the truth what he spoke, as he would answer it before God, and spoke so many words, and so fast that neither he nor the Sheriff could be understood.

The Sentence being read, the Divines did admonish him to leave all Earthly thoughts, to implore the assistance of Heaven, and to resign his Soul to the Eternal providence of the Almighty, and his Body to what the Law had ordained of it, he made some Prayer to God, and bound his Eyes with his own Handkarchief, and asked the Executioner in what place he was to put himself, the Executioner pointing with his finger, said, there my Lord; he pulled off his Handkarchief in a rage, and where is that there, said he? thou seest I am blind fold, and thou shewest me as if I could see; he bound himself again, and bid the Executioner to dispatch quickly: The Executioner told him he ought to kneel, for fear he should do something amiss. No, no, said he, I shall not stir, if thou canst not do it at one blow do it at thirty, he was intreated again to kneel, which he did, and spoke these Imperious words, dispatch, dispatch, then rose up again, and untied his Handkarchief, and by casting his Eyes upon the Executioner, made the people believe, that either he had a mind to seize upon the Sword, or that he was terribly afrighted by the approaches of Death, and began again his former complaints, is there no pardon? must I die so miserably? after so many services. The Executioner intreated him to suffer his hairs behind to be cut off; he began to swear again fearfully, that if he toucht him otherwise than with the Sword, he would strangle him. The Divines told him that he was too carefull of his Body, he would hear no more of that, but fell into a rage, and swore, that he would not be toucht by so Infamous a Person as long as he was alive, that if they did provoke him too much, he would strangle half the Company, and oblige the other half to kill him, those that were upon the Scaffold went down and left him with the Executioner, who repented himself heartily that he had taken the care of him unbound.

The Divines went up again upon the Scaffold, and desired him for the love of God to resolve to step over that pass, which was necessary for every man to do, and with some few other words, whispered into his ears, did calm him a little, and made him resolve to undergo the Execution, after he had made many complaints, and shewed great fears of dying. A strange thing that as stout and valiant a man as ever was born, who had so many times cast himself amongst the greatest dangers, without any fear or apprehension, as if there was no death for him, should shew himself now so fearful at the coming of it; we may judge by this, that the apprehension of death is incomparably greater when it cometh upon a cold blood, and those that know what his Chirurgion was wont to say, shall less wonder at it; for he said, that the Duke of *Biron* used to wonder at himself, that being not afraid of the thrust of a Sword, nevertheless he was very timerous at the pricking of a Launcet, when he had occasion to be let blood: Whereupon we must confess, that the greatest courage, and most undaunted stoutness of a man, is nothing in comparison of human Natures weakness.

The Divines judging him to be out of fear, gave him his last absolution, he kneeled again, and cried aloud three times, *My God, my God, my God, have Mercy upon me*, then turning to the Executioner, he took the headband that he had in his hand, and intreated *Baranton* to do him that last curtesie as to lift up his hairs behind, which *Baranton* did, and the Duke himself did tie the Handkarchief about his Eyes. The Divines seeing him in that good disposition, did assure him, that he was ready to go to Heaven, and to see God, and to enjoy his Glory. Yes, said he, Heaven is open to receive my Soul, and so stooped his neck for the Executioner to do his office. The Executioner considering, that he had untied himself three times before, and might do so again for the fourth, thought fitting to entertain him with fair words, to desire his forgiveness, and to put him in mind of saying his last Prayer, in the mean time he beckened to his man, who was at the foot of the Scaffold, to reach him the Sword, which no sooner was in his hand, but the Duke of *Birons* Head was off his Shoulders, it fell from the Scaffold to the ground, and was thrown again by the Executioners man upon the Scaffold, the Body was stript to its Shirt, and wraped in a Sheet, and the same day buried, about nine of the Clock at night, in St. *Pauls* Church, without any shew or Ceremony. Thus ended the Tragical History of the Duke of *Biron*.

Now follows the two last Verses of this Prophecie.

A Post overtaken in the Countrey, And the Scrivener shall cast himself into the Water.

Which as we have said before, were concerning *Nicolas L'oste*, Secretary to the Lord *Villeroy*, chief Secretary of State. The History therefore is thus.

The *French* Embassador at *Madrid*, complained once to *Henry* the IV. he was so ill informed, and so late of Affairs, that the King of *Spain*'s Ministers knew them before him: The King was a great while troubled before he could discover the spring of that infidelity, at last it came out in this manner. *Villeroy* that great Oracle of *France,* and the most confident Secretary to the King, had among his servants one *Nicolas l'Oste,* born at *Orleans,* in whom he did confide so much the more, because his Father had been the most part of his life in his service.

The Lord *Rochepot* going Embassador into *Spain, Oste* desired to be admitted into his Family, to serve him as his secretary, that he might the better fit himself for publick employment. *Villeroy*'s commendation got him easily that employment, by which in a few Months he became so capable of the *Spanish* Tongue and manners, that no body could have distinguished him from a natural *Spaniard.* The Embassador having sworn in the name of the most Christian King the treaty of Peace made at *Veruins,* the King of *Spain* presented him with a rich Chain of Jewels, and with six other of Gold, valued at 150. Crowns apiece, to bestow upon as many of his own servants as he should think fit.

The pride and presumption of this young man was such as to perswade him he deserved one of them, and chiefly because one of his fellows was thought worthy of it, but his Master did not think so, and thus he was neglected.

Thus envy and jealousie were the Windows by which the Devil crept into his soul; the vanity, lying, pride, and debauchery gave him a full admittance, he had spent all his Money to buy the love of a Courtisane, and wanted means to follow that course which he had no mind to leave off. His Masters neglecting of him, had extraordinarily vexed him, but he comforted himself that he knew his secrets, and that in revealing them to the King of *Spains* Ministers he shot two Birds with one shot; for he should avenge himself of that contempt he had received, and should have a way to continue his amorous expences. With that intention he made himself known to *Don Franchese* one of the Secretaries of State, and told him what means he had to serve the King of *Spain,* and to shew him proofs of that service and affection he had vowed to him long before, by imparting to him all the Letters that the Embassador did both send and receive from the King his Master.

Don Franchese heard this proposition as from a young man, whose Brains were not well settled, or perhaps did abhor such infidelity, therefore told him coldly, that the Catholick King was in so good amity with the most Christian one, that he desired to know no more of his business, than what his Embassador should tell him.

L'Oste did not despond for all this, but went to *Don Ydiaques* another Secretary of State, who knowing how important it is for a Prince to know the secrets of his Neighbours, and that the slighting of such an offer would be prejudicial to the King his Masters Service, did hearken unto this Traitor, approved of his design, and exhorted him to persevere in the good affection he shewed to the King of *Spains* service, promised to acquaint the King with it, and to procure him such a reward, as he should have reason to be satisfied with.

The Councel agreed that *L'Oste* should be incouraged, and *Don Ydiaques,* presented him to the Duke of *Lerma,* to whom he shewed the Alphabet of Cyphers, with which his Master writ his Letters into *France,* and for a further proof unciphered the last Letter that the King of *France* had sent. The Duke exhorted him to continue his good Will, gave him 1200. Crowns for an earnest of the Bargain, with a promise of as much for a yearly pension, besides a considerable gratification he was to expect from the King.

Since that time the *French* Embassador received no Letters but they were presently imparted to the *Spanish* Councel: But the Lord *la Rochepot* being called back into *France,* *L'Oste* lost the conveniency of prosecuting his Treasons, and consequently the hopes of his promised reward, therefore sought means to come again into his first Masters, that is, *Villeroy*'s service, but he was a while kept back from it by reason of a difference between his Mother and *Villeroy,* about some rest of Accounts; but *L'Oste* had rather take that loss upon him than to be deprived of that occasion. The Embassador himself gave him a large Testimony Of his ability and faithfulness, and was Instrumental for his re-admission into that service.

Thus being re-established, he became more diligent and sedulous than ever before, and not only writ more Letters than any of his fellows, but also offered them his service to help them, that he might have a more perfect knowledge of all transactions, and so impart them to the *Spaniard*, and so visited and conferred with *Taxis* the *Spanish* Embassador at *Paris*, and after that with his successor, *Don Baltazar de Cuniga*, with so much cunning and secrecy, that the Councel of *Spain* received his Letters, before *des Barreaux* the *French* Embassador at *Madrid*, could receive those of the King.

Des Barreaux sent word to the King, that when he propounded any thing, according to his Majesties command, to the Councel of *Spain*, he found them always preadvised, and could not find out by what means; certainly said the King, there must be some in my Councel that keep a strict intelligence with the *Spaniard*, and I can not tell whom to suspect. Providence doth often draw good effects out of the worse causes, and permitteth that the wicked should disclose one anothers wickedness, as a Nail driveth out another. *Loste* had revealed himself familiarly to one *Raffis*, formerly Secretary to the Lord *Lansac*, a fugitive into *Spain*, for many Treasons, and exempted from pardon; but the *Spaniard* had begun to cut him short of his former Pensions, since the Treason of the Baron of *Fontanelles*, Governour of *Dornavenest* in *Brittanny*, in which the said *Raffis* had been a principal Actor, though in vain, so that since, the Councel of *Spain* looked upon him as an unprofitable servant, and withdrew their Pension.

Raffis finding himself near a great want and misery, thought this occasion might be a means to prevent it, and to procure his return into his native Countrey, by doing so great a service to his Prince; therefore he went to one of the *French* Embassadors most faithful servants, and told him his grief, for having had a share in so many Treasons and Rebellions in *France*, which he acknowledged God had into his particular protection, that he was resolved to blot out the memory of them by a notable service done to the King and Kingdom, but that could not be, unless he had first obtained pardon for all his former misdemeanors.

This being told to the Embassadour, he heard *Raffis*, who told him in general that the King was betrayed, and his most secret Councel bewrayed, but that he could not name the Traitor, no not to his Majesty himself, before he had his pardon: that being done, he would wholly withdraw himself from those whom he knew certainly to be enemies to the Kingdom. The Embassadour sent an express to the King to give him notice of it. The King sent him full power to treat with *Raffis*, with promiss to ratifie whatsoever he should promiss to *Raffis*; *Raffis* could not make good his accusation, but by two Letters written by *Loste*, to a great friend of his, named *Blas*, which Letters he knew to be in a Box of *Blas*, who lodged with him; therefore upon some pretext or another, they found means to send *Blas* as far as l'*Escurial*. In his absence *Raffis* and *Descardes* Secretary to the Embassadour, broke open the Box, and took out the Letters, by which *Loste* did much magnifie the liberalities of *Spain*, as being above his desert and expectation; with this proofs and the Embassadors Letters, *Raffis* fained to go to a Monastery near *Madrid*, and there make his devotions upon Palm-Sunday, as he was wont to do, but he went directly to *Bayone*, where he met with *Discardes* upon a set day. *Blas* came back after Palm-Sunday, and finding his Box open, and his companion run away, he suspected the matter, and gave notice of it to the *Spanish* Ministers, who presently dispatched two Courriers to the *Spanish* Embassador at *Paris*, to give him notice that a man was gone from *Madrid*; who would discover *Loste* and his practises, therefore he should give him notice of it, and bid him look to himself, and that in case he should be taken, to keep secresie.

Descardes and *Raffis* came to *Paris* the *Wensday* after Easter, and carried themselves with all faithfulness in this occasion, but not with all the prudence that could have been desired. *Villeroy* was going the same day to lie at his own House, between *Paris* and *Fountain-bleau*, where the Court was then; they met with him at *Juvisy*, and waited on him as far as *Villeroy*, but told him nothing of the occasion of their coming by the way, till they presented him with the Embassadors Letters, which was a notable fault, for he would certainly have neglected all other business to secure his man, who was then doing his devotions at the Charter-house of *Paris*.

The next day *Villeroy* was the first that told the King of the coming of *Raffis*, and of the perfidiousness of his own servant. As he was going back to his Lodging, notice was given him that two *Spanish* Courtiers were arrived at the Post-house; he commanded one of the Commissioners of the Post-house, that he should cause them to withdraw into a Room, and that no body should speak with them; he charged also *Descardes*, that he should spy the coming of *Loste*, that he should keep him close company, and send him presently notice of his arrival. The Commissioner and *Descardes* did commit here another great fault, for *Loste* being come to the Post-house about noon, this silly Commissioner told him that there were arrived two *Spanish* Courtiers who asked for him, that they had Letters for him, and more then that, suffered him to go into their Chamber and see them, he saluted them, and one of them whispered him in the ear that he was undone if he did not save himself presently, and that *Raffis* had discovered him; fear and astonishment with his guilty conscience, persuaded him easily to look to himself.

Nevertheless, he settled his countenance the best he could, he went out with an intention to take his Horse again, which he had sent before, and so save himself; *Descardes* and *Raffis* perceived him, *Descardes* came and saluted him, and thinking perhaps that he was strong enough to give an account of him, neglected to send word to *Villeroy*, who was then in his Closet with the Bishop of *Chartres*; *Descardes* presence was a great thorn in *Loste*'s foot, to be rid of him, he said he was going to his Master, who stayed for him; *Descardes* offered to accompany him: he answered, he had not dined, and that believing it was past Dinner time at home, he would go into some Cabaret to look for a Dinner, the other answered I have not dinned neither, we shall dine together. *Loste* found another excuse, and said my Boots hurt me, I pray give me leave that I may go and pull them off; *Descardes* answered, he must needs drink with him. Thus arguing together, they came to *Villeroy*'s Lodging, where *Descardes* thinking to have him sure, left him in the Room, not knowing that the *Spanish* Courtiers had talked with him, and came near the Closet to give notice of it to *Villeroy*; but as soon as he saw himself rid of *Descardes*, he went down into the Stable, and finding his Horse yet Sadled he Mounted, and with all speed rid to *Paris*; *Villeroy* in the mean time having notice that his man was come, he commanded they should bring them in; but he was not to be found, nor his Horse neither, no body knowing which way he was gone. *Villeroy* told the King that his man was escaped, they sent after him on all sides, and *Villeroy* particularly sent all his Servants after into all the ways. *Loste* coming to *Paris* about nine of the Clock at night, went to take counsel of the *Spanish* Embassadour, and before day, went out habited like a *Spaniard*, with the Embassadors Steward, and took his way towards *Meaux*, with an intent to get into *Luxembourg* by Poste.

That every one might endeavour the apprehending of that Traitor, it was spread abroad that one of *Villeroy*'s Secretaries had attempted upon the Kings Person, and notice was given of his Stature, Age, Cloaths and Horse. The Sheriffs of every Countrey were in quest, and all Post-Masters were forbidden to let out any Horses, but that of *Meaux* had notice of it too late; *Loste* was got on Horseback already, but assoon as he began to gallop, his Horse fell to the ground, and was an ill *Omen* to the Rider; he got up again, and shewed so much fearfulness in his Countenance, that the Postillion himself thought he had committed some notorious villany, which he did run for. Being come home, he gave notice of it to his Master, who suspecting him to be the man enquired off, he gave notice of it to the Sheriff, who presently made after him at the second Ferry of *la Ferte soubs Jouare*, where he was Crossing the River; the Sheriff cried after the Ferry man to come back, but the fear of his life, which the two run aways put him into, prevailed upon him, above the Sheriffs commands, being got over, and judging that their Post-Horses should be quickly overtaken by those of the Sheriff, they forsook them and the Postillion; and trusted to their heels in the darkness of the night among the Bushes and Brambles that are upon the River *Marne*. The Sheriff scattered his men all about, caused fires to be made, and raised up all the Countrey people thereabout; the *Spaniard* ran over the Champion Countrey, and *Loste* went from Bush to Bush, and whether accidentally or wilfully he fell into the River *Marne*, where he was drowned; the next day his Hat was found between two posts, and his body two days after not far from that place.

Thus you may plainly see the full event of those two famous Prophecies, contained in this sixth Stanza.

VII.

French.

La Sangsue au Loup se joindra, Lors qu'en Mer le bled defaudra, Mais le grand Prince sans envie, Par Ambassade luy donra, De son bled pour luy donner vie, Pour un besoing s'en pourvoira.
English.

The Leech will joyn it self to the Wolf, When in the Sea Corn shall be wanting, But the great Prince without envy, By Embassy shall give him, Of his Corn to give him life, Of which in his need he shall make provision.

ANNOT.

By the *Leech* is understood the *Spaniard*. By the *Wolf* is meant the *French*, by reason of the multitude of those Creatures in that Kingdom; the meaning therefore of this Prophecy is, that there should be a great famine in *Spain*, wherein the *Spaniard* should be constrained to make his application to the *French* for relief of Corn, which should be granted him. This happened in the year 1665 for you must understand that most of these last Prophecies were to be fulfilled in the Reign of *Henry* IV.

VIII.

French.

Un peu devant l'ouvert commerce, Ambassadeur viendra de Perse, Nouvelle au Franc Pais porter, Mais non receu vaine esperance, A son grand Dieu sera l'offense, Feignant de le vouloir quitter.
English.

A little before that Trade shall be open, An Embassador shall come from *Persia*, To bring news into *France*, But he shall not be received, O vain hope! To his great God shall the offence be, Faining that he would leave him.

ANNOT.

In the year 1608. the year before the Truce was concluded between the *Spaniard* and the *Hollanders*, by which all free Commerce was opened through *Europe*. The King of *Persia* being then in War with the great *Turk*, sent an Embassador to all the Christian Princes, and chiefly into *France*, to move them to make a diversion in so fit a time, but he could prevail nothing, and went back again *re infecta*, which he thought to be a great injury done to his Prophet *Mahomet*.

IX.

French.

Deux Estendars du costé de l'Auvergne, Senestre pris, pour un temps prison regne, Et un Dame enfant voudra mener, An Censuart, mais discouvert l'affaire, Danger de mort, murmure sur la Terre, Germain, Bastille, Frere & Sœur prisonier. English.

Two Standards in the County of *Auvergne*, The left one taken, for a while Prison shall reign, And a Lady shall endeavour to carry a child To the Censuart, but the plot being discovered, Danger of Death, murmur upon Earth, Own Brother, *Bastille*, Brother and Sister prisoners.

This Stanza being most obscure and difficult, cannot be understood so well by parcels, as by laying down the whole *Synopsis* of it, which I do the more willingly, because I think it will be delightful to the Reader, and that the whole being known, the meaning of every particular will easily be understood.

Charles the IX. King of *France*, the last of the House of *Valois* left only one natural Son, called the Earl of *Auvergne*, who had a Sister by the Mothers side, that was called *Henrietta de Balzac* Duchess of *Verneuil*, once Mistriss to *Henry* the IV. by whom she had upon promiss of marriage one Son, at this time Duke of *Verneuil*, and Governour of *Languedoc*; but this promiss being made void by Act of Parliament, *Henry* IV. married *Mary* of *Medicis*, by which he had issue *Lewis* the XIII. and other children: now upon the discontent of the Marshal of *Biron*, the Dutchess of *Verneuil*, the Earl of *Auvergne* her Brother, and their party joyned with him for the promoting of the Duke of *Verneuil*'s interest to the Crown, whereupon the King sent for the Earl of *Auvergne*, who was then in his County a hundred Leagues from *Paris*; but the Earl trusting more the good will of the Citizens of *Clermont* in *Auvergne* who loved him, then to the Kings Clemency, neglected to come, whereupon the King sent again the Lord d'*Escures*, with a pardon for what was past; he promised to come when he should see his pardon Signed and Sealed in good form; the King was offended at his proceeding, and took it very ill that a Subject of his would capitulate with him, who intended to deal plainly and sincerely; the King nevertheless past that over for many considerations, one of them was that the Earl was of the blood of *France*, and brother by the Mother to one that had been his Mistress, besides that he was a Prince endowed with many good qualities, most of which did Sympathise with those of the King, thus the King sent him his Pardon as well for what was past, as for the present, but with this proviso that he should come; for all this, he did not stir out of *Clermont*; the King seeing that, did resolve to have him at any rate: there was several propositions made for to take him: at Hunting, at running of the Ring, at some Banquet, in the Fields, in the City; all these ways might be suspected by the Earl, but a new one was found out, of which he himself was the Author; the Troop of the Duke of *Vendosme* was preparing for to Muster, the Earl intreated d'*Eurre* Lieutenant of the said company, that it might be in the Fields by *Clermont* towards *Nonnain*, because he intended to take revenge in the behalf of a Lady, upon the Inhabitants of that place. The King sent directions and orders to d'*Eurre*, how he should govern himself in that action, and gave him for Associates, *la Boulaye*, Lieutenant of the Marquess of *Verneuil*'s Troop, and *Nerestan* Colonel of a Foot Regiment. By the Kings advice they imparted the business to the Viscount of *Pont du Chasteau*, to the Baron of *Canillac* and some others, that had authority in that Province, and were devoted to the Kings service, and all keeping religiously the Laws of silence. The 12 of *November* the Troop met at the Rendezvous; the Earl came thither by times with two only of his followers, thinking that the Troop should not be ready so soon, and so he should have pretext either to go back to *Clermont*, or to go on further to visit his Mistress. The prudence and diligence of those that managed the business did prevent him, and begot a suspition in him, for he was seen to truss up his Cloak and to try whither his sword did not stick to the Scabbard. D'*Eurre* went to him, and having complemented him rode on his left hand, while the Troop was setting in order; *Nerestan* came to salute him on the other side, and rode on his right hand, being followed by three stout Souldiers, habited like Lackeys, and appointed for this action. The Viscount of *du Pont du Chasteau* and his brother rode out of the Troop and encompassed him on all sides. One of the Souldiers laid hold on the Horses Bridle; d'*Eurre* at the same time laid hold on his Swords Hilt, saying, my Lord, we are commanded by the King to give him an account of your person, and we intreat you to submit unto his Majesties good pleasure, that we may have no occasion to use you otherways then we desire. *Maison-ville* and *Liverne* who were his two followers drew their Swords, thinking to make him way to escape, but some shot spent upon them, made them presently retire and run away. He was put upon a Trumpeters Nag as far as *Briare*, and thence conducted to *Montargis* in a Coach, and afterwards by water to *Paris* and put in the Bastille.

By this History, and the explication of the word *Censuart*, which is an ancient word derived from the Latine word *Censor*; and taken here for the Kingly office, the whole Prophecy is easily understood, and obvious to the meanest capacity.

X.

French.

Embassadeur pour une Dame, A son Vaissau mettra la rame, Pour prier le grand Medecin, Que de l'Oster de telle peine, Mais a ce s'opposera Roine, Grand peine avant qu'en voir la fin. English.

An Embassador for a Lady, Shall set Oares to his Ship, To intreat the great Physition, To take her out of such pain, But a Queen shall oppose it, A great deal of trouble before the end of it.

ANNOT.

This Prophecy is concerning *Mary Stuart* Queen of *Scots* put in Prison by Queen *Elizabeth*, who is called here the opponant Queen, to the Embassy that the said Queen of *Scots* sent for relief to the King of *France*, called here the great Physitian.

XI.

French.

Durant le Siecle on verra deux ruisseaux, Tout un terrouer inonder de leurs eaux, Et submerger par Ruisseaux & Fontaines, Coups, & Monfrein, Beccoyran & Alais, Par le Gardon bien souvent travaillez, Six cens & quattre, Ales & trente Moines. English.

In this Age two Rivolets shall be seen, To overflow a whole Countrey with their waters, And to drown by Rivolets and Fountains, *Coups*, and *Monfrein*, *Beccoiran* and *Alais*, By the *Gardon* often troubled, Six hundred and four *Alais*, and thirty Monks.

ANNOT.

An Age is the space of one hundred years, the meaning therefore of this is, that within the Age following, his Prophecies namely as he saith after, in the year 1664. there shall be great Inundation in *Languedoc*, caused by the overflowing of two small Rivers, besides that of *Gardon*, which Inundation shall drown these following places, *Coups*, *Monfrein*, *Becoyran* and *Alais*, besides, and Abbey wherein there was 30. Monks, but of this I could find nothing in the History, therefore those that live about those places must make it good.

XII.

Six cens & cinq tres grand nouvelle, De deux Seigneurs la grand querelle, Proche de Gevaudan sera, En une Eglise apres l'offrande, Meuttre commis, prestre de mande, Tremblant de peur se sauvera. English.

In six hundred and five shall be great news; The quarrel of two great Lords, Shall be near *Gevaudan,* In a Church after the Offering, A murder committed, the Priest shall ask, And quaking for fear, shall save himself.

ANNOT.

This (like the former) is a particuler accident, of which the publick History taketh no notice; it seemeth that in the year 1665. in *Gevaudan,* a Province of *France* near *Languedoc,* there was a great quarrel between two Lords who meeting at Church, did about the time of the Offering set one upon another, and one of them was killed, whereupon the Priest being terrified, ran away.

XIII.

French.

L'aventurier, six cens, & six ou neuf, Sera surpris par fiel mis dans un Oeuf, Et peu apres sera hors de puissance, Par le puissant Empereur General, Qu'ou Monde nest an pereil ny esgal, Dont un chascun luy rend obeissance. English.

The adventurer, six hundred, six or nine, Shall be surprised by Gall put into an Egge, And a little while after shall be out of power, By the potent Emperour General, To whom in the world there is not his like or equal, Wherefore every one yieldeth obedience to him.

ANNOT.

This Prophecie was concerning the Duke of *Savoy* and *Henry* the IV. for about that time mentioned by the Author, after the death of Marshal *de Biron,* who sided with the Duke of *Savoy* (which death is called here Gall put into an Egg;) the Duke of *Savoy* refused to perform the treaty concerning the restitution of the Marquisate of *Saluces,* wherefore *Henry* the IV. went and subdued most of his Countrey, and compelled him to give the Province of *Bresse* instead of the said Marquisate.

XIV.

French.

Au grand Siege encor grand forfaits, Recommenceant plus que jamais, Six cens & cinq sur la verdure, La prise & reprise sera, Soldats es Champs jusqu' en froidure, Puis apres recommencera.
English.

At the great Siege yet great misdemeanors, Beginning again more than ever, Six hundred and five about the Spring, The taking and retaking shall be, Souldiers in the fields till Winter, And after that shall begin again.

ANNOT.

This Stanza is about the same subject as the precedent. By the great Siege here is meant the Siege of *Montpelian*, the strongest place in *Savoy*, which *Henry* the IV. took, and by it compelled the Duke of *Savoy* to an agreement. The rest is easie.

XV.

French.

Nouveau esleu Patron du grand Vaisseau, Verra long temps briller le grand flambeau, Qui sert de Lampe a ce grand territoire, Et auquel temps Armées soubs son nom, Jointes a celles de l'heureux de Bourbon, Levant, Ponant, & Couchant sa memoire. English.

The new elected Master of the great Ship, Shall a great while see the great light shine, Which serveth for a Lamp to this great Territory, And at which time Armies under his name, Joyned with those of happy of *Bourbon*, East, West, and North his memory shall be.

ANNOT.

The three first Verses are concerning *Clement* the VIII. who was elected Pope about that time, and was Instrumental to make a Peace between the King of *France* and the Duke of *Savoy*, and was Pope a good while.

By the great Ship is meant the Church, of which he is called Master. The rest is easie.

XVI.

French.

En Octobre Six cens & cinq, Pour voieur du Monstre Marin, Prendra du Souverain le cresme, Ou en six cens & six en Juin, Grand joye aux Grands & au Commun, Grand faits apres ce grand Baptesme. English.

In *October* six hundred and five, The Purveyor of the Sea Monster, Shall take the unction of the Sovereign, Or in six hundred and six in *June*, Great joy shall be to the Great ones, and to the Commons, Great feats shall be after this great Baptism.

In the year 1606. the 14 of *September*, instead of which the printer hath put *October*, the Dolphin of *France, Lewis* the XIII. son to *Henry* the IV. was Christened with his two Sisters at *Fountainbleau*, and because the Ceremonies were extraordinary, and our Author calleth this a great Baptism, it will not be amiss for the satisfaction of the curious Reader, to give here succinctly a description of it.

In the great quadrangle of the Castles Yard, was erected a great Theatre, all spread and hanged with most rich Carpets and Hangings, in the middle of which Theatre was a square of thirty foot on each side, with rails about it, all covered with Carpets, in the front of it was erected an Altar, adorned with the Ornaments belonging to the Order of the Holy Ghost, behind the Table was a Footstool of three steps, spread with Carpets, and in the middle of the Footstool was a kind of a Stand, covered with a Silver Cloth, upon which were the Fount, covered with a most exquisite Towel, and a Canopy over it, on both sides of the Altars were two Scaffolds for two Quires of Musick, and a little lower on the right hand a Bench covered with Carpets for the Prelates to sit, among which were three Archbishops, nine Bishops and three Abbots, on the left hand were the Lords of the Councel, and before the Altar was the Cardinal of *Gondy*, encompassed with Almoners and Chaplains, and a great multitude of spectators seated upon Benches, in form of a Theatre, round about the Theatre were the guard of *Switzers*, having every one a Torch in his hand.

The Dolphin and his Sisters were in their Chambers upon Beds of State, with their Robes lined with Hermines, and were brought to the quadrangle, the waiting Gentlemen going before with Torches in their hands, with the Bed Chamber men, and Gentlemen of the Chamber, five Drums, Waits, and Trumpeters, Heralds, and the Knights of the Holy Ghost, with the three Honours; in the first, for the youngest Daughter, the Ewer, the Bason, the Pillow, the Wax Taper, the Chrisme, the Saltseller, were carryed by the Baron, Son to Marshal *de la Chastre*, by the Lords *Montigny, la Rochepot, Chemerand, Liencourt, Fervacques*, and the Lady was carryed by the Marshal of *Bois Dauphin*, followed by *Charles* Duke of *Lorrain* Godfather, and of *Don Juan de Medicis*, Brother to the great Duke of *Tuscany*, representing *Christian*, Daughter to the Duke of *Lorrain*, and Wife of the great Duke. After that followed the Dutches of *Guise*, the Countesses of *Guiche*, of *Saulx*, the Marchioness *Monlaur*, and other Ladies.

The Marshals of *Laverdin*, and of *la Chastre*, the Dukes of *Silly*, of *Monbazon*, of *Espernon*, of *Esguillon* did the same office for the elder Lady. The Lord of *Ragny* carryed her for *Diana* Dutchess of *Angoulesme*, who did represent the *Infanta, Clara, Eugenia, Eusabella*, Archidutchess of *Austria*, followed by the Dutchess of *Rohan, Montmorency, Mayenne*.

The third Honour for the Dolphin was carried by the Earl of *Vaudemont*, the Knight of *Vendosme* his elder Brother, the Duke of *Mensier*, the Earl of *Soissons*, and the Prince of *County*, all three Princes of the Blood, and the Dolphin was carryed by the Lord *Souvray* his Governour, in the room of the Prince of *Condé*, first Prince of the Blood, who because of his sickness could do him no other service then to hold him by the hand. The Duke of *Guise* carryed his Train, and the Cardinal of *Joyouse* followed him, representing the Pope *Paul* the V. then followed *Eleonor* Wife to *Vincent* Duke of *Mantua*, and the Princess of the Blood, all richly attired.

The Dolphin being brought upon the Table of the quadrangle, the Cardinal of *Gondy* appointed for this Ceremony, came near him; and having heard him answer pertinently to the questions asked by the Almoner according to the usual forms, and to say the Lords Prayer and the Creed in Latine, he was exercised, appointed, and by the Cardinal of *Joyouse Legat*, named *Lewis*.

The Ladies were afterwards brought upon the Table, and the eldest, named *Elizabeth* by the Dutchess of *Angoulesme*, representing the Archidutchess her Godmother, without any Godfather.

The youngest was named by *Don Juan* of *Medicis* (representing the great Dutchess) *Christierne*.

At Supper the King was waited upon by the Princess of his Blood; the Prince of *Condé* served for Pantler, the Prince of *Compty* for Cupbearer, the Duke of *Monpensier* for Squire Carver, the Earl of *Soissons* for high Steward, the Duke of *Guise* and the Earl of *Vondemont* waited upon the Queen, and the Duke of *Sully* waited upon the Legat. The Godfathers sat, and after them the Princesses, Ladies and Lords of high quality, at the great Ball the Duke of *Lorrain* did precede by the Kings order, for the only consideration that he was Godfather.

The next day there was a runing at the Ring, and at night the Duke of *Sully* caused an artificial Castle to be assaulted with an innumerable quantity of Squibs, Chambers, Canon shots, and other Fire Works, but never any thing was seen more incredible or wonderful, then the beauty, ornament and lustre of the Princesses and Ladies of the Court; The Eyes could not stedfastly behold the splendor of the Gold, nor the brightness of the Silver, nor the glittering of Jewels; the Princes and Lords did out vie one another who should be most richly attired, among the rest the Duke of *Espernon* had a Sword valued at 30000. Crowns, and upon the Queens Gown were 32000. Pearls, and 3000. Diamonds.

XVII.

French.

Au mesme temps un grand endurera, Joyeux, malsain, l'an complet ne verra, Et quelques uns qui Seront de la feste, Feste pour un feulement, a ce jour, Mais peuapres sans faire long sejour, Deux se donront l'un l'autre de la teste. **English.**

At the same time a great one shall suffer, Joyful, sickly, shall not see the year compleat, And some others who shall be of the feast, A feast for one only at that day, But a little while after without long delay, Two shall knock one another in the head.

ANNOT.

This Stanza hath relation to the precedent, for about the time of, or a little before that famous Christning died Pope *Leo* the IX. formerly called Cardinal of *Florence*, who did not live a whole year in the papacy; and is called here *Joyful, Sickly*, because though infirm, he did much rejoyce in the obtaining of it; those others that were of the Feast, were some Cardinals of his party, who died also within the same year.

The two last Verses signifie the differences that happened, between *Paul* V. his Successor, and the Common-wealth of *Venice* presently after his death.

XVIII.

French.

Considerant la triste Philomele, Qu'en pleurs & cris sa plainte renouvelle, Racourcissant par tel moyen ses jours, Six cens & cinq elle en verra l'yssue, De son tourment, ia la toile tissue, Por son moien senestre aura secours. **English.**

Considering the sad *Philomela*, Who in tears and cries reneweth her complaint, Shortning by such means her days, Six hundred and five shall see the end, Of her torment, then the Cloath Woven, By her sinister means shall have help.

ANNOT.

This sad *Philomela* was *Henrietta* of *Balzac* Daughter to *Francis* of *Balzac*, Marquess of *Entragues*, and Mistress to *Henry* the IV. who being found guilty of a Conspiracy against the State, was confined to the Abbey of the Nuns of *Beaumont lez Tours*, where she was seven Months, after which the King taking pitty of her, passed a Declaration, wherein in respect of his former Love, and of the Children that he had by her, he forgave her all what was past, did abolish and suppress for ever the Memory of the Crime that she was accused off, and did dispense her from appearing before the Parliament, who in her absence did Register her Letters of Pardon the 6. of *September* 1605. Thus Reader you may see how punctual was our Author in his Prognostications.

XIX.

French.

Six cens & cinq, six cens & six & sept. Nous monstrera jusques l'an dixsept, Du boutefeu l'Ire, haine & envie, Soubs l'Olivier d'assez long temps caché, Le Crocodil sur la Terre a caché, Ce qui estoit mort sera pour lors en vie. English.

Six hundred and five, six hundred and six and seven, Will shew us unto the year seventeen, The anger of the bontefeu, his hatred and envy, Under the Olive-Tree a great while hidden, The Crocodile upon the ground hath hidden, What was dead, shall then be alive.

ANNOT.

This Stanza is so difficult, signifieth nothing but the confusions that have happened in *France* from the year 1605. to the year 1617. which would be too tedious and prolix here to relate, the Reader may see them in the *French* History.

XX.

French.

Celuy qui a par plusieurs fois, Tenu la Cage & puis les bois, Rentre a son premier estre, Vie sauve pen apres sortir, Ne se scachant encor cognoistre, Cherchera subject pour mourir. English.

He that hath many times, Been in the Cage and in the Woods, Cometh again to his first being, And shall go out a little after with his life safe, And not able yet to know himself, Shall seek a subject to be put to death.

ANNOT.

This is yet concerning the Earl of *Auvergne* half Brother to the Dutchess of *Verneuil*, who for his misdemeanours having been put several times in the Bastille, and set free again, nevertheless was attempting still some new thing, which might have endangered his life.

XXI.

French.

L'Autheur des maux commencera Regner, En l'an fix cens & sept sans espargner, Tous les subjects qui sont a la Sangsüe, Et puis apres s'en viendra peu a peu, Au franc Païs rallumer son feu, S'en retournant d'ou elle est issue. English.

The Author of evils shall begin to Reign, In the year six hundred and seven, without sparing, All the subjects that belong to the Leech, And afterwards shall come by little and little, To the free Countrey to kindle again his fire, Going back again from whence it came.

ANNOT.

The Author being a zealous Roman Catholick, calls here the *Hollanders* the Authors of evils, who in the year 1607 and 1608. made a grievous War, and had several successes against the *Spaniard*, with the help of the *French* and *English*, till the year 1609. when by the mediation of the *French* and *English* Embassadors, the Truce was concluded at *Antwerp*, between the Arch-duke and the States of the *United Provinces*, the Articles of it to the number of 38. were solemnly proclaimed and published the ninth of *April*, and ratified by the King of *Spain* in the Month of *July* next ensuing.

XXII.

French.

Cil qui dira descouvrisant l'affaire, Comme du mort, la mort pourra bien faire, Coups de Poniards par un qu'auront induits, Sa fin sera pis qu'il n'aura fait faire, La fin conduit les homines sur la Terre, Gueté par tout, tant le jour que la nuit. English.

He that shall say discovering the business, How of the dead, can make a death well, Strokes of a Dagger by one that hath been induced to it, His end shall be worse then he hath caused to be done, The end leadeth all men upon the Earth, Espied every where, as well by day as by night.

ANNOT.

This Stanza is wholly abstruse and Enigmatical, therefore I will not pretend to expound it, but leave the interpretation to those that have more time and leasure then I.

XXIII.

French.

Quand la grand Nef, la prove & Gouvernail, Du franc Pais, & son Esprit vital, Descueils & slots par la Mer Secovée, Six cens & sept & dix cœur assiegé, Et des reflux de son corps afflegé, Sa vie estant sur ce mal renovée. English.

When the great Ship, the Prow, and Rudder, Of the *French* Countrey, and her vital Spirit, Being tossed by Baks and Waves, Six hundred and seven, and ten, a heart beset, And by the ebbing of his body afflicted, Her life being upon this, evil knotted again.

ANNOT.

This Stanza signifieth the great troubles that were in *France* from the year 1610 in which *Henry* the IV. died, to the year 1617. in which the Marshal d'*Ancre* was killed.

This man was named *Concino Concini* a *Florentine* born, who in a little time was grown very great, and from a base extraction had ascended to the dignity of Marshal of *France*, by the favour of the Queen Regent *Mary* of *Medicis*, and grew so rich, that he offered to the King to maintain at his own charge 6000. foot, and 800. Horses for four Months together; he had made himself Master of many strong Places in *Picardy* and *Normandy*, went about to buy the Government of several Provinces, did dispose of the Kings Exchequer at his pleasure, and spent vast sums of money at his Masters charge. His insolencies were the cause of his ruine, when he thought least of it; for he threatned every one with words and deeds, so far as to say, that he would cause them to eat up their fingers, that should oppose his Will, and so caused many Officers and Souldiers of the contrary party to be put to death. The King *Lewis* the XIII. was particularly informed of the unsufferable pride and misdemeanors of this Marshal, and that his design was to keep up the War in *France*, to continue his Authority and Power; therefore the King commanded *Vitry*, the Captain of his Guards, to apprehend him. This was a difficult thing, because that the Marshal (besides his Menial servants) had always twelve Guards wearing his Livery, that were desperate fellows; there was also another difficulty, because no body could tell, when or at what time he would come to the *Louvre*; nevertheless at last he came to it, upon the 24. of *April* 1617. attended with a great Train and his Guards; the great Gate was opened to him, and presently shut again, *Vitry* drew near to him, and holding his staff to him, said, *I arrest you in the Kings name*, upon these words the Marshal stept back, as if it were to make resistance, saying, *Me?* whereupon those that were with *Vitry* shot three Pistols at him, one did hit him in the Heart, the other in the Head, and the third in the Belly, so that he fell down dead immediately upon his left side, a certain Lord that was on his right hand speaking with him, fell down also without any hurt, but his followers seeing him dead run away.

This death was the cause of great alteration, in the publick Government. The body of the said Marshal was buried at St. *Germain de l'Auxerrois*, but the people digged it out, and dragged it to the new Bridge, where they hanged it by the feet upon a Gibbet, having cut off his Nose, his Ears and his privy parts, then they took him down, and dragged him through the Town, and afterwards burnt it. Thus did perish he that was worth about two Millions of Pounds Sterling, and pretended to make his house perpetual and Sovereign. The new Officers that had governed the State from the 24 of *November* to the 24 of *April* 1617. were arrested in their houses, and the old ones put in again, and the Princes called back again to the Court.

XXIV.

French.

Le Mercurial non de trop longue vie, Six cens & huit & vingt, grand maladie, Et encor pis danger de feu & d'eau, Son grand amy lors luy sera contraire, De tels hazards se pourroit bien distraire, Mais bref, le ser luy sera son Tombeau. **English.**

The *Mercurial* not too long lived, Six hundred and eight and twenty, a great sickness, And what is worse a danger of fire and water, His great friend then shall be against him, He might well avoid those dangers, But a little after, the Iron shall make his Sepulcher.

This is concerning *Lewis* the XIII. King of *France*, who fell dangerously sick of the Plague at *Lions*, about the year 1628. after that went with his Army into *Savoy*, where he escaped many dangers of fire and water. As for the Verse it must not be understood, as if he had been killed, but that the cares he took about his Armies should shorten his days. The fourth Verse is to be understood of the Lord *Bellingham*, then favorite to the King, who forsook him in his sickness, for which he was afterwards disgraced, and could never come into favour again.

XXV.

French.

Six cens & six, six cens & neuf, Un Chancelier gros comme un Bœuf Vieux comme le Phœnix du Monde, En ce Terroir plus ne luira, De la Nef doubly passera, Au Champs Elysiens faire ronde.
English.

Six hundred and six, six hundred and nine, A Chancellor big as an Oxe, Old as the *Phœnix* of the World, Shall shine no more in this Countrey, Shall pass from the Ship of forgetfulness, Into the *Elysian* Fields to go the round.

ANNOT.

Six and nine joyned together makes 15. the meaning of this therefore is, that about the year 1615. should die the Chancellor of *France*, who was then *Nicolas Brulart* Lord of *Sillery* a very corpulent man.

XXVI.

French.

Deux freres sont de l'ordre Ecclesiastique, Dont l'un prendra pour la France la pique, Encor un coup si l'an six cens & six, N'est afflige d'une grand maladie, Les Armes en main jusques six cens & dix, Gueres plus loing ne s'estendant sa vie. English.

Two Brothers are of the Ecclesiastical Order, One of which shall take up the Pike for *France*, Once more, is in the year six hundred and six, He be not afflicted with a great sickness, The Weapons in his hands till six hundred and ten, His Life shall reach not much further.

ANNOT.

In the year 1606. there was two Brothers of the House of *Joyeuse*, one called *Francis* Cardinal of *Joyeuse*, and the other a Capuchin Frier, the rest of the Brothers being dead without issue; Father Angel got a dispensation from the Pope to go out of his Covent, and to Marry, that the Family might not be extinguished, and so turned Courtier and Souldier again, till he had got a Daughter, who was afterwards married to the Duke of *Guise*; after that, remembring his Vows, he turned Capuchin again, and a little while after died, coming from *Rome* to *Paris*.

XXVII.

French.

Celeste seu du costé d'Occident, Et du Midy courir jusqu'au Levant, Vers demy morts sans point trouver racine, Troisiesme Age a Mars le Belliqueux, Des Escarboucles on verra briller feux, Age Escarboucle, & a la fin famine. English.

A Cœlestial fire on the West side, And from the South shall run to the East, Warm, half dead, and incapable to find Roots, The third Age to *Mars* the Warriour, Out of *Carbuncles* fires shall be seen to shine, The Age shall be a *Carbuncle*, but in the end famine.

ANNOT.

This signifies nothing but the troubles that were all *France* over, from the year 1620. to the year 1628. when *Rochel* was taken, and the great famine that was in the year 1626.

XXVIII.

French.

L'An mil six cens & neuf ou quatorziesme Le vieux Charon sera Pasques en Caresme, Six cens & six par escrit le mettra, Le Medecin de tout cecy s'estonne, A mesme temps assigné en personne, Mais pour certain l'un deux comparoistra. English.

In the year a thousand six hundred and nine or fourteen, The old *Charon* shall Celebrate *Easter* in Lent, Six hundred and six shall put it in writing, The Physician wondereth at all this. At the same time being Cited in person, But for certain, one of them shall appear.

ANNOT.

This signifieth that about the time mentioned by the Author, some great one should be very sick in Lent, and should eat flesh, which is called here to *Celebrate Easter in Lent*; and that his Physician wondering at it should fall sick himself, and that without fail, one of them two should die.

XXIX.

French.

Le Griffon Se peut apprester, Pour a l'ennemy resister, Er renforcer bien son Armée, Autrement l'Elephant viendra, Qui d'un abord le surprendra, Six cens & huit, Mer enflammée. English.

The Griffin may prepare himself, To resist the Enemy, And to strengthen his Army, Otherways the Elephant shall come, Who on a sudden shall surprise him. Six hundred and eight, the Sea shall be inflamed.

ANNOT.

By the Griffin was meant the *Hollanders*, who were warned here to beware of the Elephant, that is, the *Spaniard*, and to strengthen their Army for fear of being surprised.

The last Verse signifieth, that in the year 1608. there should be a notable Sea-fight, which was then frequent enough between the said *Hollanders* and *Spaniard*.

XXX.

French.

Dans peu de temps Medicin du grand mal, Et la Sangsue d'ordre & rang inegal, Mettront le feu a la branche d'Olive, Poste courir d'un & d'autre costé, Et par tel feu leur Empire accosté, Se rallumant du franc finy salive. English.

Within a little while the Physician of the great disease, And the Leech, of order and rank unequal, Shall set fire to the branch of Olive, Posts shall run to and fro, And with such fire their Empire acquainted, Shall kindle again with the *French* finished spittle.

ANNOT.

By the Physitian of the great disease, is meant the King of *France*; and the Leech the King of *Spain*, so that it is foretold here, how they shall set fire to the branch of Olive, that is, shall break the Peace and fall to War, which in the year 1636. when upon the imprisoning of the Archbishop of *Triers* by the King of *Spain*, because he had put himself under the *French* Protection, the King of *France* sent an Army of 40000. men in the *Low-Countreys*, to come with the Prince of *Orange* at *Mastricht*, which quarrel hath continued till the Marriage of the King of *France* with the Infanta of *Spain*, Daughter to *Philip* the IV. The last Verse is forced in, only to make up the rime.

XXXI.

French.

Celuy qui a les hazards surmouté, Qui fer, feu, eau, na jamais redouté, Et du Pais bien proche du Basacle, D'un coup de fer tout le Monde eftonné, Par Crocodil estrangement donné, Peuple ravy de voir un tel spectacle. English.

He that hath overcome the dangers, That hath never feared Iron, Fire nor Water, And of the Countrey near the *Basacle*, By a stroke of Iron (all the World being astonished), By a Crocodile strangely given, People will wonder to see such a spectacle.

ANNOT.

This Prophecy may admit of two Interpretations; the first, that *Henry* the IV. who was born in the Province of *Bearn*, not far from *Thoulouze*, the chief City of *Languedoc*, wherein there is a place upon the River called *Basacle*, where the Mills are, who was stobbed with a knife by *Francis Ravillac* in the year 1610.

The other is of the last Duke of *Montmorency*, who being Governour of *Languedoc*, took up Arms against the King, in the behalf of the Duke of *Orleans*, for which he was beheaded at *Thoulouse* at the solicitation of Cardinal *Richelieu*, which happened about the year 1632.

XXXII.

French.

Vin a foison tres-bon pour les Gendarmes, Pleurs & soupirs plaintes, cris, & alarmes, Le Ciel fer ses Tonnerres pleuvoir, Feu, eau, & sang le tout meslé ensemble, Le Ciel de Sol en fremit & en tremble, Vivant na veu ce quil pourra bien voir. English.

Plenty of Wine, very good for Troopers, Tears, and sighs, complaints, cries, and alarums, Heaven shall cause its Thunders to rain, Fire, water and blood, all mixed together, The Suns Heaven, quaketh and shaketh for it, No living man hath seen what he may see then.

ANNOT.

This great plenty of Wine happened in the year 1634. at which time there was in *France* such plenty of Grapes, that half of them perished for want of Vessels to put them in, and I remember very well, that then whosoever would bring a Poinchon Vessel, which is the third part of a Tun, might have it filled with Grapes for half a Crown, and that being my self at that time at a Town of *Burgundy*, called *Beaune*, where the best Wine of *France* groweth, four of us had one Pottle of Wine *English* measure for one half penny. The rest signifieth no more but the miseries that happened in *Germany*, by the Wars that the King of *Sweden* brought in about the same time.

XXXIII.

French.

Bien peu apres sera tres-grand misere, De pou de Bled qui sera sur la Terre, De Dauphiné, Provence & Vivarois, Au Vivarois est un pauvre presage, Pere du fils sera Antrophophage, Et mangeront Racine & gland du Bois. English.

A little after shall be a great misery, Of the scarcity of Corn that shall be upon the ground Of *Dauphine*, *Provence*, and *Vivarois*, In *Vivarois* is a poor presage, Father of son shall be Antropophage, And shall eat Roots and Acorns of the Wood.

ANNOT.

This came to pass when the Duke of *Rohan* headed the Protestant party, and made those Provinces the seat of the Civil Wars in *France*, about the year 1640. or 1642.

XXXIV.

French.

Princes & Seigneurs tous se feront la guerre, Cousin Germain, le Frere avec le Frere, Finy l'Arby de l'heureux de Bourbon, De Hierusalem les Princes aimables, Du fait commis enorme & execrable, Se ressentiront sur la bourse sans fond. English.

Princes and Lords shall war one against another Cousin German, the Brother against the Brother, The Arby finished of the happy *Bourbon*, The Princes of *Hierusalem* so lovely, Of the enormous and execrable fact committed Shall ressent upon the bottomless Purse.

ANNOT.

This foretelleth of the Wars that were to be between the Princes and Lords a little after the death of *Henry* the IV. when the Marshal d'*Ancre* took upon him the administration of affairs by the favour of the Queen Regent *Mary* of *Medicis*.

XXXV.

French.

Dame par mort grandement atristée, Mere & tutrice au lang qui la quittée, Dame & Seigneurs faits enfants Orphelins, Par les Aspics & par les Crocodiles, Seront surpris forts bourgs, Chasteaux & Villes, Dieu tout puissant les garde des malins. English.

A Lady by death greatly afflicted, Mother and Tutor to the Blood that hath left her, Ladies and

Lords made Orphans, By Asps and by Crocodiles, Shall strong holds, Castles and Towns be surprised, God Almighty keep them from the wicked.

ANNOT.

That great Lady afflicted by death, and Mother and Tutor to the Blood that left her was *Mary* of *Medicis*, Wife to *Henry* the IV. who after the death of her Husband was much troubled in her regency by her own Son *Lewis* the XIII. and several great Lords of his party whence did follow the Battle of *Pont de Cé.*

XXXVI.

French.

La grand rumeur qui sera par la France, Les impuissans voudront avoir puissance, Langue emmiellée & vrais Cameleons, De boutefeus, allumeurs de chandelles, Pyes & Geais, rapporteurs de nouvelles, Dont la morsure semblera Scorpions. English.

The great rumor that shall be through *France*, The impuissants would fain have power, Honey Tongues, and true Camelions, Bourefeux, and lighters of Candles, Magpies and Jays, carriers of news, Whose biting shall be like that of Scorpions.

ANNOT.

This hath a relation to the precedent, and expresseth further the misery of those times.

XXXVII.

French.

Foible & puissant seront en grand discord, Plusieurs mourront avant faire l'accord, Foible ou puissant vainqueur se fera dire, Le plus puissant au jeune cedera, Et le plus vieux des deux decedera, Lors que l'un d'eux envahira l'Empire. English.

The Weak and powerfull shall be at great variance, Many shall die before they agree, The weak shall cause the powerful to call him Victor, The most potent shall yield to the younger, And the older of the two shall die, When one of the two shall invade the Empire.

ANNOT.

This Prophecie is not come to pass yet (for all I know) therefore I leave the interpretation to every ones liberty.

XXXVIII.

French.

Par Eau, & par fer & par grand maladie, Le Pourvoieur a l'hazard de sa vie, Scaura combien vaut le Quintal de Bois, Six cens & quinze ou le dixneufiesme, On gravera d'un grand Prince cinquiesme, L'Immortel nom sur le pied de la Croix. **English.**

By Water, by Fire, and by great sickness, The Purveyor to the hazard of his life, Shall know how much is worth the Quintal of Wood, Six hundred and fifteen, or the nineteen, There shall be graven of a great Prince the fifth, The immortal name upon the foot of the Cross.

ANNOT.

By the Purveyor is meant the King of *France*, as we have said before.

The great Prince the V. was *Paul* the V. who was foretold he should die about the year 1615. 1619.

XXXIX.

French.

Le Pourvoieur de Monstre sans pareil, Se sera voir ainsy que le Soleil, Montant le long la ligne Meridienne, En poursuivant l'Elephant & le Loup, Nul Empereur ne fit jamais tel coup, Et rien plus pis a ce Prince n'avienne. **English.**

The Purveyor of the Monster without equal, Shall shew himself like the Sun, Ascending in the Meridional line, In persecuting the Elephant and the Wolf, No Emperour did ever such an act, I wish nothing worse may happen to that Prince.

ANNOT.

This is a Prophecie of the glorious success that *Lewis* the XIII. was to have against the *Spaniard* in *Italy*, and the Protestant party at home.

XL.

French.

Ce qu'en vivant le Pere n'avoit sceu, Il acquerra ou par guerre ou par feu, Et Combatra la sangsue irritée, Ou jouira de son bien paternel, Et savory du grand Dieu Eternel, Aura bien tost sa Province heritée. **English.**

That which while he lived the father did not know, He shall get it either by Water or by Fire, And shall fight with the angry Leech, Or shall enjoy his Paternal goods, And be favorised by the great Eternal God, Shall quickly become Heir of his Province.

This concerneth the present King of *France Lewis* the XIV. who hath lately got by Fire and Sword those Provinces in the *Low Countreys*, to which he laid claim by his Wives Title, which his father never knew nor attempted.

XLI.

French.

Vaisseaux Galeres avec leur Estendar, Sentrebattront pres du Mont Gilbatar, Et lors sera forfait a Pampelonne, Qui pour son bien souffrira mille maux, Par plusieurs fois soustiendra les assaux, Mais a la fin unie a la Coronne. English.

Ships and Galleys with their Standard, Shall fight near the Mountain *Gilbatar,* And then shall be endeavoured against *Pampelonne,* Which for her good shall suffer a thousand evils, And many times shall resist the assaults; But at last shall be united to the Crown.

ANNOT.

This Prophecieth the reduction of the City of *Pampelona*, the chief City of the Kingdom of *Navarre*, under the obedience of the King of *France* and *Navarre*.

XLII.

French.

La grand Cité ou est le premier homme, Bien amplement la ville ie vous nomme, Tout en alarme, & le Soldat es Champs, Par Fer & Eau grandement affligée, Et a la fin des Francois soulagée, Mais ce sera des six cens & dix ans. English.

The great City where the first man is, Fully I name the Town to you, Shall be alarmed and the Souldier in the field, Shall be by Fire and Water greatly afflicted, And at last shall be helped by the *French,* But it shall be from six hundred and ten years.

ANNOT.

That great City where the first man is, is *Amsterdam*, because the first Letter and the last Sylable of it maketh *Adam*: But of her affliction by Fire and Water, and of her being relieved by the *French* in the year 1610. I can find nothing in the History; those that are better furnished with Books than I am, may chance to satisfie themselves and others, better than I can do.

XLIII.

Le petit coin Provinces mutinées, Par forts Chasteaux se verront dominées, Encor un coup par la gent Militaire, Dans bref seront fortement assiegez, Mais il seront d'un tres grand soulagez, Qui aura fait entrée dans Beaucaire. English.

The little corner, Provinces revolted, By strong Castles, shall see themselves commanded, Once more by the Military Troops, Within a little while shall be strongly Besieged, But shall be helped by a great one, That hath made his entry in *Beaucaire.*

ANNOT.

This little Corner and Provinces revolted are *Holland,* and the rest of the United Provinces, who are threatned here with many troubles, as they did suffer till the Peace of *Munster.*

That great man that helped them, was the King of *France.*

XLIV.

French.

La belle Rose en la France admirée, D'un tres-grand Prince a la fin desirée, Six cens & dix lors naistront ses amours, Cinq ans apres sera d'un grand blessée, Du tract d'Amour elle sera enlassée, Si a quinze ans du Ciel recoit secours. English.

The faire Rose admired in *France,* Shall at last be desired by a great Prince, Six hundred and ten, then shall her love begin, Five years after she shall be wounded, With the love of a great one she shall be intangled, If at five years she receiveth help from Heaven.

ANNOT.

This Prophecy was concerning the Match between *Lewis* the XIII. and *Ann* of *Austria* Infanta of *Spain,* who were both Married very young.

XLV.

French.

De coup de fer tout le Monde estonné, Par Crocodil estrangement donné, A un bien grand, parent de la Sangsue, Et peu apres sera un autre coup, De guet a pens commis contre le Loup, Et de tels faits on en verra l'yssue. English.

All the World being astonished at a blow of Iron, Strangely given by a Crocodile, To a great one, kin to the *Leech,* And a little while after another blow, On purpose given against the Wolf, And of such deeds the end shall be seen.

ANNOT.

I think this needeth no further explication, then that I have given upon the 31. Stanza.
XLVI.

French.

Les Pourvoieux mettra tout en desroute, Sangsue & Loup, en mon dire escoute, Quand Mars sera au Signe du Mouton, Joint a Saturne, Saturne a la Lune, Alors sera ta plus grande infortune, Le Soleil lors en exaltation. English.

The Purveyor shall put all in disorder, Leech and Wolf, do ye hearken to me, When *Mars* shall be in the Sign of *Aries*, Joyned with *Saturn*, and *Saturn* with the Moon, Then shall be thy greatest misfortune, The Sun being then in its exaltation.

ANNOT.

This is plain, if you remember that by the Purveyor is meant the King of *France*, by the Leech the King of *Spain*, and by the Wolf the Duke of *Savoy*.
XLVII.

French.

Le grand d'Hongrie ira dans la Nacelle, Le nouveau né sera guerre nouvelle, A son voisin, qu'il tiendra assiegé, Et le noireau avec son Altesse, Ne souffrira que par trop on le presse, Durant trois ans ses gens tiendra rangé. English.

The great one of *Hungary* shall go in the Boat, The new born shall make a new War, To his Neighbour, whom he shall Besiege, And the black one with his Highness, Shall not suffer to be overpressed, During three years he shall keep his Men in order.

ANNOT.

This is concerning the King of *Bohemia*, and his War with the Emperour, who is called here the *great one of Hungary*, because he is King of it; *the black one with his Highness*, is the Palsgrave, who after three years broils was defeated at the Battle of *Prage*.
XLVIII.

French.

Du vieux Charon on verra le Phœnix, Estre premier & dernier des fils, Reluire en France, & d'un chascun aimable, Regner long temps, avec tous les honneurs, Qu'auront jamais eu ses Predecesseurs, Dont il rendra sa gloire memorable. English.

The Phœnix of the old *Charon* shall be seen, To be the first and last of the Sons, To shine in

France, beloved of every one, To Reign a great while with all the honours, That ever his Predecessors had, By which he shall make his glory memorable.

ANNOT.

No doubt but this is meant of some King of *France*, which is to come.

XLIX.

French.

Venus & Sol, Jupiter & Mercure, Augmenteront le genre de nature, Grande Alliance en France se fera, Et du Midy la Sangsue de mesme, Le feu esteint par ce remede extreme; En Terre ferme Olivier plantera. English.

Venus and *Sol*, *Jupiter* and *Mercury*, Shall augment humane kind, A great Alliance shall be made in *France*, And on the South the Leech shall do the same, The fire extinguished by this extreme remedy, Shall plant the Olive-Tree in a firm ground.

ANNOT.

By the consent of all Astronomers, those four benigne Planets augment generation.

That great Alliance mentioned here, by which the fire was extinguished, and the Olive-Tree planted in a firm ground, is the Marriage of the present King of *France*, *Lewis*, the XIV. with the Infanta of *Spain*, by which all differences were composed, and the Peace firmly settled.

L.

French.

Un peu devant ou apres l'Angleterre, Par mort de Loup mise aussy bas que terre, Verra le feu resister contre l'eau, Le rallumant avecque telle force, Du sang humain, dessus l'humaine escorce, Faute de pain, bondance de cousteau. English.

A little while before or after, *England*, By the death of the Wolf being put as low as the ground, Shall see the fire resist against the water, Kindling it again with such force, Of humane blood, upon the humane bark, That want of bread and abundance of knives shall be.

ANNOT.

The meaning is, that a little while after or before the said match mentioned in the foregoing: *England* was or should be brought as low as the ground, and that there should be abundance of humane blood spilled, and a great decay of Trade, with Wars, which is that he calleth, Want of Bread and abundance of knives.

LI.

French.

La Ville qu'avoit en ses ans, Combatu l'Injure du temps, Qui de son Vainqueur tient la vie, Celuy qui premier la surprit, Que peu apres Francois reprit, Par Combats encore affoible. English.

The City that had in her years, Resisted the injury of the times, And oweth her life to him that overcame her, Being the first that surprised it, Which a little while after *Francis* took again, Being yet weakened with fightings.

LII.

French.

La grand Cité qui n'a Pain a demy, Encor un coup la saint Barthelemy, Engravera au profond de son Ame, Nismes, Rochelle, Geneve & Montpelier, Castres, Lion, Mars entrant au Belier, S'entrebattront le tout pour une Dame. English.

The great City that hath not bread half enough, Shall once more engrave In the bottom of her soul St. *Bartholomew*'s day, *Nismes, Rochel, Geneva* and *Montpelier, Castres, Lion, Mars* coming into *Aries*, Shall fight one against another, and all for a Lady.

ANNOT.

That great City mentioned here, is *Paris*, which is threatned of another St. *Bartholomew*'s day, which was fatal to the Protestants in *France*, for upon that day in the year 1572. there was a general Massacre made of them through all *France*, insomuch, that in *Paris* alone there was above ten thousand slain.

As for those Towns here named that are to fight about a Lady, I cannot guess what Lady it should be, unless he meaneth the *Roman* Church.

LIII.

French.

Plusieurs mourront avant que Phœnix meure, Jusques six cens septante est sa demeure, Passé quinze ans, vingt & un, trente neuf, Le premier est Subjet a maladie, Et le second au fer, danger de vie, Au feu a l'eau est subjet a trenteneuf. English.

Many shall die before that Phœnix dieth, Till six hundred and seventy he shall remain, Above fifteen years, one and twenty, thirty nine, The first shall be subject to sickness, And the second to Iron, a danger of life, Thirty nine shall be subject to fire and water.

ANNOT.

By the Phœnix is meant a Pope, because there is but one of that kind at once, the meaning of the rest is unknown to me.

LIV.

French.

Six cens & quinze vingt, grand Dame mourra, Et peu apres un fort long temps pleuvra, Plusieurs Pais Flandres & l'Angleterre, Seront par seu & par fer affligez, De leurs Voisins longuement assiegez, Contraints seront de leur faire la Guerre. English.

Six hundred and fifteen, and twenty, a great Lady shall die, And a little after it shall rain for a great while, Many Countreys as *Flanders* and *England*, Shall by fire and Iron be afflicted, And a good while Besieged by their Neighbours, So that they shall be constrained to make War against them.

ANNOT.

What that great Lady was, that should die in the year 653. is not easie to guess, there being many in every Countrey that died that year. The rest is easie, and we have seen the truth of it in our days, and may see it hereafter.

LV.

French.

Un peu devant ou apres tres grand' Dame, Son ame au Ciel, & son corps soubs la lame, De plusieurs gens regretée sera, Tous ses parens seront en grand tristesse, Pleurs & souspirs d'une Dame en jeunesse, Et a deux grands le dueil delaissera. English.

A little while before, or after, a very great Lady, Her soul in Heaven, and her body in the Grave, Shall be lamented by many, All her kindred shall be in great mourning, Tears and sighs of a Lady in her youth, And shall leave the mourning to two great ones.

ANNOT.

This may be understood of the death of *Anna* of *Austria*, Queen of *France*, who left in mourning two great ones, *viz.* her two Sons *Lewis* the XIV. King of *France*, and *Philip* of *Bourbon* Duke of *Orleans*.

Or of the death of the Queen Dowager of *England*, *Henrietta Maria*, who also was much lamented, and left in mourning two great ones, *viz. Charles* the II. King of *England*, and *James* Duke of *York* his Brother.

LVI.

French.

Tost l'Elephant de toutes parts verra, Quand Pourvoyeur au Griffon se joindra, Sa ruine proche, & Mars qui tousiour gronde, Fera grands faits aupres de Terre Sainte, Grands Estendars sur la Terre & sur l'Onde, Si la Nef a esté, de deux frere enceinte. English.

Shortly the Elephant on all sides shall see, When the Purveyor shall joyn with the Griffin, His ruine at hand, and *Mars* which always grumbleth, Shall do great feats near the *Holy Land*, Great Standarts upon the Earth and the Sea, If the Ship hath been with Child of two Brothers.

ANNOT.

  The Elephant is the Emperor, the Purveyor the King of *France*, the Griffin the *Hollanders*; the meaning then is that the Emperor shall go to ruine, when the *French* and the *Hollanders* shall joyn together.
  And that there shall be great Wars and Fightings in the Holy Lands, both by Sea and Land, when two Brothers of great quality shall go in one Ship.

LVII.

French.

Peu apres l'Alliance faite, Avant solemnises la Feste, L'Empereur le tout troublera, Et la nouvelle Mariée, Au Franc Païs par sort liée, Dans peu de temps apres mourra. English.

A little after the Alliance made, Before the Feast be Solemnized, The Emperor shall trouble all, And the new Bride, Being by fate tied to the *French* Countrey, A little while after shall die.

ANNOT.

  This is concerning a match that shall be made between the *French* King, and some Lady of another Countrey, which Match shall be disturbed by the Emperour, and the Bride shall die a little while after her Marriage.

LVIII.

French.

Sangsue en peu de temps mourra, Sa mort bon signe nous donra, Pour l'accroissement de la France, Alliances se trouveront, Deux grands Roiaumes se joindront, Francois aura sur eux puissance. English.

The Leech within a little while shall die, His death shall be a good sign to us, For the augmentation of *France*, Alliances shall be found, Two great Kingdoms shall joyn together, The *French* shall have power over them.

ANNOT.

The *Leech* was *Philip* the IV. the last King of *Spain*, who died a little while after he had Married his Daughter to *Lewis* the XIV. now King of *France*, by which Marriage the Peace was made between the two Kingdoms, in the Island of the *Conference*, upon the Borders of *France* and *Spain*. By his death and that Match is foretold the encrease and happy condition of the Kingdom of *France*.

Printed in Great Britain
by Amazon

86538413R00280